P9-CMO-029

The Annotated
LOLITA

A Partial Listing of
Books by Vladimir Nabokov

Ada, a novel
Bend Sinister, a novel
The Defense, a novel
Despair, a novel
Eugene Onegin, by Aleksandr Pushkin,
   translated from the Russian, with a
   Commentary
The Eye, a novel
The Gift, a novel
Invitation to a Beheading, a novel
King, Queen, Knave, a novel
Laughter in the Dark or *Camera Obscura*,
   a novel
Lolita, a novel
Nabokov's Dozen, a collection of short stories
Nabokov's Quartet, a collection of short stories
Nikolai Gogol, a critical biography
Pale Fire, a novel
Pnin, a novel
Podvig, a novel
Poems
The Real Life of Sebastian Knight, a novel
The Song of Igor's Campaign, Anon.,
   translated from Old Russian
Speak, Memory or *Conclusive Evidence*,
   a memoir
Spring in Fialta and Other Stories
Three Russian Poets, verse translation from
   the Russian
The Waltz Invention, a drama

Books by Alfred Appel, Jr.

The Annotated Lolita
"Tri-Quarterly" Nabokov Festschrift (co-editor)
*Vladimir Nabokov: A Collection of Critical
   Essays* (editor)
Vladimir Nabokov (in preparation)

This edition of LOLITA is published by special arrangement
with G.P. PUTNAM'S SONS, New York

VLADIMIR NABOKOV

The Annotated

LOLITA

Edited, with
preface, introduction and notes by

ALFRED APPEL, JR.

McGraw-Hill Book Company · New York · Toronto

LOLITA

Copyright © by Vladimir Nabokov 1955.
All rights reserved.
Library of Congress Catalog Card Number: 58-10755

This edition copyright © 1970 by McGraw-Hill, Inc.
All rights reserved.
Printed in the United States of America.
No part of this publication may be
reproduced, stored in a retrieval system, or
transmitted, in any form or by any means,
electronic, mechanical, photocopying,
recording or otherwise, without the prior
written permission of McGraw-Hill, Inc.

Library of Congress Catalog Card Number: 75-95819
07-045729-8
07-045730-1

7 8 9 10   KPKP   83210

To Véra

ACKNOWLEDGMENTS

I would like to thank the following for permission to quote: Vladimir Nabokov and *The New Yorker*, in whose pages the poems first appeared, for "A Discovery" and "Ode to a Model," Copyright © 1943, 1955 by Vladimir Nabokov; G.P. Putnam's Sons for passages from *Pale Fire* by Vladimir Nabokov, Copyright © 1962 by G.P. Putnam's Sons; G.P. Putnam's Sons for passages from *The Gift* by Vladimir Nabokov, Copyright © 1963 by G.P. Putnam's Sons; New Directions, for passages from *The Real Life of Sebastian Knight* by Vladimir Nabokov, Copyright by New Directions, 1941; and Little, Brown and Co., for passages from *Nabokov: His Life in Art* by Andrew Field, Copyright © 1967 by Andrew Field. Part II of my own article, "Nabokov's Puppet Show," is reprinted by permission of *The New Republic*, Copyright © 1967 by Harrison-Blaine of New Jersey, Inc. The University of Wisconsin Press has kindly allowed me to reprint portions of my article, "*Lolita*: The Springboard of Parody," *Wisconsin Studies in Contemporary Literature*, VIII (Spring 1967), and passages from "An Interview with Vladimir Nabokov," *ibid*. (© 1967 by the Regents of the University of Wisconsin). I also wish to acknowledge the assistance of Karen Appel, Frank Cady, Eli Cohen, Patricia McKea, Raymond Nelson, Professor Fred C. Robinson, and Bruce Sattler.

—A. A.

PREFACE

In the decade since its American publication (in 1958), Vladimir Nabokov's *Lolita* has emerged as a classic of contemporary literature. This annotated edition is designed for the general reader and particularly for use in college literature courses. It has developed out of my own experiences in teaching and writing about *Lolita*, which have demonstrated that many readers are more troubled by Humbert Humbert's use of language and lore than by his abuse of Lolita and law. Their sense of intimidation is not unwarranted; *Lolita* is surely the most allusive and linguistically playful novel in English since *Ulysses* (1922) and *Finnegans Wake* (1939), and, if its involuted and constantly evolving means bring to mind any previous novel, it should be that most elusive of works, *The Confidence-Man* (1857) by Herman Melville. As with Joyce and Melville, the reader of *Lolita* attempts to arrive at some sense of its overall "meaning," while at the same time having to struggle, often page by page, with the difficulties posed by the recondite materials and rich, elaborate verbal textures. The main purpose of this edition is to solve such local problems and to show how they contribute to the total design of the novel. Neither the Introduction nor the Notes attempts a total interpretation of *Lolita*.

The annotations keep in mind the specific needs of college students. Many kinds of allusions are identified: literary, historical, mythological, Biblical, anatomical, zoological, botanical, and geographical. Writers and artists long out of fashion (e.g., Maeterlinck) receive fuller treatment than more familiar names. Selective cross references to identical or related allusions in other Nabokov works will help to place *Lolita* in a wider context and, one hopes, may be of some assistance to future critics of Nabokov. Many of the novel's most important motifs are limned by brief cross-references. Humbert's vocabulary is extraordinary, its range enlarged by the many portmanteau words he creates. Puns, coinages, and comic etymologies, as well as foreign, archaic, rare, or unusual words are defined. Although some of the "unusual" words are in collegiate dictionaries, they are nevertheless annotated as a matter of convenience. Not every neologism is identified (e.g., "truckster"), but many that should be obvious enough *are* noted, because the rapidly moving eye may well miss the vowel on which such a pun depends (speed-readers of the world, beware! *Lolita* is not the book for you). Because many American students have little or no French, virtually all the interpolations in French are translated. In a few instances, readers may feel an annotation belabors the obvious; I well remember my own resentment, as a college sophomore, when a textbook reference to Douglas MacArthur was garnished by the footnote "Famous American general (1880–)." Yet the commonplace may turn out to be obscure. For instance, early in *Lolita* Humbert mentions that his first wife Valeria was "deep in *Paris-Soir*" (p. 28). When I asked a Stanford University class of some eighty students if they knew what *Paris-Soir* was, sixty of them had no idea, twenty reasonably guessed it to be a magazine or newspaper, but no one knew specifically that it was a newspaper which featured lurid reportage, and that the detail formulates Valeria's puerility and Humbert's contempt for her. Several notes are thus predicated on the premise that one epoch's "popular culture" may be another's esoterica (see Notes 150/1 and 256/6).

Most of the Introduction is drawn from parts of my previously published articles in *The New Republic* ("Nabokov's Puppet Show—Part II," CLVI [January 21, 1967], 25–32), *Wisconsin Studies in Contemporary Literature* (1967), *The Denver Quarterly* (1968), and *Tri Quarterly* (1970). Many Notes are adapted from the two middle articles and my interview with Nabokov in *Wisconsin Studies* (see bibliography for full entries). This edition was completed more than two years ago, save for eleventh-hour allusions to *Ada*, but the vagaries and vagrancies of publishing delayed its appearance. In the meantime, Carl R. Proffer's excellent *Keys to Lolita* was published (1968). Two enchanted hunters (see Note 110/2) working independently of each other, Mr. Proffer and I arrived at many similar identifications, and, excepting those which are readily apparent, I have tried to indicate where he has anticipated me.

The text is that of the 1958 Putnam's edition. Nabokov and the editor have made many corrections in the text, all identified in the Notes. Like the 1958 edition, this variorum edition concludes with Nabokov's Afterword, which, along with its Notes, should be read in conjunction with the Introduction (where the reader will be offered exact instructions as to this procedure).

Given the length of the Notes and the fact that they are at the back of the book, the reader would do well to consider the question of how best to use these annotations. An old reader familiar with *Lolita* can approach the apparatus as a separate unit, but the perspicacious student who keeps turning back and forth from text to Notes risks vertigo. A more balanced method is to read through a chapter and then read its annotations, or vice versa. Each reader, however, has to decide for himself which is the most comfortable procedure. In a more perfect world, this edition would be in two volumes, text in one, Notes in the other; placed adjacent to one another, they could be read concurrently. Charles Kinbote in his Foreword to *Pale Fire* (1962) suggests a solution that closely approximates this arrangement, and the reader is directed to his sensible remarks, which serve this edition in place of a note on the text.

Although there are almost nine hundred notes to this text, the initial annotated edition of a work should never be offered as "definitive" and that claim will not be made here. As it is, *The Annotated Lolita* is the first annotated edition of a modern novel to have been published during its author's lifetime—*A Tale of a Tub* for our time. Vladimir Nabokov has occasionally been consulted and, in some cases, has commented on the annotations. In such instances his contribution is acknowledged. He wants me to mention that in several instances his interpretation of *Lolita* does not necessarily coincide with mine, and I have tried to point out such cases; the literary allusions, however, have been deemed accurate.

This edition, then, is analogous to what *Pale Fire* might have been like if poor John Shade had been given the opportunity to comment on Charles Kinbote's Commentary. Of course, the annotator and editor of a novel written by the creator of Kinbote and John Ray, Jr., runs the real risk of being mistaken for another fiction, when at most he resembles those gentlemen only figuratively. But the annotator exists; he is a veteran and a father, a teacher and taxpayer, and has not been invented by Vladimir Nabokov.

CONTENTS

Preface   ix

Introduction   xv

Selected Bibliography
1. Checklist of Nabokov's writing   lxxii
2. Criticism of *Lolita*   lxxiv

In Place of a Note on the Text—from *Pale Fire*   1

Lolita
Foreword   5
Part One   9
Part Two   145
Vladimir Nabokov: On a Book
    Entitled *Lolita*   313

Notes   321

INTRODUCTION

1. NABOKOV'S PUPPET SHOW

I have tried my best to show the workings of the book, at least some of its workings. Its charm, humour and pathos can only be appreciated by direct reading. But for enlightenment of those who felt baffled by its habit of metamorphosis, or merely disgusted at finding something incompatible with the idea of a "nice book" in the discovery of a book's being an utterly new one, I should like to point out that *The Prismatic Bezel* can be thoroughly enjoyed once it is understood that the heroes of the book are what can be loosely called "methods of composition." It is as if a painter said: look, here I'm going to show you not the painting of a landscape, but the painting of different ways of painting a certain landscape, and I trust their harmonious fusion will disclose the landscape as I intend you to see it.

Vladimir Nabokov, *The Real Life of Sebastian Knight* [1]

Vladimir Vladimirovich Nabokov was born on April 23, 1899, in St. Petersburg, Russia. The rich and aristocratic Nabokovs were not the "White Russian" stock figures of Western liberal demonology—all monocles, Fabergé snuffboxes, and reactionary opinions —but rather a family with a long tradition of high culture and pub-

[1] New York, 1941, p. 95. Henceforth, page references will be placed in parentheses in the text, and pertain to the hardcover editions of Nabokov's books.

lic service. Nabokov's grandfather was Minister of Justice under two tsars and implemented the court reforms, while Nabokov's father was a distinguished jurist, a foe of anti-Semitism, a prolific journalist and scholar, a leader of the opposition party (the Kadets), and a member of the first parliament (Duma). In 1919 he took his family into exile, co-editing a liberal émigré daily in Berlin until his death in 1922 (at age fifty-two), at a political meeting, where he was shot while trying to shield the speaker from two monarchist assassins. Young Nabokov went to Trinity College, Cambridge, in 1922 taking an honors degree in Slavic and Romance Languages. For the next eighteen years he lived in Germany and France, writing prolifically in Russian. The spectral émigré communities of Europe were not large enough to sustain a writer, and Nabokov supported himself through translations, public readings of his works, lessons in English and tennis, and, fittingly, the first Russian crossword puzzles, which he composed for a daily émigré paper. In 1940 he and his wife and son moved to the United States, and Nabokov began to write in English. The frequently made comparison with Joseph Conrad denies Nabokov his signal achievement; for the Polish-born author was thirty when he started to write in English, and, unlike the middle-aged Nabokov, he had not written anything in his native language, let alone nine novels.

In America, Nabokov lectured on Russian literature at Wellesley (1941–1948) and Cornell (1948–1958), where his Masterpieces of European Fiction course proved immensely popular. While at Wellesley he also worked on Lepidoptera in the Museum of Comparative Zoology at Harvard. Nabokov's several books in English had meanwhile earned him the quiet respect of discerning readers, but *Lolita* was the first to attract wide attention. Its best-sellerdom and film sale in 1958 enabled Nabokov to resign his teaching position and devote himself to his writing. Since 1960 he has lived in Montreux, Switzerland, where he is now working on a new novel (entitled *Transparent Things*) and a history of the butterfly in Western art, and planning for the future publication of several works, including his Cornell lectures, his screenplay of *Lolita* (only parts of which were used in Stanley Kubrick's 1962 film), and a selection of his Russian poems, translated by Nabokov and to be published together with his chess problems.

Lolita made Lolita famous, rather than Nabokov. Although praised by influential critics, *Lolita* was treated as a kind of miracle of spontaneous generation, for Nabokov's *oeuvre* was like an iceberg, the massive body of his Russian novels, stories, plays, and poems remaining untranslated and out of sight, lurking beneath the visible peaks of *Lolita* and *Pnin* (1957). But in the eleven years since Putnam's published *Lolita*, twenty-one Nabokov titles have appeared, including seven works translated from the Russian, three out-of-print novels, two collections of stories, *Pale Fire* (1962), the monumental four-volume translation of Pushkin's *Eugene Onegin* (1964), *Speak, Memory: An Autobiography Revisited* (1966)—a considerably revised and expanded version of the memoir first issued in 1951 as *Conclusive Evidence*—and *Ada* (1969), his fifteenth novel, whose publication celebrated his seventieth birthday. The publication of *Mashenka* (1926) and *The Exploit* (1931), now being Englished by his son Dmitri, will complete the translation of his Russian novels.

This extraordinary outburst of Nabokoviana highlights the resolute and indomitable spirit of the man who published his masterpieces, *Lolita, Pale Fire,* and *Ada,* at the ages of fifty-six, sixty-three, and seventy, respectively. Nabokov endured the exigencies of being an émigré writer when the Western world seemed interested only in his inferior Soviet contemporaries, and has emerged not only as a major Russian writer, but as the most important living American novelist. No doubt some academic pigeonholers still worry about Nabokov's nationality and where to "place" him, but John Updike solved this synthetic problem when he described Nabokov as "the best writer of English prose at present holding American citizenship." [1] Not since Henry James, an émigré in his own right, has an American citizen created so formidable a corpus of work.

Nabokov's pronounced antipathy to Freud and the novel of society will continue to alienate some critics, but there is a reason for

[1] John Updike, "Grandmaster Nabokov," *New Republic,* CLI (September 26, 1964), 15. Reprinted in Updike's *Assorted Prose* (New York, 1965).

the delay in achieving his proper status more basic than the unavailability of his books or his failure to conform to some accepted school or *Zeitgeist* pattern: readers trained on the tenets of formalist criticism have simply not known what to make of works which resist the search for ordered mythic and symbolic "levels of meaning" and depart completely from post-Jamesian requisites for the "realistic" or "impressionistic" novel—that a fiction be the impersonal product of a pure aesthetic impulse, a self-contained illusion of reality rendered from a consistently held point of view and through a central intelligence from which all authorial comment has been exorcised. Quite the opposite happens in Nabokov's fiction: his art is artifice or nothing; and the fantastic, a-realistic, and involuted forms toward which even his earliest fictions evolve make it clear that Nabokov has always gone his own way, and it has not been the way of the novel's Great Tradition according to F. R. Leavis. But Nabokov's present eminence signals a radical shift in opinions about the novel and the novelist's ethical responsibilities. A future historian of the novel may one day claim that it was Nabokov, more than any novelist now living, who kept alive an exhausted art form not only by demonstrating new possibilities for it, but by reminding us, through his example, of the variegated aesthetic resources of his great forebears, such as Sterne and the Joyce who was a parodist rather than a symbolist.

In addition to its qualities as a memoir, *Speak, Memory* serves, along with Chapter Five in *Gogol* (1944), as the ideal introduction to Nabokov's art, for some of the most lucid criticism of Nabokov is found in his own books. His most overtly parodic novels spiral in upon themselves and provide their own commentary; sections of *The Gift* (1937–1938) and *The Real Life of Sebastian Knight* (1941) limpidly describe the narrative strategies of later novels. Nabokov's preoccupations are perhaps best projected by bringing together the opening and closing sentences of *Speak, Memory:* "The cradle rocks above an abyss, and common sense tells us that our existence is but a brief crack of light between two eternities of darkness." At the end of the book he describes how he and his wife first perceived, through the stratagems thrown up to confound the eye, the ocean liner waiting to take them and their son to America: "It was most satisfying to make out among the jumbled angles of roofs and walls, a splendid ship's funnel, showing from behind the clothes-line as something in a scrambled picture—Find What the Sailor Has Hidden—that the finder cannot unsee once it has been seen." *The Eye* (1930) is well titled; the apprehension of "reality" (a word that Nabokov says must always have quotes around it) is first of all a miracle of vision, and our existence is a sequence of attempts to unscramble the "pictures" glimpsed in that "brief crack of light." Both art and nature are to Nabokov "a game of intricate enchant-ment and deception," and the process of reading and rereading his novels is a game of perception, like those E. H. Gombrich writes about in *Art and Illusion*—everything is *there*, in sight (no symbols lurking in murky depths), but one must penetrate the *trompe-l'oeil*, which eventually reveals something totally different from what one had expected. This is how Nabokov seems to envision the game of life and the effect of his novels: each time a "scrambled picture" has been discerned "the finder cannot unsee" it; consciousness has been expanded or created.

The word "game" commonly denotes frivolity and an escape from the exigencies of the world, but Nabokov confronts the void by virtue of his play-concept. His "game of worlds" (to quote John Shade in *Pale Fire*) proceeds within the terrifyingly immuta-ble limits defined by the "two eternities of darkness" and is a search for order—for "some kind / Of correlated pattern in the game"—which demands the full consciousness of its players. The author and the reader are the "players," and when in *Speak, Mem-ory* Nabokov describes the composition of chess problems he is also telescoping his fictional practices. If one responds to the author's "false scents" and "specious lines of play," best effected by parody, and believes, say, that Humbert's confession is "sincere" and that he exorcises his guilt, or that the narrator of *Pnin* is really per-plexed by Pnin's animosity toward him, or that a Nabokov book is an illusion of a reality proceeding under the natural laws of our world—then one has not only lost the game to the author, but most likely is not faring too well in the "game of worlds," one's own un-scrambling of pictures.

Speak, Memory rehearses the major themes of Nabokov's fiction: the confrontation of death; the withstanding of exile; the nature of the creative process; the search for complete consciousness and the "free world of timelessness." In the first chapter he writes, "I have journeyed back in thought—with thought hopelessly tapering off as I went—to remote regions where I groped for some secret outlet only to discover that the prison of time is spherical and without exits." Nabokov's protagonists live in claustrophobic, cell-like rooms; and Humbert, Cincinnatus in *Invitation to a Beheading* (1936), and Krug in *Bend Sinister* (1947) are all indeed imprisoned. The struggle to escape from this spherical prison (Krug is Russian for "circle") assumes many forms throughout Nabokov; and his own desperate and sometimes ludicrous attempts, as described in *Speak, Memory*, are variously parodied in the poltergeist machinations of *The Eye*, in Hazel Shade's involvement with "a domestic ghost" and her spirit-writing in the haunted barn in *Pale Fire*, and in "The Vane Sisters" (in *Nabokov's Quartet* [1966]), where an acrostic in the final paragraph reveals that two vivid images from the story's opening paragraphs were dictated by the dead Vane sisters.

Although *Speak, Memory* clearly illuminates the self-parodic content of Nabokov's fiction, no one has fully recognized the aesthetic implications of these transmutations or the extent to which Nabokov has consciously projected his own life in his fiction. To be sure, this is dangerous talk, easily misunderstood. Of course Nabokov does not write the kind of thinly disguised transcription of personal experience which too often passes for fiction. But it is crucial to an understanding of his art to realize how often his novels are improvisations on an autobiographic theme, and in *Speak, Memory* Nabokov good-naturedly anticipates his critics: "The future specialist in such dull literary lore as auto-plagiarism will like to collate a protagonist's experience in my novel *The Gift* with the original event." Further on he comments on his habit of bestowing "treasured items" from his past on his characters. But it is more than mere "items" that Nabokov has transmogrified in the "artificial world" of his novels, as a dull specialist discovers by comparing Chapters Eleven and Thirteen of *Speak, Memory* with *The Gift*, or, since it is Nabokov's overriding subject, by comparing the attitudes toward exile expressed in *Speak, Memory* with the treatment it is given in his fiction. The reader of his memoir learns that Nabokov's great-grandfather explored and mapped Nova Zembla (where Nabokov's River is named after him), and in *Pale Fire* Kinbote believes himself to be the exiled king of Zembla. His is both a fantastic vision of Nabokov's opulent past as entertained by a madman, and the vision of a poet's irreparable loss, expressed otherwise by Nabokov in 1945: "Beyond the seas where I have lost a sceptre, / I hear the neighing of my dappled nouns" ("An Evening of Russian Poetry"). Nabokov's avatars do not grieve for "lost banknotes." Their circumstances, though exacerbated by adversity, are not exclusive to the émigré. Exile is a correlative for all human loss, and Nabokov records with infinite tenderness the constrictions the heart must suffer; even in his most parodic novels, such as *Lolita*, he makes audible through all the playfulness a cry of pain. "Pity," says John Shade, "is the password." Nabokov's are emotional and spiritual exiles, turned back upon themselves, trapped by their obsessive memories and desires in a solipsistic "prison of mirrors" where they cannot distinguish the glass from themselves (to use another prison trope, drawn from the story "The Assistant Producer" [1943], in *Nabokov's Dozen* [1958]).

The transcendence of solipsism is a central concern in Nabokov. He recommends no escape, and there is an unmistakable moral resonance in his treatment of the theme: it is only at the outset of *Lolita* that Humbert can say that he had Lolita "safely solipsized." The coldly unromantic scrutiny which his exiles endure is often overlooked by critics. In *Pnin* the gentle, addlepated professor is seen in a new and harsh light in the final chapter, when the narrator assumes control and makes it clear that he is inheriting Pnin's job but not, he would hope, his existence. John Shade asks us to pity "the exile, the old man / Dying in a motel," and we do; but in the Commentary, Kinbote says that a "king who sinks his identity in the mirror of exile is guilty of [a regicide]." "The past [is] the past," Lolita tells Humbert toward the end of that novel (p. 274), when he asks her to relive what had always been inexorably lost. As a book about the spell exerted by the past, *Lolita* is Nabokov's own parodic answer to his previous book, the first edition of *Speak*,

Memory. Mnemosyne is now seen as a black muse, nostalgia as a grotesque cul-de-sac. *Lolita* is the last book one would offer as "autobiographical," but even in its totally created form it connects with the deepest reaches of Nabokov's soul. Like the poet Fyodor in *The Gift*, Nabokov could say that while he keeps everything "on the very brink of parody . . . there must be on the other hand an abyss of seriousness, and I must make my way along this narrow ridge between my own truth and a caricature of it" (p. 212).

An autobiographic theme submitted to the imagination thus takes on a new life: frozen in art, halted in space, now timeless, it can be lived with. When the clownish Gradus assassinates John Shade by mistake, in a novel published forty years after Nabokov's father was similarly murdered, one may remember the butterfly which the seven-year-old Nabokov caught and then lost, but which was "finally overtaken and captured, after a forty-year race, on an immigrant dandelion . . . near Boulder" (*Speak, Memory*, p. 120). One recognizes how art makes life possible for Nabokov, and why he calls *Invitation to a Beheading* a "violin in a void." His art records a constant process of becoming—the evolution of the artist's self through artistic creation—and the cycle of insect metamorphosis is Nabokov's controlling metaphor for the process, provided by a lifetime of biological investigations which established in his mind "links between butterflies and the central problems of nature." Significantly, a butterfly or moth will often appear at the end of a Nabokov novel, when the artistic "cycle" of that book is complete.

Speak, Memory only reinforces what is suggested by Nabokov's visibly active participation in the life of his fiction, as in *Invitation to a Beheading* when Cincinnatus strains to look out of his barred window and sees on the prison wall the telling, half-erased inscription, "You cannot see anything. I tried it too" (p. 29), written in the neat, recognizable hand of the "prison director"—that is, the author—whose intrusions involute the book and deny it any reality except that of "book." The word "involution" may trouble some readers, but one has only to extend the dictionary definition. An involuted work turns in upon itself, is self-referential, conscious of its status as a fiction, and "*allégorique de lui-même*"—allegorical of itself, to use Mallarmé's description of one of his own poems.

An ideally involuted sentence would simply read, "I am a sentence," and John Barth's recent short stories "Title," "Life-Story," and "Menelaiad" (in *Lost in the Funhouse*, 1968) come as close to this dubious ideal as any fiction possibly can. The components of "Title," for example, sustain a miraculous discussion among themselves, sometimes even addressing the author: "Once upon a time you were satisfied with incidental felicities and niceties of technique."

Characters in involuted works often recognize that their authenticity is more than suspect. In Raymond Queneau's *Les Enfants du Limon* (1938), Chambernac is a lycée headmaster who has been collecting material for a monumental work on "literary madmen," *L'Encyclopédie des sciences inexactes*. By the last chapter he has abandoned hope of getting it published, but he then is approached in a café by *"un type"* (Queneau, as it turns out, who identifies himself by name) and offers to turn the manuscript over for use in a novel Queneau is writing, one of whose characters is a headmaster, and so forth. A similar infinite regress exists in Chapter Four of Lewis Carroll's *Through the Looking-Glass* (1872), the creator's (and Creator's) role now played by the sleeping Red King. When Alice moves to waken the King, Tweedledee stops her:

> "He's dreaming now," said Tweedledee: "and what do you think he's dreaming about?"
>
> Alice said, "Nobody can guess that."
>
> "Why, about *you!*" Tweedledee exclaimed, clapping his hands triumphantly. "And if he left off dreaming about you, where do you suppose you'd be?"
>
> "Where I am now, of course," said Alice.
>
> "Not you!" Tweedledee retorted contemptuously. "You'd be nowhere. Why you're only a sort of thing in his dream!"
>
> "If that there King was to wake," added Tweedledum, "you'd go out—bang!—just like a candle!"
>
> "I shouldn't!" Alice exclaimed indignantly. "Besides, if *I'm* only a sort of thing in his dream, what are *you*, I should like to know?"
>
> "Ditto," said Tweedledum.
>
> "Ditto, ditto!" cried Tweedledee.
>
> He shouted this so loud that Alice couldn't help saying "Hush! You'll be waking him, I'm afraid, if you make so much noise."

"Well, it's no use *your* talking about waking him," said Twee-dledum, "when you're only one of the things in his dream. You know very well you're not real."

"I *am* real!" said Alice, and began to cry.

A similar discussion occurs in Samuel Beckett's *Endgame* (1957). "What is there to keep me here?" asks Clov. "The dialogue," answers Hamm. More like the Tweedles than Alice are the three aging characters in Queneau's *Le Chiendent* (1933). Having survived the long destructive Franco-Etruscan war, by the final pages they are ready for anything. When the queen is complimented, she says, "It wasn't I who said that.... It's in the book." Asked "What book?," she replies, "Well, this one. The one we're in now, which repeats what we say as we say it and which follows us and tells about us, a genuine blotter which has been stuck on our lives." [1] They then discuss the novel of which they are a part and agree to try to annihilate time and begin all over again. They go back to Paris, back in time. The last two sentences of the book are the first two sentences.

Although the philosophical implications are somewhat less interesting, the most patent examples of involution are found in comic books, comic strips, and animated cartoons. The creatures in cartoons used to be brought to life before one's eyes: first, the *tabula rasa* of an empty screen, which is then seen to be a drawing board, over which the artist's brush sweeps, a few strokes creating the characters, who only then begin to move. Or the convention of the magical ink bottle, framing the action fore and aft. The characters are sucked back into the bottle at the end, just as they had spilled out of it at the start. These devices describe the process of *Le Chiendent*, where one sees a silhouette from the first page fleshed-out more and more as the novel progresses, or Alain Robbe-Grillet's *Dans le labyrinthe* (*In the Labyrinth*, 1959), where in the stillness of his room the narrator contemplates several objects, including a steel engraving, which is then "animated," a fiction spinning out of it. "We create ourselves in time," says one of the characters at the

[1] Raymond Queneau, *Le Chiendent* (Paris, 1933), p. 294. The above translations are mine—A.A.

end of *Le Chiendent*, "and the old book snatches us up right away with its funny little scrawl [handwriting]." [1]

In involuted works, characters readily communicate with their creators, though the relationship is not always ideal. One may recall an early *Bugs Bunny* animated cartoon (c. 1943) in which there is a wild running battle between the rabbit and the artist, whose visible hand alternately wields an eraser and a drawing pencil, terrible weapons which at one moment remove the rabbit's feet so that he cannot escape, and at another give him a duck's bill so that he cannot talk back, not unlike the lot of the characters in *Invitation to a Beheading*, who are taken apart, rearranged, and reassembled at will. But characters are not always as uncomplaining as Cincinnatus. In the next-to-last box of a 1936 daily strip, Chester Gould pictured his hero trapped horribly in a mine shaft, its entrance blocked by a huge boulder. The balloon above Dick Tracy's stricken face said, "Gould, you have gone too far." The concluding box was to have shown a kindly eraser-bearing hand, descending to remove the boulder; but *The Chicago Tribune*'s Captain Patterson, no doubt a disciple of Dr. Leavis, thought Gould had indeed gone too far, and rejected that strip. Considerably less desperate is Shakespeare's direct address to Joyce in Nighttown: "How my Oldfellow chokit his Thursdaymomun," that moment being Bloomsday, this book, and Joyce's stab at greatness. [2] "O Jamesy let me up out of this," pleads Molly Bloom to Joyce, [3] and in the hallucinated Nighttown section the shade of Virag says, "That suits your book, eh?" When in acknowledgment his throat is made to twitch, Virag says, "Slapbang! There he goes again." [4] Virag is quite right to speak directly to Joyce, because the phantasmagoria of Nighttown are the artist's. Virag accepts the truth that he is another's creation, and does so far more gracefully than Alice or poor Krug in Nabokov's *Bend Sinister*, who is instantaneously rendered insane by the realization. On the other hand, this perception steels Cincin-

[1] *ibid.*
[2] James Joyce, *Ulysses* (New York, 1961), p. 567.
[3] *ibid.*, p. 769.
[4] *ibid.*, p. 513.

natus, who is waiting to be beheaded, since it means he cannot really "die."

Nabokov's remarks on Gogol help to underscore this analogical definition of involution. "All reality is a mask," he writes (p. 148), and Nabokov's narratives are masques, stagings of his own inventions rather than re-creations of the naturalistic world. But, since the latter is what most readers expect and demand of fiction, many still do not understand what Nabokov is doing. They are not accustomed to "the allusions to something else behind the crudely painted screens" (p. 142), where the "real plots behind the obvious ones are taking place." There are thus at least two "plots" in all of Nabokov's fiction: the characters in the book, and the consciousness of the creator above it—the "real plot" which is visible in the "gaps" and "holes" in the narrative. These are best described in Chapter Fourteen of *Speak, Memory*, when Nabokov discusses "the loneliest and most arrogant" of the émigré writers, Sirin (his émigré pen name): "The real life of his books flowed in his figures of speech, which one critic [Nabokov?] has compared to windows giving upon a contiguous world . . . a rolling corollary, the shadow of a train of thought." The contiguous world is the mind and spirit of the author, whose identity, psychic survival, and "manifold awareness" are ultimately both the subject and the product of the book. In whatever way they are opened, the "windows" always reveal that "the poet (sitting in a lawn chair, at Ithaca, N.Y.) is the nucleus" of everything.

From its birth in *King, Queen, Knave* (1928), to its full maturation in *Invitation to a Beheading* (1936), to its apotheosis in the "involute abode" of *Pale Fire* (1962), the strategy of involution has determined the structure and meaning of Nabokov's novels. One must always be aware of the imprint of "that master thumb," to quote Frank Lane in *Pale Fire*, "that made the whole involuted boggling thing one beautiful straight line," for only then does it become possible to see how the "obvious plots" spiral in and out of the "real" ones. Although other writers have created involuted works, Nabokov's self-consciousness is supreme; and the range and scale of his effects, his mastery and control, make him unique. Not including autobiographic themes, the involution is achieved in six basic ways, all closely interrelated, but schematized here for the sake of clarity:

PARODY. As willful artifice, parody provides the main basis for Nabokov's involution, the "springboard for leaping into the highest region of serious emotion," as the narrator of *The Real Life of Sebastian Knight* says of Knight's novels. Because its referents are either other works of art or itself, parody denies the possibility of a naturalistic fiction. Only an authorial sensibility can be responsible for the texture of parody and self-parody; it is a verbal vaudeville, a series of literary impersonations performed by the author. When Nabokov calls a character or even a window shade "a parody," it is in the sense that his creation can possess no other "reality." In a novel such as *Lolita*, which has the fewest "gaps" of any novel after *Despair* (1934), and is seemingly his most realistic, the involution is sustained by the parody and the verbal patterning.

COINCIDENCE. *Speak, Memory* is filled with examples of Nabokov's love of coincidence. Because they are drawn from his life, these incidents demonstrate how Nabokov's imagination responds to coincidence, using it in his fiction to trace the pattern of a life's design, to achieve shattering interpenetrations of space and time. "Some law of logic," writes Nabokov in *Ada* (1969), "should fix the number of coincidences, in a given domain, after which they cease to be coincidences, and form, instead, the living organism of a new truth" (p. 368). Humbert goes to live in Charlotte Haze's house at 342 Lawn Street; he and Lolita inaugurate their illicit cross-country tour in room 342 of The Enchanted Hunters hotel; and in one year on the road they register in 342 motels and hotels. Given the endless mathematical combinations possible, the numbers seem to signal his entrapment by McFate (to use Humbert's personification). But they are also a patent, purposeful contrivance, like the copy of the 1946 *Who's Who in the Limelight* which Humbert would have us believe he found in the prison library on the night previous to his writing the chapter we are now reading. The yearbook not only prefigures the novel's action, but under Lolita's mock-entry of "Dolores Quine" we are informed that she "Made

New York debut in 1904 in *Never Talk to Strangers*"—and in the closing paragraph of the novel, almost three hundred pages later, Humbert advises the absent Lolita, "Do not talk to strangers," a detail that exhibits extraordinary narrative control for an allegedly unrevised, first-draft confessional, written during fifty-six chaotic days. Clearly, "Someone else is in the know," to quote a mysterious voice that interrupts the narration of *Bend Sinister*. It is no coincidence when coincidences extend from book to book. Creations from one "reality" continually turn up in another: the imaginary writer Pierre Delalande is quoted in *The Gift* and provides the epigraph for *Invitation to a Beheading* (inadvertently omitted from the paperback edition); Pnin and another character mention "Vladimir Vladimirovich" and dismiss his entomology as an affectation; "Hurricane Lolita" is mentioned in *Pale Fire*, and Pnin is glimpsed in the university library. Mythic or prosaic names and certain fatidic numbers recur with slight variation in many books, carrying no burden of meaning whatsoever other than the fact that someone beyond the work is repeating them, that they are all part of one master pattern.

PATTERNING. Nabokov's passion for chess, language, and lepidoptery has inspired the most elaborately involuted patterning in his work. Like the games implemented by parody, the puns, anagrams, and spoonerisms all reveal the controlling hand of the logomachist; thematically, they are appropriate to the prison of mirrors. Chess motifs are woven into several narratives, and even in *The Defense* (1930), a most naturalistically ordered early novel, the chess patterning points to forces beyond Grandmaster Luzhin's comprehension ("Thus toward the end of Chapter Four an unexpected move is made by me in a corner of the board," writes Nabokov in the Foreword). The importance of the lepidopteral motif has already been suggested, and it spirals freely in and out of Nabokov's books: in *Invitation to a Beheading*, just before he is scheduled to die, Cincinnatus gently strokes a giant moth; in *Pale Fire* a butterfly alights on John Shade's arm the minute before he is killed; in *Ada*, when Van Veen arrives for a duel, a transparent white butterfly floats past and Van is certain he has only minutes to live; in the final chapter of *Speak, Memory* Nabokov recalls seeing in Paris, just before the war, a live butterfly being promenaded on a leash of thread; at the end of *Bend Sinister* the masked author intrudes and suspends the "obvious plot," and as the book closes he looks out of the window and decides, as a moth twangs against the screen, that it is "A good night for mothing." *Bend Sinister* was published in 1947, and it is no accident that in Nabokov's next novel (1955) Humbert meets Lolita back in 1947, thus sustaining the author's "fictive time" without interruption and enabling him to pursue that moth's lovely diurnal Double through the substratum of the new novel in the most fantastic butterfly hunt of his career. "I confess I do not believe in time," writes Nabokov at the end of the ecstatic butterfly chapter in *Speak, Memory*. "I like to fold my magic carpet, after use, in such a way as to superimpose one part of the pattern upon another."

THE WORK-WITHIN-THE-WORK. The self-referential devices in Nabokov, mirrors inserted into the books at oblique angles, are clearly of the author's making, since no point of view within the fiction could possibly account for the dizzying inversions they create. The course of *The Real Life of Sebastian Knight*, which purports to be an attempt to gather material for a proposed literary biography of the narrator's half brother but ends by obfuscating even the narrator's identity, is refracted in Knight's first novel, *The Prismatic Bezel*, "a rollicking parody of the setting of a detective tale." Like an Elizabethan play-within-a-play, Quilty's play within *Lolita*, *The Enchanted Hunters*, offers a "message" that can be taken seriously as a commentary on the progression of the entire novel; and *Who's Who in the Limelight* and the class list of the Ramsdale school magically mirror the action taking place around them, including, by implication, the writing of *Lolita*. The a-novelistic components of *Pale Fire*—Foreword, Poem, Commentary, and Index—create a mirror-lined labyrinth of involuted cross references, a closed cosmos that can only be of the author's making, rather than the product of an "unreliable" narrator. *Pale Fire* realizes the ultimate possibilities of works within works, already present twenty-four years earlier in the literary biography that serves as the fourth chapter of *The Gift*. If it is disturbing to discover that the characters in *The Gift* are also the readers of Chapter Four, this is because it suggests, as Jorge Luis Borges says of the play within *Hamlet*, "that if the characters of a fictional work can be readers or spectators, we, its readers or spectators, can be fictitious." [1]

THE STAGING OF THE NOVEL. Nabokov wrote the screenplay of *Lolita*, as well as nine plays in Russian, including one of his several forays into science fiction, *The Waltz Invention* (1938), which was translated and published in 1966. It is not surprising, then, that his novels should proliferate with "theatrical" effects that serve his play-spirit exceedingly well. Problems of identity can be investigated poetically by trying on and discarding a series of masks. And, too, what better way to demonstrate that everything in a book is being manipulated than by seeming to *stage* it? In *Invitation to a Beheading*, "A Summer thunderstorm, simply yet tastefully staged, was performed outside." When Quilty finally dies in *Lolita*, Humbert says, "This was the end of the ingenious play staged for me by Quilty"; and in *Laughter in the Dark* (1932), "The stage manager whom Rex had in view was an elusive, double, triple, self-reflecting Proteus." Nabokov the protean impersonator is always a masked presence in his fiction: as impresario, scenarist, director, warden, dictator, landlord, and even as bit player (the seventh Hunter in Quilty's play within *Lolita*, a Young Poet who insists that everything in the play is his invention)—to name only a few of the disguises he has donned as a secret agent who moves among his own creations like Prospero in *The Tempest*. Shakespeare is very much an ancestor (he and Nabokov even share a birthday), and the creaking, splintering noise made by the stage setting as it disintegrates at the end of *Invitation to a Beheading* is Nabokov's version of the snapping of Prospero's wand and his speech to the players ("Our revels now are ended. These our actors, /As I foretold you, were all spirits and /Are melted into air, into thin air"; IV. i).

[1] J. L. Borges, "Partial Magic in the *Quixote*," in *Labyrinths* (New York, 1964), p. 196.

[xxx]

AUTHORIAL VOICE. All the involuted effects spiral into the authorial voice—"an anthropomorphic deity impersonated by me," Nabokov calls it—which intrudes continually in all of his novels after *Despair*, most strikingly at the end, when it completely takes over the book (*Lolita* is a notable exception). It is this "deity" who is responsible for everything: who begins a narrative only to stop and retell the passage differently; halts a scene to "rerun" it on the chapter's screen, or turns a reversed lantern slide around to project it properly; intrudes to give stage directions, to compliment or exhort the actors, to have a prop moved; who reveals that the characters have "cotton-padded bodies" and are the author's puppets, that all is a fiction; and who widens the "gaps" and "holes" in the narrative until it breaks apart at "the end," when the vectors are removed, the cast of characters is dismissed, and even the fiction fades away—at most leaving behind an imprint on space in the form of a précis of "an old-fashioned [stage] melodrama" the "deity" may one day write, and which describes (as in the case of *Pale Fire*) the book we've just finished reading.

The vertiginous conclusion of a Nabokov novel calls for a complicated response which many readers, after a lifetime of realistic novels, are incapable of making. Children, however, are aware of other possibilities, as their art reveals. My own children, then three and six years old, reminded me of this two summers ago when they inadvertently demonstrated that, unless they change, they will be among Nabokov's ideal readers. One afternoon my wife and I built them a puppet theater. After propping the theater on the top edge of the living room couch, I crouched down behind it and began manipulating the two hand puppets in the stage above me. The couch and the theater's scenery provided good cover, enabling me to peer over the edge and watch the children immediately become engrossed in the show, and then virtually mesmerized by my improvised little story that ended with a patient father spanking an impossible child. But the puppeteer, carried away by his story's violent climax, knocked over the entire theater, which clattered onto the floor, collapsing into a heap of cardboard, wood, and cloth—leaving me crouched, peeking out at the room, my head now visible over the couch's rim, my puppeted hands, with their naked wrists, poised in mid-air. For several moments my children remained in their open-mouthed trance, still in the story, staring at the space where the theater had been, not seeing me at all. Then they did the kind of double take that a comedian might take a lifetime to perfect, and began to laugh uncontrollably, in a way I had never seen before—and not so much at my clumsiness, which was nothing new, but rather at those moments of total involvement in a nonexistent world, and at what its collapse implied to them about the authenticity of the larger world, and about their daily efforts to order it and their own fabricated illusions. They were laughing, too, over their sense of what the vigorous performance had meant to me; but they saw how easily they could be tricked and their trust belied, and the shrillness of their laughter finally suggested that they recognized the frightening implications of what had happened, and that only laughter could steel them in their new awareness.

When in 1966 I visited Vladimir Nabokov for four days in Montreux, to interview him for *Wisconsin Studies* and in regard to my critical study of his work, I told him about this incident, and how for me it defined literary involution and the response which he hoped to elicit from his readers at "the end" of a novel. "Exactly, exactly," he said as I finished. "You must put that in your book."

In parodying the reader's complete, self-indulgent identification with a character, which in its mindlessness limits consciousness, Nabokov is able to create the detachment necessary for a multiform, spatial view of his novels. The "two plots" in Nabokov's puppet show are thus made plainly visible as a description of the total design of his work, which reveals that in novel after novel his characters try to escape from Nabokov's prison of mirrors, struggling toward a self-awareness that only their creator has achieved by creating them—an involuted process which connects Nabokov's art with his life, and clearly indicates that the author himself is not in this prison. He is its creator, and is *above* it, in control of a book, as in one of those Saul Steinberg drawings (greatly admired by Nabokov) that show a man drawing the very line that gives him "life," in the fullest sense. But the process of Nabokov's involution, the global perspective which he invites us to share with him, is best described in *Speak, Memory*, Chapter Fifteen, when he comments on the disinclination of

> ... physicists to discuss the outside of the inside, the whereabouts of the curvature; for every dimension presupposes a medium within which it can act, and if, in the spiral unwinding of things, space warps into something akin to time, and time, in its turn, warps into something akin to thought, then, surely, another dimension follows—a special Space maybe, not the old one, we trust, unless spirals become vicious circles again.

The ultimate detachment of an "outside" view of a novel inspires our wonder and enlarges our potential for compassion because, "in the spiral unwinding of things," such compassion is extended to include the mind of an author whose deeply humanistic art affirms man's ability to confront and order chaos.

2. *BACKGROUNDS OF* LOLITA

Critics too often treat Nabokov's twelfth novel as a special case quite apart from the rest of his work, when actually it concerns, profoundly and in their darkest and yet most comic form, the themes which have always occupied him. Although *Lolita* may still be a shocking novel to several aging non-readers, the exact circumstances of its troubled publication and reception may not be familiar to younger readers. After four American publishers refused it, Madame Ergaz, of Bureau Littéraire Clairouin, Paris, submitted *Lolita* to Maurice Girodias' Olympia Press in Paris.[1] Although Girodias must be credited with the publication of several estimable if controversial works by writers such as Jean Genet, his main fare was the infamous Travellers Companion series, the green-backed books once so familiar and dear to the eagle-eyed inspectors of the U.S. Customs. But Nabokov did not know this and, because of one of Girodias' previous publishing ventures, the "Editions du Chêne," thought him a publisher of "fine editions." Cast in two

[1] See Nabokov's article *"Lolita* and Mr. Girodias," *Evergreen Review*, XI (February 1967), 37–41.

volumes and bound in the requisite green, *Lolita* was quietly published in Paris in September 1955.

Because it seemed to confirm the judgment of those nervous American publishers, the Girodias imprimatur became one more obstacle for *Lolita* to overcome, though the problem of its alleged pornography indeed seems remote today, and was definitively settled in France not long after its publication. I was Nabokov's student at Cornell in 1953–1954, at a time when most undergraduates did not know he was a writer. Drafted into the army a year later, I was sent overseas to France. On my first pass to Paris I naturally went browsing in a Left Bank bookstore. An array of Olympia Press books, daringly displayed above the counter, seemed most inviting—and there, between copies of *Until She Screams* and *The Sexual Life of Robinson Crusoe*, I found *Lolita*. Although I thought I knew all of Nabokov's works in English (and had searched through out-of-print stores to buy each of them), this title was new to me; and its context and format were more than surprising, even if in those innocent pre–Grove Press days the semi-literate wags on fraternity row had dubbed Nabokov's Literature 311–312 lecture course "Dirty Lit" because of such readings as *Ulysses* and *Madame Bovary* (the keenest campus wits invariably dropped the *B* when mentioning the latter). I brought *Lolita* back to my base, which was situated out in the woods. Passes were hard to get and new Olympia titles were always in demand in the barracks. The appearance of a new girl in town thus caused a minor clamor. "Hey, lemme read your dirty book, man!" insisted "Stockade Clyde" Carr, who had justly earned his sobriquet, and to whose request I acceded at once. "Read it aloud, Stockade," someone called, and skipping the Foreword, Stockade Clyde began to make his remedial way through the opening paragraph. " 'Lo ... lita, light ... of my life, fire of my ... loins. My sin, my soul ... Lo-lee-ta: The ... tip of the ... tongue ... taking ... a trip ...' —*Damn!*" yelled Stockade, throwing the book against the wall. "*It's God-damn Litachure!!*" Thus the Instant Pornography Test, known in psychological-testing circles as the "IPT." Although infallible, it has never to my knowledge been used in any court case.

At a double remove from the usual review media, *Lolita* went generally unnoticed during its first six months. But in the winter of 1956 Graham Greene in England recommended *Lolita* as one of the best books of 1955, incurring the immediate wrath of a columnist in the *Sunday Express*, which moved Greene to respond in *The Spectator*. Under the heading of "Albion" (suggesting a quaint tempest in an old teapot), *The New York Times Book Review* of February 26, 1956, alluded briefly to this exchange, calling *Lolita* "a long French novel" and not mentioning Nabokov by name. Two weeks later, noting "that our mention of it created a flurry of mail," *The Times* devoted two-thirds of a column to the subject, quoting Greene at some length. Thus began the underground existence of *Lolita*, which became public in the summer of 1957 when the *Anchor Review* in New York devoted 112 of its pages to Nabokov. Included were an excellent introduction by F. W. Dupee, a long excerpt from the novel, and Nabokov's Afterword, "On a Book Entitled *Lolita*." When Putnam's brought out the American edition in 1958 they were able to dignify their full-page advertisements with an array of statements by respectable and even distinguished literary names, though *Lolita*'s fast climb to the top of the best-seller list was not exclusively the result of their endorsements or the novel's artistry. "Hurricane / Lolita swept from Florida to Maine" (to quote John Shade in *Pale Fire* [l. 680]), also creating storms in England and Italy, and in France, where it was banned on three separate occasions. Although it never ran afoul of the law in this country, there were predictably some outraged protests, including an editorial in *The New Republic;* but, since these at best belong to social rather than literary history, they need not be detailed here, with one exception. Orville Prescott's review in the daily *New York Times* of August 18, 1958, has a charm that should be preserved: " 'Lolita,' then, is undeniably news in the world of books. Unfortunately, it is bad news. There are two equally serious reasons why it isn't worth any adult reader's attention. The first is that it is dull, dull, dull in a pretentious, florid and archly fatuous fashion. The second is that it is repulsive." [1] Pres-

---

[1] In a manner similar to Joyce's, Nabokov four years later paid his respects to Prescott, though not by name, by having the assassin Gradus carefully read *The New York Times:* "A hack reviewer of new books for tourists, reviewing his

cott's remarks complement those of an anonymous reviewer in *The Southern Quarterly Review* (January 1852), who found an earlier, somewhat different treatment of the quest theme no less intolerable: "The book is sad stuff, dull and dreary, or ridiculous. Mr. Melville's Quakers are the wretchedest dolts and drivellers, and his Mad Captain, who pursues his personal revenges against the fish who has taken off his leg, at the expense of ship, crew and owners, is a monstrous bore. . . ."

Not surprisingly, Humbert Humbert's obsession has moved commentators to search for equivalent situations in Nabokov's earlier work, and they have not been disappointed. In *The Gift* (written between 1935 and 1937), some manuscript pages on the desk of the young poet Fyodor move a character to say:

> "Ah, if only I had a tick or two, what a novel I'd whip off! From real life. Imagine this kind of thing: an old dog—but still in his prime, fiery, thirsting for happiness—gets to know a widow, and she has a daughter, still quite a little girl—you know what I mean —when nothing is formed yet but already she has a way of walking that drives you out of your mind—A slip of a girl, very fair, pale, with blue under the eyes—and of course she doesn't even look at the old goat. What to do? Well, not long thinking, he ups and marries the widow. Okay. They settle down the three of them. Here you can go on indefinitely—the temptation, the eternal torment, the itch, the mad hopes. And the upshot—a miscalculation. Time flies, he gets older, she blossoms out—and not a sausage. Just walks by and scorches you with a look of contempt. Eh? D'you feel here a kind of Dostoevskian tragedy? That story, you see, happened to a great friend of mine, once upon a time in fairyland when Old King Cole was a merry old soul. . . ." (pp. 198–199)

Although the passage [1] seems to anticipate *Lolita* ("It's queer, I seem to remember my future works," says Fyodor [p. 206]), *Laughter in the Dark* (1932) is mentioned most often in this regard, since Albinus Kretschmar sacrifices everything, including his eyesight,

---

own tour through Norway, said that the fjords were too famous to need (his) description, and that all Scandinavians loved flowers" (*Pale Fire*, p. 275). This was actually culled from the newspaper.

[1] Also pointed out by Andrew Field, in *Nabokov: His Life in Art* (Boston, 1967), p. 325, and Carl R. Proffer, *Keys to Lolita* (Bloomington, 1968), p. 3.

for a girl, and loses her to a hack artist, Axel Rex. "Yes," agrees Nabokov, "some affinities between Rex and Quilty exist, as they do between Margot and Lo. Actually, of course, Margot was a common young whore, not an unfortunate little Lolita [and, technically speaking, no nymphet at all—A.A.]. Anyway I do not think that those recurrent sexual oddities and morbidities are of much interest or importance. My Lolita has been compared to Emmie in *Invitation*, to Mariette in *Bend Sinister*, and even Colette in *Speak, Memory*...." (*Wisconsin Studies* interview, see Bibliography). Nabokov is justly impatient with those who hunt for Ur-Lolitas, for a preoccupation with specific "sexual morbidities" obscures the more general context in which these oddities should be seen, and his Afterword offers an urgent corrective. The reader of this Introduction should turn to that Afterword, "On a Book Entitled *Lolita*," but not before placing a bookmark here, one substantial enough to remind him to return—a brightly colored piece of clothing would be suitable (the Notes to page 318 are particularly recommended). Now please turn to page 313. ☞

Having just completed the Afterword, the serious reader is familiar with Nabokov's account of *Lolita*'s origins. That "initial shiver of inspiration" resulted in a short story, "The Magician" ("Volshebnik"), written in Russian in 1939, but never published. Nabokov excerpted two passages for Andrew Field's critical study.[1] In the first, the magician sees the young girl for the first time in the Tuileries Gardens:

> A girl of twelve (he determined age with an unerring eye), dressed in a violet frock, was moving step by step her roller skates, which did not work on the gravel—lifting each in turn and bringing it down with a crunch—as she advanced at a kind of Japanese tread, through the striped rapture of the sun, toward his bench. Later (as long as that "later" endured) it would seem to him that right then, at one glance he had taken her measure from head to foot: the animation of her reddish-brown curls which had been recently trimmed, the lightness of her large vacant eyes which somehow brought to mind a semi-translucent gooseberry, the gay warm color of her face, her pink mouth, just barely open so that her two large front teeth were resting

[1] Quoted by Field, *op. cit.*, pp. 328–329.

lightly on the cushion of her lower lip, the summer tan of her bare arms with sleek fox-like little hairs running along the forearms, the vague tenderness of her still narrow but already not at all flat chest, the movement of the folds in her skirt, their short sweep and light fall back into place, the slenderness and glow of her careless legs, the sturdy straps of her roller skates. She stopped in front of the amiable woman sitting beside him who, turning to rummage in something which she had by her right hand side, found and held out to the little girl a piece of chocolate on a piece of bread. Chewing rapidly, she undid the straps with her free hand, shook off all the heaviness of steel soles on solid wheels —and, descending to us on earth, having straightened up with a sudden sensation of heavenly nakedness which took a moment to grow aware of being shaped by shoes and socks, she rushed off.

According to Field, Arthur makes no sexual advances until almost the final page, soon after the girl's mother has died:

"Is this where I sleep?" the little girl asked indifferently, and when, struggling with the shutters so as to further close the slits between them, he answered, yes, she looked at her cap which she was holding in her hand and limply tossed it onto the broad bed.

"Well," he said after the old porter who had lugged in their suitcases had left, and there remained only the beating of his heart and the distant shiver of the night, "Well ... Now to bed."

Unsteady in her drowsiness, she stumbled against the edge of the armchair, and, then, simultaneously sitting down, he drew her to him by encircling her hip; she, arching her body, grew up like an angel, strained all her muscles for a moment, took still another half-step, and then lightly sank down in his lap. "My darling, my poor little girl," he murmured in a sort of general mist of pity, tenderness, and desire, observing her sleepiness, fuzziness, her wan smile, fondling her through her dark dress, feeling the stripe of the orphan's garter through its thin wool, thinking about her defenselessness, her state of abandonment, her warmth, enjoying the animated weight of her legs which sprawled loose and then again, with an ever so light bodily rustle, hunched themselves up higher —and she slowly wound one dreamy tight-sleeved arm around the back of his neck, immersing him in the chestnut odor of her soft hair.

But Arthur fails as both a magician and lover, and soon afterwards dies in a manner which Nabokov will transfer to Charlotte Haze. While the scene clearly foreshadows the first night at The Enchanted Hunters hotel, its straightforward action and solemn tone are quite different, and it compresses into a few paragraphs what will later occupy almost two chapters (pp. 121–135). Arthur's enjoyment of the girl's "animated weight" suggests the considerably more combustible lap scene in *Lolita* (pp. 60–63), perhaps the most erotic interlude in the novel—but it only *suggests* it. Aside from such echoes, one must assume, on the evidence of these two long passages, that little beyond the basic idea of the tale subsists in *Lolita;* and the telling is quite literally a world apart.

"The Magician" went unpublished not because of the forbidding subject matter, but rather, says Nabokov, because the girl possessed little "semblance of reality." [1] In 1949, after moving from Wellesley to Cornell, he became involved in a "new treatment of the theme, this time in English." Although *Lolita* "developed slowly," taking five years to complete, Nabokov had everything in mind quite early. As is customary with him, however, he did not write it in exact chronological sequence. Humbert's confessional diary was composed at the outset of this "new treatment," followed by Humbert and Lolita's first journey westward, and the climactic scene in which Quilty is killed ("His death had to be clear in my mind in order to control his earlier appearances," says Nabokov). Nabokov next filled in the gaps of Humbert's early life, and then proceeded ahead with the rest of the action, more or less in chronological order. Humbert's final interview with Lolita was composed at the very end, in 1954, followed only by John Ray's Foreword.

Especially new in this treatment was the shift from the third person to the first person, which created—obviously—the always formidable narrative problem of having an obsessed and even mad character meaningfully relate his own experience, a problem compounded in this specific instance by the understandable element of

[1] One should remember that the story would have been read by a Russian émigré audience, notes Andrew Field. Strongly erotic (as opposed to pornographic) themes have been used "seriously" far more frequently by Russian writers than by their English and American counterparts. Field points to Dostoevsky (the suppressed chapter of *The Possessed*), Leskov, Sologub, Kuzmin, Rozanov, Kuprin, Pilnyak, Babel, and Bunin (*ibid.*, p. 332). Field also summarizes the plots of two early, untranslated Nabokov stories which treat sexual themes, "A Fairytale" (1926) and "A Dashing Fellow" (c. 1936); (*ibid.*, pp. 333–334).

self-justification which his perversion would necessarily occasion, and by the fact that Humbert is a dying man. One wonders whether Thomas Mann would have been able to make *Death in Venice* an allegory about art and the artist if Aschenbach had been its narrator. While many of Nabokov's other principal characters are victims (Luzhin, Pnin, Albinus), none of them tells his own story; and it is only Humbert who is both victim and victimizer, thus making him unique among Nabokov's first-person narrators (discounting Hermann, the mad and murderous narrator of *Despair*, who is too patently criminal to qualify properly as victim). By having Humbert tell the tale, Nabokov created for himself the kind of challenge best described in Chapter Fourteen of *Speak, Memory* when, in a passage written concurrently with the early stages of *Lolita*, he compares the composition of a chess problem to "the writing of one of those incredible novels where the author, in a fit of lucid madness, has set himself certain unique rules that he observes, certain nightmare obstacles that he surmounts, with the zest of a deity building a live world from the most unlikely ingredients—rocks, and carbon, and blind throbbings." [1]

In addition to such obstacles, the novel also developed slowly because of an abundance of materials as unfamiliar as they were unlikely. It had been difficult enough to "invent Russia and Western Europe," let alone America, and at the age of fifty Nabokov now had to set about obtaining "such local ingredients as would allow me to inject a modicum of average 'reality' (one of the few words which mean nothing without quotes) into the brew of individual fancy." "What was most difficult," he recently told an interviewer, "was putting myself ... I am a normal man, you see." [2] Research was thus called for, and in scholarly fashion Nabokov followed newspaper stories involving pedophilia (incorporating some into the novel), read case studies, and, like Margaret Mead coming home to roost, even did research in the field: "I travelled in school buses to listen to the talk of schoolgirls. I went to school on the

[1] And speaking specifically of the writing of *Lolita*, he says, "She was like the composition of a beautiful puzzle—its composition and its solution at the same time, since one is a mirror view of the other, depending on the way you look."
[2] Penelope Gilliatt, "Nabokov," *Vogue*, No. 2170 (December 1966), p. 280.

pretext of placing our daughter. We have no daughter. For Lolita, I took one arm of a little girl who used to come to see Dmitri [his son], one kneecap of another," [1] and thus a nymphet was born.

Perspicacious "research" aside, it was a remarkable imaginative feat for a European émigré to have re-created America so brilliantly, and in so doing to have become an American writer. Of course, those critics and readers who marvel at Nabokov's accomplishment may not realize that he physically knows America better than most of them. As he says in *Speak, Memory*, his adventures as a "lepist" carried him through two hundred motel rooms in forty-six states, that is, along all the roads traveled by Humbert and Lolita. Yet of all of Nabokov's novels, *Lolita* is the most unlikely one for him to have written, given his background and the rarefied nature of his art and avocations. "It was hardly foreseeable," writes Anthony Burgess, "that so exquisite and scholarly an artist should become America's greatest literary glory, but now it seems wholly just and inevitable." [2] It was even less foreseeable that Nabokov would realize better than any contemporary the hopes expressed by Constance Rourke in *American Humor* (1931) for a literature that would achieve an instinctive alliance between native materials and old world traditions, though the literal alliance in *Lolita* is perhaps more intimate than even Miss Rourke might have wished. But to know Nabokov at all personally is first to be impressed by his intense and immense curiosity, his uninhibited and imaginative response to everything around him. To paraphrase Henry James's famous definition of the artist, Nabokov is truly a man on whom nothing is lost—except that in Nabokov's instance it is *true*, whereas James and many American literary intellectuals after him have been so self-conscious in their mandarin "seriousness" and consequently so narrow in the range of their responses that they have often overlooked the sometimes extraordinarily uncommon qualities of the commonplace.

Nabokov's responsiveness is characterized for me by the last evening of my first visit to Montreux in September 1966. During my

---

[1] *Ibid.*
[2] Anthony Burgess, "Poet and Pedant," *The Spectator*, March 24, 1967, p. 336. Reprinted in *Urgent Copy* (New York, 1969).

two hours of conversation with the Nabokovs in their suite after dinner, Nabokov tried to imagine what the history of painting might have been like if photography had been invented in the Middle Ages; spoke about science fiction; asked me if I had noticed what was happening in *Li'l Abner* and then compared it, in learned fashion, with an analogous episode of a dozen years back; noted that a deodorant stick had been found among the many days' siege provisions which the Texas sniper had with him on the tower; discoursed on a monstrous howler in the translation of Bely's *St. Petersburg;* showed me a beautifully illustrated book on hummingbirds, and then discussed the birdlife of Lake Geneva; talked admiringly and often wittily of the work of Borges, Updike, Salinger, Genet, Andrei Sinyavsky ("Abram Tertz"), Burgess, and Graham Greene, always making precise critical discriminations; recalled his experiences in Hollywood while working on the screenplay of *Lolita,* and his having met Marilyn Monroe at a party ("A delightful actress. Delightful," he said. "Which is your favorite Monroe film?"); talked of the Soviet writers he admired, summarizing their stratagems for survival; and defined for me exactly what kind of beetle Kafka's Gregor Samsa was in *The Metamorphosis* ("It was a domed beetle, a scarab beetle with wing-sheaths, and neither Gregor nor his maker realized that when the room was being made by the maid, and the window was open, he could have flown out and escaped and joined the other happy dung beetles rolling the dung balls on rural paths"). And did I know how a dung beetle laid its eggs? Since I did not, Nabokov rose and imitated the process, bending his head toward his waist as he walked slowly across the room, making a dung-rolling motion with his hands until his head was buried in them and the eggs were laid. When Lenny Bruce's name somehow came up, both Nabokov and his wife commented on how sad they had been to hear of Bruce's death; he had been a favorite of theirs. But they disagreed about where it was that they had last seen Bruce; Mrs. Nabokov thought it had been on Jack Paar's television show, while her husband—the scientist, linguist, and author of fifteen novels, who has written and published in three languages, and whose vast erudition is most clearly evidenced by the four-volume translation of Pushkin's *Eu-*

gene Onegin, with its two volumes of annotations and one-hundred-page "Note on Prosody"—held out for the Ed Sullivan show.

Not only is nothing lost on Nabokov, but, like the title character in Borges's story "Funes the Memorious," he seems to remember everything. At dinner the first evening of my 1966 visit, we reminisced about Cornell and his courses there, which were extraordinary and thoroughly Nabokovian, even in the smallest ways (witness the "bonus system" employed in examinations, allowing students two extra points per effort whenever they could garnish an answer with a substantial and accurate quotation ["a gem"] drawn from the text in question). Skeptically enough, I asked Nabokov if he remembered my wife, Nina, who had taken his Literature 312 course in 1955, and I mentioned that she had received a grade of 96. Indeed he did, since he had always asked to meet the students who performed well, and he described her accurately (seeing her in person in 1968, he remembered where she had sat in the lecture hall). On the night of my departure I asked Nabokov to inscribe my Olympia Press first edition of *Lolita.* With great rapidity he not only signed and dated it, but added two elegant drawings of recently discovered butterflies, one identified as *"Flammea palida"* ("Pale Fire") and, below it, a considerably smaller species, labeled "Bonus bonus." [1] Delighted but in part mystified, I inquired, "Why 'Bonus bonus'?" Wrinkling his brow and peering over his eyeglasses, a parody of a professor, Nabokov replied in a mock-stentorian voice, "Now your wife has 100!" After four days and some twelve hours of conversation, and within an instant of my seemingly unrelated request, my prideful but passing comment had come leaping out of storage. So too has Nabokov's memory been able to draw on a lifetime of reading—a lifetime in the most literal sense.

When asked what he had read as a boy, Nabokov replied: "Between the ages of ten and fifteen in St. Petersburg, I must have read more fiction and poetry—English, Russian, and French—than in any other five-year period of my life. I relished especially the works of Wells, Poe, Browning, Keats, Flaubert, Verlaine, Rim-

[1] A photograph of these drawings appears in *Time,* May 23, 1969, p. 83.

baud, Chekhov, Tolstoy, and Alexander Blok. On another level, my heroes were the Scarlet Pimpernel, Phileas Fogg, and Sherlock Holmes. In other words, I was a perfectly normal trilingual child in a family with a large library. At a later period, in Cambridge, England, between the ages of twenty and twenty-three, my favorites were Housman, Rupert Brooke, Joyce, Proust, and Pushkin. Of these top favorites, several—Poe, Verlaine, Jules Verne, Emmuska Orczy, Conan Doyle, and Rupert Brooke—have faded away, have lost the glamour and thrill they held for me. The others remain intact and by now are probably beyond change as far as I am concerned" (*Playboy* interview). The Notes to this edition will demonstrate that Nabokov has managed to invoke in his fiction the most distant of enthusiasms: a detective story read in early youth, a line from Verlaine, a tennis match seen at Wimbledon forty years before. All are clear in his mind, and, recorded in *Lolita*, memory negates time.

When queried about Nabokov, friends and former colleagues at Cornell invariably comment on the seemingly paradoxical manner in which the encyclopedic Nabokov mind could be enthralled by the trivial as well as the serious. One professor, at least twenty years Nabokov's junior and an instructor when he was there, remembers how Nabokov once asked him if he had ever watched a certain soap opera on television. Soap operas are of course ultimately comic if not fantastic in the way they characterize the life of the typical middle-class housewife as an uninterrupted series of crises and disasters; but missing the point altogether, suspecting a deadly leg-pull and supposing that with either answer he would lose (one making him a fool, the other a snob), Nabokov's young colleague had been reduced to a fit of wordless throat-clearing. Recalling it ten years later, he seemed disarmed all over again. On easier terms with Nabokov was Professor M. H. Abrams, who warmly recalls how Nabokov came into a living room where a faculty child was absorbed in a television western. Immediately engaged by the program, Nabokov was soon quaking with laughter over the furiously climactic fight scene. Just such idle moments, if not literally this one, inform the hilarious burlesque of the comparable "obligatory scene" in *Lolita*, the tussle of Humbert and

Quilty which leaves them "panting as the cowman and the sheep-man never do after their battle" (p. 301).

Even though he had academic tenure at Cornell, the Nabokovs never owned a house, and instead always rented, moving from year to year, a mobility he bestowed on refugee Humbert. "The main reason [for never settling anywhere permanently], the background reason, is, I suppose, that nothing short of a replica of my childhood surroundings would˙ have satisfied me," says Nabokov. "I would never manage to match my memories correctly—so why trouble with hopeless approximations? Then there are some special considerations: for instance, the question of impetus, the habit of impetus. I propelled myself out of Russia so vigorously, with such indignant force, that I have been rolling on and on ever since. True, I have lived to become that appetizing thing, a 'full professor,' but at heart I have always remained a lean 'visiting lecturer.' The few times I said to myself anywhere: 'Now that's a nice spot for a permanent home,' I would immediately hear in my mind the thunder of an avalanche carrying away the hundreds of far places which I would destroy by the very act of settling in one particular nook of the earth. And finally, I don't much care for furniture, for tables and chairs and lamps and rugs and things—perhaps because in my opulent childhood I was taught to regard with amused contempt any too-earnest attachment to material wealth, which is why I felt no regret and no bitterness when the Revolution abolished that wealth" (*Playboy* interview).

Professor Morris Bishop, Nabokov's best friend at Cornell, who was responsible for his shift from Wellesley to Ithaca, recalls visiting the Nabokovs just after they had moved into the appallingly vulgar and garish home of an absented professor of Agriculture. "I couldn't have lived in a place like that," says Bishop, "but it delighted him. He seemed to relish every awful detail." Although Bishop didn't realize it then, Nabokov was learning about Charlotte Haze by renting her house, so to speak, by reading her books and living with her pictures and "wooden thingamabob[s] of commercial Mexican origin." These annual moves, however dismal their circumstances, constituted a field trip enabling entomologist Nabokov to study the natural habitat of Humbert's prey. Bishop also remembers that Nabokov read the New York *Daily News* for its crime stories,[1] and, for an even more concentrated dose of bizarrerie, Father Divine's newspaper, *New Day*—all of which should recall James Joyce, with whom Nabokov has so much else in common. Joyce regularly read *The Police Gazette*, the shoddy magazine *Tit-bits* (as does Bloom), and all the Dublin newspapers; attended burlesque shows, knew by heart most of the vulgar and comically obscene songs of the day, and was almost as familiar with the work of the execrable lady lending-library novelists of the *fin de siècle* as he was with the classics; and when he was living in Trieste and Paris and writing *Ulysses*, relied on his Aunt Josephine to keep him supplied with the necessary sub-literary materials. Of course, Joyce's art depends far more than Nabokov's on the vast residue of erudition and trivia which Joyce's insatiable and equally encyclopedic mind was able to store.

Nabokov is very selective, whereas Joyce collected almost at random and then ordered in art the flotsam and jetsam of everyday life. That Nabokov does not equal the older writer in this respect surely points to a conscious choice on Nabokov's part, as his Cornell lectures on *Ulysses* suggest.[2] In singling out the flaws in what is to him the greatest novel of the century, Nabokov stressed the "needless obscurities baffling to the less-than-brilliant reader," such as "local idiosyncrasies" and "untraceable references." Yet Nabokov has also practiced the art of assemblage, incorporating in the rich textures of *Bend Sinister*, *Lolita*, *Pale Fire*, and *Ada* a most "Joycean" profusion of rags, tags, and oddments, both high and low, culled from books or drawn from "real life." Whatever the respective scales of their efforts in this direction, Nabokov and Joyce are (with Queneau and Borges) among the few modern fiction writers who have made aesthetic capital out of their learning.

[1] In *Pale Fire*, Charles Kinbote spies John Shade seated in his car, "reading a tabloid newspaper which I had thought no poet would deign to touch" (p. 22).
[2] The course in question is Literature 311–312, "Masterpieces of European Fiction," MWF, 12 (first term: Jane Austen's *Mansfield Park*, Gogol's *Dead Souls*, Dickens' *Bleak House*, Flaubert's *Madame Bovary*, and Tolstoy's *The Death of Ivan Ilyich;* second term: Tolstoy's *Anna Karenina*, Stevenson's *Dr. Jekyll and Mr. Hyde*, Gogol's *The Overcoat*, Kafka's *The Metamorphosis*, Proust's *Swann's Way*, and *Ulysses*, in that order). The quotations are from the annotator's class notes of 1953–1954.

[xlvi]

Both include in their novels the compendious stuff one associates with the bedside library, the great literary anatomies such as Burton's *Anatomy of Melancholy* or Dr. Johnson's *Dictionary*, or those unclassifiable masterpieces such as *Moby-Dick, Tristram Shandy,* and *Gargantua and Pantagruel*, in which the writer makes fictive use of all kinds of learning, and exercises the anatomist's penchant for collage effected out of verbal trash and bizarre juxtapositions—for the digression, the catalogue, the puzzle, pun, and parody, the gratuitous bit of lore included for the pleasure it can evoke, and for the quirky detail that does not contribute to the book's verisimilar design but nevertheless communicates vividly a sense of what it was like to be alive at a given moment in time. A hostile review of Nabokov's *Eugene Onegin* offered as typical of the Commentary's absurdities its mention of the fact that France exported to Russia some 150,000 bottles of champagne per annum; but the detail happens to telescope brilliantly the Francophilia of early nineteenth-century Russia, and is an excellent example of the anatomist's imaginative absorption of significant trivia and a justification of his methods. M. H. Abrams recalls how early one Monday morning he met Nabokov entering the Cornell Library, staggering beneath a run of *The Edinburgh Review*, which Nabokov had pored over all weekend in Pushkin's behalf. "Marvelous ads!" explained Nabokov, "simply marvelous!" It was this spirit that enabled Nabokov to create in the two volumes of *Onegin* Commentary a marvelous literary anatomy in the tradition of Johnson, Sterne, and Joyce—an insomniac's delight, a monumental, wildly inclusive, yet somehow elegantly ordered ragbag of humane discourse, in its own right a transcending work of imagination.

Nabokov was making expressive use of unlikely bits and pieces in his novels as early as *The Defense* (1930), as when Luzhin's means of suicide is suggested by a movie still, lying on The Veritas film company's display table, showing "a white-faced man with his lifeless features and big American glasses, hanging by his hands from the ledge of a skyscraper—just about to fall off into the abyss"—a famous scene from Harold Lloyd's 1923 silent film, *Safety Last*. Although present throughout his work of the 'thirties, and culminating logically in *The Gift*, his last novel in Russian,

Nabokov's penchant for literary anatomy was not fully realized until after he had been exposed to the polar extremes of American culture and American university libraries. Thus the richly variegated but sometimes crowded texture of *Bend Sinister* (1947), Nabokov's first truly "American" novel,[1] looks forward to *Lolita*, his next novel. *Bend Sinister*'s literary pastiche is by turns broad and hermetic. Titles by Remarque and Sholokov are combined to produce *All Quiet on the Don*, and Chapter Twelve offers this "famous American poem":

> A curious sight—these bashful bears,
> These timid warrior whalemen
>
> And now the time of tide has come;
> The ship casts off her cables
>
> It is not shown on any map;
> True places never are
>
> This lovely light, it lights not me;
> All loveliness is anguish—

No poem at all, it is formed, says Nabokov, by random "iambic incidents culled from the prose of *Moby-Dick*." Such effects receive their fullest orchestration in *Lolita*, as the Notes to this volume will suggest.

If the *Onegin* Commentary (1964) is the culmination, then *Lolita* represents the apogee in fiction of Nabokov's proclivities as anatomist, and as such is a further reminder that the novel extends and develops themes and methods present in his work all along. Ranging from Dante to *Dick Tracy*, the allusions, puns, parodies, and pastiches in *Lolita* are controlled with a mastery unequaled by any writer since Joyce (who died in 1941). Readers should not be disarmed by the presence of so many kinds of "real" materials in a novel by a writer who believes so passionately in the primacy of the imagination; as Kinbote says in *Pale Fire*, " 'reality' is neither the subject nor the object of true art which creates its own special

[1] Although published in New York in 1941, a year after Nabokov's emigration, *The Real Life of Sebastian Knight* was in fact written in Paris in 1938 (in English). Students of chronology should also note that *Lolita* precedes *Pnin* (1957). The date of the former's American publication (1958) has proved misleading.

reality having nothing to do with the average 'reality' perceived by the communal eye" (p. 130).

By his example, Nabokov has reminded younger American writers of the fictional nature of reality. When Terry Southern in *The Magic Christian* (1960) lampoons the myth of American masculinity and its attendant deification of the athlete by having his multimillionaire trickster, Guy Grand, fix the heavyweight championship fight so that the boxers grotesquely enact in the ring a prancing and mincing charade of homosexuality, causing considerable psychic injury to the audience, his art, such as it is, is quite late in imitating life. A famous athlete of the 'twenties was well-known as an invert, and Humbert mentions him twice, never by his real name, though he does call him "Ned Litam" (p. 234)—a simple anagram of "Ma Tilden"—which turns out to be one of the actual pseudonyms chosen by Tilden himself, under which he wrote stories and articles. Like the literary anatomists who have preceded him, Nabokov knows that what is so extraordinary about "reality" is that too often even the blackest of imaginations could not have invented it; and by taking advantage of this fact in *Lolita* he has, along with Nathanael West, defined with absolute authority the inevitable mode, the dominant dark tonalities—if not the contents—of the American comic novel.

Although Humbert clearly delights in many of the absurdities around him, the anatomist's characteristic vivacity is gone from the pages which concern Charlotte Haze, and not only because she is repugnant to Humbert in terms of the "plot," but rather because to Nabokov she is the definitive artsy-craftsy suburban lady—the culture-vulture, that travesty of Woman, Love, and Sexuality. In short, she is the essence of American *poshlust*, to use the "one pitiless [Russian] word" which, writes Nabokov in *Gogol*, is able to express "the idea of a certain widespread defect for which the other three European languages I happen to know possess no special term." *Poshlust*: "the sound of the 'o' is as big as the plop of an elephant falling into a muddy pond and as round as the bosom of a bathing beauty on a German picture postcard" (p. 63). More precisely, it "is not only the obviously trashy but also the falsely important, the falsely beautiful, the falsely clever, the falsely attractive" (p. 70).[1] It is an amalgam of pretentiousness and philistine vulgarity. In the spirit of Mark Twain describing the contents of the Grangerford household in *Huckleberry Finn* (earlier American *poshlust*), Humbert eviscerates the muddlecrass (to wax Joycean) world of Charlotte and her friends, reminding us that Humbert's long view of America is not an altogether genial one.

In the course of showing us our landscape in all its natural beauty, Humbert satirizes American songs, ads, movies, magazines, brand names, tourist attractions, summer camps, Dude Ranches, hotels, and motels, as well as the Good-Housekeeping Syndrome (*Your Home Is You* is one of Charlotte Haze's essential volumes) and the cant of progressive educationists and child-guidance pontificators.[2] Nabokov offers us a grotesque parody of a "good relationship," for Humbert and Lo are "pals" with a vengeance; *Know Your Own Daughter* is one of the books which Humbert consults (the title exists). Yet Humbert's terrible demands notwithstanding, she is as insensitive as children are to their parents; sexuality aside, she demands anxious parental placation in a too typically American way, and, since it is Lolita "to whom ads were dedicated: the ideal consumer, the subject and object of every foul poster" (p. 150), she affords Nabokov an ideal opportunity to comment on the Teen and Sub-teen Tyranny. "Tristram in Movielove," remarks Humbert, and Nabokov has responded to those various travesties of behavior which too many Americans recognize as tenable examples of reality. A gloss on this aspect of *Lolita* is provided by "Ode to a Model," a poem which Nabokov published the same year as the Olympia Press edition of *Lolita* (1955):

> I have followed you, model,
> in magazine ads through all seasons,
> from dead leaf on the sod
> to red leaf on the breeze,

[1] For Nabokov's most recent description of *poshlost* (as he now transliterates it), see his interview, *Paris Review*, No. 41 (Summer-Fall 1967), 103–104.

[2] Satirized too is the romantic myth of the child, extending from Wordsworth to Salinger. "The McCoo girl?" responds Lolita kindly. "Ginny McCoo? Oh, she's a fright. And mean. And lame. Nearly died of polio." If the origin of modern sentimentality about the child's innocence can be dated at 1760, with the publication of *Mother Goose's Melodies*, then surely *Lolita* marks its death in 1955.

[1]

from your lily-white armpit
to the tip of your butterfly eyelash,
charming and pitiful,
silly and stylish.

Or in kneesocks and tartan
standing there like some fabulous symbol,
parted feet pointed outward
—pedal form of akimbo.

On a lawn, in a parody
of Spring and its cherry-tree,
near a vase and a parapet,
virgin practising archery.

Ballerina, black-masked,
near a parapet of alabaster.
"Can one"—somebody asked—
"rhyme 'star' and 'disaster'?"

Can one picture a blackbird
as the negative of a small firebird?
Can a record, run backward,
turn 'repaid' into 'diaper'?

Can one marry a model?
Kill your past, make you real, raise a family,
by removing you bodily
from back numbers of Sham?

Although Nabokov has called attention to the elements of parody
in his work, he has repeatedly denied the relevance of satire. One
can understand why he says, "I have neither the intent nor the temperament of a moral or social satirist" (*Playboy* interview), for
he eschews the overtly moral stance of the satirist who offers
"to mend the world." Humbert's "satires" are too often effected
with an almost loving care. Lolita is indeed an "ideal consumer,"
but she herself is consumed, pitifully, and there is, as Nabokov has
said, "a queer, tender charm about that mythical nymphet." Moreover, since Humbert's desperate tourism is undertaken in order to
distract and amuse Lolita and to outdistance his enemies, real and
imagined, the "invented" American landscape also serves a quite
functional thematic purpose in helping to dramatize Humbert's

total and terrible isolation. Humbert and Lolita, each in his way, are captives of the other, imprisoned together in a succession of bedrooms and cars, but so distant from one another that they can share nothing of what they see—making Humbert seem as alone during the first trip West as he will be on the second, when she has left him and the car is an empty cell.

Nabokov's denials notwithstanding, many of Humbert's observations of American morals and mores *are* satirical, the product of his maker's moral sensibility; but the novel's greatness does not depend on the profundity or extent of its "satire," which is over-emphasized by readers who fail to recognize the extent of the parody, its full implications, or the operative distinction made by Nabokov: "satire is a lesson, parody is a game." Like Joyce, Nabokov has shown how parody may inform a high literary art, and parody figures in the design of each of his novels. *The Eye* parodies the nineteenth-century Romantic tale, such as V. F. Odoevsky's "The Brigadier" (1844), which is narrated by a ghost who has awakened after death to view his old life with new clarity, while *Laughter in the Dark* is a mercilessly cold mocking of the convention of the love triangle; *Despair* is cast as the kind of "cheap mystery" story the narrator's banal wife reads, though it evolves into something quite different; and *The Gift* parodies the major nineteenth-century Russian writers. *Invitation to a Beheading* is cast as a mock anti-utopian novel, as though Zamiatin's *We* (1920) had been re-staged by the Marx Brothers. *Pnin* masquerades as an "academic novel" and turns out to parody the possibility of a novel's having a "reliable" narrator. Pnin's departure at the end mimics Chichikov's orbital exit from *Dead Souls* (1842), just as the last paragraph of *The Gift* conceals a parody of a Pushkin stanza. The texture of Nabokov's parody is unique because, in addition to being a master parodist of literary styles, he is able to make brief references to another writer's themes or devices which are so telling in effect that Nabokov need not burlesque that writer's style. He not only parodies narrative clichés and outworn subject matter, but genres and prototypes of the novel; *Ada* parodically surveys nothing less than the novel's evolution. Because Chapter Four of *The Gift* is a mock literary biography, it anticipates the themes of Nabokov's major achievements, for he is continuously parodying the search for a verifiable truth—the autobiography, the biography, the exegesis, the detective story—and these generic "quests" will coalesce in one work, especially when the entire novel is conceptually a parody, as in *Lolita* and *Pale Fire*.

In form, *Pale Fire* is a grotesque scholarly edition, while *Lolita* is a burlesque of the confessional mode, the literary diary, the Romantic novel that chronicles the effects of a debilitating love, the *Doppelgänger* tale, and, in parts, a Duncan Hines tour of America conducted by a guide with a black imagination, a parodic case study, and, as the narrator of *The Real Life of Sebastian Knight* says of his half brother's first novel, *The Prismatic Bezel*, "It is also a wicked imitation of many other . . . literary habit[s]." Knight's procedures summarize Nabokov's:

> As often was the way with Sebastian Knight he used parody as a kind of springboard for leaping into the highest region of serious emotion. J. L. Coleman has called it "a clown developing wings, an angel mimicking a tumbler pigeon," and the metaphor seems to me very apt. Based cunningly on a parody of certain tricks of the literary trade, *The Prismatic Bezel* soars skyward. With something akin to fanatical hate Sebastian Knight was ever hunting out the things which had once been fresh and bright but which were now worn to a thread, dead things among living ones; dead things shamming life, painted and repainted, continuing to be accepted by lazy minds serenely unaware of the fraud. (p. 91)

"But all this obscure fun is, I repeat, only the author's springboard" (p. 92), says the narrator, whose tone is justifiably insistent, for although Nabokov is a virtuoso of the minor art of literary burlesque, which is at best a kind of literary criticism, he knows that the novelist who uses parody is under an obligation to engage the reader emotionally in a way that Max Beerbohm's *A Christmas Garland* (1912) does not. The description of *The Prismatic Bezel* and the remainder of Chapter Ten in *The Real Life of Sebastian Knight* indicate that Nabokov is fully aware of this necessity, and, like Knight, he has succeeded in making parody a "springboard." There is thus an important paradox implicit in Nabokov's most audacious parodies: *Lolita* makes fun of Dostoevsky's *Notes from*

Underground (1864), but Humbert's pages are indeed notes from underground in their own right, and Clare Quilty is both a parody of the Double as a convention of modern fiction, and a Double who formulates the horror in Humbert's life.

With the possible exception of Joyce, Nabokov is alone among modern writers in his ability to make parody and pathos converge and sometimes coincide. Joyce comes closest to this in *Ulysses* (1922), not in the coldly brilliant "Oxen of the Sun" section, but in the "Cyclops" episode in Barney Kiernan's pub, which oscillates between parodic passages and a straightforward rendering of the dialogue and action; in the "Nausicäa" episode on the beach, which first projects Gerty MacDowell's point of view in a style parodying sentimental ladies' magazine fiction, and midway shifts to Bloom's non-parodic stream-of-consciousness; and in parts of the "Hades" Nighttown section, especially the closing apparition of Bloom's dead son, Rudy. Nabokov has gone beyond Joyce in developing parody as a novelistic form, for in *Lolita* and *Pale Fire*, which are totally parodic in form and may be the finest comic novels since *Ulysses*, the parody and pathos are always congruent, rather than adjacent to one another—as though the entire "Nausicäa" or "Cyclops" episodes were cast as parody, without in any way diminishing our sense of Bloom's suffering, or that Joyce had been able to express something of the humanity of Bloom or Mrs. Purefoy in the "Oxen of the Sun" *tour de force*. Nabokov has summarized in a phrase his triumph in *Lolita* and *Pale Fire*. Just before Humbert takes Lolita into their room at The Enchanted Hunters hotel in what is to be the most crucial event in his life, Humbert comments, "Parody of a hotel corridor. Parody of silence and death" (p. 121). To paraphrase Marianne Moore's well-known line that poetry is "imaginary gardens with real toads in them," Nabokov's "poem" is a parody of death with real suffering in it. With characteristic self-awareness, Nabokov defines in *The Gift* the essence of his own art: "The spirit of parody always goes along with genuine poetry."

This spirit in Nabokov represents not merely a set of techniques, but, as suggested above, an attitude toward experience, a means of discovering the nature of experience. *The Prismatic Bezel* is aptly titled: a "bezel" is the sloping edge on a cutting tool or the oblique side of a gem, and the luminous bezel of Nabokov's parody can cut in any direction, often turning in upon itself as self-parody.

To stress the satiric (rather than parodic) elements of *Lolita* above all others is as limited a response as to stop short with its sexual content. "Sex as an institution, sex as a general notion, sex as a problem, sex as a platitude—all this is something I find too tedious for words," Nabokov told an interviewer from *Playboy*, and his Cornell lectures on Joyce further indicate that he is not interested in sexual oddities for their own sake. On May 10, 1954, in his opening lecture on *Ulysses* (delivered, as it turns out, at the time he was completing *Lolita*), Nabokov said of Leopold Bloom, "Joyce intended the portrait of an ordinary person. [His] sexual deportment [is] extremely perverse . . . Bloom indulges in acts and dreams subnormal in an evolutionary sense, affecting both individual and species. . . . In Bloom's (and Joyce's) mind, the theme of sex is mixed with theme of latrine. Supposed to be ordinary citizen: mind of ordinary citizen does not dwell where Bloom's does. Sexual affairs heap indecency upon indecency . . ." Coming from the creator of Humbert Humbert, the fervent tone and the rather old-fashioned sense of normalcy may seem unexpected. On May 28, the last class of the term and concluding lecture on Joyce, he discussed the flaws in *Ulysses*, complaining that there is an "Obnoxious, overdone preoccupation with sex organs, as illustrated in Molly's stream-of-consciousness. Perverse attitudes exhibited." [1] In spite of the transcriptions in notebookese, one gets a firm idea of Nabokov's attitude toward the explicit detailing of sexuality, and his remarks imply a good deal about his intentions in *Lolita*. The "nerves of the novel" revealed in the Afterword underscore these intentions by generalizing Humbert's passion (p. 318). That the seemingly inscrutable Nabokov would even write this essay, let alone reprint it in magazines and append it to the twenty-five translations of *Lolita*, surely suggests the dismay he must have felt to see how many readers, including some old friends, had taken the book solely on an erotic level. Those exposed "nerves" should make it clear that insofar as it has a definable subject, *Lolita* is not merely about pe-

[1] From the annotator's class notes, 1953–1954.

dophilia. As Humbert says, rather than describing the details of the seduction at The Enchanted Hunters hotel, "Anybody can imagine those elements of animality. A greater endeavor lures me on: to fix once for all the perilous magic of nymphets" (p. 136). Humbert's desires are those of a poet as well as a pervert, and not surprisingly, since they reflect, darkly, in a crooked enough mirror, the artistic desires of his creator.

Humbert's is a nightmare vision of the ineffable bliss variously sought by one Nabokov character after another. For a resonant summary phrase, one turns to *Agaspher* (1923), a verse drama written when Nabokov was twenty-four. An adaptation of the legend of the Wandering Jew, only its Prologue was published. Tormented by "dreams of earthly beauty," Nabokov's wanderer exclaims, "I shall catch you / catch you, Maria my inexpressible dream / from age to age!" [1] Near the end of another early work, the novel *King, Queen, Knave* (1928), an itinerant photographer walks down the street, ignored by the crowd, "yelling into the wind: 'The artist is coming! The divinely favored, *der gottbegnadete* artist is coming!' "—a yell that ironically refers to the novel's unrealized artist, businessman Dreyer, and anticipates and announces the arrival of such future avatars of the artist as the chessplayer Luzhin in *The Defense* (1930), the butterfly collector Pilgram in "The Aurelian" (1931), the daydreaming art dealer and critic Albinus Kretschmar in *Laughter in the Dark* (1932), the imprisoned and doomed Cincinnatus in *Invitation to a Beheading* (1935–1936), who struggles to write, the inventor Salvator Waltz in *The Waltz Invention* (1938), and the philosopher Krug in *Bend Sinister* (1947), as well as poets *manqués* such as Humbert Humbert in *Lolita* (1955), and such genuine yet only partially fulfilled artists as Fyodor Godunov-Cherdyntsev in *The Gift* (1937–1938), Sebastian Knight in *The Real Life of Sebastian Knight* (1941), and John Shade in *Pale Fire* (1962). When perceived by the reader, the involuted design of each novel reveals that these characters all exist in a universe of fiction arrayed around the consciousness of Vladimir Nabokov, the only artist of major stature who appears in Nabokov's work.

[1] Translated and quoted by Andrew Field, *op. cit.*, p. 79.

Some readers, however, may feel that works that are in part about themselves are limited in range and significance, too special, too hermetic. But the creative process is fundamental; perhaps nothing is *more* personal by implication and hence more relevant than fictions concerning fiction; identity, after all, is a kind of artistic construct, however imperfect the created product. If the artist does indeed embody in himself and formulate in his work the fears and needs and desires of the race, then a "story" about his mastery of form, his triumph in art is but a heightened emblem of all of our own efforts to confront, order, and structure the chaos of life, and to endure, if not master, the demons within and around us. "I am thinking of aurochs and angels, the secret of durable pigments, prophetic sonnets, the refuge of art," says Humbert in the closing moments of *Lolita*, and he speaks for more than one of Nabokov's characters.

It was the major émigré poet and critic Vladislav Khodasevich who first pointed out, more than thirty years ago, that whatever their occupations may be, Nabokov's protagonists represent the artist, and that Nabokov's principal works in part concern the creative process.[1] Khodasevich died in 1939, and until recently, his criticism remained untranslated. If it *had* been available earlier, Nabokov's English and American readers would have recognized his deep seriousness at a much earlier date. This is especially true of *Lolita*, where Nabokov's constant theme is masked, but not obscured, by the novel's ostensible subject, sexual perversion. But what may have been a brilliant formulation in the 'thirties should be evident enough by now, and not because so many other critics have said it of Nabokov, but rather because it has become a commonplace of recent criticism to note that a work of art is about itself (Wordsworth, Mallarmé, Proust, Joyce, Yeats, Queneau, Borges, Barth, Claude Mauriac, Robbe-Grillet, Picasso, Saul Steinberg, and Fellini's great film, *8½*—to name but a baker's dozen). What is not so clear is how Nabokov's artifice and strategies of involution reveal the "second plot" in his fiction, the "contiguous

---

[1] Vladislav Khodasevich, "On Sirin" (1937), translated by Michael H. Walker, edited by Simon Karlinsky and Robert P. Hughes, *TriQuarterly*, No. 17 (Winter 1970).

world" of the author's mind; what it has meant to that mind to have created a fictional world; and what the effect of those strategies is upon the reader, whose illicit involvement with that fiction constitutes a "third plot," and who is manipulated by Nabokov's dizzying illusionistic devices to such an extent that he too can be said to become, at certain moments, another of Vladimir Nabokov's creations.

3. THE ARTIFICE OF LOLITA

Although *Lolita* has received much serious attention (see this edition's selected bibliography), the criticism which it has elicited usually forces a thesis which does not and in fact cannot accommodate the total design of the novel. That intricate design, described in the Notes to this edition, makes *Lolita* one of the few supremely original novels of the century. It is difficult to imagine, say, that *Lord Jim* could have been achieved without the example of Henry James's narrative strategies, or that *The Sound and the Fury* would be the same novel if Faulkner had not read *Ulysses*. But like *The Castle, Remembrance of Things Past, Ulysses, Finnegans Wake,* and *Pale Fire, Lolita* is one of those transcendent works of the imagination which defy the neat continuum maintained so carefully by literary historians. At most, it is one of those works which create their own precursors, to use Jorge Luis Borges's winning phrase.

Because Nabokov continually parodies the conventions of "realistic" and "impressionistic" fiction, readers must accept or reject him on his own terms. Many of his novels become all but meaningless in any other terms. At the same time, however, even Nabokov's most ardent admirers must sometimes wonder about the smaller, more hermetic components of Nabokov's artifice—the multifarious puns, allusions, and butterfly references which proliferate in novels such as *Pale Fire* and *Lolita.* Are they organic? Do they coalesce to form any meaningful pattern? Humbert's wide-ranging literary allusions more than "challenge [our] scholarship," as H.H. says of Quilty's similar performance. Several of Humbert's allusions are woven so subtly into the texture of the narrative as to elude all but the most compulsive exegetes. Many allusions, however, are direct and available, and these are most frequently to nineteenth-century writers; an early Note will suggest that this is of considerable importance. But unlike the allusions, which are sometimes only a matter of fun, the patterned verbal cross references are always fundamental, defining a dimension of the novel that has escaped critical notice.

The verbal *figurae* in *Lolita* limn the novel's involuted design and establish the basis of its artifice. As indicated in the Foreword, no total interpretation of *Lolita* will be propounded here. The following remarks on artifice and game are *not* intended to suggest that this "level" of the novel is the most important; they are offered because no one has yet recognized the magnitude of this verbal patterning, or its significance.[1] Just as Nabokov's Afterword was read in advance of the novel, so the following pages might well be re-read after the annotations, many of which they anticipate.

Although *Lolita* is less dramatically anti-realistic than *Pale Fire*, in its own way it is as grandly labyrinthine and as much a work of artifice as that more ostentatiously tricky novel. This is not immediately apparent because Humbert is Nabokov's most "humanized" character since Luzhin (1930), and *Lolita* the first novel since the early 'thirties in which "the end" remains intact. Moreover, Nabokov has said that "The Magician," the 1939 story containing the central idea of *Lolita*, went unpublished *not* because of its subject matter but rather because "The little girl wasn't alive. She hardly spoke. Little by little I managed to give her some semblance of reality." It may seem anomalous for puppeteer Nabokov, creator of the sham worlds of *Invitation to a Beheading* and *Bend Sinister*, to worry this way about "reality" (with or without quotation marks); yet one extreme does not preclude the other in Nabokov, and the originality of *Lolita* derives from this very paradox. The puppet theater never collapses, but everywhere there are fissures, if

---

[1] I have elsewhere discussed the novel as a novel, as well as an artifice; see my article "*Lolita*: The Springboard of Parody," *Wisconsin Studies in Contemporary Literature*, VIII (Spring 1967), 204–241. Reprinted in L.S. Dembo, ed., *Nabokov: The Man and His Work* (Madison, 1967), pp. 106–143. Especially see pp. 125–131 and 139–141.

not gaps, in the structure, crisscrossing in intricate patterns and visible to the discerning eye—that is, the eye trained on Nabokov fictions and thus accustomed to novelistic *trompe-l'oeil*. *Lolita* is a great novel to the same extent as Nabokov is able to have it both ways, involving the reader on the one hand in a deeply moving yet outrageously comic story, rich in verisimilitude, and on the other engaging him in a game made possible by the interlacings of verbal figurations which undermine the novel's realistic base and distance the reader from its dappled surface, which then assumes the aspect of a gameboard (the figurations are detailed in the Notes).

As a lecturer, Nabokov was a considerable Thespian, able to manipulate audiences in a similar manner. His rehearsal of Gogol's death agonies remains in one's mind: how the hack doctors alternately bled him and purged him and plunged him into icy baths, Gogol so frail that his spine could be felt through his stomach, the six fat white bloodletting leeches clinging to his nose, Gogol begging to have them removed—*"Please lift them, lift them, keep them away!"*—and, sinking behind the lectern, now a tub, Nabokov for several moments *was* Gogol, shuddering and shivering, his hands held down by a husky attendant, his head thrown back in pain and terror, nostrils distended, eyes shut, his beseechments filling the large lecture hall. Even the sea of C-minuses in the back of the room could not help being moved. And then, after a pause, Nabokov would very quietly say, in a sentence taken word-for-word from his *Gogol*, "Although the scene is unpleasant and has a human appeal which I deplore, it is necessary to dwell upon it a little longer in order to bring out the curiously physical side of Gogol's genius."

A great deal has been written about "unreliable narrators," but too little about unreliable readers. Although editor John Ray, Jr., serves fair enough warning to those "old-fashioned readers who wish to follow the destinies of 'real' people beyond the 'true story,'" virtually every "move" in the "true story" of *Lolita* seems to be structured with their predictable responses in mind; and the game-element depends on such reflexive action, for it tests the reader in so many ways. By calling out "Reader! *Bruder!*" (p. 264), Humbert echoes *Au Lecteur*, the prefatory poem in *Les*

Fleurs du mal ("Hypocrite reader!—My fellow man—My brother!"); and, indeed, the entire novel constitutes an ironic up-ending of Baudelaire and a good many other writers who would enlist the reader's full participation in the work. "I want my learned readers to participate in the scene I am about to replay," says Humbert (p. 59), but such illicit participation will find the reader in constant danger of check, or even rougher treatment: "As greater authors than I have put it: 'Let readers imagine' etc. On second thought, I may as well give those imaginations a kick in the pants" (p. 67). Humbert addresses the reader directly no less than twenty-seven times,[1] drawing him into one trap after another. In Nabokov's hands the novel thus becomes a gameboard on which, through parody, he assaults his readers' worst assumptions, pretentions, and intellectual conventions, realizing and formulating through game his version of Flaubert's dream of an *Encyclopédie des idées reçues*, a *Dictionary of Accepted Ideas*.

"Satire is a lesson, parody is a game," says Nabokov, and although the more obvious sallies in *Lolita* could be called satiric (e.g., those against Headmistress Pratt), the most telling are achieved through the games implemented by parody. By creating a surface that is rich in "psychological" clues, but which finally re-

[1] See pp. 6, 36, 50, 59, 67, 89, 98, 106, 131, 139, 141, 156, 159, 167, 169, 186, 192, 205, 212, 218, 228, 249, 252, 255, 259, 260, and 287—not to mention Humbert's several interjections to the jury (p. 134 is typical), to mankind in general ("Human beings, attend!" [p. 126]), and to his car ("Hi, Melmoth, thanks a lot, old fellow" [p. 309]). One waxes statistical here because H.H.'s direct address is an important part of the narrative, and important too in the way that it demonstrates a paradoxically new technique. In regard to literary forms and devices, there is almost nothing new under the sun (to paraphrase a poet); it is contexts and combinations that are continually being made new. One epoch's realism is another's surrealism. To the Elizabethan playgoer or the reader of Cervantes, the work-within-the-work was a convention; to an audience accustomed to nineteenth-century realism, it is fantastic, perplexing, and strangely affecting. The same can be said of the reintroduction of "old-fashioned" direct address, revived and transmogrified at a moment in literary history when the post-Jamesian novelists seemed to have forever ruled out such self-conscious devices by refining the newer "impressionistic" conventions (the effaced narrator, the "central intelligence," the consistent if "unreliable" narrative *persona*, and so forth). "This new technique is that of the deliberate anachronism," writes J.L. Borges in "Pierre Menard, Author of the *Quixote*," an essential text on the subject (*Labyrinths*, p. 44); and cinematic equivalents are readily available in the work of the recent directors who have reintroduced silent film techniques (notably François Truffaut, Jean-Luc Godard, and Richard Lester).

sists and then openly mocks the interpretations of depth psychology, Nabokov is able to dispatch any Freudians who choose to "play" in the blitzkrieg game that is the novel's first sixty-or-so pages. The traps are baited with tempting "false scents" drawn from what Nabokov in *Speak, Memory* calls the "police state of sexual myth." The synthetic incest of Humbert and Lolita seems to suggest a classical Oedipal situation, but Humbert later calls it a "parody of incest." Nabokov further implies that the story works out the "transference" theory, whereby the daughter transfers her affections to another, similar man, but not her father, thus exorcising her Oedipal tension. If Freudians have interpreted Lolita's elopement with Quilty in this way, then they stop short in the hospital scene when Humbert says of the nurse, "I suppose Mary thought comedy father Professor Humbertoldi was interfering with the romance between Dolores and her father-substitute, rolypoly Romeo" (p. 245). The boyish qualities of a nymphet tempt the reader into interpreting Humbert's quest as essentially homosexual, but we may be less absolute in our judgment and practice of pop psychoanalysis when Humbert tells how during one of his incarcerations he trifled with psychiatrists, "teasing them with fake 'primal scenes.'" "By bribing a nurse I won access to some files and discovered, with glee, cards calling me 'potentially homosexual'" (p. 36). If the clinical-minded have accepted Humbert's explanation of the adolescent "trauma" which accounts for his pedophilia —interrupted coitus—then they should feel the force of the attack and their own form of loss when Lolita must leave Quilty's play "a week before its natural climax" (p. 211). Humbert's "trauma" affords a further trap for the clinical mind, for the incident seems to be a sly fictive transmutation of Nabokov's own considerably more innocent childhood infatuation with Colette (Chapter Seven, *Speak, Memory*); and such hints as the butterfly and the *Carmen* allusions shared by that chapter and *Lolita* only reinforce the more obvious similarities. When earnest readers, nurtured on the "standardized symbols of the psychoanalytic racket" (p. 287), leap to make the association between the two episodes—as several have done—and immediately conclude that *Lolita* is autobiographical in the most literal sense, then the trap has been sprung: their wantonly reductive gesture justifies the need for just such a parody as Nabokov's. With a cold literary perversity, Nabokov has demonstrated the falseness of their "truth"; the implications are considerable. Even the exegetic act of searching for the "meaning" of *Lolita* by trying to unfold the butterfly pattern becomes a parody of the expectations of the most sophisticated reader, who finds he is chasing a mocking inversion of the "normal" Freudian direction of symbols which, once identified, may still remain mysterious, explain very little, or, like the game of Word Golf in *Pale Fire*, reveal nothing.

Until almost the end of *Lolita*, Humbert's fullest expressions of "guilt" and "grief" are qualified, if not undercut completely, and these passages represent another series of traps in which Nabokov again parodies the reader's expectations by having Humbert the penitent say what the reader wants to hear: "I was a pentapod monster, but I loved you. I was despicable and brutal, and turpid, and everything" (p. 286). Eagerly absorbing Humbert's "confession," the reader suddenly stumbles over the rare word "turpid," and then is taken unawares by the silly catchall "and everything," which renders absurd the whole cluster, if not the reader. It *is* easy to confess, but the moral vocabulary we employ so readily may go no deeper than Humbert's parody of it.

Humbert's own moral vocabulary would seem to find an ideally expressive vehicle in the person of Clare Quilty. Throughout the narrative Humbert is literally and figuratively pursued by Quilty, who is by turns ludicrous and absurd, sinister and grotesque. For a while Humbert is certain that his "shadow" and nemesis is his Swiss cousin, Detective Trapp, and when Lolita agrees and says, "Perhaps he is Trapp," she is summarizing Quilty's role in the novel (p. 221). Quilty is so ubiquitous because he formulates Humbert's entrapment, his criminal passion, his sense of shame and self-hate. Yet Quilty embodies both "the truth and a caricature of it," for he is at once a projection of Humbert's guilt and a parody of the psychological Double; "Lolita was playing a double game," says Humbert (p. 245), punningly referring to Lolita's tennis, the *Doppelgänger* parody, and the function of parody as game.

The Double motif figures prominently throughout Nabokov,

from the early 'thirties in *Despair* and *Laughter in the Dark* (where the Albinus–Axel Rex pairing rehearses the Humbert–Quilty doubling), to *The Real Life of Sebastian Knight* and on through *Bend Sinister*, the story "Scenes from the Life of a Double Monster," *Lolita, Pnin,* and *Pale Fire,* which offers a monumental doubling (or, more properly, tripling). It is probably the most intricate and profound of all *Doppelgänger* novels, written at precisely the time when it seemed that the Double theme had been exhausted in modern literature, and this achievement was very likely made possible by Nabokov's elaborate parody of the theme in *Lolita,* which renewed his sense of the artistic efficacy of another literary "thing which had once been fresh and bright but which was now worn to a thread" (*Sebastian Knight,* p. 91).

By making Clare Quilty too clearly guilty,[1] Nabokov is assaulting the convention of the good and evil "dual selves" found in the traditional Double tale. Humbert would let some of us believe that when he kills Quilty in Chapter Thirty-five, Part Two, the good poet has exorcised the bad monster, but the two are finally not to be clearly distinguished: when Humbert and Quilty wrestle, "I rolled over him. We rolled over me. They rolled over him. We rolled over us." Although the parody culminates in this "silent, soft, formless tussle on the part of two literati" (p. 301), it is sustained throughout the novel. In traditional *Doppelgänger* fiction the Double representing the reprehensible self is often described as an ape. In Dostoevsky's *The Possessed* (1871), Stavrogin tells Verkhovensky, "you're my ape"; in Stevenson's *Dr. Jekyll and Mr. Hyde* (1886), Hyde plays "apelike tricks," attacks and kills with "apelike fury" and "apelike spite"; and in Poe's "The Murders in the Rue Morgue" (1845), the criminal self is literally an ape. But "good" Humbert undermines the doubling by often calling himself an ape, rather than Quilty, and when the two face one another, Quilty also calls Humbert an ape. This transference is forcefully underscored when Humbert refers to himself as running along like "Mr. Hyde," his "talons still tingling" (p. 208). In Conrad's *Heart of Darkness* (1902), Kurtz is Marlow's "shadow" and "shade." Although Humbert calls Quilty his "shadow," the pun on Humbert's

---

[1] The pun is also pointed out by Page Stegner in *Escape into Aesthetics: The Art of Vladimir Nabokov* (New York, 1966), p. 104.

name (*ombre* = shadow) suggests that he is as much a shadow as Quilty, and like the shadow self who pursues the professor in Hans Christian Andersen's "The Shadow" (1850), Humbert is dressed all in black. Quilty in fact first regards Humbert as possibly being "some familiar and innocuous hallucination" of his own (p. 296); and in the novel's closing moments the masked narrator addresses Lolita and completes this transferral: "And do not pity C.Q. One had to choose between him and H.H., and one wanted H.H. to exist at least a couple of months longer, so as to have him make you live in the minds of later generations." The book might have been told by "C.Q.," the doubling reversed; "H.H." is simply a better artist, more likely to possess the "secret of durable pigments."

If the Humbert-Quilty doubling is a conscious parody of "William Wilson" (1839), it is with good reason, for Poe's story is unusual among *Doppelgänger* tales in that it presents a reversal of the conventional situation: the weak and evil self is the main character, pursued by the moral self, whom he kills. Nabokov goes further and with one vertiginous sweep stands the convention on its head: in terms of the nineteenth-century Double tale, it should not even be necessary to kill Quilty and what he represents, for Humbert has already declared his love for Lolita *before* he goes to Quilty's Pavor Manor, and, in asking the no longer nymphic Lolita to go away with him, he has transcended his obsession. Although Humbert's unqualified expression of "guilt" (p. 310) comes at the end of the novel, in the chronology of events it too occurs before he kills Quilty. As a "symbolic" act, the killing is gratuitous; the parodic design is complete.

Quilty rightly balks at his symbolic role: "I'm not responsible for the rapes of others. Absurd!" he tells Humbert, and his words are well taken, for in this scene Humbert *is* trying to make him totally responsible, and the poem which he has Quilty read aloud reinforces his effort, and again demonstrates how a Nabokov parody moves beyond the "obscure fun" of stylistic imitation to connect with the most serious region of the book. It begins as a parody of Eliot's "Ash Wednesday" but ends by undercutting all the confessing in which "remorseful" Humbert has just been engaged: "because of all you did / because of all I did not / you have to die" (p. 302). Since Quilty has been described as "the American Maeterlinck," it goes without saying that his ensuing death scene should be extravagantly "symbolic." Because one is not easily rid of an "evil" self, Quilty, indomitable as Rasputin, is almost impossible to kill; but the idea of exorcism is rendered absurd by his comically prolonged death throes, which, in the spirit of Canto V of *The Rape of the Lock*, burlesque the gore and rhetoric of literary death scenes ranging from the Elizabethan drama to the worst of detective novels. Quilty returns to the scene of the crime—a bed—and it is here that Humbert finally corners him. When Humbert fires his remaining bullets at close range, Quilty "lay back, and a big pink bubble with juvenile connotations formed on his lips, grew to the size of a toy balloon, and vanished" (p. 306). The last details emphasize the mock-symbolic association with Lolita; the monstrous self that has devoured Lolita, bubble gum, childhood, and all, is "symbolically" dead, but as the bubble explodes, so does the Gothic *Doppelgänger* convention, with all its own "juvenile connotations" about identity, and we learn shortly that Humbert is still "all covered with Quilty." Guilt is not to be exorcised so readily—McFate is McFate, to coin a Humbertism—and the ambiguities of human experience and identity are not to be reduced to mere "dualities." Instead of the successful integration of a neatly divisible self, we are left with "Clare Obscure" and "quilted Quilty," the patchwork self (p. 308). Quilty refuses to die, just as the recaptured nose in Gogol's extraordinary Double story of that name (1836) would not at first stick to its owner's face. The reader who has expected the solemn moral-ethical absolutes of a Poe, Dostoevsky, Mann, or Conrad *Doppelgänger* fiction instead discovers himself adrift in a fantastic, comic cosmos more akin to Gogol's. Having hoped that Humbert would master his "secret sharer," we find instead that his quest for his "slippery self" figuratively resembles Major Kovaliov's frantic chase after his own nose through the spectral streets of St. Petersburg, and that Humbert's "quest" has its mock "ending" in a final confrontation that, like the end of "The Overcoat" (1842), is not a confrontation at all.

The parodic references to R.L. Stevenson suggest that Nabokov had in mind Henry Jekyll's painfully earnest discovery of the "truth" that "man is not only one, but truly two. I say two, because the state of my own knowledge does not pass beyond that point. Others will follow, others will outstrip me on the same lines." The "serial selves" of *Pale Fire* "outstrip" Stevenson and a good many other writers, and rather than undermining Humbert's guilt, the Double parody in *Lolita* locks Humbert within that prison of mirrors where the "real self" and its masks blend into one another, the refracted outlines of good and evil becoming terrifyingly confused.

Humbert's search for the whereabouts and identity of Detective Trapp (Quilty) invites the reader to wend his way through a labyrinth of clues in order to solve this mystery, a process which both parallels and parodies the Poe "tale of ratiocination." When Humbert finds Lolita and presses her for her abductor's name,

> She said really it was useless, she would never tell, but on the other hand, after all—"Do you really want to know who it was? Well it was—"
> And softly, confidentially, arching her thin eyebrows and puckering her parched lips, she emitted, a little mockingly, somewhat fastidiously, not untenderly, in a kind of muted whistle, the name that the astute reader has guessed long ago.
> Waterproof. Why did a flash from Hourglass Lake cross my consciousness? I, too, had known it, without knowing it, all along. There was no shock, no surprise. Quietly the fusion took place, and everything fell into order, into the pattern of branches that I have woven throughout this memoir with the express purpose of having the ripe fruit fall at the right moment; yes, with the express and perverse purpose of rendering—she was talking but I sat melting in my golden peace—of rendering that golden and monstrous peace through the satisfaction of logical recognition, which my most inimical reader should experience now. (pp. 273–274)

Even here Humbert withholds Quilty's identity, though the "astute reader" may recognize that "Waterproof" is a clue which leads back to an early scene at the lake, in which Charlotte had said that Humbert's watch was waterproof and Jean Farlow had alluded to Quilty's Uncle Ivor (by his first name only), and then had almost mentioned Clare Quilty by name: Ivor "told me a completely indecent story about his nephew. It appears—" But she is interrupted and the chapter ends (p. 91). This teasing exercise in ratiocination—"peace" indeed!—is the detective trap, another parody of the reader's assumptions and expectations, as though even the most astute reader could ever fully discover the identity of Quilty, Humbert, or of himself.

Provided with Quilty's name, Humbert now makes his way to Pavor Manor, that latter-day House of Usher, where the extended and variegated parodies of Poe are laid to rest. All the novel's parodic themes are concluded in this chapter. Its importance is telescoped by Humbert's conclusion: "This, I said to myself, was the end of the ingenious play staged for me by Quilty" (p. 307). In form, of course, this bravura set piece is not a play; but, as a summary parodic commentary on the main action, it does function in the manner of an Elizabethan play-within-the-play, and its "staging" underscores once more the game-element central to the book.

Simultaneous with these games is a fully novelistic process that shows Humbert traveling much further than the 27,000 miles he and Lolita literally traverse. Foolish John Ray describes Humbert's as "a tragic tale tending unswervingly to nothing less than a moral apotheosis" (p. 7) and, amazingly enough, he turns out to be right. The reader sees Humbert move beyond his obsessional passion to a not altogether straightforward declaration of genuine love (pp. 279–280) and, finally, to a realization of the loss suffered not by him but by Lolita (pp. 309–310). It is expressed on the next to the last page in a long and eloquent passage that, for the first time in the novel, is in no way undercut by parody or qualified by irony. Midway through this "last mirage of wonder and hopelessness," the reader is invoked again, because Humbert's moral apotheosis, so uniquely straightforward, constitutes the end game and Nabokov's final *trompe-l'oeil*. If the reader has long since decided that there is no "moral reality" in the novel, and in his sophisticated way has accepted that, he may well miss this unexpected move in the farthest corner of the board and lose the game after all. It is the last time the reader will be addressed directly, for the game is about over, as is the novel.

In addition to sustaining the game-element, the authorial patterning reminds us that *Lolita* is but one part of that universe of fiction arrayed around the consciousness of Nabokov, who would join Humbert in his lament that words do indeed have their limitations, and that "the past is the past"; to live in it, as Humbert tried, is to die. That the author of *Speak, Memory* should suggest this surely establishes the moral dimension of Lolita; and in the light of Johan Huizinga's remark that "Play is outside the range of good and bad," [1] *Lolita* becomes an even more extraordinary achievement.

When in *The Gift* Nabokov writes of Fyodor's poem, "At the same time he had to take great pains not to lose either his control of the game, or the viewpoint of the plaything," he is defining the difficulties he faced in writing novels whose full meaning depends on the reader's having a spatial view of the book. It should be evident by now how the parody and patterning create the distance necessary for a clear view of the "plaything," and Nabokov reinforces one's sense of the novel-as-gameboard by having an actual game in progress within *Lolita:* the seemingly continuous match between Humbert and Gaston Godin—a localized, foreground action which in turn telescopes both the Humbert-Quilty "Double game" being played back and forth across the gameboard of America and the overriding contest waged above the novel, between the author and the reader. [2]

[1] Johan Huizinga, *Homo Ludens: A Study of the Play Element in Culture* (Boston, 1955 [1st ed. 1944]), p. 11. An excellent introduction to Nabokov, even if he is not mentioned.

[2] This aspect of *Lolita* is nicely visualized in Tenniel's drawing of a landscaped chessboard (or chessbored landscape) for Chapter Two of Lewis Carroll's *Through the Looking-Glass,* in which a chess game is literally woven into the narrative. For more on Carroll and Nabokov, see Note 133/1.

Humbert and Gaston play chess "two or three times weekly" in Humbert's study, and several times Nabokov carefully links Lolita with the Queen in their game (pp. 184–185). One evening while they are playing, Humbert gets a telephone call from Lolita's music teacher informing him that Lolita has again missed her lesson, the boldest lie he has caught her in, indicating that he is soon to lose her:

> As the reader may well imagine, my faculties were now impaired, and a move or two later, with Gaston to play, I noticed through the film of my general distress that he could collect my queen; he noticed it too, but thinking it might be a trap on the part of his tricky opponent, he demurred for quite a minute, and puffed and wheezed, and shook his jowls, and even shot furtive glances at me, and made hesitating half-thrusts with his pudgily bunched fingers—dying to take that juicy queen and not daring—and all of a sudden he swooped down upon it (who knows if it did not teach him certain later audacities?), and I spent a dreary hour in achieving a draw. (pp. 204–205)

In their respective ways, all the players want to capture "that juicy queen": poor homosexual Gaston, quite literally; pornographer Quilty, for only one purpose; pervert and poet Humbert, in two ways, first carnally but then artistically, out of love; and the common reader, who would either rescue Lolita by judging and condemning Humbert, or else participate vicariously, which would make him of Quilty's party—though there is every reason to think that the attentive reader will sooner or later share Humbert's perspective: "In my chess sessions with Gaston I saw the board as a square pool of limpid water with rare shells and stratagems rosily visible upon the smooth tessellated bottom, which to my confused adversary was all ooze and squid-cloud" (p. 235).

Humbert is being too modest at the outset of *Lolita* when he says "it is only a game," for it is one in which everything on the board "breath[es] with life," as Nabokov writes of the match between Luzhin and Turati in *The Defense*. Radical and dizzying shifts in focus are created in the reader's mind as he oscillates between a sense that he is by turns confronting characters in a novel and pieces in a game—as if a telescope were being spun 360 degrees on its axis, allowing one to look alternately through one end and then the other. The various "levels" of *Lolita* are of course not the New Criticism's "levels of meaning," for the telescopic and global views of the "plaything" should enable one to perceive these levels or dimensions as instantaneous—as though, to adapt freely an image used by Mary McCarthy to describe *Pale Fire*, one were looking down on three or more games being played simultaneously by two chess masters on several separate glass boards, each arranged successively above the other.[1] A first reading of *Lolita* rarely affords this limpid, multiform view, and for many reasons, the initially disarming and distractive quality of its ostensible subject being foremost. But the uniquely exhilarating experience of rereading it on its own terms derives from the discovery of a totally new book in place of the old, and the recognition that its habit of metamorphosis has happily described the course of one's own perceptions. What Jorge Luis Borges says of Pierre Menard, author of the *Quixote*, surely holds for Vladimir Nabokov, the author of *Lolita:* he "has enriched, by means of a new technique, the halting and rudimentary art of reading." [2]

ALFRED APPEL, JR.

Palo Alto, California
January 31, 1968

[1] Mary McCarthy, "Vladimir Nabokov's *Pale Fire*," *Encounter*, XIX (October 1962), p. 76.
[2] Borges, "Pierre Menard, Author of the *Quixote*," *op. cit.*, p. 44.

SELECTED BIBLIOGRAPHY

1. CHECKLIST OF NABOKOV'S WRITING

*Denotes a Russian work that has been translated; date following a title indicates year of magazine serialization; parentheses contain date of translation into English.

**Denotes work written in English. No asterisk indicates work is in Russian.

Not included below are Nabokov's twenty major entomological papers in English, nor the vast amount of writing that remains untranslated and uncollected from the 'twenties and 'thirties, including approximately 100 poems, seven plays, several short stories, fifty literary reviews and essays, and numerous translations of Rimbaud, Verlaine, Yeats, Brooke, Shakespeare, Musset, and others. Andrew Field's Nabokov: His Life in Art (Boston, 1967), contains a comprehensive bibliography.

Poems. St. Petersburg, 1916. 67 poems, privately printed.

Two Paths. Petrograd, 1918. 12 poems by Nabokov and 8 by Andrei Balashov.

The Empyrean Path. Berlin, 1923. 147 poems.

The Cluster. Berlin, 1923. 35 poems.

Carroll. Alice in Wonderland. Berlin, 1923. Translation.

Mashenka. Berlin, 1926 (New York, 1970, as Mary). A novel.

*King, Queen, Knave. Berlin, 1928 (New York, 1968). New York, 1969, a facsimile of the Russian first edition. A novel.

*The Defense. 1929. Berlin, 1930 (New York, 1964). A novel.

The Return of Chorb: Stories and Poems. Berlin, 1930. 15 stories and 24 poems dated 1924–1928.

*The Eye. 1930 (New York, 1965). A short novel.

The Exploit. 1931. Paris, 1932 (New York, 1971, as *Glory*). A novel.

*Camera Obscura. Paris and Berlin, 1932 (London, 1936; rev., New York, 1938, as *Laughter in the Dark*). A novel.

*Despair. 1934. Berlin, 1936 (London, 1937; rev., New York, 1966). A novel.

*Invitation to a Beheading. 1935–1936. Berlin and Paris, 1938 (New York, 1959). Paris, 1966, a reprint of the Russian edition. A novel.

*The Gift. 1937–1938. New York, 1952, in Russian (New York, 1963). A novel.

The Eye. Paris, 1938. Short novel and 12 stories.

The Event. 1938. Drama in 3 acts.

*The Waltz Invention. 1938 (New York, 1966). Drama in 3 acts.

Solus Rex. An unfinished novel. Sections published, 1940 and 1942.

**The Real Life of Sebastian Knight. Norfolk, Conn., 1941. A novel.

**Three Russian Poets: Translations of Pushkin, Lermontov, and Tiutchev. Norfolk, Conn., 1944.

**Nikolai Gogol. Norfolk, Conn., 1944. A critical study.

**Nine Stories. Norfolk, Conn., 1947. 4 are translated from the Russian.

**Bend Sinister. New York, 1947. A novel.

**Conclusive Evidence. New York, 1951. A memoir.

Poems 1929–1951. Paris, 1952, in Russian. 15 poems.

Other Shores. New York, 1954. A Russian version of *Conclusive Evidence*, rewritten and expanded rather than translated.

**Lolita. Paris, 1955 (New York, 1958). A novel.

Spring in Fialta and Other Stories. New York, 1956, in Russian. 13 stories, 4 of which have been translated into English elsewhere.

**Pnin. New York, 1957. A novel.

**Lermontov. A Hero of Our Time. New York, 1958. A translation.

**Nabokov's Dozen. New York, 1958. *Nine Stories* and 4 more.

**Poems. New York, 1959. 14 poems.

**Lolita. Hollywood, 1960. An unpublished screenplay.

**The Song of Igor's Campaign. New York, 1960. A translation of the twelfth-century epic.

**Pale Fire. New York, 1962. A novel.

**Pushkin, *Eugene Onegin*. New York, 1964. Translation and Commentary in 4 volumes.

* *Nabokov's Quartet*. New York, 1966. One story was originally written in English.

**Speak, Memory. New York, 1966. Definitive version of memoir originally published as *Conclusive Evidence*, including *Other Shores* and new material.

Lolita. New York, 1967. A translation into Russian.

**Nabokov's Congeries, Page Stegner, ed. New York, 1968. An anthology.

**Ada. New York, 1969. A novel.

**The Annotated Lolita. New York, 1970. Alfred Appel, Jr., Preface, Introduction, and Notes.

* *Poems and Problems*. New York, 1971. Includes text of *Poems*, translations of Russian poems, and chess problems.

2. *CRITICISM OF* LOLITA

Aldridge, A. Owen, "Lolita and *Les Liaisons Dangereuses*," *Wisconsin Studies in Contemporary Literature*, II (Fall 1961), 20–26.

Amis, Kingsley, "She Was a Child and I Was a Child," *The Spectator*, No. 6854 (November 6, 1959), 635–636.

Appel, Alfred, Jr., "An Interview with Vladimir Nabokov," in the Special all-Nabokov number, *Wisconsin Studies*, VIII (Spring 1967), 127–152. Reprinted in L. S. Dembo, ed., *Nabokov: The Man and His Work*. Madison: University of Wisconsin Press, 1967. Pp. 19–44.

———, "The Art of Nabokov's Artifice," *Denver Quarterly*, III (Summer 1968), 25–37.

———, "*Lolita*: The Springboard of Parody," *Wisconsin Studies, op. cit.*, 204–241. Reprinted in Dembo. Pp. 106–143.

Brenner, Conrad, "Nabokov: The Art of the Perverse," *New Republic*, CXXXVIII (June 23, 1958), 18–21.

Bryer, Jackson R. and Thomas J. Bergin, Jr., "Vladimir Nabokov's Critical Reputation in English: A Note and a Checklist," *Wisconsin Studies, op. cit.*, 312–364. Reprinted in Dembo, *op. cit.* Pp. 225–274.

Butler, Diana, "Lolita Lepidoptera," *New World Writing*, No. 16 (1960), 58–84.

Dupee, F.W., "*Lolita* in America," *Encounter*, XII (February 1959), 30–35. Reprinted in *Columbia University Forum*, II (Winter 1959), 35–39.

———, "A Preface to *Lolita*," *Anchor Review*, No. 2 (1957), 1–13. Reprinted in his *"The King of the Cats" and Other Remarks on Writers and Writing*. New York: Farrar, Straus and Giroux, 1965. Pp. 117–141. Includes review of *The Gift*.

Fiedler, Leslie A., "The Profanation of the Child," *New Leader*, XLI (June 23, 1958), 26–29.

Field, Andrew, *Nabokov: His Life in Art*. Boston: Little, Brown, 1967. Pp. 323–351.

Girodias, Maurice, "Lolita, Nabokov, and I," *Evergreen Review*, IX (September 1965), 44–47, 89–91. Account of first publication of *Lolita*; for Nabokov's rejoinder, see *"Lolita* and Mr. Girodias," *Evergreen Review*, XI (February 1967), 37–41.

Gold, Herbert, "The Art of Fiction XL: Vladimir Nabokov, An Interview," *Paris Review*, No. 41 (Summer-Fall 1967), 92–111.

Green, Martin, "The Morality of *Lolita*," *Kenyon Review*, XXVIII (June 1966), 352–377.

Hicks, Granville, " 'Lolita' and Her Problems," *Saturday Review*, XLI (August 16, 1958), 12, 38.

Hollander, John, "The Perilous Magic of Nymphets," *Partisan Review*, XXIII (Fall 1956), 557–560. Reprinted in Richard Kostelanetz, ed., *On Contemporary Literature*. New York: Avon Books, 1964. Pp. 477–480.

Josipovici, G.D., "Lolita: Parody and the Pursuit of Beauty," *Critical Quarterly*, VI (Spring 1964), 35–48.

Kael, Pauline, "Lolita," in *I Lost It at the Movies*. New York: Bantam Books, 1966. Pp. 183–188. Reprinted in Andrew Sarris, ed., *The Film*. Indianapolis and New York: Bobbs-Merrill, 1968. Pp. 11–14. The most interesting review of the film version of *Lolita*.

Meyer, Frank S., "The Strange Fate of 'Lolita'—A Lance into Cotton Wool," *National Review*, VI (November 22, 1958), 340–341.

Mitchell, Charles, "Mythic Seriousness in *Lolita*," *Texas Studies in Literature and Language*, V (Autumn 1963), 329–343.

Nemerov, Howard, "The Morality of Art," *Kenyon Review*, XIX (Spring 1957), 313–314, 316–321. Reprinted in his *Poetry and Fiction: Essays*. New Brunswick, N.J.: Rutgers University Press, 1963. Pp. 260–269.

Phillips, Elizabeth, "The Hocus-Pocus of *Lolita*," *Literature and Psychology*, X (Summer 1960), 97–101.

"*Playboy* Interview: Vladimir Nabokov," *Playboy*, XI (January 1964), 35–41, 44–45. Reprinted in *The Twelfth Anniversary Playboy Reader.* Chicago: Playboy Press, 1965.

Prescott, Orville, "Books of The Times," *New York Times*, August 18, 1958, p. 17.

Proffer, Carl R., *Keys to Lolita.* Bloomington: Indiana University Press, 1968.

Rougemont, Denis de, "*Lolita,* or Scandal." In *Love Declared—Essays on the Myths of Love,* tr. Richard Howard. New York: Pantheon Books, 1963. Pp. 48–54.

Schickel, Richard, "Nabokov's Artistry," *The Progressive*, XXII (November 1958), 46, 48–49.

———, "A Review of a Novel You Can't Buy," *The Reporter*, XVII (November 28, 1957), 45–47.

Smith, Peter Duval, "Vladimir Nabokov on His Life and Work," *The Listener*, LXVIII (November 22, 1962), 856–858. Text of BBC television interview. Reprinted in *Vogue*, CXLI (March 1, 1963), 152–155.

Stegner, Page, *Escape into Aesthetics: The Art of Vladimir Nabokov.* New York: Dial Press, 1966. Pp. 102–115.

Trilling, Lionel, "The Last Lover—Vladimir Nabokov's 'Lolita,'" *Griffin*, VII (August 1958), 4–21. Reprinted in *Encounter*, XI (October 1958), 9–19.

West, Rebecca, "'Lolita': A Tragic Book with a Sly Grimace," *London Sunday Times*, November 8, 1959, p. 16.

IN PLACE OF A NOTE ON THE TEXT

Shade's poem is, indeed, that sudden flourish of magic: my gray-haired friend, my beloved old conjurer, put a pack of index cards into his hat—and shook out a poem.

To this poem we now must turn. My Foreword has been, I trust, not too skimpy. Other notes, arranged in a running commentary, will certainly satisfy the most voracious reader. Although those notes, in conformity with custom, come after the poem, the reader is advised to consult them first and then study the poem with their help, rereading them of course as he goes through its text, and perhaps, after having done with the poem, consulting them a third time so as to complete the picture. I find it wise in such cases as this to eliminate the bother of back-and-forth leafings by either cutting out and clipping together the pages with the text of the thing, or, even more simply, purchasing two copies of the same work which can then be placed in adjacent positions on a comfortable table—not like the shaky little affair on which my typewriter is precariously enthroned now, in this wretched motor lodge, with that carrousel inside and outside my head, miles away from New Wye. Let me state that without my notes Shade's text simply has no human reality at all since the human reality of such a poem as his (being too skittish and reticent for an autobiographical work), with the omission of many pithy lines carelessly rejected by him, has to depend entirely on the reality of its author and his surroundings, attachments and so forth, a reality that only my notes can provide. To this statement my dear poet would probably not have subscribed, but, for better or worse, it is the commentator who has the last word.

—CHARLES KINBOTE, *Pale Fire*

LOLITA

FOREWORD

*"Lolita, or the Confession of a White Widowed Male,"
such were the two titles under which the writer of the present
note received the strange pages it preambulates. "Humbert
Humbert," their author, had died in legal captivity, of coronary
thrombosis, on November 16, 1952, a few days before his trial
was scheduled to start. His lawyer, my good friend and relation,
Clarence Choate Clark, Esq., now of the District of Columbia
bar, in asking me to edit the manuscript, based his request on a
clause in his client's will which empowered my eminent cousin
to use his discretion in all matters pertaining to the preparation
of "Lolita" for print. Mr. Clark's decision may have been
influenced by the fact that the editor of his choice had just been
awarded the Poling Prize for a modest work ("Do the Senses
make Sense?") wherein certain morbid states and perversions
had been discussed.*

*My task proved simpler than either of us had anticipated.
Save for the correction of obvious solecisms and a careful sup-
pression of a few tenacious details that despite "H.H." 's own
efforts still subsisted in his text as signposts and tombstones
(indicative of places or persons that taste would conceal and
compassion spare), this remarkable memoir is presented intact.
Its author's bizarre cognomen is his own invention; and, of
course, this mask—through which two hypnotic eyes seem to
glow—had to remain unlifted in accordance with its wearer's
wish. While "Haze" only rhymes with the heroine's real sur-*

1 *name, her first name is too closely interwound with the inmost fiber of the book to allow one to alter it; nor (as the reader will perceive for himself) is there any practical necessity to do so.*
2 *References to "H.H." 's crime may be looked up by the*
3 *inquisitive in the daily papers for September–October 1952; its cause and purpose would have continued to remain a complete mystery, had not this memoir been permitted to come under my reading lamp.*

For the benefit of old-fashioned readers who wish to follow
4 *the destinies of the "real" people beyond the "true" story, a few details may be given as received from Mr. "Windmuller," of "Ramsdale," who desires his identity suppressed so that "the long shadow of this sorry and sordid business" should not reach the community to which he is proud to belong. His daughter,*
5 *"Louise," is by now a college sophomore. "Mona Dahl" is a student in Paris. "Rita" has recently married the proprietor of a*
6 *hotel in Florida. Mrs. "Richard F. Schiller" died in childbed,*
7 *giving birth to a stillborn girl, on Christmas Day 1952, in Gray*
8 *Star, a settlement in the remotest Northwest. "Vivian Dark-*
9 *bloom" has written a biography, "My Cue," to be published shortly, and critics who have perused the manuscript call it her best book. The caretakers of the various cemeteries involved report that no ghosts walk.*

Viewed simply as a novel, "Lolita" deals with situations and emotions that would remain exasperatingly vague to the reader
10 *had their expression been etiolated by means of platitudinous evasions. True, not a single obscene term is to be found in the whole work; indeed, the robust philistine who is conditioned by modern conventions into accepting without qualms a lavish array of four-letter words in a banal novel, will be quite shocked by their absence here. If, however, for this paradoxical prude's comfort, an editor attempted to dilute or omit scenes that a certain type of mind might call "aphrodisiac" (see in this respect the monumental decision rendered December 6, 1933, by Hon. John M. Woolsey in regard to another, considerably*
11 *more outspoken, book), one would have to forego the publication of "Lolita" altogether, since those very scenes that one might*

ineptly accuse of a sensuous existence of their own, are the most strictly functional ones in the development of a tragic tale tending unswervingly to nothing less than a moral apotheosis. The cynic may say that commercial pornography makes the same claim; the learned may counter by asserting that "H.H." 's impassioned confession is a tempest in a test tube; that at least 12% of American adult males—a "conservative" estimate according to Dr. Blanche Schwarzmann (verbal communication) —enjoy yearly, in one way or another, the special experience "H.H." describes with such despair; that had our demented diarist gone, in the fatal summer of 1947, to a competent psychopathologist, there would have been no disaster; but then, neither would there have been this book.

This commentator may be excused for repeating what he has stressed in his own books and lectures, namely that "offensive" is frequently but a synonym for "unusual"; and a great work of art is of course always original, and thus by its very nature should come as a more or less shocking surprise. I have no intention to glorify "H.H." No doubt, he is horrible, he is abject, he is a shining example of moral leprosy, a mixture of ferocity and jocularity that betrays supreme misery perhaps, but is not conducive to attractiveness. He is ponderously capricious. Many of his casual opinions on the people and scenery of this country are ludicrous. A desperate honesty that throbs through his confession does not absolve him from sins of diabolical cunning. He is abnormal. He is not a gentleman. But how magically his singing violin can conjure up a tendresse, a compassion for Lolita that makes us entranced with the book while abhorring its author!

As a case history, "Lolita" will become, no doubt, a classic in psychiatric circles. As a work of art, it transcends its expiatory aspects; and still more important to us than scientific significance and literary worth, is the ethical impact the book should have on the serious reader; for in this poignant personal study there lurks a general lesson; the wayward child, the egotistic mother, the panting maniac—these are not only vivid characters in a unique story: they warn us of dangerous trends; they point out potent evils. "Lolita" should make all of us—parents, social workers, educators—apply ourselves with still greater vigilance and vision to the task of bringing up a better generation in a safer world.

1 Widworth, Mass.   John Ray, Jr., Ph.D.
2 August 5, 1955

PART ONE

1

Lolita, light of my life, fire of my loins. My sin, my soul. 1
Lo-lee-ta: the tip of the tongue taking a trip of three steps 2
down the palate to tap, at three, on the teeth. Lo. Lee. Ta.

She was Lo, plain Lo, in the morning, standing four feet ten in 3
one sock. She was Lola in slacks. She was Dolly at school. She was 4
Dolores on the dotted line. But in my arms she was always Lolita. 5

Did she have a precursor? She did, indeed she did. In point of
fact, there might have been no Lolita at all had I not loved, one 6
summer, a certain initial girl-child. In a princedom by the sea. 7
Oh when? About as many years before Lolita was born as my age
was that summer. You can always count on a murderer for a
fancy prose style.

Ladies and gentlemen of the jury, exhibit number one is what
the seraphs, the misinformed, simple, noble-winged seraphs, en- 8
vied. Look at this tangle of thorns. 9

2

I was born in 1910, in Paris. My father was a gentle, easy-going
person, a salad of racial genes: a Swiss citizen, of mixed French
and Austrian descent, with a dash of the Danube in his veins. I
am going to pass around in a minute some lovely, glossy-blue
picture-postcards. He owned a luxurious hotel on the Riviera. His
father and two grandfathers had sold wine, jewels and silk, respectively. At thirty he married an English girl, daughter of

1 Jerome Dunn, the alpinist, and granddaughter of two Dorset parsons, experts in obscure subjects—paleopedology and Aeolian
2 harps, respectively. My very photogenic mother died in a freak accident (picnic, lightning) when I was three, and, save for a pocket of warmth in the darkest past, nothing of her subsists within the hollows and dells of memory, over which, if you can still stand my style (I am writing under observation), the sun of my infancy had set: surely, you all know those redolent remnants of day suspended, with the midges, about some hedge in bloom or suddenly entered and traversed by the rambler, at the bottom
3 of a hill, in the summer dusk; a furry warmth, golden midges.
4 My mother's elder sister, Sybil, whom a cousin of my father's had married and then neglected, served in my immediate family as a kind of unpaid governess and housekeeper. Somebody told me later that she had been in love with my father, and that he had lightheartedly taken advantage of it one rainy day and forgotten it by the time the weather cleared. I was extremely fond of her, despite the rigidity—the fatal rigidity—of some of her rules. Perhaps she wanted to make of me, in the fullness of time, a better widower than my father. Aunt Sybil had pink-rimmed azure eyes and a waxen complexion. She wrote poetry. She was poetically superstitious. She said she knew she would die soon after my sixteenth birthday, and did. Her husband, a great traveler in perfumes, spent most of his time in America, where eventually he founded a firm and acquired a bit of real estate.

I grew, a happy, healthy child in a bright world of illustrated books, clean sand, orange trees, friendly dogs, sea vistas and smil-
5 ing faces. Around me the splendid Hotel Mirana revolved as a kind of private universe, a whitewashed cosmos within the blue greater one that blazed outside. From the aproned pot-scrubber to the flanneled potentate, everybody liked me, everybody petted me. Elderly American ladies leaning on their canes listed toward me like towers of Pisa. Ruined Russian princesses who could not pay my father, bought me expensive bonbons. He, *mon cher petit*
6 *papa*, took me out boating and biking, taught me to swim and
7 dive and water-ski, read to me *Don Quixote* and *Les Misérables*, and I adored and respected him and felt glad for him whenever

I overheard the servants discuss his various lady-friends, beautiful and kind beings who made much of me and cooed and shed precious tears over my cheerful motherlessness.

I attended an English day school a few miles from home, and there I played rackets and fives, and got excellent marks, and was on perfect terms with schoolmates and teachers alike. The only definite sexual events that I can remember as having occurred before my thirteenth birthday (that is, before I first saw my little Annabel) were: a solemn, decorous and purely theoretical talk about pubertal surprises in the rose garden of the school with an American kid, the son of a then celebrated motion-picture actress whom he seldom saw in the three-dimensional world; and some interesting reactions on the part of my organism to certain photographs, pearl and umbra, with infinitely soft partings, in Pichon's sumptuous *La Beauté Humaine* that I had filched from under a mountain of marble-bound *Graphics* in the hotel library. Later, in his delightful debonair manner, my father gave me all the information he thought I needed about sex; this was just before sending me, in the autumn of 1923, to a *lycée* in Lyon (where we were to spend three winters); but alas, in the summer of that year, he was touring Italy with Mme de R. and her daughter, and I had nobody to complain to, nobody to consult.

3

Annabel was, like the writer, of mixed parentage: half-English, half-Dutch, in her case. I remember her features far less distinctly today than I did a few years ago, before I knew Lolita. There are two kinds of visual memory: one when you skillfully recreate an image in the laboratory of your mind, with your eyes open (and then I see Annabel in such general terms as: "honey-colored skin," "thin arms," "brown bobbed hair," "long lashes," "big bright mouth"); and the other when you instantly evoke, with shut eyes, on the dark innerside of your eyelids, the objective, absolutely optical replica of a beloved face, a little ghost in natural colors (and this is how I see Lolita).

Let me therefore primly limit myself, in describing Annabel, to saying she was a lovely child a few months my junior. Her parents were old friends of my aunt's, and as stuffy as she. They had rented a villa not far from Hotel Mirana. Bald brown Mr. Leigh and fat, powdered Mrs. Leigh (born Vanessa van Ness). How I loathed them! At first, Annabel and I talked of peripheral affairs. She kept lifting handfuls of fine sand and letting it pour through her fingers. Our brains were turned the way those of intelligent European preadolescents were in our day and set, and I doubt if much individual genius should be assigned to our interest in the plurality of inhabited worlds, competitive tennis, infinity, solipsism and so on. The softness and fragility of baby animals caused us the same intense pain. She wanted to be a nurse in some famished Asiatic country; I wanted to be a famous spy.

All at once we were madly, clumsily, shamelessly, agonizingly in love with each other; hopelessly, I should add, because that frenzy of mutual possession might have been assuaged only by our actually imbibing and assimilating every particle of each other's soul and flesh; but there we were, unable even to mate as slum children would have so easily found an opportunity to do. After one wild attempt we made to meet at night in her garden (of which more later), the only privacy we were allowed was to be out of earshot but not out of sight on the populous part of the *plage*. There, on the soft sand, a few feet away from our elders, we would sprawl all morning, in a petrified paroxysm of desire, and take advantage of every blessed quirk in space and time to touch each other: her hand, half-hidden in the sand, would creep toward me, its slender brown fingers sleepwalking nearer and nearer; then, her opalescent knee would start on a long cautious journey; sometimes a chance rampart built by younger children granted us sufficient concealment to graze each other's salty lips; these incomplete contacts drove our healthy and inexperienced young bodies to such a state of exasperation that not even the cold blue water, under which we still clawed at each other, could bring relief.

Among some treasures I lost during the wanderings of my

adult years, there was a snapshot taken by my aunt which showed Annabel, her parents and the staid, elderly, lame gentleman, a Dr. Cooper, who that same summer courted my aunt, grouped around a table in a sidewalk café. Annabel did not come out well, caught as she was in the act of bending over her *chocolat glacé*, and her thin bare shoulders and the parting in her hair were about all that could be identified (as I remember that picture) amid the sunny blur into which her lost loveliness graded; but I, sitting somewhat apart from the rest, came out with a kind of dramatic conspicuousness: a moody, beetle-browed boy in a dark sport shirt and well-tailored white shorts, his legs crossed, sitting in profile, looking away. That photograph was taken on the last day of our fatal summer and just a few minutes before we made our second and final attempt to thwart fate. Under the flimsiest of pretexts (this was our very last chance, and nothing really mattered) we escaped from the café to the beach, and found a desolate stretch of sand, and there, in the violet shadow of some red rocks forming a kind of cave, had a brief session of avid caresses, with somebody's lost pair of sunglasses for only witness. I was on my knees, and on the point of possessing my darling, when two bearded bathers, the old man of the sea and his brother, came out of the sea with exclamations of ribald encouragement, and four months later she died of typhus in Corfu.

4

I leaf again and again through these miserable memories, and keep asking myself, was it then, in the glitter of that remote summer, that the rift in my life began; or was my excessive desire for that child only the first evidence of an inherent singularity? When I try to analyze my own cravings, motives, actions and so forth, I surrender to a sort of retrospective imagination which feeds the analytic faculty with boundless alternatives and which causes each visualized route to fork and re-fork without end in the maddeningly complex prospect of my past. I am convinced, however, that in a certain magic and fateful way Lolita began with Annabel.

I also know that the shock of Annabel's death consolidated the frustration of that nightmare summer, made of it a permanent obstacle to any further romance throughout the cold years of my youth. The spiritual and the physical had been blended in us with a perfection that must remain incomprehensible to the matter-of-fact, crude, standard-brained youngsters of today. Long after her death I felt her thoughts floating through mine. Long before we met we had had the same dreams. We compared notes. We found strange affinities. The same June of the same year (1919) a stray canary had fluttered into her house and mine, in two widely separated countries. Oh, Lolita, had *you* loved me thus!

I have reserved for the conclusion of my "Annabel" phase the account of our unsuccessful first tryst. One night, she managed to deceive the vicious vigilance of her family. In a nervous and slender-leaved mimosa grove at the back of their villa we found a perch on the ruins of a low stone wall. Through the darkness and the tender trees we could see the arabesques of lighted windows which, touched up by the colored inks of sensitive memory, appear to me now like playing cards—presumably because a bridge game was keeping the enemy busy. She trembled and twitched as I kissed the corner of her parted lips and the hot lobe of her ear. A cluster of stars palely glowed above us, between the silhouettes of long thin leaves; that vibrant sky seemed as naked as she was under her light frock. I saw her face in the sky, strangely distinct, as if it emitted a faint radiance of its own. Her legs, her lovely live legs, were not too close together, and when my hand located what it sought, a dreamy and eerie expression, half-pleasure, half-pain, came over those childish features. She sat a little higher than I, and whenever in her solitary ecstasy she was led to kiss me, her head would bend with a sleepy, soft, drooping movement that was almost woeful, and her bare knees caught and compressed my wrist, and slackened again; and her quivering mouth, distorted by the acridity of some mysterious potion, with a sibilant intake of breath came near to my face.

She would try to relieve the pain of love by first roughly rubbing her dry lips against mine; then my darling would draw away with a nervous toss of her hair, and then again come darkly near and let me feed on her open mouth, while with a generosity that was ready to offer her everything, my heart, my throat, my entrails, I gave her to hold in her awkward fist the scepter of my passion.

I recall the scent of some kind of toilet powder—I believe she stole it from her mother's Spanish maid—a sweetish, lowly, musky perfume. It mingled with her own biscuity odor, and my senses were suddenly filled to the brim; a sudden commotion in a nearby bush prevented them from overflowing—and as we drew away from each other, and with aching veins attended to what was probably a prowling cat, there came from the house her mother's voice calling her, with a rising frantic note—and Dr. Cooper ponderously limped out into the garden. But that mimosa grove—the haze of stars, the tingle, the flame, the honeydew, and the ache remained with me, and that little girl with her seaside limbs and ardent tongue haunted me ever since—until at last, twenty-four years later, I broke her spell by incarnating her in another.

5

The days of my youth, as I look back on them, seem to fly away from me in a flurry of pale repetitive scraps like those morning snow storms of used tissue paper that a train passenger sees whirling in the wake of the observation car. In my sanitary relations with women I was practical, ironical and brisk. While a college student, in London and Paris, paid ladies sufficed me. My studies were meticulous and intense, although not particularly fruitful. At first, I planned to take a degree in psychiatry as many *manqué* talents do; but I was even more *manqué* than that; a peculiar exhaustion, I am so oppressed, doctor, set in; and I switched to English literature, where so many frustrated poets end as pipe-smoking teachers in tweeds. Paris suited me. I dis-

1 cussed Soviet movies with expatriates. I sat with uranists in the
2 Deux Magots. I published tortuous essays in obscure journals. I
3 composed pastiches:

> ... Fräulein von Kulp
> may turn, her hand upon the door;
> I will not follow her. Nor Fresca. Nor
> that Gull.

4 A paper of mine entitled "The Proustian theme in a letter
from Keats to Benjamin Bailey" was chuckled over by the six
or seven scholars who read it. I launched upon an *"Histoire
5 abrégée de la poésie anglaise"* for a prominent publishing firm,
and then started to compile that manual of French literature for
English-speaking students (with comparisons drawn from English
writers) which was to occupy me throughout the forties—
and the last volume of which was almost ready for press by the
time of my arrest.

I found a job—teaching English to a group of adults in
Auteuil. Then a school for boys employed me for a couple of
winters. Now and then I took advantage of the acquaintances I
had formed among social workers and psychotherapists to visit
in their company various institutions, such as orphanages and
reform schools, where pale pubescent girls with matted eyelashes
could be stared at in perfect impunity remindful of that granted
one in dreams.

Now I wish to introduce the following idea. Between the age
limits of nine and fourteen there occur maidens who, to certain
bewitched travelers, twice or many times older than they, reveal
6 their true nature which is not human, but nymphic (that is,
demoniac); and these chosen creatures I propose to designate as
"nymphets."

It will be marked that I substitute time terms for spatial ones.
In fact, I would have the reader see "nine" and "fourteen" as the
boundaries—the mirrory beaches and rosy rocks—of an enchanted
island haunted by those nymphets of mine and surrounded by
a vast, misty sea. Between those age limits, are all girl-children
nymphets? Of course not. Otherwise, we who are in the know,

we lone voyagers, we nympholepts, would have long gone insane. Neither are good looks any criterion; and vulgarity, or at least what a given community terms so, does not necessarily impair certain mysterious characteristics, the fey grace, the elusive, shifty, soul-shattering, insidious charm that separates the nymphet from such coevals of hers as are incomparably more dependent on the spatial world of synchronous phenomena than on that intangible island of entranced time where Lolita plays with her likes. Within the same age limits the number of true nymphets is strikingly inferior to that of provisionally plain, or just nice, or "cute," or even "sweet" and "attractive," ordinary, plumpish, formless, cold-skinned, essentially human little girls, with tummies and pigtails, who may or may not turn into adults of great beauty (look at the ugly dumplings in black stockings and white hats that are metamorphosed into stunning stars of the screen). A normal man given a group photograph of school girls or Girl Scouts and asked to point out the comeliest one will not necessarily choose the nymphet among them. You have to be an artist and a madman, a creature of infinite melancholy, with a bubble of hot poison in your loins and a super-voluptuous flame permanently aglow in your subtle spine (oh, how you have to cringe and hide!), in order to discern at once, by ineffable signs—the slightly feline outline of a cheekbone, the slenderness of a downy limb, and other indices which despair and shame and tears of tenderness forbid me to tabulate—the little deadly demon among the wholesome children; *she* stands unrecognized by them and unconscious herself of her fantastic power.

Furthermore, since the idea of time plays such a magic part in the matter, the student should not be surprised to learn that there must be a gap of several years, never less than ten I should say, generally thirty or forty, and as many as ninety in a few known cases, between maiden and man to enable the latter to come under a nymphet's spell. It is a question of focal adjustment, of a certain distance that the inner eye thrills to surmount, and a certain contrast that the mind perceives with a gasp of perverse delight. When I was a child and she was a child, my little Annabel was no nymphet to me; I was her equal, a faunlet in my own right, on that same enchanted island of time; but today, in September 1952, after twenty-nine years have elapsed, I think I can distinguish in her the initial fateful elf in my life. We loved each other with a premature love, marked by a fierceness that so often destroys adult lives. I was a strong lad and survived; but the poison was in the wound, and the wound remained ever open, and soon I found myself maturing amid a civilization which allows a man of twenty-five to court a girl of sixteen but not a girl of twelve.

No wonder, then, that my adult life during the European period of my existence proved monstrously twofold. Overtly, I had so-called normal relationships with a number of terrestrial women having pumpkins or pears for breasts; inly, I was consumed by a hell furnace of localized lust for every passing nymphet whom as a law-abiding poltroon I never dared approach. The human females I was allowed to wield were but palliative agents. I am ready to believe that the sensations I derived from natural fornication were much the same as those known to normal big males consorting with their normal big mates in that routine rhythm which shakes the world. The trouble was that those gentlemen had not, and I *had*, caught glimpses of an incomparably more poignant bliss. The dimmest of my pollutive dreams was a thousand times more dazzling than all the adultery the most virile writer of genius or the most talented impotent might imagine. My world was split. I was aware of not one but two sexes, neither of which was mine; both would be termed female by the anatomist. But to me, through the prism of my senses, "they were as different as mist and mast." All this I rationalize now. In my twenties and early thirties, I did not understand my throes quite so clearly. While my body knew what it craved for, my mind rejected my body's every plea. One moment I was ashamed and frightened, another recklessly optimistic. Taboos strangulated me. Psychoanalysts wooed me with pseudoliberations of pseudolibidoes. The fact that to me the only objects of amorous tremor were sisters of Annabel's, her handmaids and girl-pages, appeared to me at times as a forerunner of insanity. At other times I would tell myself that it was all a question of attitude, that there was really nothing wrong in being moved to distraction by girl-children. Let me remind my reader that in England, with the passage of the Children and Young Person Act in 1933, the term "girl-child" is defined as "a girl who is over eight but under fourteen years" (after that, from fourteen to seventeen, the statutory definition is "young person"). In Massachusetts, U.S., on the other hand, a "wayward child" is, technically, one "between seven and seventeen years of age" (who, moreover, habitually associates with vicious or immoral persons). Hugh Broughton, a writer of controversy in the reign of James the First, has proved that Rahab was a harlot at ten years of age. This is all very interesting, and I daresay you see me already frothing at the mouth in a fit; but no, I am not; I am just winking happy thoughts into a little tiddle cup. Here are some more pictures. Here is Virgil who could the nymphet sing in single tone, but probably preferred a lad's perineum. Here are two of King Akhnaten's and Queen Nefertiti's pre-nubile Nile daughters (that royal couple had a litter of six), wearing nothing but many necklaces of bright beads, relaxed on cushions, intact after three thousand years, with their soft brown puppybodies, cropped hair and long ebony eyes. Here are some brides of ten compelled to seat themselves on the fascinum, the virile ivory in the temples of classical scholarship. Marriage and cohabitation before the age of puberty are still not uncommon in certain East Indian provinces. Lepcha old men of eighty copulate with girls of eight, and nobody minds. After all, Dante fell madly in love with his Beatrice when she was nine, a sparkling girleen, painted and lovely, and bejeweled, in a crimson frock, and this was in 1274, in Florence, at a private feast in the merry month of May. And when Petrarch fell madly in love with his Laureen, she was a fair-haired nymphet of twelve running in the wind, in the pollen and dust, a flower in flight, in the beautiful plain as descried from the hills of Vaucluse.

But let us be prim and civilized. Humbert Humbert tried hard to be good. Really and truly, he did. He had the utmost respect for ordinary children, with their purity and vulnerability, and under no circumstances would he have interfered with the innocence of a child, if there was the least risk of a row. But how his heart beat when, among the innocent throng, he espied a demon child, *"enfant charmante et fourbe,"* dim eyes, bright lips, ten years in jail if you only show her you are looking at her. So life went. Humbert was perfectly capable of intercourse with Eve, but it was Lilith he longed for. The bud-stage of breast development appears early (10.7 years) in the sequence of somatic changes accompanying pubescence. And the next maturational item available is the first appearance of pigmented pubic hair (11.2 years). My little cup brims with tiddles.

A shipwreck. An atoll. Alone with a drowned passenger's shivering child. Darling, this is only a game! How marvelous were my fancied adventures as I sat on a hard park bench pretending to be immersed in a trembling book. Around the quiet scholar, nymphets played freely, as if he were a familiar statue or part of an old tree's shadow and sheen. Once a perfect little beauty in a tartan frock, with a clatter put her heavily armed foot near me upon the bench to dip her slim bare arms into me and tighten the strap of her roller skate, and I dissolved in the sun, with my book for fig leaf, as her auburn ringlets fell all over her skinned knee, and the shadow of leaves I shared pulsated and melted on her radiant limb next to my chameleonic cheek. Another time a red-haired school girl hung over me in the *métro*, and a revelation of axillary russet I obtained remained in my blood for weeks. I could list a great number of these one-sided diminutive romances. Some of them ended in a rich flavor of hell. It happened for instance that from my balcony I would notice a lighted window across the street and what looked like a nymphet in the act of undressing before a co-operative mirror. Thus isolated, thus removed, the vision acquired an especially keen charm that made me race with all speed toward my lone gratification. But abruptly, fiendishly, the tender pattern of nudity I had adored would be transformed into the disgusting lamp-lit bare arm of a man in his underclothes reading his paper by the open window in the hot, damp, hopeless summer night.

Rope-skipping, hopscotch. That old woman in black who sat down next to me on my bench, on my rack of joy (a nymphet was groping under me for a lost marble), and asked if I had stomachache, the insolent hag. Ah, leave me alone in my pubescent park, in my mossy garden. Let them play around me forever. Never grow up.

6

A propos: I have often wondered what became of those nymphets later? In this wrought-iron world of criss-cross cause and effect, could it be that the hidden throb I stole from them did not affect *their* future? I had possessed her—and she never knew it. All right. But would it not tell sometime later? Had I not somehow tampered with her fate by involving her image in my voluptas? Oh, it was, and remains, a source of great and terrible wonder.

I learned, however, what they looked like, those lovely, maddening, thin-armed nymphets, when they grew up. I remember walking along an animated street on a gray spring afternoon somewhere near the Madeleine. A short slim girl passed me at a rapid, high-heeled, tripping step, we glanced back at the same moment, she stopped and I accosted her. She came hardly up to my chest hair and had the kind of dimpled round little face French girls so often have, and I liked her long lashes and tight-fitting tailored dress sheathing in pearl-gray her young body which still retained—and that was the nymphic echo, the chill of delight, the leap in my loins—a childish something mingling with the professional *frétillement* of her small agile rump. I asked her price, and she promptly replied with melodious silvery precision (a bird, a very bird!) "*Cent.*" I tried to haggle but she saw the awful lone longing in my lowered eyes, directed so far down at her round forehead and rudimentary hat (a band, a posy); and with one beat of her lashes: "*Tant pis,*" she said, and made as if to move away. Perhaps only three years earlier I might have seen her coming home from school! That evocation settled the matter. She led me up the usual steep stairs, with the usual bell clearing the way for the *monsieur* who might not care

to meet another *monsieur,* on the mournful climb to the abject room, all bed and *bidet.* As usual, she asked at once for her *petit*
1 *cadeau,* and as usual I asked her name (Monique) and her age (eighteen). I was pretty well acquainted with the banal way of
2 streetwalkers. They all answer *"dix-huit"*—a trim twitter, a note of finality and wistful deceit which they emit up to ten times per day, the poor little creatures. But in Monique's case there could be no doubt she was, if anything, adding one or two years to her age. This I deduced from many details of her compact, neat, curiously immature body. Having shed her clothes with fascinating rapidity, she stood for a moment partly wrapped in the dingy gauze of the window curtain listening with infantile pleasure, as pat as pat could be, to an organ-grinder in the dust-brimming courtyard below. When I examined her small hands and drew her attention to their grubby fingernails, she said with
3 a naïve frown *"Oui, ce n'est pas bien,"* and went to the wash-basin, but I said it did not matter, did not matter at all. With her brown bobbed hair, luminous gray eyes and pale skin, she looked perfectly charming. Her hips were no bigger than those of a squatting lad; in fact, I do not hesitate to say (and indeed this is the reason why I linger gratefully in that gauze-gray room of memory with little Monique) that among the eighty or so
4 *grues* I had had operate upon me, she was the only one that gave me a pang of genuine pleasure. *"Il était malin, celui qui a*
5 *inventé ce truc-là,"* she commented amiably, and got back into her clothes with the same high-style speed.

I asked for another, more elaborate, assignment later the same evening, and she said she would meet me at the corner café at
6 nine, and swore she had never *posé un lapin* in all her young life. We returned to the same room, and I could not help saying how very pretty she was to which she answered demurely: *"Tu es*
7 *bien gentil de dire ça"* and then, noticing what I noticed too in the mirror reflecting our small Eden—the dreadful grimace of clenched-teeth tenderness that distorted my mouth—dutiful little Monique (oh, she had been a nymphet all right!) wanted to know if she should remove the layer of red from her lips *avant*
8 *qu'on se couche* in case I planned to kiss her. Of course, I

planned it. I let myself go with her more completely than I had with any young lady before, and my last vision that night of long-lashed Monique is touched up with a gaiety that I find seldom associated with any event in my humiliating, sordid, taciturn love life. She looked tremendously pleased with the bonus of fifty I gave her as she trotted out into the April night drizzle with Humbert Humbert lumbering in her narrow wake. Stopping before a window display she said with great gusto: *"Je vais m'acheter des bas!"* and never may I forget the way her Parisian childish lips exploded on *"bas,"* pronouncing it with an appetite that all but changed the "a" into a brief buoyant bursting "o" as in *"bot."*

I had a date with her next day at 2.15 P.M. in my own rooms, but it was less successful, she seemed to have grown less juvenile, more of a woman overnight. A cold I caught from her led me to cancel a fourth assignment, nor was I sorry to break an emotional series that threatened to burden me with heart-rending fantasies and peter out in dull disappointment. So let her remain, sleek, slender Monique, as she was for a minute or two: a delinquent nymphet shining through the matter-of-fact young whore.

My brief acquaintance with her started a train of thought that may seem pretty obvious to the reader who knows the ropes. An advertisement in a lewd magazine landed me, one brave day, in the office of a Mlle Edith who began by offering me to choose a kindred soul from a collection of rather formal photographs in a rather soiled album (*"Regardez-moi cette belle brune!"*). When I pushed the album away and somehow managed to blurt out my criminal craving, she looked as if about to show me the door; however, after asking me what price I was prepared to disburse, she condescended to put me in touch with a person *qui pourrait arranger la chose.* Next day, an asthmatic woman, coarsely painted, garrulous, garlicky, with an almost farcical Provençal accent and a black mustache above a purple lip, took me to what was apparently her own domicile, and there, after explosively kissing the bunched tips of her fat fingers to signify the delectable rosebud quality of her merchandise, she theatrically drew aside a curtain to reveal what I judged was that part of the room where a large and unfastidious family usually slept. It was now empty save for a monstrously plump, sallow, repulsively plain girl of at least fifteen with red-ribboned thick black braids who sat on a chair perfunctorily nursing a bald doll. When I shook my head and tried to shuffle out of the trap, the woman, talking fast, began removing the dingy woolen jersey from the young giantess' torso; then, seeing my determination to leave,

1 she demanded *son argent*. A door at the end of the room was opened, and two men who had been dining in the kitchen joined in the squabble. They were misshapen, bare-necked, very swarthy and one of them wore dark glasses. A small boy and a begrimed, bowlegged toddler lurked behind them. With the insolent logic of a nightmare, the enraged procuress, indicating the man in

2 glasses, said he had served in the police, *lui*, so that I had better do as I was told. I went up to Marie—for that was her stellar

3 name—who by then had quietly transferred her heavy haunches to a stool at the kitchen table and resumed her interrupted soup while the toddler picked up the doll. With a surge of pity dramatizing my idiotic gesture, I thrust a banknote into her indifferent hand. She surrendered my gift to the ex-detective, whereupon I was suffered to leave.

7

I do not know if the pimp's album may not have been another link in the daisy-chain; but soon after, for my own safety, I decided to marry. It occurred to me that regular hours, home-cooked meals, all the conventions of marriage, the prophylactic routine of its bedroom activities and, who knows, the eventual flowering of certain moral values, of certain spiritual substitutes, might help me, if not to purge myself of my degrading and dangerous desires, at least to keep them under pacific control. A little money that had come my way after my father's death (nothing very grand—the Mirana had been sold long before), in addition to my striking if somewhat brutal good looks, allowed me to enter upon my quest with equanimity. After considerable deliberation, my choice fell on the daughter of a Polish doctor: the good man happened to be treating me for spells of dizziness and tachycardia. We played chess: his daughter watched me from behind her easel, and inserted eyes or knuckles borrowed from me into the cubistic trash that accomplished misses then painted instead of lilacs and lambs. Let me repeat with quiet force: I was, and still am, despite *mes malheurs*, an exceptionally handsome male; slow-moving, tall, with soft dark hair and a gloomy but all the more seductive cast of demeanor. Exceptional virility often reflects in the subject's displayable features a sullen and congested something that pertains to what he has to conceal. And this was my case. Well did I know, alas, that I could obtain at the snap of my fingers any adult female I chose; in fact, it had become quite a habit with me of not being too attentive to women lest they come toppling, bloodripe, into my cold lap. Had I been a *français moyen* with a taste for flashy ladies, I might have easily found, among the many crazed beauties that lashed my grim rock, creatures far more fascinating than Valeria. My choice, however, was prompted by considerations whose essence was, as I realized too late, a piteous compromise. All of which goes to show how dreadfully stupid poor Humbert always was in matters of sex.

8

Although I told myself I was looking merely for a soothing presence, a glorified *pot-au-feu*, an animated merkin, what really attracted me to Valeria was the imitation she gave of a little girl. She gave it not because she had divined something about me; it was just her style—and I fell for it. Actually, she was at least in her late twenties (I never established her exact age for even her passport lied) and had mislaid her virginity under circumstances that changed with her reminiscent moods. I, on my part, was as naïve as only a pervert can be. She looked fluffy and frolicsome, dressed *à la gamine*, showed a generous amount of smooth leg, knew how to stress the white of a bare instep by the black of a velvet slipper, and pouted, and dimpled, and romped, and dirndled, and shook her short curly blond hair in the cutest and tritest fashion imaginable.

1   After a brief ceremony at the *mairie*, I took her to the new apartment I had rented and, somewhat to her surprise, had her wear, before I touched her, a girl's plain nightshirt that I had managed to filch from the linen closet of an orphanage. I derived some fun from that nuptial night and had the idiot in hysterics by sunrise. But reality soon asserted itself. The bleached curl

2   revealed its melanic root; the down turned to prickles on a shaved shin; the mobile moist mouth, no matter how I stuffed it with love, disclosed ignominiously its resemblance to the corresponding part in a treasured portrait of her toadlike dead mama; and presently, instead of a pale little gutter girl, Humbert Humbert had on his hands a large, puffy, short-legged, big-

3   breasted and practically brainless *baba*.

This state of affairs lasted from 1935 to 1939. Her only asset was a muted nature which did help to produce an odd sense of comfort in our small squalid flat: two rooms, a hazy view in one window, a brick wall in the other, a tiny kitchen, a shoe-shaped bath tub, within which I felt like Marat but with no white-

4   necked maiden to stab me. We had quite a few cozy evenings

5   together, she deep in her *Paris-Soir*, I working at a rickety table. We went to movies, bicycle races and boxing matches. I appealed to her stale flesh very seldom, only in cases of great urgency and despair. The grocer opposite had a little daughter whose shadow drove me mad; but with Valeria's help I did find after all some legal outlets to my fantastic predicament. As to cooking, we tacitly dismissed the *pot-au-feu* and had most of our meals at a crowded place in rue Bonaparte where there were wine stains on the table cloth and a good deal of foreign babble. And next door, an art dealer displayed in his cluttered window a splendid, flamboyant, green, red, golden and inky blue, ancient American estampe—a locomotive with a gigantic smokestack, great baroque lamps and a tremendous cowcatcher, hauling its mauve coaches

through the stormy prairie night and mixing a lot of spark-studded black smoke with the furry thunder clouds.

These burst. In the summer of 1939 *mon oncle d'Amérique* died bequeathing me an annual income of a few thousand dollars on condition I came to live in the States and showed some interest in his business. This prospect was most welcome to me. I felt my life needed a shake-up. There was another thing, too: moth holes had appeared in the plush of matrimonial comfort. During the last weeks I had kept noticing that my fat Valeria was not her usual self; had acquired a queer restlessness; even showed something like irritation at times, which was quite out of keeping with the stock character she was supposed to impersonate. When I informed her we were shortly to sail for New York, she looked distressed and bewildered. There were some tedious difficulties with her papers. She had a Nansen, or better say Nonsense, passport which for some reason a share in her husband's solid Swiss citizenship could not easily transcend; and I decided it was the necessity of queuing in the *préfecture*, and other formalities, that had made her so listless, despite my patiently describing to her America, the country of rosy children and great trees, where life would be such an improvement on dull dingy Paris.

We were coming out of some office building one morning, with her papers almost in order, when Valeria, as she waddled by my side, began to shake her poodle head vigorously without saying a word. I let her go on for a while and then asked if she thought she had something inside. She answered (I translate from her French which was, I imagine, a translation in its turn of some Slavic platitude): "There is another man in my life."

Now, these are ugly words for a husband to hear. They dazed me, I confess. To beat her up in the street, there and then, as an honest vulgarian might have done, was not feasible. Years of secret sufferings had taught me superhuman self-control. So I ushered her into a taxi which had been invitingly creeping along the curb for some time, and in this comparative privacy I quietly suggested she comment her wild talk. A mounting fury was suffocating me—not because I had any particular fondness for that

[29]

figure of fun, *Mme Humbert*, but because matters of legal and illegal conjunction were for me alone to decide, and here she was, Valeria, the comedy wife, brazenly preparing to dispose in her own way of my comfort and fate. I demanded her lover's name. I repeated my question; but she kept up a burlesque babble, discoursing on her unhappiness with me and announc-
1 ing plans for an immediate divorce. *"Mais qui est-ce?"* I shouted at last, striking her on the knee with my fist; and she, without even wincing, stared at me as if the answer were too simple for words, then gave a quick shrug and pointed at the thick neck of the taxi driver. He pulled up at a small café and introduced himself. I do not remember his ridiculous name but after all those years I still see him quite clearly—a stocky White Russian ex-colonel with a bushy mustache and a crew cut; there were thousands of them plying that fool's trade in Paris. We sat down at a table; the Tsarist ordered wine; and Valeria, after applying a wet napkin to her knee, went on talking—*into* me rather than to me; she poured words into this dignified receptacle with a volubility I had never suspected she had in her. And every now and then she would volley a burst of Slavic at her stolid lover. The situation was preposterous and became even more so when the taxi-colonel, stopping Valeria with a possessive smile, began to unfold *his* views and plans. With an atrocious accent to his careful French, he delineated the world of love and work into which he proposed to enter hand in hand with his child-wife Valeria. She by now was preening herself, between him and me, rouging her pursed lips, tripling her chin to pick at her blouse-bosom and so forth, and he spoke of her as if she were absent, and also as if she were a kind of little ward that was in the act of being transferred, for her own good, from one wise guardian to another even wiser one; and although my helpless wrath may have exaggerated and disfigured certain impressions, I can swear that he actually consulted me on such things as her diet, her periods, her wardrobe and the books she had read or should read. "I think," he said, "she will like *Jean Christophe?*"
2 Oh, he was quite a scholar, Mr. Taxovich.

I put an end to this gibberish by suggesting Valeria pack up her few belongings immediately, upon which the platitudinous colonel gallantly offered to carry them into the car. Reverting to his professional state, he drove the Humberts to their residence and all the way Valeria talked, and Humbert the Terrible deliberated with Humbert the Small whether Humbert Humbert should kill her or her lover, or both, or neither. I remember once handling an automatic belonging to a fellow student, in the days (I have not spoken of them, I think, but never mind) when I toyed with the idea of enjoying his little sister, a most diaphanous nymphet with a black hair bow, and then shooting myself. I now wondered if Valechka (as the colonel called her) was really worth shooting, or strangling, or drowning. She had very vulnerable legs, and I decided I would limit myself to hurting her very horribly as soon as we were alone.

But we never were. Valechka—by now shedding torrents of tears tinged with the mess of her rainbow make-up,—started to fill anyhow a trunk, and two suitcases, and a bursting carton, and visions of putting on my mountain boots and taking a running kick at her rump were of course impossible to put into execution with the cursed colonel hovering around all the time. I cannot say he behaved insolently or anything like that; on the contrary, he displayed, as a small sideshow in the theatricals I had been inveigled in, a discreet old-world civility, punctuating his movements with all sorts of mispronounced apologies (*j'ai demannde pardonne*—excuse me—*est-ce que j'ai puis*—may I—   1 and so forth), and turning away tactfully when Valechka took down with a flourish her pink panties from the clothesline above the tub; but he seemed to be all over the place at once, *le gredin*,   2 agreeing his frame with the anatomy of the flat, reading in my chair my newspaper, untying a knotted string, rolling a cigarette, counting the teaspoons, visiting the bathroom, helping his moll to wrap up the electric fan her father had given her, and carrying streetward her luggage. I sat with arms folded, one hip on the window sill, dying of hate and boredom. At last both were out of the quivering apartment—the vibration of the door I had slammed after them still rang in my every nerve, a poor substitute for the backhand slap with which I ought to have hit her across the cheekbone according to the rules of the movies. Clumsily playing my part, I stomped to the bathroom to check if they had taken my English toilet water; they had not; but I noticed with a spasm of fierce disgust that the former Counselor of the Tsar, after thoroughly easing his bladder, had not flushed the toilet. That solemn pool of alien urine with a soggy, tawny cigarette butt disintegrating in it struck me as a crowning insult, and I wildly looked around for a weapon. Actually I daresay it was nothing but middle-class Russian courtesy (with an oriental tang, perhaps) that had prompted the good colonel (Maximovich! his name suddenly taxies back to me), a very formal person as they all are, to muffle his private need in decorous silence so as not to underscore the small size of his host's domicile with the rush of a gross cascade on top of his own hushed trickle. But this did not enter my mind at the moment, as groaning with rage I ransacked the kitchen for something better than a broom. Then, canceling my search, I dashed out of the house with the heroic decision of attacking him barefisted; despite my natural vigor, I am no pugilist, while the short but broad-shouldered Maximovich seemed made of pig iron. The void of the street, revealing nothing of my wife's departure except a rhinestone button that she had dropped in the mud after preserving it for three unnecessary years in a broken box, may have spared me a bloody nose. But no matter. I had my little revenge in due time. A man from Pasadena told me one day that Mrs. Maximovich née Zborovski had died in childbirth around 1945; the couple had somehow got over to California and had been used there, for an excellent salary, in a year-long experiment conducted by a distinguished American ethnologist. The experiment dealt with human and racial reactions to a diet of bananas and dates in a constant position on all fours. My informant, a doctor, swore he had seen with his own eyes obese Valechka and her colonel, by then gray-haired and also quite corpulent, diligently crawling about the well-swept floors of a brightly lit set of rooms (fruit in one, water in another, mats in a third and so on) in the company of several other hired quadrupeds, selected from indigent and helpless groups. I tried to

find the results of these tests in the *Review of Anthropology;*
but they appear not to have been published yet. These scientific
products take of course some time to fructuate. I hope they will   1
be illustrated with good photographs when they do get printed,
although it is not very likely that a prison library will harbor
such erudite works. The one to which I am restricted these days,
despite my lawyer's favors, is a good example of the inane eclecti-
cism governing the selection of books in prison libraries. They
have the Bible, of course, and Dickens (an ancient set, N. Y.,
G. W. Dillingham, Publisher, MDCCCLXXXVII); and the
Children's Encyclopedia (with some nice photographs of sun-
shine-haired Girl Scouts in shorts), and *A Murder Is Announced*
by Agatha Christie; but they also have such coruscating trifles as   2
A Vagabond in Italy by Percy Elphinstone, author of *Venice*   3
Revisited, Boston, 1868, and a comparatively recent (1946)
Who's Who in the Limelight—actors, producers, playwrights,
and shots of static scenes. In looking through the latter volume,
I was treated last night to one of those dazzling coincidences
that logicians loathe and poets love. I transcribe most of the   4
page:

    Pym, Roland. Born in Lundy, Mass., 1922. Received stage   5
training at Elsinore Playhouse, Derby, N.Y. Made debut in   6
Sunburst. Among his many appearances are *Two Blocks from*   7
Here, The Girl in Green, Scrambled Husbands, The Strange
Mushroom, Touch and Go, John Lovely, I Was Dreaming   8
of You.
    Quilty, Clare, American dramatist. Born in Ocean City,   9
N.J., 1911. Educated at Columbia University. Started on a
commercial career but turned to playwriting. Author of *The*
Little Nymph, The Lady Who Loved Lightning (in col-   10, 11
laboration with Vivian Darkbloom), *Dark Age, The Strange*   12, 13
Mushroom, Fatherly Love, and others. His many plays for   14
children are notable. *Little Nymph* (1940) traveled 14,000
miles and played 280 performances on the road during the
winter before ending in New York. Hobbies: fast cars, pho-   15
tography, pets.   16
    Quine, Dolores. Born in 1882, in Dayton, Ohio. Studied   17

for stage at American Academy. First played in Ottawa in
1900. Made New York debut in 1904 in *Never Talk to
Strangers*. Has disappeared since in [a list of some thirty
plays follows].

How the look of my dear love's name even affixed to some
old hag of an actress, still makes me rock with helpless pain!
Perhaps, she might have been an actress too. Born 1935. Appeared
(I notice the slip of my pen in the preceding paragraph, but
please do not correct it, Clarence) in *The Murdered Playwright*.
Quine the Swine. Guilty of killing Quilty. Oh, my Lolita, I
have only words to play with!

9

Divorce proceedings delayed my voyage, and the gloom of yet
another World War had settled upon the globe when, after a
winter of ennui and pneumonia in Portugal, I at last reached
the States. In New York I eagerly accepted the soft job fate
offered me: it consisted mainly of thinking up and editing perfume ads. I welcomed its desultory character and pseudoliterary
aspects, attending to it whenever I had nothing better to do. On
the other hand, I was urged by a war-time university in New
York to complete my comparative history of French literature
for English-speaking students. The first volume took me a couple
of years during which I put in seldom less than fifteen hours of
work daily. As I look back on those days, I see them divided
tidily into ample light and narrow shade: the light pertaining to
the solace of research in palatial libraries, the shade to my excruciating desires and insomnias of which enough has been said.
Knowing me by now, the reader can easily imagine how dusty
and hot I got, trying to catch a glimpse of nymphets (alas, always
remote) playing in Central Park, and how repulsed I was by the
glitter of deodorized career girls that a gay dog in one of the
offices kept unloading upon me. Let us skip all that. A dreadful

breakdown sent me to a sanatorium for more than a year; I went back to my work—only to be hospitalized again.

Robust outdoor life seemed to promise me some relief. One of my favorite doctors, a charming cynical chap with a little brown beard, had a brother, and this brother was about to lead an expedition into arctic Canada. I was attached to it as a "recorder of psychic reactions." With two young botanists and an old carpenter I shared now and then (never very successfully) the favors of one of our nutritionists, a Dr. Anita Johnson—who was soon flown back, I am glad to say. I had little notion of what object the expedition was pursuing. Judging by the number of meteorologists upon it, we may have been tracking to its lair (somewhere on Prince of Wales' Island, I understand) the wandering and wobbly north magnetic pole. One group, jointly with the Canadians, established a weather station on Pierre Point in Melville Sound. Another group, equally misguided, collected plankton. A third studied tuberculosis in the tundra. Bert, a film photographer—an insecure fellow with whom at one time I was made to partake in a good deal of menial work (he, too, had some psychic troubles)—maintained that the big men on our team, the real leaders we never saw, were mainly engaged in checking the influence of climatic amelioration on the coats of the arctic fox.

We lived in prefabricated timber cabins amid a Pre-Cambrian world of granite. We had heaps of supplies—the *Reader's Digest*, an ice cream mixer, chemical toilets, paper caps for Christmas. My health improved wonderfully in spite or because of all the fantastic blankness and boredom. Surrounded by such dejected vegetation as willow scrub and lichens; permeated, and, I suppose, cleansed by a whistling gale; seated on a boulder under a completely translucent sky (through which, however, nothing of importance showed), I felt curiously aloof from my own self. No temptations maddened me. The plump, glossy little Eskimo girls with their fish smell, hideous raven hair and guinea pig faces, evoked even less desire in me than Dr. Johnson had. Nymphets do not occur in polar regions.

I left my betters the task of analyzing glacial drifts, drumlins,

1, 2 and gremlins, and kremlins, and for a time tried to jot down what I fondly thought were "reactions" (I noticed, for instance, that dreams under the midnight sun tended to be highly colored, and this my friend the photographer confirmed). I was also supposed to quiz my various companions on a number of important matters, such as nostalgia, fear of unknown animals, food-fantasies, nocturnal emissions, hobbies, choice of radio programs, changes in outlook and so forth. Everybody got so fed up with this that I soon dropped the project completely, and only toward the end of my twenty months of cold labor (as one of the botanists jocosely put it) concocted a perfectly spurious and very racy report that the reader will find published in the *Annals of Adult Psychophysics* for 1945 or 1946, as well as in the issue of *Arctic Explorations* devoted to that particular expedition; which, in conclusion, was not really concerned with Victoria Island copper or anything like that, as I learned later from my genial doctor; for the nature of its real purpose was what is termed "hush-hush," and so let me add merely that whatever it was, that purpose was admirably achieved.

3 The reader will regret to learn that soon after my return to civilization I had another bout with insanity (if to melancholia and a sense of insufferable oppression that cruel term must be applied). I owe my complete restoration to a discovery I made while being treated at that particular very expensive sanatorium. I discovered there was an endless source of robust enjoyment in trifling with psychiatrists: cunningly leading them on; never letting them see that you know all the tricks of the trade; inventing for them elaborate dreams, pure classics in style (which make *them*, the dream-extortionists, dream and wake up shrieking); teasing them with fake "primal scenes"; and never allowing them the slightest glimpse of one's real sexual predicament. By bribing a nurse I won access to some files and discovered, with glee, cards calling me "potentially homosexual" and "totally impotent." The sport was so excellent, its results—in *my* case—so ruddy that I stayed on for a whole month after I was quite well (sleeping admirably and eating like a schoolgirl). And then I added another week just for the pleasure of taking on a power-

ful newcomer, a displaced (and, surely, deranged) celebrity, known for his knack of making patients believe they had witnessed their own conception.

10

Upon signing out, I cast around for some place in the New England countryside or sleepy small town (elms, white church) where I could spend a studious summer subsisting on a compact boxful of notes I had accumulated and bathing in some nearby lake. My work had begun to interest me again—I mean my scholarly exertions; the other thing, my active participation in my uncle's posthumous perfumes, had by then been cut down to a minimum.

One of his former employees, the scion of a distinguished family, suggested I spend a few months in the residence of his impoverished cousins, a Mr. McCoo, retired, and his wife, who wanted to let their upper story where a late aunt had delicately dwelt. He said they had two little daughters, one a baby, the other a girl of twelve, and a beautiful garden, not far from a beautiful lake, and I said it sounded perfectly perfect.

I exchanged letters with these people, satisfying them I was housebroken, and spent a fantastic night on the train, imagining in all possible detail the enigmatic nymphet I would coach in French and fondle in Humbertish. Nobody met me at the toy station where I alighted with my new expensive bag, and nobody answered the telephone; eventually, however, a distraught Mc-Coo in wet clothes turned up at the only hotel of green-and-pink Ramsdale with the news that his house had just burned down—possibly, owing to the synchronous conflagration that had been raging all night in my veins. His family, he said, had fled to a farm he owned, and had taken the car, but a friend of his wife's, a grand person, Mrs. Haze of 342 Lawn Street, offered to accommodate me. A lady who lived opposite Mrs. Haze's had lent McCoo her limousine, a marvelously old-fashioned, square-topped affair, manned by a cheerful Negro. Now, since the only reason for my coming at all had vanished, the aforesaid arrangement seemed preposterous. All right, his house would have to be completely rebuilt, so what? Had he not insured it sufficiently? I was angry, disappointed and bored, but being a polite European, could not refuse to be sent off to Lawn Street in that funeral car, feeling that otherwise McCoo would devise an even more elaborate means of getting rid of me. I saw him scamper away, and my chauffeur shook his head with a soft chuckle. En route, I swore to myself I would not dream of staying in Ramsdale under any circumstance but would fly that very day to the Bermudas or the Bahamas or the Blazes. Possibilities of sweetness on technicolor beaches had been trickling through my spine for some time before, and McCoo's cousin had, in fact, sharply diverted that train of thought with his well-meaning but as it transpired now absolutely inane suggestion.

Speaking of sharp turns: we almost ran over a meddlesome suburban dog (one of those who lie in wait for cars) as we swerved into Lawn Street. A little further, the Haze house, a white-frame horror, appeared, looking dingy and old, more gray than white—the kind of place you know will have a rubber tube affixable to the tub faucet in lieu of shower. I tipped the chauffeur and hoped he would immediately drive away so that I might double back unnoticed to my hotel and bag; but the man merely crossed to the other side of the street where an old lady was calling to him from her porch. What could I do? I pressed the bell button.

A colored maid let me in—and left me standing on the mat while she rushed back to the kitchen where something was burning that ought not to burn.

The front hall was graced with door chimes, a white-eyed wooden thingamabob of commercial Mexican origin, and that banal darling of the arty middle class, van Gogh's "Arlésienne." A door ajar to the right afforded a glimpse of a living room, with some more Mexican trash in a corner cabinet and a striped sofa along the wall. There was a staircase at the end of the hallway, and as I stood mopping my brow (only now did I realize how hot it had been out-of-doors) and staring, to stare at something, at an old gray tennis ball that lay on an oak chest, there came from the upper landing the contralto voice of Mrs. Haze, who leaning over the banisters inquired melodiously, "Is that Monsieur Humbert?" A bit of cigarette ash dropped from there in addition. Presently, the lady herself—sandals, maroon slacks, yellow silk blouse, squarish face, in that order—came down the steps, her index finger still tapping upon her cigarette.

I think I had better describe her right away, to get it over with. The poor lady was in her middle thirties, she had a shiny forehead, plucked eyebrows and quite simple but not unattractive features of a type that may be defined as a weak solution of Marlene Dietrich. Patting her bronze-brown bun, she led me into the parlor and we talked for a minute about the McCoo fire and the privilege of living in Ramsdale. Her very wide-set sea-green eyes had a funny way of traveling all over you, carefully avoiding your own eyes. Her smile was but a quizzical jerk of one eyebrow; and uncoiling herself from the sofa as she talked, she kept making spasmodic dashes at three ashtrays and the near fender (where lay the brown core of an apple); whereupon she would sink back again, one leg folded under her. She was, obviously, one of those women whose polished words may reflect a book club or bridge club, or any other deadly conventionality, but never her soul; women who are completely devoid of humor; women utterly indifferent at heart to the dozen or so possible subjects of a parlor conversation, but very particular about the rules of such conversations, through the sunny cellophane of which not very appetizing frustrations can be readily distinguished. I was perfectly aware that if by any wild chance I became her lodger, she would methodically proceed to do in regard to me what taking a lodger probably meant to her all along, and I would again be enmeshed in one of those tedious affairs I knew so well.

But there was no question of my settling there. I could not be happy in that type of household with bedraggled magazines on every chair and a kind of horrible hybridization between the comedy of so-called "functional modern furniture" and the

1

tragedy of decrepit rockers and rickety lamp tables with dead lamps. I was led upstairs, and to the left—into "my" room. I inspected it through the mist of my utter rejection of it; but I did discern above "my" bed René Prinet's "Kreutzer Sonata." And she called that servant maid's room a "semi-studio"! Let's get out of here at once, I firmly said to myself as I pretended to deliberate over the absurdly, and ominously, low price that my wistful hostess was asking for board and bed.

Old-world politeness, however, obliged me to go on with the ordeal. We crossed the landing to the right side of the house (where "I and Lo have our rooms"—Lo being presumably the maid), and the lodger-lover could hardly conceal a shudder when he, a very fastidious male, was granted a preview of the only bathroom, a tiny oblong between the landing and "Lo's" room, with limp wet things overhanging the dubious tub (the question mark of a hair inside); and there were the expected coils of the rubber snake, and its complement—a pinkish cozy, coyly covering the toilet lid.

"I see you are not too favorably impressed," said the lady letting her hand rest for a moment upon my sleeve: she combined a cool forwardness—the overflow of what I think is called "poise"—with a shyness and sadness that caused her detached way of selecting her words to seem as unnatural as the intonation of a professor of "speech." "This is not a neat household, I confess," the doomed dear continued, "but I assure you [she looked at my lips], you will be very comfortable, very comfortable, indeed. Let me show you the garden" (the last more brightly, with a kind of winsome toss of the voice).

Reluctantly I followed her downstairs again; then through the kitchen at the end of the hall, on the right side of the house— the side where also the dining room and the parlor were (under "my" room, on the left, there was nothing but a garage). In the kitchen, the Negro maid, a plump youngish woman, said, as she took her large glossy black purse from the knob of the door leading to the back porch: "I'll go now, Mrs. Haze." "Yes, Louise," answered Mrs. Haze with a sigh. "I'll settle with you Friday." We passed on to a small pantry and entered the dining room, parallel to the parlor we had already admired. I noticed a white sock on the floor. With a deprecatory grunt, Mrs. Haze stooped without stopping and threw it into a closet next to the pantry. We cursorily inspected a mahogany table with a fruit vase in the middle, containing nothing but the still glistening stone of one plum. I groped for the timetable I had in my pocket and surreptitiously fished it out to look as soon as possible for a train. I was still walking behind Mrs. Haze through the dining room when, beyond it, there came a sudden burst of greenery— "the piazza," sang out my leader, and then, without the least warning, a blue sea-wave swelled under my heart and, from a mat in a pool of sun, half-naked, kneeling, turning about on her knees, there was my Riviera love peering at me over dark glasses.   1

It was the same child—the same frail, honey-hued shoulders, the same silky supple bare back, the same chestnut head of hair. A polka-dotted black kerchief tied around her chest hid from my aging ape eyes, but not from the gaze of young memory, the juvenile breasts I had fondled one immortal day. And, as if I were the fairy-tale nurse of some little princess (lost, kidnaped,   2 discovered in gypsy rags through which her nakedness smiled at the king and his hounds), I recognized the tiny dark-brown mole on her side. With awe and delight (the king crying for joy, the trumpets blaring, the nurse drunk) I saw again her lovely in-drawn abdomen where my southbound mouth had briefly paused; and those puerile hips on which I had kissed the crenu-lated imprint left by the band of her shorts—that last mad im-mortal day behind the "Roches Roses." The twenty-five years I   3 had lived since then, tapered to a palpitating point, and vanished.

I find it most difficult to express with adequate force that flash, that shiver, that impact of passionate recognition. In the course of the sun-shot moment that my glance slithered over the kneeling child (her eyes blinking over those stern dark spectacles —the little Herr Doktor who was to cure me of all my aches) while I passed by her in my adult disguise (a great big hand-some hunk of movieland manhood), the vacuum of my soul managed to suck in every detail of her bright beauty, and these I checked against the features of my dead bride. A little later, of

1 course, she, this *nouvelle*, this Lolita, *my* Lolita, was to eclipse completely her prototype. All I want to stress is that my discovery of her was a fatal consequence of that "princedom by the sea" in my tortured past. Everything between the two events was but a series of gropings and blunders, and false rudiments of joy. Everything they shared made one of them.

I have no illusions, however. My judges will regard all this as a
2 piece of mummery on the part of a madman with a gross liking
3, 4 for the *fruit vert*. *Au fond, ça m'est bien égal*. All I know is that while the Haze woman and I went down the steps into the breathless garden, my knees were like reflections of knees in rippling water, and my lips were like sand, and—

"That was my Lo," she said, "and these are my lilies."

"Yes," I said, "yes. They are beautiful, beautiful, beautiful!"

11

Exhibit number two is a pocket diary bound in black imitation
5 leather, with a golden year, 1947, *en escalier*, in its upper left-hand corner. I speak of this neat product of the Blank Blank Co.,
6 Blankton, Mass., as if it were really before me. Actually, it was destroyed five years ago and what we examine now (by courtesy of a photographic memory) is but its brief materialization, a
7 puny unfledged phœnix.

I remember the thing so exactly because I wrote it really twice. First I jotted down each entry in pencil (with many erasures and corrections) on the leaves of what is commercially known as a "typewriter tablet"; then, I copied it out with obvious abbreviations in my smallest, most satanic, hand in the little black book just mentioned.

May 30 is a Fast Day by Proclamation in New Hampshire but not in the Carolinas. That day an epidemic of "abdominal flu" (whatever that is) forced Ramsdale to close its schools for the summer. The reader may check the weather data in the Ramsdale *Journal* for 1947. A few days before that I moved into the

Haze house, and the little diary which I now propose to reel off (much as a spy delivers by heart the contents of the note he swallowed) covers most of June.

Thursday. Very warm day. From a vantage point (bathroom window) saw Dolores taking things off a clothesline in the apple-green light behind the house. Strolled out. She wore a plaid shirt, blue jeans and sneakers. Every movement she made in the dappled sun plucked at the most secret and sensitive chord of my abject body. After a while she sat down next to me on the lower step of the back porch and began to pick up the pebbles between her feet—pebbles, my God, then a curled bit of milk-bottle glass resembling a snarling lip—and chuck them at a can. *Ping.* You can't a second time—you can't hit it—this is agony—a second time. *Ping.* Marvelous skin—oh, marvelous: tender and tanned, not the least blemish. Sundaes cause acne. The excess of the oily substance called sebum which nourishes the hair follicles of the skin creates, when too profuse, an irritation that opens the way to infection. But nymphets do not have acne although they gorge themselves on rich food. God, what agony, that silky shimmer above her temple grading into bright brown hair. And the little bone twitching at the side of her dust-powdered ankle. "The McCoo girl? Ginny McCoo? Oh, she's a fright. And mean. And lame. Nearly died of polio." Ping. The glistening tracery of down on her forearm. When she got up to take in the wash, I had a chance of adoring from afar the faded seat of her rolled-up jeans. Out of the lawn, bland Mrs. Haze, complete with camera, grew up like a fakir's fake tree and after some heliotropic fussing—sad eyes up, glad eyes down —had the cheek of taking my picture as I sat blinking on the steps, Humbert le Bel.

Friday. Saw her going somewhere with a dark girl called Rose. Why does the way she walks—a child, mind you, a mere child! —excite me so abominably? Analyze it. A faint suggestion of turned in toes. A kind of wiggly looseness below the knee prolonged to the end of each footfall. The ghost of a drag. Very infantile, infinitely meretricious. Humbert Humbert is also infinitely moved by the little one's slangy speech, by her harsh high voice. Later heard her volley crude nonsense at Rose across the fence. Twanging through me in a rising rhythm. Pause. "I must go now, kiddo."

Saturday. (Beginning perhaps amended.) I know it is madness to keep this journal but it gives me a strange thrill to do so; and only a loving wife could decipher my microscopic script. Let me state with a sob that today my L. was sun-bathing on the so-called "piazza," but her mother and some other woman were around all the time. Of course, I might have sat there in the rocker and pretended to read. Playing safe, I kept away, for I was afraid that the horrible, insane, ridiculous and pitiful tremor
1 that palsied me might prevent me from making my *entrée* with any semblance of casualness.

2 *Sunday.* Heat ripple still with us; a most favonian week. This time I took up a strategic position, with obese newspaper and new pipe, in the piazza rocker *before* L. arrived. To my intense disappointment she came with her mother, both in two-piece bathing suits, black, as new as my pipe. My darling, my sweetheart stood for a moment near me—wanted the funnies—and she smelt almost exactly like the other one, the Riviera one, but more intensely so, with rougher overtones—a torrid odor that at once set my manhood astir—but she had already yanked out of
3 me the coveted section and retreated to her mat near her phocine mamma. There my beauty lay down on her stomach, showing me, showing the thousand eyes wide open in my eyed blood, her slightly raised shoulder blades, and the bloom along the incurvation of her spine, and the swellings of her tense narrow nates clothed in black, and the seaside of her schoolgirl thighs. Silently, the seventh-grader enjoyed her green-red-blue comics. She was
4 the loveliest nymphet green-red-blue Priap himself could think up. As I looked on, through prismatic layers of light, dry-lipped, focusing my lust and rocking slightly under my newspaper, I felt that my perception of her, if properly concentrated upon, might be sufficient to have me attain a beggar's bliss immediately;
5 but, like some predator that prefers a moving prey to a motionless one, I planned to have this pitiful attainment coincide with one of the various girlish movements she made now and then as

she read, such as trying to scratch the middle of her back and revealing a stippled armpit—but fat Haze suddenly spoiled everything by turning to me and asking me for a light, and starting a make-believe conversation about a fake book by some popular fraud.

Monday. Delectatio morosa. I spend my doleful days in dumps and dolors. We (mother Haze, Dolores and I) were to go to Our Glass Lake this afternoon, and bathe, and bask; but a nacreous morn degenerated at noon into rain, and Lo made a scene.

The median age of pubescence for girls has been found to be thirteen years and nine months in New York and Chicago. The age varies for individuals from ten, or earlier, to seventeen. Virginia was not quite fourteen when Harry Edgar possessed her. He gave her lessons in algebra. *Je m'imagine cela.* They spent their honeymoon at Petersburg, Fla. "Monsieur Poe-poe," as that boy in one of Monsieur Humbert Humbert's classes in Paris called the poet-poet.

I have all the characteristics which, according to writers on the sex interests of children, start the responses stirring in a little girl: clean-cut jaw, muscular hand, deep sonorous voice, broad shoulder. Moreover, I am said to resemble some crooner or actor chap on whom Lo has a crush.

Tuesday. Rain. Lake of the Rains. Mamma out shopping. L., I knew, was somewhere quite near. In result of some stealthy maneuvering, I came across her in her mother's bedroom. Prying her left eye open to get rid of a speck of something. Checked frock. Although I do love that intoxicating brown fragrance of hers, I really think she should wash her hair once in a while. For a moment, we were both in the same warm green bath of the mirror that reflected the top of a poplar with us in the sky. Held her roughly by the shoulders, then tenderly by the temples, and turned her about. "It's right there," she said, "I can feel it." "Swiss peasant would use the top of her tongue." "Lick it out?" "Yeth. Shly try?" "Sure," she said. Gently I pressed my quivering sting along her rolling salty eyeball. "Goody-goody," she said nictating. "It *is* gone." "Now the other?" "You dope," she began,

[45]

"there is noth—" but here she noticed the pucker of my approaching lips. "Okay," she said co-operatively, and bending toward her warm upturned russet face somber Humbert pressed his mouth to her fluttering eyelid. She laughed, and brushed past me out of the room. My heart seemed everywhere at once. Never in my life—not even when fondling my child-love in France—never—

Night. Never have I experienced such agony. I would like to describe her face, her ways—and I cannot, because my own desire for her blinds me when she is near. I am not used to being with nymphets, damn it. If I close my eyes I see but an immobilized fraction of her, a cinematographic still, a sudden smooth nether loveliness, as with one knee up under her tartan skirt she sits tying her shoe. "Dolores Haze, *ne montrez pas vos zhambes*" (this is her mother who thinks she knows French).

A poet *à mes heures*, I composed a madrigal to the soot-black lashes of her pale-gray vacant eyes, to the five asymmetrical freckles of her bobbed nose, to the blond down of her brown limbs; but I tore it up and cannot recall it today. Only in the tritest of terms (diary resumed) can I describe Lo's features: I might say her hair is auburn, and her lips as red as licked red candy, the lower one prettily plump—oh, that I were a lady writer who could have her pose naked in a naked light! But instead I am lanky, big-boned, wooly-chested Humbert Humbert, with thick black eyebrows and a queer accent, and a cesspoolful of rotting monsters behind his slow boyish smile. And neither is she the fragile child of a feminine novel. What drives me insane is the twofold nature of this nymphet—of every nymphet, perhaps; this mixture in my Lolita of tender dreamy childishness and a kind of eerie vulgarity, stemming from the snub-nosed cuteness of ads and magazine pictures, from the blurry pinkness of adolescent maidservants in the Old Country (smelling of crushed daisies and sweat); and from very young harlots disguised as children in provincial brothels; and then again, all this gets mixed up with the exquisite stainless tenderness seeping through the musk and the mud, through the dirt and the death, oh God, oh God. And what is most singular is that she, *this* Lolita, *my* Lolita, has individualized the writer's ancient lust, so that above and over everything there is—Lolita.

Wednesday. "Look, make Mother take you and me to Our Glass Lake tomorrow." These were the textual words said to me by my twelve-year-old flame in a voluptuous whisper, as we happened to bump into one another on the front porch, I out, she in. The reflection of the afternoon sun, a dazzling white diamond with innumerable iridescent spikes quivered on the round back of a parked car. The leafage of a voluminous elm played its mellow shadows upon the clapboard wall of the house. Two poplars shivered and shook. You could make out the formless sounds of remote traffic; a child calling "Nancy, Nan-cy!" In the house, Lolita had put on her favorite "Little Carmen" record which I used to call "Dwarf Conductors," making her snort with mock derision at my mock wit.

Thursday. Last night we sat on the piazza, the Haze woman, Lolita and I. Warm dusk had deepened into amorous darkness. The old girl had finished relating in great detail the plot of a movie she and L. had seen sometime in the winter. The boxer had fallen extremely low when he met the good old priest (who had been a boxer himself in his robust youth and could still slug a sinner). We sat on cushions heaped on the floor, and L. was between the woman and me (she had squeezed herself in, the pet). In my turn, I launched upon a hilarious account of my arctic adventures. The muse of invention handed me a rifle and I shot a white bear who sat down and said: Ah! All the while I was acutely aware of L.'s nearness and as I spoke I gestured in the merciful dark and took advantage of those invisible gestures of mine to touch her hand, her shoulder and a ballerina of wool and gauze which she played with and kept sticking into my lap; and finally, when I had completely enmeshed my glowing darling in this weave of ethereal caresses, I dared stroke her bare leg along the gooseberry fuzz of her shin, and I chuckled at my own jokes, and trembled, and concealed my tremors, and once or twice felt with my rapid lips the warmth of her hair as I treated her to a quick nuzzling,

[47]

humorous aside and caressed her plaything. She, too, fidgeted a good deal so that finally her mother told her sharply to quit it and sent the doll flying into the dark, and I laughed and addressed myself to Haze across Lo's legs to let my hand creep up my nymphet's thin back and feel her skin through her boy's shirt.

But I knew it was all hopeless, and was sick with longing, and my clothes felt miserably tight, and I was almost glad when her mother's quiet voice announced in the dark: "And now we all think that Lo should go to bed." "I think you stink," said Lo. "Which means there will be no picnic tomorrow," said Haze. "This is a free country," said Lo. When angry Lo with a Bronx cheer had gone, I stayed on from sheer inertia, while Haze smoked her tenth cigarette of the evening and complained of Lo.

She had been spiteful, if you please, at the age of one, when she used to throw her toys out of her crib so that her poor mother should keep picking them up, the villainous infant! Now, at twelve, she was a regular pest, said Haze. All she wanted from life was to be one day a strutting and prancing baton twirler or a jitterbug. Her grades were poor, but she was better adjusted in her new school than in Pisky (Pisky was the Haze home town in the Middle West. The Ramsdale house was her late mother-in-law's. They had moved to Ramsdale less than two years ago). "Why was she unhappy there?" "Oh," said Haze, "poor me should know, I went through that when *I* was a kid: boys twisting one's arm, banging into one with loads of books, pulling one's hair, hurting one's breasts, flipping one's skirt. Of course, moodiness is a common concomitant of growing up, but Lo exaggerates. Sullen and evasive. Rude and defiant. Stuck Viola, an Italian schoolmate, in the seat with a fountain pen. Know what I would like? If you, monsieur, happened to be still here in the fall, I'd ask you to help her with her home-work—you seem to know everything, geography, mathematics, French." "Oh, everything," answered monsieur. "That means," said Haze quickly, "you'll *be* here!" I wanted to shout that I would stay on eternally if only I could hope to caress now and then my incipient pupil. But I was wary of Haze. So I just grunted and stretched my limbs nonconcomitantly (*le mot juste*) and presently went up to my room. The woman, however, was evidently not prepared to call it a day. I was already lying upon my cold bed both hands pressing to my face Lolita's fragrant ghost when I heard my indefatigable landlady creeping stealthily up to my door to whisper through it—just to make sure, she said, I was through with the Glance and Gulp magazine I had borrowed the other day. From her room Lo yelled *she* had it. We are quite a lending library in this house, thunder of God.

Friday. I wonder what my academic publishers would say if I were to quote in my textbook Ronsard's "*la vermeillette fente*" or Remy Belleau's "*un petit mont feutré de mousse délicate, tracé sur le milieu d'un fillet escarlatte*" and so forth. I shall probably have another breakdown if I stay any longer in this house, under the strain of this intolerable temptation, by the side of my darling—my darling—my life and my bride. Has she already been initiated by mother nature to the Mystery of the Menarche? Bloated feeling. The Curse of the Irish. Falling from the roof. Grandma is visiting. "Mr. Uterus [I quote from a girls' magazine] starts to build a thick soft wall on the chance a possible baby may have to be bedded down there." The tiny madman in his padded cell.

Incidentally: if I ever commit a serious murder . . . Mark the "if." The urge should be something more than the kind of thing that happened to me with Valeria. Carefully mark that *then* I was rather inept. If and when you wish to sizzle me to death, remember that only a spell of insanity could ever give me the simple energy to be a brute (all this amended, perhaps). Sometimes I attempt to kill in my dreams. But do you know what happens? For instance I hold a gun. For instance I aim at a bland, quietly interested enemy. Oh, I press the trigger all right, but one bullet after another feebly drops on the floor from the sheepish muzzle. In those dreams, my only thought is to conceal the fiasco from my foe, who is slowly growing annoyed.

At dinner tonight the old cat said to me with a sidelong gleam of motherly mockery directed at Lo (I had just been describing, in a flippant vein, the delightful little toothbrush mustache I had not quite decided to grow): "Better don't, if somebody is not to go absolutely dotty." Instantly Lo pushed her plate of boiled fish away, all but knocking her milk over, and bounced out of the dining room. "Would it bore you very much," quoth Haze, "to come with us tomorrow for a swim in Our Glass Lake if Lo apologizes for her manners?"

Later, I heard a great banging of doors and other sounds coming from quaking caverns where the two rivals were having a ripping row.

She has not apologized. The lake is out. It might have been fun.

Saturday. For some days already I had been leaving the door ajar, while I wrote in my room; but only today did the trap work. With a good deal of additional fidgeting, shuffling, scraping—to disguise her embarrassment at visiting me without having been called—Lo came in and after pottering around, became interested in the nightmare curlicues I had penned on a sheet of paper. Oh no: they were not the outcome of a belle-lettrist's inspired pause between two paragraphs; they were the hideous hieroglyphics (which she could not decipher) of my fatal lust. As she bent her brown curls over the desk at which I was sitting, Humbert the Hoarse put his arm around her in a miserable imitation of blood-relationship; and still studying, somewhat shortsightedly, the piece of paper she held, my innocent little visitor slowly sank to a half-sitting position upon my knee. Her adorable profile, parted lips, warm hair were some three inches from my bared eyetooth; and I felt the heat of her limbs through her rough tomboy clothes. All at once I knew I could kiss her throat or the wick of her mouth with perfect impunity. I knew she would let me do so, and even close her eyes as Hollywood teaches. A double vanilla with hot fudge —hardly more unusual than that. I cannot tell my learned reader (whose eyebrows, I suspect, have by now traveled all the way to the back of his bald head), I cannot tell him how the knowledge came to me; perhaps my ape-ear had unconsciously caught some slight change in the rhythm of her respiration—for now she was not really looking at my scribble, but waiting with curiosity and composure—oh, my limpid nymphet! —for the glamorous lodger to do what he was dying to do. A modern child, an avid reader of movie magazines, an expert in dream-slow close-ups, might not think it too strange, I guessed, if a handsome, intensely virile grown-up friend—too late. The house was suddenly vibrating with voluble Louise's voice telling Mrs. Haze who had just come home about a dead something she and Leslie Tomson had found in the basement, and little Lolita was not one to miss such a tale.

Sunday. Changeful, bad-tempered, cheerful, awkward, grace-ful with the tart grace of her coltish subteens, excruciatingly desirable from head to foot (all New England for a lady-writer's pen!), from the black ready-made bow and bobby pins holding her hair in place to the little scar on the lower part of her neat calf (where a roller-skater kicked her in Pisky), a couple of inches above her rough white sock. Gone with her mother to the Hamiltons—a birthday party or something. Full-skirted ging-ham frock. Her little doves seem well formed already. Pre-cocious pet!

Monday. Rainy morning. *"Ces matins gris si doux . . ."* My white pajamas have a lilac design on the back. I am like one of those inflated pale spiders you see in old gardens. Sitting in the middle of a luminous web and giving little jerks to this or that strand. *My* web is spread all over the house as I listen from my chair where I sit like a wily wizard. Is Lo in her room? Gently I tug on the silk. She is not. Just heard the toilet paper cylinder make its staccato sound as it is turned; and no footfalls has my outflung filament traced from the bathroom back to her room. Is she still brushing her teeth (the only sanitary act Lo performs with real zest)? No. The bathroom door has just slammed, so one has to feel elsewhere about the house for the beautiful warm-colored prey. Let us have a strand of silk descend the stairs. I satisfy myself by this means that she is not in the kitchen—not banging the refrigerator door or screech-ing at her detested mamma (who, I suppose, is enjoying her third, cooing and subduedly mirthful, telephone conversation of the morning). Well, let us grope and hope. Ray-like, I glide in thought to the parlor and find the radio silent (and mamma still talking to Mrs. Chatfield or Mrs. Hamilton, very softly, flushed, smiling, cupping the telephone with her free hand, denying by implication that she denies those amusing rumors, rumor, roomer, whispering intimately, as she never does, the clear-cut lady, in face to face talk). So my nymphet is not in the house at all! Gone! What I thought was a prismatic weave turns out to be but an old gray cobweb, the house is empty, is dead. And then comes Lolita's soft sweet chuckle through my half-open door "Don't tell Mother but I've eaten *all* your bacon." Gone when I scuttle out of my room. Lolita, where are you? My breakfast tray, lovingly prepared by my landlady, leers at me toothlessly, ready to be taken in. Lola, Lolita!

Tuesday. Clouds again interfered with that picnic on that unattainable lake. Is it Fate scheming? Yesterday I tried on before the mirror a new pair of bathing trunks.

Wednesday. In the afternoon, Haze (common-sensical shoes, tailor-made dress), said she was driving downtown to buy a present for a friend of a friend of hers, and would I please come too because I have such a wonderful taste in textures and perfumes. "Choose your favorite seduction," she purred. What could Humbert, being in the perfume business, do? She had me cornered between the front porch and her car. "Hurry up," she said as I laboriously doubled up my large body in order to crawl in (still desperately devising a means of escape). She had started the engine, and was genteelly swearing at a backing and turning truck in front that had just brought old invalid Miss Opposite a brand new wheel chair, when my Lolita's sharp voice came from the parlor window: "You! Where are you going? I'm coming too! Wait!" "Ignore her," yelped Haze (killing the motor); alas for my fair driver; Lo was already pulling at the door on my side. "This is intolerable," began Haze; but Lo had scrambled in, shivering with glee. "Move your bottom, you," said Lo. "Lo!" cried Haze (sideglancing at me, hoping I would throw rude Lo out). "And behold," said Lo (not for the first time), as she jerked back, as I jerked back, as the car leapt forward. "It is intolerable," said Haze, violently getting into second, "that a child should be so ill-mannered. And so very persevering. When she knows she is unwanted. And needs a bath."

My knuckles lay against the child's blue jeans. She was bare-footed; her toenails showed remnants of cherry-red polish and there was a bit of adhesive tape across her big toe; and, God, what would I not have given to kiss then and there those delicate-boned, long-toed, monkeyish feet! Suddenly her hand slipped into mine and without our chaperon's seeing, I held, and stroked, and squeezed that little hot paw, all the way to the store. The wings of the driver's Marlenesque nose shone, having shed or burned up their ration of powder, and she kept up an elegant monologue anent the local traffic, and smiled in profile, and pouted in profile, and beat her painted lashes in profile, while I prayed we would never get to that store, but we did.

I have nothing else to report, save, *primo:* that big Haze had little Haze sit behind on our way home, and *secundo:* that the lady decided to keep Humbert's Choice for the backs of her own shapely ears.

Thursday. We are paying with hail and gale for the tropical beginning of the month. In a volume of the *Young People's Encyclopedia,* I found a map of the States that a child's pencil had started copying out on a sheet of lightweight paper, upon the other side of which, counter to the unfinished outline of Florida and the Gulf, there was a mimeographed list of names referring, evidently, to her class at the Ramsdale school. It is a poem I know already by heart.

> Angel, Grace
> Austin, Floyd
> Beale, Jack
> Beale, Mary
> Buck, Daniel
> Byron, Marguerite
> Campbell, Alice
> Carmine, Rose
> Chatfield, Phyllis

Clarke, Gordon
Cowan, John
Cowan, Marion
Duncan, Walter
Falter, Ted
Fantasia, Stella
Flashman, Irving
Fox, George
Glave, Mabel
Goodale, Donald
Green, Lucinda
Hamilton, Mary Rose
Haze, Dolores
Honeck, Rosaline
Knight, Kenneth
McCoo, Virginia
McCrystal, Vivian
McFate, Aubrey
Miranda, Anthony
Miranda, Viola
Rosato, Emil
Schlenker, Lena
Scott, Donald
Sheridan, Agnes
Sherva, Oleg
Smith, Hazel
Talbot, Edgar
Talbot, Edwin
Wain, Lull
Williams, Ralph
Windmuller, Louise

A poem, a poem, forsooth! So strange and sweet was it to discover this "Haze, Dolores" (she!) in its special bower of names, with its bodyguard of roses—a fairy princess between her two maids of honor. I am trying to analyze the spine-thrill of delight it gives me, this name among all those others. What is it that excites me almost to tears (hot, opalescent, thick tears that poets and lovers shed)? What is it? The tender anonymity of this name with its formal veil ("Dolores") and that abstract transposition of first name and surname, which is like a pair of new pale gloves or a mask? Is "mask" the keyword? Is it because there is always delight in the semitranslucent mystery, the flowing charshaf, through which the flesh and the eye you alone are elected to know smile in passing at you alone? Or is it because I can imagine so well the rest of the colorful classroom around my dolorous and hazy darling: Grace and her ripe pimples; Ginny and her lagging leg; Gordon, the haggard masturbator; Duncan, the foul-smelling clown; nail-biting Agnes; Viola, of the blackheads and the bouncing bust; pretty Rosaline; dark Mary Rose; adorable Stella, who has let strangers touch her; Ralph, who bullies and steals; Irving, for whom I am sorry. And there she is there, lost in the middle, gnawing a pencil, detested by teachers, all the boys' eyes on her hair and neck, *my* Lolita.

Friday. I long for some terrific disaster. Earthquake. Spectacular explosion. Her mother is messily but instantly and permanently eliminated, along with everybody else for miles around. Lolita whimpers in my arms. A free man, I enjoy her among the ruins. Her surprise, my explanations, demonstrations, ullulations. Idle and idiotic fancies! A brave Humbert would have played with her most disgustingly (yesterday, for instance, when she was again in my room to show me her drawings, schoolartware); he might have bribed her—and got away with it. A simpler and more practical fellow would have soberly stuck to various commercial substitutes—if you know where to go, I don't. Despite my manly looks, I am horribly timid. My romantic soul gets all clammy and shivery at the thought of running into some awful indecent unpleasantness. Those ribald sea monsters. *"Mais allez-y, allez-y!"* Annabel skipping on one foot to get into her shorts, I seasick with rage, trying to screen her.

Same date, later, quite late. I have turned on the light to take down a dream. It had an evident antecedent. Haze at dinner had benevolently proclaimed that since the weather bureau promised a sunny weekend we would go to the lake Sunday after church. As I lay in bed, erotically musing before trying to go to sleep, I thought of a final scheme how to profit by the picnic to come. I was aware that mother Haze hated my darling for her being sweet on me. So I planned my lake day with a view to satisfying the mother. To her alone would I talk; but at some appropriate moment I would say I had left my wrist watch or my sunglasses in that glade yonder—and plunge with my nymphet into the wood. Reality at this juncture withdrew, and the Quest for the Glasses turned into a quiet little orgy with a singularly knowing, cheerful, corrupt and compliant Lolita behaving as reason knew she could not possibly behave. At 3 A.M. I swallowed a sleeping pill, and presently, a dream that was not a sequel but a parody revealed to me, with a kind of meaningful clarity, the lake I had never yet visited: it was glazed over with a sheet of emerald ice, and a pockmarked Eskimo was trying in vain to break it with a pickaxe, although imported mimosas and oleanders flowered on its gravelly banks. I am sure Dr. Blanche Schwarzmann would have paid me a sack of schillings for adding such a libidream to her files. Unfortunately, the rest of it was frankly eclectic. Big Haze and little Haze rode on horseback around the lake, and I rode too, dutifully bobbing up and down, bowlegs astraddle although there was no horse between them, only elastic air—one of those little omissions due to the absent-mindedness of the dream agent.

Saturday. My heart is still thumping. I still squirm and emit low moans of remembered embarrassment.

Dorsal view. Glimpse of shiny skin between T-shirt and white gym shorts. Bending, over a window sill, in the act of tearing off leaves from a poplar outside while engrossed in torrential talk with a newspaper boy below (Kenneth Knight, I suspect) who had just propelled the Ramsdale *Journal* with a very precise thud onto the porch. I began creeping up to her—"crippling" up to her, as pantomimists say. My arms and legs were convex surfaces between which—rather than upon which—I slowly progressed by some neutral means of locomotion: Humbert the Wounded Spider. I must have taken hours to reach her: I seemed to see her through the wrong end of a telescope, and toward her taut little rear I moved like some paralytic, on soft distorted limbs, in terrible concentration. At last I was right behind her when I had the unfortunate idea of blustering a trifle—shaking her by the scruff of the neck and that sort of thing to cover my real *manège*, and she said in a shrill brief whine: "Cut it out!"— most coarsely, the little wench, and with a ghastly grin Humbert the Humble beat a gloomy retreat while she went on wisecracking streetward.

But now listen to what happened next. After lunch I was reclining in a low chair trying to read. Suddenly two deft little hands were over my eyes: she had crept up from behind as if re-enacting, in a ballet sequence, my morning maneuver. Her fingers were a luminous crimson as they tried to blot out the sun, and she uttered hiccups of laughter and jerked this way and that as I stretched my arm sideways and backwards without otherwise changing my recumbent position. My hand swept over her agile giggling legs, and the book like a sleigh left my lap, and Mrs. Haze strolled up and said indulgently: "Just slap her hard if she interferes with your scholarly meditations. How I love this garden [no exclamation mark in her tone]. Isn't it divine in the sun [no question mark either]." And with a sign of feigned content, the obnoxious lady sank down on the grass and looked up at the sky as she leaned back on her splayed-out hands, and presently an old gray tennis ball bounced over her, and Lo's voice came from the house haughtily: "*Pardonnez*, Mother. I was not aiming at *you*." Of course not, my hot downy darling.

12

This proved to be the last of twenty entries or so. It will be seen from them that for all the devil's inventiveness, the scheme remained daily the same. First he would tempt me—and then thwart me, leaving me with a dull pain in the very root of my being. I knew exactly what I wanted to do, and how to do it, without impinging on a child's chastity; after all, I had had *some* experience in my life of pederosis; had visually possessed dappled nymphets in parks; had wedged my wary and bestial way into the hottest, most crowded corner of a city bus full of strap-hanging school children. But for almost three weeks I had been interrupted in all my pathetic machinations. The agent of these interruptions was usually the Haze woman (who, as the reader will mark, was more afraid of Lo's deriving some pleasure from me than of my enjoying Lo). The passion I had developed for that nymphet—for the first nymphet in my life that could be reached at last by my awkward, aching, timid claws—would have certainly landed me again in a sanatorium, had not the devil realized that I was to be granted some relief if he wanted to have me as a plaything for some time longer.

The reader has also marked the curious Mirage of the Lake. It would have been logical on the part of Aubrey McFate (as I would like to dub that devil of mine) to arrange a small treat for me on the promised beach, in the presumed forest. Actually, the promise Mrs. Haze had made was a fraudulent one: she had not told me that Mary Rose Hamilton (a dark little beauty in her own right) was to come too, and that the two nymphets would be whispering apart, and playing apart, and having a good time all by themselves, while Mrs. Haze and her handsome lodger conversed sedately in the seminude, far from prying eyes. Incidentally, eyes did pry and tongues did wag. How queer life is! We hasten to alienate the very fates we intended to woo. Before my actual arrival, my landlady had planned to have an old spinster, a Miss Phalen, whose mother had been cook in Mrs. Haze's family, come to stay in the house with Lolita and me, while Mrs. Haze, a career girl at heart, sought some suitable job in the nearest city. Mrs. Haze had seen the whole situation very clearly: the bespectacled, round-backed Herr Humbert coming with his Central-European trunks to gather dust in his corner behind a heap of old books; the unloved ugly little daughter firmly supervised by Miss Phalen who had already once had my Lo under her buzzard wing (Lo recalled that 1944 summer with an indignant shudder); and Mrs. Haze herself engaged as a receptionist in a great elegant city. But a not too complicated event interfered with that program. Miss Phalen broke her hip in Savannah, Ga., on the very day I arrived in Ramsdale.

[58]

The Sunday after the Saturday already described proved to be as bright as the weatherman had predicted. When putting the breakfast things back on the chair outside my room for my good landlady to remove at her convenience, I gleaned the following situation by listening from the landing across which I had softly crept to the bannisters in my old bedroom slippers— the only old things about me.

There had been another row. Mrs. Hamilton had telephoned that her daughter "was running a temperature." Mrs. Haze informed *her* daughter that the picnic would have to be postponed. Hot little Haze informed big cold Haze that, if so, she would not go with her to church. Mother said very well and left.

I had come out on the landing straight after shaving, soapy-earlobed, still in my white pajamas with the cornflower blue (not the lilac) design on the back; I now wiped off the soap, perfumed my hair and armpits, slipped on a purple silk dressing gown, and, humming nervously, went down the stairs in quest of Lo.

I want my learned readers to participate in the scene I am about to replay; I want them to examine its every detail and see for themselves how careful, how chaste, the whole wine-sweet event is if viewed with what my lawyer has called, in a private talk we have had, "impartial sympathy." So let us get started. I have a difficult job before me.

Main character: Humbert the Hummer. Time: Sunday morning in June. Place: sunlit living room. Props: old, candy-striped davenport, magazines, phonograph, Mexican knickknacks (the late Mr. Harold E. Haze—God bless the good man—had engendered my darling at the siesta hour in a blue-washed room, on a honeymoon trip to Vera Cruz, and mementoes, among these Dolores, were all over the place). She wore that day a pretty print dress that I had seen on her once before, ample in the skirt, tight in the bodice, short-sleeved, pink, checkered with darker pink, and, to complete the color scheme, she had painted her lips and was holding in her hollowed hands a beautiful, banal, Eden-red apple. She was not shod, however, for church. And her white Sunday purse lay discarded near the phonograph.

My heart beat like a drum as she sat down, cool skirt ballooning, subsiding, on the sofa next to me, and played with her glossy fruit. She tossed it up into the sun-dusted air, and caught it— it made a cupped polished *plop.*

Humbert Humbert intercepted the apple.

"Give it back," she pleaded, showing the marbled flush of her palms. I produced Delicious. She grasped it and bit into it, and my heart was like snow under thin crimson skin, and with the monkeyish nimbleness that was so typical of that American nymphet, she snatched out of my abstract grip the magazine I had opened (pity no film had recorded the curious pattern, the monogrammic linkage of our simultaneous or overlapping moves). Rapidly, hardly hampered by the disfigured apple she held, Lo flipped violently through the pages in search of something she wished Humbert to see. Found it at last. I faked interest by bringing my head so close that her hair touched my temple and her arm brushed my cheek as she wiped her lips with her wrist. Because of the burnished mist through which I peered at the picture, I was slow in reacting to it, and her bare knees rubbed and knocked impatiently against each other. Dimly there came into view: a surrealist painter relaxing, supine, on a beach, and near him, likewise supine, a plaster replica of the Venus di Milo, half-buried in sand. Picture of the Week, said the legend. I whisked the whole obscene thing away. Next moment, in a sham effort to retrieve it, she was all over me. Caught her by her thin knobby wrist. The magazine escaped to the floor like a flustered fowl. She twisted herself free, recoiled, and lay back in the right-hand corner of the davenport. Then, with perfect simplicity, the impudent child extended her legs across my lap.

By this time I was in a state of excitement bordering on insanity; but I also had the cunning of the insane. Sitting there, on the sofa, I managed to attune, by a series of stealthy movements, my masked lust to her guileless limbs. It was no easy matter to divert the little maiden's attention while I performed the obscure adjustments necessary for the success of the trick.

Talking fast, lagging behind my own breath, catching up with it, mimicking a sudden toothache to explain the breaks in my patter —and all the while keeping a maniac's inner eye on my distant golden goal, I cautiously increased the magic friction that was doing away, in an illusional, if not factual, sense, with the physically irremovable, but psychologically very friable texture of the material divide (pajamas and robe) between the weight of two sunburnt legs, resting athwart my lap, and the hidden tumor of an unspeakable passion. Having, in the course of my patter, hit upon something nicely mechanical, I recited, garbling them slightly, the words of a foolish song that was then popular—O my Carmen, my little Carmen, something, something, those something nights, and the stars, and the cars, and the bars, and the barmen; I kept repeating this automatic stuff and holding her under its special spell (spell because of the garbling), and all the while I was mortally afraid that some act of God might interrupt me, might remove the golden load in the sensation of which all my being seemed concentrated, and this anxiety forced me to work, for the first minute or so, more hastily than was consensual with deliberately modulated enjoyment. The stars that sparkled, and the cars that parkled, and the bars, and the barmen, were presently taken over by her; her voice stole and corrected the tune I had been mutilating. She was musical and apple-sweet. Her legs twitched a little as they lay across my live lap; I stroked them; there she lolled in the right-hand corner, almost asprawl, Lola the bobby-soxer, devouring her immemorial fruit, singing through its juice, losing her slipper, rubbing the heel of her slipperless foot in its sloppy anklet, against the pile of old magazines heaped on my left on the sofa—and every movement she made, every shuffle and ripple, helped me to conceal and to improve the secret system of tactile correspondence between beast and beauty—between my gagged, bursting beast and the beauty of her dimpled body in its innocent cotton frock.

Under my glancing finger tips I felt the minute hairs bristle ever so slightly along her shins. I lost myself in the pungent but healthy heat which like summer haze hung about little Haze. Let her stay, let her stay... As she strained to chuck the core

1

2

of her abolished apple into the fender, her young weight, her shameless innocent shanks and round bottom, shifted in my tense, tortured, surreptitiously laboring lap; and all of a sudden a mysterious change came over my senses. I entered a plane of being where nothing mattered, save the infusion of joy brewed within my body. What had begun as a delicious distension of my innermost roots became a glowing tingle which *now* had reached that state of absolute security, confidence and reliance not found elsewhere in conscious life. With the deep hot sweetness thus established and well on its way to the ultimate convulsion, I felt I could slow down in order to prolong the glow. Lolita

1 had been safely solipsized. The implied sun pulsated in the supplied poplars; we were fantastically and divinely alone; I watched her, rosy, gold-dusted, beyond the veil of my controlled delight, unaware of it, alien to it, and the sun was on her lips, and her lips were apparently still forming the words of the Carmenbarmen ditty that no longer reached my consciousness. Everything was now ready. The nerves of pleasure had been laid bare.

2 The corpuscles of Krause were entering the phase of frenzy. The least pressure would suffice to set all paradise loose. I had ceased to be Humbert the Hound, the sad-eyed degenerate cur clasping the boot that would presently kick him away. I was above the tribulations of ridicule, beyond the possibilities of retribution. In

3 my self-made seraglio, I was a radiant and robust Turk, deliberately, in the full consciousness of his freedom, postponing the moment of actually enjoying the youngest and frailest of his slaves. Suspended on the brink of that voluptuous abyss (a nicety of physiological equipoise comparable to certain techniques in the arts) I kept repeating chance words after her—barmen, alarmin', my charmin', my carmen, ahmen, ahahamen—as one talking and laughing in his sleep while my happy hand crept up her sunny leg as far as the shadow of decency allowed. The day before she had collided with the heavy chest in the hall and— "Look, look!"—I gasped—"look what you've done, what you've done to yourself, ah, look"; for there was, I swear, a yellowish-violet bruise on her lovely nymphet thigh which my huge hairy hand massaged and slowly enveloped—and because of her very

[62]

perfunctory underthings, there seemed to be nothing to prevent my muscular thumb from reaching the hot hollow of her groin —just as you might tickle and caress a giggling child—just that— and: "Oh it's nothing at all," she cried with a sudden shrill note in her voice, and she wiggled, and squirmed, and threw her head back, and her teeth rested on her glistening underlip as she half-turned away, and my moaning mouth, gentlemen of the jury, almost reached her bare neck, while I crushed out against her left buttock the last throb of the longest ecstasy man or monster had ever known.

Immediately afterward (as if we had been struggling and now my grip had eased) she rolled off the sofa and jumped to her feet—to her foot, rather—in order to attend to the formidably loud telephone that may have been ringing for ages as far as I was concerned. There she stood and blinked, cheeks aflame, hair awry, her eyes passing over me as lightly as they did over the furniture, and as she listened or spoke (to her mother who was telling her to come to lunch with her at the Chatfields—neither Lo nor Hum knew yet what busybody Haze was plotting), she kept tapping the edge of the table with the slipper she held in her hand. Blessed be the Lord, she had noticed nothing!

With a handkerchief of multicolored silk, on which her listening eyes rested in passing, I wiped the sweat off my forehead, and, immersed in a euphoria of release, rearranged my royal robes. She was still at the telephone, haggling with her mother (wanted to be fetched by car, my little Carmen) when, singing louder and louder, I swept up the stairs and set a deluge of steaming water roaring into the tub.

At this point I may as well give the words of that song hit in full—to the best of my recollection at least—I don't think I ever had it right. Here goes:

> O my Carmen, my little Carmen!
> Something, something those something nights,
> And the stars, and the cars, and the bars, and the
> [barmen—
> And, O my charmin', our dreadful fights.

And the something town where so gaily, arm in
Arm, we went, and our final row,
And the gun I killed you with, O my Carmen,
The gun I am holding now.

1 (Drew his .32 automatic, I guess, and put a bullet through his
moll's eye.)

14

I had lunch in town—had not been so hungry for years. The
house was still Lo-less when I strolled back. I spent the afternoon musing, scheming, blissfully digesting my experience of the
morning.

I felt proud of myself. I had stolen the honey of a spasm without impairing the morals of a minor. Absolutely no harm done.
The conjurer had poured milk, molasses, foaming champagne
into a young lady's new white purse; and lo, the purse was intact.
Thus had I delicately constructed my ignoble, ardent, sinful
dream; and still Lolita was safe—and I was safe. What I had
madly possessed was not she, but my own creation, another,
fanciful Lolita—perhaps, more real than Lolita; overlapping, en-
casing her; floating between me and her, and having no will, no
consciousness—indeed, no life of her own.

The child knew nothing. I had done nothing to her. And
nothing prevented me from repeating a performance that affected her as little as if she were a photographic image rippling
upon a screen and I a humble hunchback abusing myself in the
dark. The afternoon drifted on and on, in ripe silence, and the
sappy tall trees seemed to be in the know; and desire, even
stronger than before, began to afflict me again. Let her come
2 soon, I prayed, addressing a loan God, and while mamma is in
the kitchen, let a repetition of the davenport scene be staged,
please, I adore her so horribly.

No: "horribly" is the wrong word. The elation with which the
vision of new delights filled me was not horrible but pathetic. I

qualify it as pathetic. Pathetic—because despite the insatiable fire of my venereal appetite, I intended, with the most fervent force and foresight, to protect the purity of that twelve-year-old child.

And now see how I was repaid for my pains. No Lolita came home—she had gone with the Chatfields to a movie. The table was laid with more elegance than usual: candlelight, if you please. In this mawkish aura, Mrs. Haze gently touched the silver on both sides of her plate as if touching piano keys, and smiled down on her empty plate (was on a diet), and said she hoped I liked the salad (recipe lifted from a woman's magazine). She hoped I liked the cold cuts, too. It had been a perfect day. Mrs. Chatfield was a lovely person. Phyllis, her daughter, was going to a summer camp tomorrow. For three weeks. Lolita, it was decided, would go Thursday. Instead of waiting till July, as had been initially planned. And stay there after Phyllis had left. Till school began. A pretty prospect, my heart.

Oh, how I was taken aback—for did it not mean I was losing my darling, just when I had secretly made her mine? To explain my grim mood, I had to use the same toothache I had already simulated in the morning. Must have been an enormous molar, with an abscess as big as a maraschino cherry.

"We have," said Haze, "an excellent dentist. Our neighbor, in fact. Dr. Quilty. Uncle or cousin, I think, of the playwright. Think it will pass? Well, just as you wish. In the fall I shall have him 'brace' her, as my mother used to say. It may curb Lo a little. I am afraid she has been bothering you frightfully all these days. And we are in for a couple of stormy ones before she goes. She has flatly refused to go, and I confess I left her with the Chatfields because I dreaded to face her alone just yet. The movie may mollify her. Phyllis is a very sweet girl, and there is no earthly reason for Lo to dislike her. Really, monsieur, I am very sorry about that tooth of yours. It would be so much more reasonable to let me contact Ivor Quilty first thing tomorrow morning if it still hurts. And, you know, I think a summer camp is so much healthier, and—well, it is all so much more *reasonable* as I say than to mope on a suburban lawn and use mamma's lipstick, and pursue shy studious gentlemen, and go into tantrums at the least provocation."

"Are you sure," I said at last, "that she will be happy there?" (lame, lamentably lame!)

"She'd better," said Haze. "And it won't be all play either. The camp is run by Shirley Holmes—you know, the woman who wrote *Campfire Girl.* Camp will teach Dolores Haze to grow in many things—health, knowledge, temper. And particularly in a sense of responsibility toward other people. Shall we take these candles with us and sit for a while on the piazza, or do you want to go to bed and nurse that tooth?"

Nurse that tooth.

15

Next day they drove downtown to buy things needed for the camp: any wearable purchase worked wonders with Lo. She seemed her usual sarcastic self at dinner. Immediately afterwards, she went up to her room to plunge into the comic books acquired for rainy days at Camp Q (they were so thoroughly sampled by Thursday that she left them behind). I too retired to my lair, and wrote letters. My plan now was to leave for the seaside and then, when school began, resume my existence in the Haze household; for I knew already that I could not live without the child. On Tuesday they went shopping again, and I was asked to answer the phone if the camp mistress rang up during their absence. She did; and a month or so later we had occasion to recall our pleasant chat. That Tuesday, Lo had her dinner in her room. She had been crying after a routine row with her mother and, as had happened on former occasions, had not wished me to see her swollen eyes: she had one of those tender complexions that after a good cry get all blurred and inflamed, and morbidly alluring. I regretted keenly her mistake about my private aesthetics, for I simply love that tinge of Botticellian pink, that raw rose about the lips, those wet, matted eyelashes; and, naturally, her bashful whim deprived me of many opportunities of specious consolation. There was, however, more to it than I thought. As we sat in the darkness of the veranda (a rude wind had put out her red candles), Haze, with a dreary laugh, said she had told Lo that her beloved Humbert thoroughly approved of the whole camp idea "and now," added Haze, "the child throws a fit; pretext: you and I want to get rid of her; actual reason: I told her we would exchange tomorrow for plainer stuff some much too cute night things that she bullied me into buying for her. You see, *she* sees herself as a starlet; *I* see her as a sturdy, healthy, but decidedly homely kid. This, I guess, is at the root of our troubles."

On Wednesday I managed to waylay Lo for a few seconds: she was on the landing, in sweatshirt and green-stained white shorts, rummaging in a trunk. I said something meant to be friendly and funny but she only emitted a snort without looking at me. Desperate, dying Humbert patted her clumsily on her coccyx, and she struck him, quite painfully, with one of the late Mr. Haze's shoetrees. "Doublecrosser," she said as I crawled downstairs rubbing my arm with a great show of rue. She did not condescend to have dinner with Hum and mum: washed her hair and went to bed with her ridiculous books. And on Thursday quiet Mrs. Haze drove her to Camp Q.

As greater authors than I have put it: "Let readers imagine" etc. On second thought, I may as well give those imaginations a kick in the pants. I knew I had fallen in love with Lolita forever; but I also knew she would not be forever Lolita. She would be thirteen on January 1. In two years or so she would cease being a nymphet and would turn into a "young girl," and then, into a "college girl"—that horror of horrors. The word "forever" referred only to my own passion, to the eternal Lolita as reflected in my blood. The Lolita whose iliac crests had not yet flared, the Lolita that today I could touch and smell and hear and see, the Lolita of the strident voice and the rich brown hair—of the bangs and the swirls at the sides and the curls at the back, and the sticky hot neck, and the vulgar vocabulary—"revolting," "super," "luscious," "goon," "drip"—*that* Lolita, *my* Lolita, poor

[67]

1 Catullus would lose forever. So how could I afford not to see her for two months of summer insomnias? Two whole months out of the two years of her remaining nymphage! Should I disguise myself as a somber old-fashioned girl, gawky Mlle Humbert, and put up my tent on the outskirts of Camp Q, in the hope that its russet nymphets would clamor: "Let us adopt that deep-voiced

2, 3 D.P.," and drag the sad, shyly smiling Berthe *au Grand Pied* to their rustic hearth. Berthe will sleep with Dolores Haze!

Idle dry dreams. Two months of beauty, two months of tenderness, would be squandered forever, and I could do nothing

4 about it, but nothing, *mais rien*.

One drop of rare honey, however, that Thursday did hold in its acorn cup. Haze was to drive her to the camp in the early morning. Upon sundry sounds of departure reaching me, I rolled out of bed and leaned out of the window. Under the poplars, the car was already athrob. On the sidewalk, Louise stood shading her eyes with her hand, as if the little traveler were already riding into the low morning sun. The gesture proved to be premature. "Hurry up!" shouted Haze. My Lolita, who was half in and about to slam the car door, wind down the glass, wave to Louise and the poplars (whom and which she was never to see again), interrupted the motion of fate: she looked up—and dashed back into the house (Haze furiously calling after her). A moment later I heard my sweetheart running up the stairs. My heart expanded with such force that it almost blotted me out. I hitched up the pants of my pajamas, flung the door open: and simultaneously Lolita arrived, in her Sunday frock, stamping, panting, and then she was in my arms, her innocent mouth melting under the ferocious pressure of dark male jaws, my palpitating darling! The next instant I heard her—alive, unraped—clatter downstairs. The motion of fate was resumed. The blond leg was pulled in, the car door was slammed—was re-slammed—and driver Haze at the violent wheel, rubber-red lips writhing in angry, inaudible speech, swung my darling away, while unnoticed by them or Louise, old Miss Opposite, an invalid, feebly but rhythmically waved from her vined veranda.

16

The hollow of my hand was still ivory-full of Lolita—full of the feel of her pre-adolescently incurved back, that ivory-smooth, sliding sensation of her skin through the thin frock that I had worked up and down while I held her. I marched into her tumbled room, threw open the door of the closet and plunged into a heap of crumpled things that had touched her. There was particularly one pink texture, sleazy, torn, with a faintly acrid odor in the seam. I wrapped in it Humbert's huge engorged heart. A poignant chaos was welling within me—but I had to drop those things and hurriedly regain my composure, as I became aware of the maid's velvety voice calling me softly from the stairs. She had a message for me, she said; and, topping my automatic thanks with a kindly "you're welcome," good Louise left an unstamped, curiously clean-looking letter in my shaking hand.

This is a confession: I love you [so the letter began; and for a distorted moment I mistook its hysterical scrawl for a schoolgirl's scribble]. Last Sunday in church—bad you, who refused to come to see our beautiful new windows!—only last Sunday, my dear one, when I asked the Lord what to do about it, I was told to act as I am acting now. You see, there is no alternative. I have loved you from the minute I saw you. I am a passionate and lonely woman and you are the love of my life.

Now, my dearest, dearest, *mon cher, cher monsieur*, you have read this; now you know. So, will you please, *at once*, pack and leave. This is a landlady's order. I am dismissing a lodger. I am kicking you out. Go! Scram! *Departez!* I shall be back by dinnertime, if I do eighty both ways and don't have an accident (but what would it matter?), and I do not wish to find you in the house. Please, please, leave at once, *now*, do not even read this absurd note to the end. Go. Adieu.

The situation, *chéri*, is quite simple. Of course, I know with *absolute certainty* that I am nothing to you, nothing at all. Oh yes, you enjoy talking to me (and kidding poor me), you have grown fond of our friendly house, of the books I like, of my lovely garden, even of Lo's noisy ways—but I am nothing to you. Right? Right. Nothing to you whatever. *But* if, after reading my "confession," you decided, in your dark romantic European way, that I am attractive enough for you to take advantage of my letter and make a pass at me, then you would be a criminal—worse than a kidnaper who rapes a child. You see, *chéri.* If you decided to stay, *if* I found you at home (which I know I won't—and that's why I am able to go on like this), the *fact* of your remaining would only mean one thing: that you want me as much as I do you: as a lifelong mate; and that you are ready to link up your life with mine forever and ever and be a father to my little girl.

Let me rave and ramble on for a teeny while more, my dearest, since I know this letter has been by now torn by you, and its pieces (illegible) in the vortex of the toilet. My dearest, *mon très, très cher*, what a world of love I have built up for you during this miraculous June! I know how reserved you are, how "British." Your old-world reticence, your sense of decorum may be shocked by the boldness of an American girl! You who conceal your strongest feelings must think me a shameless little idiot for throwing open my poor bruised heart like this. In years gone by, many disappointments came my way. Mr. Haze was a splendid person, a sterling soul, but he happened to be twenty years my senior, and—well, let us not gossip about the past. My dearest, your curiosity must be well satisfied if you have ignored my request and read this letter to the bitter end. Never mind. Destroy it and go. Do not forget to leave the key on the desk in your room. And some scrap of address so that I could refund the twelve dollars I owe you till the end of the month. Good-bye, dear one. Pray for me—if you ever pray.

C.H.

What I present here is what I remember of the letter, and what I remember of the letter I remember verbatim (including that awful French). It was at least twice longer. I have left out a lyrical passage which I more or less skipped at the time, concerning Lolita's brother who died at 2 when she was 4, and how much I would have liked him. Let me see what else can I say?

Yes. There is just a chance that "the vortex of the toilet" (where the letter did go) is my own matter-of-fact contribution. She probably begged me to make a special fire to consume it.

My first movement was one of repulsion and retreat. My second was like a friend's calm hand falling upon my shoulder and bidding me take my time. I did. I came out of my daze and found myself still in Lo's room. A full-page ad ripped out of a slick magazine was affixed to the wall above the bed, between a crooner's mug and the lashes of a movie actress. It represented a dark-haired young husband with a kind of drained look in his Irish eyes. He was modeling a robe by So-and-So and holding a bridgelike tray by So-and-So, with breakfast for two. The legend, by the Rev. Thomas Morell, called him a "conquering hero." 1 The thoroughly conquered lady (not shown) was presumably propping herself up to receive her half of the tray. How her bedfellow was to get under the bridge without some messy mishap was not clear. Lo had drawn a jocose arrow to the haggard lover's face and had put, in block letters: H.H. And indeed, despite a difference of a few years, the resemblance was striking. Under this was another picture, also a colored ad. A distinguished playwright was solemnly smoking a Drome. He always smoked Dromes. The 2 resemblance was slight. Under this was Lo's chaste bed, littered with "comics." The enamel had come off the bedstead, leaving black, more or less rounded, marks on the white. Having convinced myself that Louise had left, I got into Lo's bed and reread the letter.

17

Gentlemen of the jury! I cannot swear that certain motions pertaining to the business in hand—if I may coin an expression—had not drifted across my mind before. My mind had not retained them in any logical form or in any relation to definitely recollected occasions; but I cannot swear—let me repeat—that I had not toyed with them (to rig up yet another expression), in my dimness of thought, in my darkness of passion. There may

have been times—there must have been times, if I know my
Humbert—when I had brought up for detached inspection the
idea of marrying a mature widow (say, Charlotte Haze) with not
one relative left in the wide gray world, merely in order to have
my way with her child (Lo, Lola, Lolita). I am even prepared
to tell my tormentors that perhaps once or twice I had cast an
appraiser's cold eye at Charlotte's coral lips and bronze hair and
dangerously low neckline, and had vaguely tried to fit her into a
plausible daydream. This I confess under torture. Imaginary torture, perhaps, but all the more horrible. I wish I might digress
1 and tell you more of the *pavor nocturnus* that would rack me at
night hideously after a chance term had struck me in the random
2 readings of my boyhood, such as *peine forte et dure* (what a
Genius of Pain must have invented that!) or the dreadful, mysterious, insidious words "trauma," "traumatic event," and "tran-
som." But my tale is sufficiently incondite already.

After a while I destroyed the letter and went to my room, and
ruminated, and rumpled my hair, and modeled my purple robe,
and moaned through clenched teeth and suddenly—Suddenly,
3 gentlemen of the jury, I felt a Dostoevskian grin dawning
(through the very grimace that twisted my lips) like a distant
and terrible sun. I imagined (under conditions of new and perfect visibility) all the casual caresses her mother's husband would
be able to lavish on his Lolita. I would hold her against me three
times a day, every day. All my troubles would be expelled, I
would be a healthy man. "To hold thee lightly on a gentle knee
and print on thy soft cheek a parent's kiss..." Well-read
4 Humbert!

Then, with all possible caution, on mental tiptoe so to speak,
5 I conjured up Charlotte as a possible mate. By God, I could make
myself bring her that economically halved grapefruit, that sugar-
less breakfast.

Humbert Humbert sweating in the fierce white light, and
howled at, and trodden upon by sweating policemen, is now
6 ready to make a further "statement" (*quel mot!*) as he turns
his conscience inside out and rips off its innermost lining. I did
not plan to marry poor Charlotte in order to eliminate her in

[72]

some vulgar, gruesome and dangerous manner such as killing her by placing five bichloride-of-mercury tablets in her preprandial sherry or anything like that; but a delicately allied, pharmacopoeial thought did tinkle in my sonorous and clouded brain. Why limit myself to the modest masked caress I had tried already? Other visions of venery presented themselves to me swaying and smiling. I saw myself administering a powerful sleeping potion to both mother and daughter so as to fondle the latter through the night with perfect impunity. The house was full of Charlotte's snore, while Lolita hardly breathed in her sleep, as still as a painted girl-child. "Mother, I swear Kenny never even *touched* me." "You either lie, Dolores Haze, or it was an incubus." No, I would not go that far.

So Humbert the Cubus schemed and dreamed—and the red sun of desire and decision (the two things that create a live world) rose higher and higher, while upon a succession of balconies a succession of libertines, sparkling glass in hand, toasted the bliss of past and future nights. Then, figuratively speaking, I shattered the glass, and boldly imagined (for I was drunk on those visions by then and underrated the gentleness of my nature) how eventually I might blackmail—no, that is too strong a word—mauvemail big Haze into letting me consort with little Haze by gently threatening the poor doting Big Dove with desertion if she tried to bar me from playing with my legal stepdaughter. In a word, before such an Amazing Offer, before such a vastness and variety of vistas, I was as helpless as Adam at the preview of early oriental history, miraged in his apple orchard.

And now take down the following important remark: the artist in me has been given the upper hand over the gentleman. It is with a great effort of will that in this memoir I have managed to tune my style to the tone of the journal that I kept when Mrs. Haze was to me but an obstacle. That journal of mine is no more; but I have considered it my artistic duty to preserve its intonations no matter how false and brutal they may seem to me now. Fortunately, my story has reached a point where I can cease insulting poor Charlotte for the sake of retrospective verisimilitude.

Wishing to spare poor Charlotte two or three hours of suspense on a winding road (and avoid, perhaps, a head-on collision that would shatter our different dreams), I made a thoughtful but abortive attempt to reach her at the camp by telephone. She had left half an hour before, and getting Lo instead, I told her—trembling and brimming with my mastery over fate—that I was going to marry her mother. I had to repeat it twice because something was preventing her from giving me her attention. "Gee, that's swell," she said laughing. "When is the wedding? Hold on a sec, the pup—That pup here has got hold of my sock. Listen—" and she added she guessed she was going to have loads of fun . . . and I realized as I hung up that a couple of hours at that camp had been sufficient to blot out with new impressions the image of handsome Humbert Humbert from little Lolita's mind. But what did it matter now? I would get her back as soon as a decent amount of time after the wedding had elapsed. "The orange blossom would have scarcely withered on the grave," as a poet might have said. But I am no poet. I am only a very conscientious recorder.

After Louise had gone, I inspected the icebox, and finding it much too puritanic, walked to town and bought the richest foods available. I also bought some good liquor and two or three kinds of vitamins. I was pretty sure that with the aid of these stimulants and my natural resources, I would avert any embarrassment that my indifference might incur when called upon to display a strong and impatient flame. Again and again resourceful Humbert evoked Charlotte as seen in the raree-show of a manly imagination. She was well groomed and shapely, this I could say for her, and she was my Lolita's big sister—this notion, perhaps, I could keep up if only I did not visualize too realistically her heavy hips, round knees, ripe bust, the coarse pink skin of her neck ("coarse" by comparison with silk and honey) and all the rest of that sorry and dull thing: a handsome woman.

The sun made its usual round of the house as the afternoon ripened into evening. I had a drink. And another. And yet another. Gin and pineapple juice, my favorite mixture, always double my energy. I decided to busy myself with our unkempt lawn. *Une petite attention.* It was crowded with dandelions, and

[74]

a cursed dog—I loathe dogs—had defiled the flat stones where a sundial had once stood. Most of the dandelions had changed from suns to moons. The gin and Lolita were dancing in me, and I almost fell over the folding chairs that I attempted to dislodge. Incarnadine zebras! There are some eructations that sound like cheers—at least, mine did. An old fence at the back of the garden separated us from the neighbor's garbage receptacles and lilacs; but there was nothing between the front end of our lawn (where it sloped along one side of the house) and the street. Therefore I was able to watch (with the smirk of one about to perform a good action) for the return of Charlotte: that tooth should be extracted at once. As I lurched and lunged with the hand mower, bits of grass optically twittering in the low sun, I kept an eye on that section of suburban street. It curved in from under an archway of huge shade trees, then sped towards us down, down, quite sharply, past old Miss Opposite's ivied brick house and high-sloping lawn (much trimmer than ours) and disappeared behind our own front porch which I could not see from where I happily belched and labored. The dandelions perished. A reek of sap mingled with the pineapple. Two little girls, Marion and Mabel, whose comings and goings I had mechanically followed of late (but who could replace my Lolita?) went toward the avenue (from which our Lawn Street cascaded), one pushing a bicycle, the other feeding from a paper bag, both talking at the top of their sunny voices. Leslie, old Miss Opposite's gardener and chauffeur, a very amiable and athletic Negro, grinned at me from afar and shouted, re-shouted, commented by gesture, that I was mighty energetic to-day. The fool dog of the prosperous junk dealer next door ran after a blue car—not Charlotte's. The prettier of the two little girls (Mabel, I think), shorts, halter with little to halt, bright hair—a nymphet, by Pan!—ran back down the street crumpling her paper bag and was hidden from this Green Goat by the frontage of Mr. and Mrs. Humbert's residence. A station wagon popped out of the leafy shade of the avenue, dragging some of it on its roof before the shadows snapped, and swung by at an idiotic pace, the sweatshirted driver roof-holding with his left hand and the junkman's dog tearing alongside. There was a smiling pause—and then, with a flutter in my breast, I witnessed the return of the Blue Sedan. I saw it glide downhill and disappear behind the corner of the house. I had a glimpse of her calm pale profile. It occurred to me that until she went upstairs she would not know whether I had gone or not. A minute later, with an expression of great anguish on her face, she looked down at me from the window of Lo's room. By sprinting upstairs, I managed to reach that room before she left it.

18

When the bride is a widow and the groom is a widower; when the former has lived in Our Great Little Town for hardly two years, and the latter for hardly a month; when Monsieur wants to get the whole damned thing over with as quickly as possible, and Madame gives in with a tolerant smile; then, my reader, the wedding is generally a "quiet" affair. The bride may dispense with a tiara of orange blossoms securing her finger-tip veil, nor does she carry a white orchid in a prayer book. The bride's little daughter might have added to the ceremonies uniting H. and H. a touch of vivid vermeil; but I knew I would not dare be too tender with cornered Lolita yet, and therefore agreed it was not worth while tearing the child away from her beloved Camp Q.

1   My *soi-disant* passionate and lonely Charlotte was in everyday life matter-of-fact and gregarious. Moreover, I discovered that although she could not control her heart or her cries, she was a woman of principle. Immediately after she had become more or less my mistress (despite the stimulants, her "nervous, eager *chéri*"—a heroic *chéri!*—had some initial trouble, for which, however, he amply compensated her by a fantastic display of old-world endearments), good Charlotte interviewed me about my relations with God. I could have answered that on that score my mind was open; I said, instead—paying my tribute to a pious platitude—that I believed in a cosmic spirit. Looking down at her fingernails, she also asked me had I not in my family a cer-

tain strange strain. I countered by inquiring whether she would still want to marry me if my father's maternal grandfather had been, say, a Turk. She said it did not matter a bit; but that, if she ever found out I did not believe in Our Christian God, she would commit suicide. She said it so solemnly that it gave me the creeps. It was then I knew she was a woman of principle.

Oh, she was very genteel: she said "excuse me" whenever a slight burp interrupted her flowing speech, called an envelope an ahnvelope, and when talking to her lady-friends referred to me as Mr. Humbert. I thought it would please her if I entered the community trailing some glamor after me. On the day of our wedding a little interview with me appeared in the Society Column of the Ramsdale *Journal*, with a photograph of Charlotte, one eyebrow up and a misprint in her name ("Hazer"). Despite this contretemps, the publicity warmed the porcelain cockles of her heart—and made my rattles shake with awful glee. By engaging in church work as well as by getting to know the better mothers of Lo's schoolmates, Charlotte in the course of twenty months or so had managed to become if not a prominent, at least an acceptable citizen, but never before had she come under that thrilling *rubrique*, and it was I who put her there, Mr. Edgar H. Humbert (I threw in the "Edgar" just for the heck of it), "writer and explorer." McCoo's brother, when taking it down, asked me what I had written. Whatever I told him came out as "several books on Peacock, Rainbow and other poets." It was also noted that Charlotte and I had known each other for several years and that I was a distant relation of her first husband. I hinted I had had an affair with her thirteen years ago but this was not mentioned in print. To Charlotte I said that society columns *should* contain a shimmer of errors.

Let us go on with this curious tale. When called upon to enjoy my promotion from lodger to lover, did I experience only bitterness and distaste? No. Mr. Humbert confesses to a certain titillation of his vanity, to some faint tenderness, even to a pattern of remorse daintily running along the steel of his conspiratorial dagger. Never had I thought that the rather ridiculous, though rather handsome Mrs. Haze, with her blind faith in the wisdom of her church and book club, her mannerisms of elocution, her harsh, cold, contemptuous attitude toward an adorable, downy-armed child of twelve, could turn into such a touching, helpless creature as soon as I laid my hands upon her which happened on the threshold of Lolita's room whither she tremulously backed repeating "no, no, please no."

The transformation improved her looks. Her smile that had been such a contrived thing, thenceforth became the radiance of utter adoration—a radiance having something soft and moist about it, in which, with wonder, I recognized a resemblance to the lovely, inane, lost look that Lo had when gloating over a new kind of concoction at the soda fountain or mutely admiring my expensive, always tailor-fresh clothes. Deeply fascinated, I would watch Charlotte while she swapped parental woes with some other lady and made that national grimace of feminine resignation (eyes rolling up, mouth drooping sideways) which, in an infantile form, I had seen Lo making herself. We had highballs before turning in, and with their help, I would manage to evoke the child while caressing the mother. This was the white stomach within which my nymphet had been a little curved fish in 1934. This carefully dyed hair, so sterile to my sense of smell and touch, acquired at certain lamplit moments in the poster bed the tinge, if not the texture, of Lolita's curls. I kept telling myself, as I wielded my brand-new large-as-life wife, that biologically this was the nearest I could get to Lolita; that at Lolita's age, Lotte had been as desirable a schoolgirl as her daughter was, and as Lolita's daughter would be some day. I had my wife unearth from under a collection of shoes (Mr. Haze had a passion for them, it appears) a thirty-year-old album, so that I might see how Lotte had looked as a child; and even though the light was wrong and the dresses graceless, I was able to make out a dim first version of Lolita's outline, legs, cheekbones, bobbed nose. Lottelita, Lolitchen.

1

So I tom-peeped across the hedges of years, into wan little windows. And when, by means of pitifully ardent, naïvely lascivious caresses, she of the noble nipple and massive thigh prepared me for the performance of my nightly duty, it was still a nymphet's scent that in despair I tried to pick up, as I bayed through the undergrowth of dark decaying forests.

I simply can't tell you how gentle, how touching my poor wife was. At breakfast, in the depressingly bright kitchen, with its chrome glitter and Hardware and Co. Calendar and cute breakfast nook (simulating that Coffee Shoppe where in their college days Charlotte and Humbert used to coo together), she would sit, robed in red, her elbow on the plastic-topped table, her cheek propped on her fist, and stare at me with intolerable tenderness as I consumed my ham and eggs. Humbert's face might twitch with neuralgia, but in her eyes it vied in beauty and animation with the sun and shadows of leaves rippling on the white refrigerator. My solemn exasperation was to her the silence of love. My small income added to her even smaller one impressed her as a brilliant fortune; not because the resulting sum now sufficed for most middle-class needs, but because even my money shone in her eyes with the magic of my manliness, and she saw our joint account as one of those southern boulevards at midday that have solid shade on one side and smooth sunshine on the other, all the way to the end of a prospect, where pink mountains loom.

Into the fifty days of our cohabitation Charlotte crammed the activities of as many years. The poor woman busied herself with a number of things she had foregone long before or had never been much interested in, as if (to prolong these Proustian intonations) by my marrying the mother of the child I loved I had enabled my wife to regain an abundance of youth by proxy. With the zest of a banal young bride, she started to "glorify the home." Knowing as I did its every cranny by heart—since those days when from my chair I mentally mapped out Lolita's course through the house—I had long entered into a sort of emotional relationship with it, with its very ugliness and dirt, and now I could almost feel the wretched thing cower in its reluctance to endure the bath of ecru and ocher and putty-buff-and-snuff that Charlotte planned to give it. She never got as far as that, thank God, but she did use up a tremendous amount of energy in washing window shades, waxing the slats of Venetian blinds, pur-

1

chasing new shades and new blinds, returning them to the store, replacing them by others, and so on, in a constant chiaroscuro of smiles and frowns, doubts and pouts. She dabbled in cretonnes and chintzes; she changed the colors of the sofa—the sacred sofa where a bubble of paradise had once burst in slow motion within me. She rearranged the furniture—and was pleased when she found, in a household treatise, that "it is permissible to separate a pair of sofa commodes and their companion lamps." With the authoress of *Your Home Is You,* she developed a hatred for little lean chairs and spindle tables. She believed that a room having a generous expanse of glass, and lots of rich wood paneling was an example of the masculine type of room, whereas the feminine type was characterized by lighter-looking windows and frailer woodwork. The novels I had found her reading when I moved in were now replaced by illustrated catalogues and homemaking guides. From a firm located at 4640 Roosevelt Blvd., Philadelphia, she ordered for our double bed a "damask covered 312 coil mattress"—although the old one seemed to me resilient and durable enough for whatever it had to support.

A Midwesterner, as her late husband had also been, she had lived in coy Ramsdale, the gem of an eastern state, not long enough to know all the nice people. She knew slightly the jovial dentist who lived in a kind of ramshackle wooden chateau behind our lawn. She had met at a church tea the "snooty" wife of the local junk dealer who owned the "colonial" white horror at the corner of the avenue. Now and then she "visited with" old Miss Opposite; but the more patrician matrons among those she called upon, or met at lawn functions, or had telephone chats with—such dainty ladies as Mrs. Glave, Mrs. Sheridan, Mrs. McCrystal, Mrs. Knight and others, seldom seemed to call on my neglected Charlotte. Indeed, the only couple with whom she had relations of real cordiality, devoid of any *arrière-pensée* or practical foresight, were the Farlows who had just come back from a business trip to Chile in time to attend our wedding, with the Chatfields, McCoos, and a few others (but not Mrs. Junk or the even prouder Mrs. Talbot). John Farlow was a middle-aged, quiet, quietly athletic, quietly successful dealer in sporting goods, who had an office at Parkington, forty miles away: it was he who got me the cartridges for that Colt and showed me how to use it, during a walk in the woods one Sunday; he was also what he called with a smile a part-time lawyer and had handled some of Charlotte's affairs. Jean, his youngish wife (and first cousin), was a long-limbed girl in harlequin glasses with two boxer dogs, two pointed breasts and a big red mouth. She painted—landscapes and portraits—and vividly do I remember praising, over cocktails, the picture she had made of a niece of hers, little Rosaline Honeck, a rosy honey in a Girl Scout uniform, beret of green worsted, belt of green webbing, charming shoulder-long curls—and John removed his pipe and said it was a pity Dolly (my Dolita) and Rosaline were so critical of each other at school, but he hoped, and we all hoped, they would get on better when they returned from their respective camps. We talked of the school. It had its drawbacks, and it had its virtues. "Of course, too many of the tradespeople here are Italians," said John, "but on the other hand we are still spared—" "I wish," interrupted Jean with a laugh, "Dolly and Rosaline were spending the summer together." Suddenly I imagined Lo returning from camp—brown, warm, drowsy, drugged—and was ready to weep with passion and impatience.

19

A few words more about Mrs. Humbert while the going is good (a bad accident is to happen quite soon). I had been always aware of the possessive streak in her, but I never thought she would be so crazily jealous of anything in my life that had not been she. She showed a fierce insatiable curiosity for my past. She desired me to resuscitate all my loves so that she might make me insult them, and trample upon them, and revoke them apostately and totally, thus destroying my past. She made me tell her about my marriage to Valeria, who was of course a scream; but I also had to invent, or to pad atrociously, a long series of mistresses for Charlotte's morbid delectation. To keep her happy, I had to present her with an illustrated catalogue of them, all nicely differentiated, according to the rules of those American ads where schoolchildren are pictured in a subtle ratio of races, with one—only one, but as cute as they make them— chocolate-colored round-eyed little lad, almost in the very middle of the front row. So I presented my women, and had them smile and sway—the languorous blond, the fiery brunette, the sensual copperhead—as if on parade in a bordello. The more popular and platitudinous I made them, the more Mrs. Humbert was pleased with the show.

Never in my life had I confessed so much or received so many confessions. The sincerity and artlessness with which she discussed what she called her "love-life," from first necking to connubial catch-as-catch-can, were, ethically, in striking contrast with my glib compositions, but technically the two sets were congeneric since both were affected by the same stuff (soap operas, psychoanalysis and cheap novelettes) upon which I drew for my characters and she for her mode of expression. I was considerably amused by certain remarkable sexual habits that the good Harold Haze had had according to Charlotte who thought my mirth improper; but otherwise her autobiography was as devoid of interests as her autopsy would have been. I never saw a healthier woman than she, despite thinning diets.

Of my Lolita she seldom spoke—more seldom, in fact, than she did of the blurred, blond male baby whose photograph to the exclusion of all others adorned our bleak bedroom. In one of her tasteless reveries, she predicted that the dead infant's soul would return to earth in the form of the child she would bear in her present wedlock. And although I felt no special urge to supply the Humbert line with a replica of Harold's production (Lolita, with an incestuous thrill, I had grown to regard as *my* child), it occurred to me that a prolonged confinement, with a nice Caesarean operation and other complications in a safe maternity ward sometime next spring, would give me a chance to be alone with my Lolita for weeks, perhaps—and gorge the limp nymphet with sleeping pills.

Oh, she simply hated her daughter! What I thought especially vicious was that she had gone out of her way to answer with great diligence the questionnaires in a fool's book she had (*A Guide to Your Child's Development*), published in Chicago. The rigmarole went year by year, and Mom was supposed to fill out a kind of inventory at each of her child's birthdays. On Lo's twelfth, January 1, 1947, Charlotte Haze, née Becker, had underlined the following epithets, ten out of forty, under "Your Child's Personality": aggressive, boisterous, critical, distrustful, impatient, irritable, inquisitive, listless, negativistic (underlined twice) and obstinate. She had ignored the thirty remaining adjectives, among which were cheerful, co-operative, energetic, and so forth. It was really maddening. With a brutality that otherwise never appeared in my loving wife's mild nature, she attacked and routed such of Lo's little belongings that had wandered to various parts of the house to freeze there like so many hypnotized bunnies. Little did the good lady dream that one morning when an upset stomach (the result of my trying to improve on her sauces) had prevented me from accompanying her to church, I deceived her with one of Lolita's anklets. And then, her attitude toward my saporous darling's letters!

DEAR MUMMY AND HUMMY,
    Hope you are fine. Thank you very much for the candy. I [crossed out and re-written again] I lost my new sweater in the woods. It has been cold here for the last few days. I'm having a time. Love.
                                    DOLLY

"The dumb child," said Mrs. Humbert, "has left out a word before 'time.' That sweater was all-wool, and I wish you would not send her candy without consulting me."

20

There was a woodlake (Hourglass Lake—not as I had thought it was spelled) a few miles from Ramsdale, and there was one week of great heat at the end of July when we drove there daily.

I am now obliged to describe in some tedious detail our last swim there together, one tropical Tuesday morning.

We had left the car in a parking area not far from the road and were making our way down a path cut through the pine forest to the lake, when Charlotte remarked that Jean Farlow, in quest of rare light effects (Jean belonged to the old school of painting), had seen Leslie taking a dip "in the ebony" (as John had quipped) at five o'clock in the morning last Sunday.

"The water," I said, "must have been quite cold."

"That is not the point," said the logical doomed dear. "He is subnormal, you see. And," she continued (in that carefully phrased way of hers that was beginning to tell on my health), "I have a very definite feeling our Louise is in love with that moron."

Feeling. "We feel Dolly is not doing as well" etc. (from an old school report).

The Humberts walked on, sandaled and robed.

"Do you know, Hum: I have one most ambitious dream," pronounced Lady Hum, lowering her head—shy of that dream— and communing with the tawny ground. "I would love to get hold of a real trained servant maid like that German girl the Talbots spoke of; and have her live in the house."

"No room," I said.

"Come," she said with her quizzical smile, "surely, *chéri*, you underestimate the possibilities of the Humbert home. We would put her in Lo's room. I intended to make a guestroom of that hole anyway. It's the coldest and meanest in the whole house."

"What are you talking about?" I asked, the skin of my cheek-bones tensing up (this I take the trouble to note only because my daughter's skin did the same when she felt that way: dis-belief, disgust, irritation).

"Are you bothered by Romantic Associations?" queried my wife—in allusion to her first surrender.

"Hell no," said I. "I just wonder where will you put your daughter when you get your guest or your maid."

"Ah," said Mrs. Humbert, dreaming, smiling, drawing out the "Ah" simultaneously with the raise of one eyebrow and a soft exhalation of breath. "Little Lo, I'm afraid, does not enter the picture at all, at all. Little Lo goes straight from camp to a good boarding school with strict discipline and some sound religious training. And then—Beardsley College. I have it all mapped out, you need not worry."

She went on to say that she, Mrs. Humbert, would have to overcome her habitual sloth and write to Miss Phalen's sister who taught at St. Algebra. The dazzling lake emerged. I said I had forgotten my sunglasses in the car and would catch up with her.

I had always thought that wringing one's hands was a fictional gesture—the obscure outcome, perhaps, of some medieval ritual; but as I took to the woods, for a spell of despair and desperate meditation, this was the gesture ("look, Lord, at these chains!") that would have come nearest to the mute expression of my mood.

Had Charlotte been Valeria, I would have known how to handle the situation; and "handle" is the word I want. In the good old days, by merely twisting fat Valechka's brittle wrist (the one she had fallen upon from a bicycle) I could make her change her mind instantly; but anything of the sort in regard to Charlotte was unthinkable. Bland American Charlotte frightened me. My lighthearted dream of controlling her through her passion for me was all wrong. I dared not do anything to spoil the image of me she had set up to adore. I had toadied to her when she was the awesome duenna of my darling, and a groveling something still persisted in my attitude toward her. The only ace I held was her ignorance of my monstrous love for her Lo. She had been annoyed by Lo's liking me; but *my* feelings she could not divine. To Valeria I might have said: "Look here, you fat fool, *c'est moi qui décide* what is good for Dolores Humbert." To Charlotte, I could not even say (with ingratiating calm): "Excuse me, my dear, I disagree. Let us give the child one more chance. Let me be her private tutor for a year or so. You once told me yourself—" In fact, I could not say anything at all to Charlotte about the child without giving myself away. Oh, you cannot imagine (as I had never imagined) what these women of principle are! Charlotte, who did not notice the falsity of all the everyday conventions and rules of behavior, and foods, and books, and people she doted upon, would distinguish at once a false intonation in anything I might say with a view to keeping Lo near. She was like a musician who may be an odious vulgarian in ordinary life, devoid of tact and taste; but who will hear a false note in music with diabolical accuracy of judgment. To break Charlotte's will, I would have to break her heart. If I broke her heart, her image of me would break too. If I said: "Either I have my way with Lolita, and you help me to keep the matter quiet, or we part at once," she would have turned as pale as a woman of clouded glass and slowly replied: "All right, whatever you add or retract, this is the end." And the end it would be.

Such, then, was the mess. I remember reaching the parking area and pumping a handful of rust-tasting water, and drinking it as avidly as if it could give me magic wisdom, youth, freedom, a tiny concubine. For a while, purple-robed, heel-dangling, I sat on the edge of one of the rude tables, under the wooshing pines. In the middle distance, two little maidens in shorts and halters came out of a sun-dappled privy marked "Women." Gum-chewing Mabel (or Mabel's understudy) laboriously, absent-mindedly, straddled a bicycle, and Marion, shaking her hair because of the flies, settled behind, legs wide apart; and, wobbling, they slowly, absently, merged with the light and shade. Lolita! Father and daughter melting into these woods! The natural solution was to destroy Mrs. Humbert. But how?

No man can bring about the perfect murder; chance, however, can do it. There was the famous dispatch of a Mme Lacour in Arles, southern France, at the close of last century. An unidentified bearded six-footer, who, it was later conjectured, had been the lady's secret lover, walked up to her in a crowded street, soon after her marriage to Colonel Lacour, and mortally stabbed her in the back, three times, while the Colonel, a small bulldog of a man, hung onto the murderer's arm. By a miraculous and beautiful coincidence, right at the moment when the operator was in the act of loosening the angry little husband's jaws (while several onlookers were closing in upon the group), a cranky Italian in the house nearest to the scene set off by sheer accident some kind of explosive he was tinkering with, and immediately the street was turned into a pandemonium of smoke, falling bricks and running people. The explosion hurt no one (except that it knocked out game Colonel Lacour); but the lady's vengeful lover ran when the others ran—and lived happily ever after.

Now look what happens when the operator himself plans a perfect removal.

I walked down to Hourglass Lake. The spot from which we and a few other "nice" couples (the Farlows, the Chatfields) bathed was a kind of small cove; my Charlotte liked it because it was almost "a private beach." The main bathing facilities (or "drowning facilities" as the Ramsdale *Journal* had had occasion to say) were in the left (eastern) part of the hourglass, and could not be seen from our covelet. To our right, the pines soon gave way to a curve of marshland which turned again into forest on the opposite side.

I sat down beside my wife so noiselessly that she started.

"Shall we go in?" she asked.

"We shall in a minute. Let me follow a train of thought."

I thought. More than a minute passed.

"All right. Come on."

"Was I on that train?"

"You certainly were."

"I hope so," said Charlotte entering the water. It soon reached the gooseflesh of her thick thighs; and then, joining her outstretched hands, shutting her mouth tight, very plain-faced in her black rubber headgear, Charlotte flung herself forward with a great splash.

Slowly we swam out into the shimmer of the lake.

On the opposite bank, at least a thousand paces away (if one could walk across water), I could make out the tiny figures of two men working like beavers on their stretch of shore. I knew exactly who they were: a retired policeman of Polish descent and the retired plumber who owned most of the timber on that side of the lake. And I also knew they were engaged in building, just for the dismal fun of the thing, a wharf. The knocks that reached us seemed so much bigger than what could be distinguished of those dwarfs' arms and tools; indeed, one suspected the director of those acrosonic effects to have been at odds with the puppet-master, especially since the hefty crack of each diminutive blow lagged behind its visual version.

The short white-sand strip of "our" beach—from which by now we had gone a little way to reach deep water—was empty on weekday mornings. There was nobody around except those two tiny very busy figures on the opposite side, and a dark-red private plane that droned overhead, and then disappeared in the blue. The setting was really perfect for a brisk bubbling murder, and here was the subtle point: the man of law and the man of water were just near enough to witness an accident and just far enough not to observe a crime. They were near enough to hear a distracted bather thrashing about and bellowing for somebody to come and help him save his drowning wife; and they were too far to distinguish (if they happened to look too soon) that the anything but distracted swimmer was finishing to tread his wife underfoot. I was not yet at that stage; I merely want to convey the ease of the act, the nicety of the setting! So there was Charlotte swimming on with dutiful awkwardness (she was a very mediocre mermaid), but not without a certain solemn pleasure (for was not her merman by her side?); and as I watched, with the stark lucidity of a future recollection (you know—trying to see things as you will remember having seen them), the glossy whiteness of her wet face so little tanned despite all her endeavors, and her pale lips, and her naked convex forehead, and the tight black cap, and the plump wet neck, I knew that all I had to do was to drop back, take a deep breath, then grab her by the ankle and rapidly dive with my captive corpse. I say corpse because surprise, panic and inexperience would cause her to inhale at once a lethal gallon of lake, while I would be able to hold on for at least a full minute, open-eyed under water. The fatal gesture passed like the tail of a falling star across the blackness of the contemplated crime. It was like some dreadful silent ballet, the male dancer holding the

ballerina by her foot and streaking down through watery twilight. I might come up for a mouthful of air while still holding
her down, and then would dive again as many times as would
be necessary, and only when the curtain came down on her
for good, would I permit myself to yell for help. And when
some twenty minutes later the two puppets steadily growing
arrived in a rowboat, one half newly painted, poor Mrs. Humbert
Humbert, the victim of a cramp or coronary occlusion, or both,
would be standing on her head in the inky ooze, some thirty
feet below the smiling surface of Hourglass Lake.

Simple, was it not? But what d'ye know, folks—I just could
not make myself do it!

She swam beside me, a trustful and clumsy seal, and all the
logic of passion screamed in my ear: Now is the time! And,
folks, I just couldn't! In silence I turned shoreward and gravely,
dutifully, she also turned, and still hell screamed its counsel,
and still I could not make myself drown the poor, slippery,
big-bodied creature. The scream grew more and more remote
as I realized the melancholy fact that neither tomorrow, nor
Friday, nor any other day or night, could I make myself put
her to death. Oh, I could visualize myself slapping Valeria's
breasts out of alignment, or otherwise hurting her—and I could
see myself, no less clearly, shooting her lover in the underbelly
and making him say "akh!" and sit down. But I could not kill
Charlotte—especially when things were on the whole not quite
as hopeless, perhaps, as they seemed at first wince on that miserable morning. Were I to catch her by her strong kicking foot;
were I to see her amazed look, hear her awful voice; were I still
to go through with the ordeal, her ghost would haunt me all
my life. Perhaps if the year were 1447 instead of 1947 I might
have hoodwinked my gentle nature by administering her some
classical poison from a hollow agate, some tender philter of death.
But in our middle-class nosy era it would not have come off the
way it used to in the brocaded palaces of the past. Nowadays
you have to be a scientist if you want to be a killer. No, no, I
was neither. Ladies and gentlemen of the jury, the majority of
sex offenders that hanker for some throbbing, sweet-moaning,

physical but not necessarily coital, relation with a girl-child, are innocuous, inadequate, passive, timid strangers who merely ask the community to allow them to pursue their practically harmless, so-called aberrant behavior, their little hot wet private acts of sexual deviation without the police and society cracking down upon them. We are not sex fiends! We do not rape as good soldiers do. We are unhappy, mild, dog-eyed gentlemen, sufficiently well integrated to control our urge in the presence of adults, but ready to give years and years of life for one chance to touch a nymphet. Emphatically, no killers are we. Poets never kill. Oh, my poor Charlotte, do not hate me in your eternal heaven among an eternal alchemy of asphalt and rubber and metal and stone—but thank God, not water, not water!

Nonetheless it was a very close shave, speaking quite objectively. And now comes the point of my perfect-crime parable.

We sat down on our towels in the thirsty sun. She looked around, loosened her bra, and turned over on her stomach to give her back a chance to be feasted upon. She said she loved me. She sighed deeply. She extended one arm and groped in the pocket of her robe for her cigarettes. She sat up and smoked. She examined her right shoulder. She kissed me heavily with open smoky mouth. Suddenly, down the sand bank behind us, from under the bushes and pines, a stone rolled, then another.

"Those disgusting prying kids," said Charlotte, holding up her big bra to her breast and turning prone again. "I shall have to speak about that to Peter Krestovski."

From the debouchment of the trail came a rustle, a footfall, and Jean Farlow marched down with her easel and things.

"You scared us," said Charlotte.

Jean said she had been up there, in a place of green concealment, spying on nature (spies are generally shot), trying to finish a lakescape, but it was no good, she had no talent whatever (which was quite true)—"And have *you* ever tried painting, Humbert?" Charlotte, who was a little jealous of Jean, wanted to know if John was coming.

He was. He was coming home for lunch today. He had dropped her on the way to Parkington and should be picking

[90]

her up any time now. It was a grand morning. She always felt
a traitor to Cavall and Melampus for leaving them roped on
such gorgeous days. She sat down on the white sand between
Charlotte and me. She wore shorts. Her long brown legs were
about as attractive to me as those of a chestnut mare. She
showed her gums when she smiled.

"I almost put both of you into my lake," she said. "I even
noticed something you overlooked. You [addressing Humbert]
had your wrist watch on in, yes, sir, you had."

"Waterproof," said Charlotte softly, making a fish mouth.

Jean took my wrist upon her knee and examined Charlotte's
gift, then put back Humbert's hand on the sand, palm up.

"You could see anything that way," remarked Charlotte
coquettishly.

Jean sighed. "I once saw," she said, "two children, male and
female, at sunset, right here, making love. Their shadows were
giants. And I told you about Mr. Tomson at daybreak. Next
time I expect to see fat old Ivor in the ivory. He is really a
freak, that man. Last time he told me a completely indecent
story about his nephew. It appears—"

"Hullo there," said John's voice.

21

My habit of being silent when displeased, or, more exactly,
the cold and scaly quality of my displeased silence, used to
frighten Valeria out of her wits. She used to whimper and wail,
saying *"Ce qui me rend folle, c'est que je ne sais à quoi tu penses
quand tu es comme ça."* I tried being silent with Charlotte—and
she just chirped on, or chucked my silence under the chin.
An astonishing woman! I would retire to my former room, now
a regular "studio," mumbling I had after all a learned opus to
write, and cheerfully Charlotte went on beautifying the home,
warbling on the telephone and writing letters. From my window,
through the lacquered shiver of poplar leaves, I could see her

crossing the street and contentedly mailing her letter to Miss Phalen's sister.

The week of scattered showers and shadows which elapsed after our last visit to the motionless sands of Hourglass Lake was one of the gloomiest I can recall. Then came two or three dim rays of hope—before the ultimate sunburst.

It occurred to me that I had a fine brain in beautiful working order and that I might as well use it. If I dared not meddle with my wife's plans for her daughter (getting warmer and browner every day in the fair weather of hopeless distance), I could surely devise some general means to assert myself in a general way that might be later directed toward a particular occasion. One evening, Charlotte herself provided me with an opening.

"I have a surprise for you," she said looking at me with fond eyes over a spoonful of soup. "In the fall we two are going to England."

I swallowed *my* spoonful, wiped my lips with pink paper (Oh, the cool rich linens of Mirana Hotel!) and said:

"I have also a surprise for you, my dear. We two are not going to England."

"Why, what's the matter?" she said, looking—with more surprise than I had counted upon—at my hands (I was involuntarily folding and tearing and crushing and tearing again the innocent pink napkin). My smiling face set her somewhat at ease, however.

"The matter is quite simple," I replied. "Even in the most harmonious of households, as ours is, not all decisions are taken by the female partner. There are certain things that the husband is there to decide. I can well imagine the thrill that you, a healthy American gal, must experience at crossing the Atlantic on the same ocean liner with Lady Bumble—or Sam Bumble, the Frozen Meat King, or a Hollywood harlot. And I doubt not that you and I would make a pretty ad for the Traveling Agency when portrayed looking—you, frankly starry-eyed, I, controlling my envious admiration—at the Palace Sentries, or Scarlet Guards, or Beaver Eaters, or whatever they are called. But I happen to be allergic to Europe, including merry old England. As you well know, I have nothing but very sad associations with the Old and rotting World. No colored ads in your magazines will change the situation."

"My darling," said Charlotte. "I really—"

"No, wait a minute. The present matter is only incidental. I am concerned with a general trend. When you wanted me to spend my afternoons sunbathing on the Lake instead of doing my work, I gladly gave in and became a bronzed glamor boy for your sake, instead of remaining a scholar and, well, an educator. When you lead me to bridge and bourbon with the charming Farlows, I meekly follow. No, please, wait. When you decorate your home, I do not interfere with your schemes. When you decide—when you decide all kinds of matters, I may be in complete, or in partial, let us say, disagreement—but I say nothing. I ignore the particular. I cannot ignore the general. I love being bossed by you, but every game has its rules. I am not cross. I am not cross at all. Don't do that. But I am one half of this household, and have a small but distinct voice."

She had come to my side and had fallen on her knees and was slowly, but very vehemently, shaking her head and clawing at my trousers. She said she had never realized. She said I was her ruler and her god. She said Louise had gone, and let us make love right away. She said I must forgive her or she would die.

This little incident filled me with considerable elation. I told her quietly that it was a matter not of asking forgiveness, but of changing one's ways; and I resolved to press my advantage and spend a good deal of time, aloof and moody, working at my book—or at least pretending to work.

The "studio bed" in my former room had long been converted into the sofa it had always been at heart, and Charlotte had warned me since the very beginning of our cohabitation that gradually the room would be turned into a regular "writer's den." A couple of days after the British Incident, I was sitting in a new and very comfortable easy chair, with a large volume in my lap, when Charlotte rapped with her ring finger and sauntered in. How different were her movements from those of my Lolita, when *she* used to visit me in her dear dirty blue jeans, smelling of orchards in nymphetland; awkward and fey, and dimly depraved, the lower buttons of her shirt unfastened. Let me tell you, however, something. Behind the brashness of little Haze, and the poise of big Haze, a trickle of shy life ran that tasted the same, that murmured the same. A great French doctor once told my father that in near relatives the faintest gastric gurgle has the same "voice."

So Charlotte sauntered in. She felt all was not well between us. I had pretended to fall asleep the night before, and the night before that, as soon as we had gone to bed, and had risen at dawn.

Tenderly, she inquired if she were not "interrupting."

"Not at the moment," I said, turning volume C of the *Girls' Encyclopedia* around to examine a picture printed "bottom-edge" as printers say.

Charlotte went up to a little table of imitation mahogany with a drawer. She put her hand upon it. The little table was ugly, no doubt, but it had done nothing to her.

"I have always wanted to ask you," she said (businesslike, not coquettish), "why is this thing locked up? Do you want it in this room? It's so abominably uncouth."

"Leave it alone," I said. I was Camping in Scandinavia.

"Is there a key?"

"Hidden."

"Oh, Hum . . ."

"Locked up love letters."

She gave me one of those wounded-doe looks that irritated me so much, and then, not quite knowing if I was serious, or how to keep up the conversation, stood for several slow pages (Campus, Canada, Candid Camera, Candy) peering at the window-pane rather than through it, drumming upon it with sharp almond-and-rose fingernails.

Presently (at Canoeing or Canvasback) she strolled up to my chair and sank down, tweedily, weightily, on its arm, in-undating me with the perfume my first wife had used. "Would his lordship like to spend the fall *here?*" she asked, pointing with her little finger at an autumn view in a conservative Eastern State. "Why?" (very distinctly and slowly). She shrugged. (Probably Harold used to take a vacation at that time. Open season. Conditional reflex on her part.)

"I think I know where that is," she said, still pointing. "There is a hotel I remember, Enchanted Hunters, quaint, isn't it? And the food is a dream. And nobody bothers anybody."

She rubbed her cheek against my temple. Valeria soon got over that.

"Is there anything special you would like for dinner, dear? John and Jean will drop in later."

I answered with a grunt. She kissed me on my underlip, and, brightly saying she would bake a cake (a tradition subsisted from my lodging days that I adored her cakes), left me to my idleness.

Carefully putting down the open book where she had sat (it attempted to send forth a rotation of waves, but an inserted pencil stopped the pages), I checked the hiding place of the key: rather self-consciously it lay under the old expensive safety razor I had used before she bought me a much better and cheaper one. Was it the perfect hiding place—there, under that razor, in the groove of its velvet-lined case? The case lay in a small trunk where I kept various business papers. Could I improve upon this? Remarkable how difficult it is to conceal things— especially when one's wife keeps monkeying with the furniture.

22

I think it was exactly a week after our last swim that the noon mail brought a reply from the second Miss Phalen. The lady wrote she had just returned to St. Algebra from her sister's funeral. "Euphemia had never been the same after breaking that hip." As to the matter of Mrs. Humbert's daughter, she wished to report that it was too late to enroll her this year; but that she, the surviving Phalen, was practically certain that if Mr. and Mrs. Humbert brought Dolores over in January, her admittance might be arranged.

Next day, after lunch, I went to see "our" doctor, a friendly fellow whose perfect bedside manner and complete reliance on a few patented drugs adequately masked his ignorance of, and indifference to, medical science. The fact that Lo would have to come back to Ramsdale was a treasure of anticipation. For this event I wanted to be fully prepared. I had in fact begun my campaign earlier, before Charlotte made that cruel decision of hers. I had to be sure when my lovely child arrived, that very night, and then night after night, until St. Algebra took her away from me, I would possess the means of putting two creatures to sleep so thoroughly that neither sound nor touch should rouse them. Throughout most of July I had been experimenting with various sleeping powders, trying them out on Charlotte, a great taker of pills. The last dose I had given her (she thought it was a tablet of mild bromides—to anoint her nerves) had knocked her out for four solid hours. I had put the radio at full blast. I had blazed in her face an olisbos-like flashlight. I had pushed her, pinched her, prodded her—and nothing had disturbed the rhythm of her calm and powerful breathing. However, when I had done such a simple thing as kiss her, she had awakened at once, as fresh and strong as an octopus (I barely escaped). This would not do, I thought; had to get something still safer. At first, Dr. Byron did not seem to believe me when I said his last prescription was no match for my insomnia. He suggested I try again, and for a moment diverted my attention by showing me photographs of his family. He had a fascinating child of Dolly's age; but I saw through his tricks and insisted he prescribe the mightiest pill extant. He suggested I play golf, but finally agreed to give me something that, he said, "would really work"; and going to a cabinet, he produced a vial of violet-blue capsules banded with dark purple at one end, which, he said, had just been placed on the market and were intended not for neurotics whom a draft of water could calm if properly administered, but only for great sleepless artists who had to die for a few hours in order to live for centuries. I love

[96]

to fool doctors, and though inwardly rejoicing, pocketed the pills with a skeptical shrug. Incidentally, I had had to be careful with him. Once, in another connection, a stupid lapse on my part made me mention my last sanatorium, and I thought I saw the tips of his ears twitch. Being not at all keen for Charlotte or anybody else to know that period of my past, I had hastily explained that I had once done some research among the insane for a novel. But no matter; the old rogue certainly had a sweet girleen.

I left in great spirits. Steering my wife's car with one finger, I contentedly rolled homeward. Ramsdale had, after all, lots of charm. The cicadas whirred; the avenue had been freshly watered. Smoothly, almost silkily, I turned down into our steep little street. Everything was somehow so right that day. So blue and green. I knew the sun shone because my ignition key was reflected in the windshield; and I knew it was exactly half past three because the nurse who came to massage Miss Opposite every afternoon was tripping down the narrow sidewalk in her white stockings and shoes. As usual, Junk's hysterical setter attacked me as I rolled downhill, and as usual, the local paper was lying on the porch where it had just been hurled by Kenny.

The day before I had ended the regime of aloofness I had imposed upon myself, and now uttered a cheerful homecoming call as I opened the door of the living room. With her cream-white nape and bronze bun to me, wearing the yellow blouse and maroon slacks she had on when I first met her, Charlotte sat at the corner bureau writing a letter. My hand still on the doorknob, I repeated my hearty cry. Her writing hand stopped. She sat still for a moment; then she slowly turned in her chair and rested her elbow on its curved back. Her face, disfigured by her emotion, was not a pretty sight as she stared at my legs and said:

"The Haze woman, the big bitch, the old cat, the obnoxious mamma, the—the old stupid Haze is no longer your dupe. She has—she has . . ."

My fair accuser stopped, swallowing her venom and her tears.

Whatever Humbert Humbert said—or attempted to say—is inessential. She went on:

"You're a monster. You're a detestable, abominable, criminal fraud. If you come near—I'll scream out the window. Get back!"

Again, whatever H.H. murmured may be omitted, I think.

"I am leaving tonight. This is all yours. Only you'll never, never see that miserable brat again. Get out of this room."

Reader, I did. I went up to the ex-semi-studio. Arms akimbo, I stood for a moment quite still and self-composed, surveying from the threshold the raped little table with its open drawer, a key hanging from the lock, four other household keys on the table top. I walked across the landing into the Humberts' bed-room, and calmly removed my diary from under her pillow into my pocket. Then I started to walk downstairs, but stopped half-way: she was talking on the telephone which happened to be plugged just outside the door of the living room. I wanted to hear what she was saying: she canceled an order for something or other, and returned to the parlor. I rearranged my respiration and went through the hallway to the kitchen. There, I opened a bottle of Scotch. She could never resist Scotch. Then I walked into the dining room and from there, through the half-open door, contemplated Charlotte's broad back.

"You are ruining my life and yours," I said quietly. "Let us be civilized people. It is all your hallucination. You are crazy, Charlotte. The notes you found were fragments of a novel. Your name and hers were put in by mere chance. Just because they came handy. Think it over. I shall bring you a drink."

She neither answered nor turned, but went on writing in a scorching scrawl whatever she was writing. A third letter, pre-sumably (two in stamped envelopes were already laid out on the desk). I went back to the kitchen.

I set out two glasses (to St. Algebra? to Lo?) and opened the refrigerator. It roared at me viciously while I removed the ice from its heart. Rewrite. Let her read it again. She will not recall details. Change, forge. Write a fragment and show it to her or leave it lying around. Why do faucets sometimes whine so horribly? A horrible situation, really. The little pillow-shaped blocks of ice—pillows for polar teddy bear, Lo—emitted rasping, crackling, tortured sounds as the warm water loosened them in their cells. I bumped down the glasses side by side. I poured in the whiskey and a dram of soda. She had tabooed my pin. Bark and bang went the icebox. Carrying the glasses, I walked through the dining room and spoke through the parlor door which was a fraction ajar, not quite space enough for my elbow.

"I have made you a drink," I said.

She did not answer, the mad bitch, and I placed the glasses on the sideboard near the telephone, which had started to ring.

"Leslie speaking. Leslie Tomson," said Leslie Tomson who favored a dip at dawn. "Mrs. Humbert, sir, has been run over and you'd better come quick."

I answered, perhaps a bit testily, that my wife was safe and sound, and still holding the receiver, I pushed open the door and said:

"There's this man saying you've been killed, Charlotte."

But there was no Charlotte in the living room.

23

I rushed out. The far side of our steep little street presented a peculiar sight. A big black glossy Packard had climbed Miss Opposite's sloping lawn at an angle from the sidewalk (where a tartan laprobe had dropped in a heap), and stood there, shining in the sun, its doors open like wings, its front wheels deep in evergreen shrubbery. To the anatomical right of this car, on the trim turf of the lawn-slope, an old gentleman with a white mustache, well-dressed—doublebreasted gray suit, polka-dotted bow-tie—lay supine, his long legs together, like a death-size wax figure. I have to put the impact of an instantaneous vision into a sequence of words; their physical accumulation in the page impairs the actual flash, the sharp unity of impression: Rug-heap, car, old man-doll, Miss O.'s nurse running with a rustle, a half-empty tumbler in her hand, back to the screened porch—where the propped-up, imprisoned, decrepit lady herself may be imagined screeching, but not loud enough to drown the rhythmical yaps of the Junk setter walking from group to group—from a bunch of neighbors already collected on the sidewalk, near the bit of checked stuff, and back to the car which he had finally run to earth, and then to another group on the lawn, consisting of Leslie, two policemen and a sturdy man with tortoise shell glasses. At this point, I should explain that the prompt appearance of the patrolmen, hardly more than a minute after the accident, was due to their having been ticketing the illegally parked cars in a cross lane two blocks down the grade; that the fellow with the glasses was Frederick Beale, Jr., driver of the Packard; that his 79-year-old father, whom the nurse had just watered on the green bank where he lay—a banked banker so to speak—was not in a dead faint, but was comfortably and methodically recovering from a mild heart attack or its possibility; and, finally, that the laprobe on the sidewalk (where she had so often pointed out to me with disapproval the crooked green cracks) concealed the mangled remains of Charlotte Humbert who had been knocked down and dragged several feet by the Beale car as she was hurrying across the street to drop three letters in the mailbox, at the corner of Miss Opposite's lawn. These were picked up and handed to me by a pretty child in a dirty pink frock, and I got rid of them by clawing them to fragments in my trouser pocket.

Three doctors and the Farlows presently arrived on the scene and took over. The widower, a man of exceptional self-control, neither wept nor raved. He staggered a bit, that he did; but he opened his mouth only to impart such information or issue such directions as were strictly necessary in connection with the identification, examination and disposal of a dead woman, the top of her head a porridge of bone, brains, bronze hair and blood. The sun was still a blinding red when he was put to bed in Dolly's room by his two friends, gentle John and dewy-eyed Jean; who, to be near, retired to the Humberts' bedroom for the night; which, for all I know, they may not have spent as innocently as the solemnity of the occasion required.

I have no reason to dwell, in this very special memoir, on the pre-funeral formalities that had to be attended to, or on the funeral itself, which was as quiet as the marriage had been. But a few incidents pertaining to those four or five days after Charlotte's simple death, have to be noted.

My first night of widowhood I was so drunk that I slept as soundly as the child who had slept in that bed. Next morning I hastened to inspect the fragments of letters in my pocket. They had got too thoroughly mixed up to be sorted into three complete sets. I assumed that "... and you had better find it because I cannot buy ..." came from a letter to Lo; and other fragments seemed to point to Charlotte's intention of fleeing with Lo to Parkington, or even back to Pisky, lest the vulture snatch her precious lamb. Other tatters and shreds (never had I thought I had such strong talons) obviously referred to an application not to St. A. but to another boarding school which was said to be so harsh and gray and gaunt in its methods (although supplying croquet under the elms) as to have earned the nickname of "Reformatory for Young Ladies." Finally, the third epistle was obviously addressed to me. I made out such items as "... after a year of separation we may ..." "... oh, my dearest, oh my ..." "... worse than if it had been a woman you kept ..." "... or, maybe, I shall die ..." But on the whole my gleanings made little sense; the various fragments of those three hasty missives were as jumbled in the palms of my hands as their elements had been in poor Charlotte's head.

That day John had to see a customer, and Jean had to feed her dogs, and so I was to be deprived temporarily of my friends' company. The dear people were afraid I might commit suicide if left alone, and since no other friends were available (Miss Opposite was incommunicado, the McCoos were busy building a new house miles away, and the Chatfields had been recently called to Maine by some family trouble of their own), Leslie and Louise were commissioned to keep me company under the pretense of helping me to sort out and pack a multitude of orphaned things. In a moment of superb inspiration I showed the kind and credulous Farlows (we were waiting for Leslie to come for his paid tryst with Louise) a little photograph of Charlotte I had found among her affairs. From a boulder she smiled through blown hair. It had been taken in April 1934, a memorable spring. While on a business visit to the States, I had had occasion to spend several months in Pisky. We met— and had a mad love affair. I was married, alas, and she was engaged to Haze, but after I returned to Europe, we corresponded through a friend, now dead. Jean whispered she had heard some rumors and looked at the snapshot, and, still looking, handed it to John, and John removed his pipe and looked at lovely and fast Charlotte Becker, and handed it back to me. Then they left for a few hours. Happy Louise was gurgling and scolding her swain in the basement.

Hardly had the Farlows gone than a blue-chinned cleric called —and I tried to make the interview as brief as was consistent with neither hurting his feelings nor arousing his doubts. Yes, I would devote all my life to the child's welfare. Here, incidentally, was a little cross that Charlotte Becker had given me when we were both young. I had a female cousin, a respectable spinster in New York. There we would find a good private school for Dolly. Oh, what a crafty Humbert!

For the benefit of Leslie and Louise who might (and did) report it to John and Jean I made a tremendously loud and beautifully enacted long-distance call and simulated a conversation with Shirley Holmes. When John and Jean returned, I completely took them in by telling them, in a deliberately wild and confused mutter, that Lo had gone with the intermediate group on a five-day hike and could not be reached.

"Good Lord," said Jean, "what shall we do?"

John said it was perfectly simple—he would get the Climax police to find the hikers—it would not take them an hour. In fact, he knew the country and—

"Look," he continued, "why don' I drive there right now, and you may sleep with Jean"—(he did not really add that but Jean supported his offer so passionately that it might be implied).

I broke down. I pleaded with John to let things remain the

way they were. I said I could not bear to have the child all around me, sobbing, clinging to me, she was so high-strung, the experience might react on her future, psychiatrists have analyzed such cases. There was a sudden pause.

"Well, you are the doctor," said John a little bluntly. "But after all I was Charlotte's friend and adviser. One would like to know what you are going to do about the child anyway."

"John," cried Jean, "she is his child, not Harold Haze's. Don't you understand? Humbert is Dolly's real father."

"I see," said John. "I am sorry. Yes, I see. I did not realize that. It simplifies matters, of course. And whatever you feel is right."

The distraught father went on to say he would go and fetch his delicate daughter immediately after the funeral, and would do his best to give her a good time in totally different surroundings, perhaps a trip to New Mexico or California—granted, of course, he lived.

So artistically did I impersonate the calm of ultimate despair, the hush before some crazy outburst, that the perfect Farlows removed me to their house. They had a good cellar, as cellars go in this country; and that was helpful, for I feared insomnia and a ghost.

Now I must explain *my* reasons for keeping Dolores away. Naturally, at first, when Charlotte had just been eliminated and I re-entered the house a free father, and gulped down the two whiskey-and-sodas I had prepared, and topped them with a pint or two of my "pin," and went to the bathroom to get away from neighbors and friends, there was but one thing in my mind and pulse—namely, the awareness that a few hours hence, warm, brown-haired, and mine, mine, mine, Lolita would be in my arms, shedding tears that I would kiss away faster than they could well. But as I stood wide-eyed and flushed before the mirror, John Farlow tenderly tapped to inquire if I was okay—and I immediately realized it would be madness on my part to have her in the house with all those busybodies milling around and scheming to take her away from me. Indeed, unpredictable Lo herself might—who knows?—show some foolish distrust of me, a sudden repugnance, vague fear and the like—and gone would be the magic prize at the very instant of triumph.

Speaking of busybodies, I had another visitor—friend Beale, the fellow who eliminated my wife. Stodgy and solemn, looking like a kind of assistant executioner, with his bulldog jowls, small black eyes, thickly rimmed glasses and conspicuous nostrils, he was ushered in by John who then left us, closing the door upon us, with the utmost tact. Suavely saying he had twins in my stepdaughter's class, my grotesque visitor unrolled a large diagram he had made of the accident. It was, as my stepdaughter would have put it, "a beaut," with all kinds of impressive arrows and dotted lines in varicolored inks. Mrs. H. H.'s trajectory was illustrated at several points by a series of those little outline figures—doll-like wee career girl or WAC—used in statistics as visual aids. Very clearly and conclusively, this route came into contact with a boldly traced sinuous line representing two consecutive swerves—one which the Beale car made to avoid the Junk dog (dog not shown), and the second, a kind of exaggerated continuation of the first, meant to avert the tragedy. A very black cross indicated the spot where the trim little outline figure had at last come to rest on the sidewalk. I looked for some similar mark to denote the place on the embankment where my visitor's huge wax father had reclined, but there was none. That gentleman, however, had signed the document as a witness underneath the name of Leslie Tomson, Miss Opposite and a few other people.

With his hummingbird pencil deftly and delicately flying from one point to another, Frederick demonstrated his absolute innocence and the recklessness of my wife: while he was in the act of avoiding the dog, *she* had slipped on the freshly watered asphalt and plunged forward whereas she should have flung herself not forward but backward (Fred showed how by a jerk of his padded shoulder). I said it was certainly not his fault, and the inquest upheld my view.

Breathing violently through jet-black tense nostrils, he shook his head and my hand; then, with an air of perfect *savoir vivre* and gentlemanly generosity, he offered to pay the funeral-home expenses. He expected me to refuse his offer. With a drunken sob of gratitude I accepted it. This took him aback. Slowly, incredulously, he repeated what he had said. I thanked him again, even more profusely than before.

In result of that weird interview, the numbness of my soul was for a moment resolved. And no wonder! I had actually seen the agent of fate. I had palpated the very flesh of fate— and its padded shoulder. A brilliant and monstrous mutation had suddenly taken place, and here was the instrument. Within the intricacies of the pattern (hurrying housewife, slippery pavement, a pest of a dog, steep grade, big car, baboon at its wheel), I could dimly distinguish my own vile contribution. Had I not been such a fool—or such an intuitive genius— to preserve that journal, fluids produced by vindictive anger and hot shame would not have blinded Charlotte in her dash to the mailbox. But even had they blinded her, still nothing might have happened, had not precise fate, that synchronizing phantom, mixed within its alembic the car and the dog and the sun and the shade and the wet and the weak and the strong and the stone. Adieu, Marlene! Fat fate's formal handshake (as reproduced by Beale before leaving the room) brought me out of my torpor; and I wept. Ladies and gentlemen of the jury— I wept.

24

The elms and the poplars were turning their ruffled backs to a sudden onslaught of wind, and a black thunderhead loomed above Ramsdale's white church tower when I looked around me for the last time. For unknown adventures I was leaving the livid house where I had rented a room only ten weeks before. The shades—thrifty, practical bamboo shades—were already down. On porches or in the house their rich textures lend modern drama. The house of heaven must seem pretty bare after that. A raindrop fell on my knuckles. I went back into the house for something or other while John was putting my bags into the car, and then a funny thing happened. I do not know if in these tragic notes I have sufficiently stressed the peculiar "sending" effect that the writer's good looks—pseudo-Celtic, attractively simian, boyishly manly—had on women of every age and environment. Of course, such announcements made in the first person may sound ridiculous. But every once in a while I have to remind the reader of my appearance much as a professional novelist, who has given a character of his some mannerism or a dog, has to go on producing that dog or that mannerism every time the character crops up in the course of the book. There may be more to it in the present case. My gloomy good looks should be kept in the mind's eye if my story is to be properly understood. Pubescent Lo swooned to Humbert's charm as she did to hiccuppy music; adult Lotte loved me with a mature, possessive passion that I now deplore and respect more than I care to say. Jean Farlow, who was thirty-one and absolutely neurotic, had also apparently developed a strong liking for me. She was handsome in a carved-Indian sort of way, with a burnt sienna complexion. Her lips were like large crimson polyps, and when she emitted her special barking laugh, she showed large dull teeth and pale gums.

She was very tall, wore either slacks with sandals or billowing skirts with ballet slippers, drank any strong liquor in any amount, had had two miscarriages, wrote stories about animals, painted, as the reader knows, lakescapes, was already nursing the cancer that was to kill her at thirty-three, and was hopelessly unattractive to me. Judge then of my alarm when a few seconds before I left (she and I stood in the hallway) Jean, with her always trembling fingers, took me by the temples, and, tears in her bright blue eyes, attempted, unsuccessfully, to glue herself to my lips.

"Take care of yourself," she said, "kiss your daughter for me."

A clap of thunder reverberated throughout the house, and she added:

"Perhaps, somewhere, some day, at a less miserable time, we may see each other again" (Jean, whatever, wherever you are, in minus time-space or plus soul-time, forgive me all this, parenthesis included).

And presently I was shaking hands with both of them in the street, the sloping street, and everything was whirling and flying before the approaching white deluge, and a truck with a mattress from Philadelphia was confidently rolling down to an empty house, and dust was running and writhing over the exact slab of stone where Charlotte, when they lifted the laprobe for me, had been revealed, curled up, her eyes intact, their black lashes still wet, matted, like yours, Lolita.

25

One might suppose that with all blocks removed and a prospect of delirious and unlimited delights before me, I would have mentally sunk back, heaving a sigh of delicious relief. *Eh bien, pas du tout!* Instead of basking in the beams of smiling Chance, I was obsessed by all sorts of purely ethical doubts and fears. For instance: might it not surprise people that Lo was so consistently debarred from attending festive and funeral functions in her immediate family? You remember—we had not had her at our wedding. Or another thing: granted it was the long hairy arm of Coincidence that had reached out to remove an innocent woman, might Coincidence not ignore in a heathen moment what its twin lamb had done and hand Lo a premature note of commiseration? True, the accident had been reported only by the Ramsdale *Journal*—not by the Parkington *Recorder* or the Climax *Herald*, Camp Q being in another state, and local deaths having no federal news interest; but I could not help fancying that somehow Dolly Haze had been informed already, and that at the very time I was on my way to fetch her, she was being driven to Ramsdale by friends unknown to me. Still more disquieting than all these conjectures and worries, was the fact that Humbert Humbert, a brand-new American citizen of obscure European origin, had taken no steps toward becoming the legal guardian of his dead wife's daughter (twelve years and seven months old). Would I ever dare take those steps? I could not repress a shiver whenever I imagined my nudity hemmed in by mysterious statutes in the merciless glare of the Common Law.

My scheme was a marvel of primitive art: I would whizz over to Camp Q, tell Lolita her mother was about to undergo a major operation at an invented hospital, and then keep moving with my sleepy nymphet from inn to inn while her mother got better and better and finally died. But as I traveled campward my anxiety grew. I could not bear to think I might not find Lolita there—or find, instead, another, scared, Lolita clamoring for some family friend: not the Farlows, thank God—she hardly knew them—but might there not be other people I had not reckoned with? Finally, I decided to make the long-distance call I had simulated so well a few days before. It was raining hard when I pulled up in a muddy suburb of Parkington, just before the Fork, one prong of which bypassed the city and led to the highway which crossed the hills to Lake Climax and Camp Q. I flipped off the ignition and for quite a minute sat in the car bracing myself for that telephone call, and staring at the rain, at the inundated sidewalk, at a hydrant: a hideous thing, really, painted a thick silver and red, extending the red stumps of its arms to be varnished by the rain which like stylized blood dripped upon its argent chains. No wonder that stopping beside those nightmare cripples is taboo. I drove up to a gasoline station. A surprise awaited me when at last the coins had satisfactorily clanked down and a voice was allowed to answer mine.

Holmes, the camp mistress, informed me that Dolly had gone Monday (this was Wednesday) on a hike in the hills with her group and was expected to return rather late today. Would I care to come tomorrow, and what was exactly—Without going into details, I said that her mother was hospitalized, that the situation was grave, that the child should not be told it was grave and that she should be ready to leave with me tomorrow afternoon. The two voices parted in an explosion of warmth and good will, and through some freak mechanical flaw all my coins came tumbling back to me with a hitting-the-jackpot clatter that almost made me laugh despite the disappointment at having to postpone bliss. One wonders if this sudden discharge, this spasmodic refund, was not correlated somehow, in the mind of McFate, with my having invented that little expedition before ever learning of it as I did now.

What next? I proceeded to the business center of Parkington and devoted the whole afternoon (the weather had cleared, the wet town was like silver-and-glass) to buying beautiful things for Lo. Goodness, what crazy purchases were prompted by the poignant predilection Humbert had in those days for check weaves, bright cottons, frills, puffed-out short sleeves, soft pleats, snug-fitting bodices and generously full skirts! Oh Lolita, you are my girl, as Vee was Poe's and Bea Dante's, and what little girl would not like to whirl in a circular skirt and scanties? Did I have something special in mind? coaxing voices asked me. Swimming suits? We have them in all shades. Dream pink, frosted aqua, glans mauve, tulip red, oolala black. What about playsuits? Slips? No slips. Lo and I loathed slips.

One of my guides in these matters was an anthropometric entry made by her mother on Lo's twelfth birthday (the reader remembers that Know-Your-Child book). I had the feeling that Charlotte, moved by obscure motives of envy and dislike, had added an inch here, a pound there; but since the nymphet had no doubt grown somewhat in the last seven months, I thought I could safely accept most of those January measurements: hip girth, twenty-nine inches; thigh girth (just below the gluteal sulcus), seventeen; calf girth and neck circumference, eleven; chest circumference, twenty-seven; upper arm girth, eight; waist, twenty-three; stature, fifty-seven inches; weight, seventy-eight pounds; figure, linear; intelligence quotient, 121; vermiform appendix present, thank God.

Apart from measurements, I could of course visualize Lolita with hallucinational lucidity; and nursing as I did a tingle on my breastbone at the exact spot her silky top had come level once or twice with my heart; and feeling as I did her warm weight in my lap (so that, in a sense, I was always "with Lolita" as a woman is "with child"), I was not surprised to discover later that my computation had been more or less correct. Having moreover studied a midsummer sale book, it was with a very knowing air that I examined various pretty articles, sport shoes, sneakers, pumps of crushed kid for crushed kids. The painted girl in black who attended to all these poignant needs of mine turned parental scholarship and precise description into commercial euphemisms, such as *"petite."* Another, much older woman, in a white dress, with a pancake make-up, seemed to be oddly impressed by my knowledge of junior fashions; perhaps I had a midget for mistress; so, when shown a skirt with two "cute" pockets in front, I intentionally put a naïve male question and was rewarded by a smiling demonstration of the way the zipper worked in the back of the skirt. I had next great fun with all kinds of shorts and briefs—phantom little Lolitas dancing, falling, daisying all over the counter. We rounded up the deal with some prim cotton pajamas in popular butcher-boy style. Humbert, the popular butcher.

There is a touch of the mythological and the enchanted in those large stores where according to ads a career girl can get a complete desk-to-date wardrobe, and where little sister can dream of the day when her wool jersey will make the boys in the back row of the classroom drool. Lifesize plastic figures of snubbed-nosed children with dun-colored, greenish, brown-dotted, faunish faces floated around me. I realized I was the only shopper in that rather eerie place where I moved about fish-like, in a glaucous aquarium. I sensed strange thoughts form in the minds of the languid ladies that escorted me from counter to counter, from rock ledge to seaweed, and the belts and the bracelets I chose seemed to fall from siren hands into transparent water. I bought an elegant valise, had my purchases put into it, and repaired to the nearest hotel, well pleased with my day.

Somehow, in connection with that quiet poetical afternoon of fastidious shopping, I recalled the hotel or inn with the seductive name of The Enchanted Hunters which Charlotte had happened to mention shortly before my liberation. With the help of a guidebook I located it in the secluded town of Briceland, a four-hour drive from Lo's camp. I could have telephoned but fearing my voice might go out of control and lapse into coy croaks of broken English, I decided to send a wire ordering a room with twin beds for the next night. What a comic, clumsy, wavering Prince Charming I was! How some of my readers will laugh at me when I tell them the trouble I had with the wording of my telegram! What should I put: Humbert and daughter? Humberg and small daughter? Homberg and immature girl? Homburg and child? The droll mistake—the "g" at the end—which eventually came through may have been a telepathic echo of these hesitations of mine.

And then, in the velvet of a summer night, my broodings over the philter I had with me! Oh miserly Hamburg! Was he not a very Enchanted Hunter as he deliberated with himself over his boxful of magic ammunition? To rout the monster of insomnia should he try himself one of those amethyst capsules? There were forty of them, all told—forty nights with a frail little sleeper at my throbbing side; could I rob myself of one such night in order to sleep? Certainly not: much too precious was each tiny plum, each microscopic planetarium with its live stardust. Oh, let me be mawkish for the nonce! I am so tired of being cynical.

26

This daily headache in the opaque air of this tombal jail is disturbing, but I must persevere. Have written more than a hundred pages and not got anywhere yet. My calendar is getting confused. That must have been around August 15, 1947. Don't think I can go on. Heart, head—everything. Lolita, Lolita, Lolita, Lolita, Lolita, Lolita, Lolita, Lolita, Lolita. Repeat till the page is full, printer.

1

27

Still in Parkington. Finally, I did achieve an hour's slumber—from which I was aroused by gratuitous and horribly exhausting congress with a small hairy hermaphrodite, a total stranger.

By then it was six in the morning, and it suddenly occurred to me it might be a good thing to arrive at the camp earlier than I had said. From Parkington I had still a hundred miles to go, and there would be more than that to the Hazy Hills and Briceland. If I had said I would come for Dolly in the afternoon, it was only because my fancy insisted on merciful night falling as soon as possible upon my impatience. But now I foresaw all kinds of misunderstandings and was all a-jitter lest delay might give her the opportunity of some idle telephone call to Ramsdale. However, when at 9.30 A.M. I attempted to start, I was confronted by a dead battery, and noon was nigh when at last I left Parkington.

I reached my destination around half past two; parked my car in a pine grove where a green-shirted, redheaded impish lad stood throwing horseshoes in sullen solitude; was laconically directed by him to an office in a stucco cottage; in a dying state, had to endure for several minutes the inquisitive commiseration of the camp mistress, a sluttish worn out female with rusty hair. Dolly she said was all packed and ready to go. She knew her mother was sick but not critically. Would Mr. Haze, I mean, Mr. Humbert, care to meet the camp counsellors? Or look at the cabins where the girls live? Each dedicated to a Disney creature? Or visit the Lodge? Or should Charlie be sent over to fetch her? The girls were just finishing fixing the Dining Room for a dance. (And perhaps afterwards she would say to somebody or other: "The poor guy looked like his own ghost.")

Let me retain for a moment that scene in all its trivial and fateful detail: hag Holmes writing out a receipt, scratching her head, pulling a drawer out of her desk, pouring change into my impatient palm, then neatly spreading a banknote over it with a bright ". . . and five!"; photographs of girl-children; some gaudy moth or butterfly, still alive, safely pinned to the wall ("nature study"); the framed diploma of the camp's dietitian; my trembling hands; a card produced by efficient Holmes with a report of Dolly Haze's behavior for July ("fair to good; keen on swimming and boating"); a sound of trees and birds, and my pounding heart . . . I was standing with my back to the open door, and then I felt the blood rush to my head as I heard her respiration and voice behind me. She arrived dragging and bumping her heavy suitcase. "Hi!" she said, and stood still, looking at me with sly, glad eyes, her soft lips parted in a slightly foolish but wonderfully endearing smile.

She was thinner and taller, and for a second it seemed to me her face was less pretty than the mental imprint I had cherished for more than a month: her cheeks looked hollowed and too much lentigo camouflaged her rosy rustic features; and that first impression (a very narrow human interval between two tiger heartbeats) carried the clear implication that all widower Humbert had to do, wanted to do, or would do, was to give this wan-looking though sun-colored little orphan *aux yeux battus* (and even those plumbaceous umbrae under her eyes bore freckles) a sound education, a healthy and happy girlhood, a clean home, nice girl-friends of her age among whom (if the fates deigned to repay me) I might find, perhaps, a pretty little *Mägdlein* for Herr Doktor Humbert alone. But "in a wink," as the Germans say, the angelic line of conduct was erased, and I overtook my prey (time moves ahead of our fancies!), and she was my Lolita again—in fact, more of my Lolita than ever. I let my hand rest on her warm auburn head and took up her bag. She was all rose and honey, dressed in her brightest gingham, with a pattern of little red apples, and her arms and legs were of a deep golden brown, with scratches like tiny dotted lines of coagulated rubies, and the ribbed cuffs of her white socks were turned down at the remembered level, and because of her childish gait, or because I had memorized her as always wearing heelless shoes, her saddle oxfords looked somehow too large and too high-heeled for her. Good-bye, Camp Q, merry Camp Q. Good-bye, plain unwholesome food, good-bye Charlie boy. In the hot car she settled down beside me, slapped a prompt fly on her lovely knee; then, her mouth working violently on a piece of chewing gum, she rapidly cranked down the window on her side and settled back again. We sped through the striped and speckled forest.

"How's Mother?" she asked dutifully.

I said the doctors did not quite know yet what the trouble

was. Anyway, something abdominal. Abominable? No, abdominal. We would have to hang around for a while. The hospital was in the country, near the gay town of Lepingville, where a great poet had resided in the early nineteenth century and where we would take in all the shows. She thought it a peachy idea and wondered if we could make Lepingville before nine P.M.

"We should be at Briceland by dinner time," I said, "and tomorrow we'll visit Lepingville. How was the hike? Did you have a marvelous time at the camp?"

"Uh-huh."

"Sorry to leave?"

"Un-un."

"Talk, Lo—don't grunt. Tell me something."

"What thing, Dad?" (she let the word expand with ironic deliberation).

"Any old thing."

"Okay, if I call you that?" (eyes slit at the road).

"Quite."

"It's a sketch, you know. When did you fall for my mummy?"

"Some day, Lo, you will understand many emotions and situations, such as for example the harmony, the beauty of spiritual relationship."

"Bah!" said the cynical nymphet.

Shallow lull in the dialogue, filled with some landscape.

"Look, Lo, at all those cows on that hillside."

"I think I'll vomit if I look at a cow again."

"You know, I missed you terribly, Lo."

"*I* did not. Fact I've been revoltingly unfaithful to you, but it does not matter one bit, because you've stopped caring for me, anyway. You drive much faster than my mummy, mister."

I slowed down from a blind seventy to a purblind fifty.

"Why do you think I have ceased caring for you, Lo?"

"Well, you haven't kissed me yet, have you?"

Inly dying, inly moaning, I glimpsed a reasonably wide shoulder of road ahead, and bumped and wobbled into the weeds. Remember she is only a child, remember she is only—

Hardly had the car come to a standstill than Lolita positively flowed into my arms. Not daring, not daring let myself go—not even daring let myself realize that *this* (sweet wetness and trembling fire) was the beginning of the ineffable life which, ably assisted by fate, I had finally willed into being—not daring really kiss her, I touched her hot, opening lips with the utmost piety, tiny sips, nothing salacious; but she, with an impatient wriggle, pressed her mouth to mine so hard that I felt her big front teeth and shared in the peppermint taste of her saliva. I knew, of course, it was but an innocent game on her part, a bit of back-fisch foolery in imitation of some simulacrum of fake romance, 1, 2 and since (as the psychotherapist, as well as the rapist, will tell 3 you) the limits and rules of such girlish games are fluid, or at least too childishly subtle for the senior partner to grasp—I was dreadfully afraid I might go too far and cause her to start back in revulsion and terror. And, as above all I was agonizingly anxious to smuggle her into the hermetic seclusion of The Enchanted Hunters, and we had still eighty miles to go, blessed intuition broke our embrace—a split second before a highway patrol car drew up alongside.

Florid and beetle-browed, its driver stared at me:

"Happen to see a blue sedan, same make as yours, pass you before the junction?"

"Why, no."

"We didn't," said Lo, eagerly leaning across me, her innocent hand on my legs, "but are you sure it was blue, because—"

The cop (what shadow of us was he after?) gave the little 4 colleen his best smile and went into a U-turn.

We drove on.

"The fruithead!" remarked Lo. "He should have nabbed *you*."

"Why me for heaven's sake?"

"Well, the speed in this bum state is fifty, and—No, don't slow down, you, dull bulb. He's gone now."

"We have still quite a stretch," I said, "and I want to get there before dark. So be a good girl."

"Bad, bad girl," said Lo comfortably. "Juvenile delickwent, but frank and fetching. That light was red. I've never seen such driving."

We rolled silently through a silent townlet.

"Say, wouldn't Mother be absolutely mad if she found out we were lovers?"

"Good Lord, Lo, let us not talk that way."

"But we *are* lovers, aren't we?"

"Not that I know of. I think we are going to have some more rain. Don't you want to tell me of those little pranks of yours in camp?"

"You talk like a book, *Dad*."

"What have you been up to? I insist you tell me."

"Are you easily shocked?"

"No. Go on."

"Let us turn into a secluded lane and I'll tell you."

"Lo, I must seriously ask you not to play the fool. Well?"

"Well—I joined in all the activities that were offered."

1   "*Ensuite?*"

"Ansooit, I was taught to live happily and richly with others and to develop a wholesome personality. Be a cake, in fact."

"Yes. I saw something of the sort in the booklet."

"We loved the sings around the fire in the big stone fireplace or under the darned stars, where every girl merged her own spirit of happiness with the voice of the group."

"Your memory is excellent, Lo, but I must trouble you to leave out the swear words. Anything else?"

"The Girl Scout's motto," said Lo rhapsodically, "is also mine. I fill my life with worthwhile deeds such as—well, never mind what. My duty is—to be useful. I am a friend to male animals. I obey orders. I am cheerful. That was another police car. I am thrifty and I am absolutely filthy in thought, word and deed."

"Now I do hope that's all, you witty child."

"Yep. That's all. No—wait a sec. We baked in a reflector oven. Isn't that terrific?"

"Well, that's better."

"We washed zillions of dishes. 'Zillions' you know is schoolmarm's slang for many-many-many-many. Oh yes, last but not least, as Mother says—Now let me see—what was it? I know: We

2   made shadowgraphs. Gee, what fun."

[116]

"*C'est bien tout?*"

"*C'est*. Except for one little thing, something I simply can't tell you without blushing all over."

"Will you tell it me later?"

"If we sit in the dark and you let me whisper, I will. Do you sleep in your old room or in a heap with Mother?"

"Old room. Your mother may have to undergo a very serious operation, Lo."

"Stop at that candy bar, will you," said Lo.

Sitting on a high stool, a band of sunlight crossing her bare brown forearm, Lolita was served an elaborate ice-cream concoction topped with synthetic syrup. It was erected and brought her by a pimply brute of a boy in a greasy bow-tie who eyed my fragile child in her thin cotton frock with carnal deliberation. My impatience to reach Briceland and The Enchanted Hunters was becoming more than I could endure. Fortunately she dispatched the stuff with her usual alacrity.

"How much cash do you have?" I asked.

"Not a cent," she said sadly, lifting her eyebrows, showing me the empty inside of her money purse.

"This is a matter that will be mended in due time," I rejoined archly. "Are you coming?"

"Say, I wonder if they have a washroom."

"You are not going there," I said firmly. "It is sure to be a vile place. Do come on."

She was on the whole an obedient little girl and I kissed her in the neck when we got back into the car.

"*Don't* do that," she said looking at me with unfeigned surprise. "Don't drool on me. You dirty man."

She rubbed the spot against her raised shoulder.

"Sorry," I murmured. "I'm rather fond of you, that's all."

We drove under a gloomy sky, up a winding road, then down again.

"Well, I'm also sort of fond of you," said Lolita in a delayed soft voice, with a sort of sigh, and sort of settled closer to me.

(Oh, my Lolita, we shall never get there!)

Dusk was beginning to saturate pretty little Briceland, its

phony colonial architecture, curiosity shops and imported shade trees, when we drove through the weakly lighted streets in search of the Enchanted Hunters. The air, despite a steady drizzle beading it, was warm and green, and a queue of people, mainly children and old men, had already formed before the box office of a movie house, dripping with jewel-fires.

"Oh, I want to see that picture. Let's go right after dinner. Oh, let's!"

"We might," chanted Humbert—knowing perfectly well, the sly tumescent devil, that by nine, when *his* show began, she would be dead in his arms.

"Easy!" cried Lo, lurching forward, as an accursed truck in front of us, its backside carbuncles pulsating, stopped at a crossing.

If we did not get to the hotel soon, immediately, miraculously, in the very next block, I felt I would lose all control over the Haze jalopy with its ineffectual wipers and whimsical brakes; but the passers-by I applied to for directions were either strangers themselves or asked with a frown "Enchanted what?" as if I were a madman; or else they went into such complicated explanations, with geometrical gestures, geographical generalities and strictly local clues (...then bear south after you hit the courthouse...) that I could not help losing my way in the maze of their well-meaning gibberish. Lo, whose lovely prismatic entrails had already digested the sweetmeat, was looking forward to a big meal and had begun to fidget. As to me, although I had long become used to a kind of secondary fate (McFate's inept secretary, so to speak) pettily interfering with the boss's generous magnificent plan—to grind and grope through the avenues of Briceland was perhaps the most exasperating ordeal I had yet faced. In later months I could laugh at my inexperience when recalling the obstinate boyish way in which I had concentrated upon that particular inn with its fancy name; for all along our route countless motor courts proclaimed their vacancy in neon lights, ready to accommodate salesmen, escaped convicts, impotents, family groups, as well as the most corrupt and vigorous couples. Ah, gentle drivers gliding through summer's black nights, what frolics, what twists of lust, you might see from your impeccable highways if Kumfy Kabins were suddenly drained of their pigments and became as transparent as boxes of glass!

The miracle I hankered for did happen after all. A man and a girl, more or less conjoined in a dark car under dripping trees, told us we were in the heart of The Park, but had only to turn left at the next traffic light and there we would be. We did not see any next traffic light—in fact, The Park was as black as the sins it concealed—but soon after falling under the smooth spell of a nicely graded curve, the travelers became aware of a diamond glow through the mist, then a gleam of lakewater appeared— and there it was, marvelously and inexorably, under spectral trees, at the top of a graveled drive—the pale palace of The Enchanted Hunters.

A row of parked cars, like pigs at a trough, seemed at first sight to forbid access; but then, by magic, a formidable convertible, resplendent, rubious in the lighted rain, came into motion—was energetically backed out by a broad-shouldered driver —and we gratefully slipped into the gap it had left. I immediately regretted my haste for I noticed that my predecessor had now taken advantage of a garage-like shelter nearby where there was ample space for another car; but I was too impatient to follow his example.

"Wow! Looks swank," remarked my vulgar darling squinting at the stucco as she crept out into the audible drizzle and with a childish hand tweaked loose the frock-fold that had stuck in the peach-cleft—to quote Robert Browning. Under the arclights enlarged replicas of chestnut leaves plunged and played on white pillars. I unlocked the trunk compartment. A hunchbacked and hoary Negro in a uniform of sorts took our bags and wheeled them slowly into the lobby. It was full of old ladies and clergymen. Lolita sank down on her haunches to caress a pale-faced, blue-freckled, black-eared cocker spaniel swooning on the floral carpet under her hand—as who would not, my heart—while I cleared my throat through the throng to the desk. There a bald porcine old man—everybody was old in that old hotel—examined my features with a polite smile, then leisurely produced my (garbled) telegram, wrestled with some dark doubts, turned his head to look at the clock, and finally said he was very sorry, he had held the room with the twin beds till half past six, and now it was gone. A religious convention, he said, had clashed with a flower show in Briceland, and—"The name," I said coldly, "is not Humberg and not Humbug, but Herbert, I mean Humbert, and any room will do, just put in a cot for my little daughter. She is ten and very tired."

The pink old fellow peered good-naturedly at Lo—still squatting, listening in profile, lips parted, to what the dog's mistress, an ancient lady swathed in violet veils, was telling her from the depths of a cretonne easy chair.

Whatever doubts the obscene fellow had, they were dispelled by that blossom-like vision. He said, he might still have a room, had one, in fact—with a double bed. As to the cot—

"Mr. Potts, do we have any cots left?" Potts, also pink and bald, with white hairs growing out of his ears and other holes, would see what could be done. He came and spoke while I unscrewed my fountain pen. Impatient Humbert!

"Our double beds are really triple," Potts cozily said tucking me and my kid in. "One crowded night we had three ladies and a child like yours sleep together. I believe one of the ladies was a disguised man [*my* static]. However—would there be a spare cot in 49, Mr. Swine?"

"I think it went to the Swoons," said Swine, the initial old clown.

"We'll manage somehow," I said. "My wife may join us later —but even then, I suppose, we'll manage."

The two pink pigs were now among my best friends. In the slow clear hand of crime I wrote: Dr. Edgar H. Humbert and daughter, 342 Lawn Street, Ramsdale. A key (342!) was half-shown to me (magician showing object he is about to palm)— and handed over to Uncle Tom. Lo, leaving the dog as she would leave me some day, rose from her haunches; a raindrop fell on Charlotte's grave; a handsome young Negress slipped open the elevator door, and the doomed child went in followed by her throat-clearing father and crayfish Tom with the bags.

Parody of a hotel corridor. Parody of silence and death. 1

"Say, it's our house number," said cheerful Lo.

There was a double bed, a mirror, a double bed in the mirror, 2 a closet door with mirror, a bathroom door ditto, a blue-dark window, a reflected bed there, the same in the closet mirror, two chairs, a glass-topped table, two bedtables, a double bed: a big panel bed, to be exact, with a Tuscan rose chenille spread, and two frilled, pink-shaded nightlamps, left and right.

I was tempted to place a five-dollar bill in that sepia palm, but thought the largesse might be misconstrued, so I placed a quarter. Added another. He withdrew. Click. *Enfin seuls.* 3

"Are we to sleep in *one* room?" said Lo, her features working in that dynamic way they did—not cross or disgusted (though plain on the brink of it) but just dynamic—when she wanted to load a question with violent significance.

"I've asked them to put in a cot. Which I'll use if you like."

"You are crazy," said Lo.

"Why, my darling?"

"Because, my dahrling, when dahrling Mother finds out she'll divorce you and strangle me."

Just dynamic. Not really taking the matter too seriously.

"Now look here," I said, sitting down, while she stood, a few feet from me, and stared at herself contentedly, not unpleasantly surprised at her own appearance, filling with her own rosy sunshine the surprised and pleased closet-door mirror.

"Look here, Lo. Let's settle this once for all. For all practical purposes I am your father. I have a feeling of great tenderness for you. In your mother's absence I am responsible for your welfare. We are not rich, and while we travel, we shall be obliged —we shall be thrown a good deal together. Two people sharing one room, inevitably enter into a kind—how shall I say—a kind—"

"The word is incest," said Lo—and walked into the closet, walked out again with a young golden giggle, opened the adjoining door, and after carefully peering inside with her strange

smoky eyes lest she make another mistake, retired to the bathroom.

I opened the window, tore off my sweat-drenched shirt,
changed, checked the pill vial in my coat pocket, unlocked the—

She drifted out. I tried to embrace her: casually, a bit of controlled tenderness before dinner.

She said: "Look, let's cut out the kissing game and get something to eat."

It was then that I sprang my surprise.

Oh, what a dreamy pet! She walked up to the open suitcase
as if stalking it from afar, at a kind of slow-motion walk, peering at that distant treasure box on the luggage support. (Was
there something wrong, I wondered, with those great gray eyes
of hers, or were we both plunged in the same enchanted mist?)
She stepped up to it, lifting her rather high-heeled feet rather
high, and bending her beautiful boy-knees while she walked
through dilating space with the lentor of one walking under
water or in a flight dream. Then she raised by the armlets a
copper-colored, charming and quite expensive vest, very slowly
stretching it between her silent hands as if she were a bemused
bird-hunter holding his breath over the incredible bird he spreads
out by the tips of its flaming wings. Then (while I stood waiting
for her) she pulled out the slow snake of a brilliant belt and
tried it on.

Then she crept into my waiting arms, radiant, relaxed, caressing me with her tender, mysterious, impure, indifferent, twilight
eyes—for all the world, like the cheapest of cheap cuties. For
that is what nymphets imitate—while we moan and die.

"What's the katter with misses?" I muttered (word-control
gone) into her hair.

"If you must know," she said, "you do it the wrong way."

"Show, wight ray."

"All in good time," responded the spoonerette.

*Seva ascendes, pulsata, brulans, kitzelans, dementissima. Ele-
vator clatterans, pausa, clatterans, populus in corridoro. Hanc
nisi mors mihi adimet nemo! Juncea puellula, jo pensavo fondis-
sime, nobserva nihil quidquam;* but, of course, in another mo-

ment I might have committed some dreadful blunder; fortunately, she returned to the treasure box.

From the bathroom, where it took me quite a time to shift back into normal gear for a humdrum purpose, I heard, standing, drumming, retaining my breath, my Lolita's "oo's" and "gee's" of girlish delight.

She had used the soap only because it was sample soap.

"Well, come on, my dear, if you are as hungry as I am."

And so to the elevator, daughter swinging her old white purse, father walking in front (nota bene: never behind, she is not a lady). As we stood (now side by side) waiting to be taken down, she threw back her head, yawned without restraint and shook her curls. 1

"When did they make you get up at that camp?"

"Half-past—" she stifled another yawn—"six"—yawn in full with a shiver of all her frame. "Half-past," she repeated, her throat filling up again.

The dining room met us with a smell of fried fat and a faded smile. It was a spacious and pretentious place with maudlin murals depicting enchanted hunters in various postures and states of enchantment amid a medley of pallid animals, dryads and trees. A few scattered old ladies, two clergymen, and a man in a sports coat were finishing their meals in silence. The dining room closed at nine, and the green-clad, poker-faced serving girls were, happily, in a desperate hurry to get rid of us. 2

"Does not he look exactly, but exactly, like Quilty?" said Lo in a soft voice, her sharp brown elbow not pointing, but visibly burning to point, at the lone diner in the loud checks, in the far corner of the room.

"Like our fat Ramsdale dentist?"

Lo arrested the mouthful of water she had just taken, and put down her dancing glass.

"Course not," she said with a splutter of mirth. "I meant the writer fellow in the Dromes ad." 3

Oh, Fame! Oh, Femina! 4

When the dessert was plunked down—a huge wedge of cherry pie for the young lady and vanilla ice cream for her protector, most of which she expeditiously added to her pie—I produced a small vial containing Papa's Purple Pills. As I look back at those seasick murals, at that strange and monstrous moment, I can only explain my behavior then by the mechanism of that dream vacuum wherein revolves a deranged mind; but at the time, it all seemed quite simple and inevitable to me. I glanced around, satisfied myself that the last diner had left, removed the stopper, and with the utmost deliberation tipped the philter into my palm. I had carefully rehearsed before a mirror the gesture of clapping my empty hand to my open mouth and swallowing a (fictitious) pill. As I expected, she pounced upon the vial with its plump, beautifully colored capsules loaded with Beauty's Sleep.

"Blue!" she exclaimed. "Violet blue. What are they made of?"

"Summer skies," I said, "and plums and figs, and the grape-blood of emperors."

"No, seriously—please."

"Oh, just Purpills. Vitamin X. Makes one strong as an ox or an ax. Want to try one?"

Lolita stretched out her hand, nodding vigorously.

I had hoped the drug would work fast. It certainly did. She had had a long long day, she had gone rowing in the morning with Barbara whose sister was Waterfront Director, as the adorable accessible nymphet now started to tell me in between suppressed palate-humping yawns, growing in volume—oh, how fast the magic potion worked!—and had been active in other ways too. The movie that had vaguely loomed in her mind was, of course, by the time we watertreaded out of the dining room, forgotten. As we stood in the elevator, she leaned against me, faintly smiling—wouldn't you like me to tell you?—half closing her dark-lidded eyes. "Sleepy, huh?" said Uncle Tom who was bringing up the quiet Franco-Irish gentleman and his daughter as well as two withered women, experts in roses. They looked with sympathy at my frail, tanned, tottering, dazed rosedarling. I had almost to carry her into our room. There, she sat down on the edge of the bed, swaying a little, speaking in dove-dull, long-drawn tones.

[124]

"If I tell you—if I tell you, will you promise [sleepy, so sleepy —head lolling, eyes going out], promise you won't make complaints?"

"Later, Lo. Now go to bed. I'll leave you here, and you go to bed. Give you ten minutes."

"Oh, I've been such a disgusting girl," she went on, shaking her hair, removing with slow fingers a velvet hair ribbon. "Lemme tell you—"

"Tomorrow, Lo. Go to bed, go to bed—for goodness sake, to bed."

I pocketed the key and walked downstairs.

28

Gentlewomen of the jury! Bear with me! Allow me to take just a tiny bit of your precious time! So this was *le grand moment*. I had left my Lolita still sitting on the edge of the abysmal 1 bed, drowsily raising her foot, fumbling at the shoelaces and showing as she did so the nether side of her thigh up to the crotch of her panties—she had always been singularly absent-minded, or shameless, or both, in matters of legshow. This, then, was the hermetic vision of her which I had locked in—after satisfying myself that the door carried no inside bolt. The key, with its numbered dangler of carved wood, became forthwith the weighty sesame to a rapturous and formidable future. It was mine, it was part of my hot hairy fist. In a few minutes—say, 2 twenty, say half-an-hour, *sicher ist sicher* as my uncle Gustave 3, 4 used to say—I would let myself into that "342" and find my nymphet, my beauty and bride, emprisoned in her crystal sleep. Jurors! If my happiness could have talked, it would have filled that genteel hotel with a deafening roar. And my only regret today is that I did not quietly deposit key "342" at the office, and leave the town, the country, the continent, the hemisphere,— indeed, the globe—that very same night.

Let me explain. I was not unduly disturbed by her self-accusatory innuendoes. I was still firmly resolved to pursue my policy of sparing her purity by operating only in the stealth of night, only upon a completely anesthetized little nude. Restraint and reverence were still my motto—even if that "purity" (incidentally, thoroughly debunked by modern science) had been slightly damaged through some juvenile erotic experience, no doubt homosexual, at that accursed camp of hers. Of course, in my old-fashioned, old-world way, I, Jean-Jacques Humbert, had taken for granted, when I first met her, that she was as unravished as the stereotypical notion of "normal child" had been since the lamented end of the Ancient World B.C. and its fascinating practices. We are not surrounded in our enlighted era by little slave flowers that can be casually plucked between business and bath as they used to be in the days of the Romans; and we do not, as dignified Orientals did in still more luxurious times, use tiny entertainers fore and aft between the mutton and the rose sherbet. The whole point is that the old link between the adult world and the child world has been completely severed nowadays by new customs and new laws. Despite my having dabbled in psychiatry and social work, I really knew very little about children. After all, Lolita was only twelve, and no matter what concessions I made to time and place—even bearing in mind the crude behavior of American schoolchildren—I still was under the impression that whatever went on among those brash brats, went on at a later age, and in a different environment. Therefore (to retrieve the thread of this explanation) the moralist in me by-passed the issue by clinging to conventional notions of what twelve-year-old girls should be. The child therapist in me (a fake, as most of them are—but no matter) regurgitated neo-Freudian hash and conjured up a dreaming and exaggerating Dolly in the "latency" period of girlhood. Finally, the sensualist in me (a great and insane monster) had no objection to some depravity in his prey. But somewhere behind the raging bliss, bewildered shadows conferred—and not to have heeded them, this is what I regret! Human beings, attend! I should have understood that Lolita had *already* proved to be something quite different from innocent Annabel, and that the nymphean evil breathing through every pore of the fey child that I had prepared for my secret delectation, would make the secrecy impossible, and the delectation lethal. I should have known (by the signs made to me by something in Lolita—the real child Lolita or some haggard angel behind her back) that nothing but pain and horror would result from the expected rapture. Oh, winged gentlemen of the jury!

And she was mine, she was mine, the key was in my fist, my fist was in my pocket, she was mine. In the course of the evocations and schemes to which I had dedicated so many insomnias, I had gradually eliminated all the superfluous blur, and by stacking level upon level of translucent vision, had evolved a final picture. Naked, except for one sock and her charm bracelet, spread-eagled on the bed where my philter had felled her—so I foreglimpsed her; a velvet hair ribbon was still clutched in her hand; her honey-brown body, with the white negative image of a rudimentary swimsuit patterned against her tan, presented to me its pale breastbuds; in the rosy lamplight, a little pubic floss glistened on its plump hillock. The cold key with its warm wooden addendum was in my pocket.

I wandered through various public rooms, glory below, gloom above: for the look of lust always is gloomy; lust is never quite sure—even when the velvety victim is locked up in one's dungeon —that some rival devil or influential god may still not abolish one's prepared triumph. In common parlance, I needed a drink; but there was no barroom in that venerable place full of perspiring philistines and period objects.

I drifted to the Men's Room. There, a person in clerical black —a "hearty party" *comme on dit*—checking with the assistance of Vienna, if it was still there, inquired of me how I had liked Dr. Boyd's talk, and looked puzzled when I (King Sigmund the Second) said Boyd was quite a boy. Upon which, I neatly chucked the tissue paper I had been wiping my sensitive finger tips with into the receptacle provided for it, and sallied lobbyward. Comfortably resting my elbows on the counter, I asked Mr. Potts was he quite sure my wife had not telephoned, and what about that cot? He answered she had not (she was dead, of course) and the cot would be installed tomorrow if we decided to stay on. From a big crowded place called The Hunters' Hall came a sound of many voices discussing horticulture or eternity. Another room, called The Raspberry Room, all bathed in light, with bright little tables and a large one with "refreshments," was still empty except for a hostess (that type of worn woman with a glassy smile and Charlotte's manner of speaking); she floated up to me to ask if I was Mr. Braddock, because if so, Miss Beard had been looking for me. "What a name for a woman," I said and strolled away.

In and out of my heart flowed my rainbow blood. I would give her till half-past-nine. Going back to the lobby, I found there a change: a number of people in floral dresses or black cloth had formed little groups here and there, and some elfish chance offered me the sight of a delightful child of Lolita's age, in Lolita's type of frock, but pure white, and there was a white ribbon in her black hair. She was not pretty, but she was a nymphet, and her ivory pale legs and lily neck formed for one memorable moment a most pleasurable antiphony (in terms of spinal music) to my desire for Lolita, brown and pink, flushed and fouled. The pale child noticed my gaze (which was really quite casual and debonair), and being ridiculously self-conscious, lost countenance completely, rolling her eyes and putting the back of her hand to her cheek, and pulling at the hem of her skirt, and finally turning her thin mobile shoulder blades to me in specious chat with her cow-like mother.

I left the loud lobby and stood outside, on the white steps, looking at the hundreds of powdered bugs wheeling around the lamps in the soggy black night, full of ripple and stir. All I would do—all I would dare to do—would amount to such a trifle . . .

Suddenly I was aware that in the darkness next to me there was somebody sitting in a chair on the pillared porch. I could not really see him but what gave him away was the rasp of a screwing off, then a discreet gurgle, then the final note of a placid screwing on. I was about to move away when his voice addressed me:

"Where the devil did you get her?"

"I beg your pardon?"

"I said: the weather is getting better."

"Seems so."

"Who's the lassie?"

"My daughter."

"You lie—she's not."

"I beg your pardon?"

"I said: July was hot. Where's her mother?"

"Dead."

"I see. Sorry. By the way, why don't you two lunch with me tomorrow. That dreadful crowd will be gone by then."

"We'll be gone too. Good night."

"Sorry. I'm pretty drunk. Good night. That child of yours needs a lot of sleep. Sleep is a rose, as the Persians say. Smoke?"   1

"Not now."

He struck a light, but because he was drunk, or because the wind was, the flame illumined not him but another person, a very old man, one of those permanent guests of old hotels—and his white rocker. Nobody said anything and the darkness returned to its initial place. Then I heard the old-timer cough and deliver himself of some sepulchral mucus.

I left the porch. At least half an hour in all had elapsed. I ought to have asked for a sip. The strain was beginning to tell. If a violin string can ache, then I was that string. But it would have been unseemly to display any hurry. As I made my way through a constellation of fixed people in one corner of the lobby, there came a blinding flash—and beaming Dr. Braddock, two orchid-ornamentalized matrons, the small girl in white, and presumably the bared teeth of Humbert Humbert sidling between the bridelike lassie and the enchanted cleric, were immortalized—insofar as the texture and print of small-town newspapers can be deemed immortal. A twittering group had   2
gathered near the elevator. I again chose the stairs. 342 was near the fire escape. One could still—but the key was already in the lock, and then I was in the room.

The door of the lighted bathroom stood ajar; in addition to that, a skeleton glow came through the Venetian blind from the outside arclights; these intercrossed rays penetrated the darkness of the bedroom and revealed the following situation.

Clothed in one of her old nightgowns, my Lolita lay on her side with her back to me, in the middle of the bed. Her lightly veiled body and bare limbs formed a Z. She had put both pillows under her dark tousled head; a band of pale light crossed her top vertebrae.

I seemed to have shed my clothes and slipped into pajamas with the kind of fantastic instantaneousness which is implied when in a cinematographic scene the process of changing is cut; and I had already placed my knee on the edge of the bed when Lolita turned her head and stared at me through the striped shadows.

Now this was something the intruder had not expected. The whole pill-spiel (a rather sordid affair, *entre nous soit dit*) had had for object a fastness of sleep that a whole regiment would not have disturbed, and here she was staring at me, and thickly calling me "Barbara." Barbara, wearing my pajamas which were much too tight for her, remained poised motionless over the little sleep-talker. Softly, with a hopeless sigh, Dolly turned away, resuming her initial position. For at least two minutes I waited and strained on the brink, like that tailor with his homemade parachute forty years ago when about to jump from the Eiffel Tower. Her faint breathing had the rhythm of sleep. Finally I heaved myself onto my narrow margin of bed, stealthily pulled at the odds and ends of sheets piled up to the south of my stone-cold heels—and Lolita lifted her head and gaped at me.

As I learned later from a helpful pharmaceutist, the purple pill did not even belong to the big and noble family of barbiturates, and though it might have induced sleep in a neurotic who believed it to be a potent drug, it was too mild a sedative to affect for any length of time a wary, albeit weary, nymphet. Whether the Ramsdale doctor was a charlatan or a shrewd old rogue, does not, and did not, really matter. What mattered, was that I had been deceived. When Lolita opened her eyes again, I realized that whether or not the drug might work later in the night, the security I had relied upon was a sham one. Slowly her head turned away and dropped onto her unfair amount of pillow. I lay quite still on my brink, peering at her rumpled hair, at the glimmer of nymphet flesh, where half a haunch and half a shoulder dimly showed, and trying to gauge the depth of her sleep by the rate of her respiration. Some time passed, nothing changed, and I decided I might risk getting a little closer to that lovely and maddening glimmer; but hardly had I moved into its warm purlieus than her breathing was suspended, and I had the odious feeling that little Dolores was wide awake and would explode in screams if I touched her with any part of my wretchedness. Please, reader: no matter your exasperation with the tenderhearted, morbidly sensitive, infinitely circumspect hero of my book, do not skip these essential pages! Imagine me; I shall not exist if you do not imagine me; try to discern the doe in me, trembling in the forest of my own iniquity; let's even smile a little. After all, there is no harm in smiling. For instance (I almost wrote "frinstance"), I had no place to rest my head, and a fit of heartburn (they call those fries "French," *grand Dieu!*) was added to my discomfort.   1

She was again fast asleep, my nymphet, but still I did not dare to launch upon my enchanted voyage. *La Petite Dormeuse ou l'Amant Ridicule.* Tomorrow I would stuff her with those   2 earlier pills that had so thoroughly numbed her mummy. In the glove compartment—or in the Gladstone bag? Should I wait a solid hour and then creep up again? The science of nympholepsy is a precise science. Actual contact would do it in one second flat. An interspace of a millimeter would do it in ten. Let us wait.

There is nothing louder than an American hotel; and, mind you, this was supposed to be a quiet, cozy, old-fashioned, homey place—"gracious living" and all that stuff. The clatter of the elevator's gate—some twenty yards northeast of my head but as clearly perceived as if it were inside my left temple—alternated with the banging and booming of the machine's various evolutions and lasted well beyond midnight. Every now and then, immediately east of my left ear (always assuming I lay on my back, not daring to direct my viler side toward the nebulous haunch of my bed-mate), the corridor would brim with cheerful, resonant and inept exclamations ending in a volley of good-nights. When *that* stopped, a toilet immediately north of my cerebellum took over. It was a manly, energetic, deep-throated toilet, and it was used many times. Its gurgle and gush and long afterflow shook the wall behind me. Then someone in a southern direction was extravagantly sick, almost coughing out his life with his liquor, and his toilet descended like a veritable Niagara, immediately beyond our bathroom. And when finally all the waterfalls had stopped, and the enchanted hunters were sound asleep, the avenue under the window of my insomnia, to the west of my wake—a staid, eminently residential, dignified alley of huge trees—degenerated into the despicable haunt of gigantic trucks roaring through the wet and windy night.

And less than six inches from me and my burning life, was nebulous Lolita! After a long stirless vigil, my tentacles moved towards her again, and this time the creak of the mattress did not awake her. I managed to bring my ravenous bulk so close to her that I felt the aura of her bare shoulder like a warm breath upon my cheek. And then, she sat up, gasped, muttered with insane rapidity something about boats, tugged at the sheets and lapsed back into her rich, dark, young unconsciousness. As she tossed, within that abundant flow of sleep, recently auburn, at present lunar, her arm struck me across the face. For a second I held her. She freed herself from the shadow of my embrace—doing this not consciously, not violently, not with any personal distaste, but with the neutral plaintive murmur of a child demanding its natural rest. And again the situation remained the same: Lolita with her curved spine to Humbert, Humbert resting his head on his hand and burning with desire and dyspepsia.

The latter necessitated a trip to the bathroom for a draft of water which is the best medicine I know in my case, except perhaps milk with radishes; and when I re-entered the strange pale-striped fastness where Lolita's old and new clothes reclined in various attitudes of enchantment on pieces of furniture that seemed vaguely afloat, my impossible daughter sat up and in clear tones demanded a drink, too. She took the resilient and cold paper cup in her shadowy hand and gulped down its contents gratefully, her long eyelashes pointing cupward, and then, with an infantile gesture that carried more charm than any carnal caress, little Lolita wiped her lips against my shoulder. She fell back on her pillow (I had subtracted mine while she drank) and was instantly asleep again.

I had not dared offer her a second helping of the drug, and had not abandoned hope that the first might still consolidate her sleep. I started to move toward her, ready for any disappointment, knowing I had better wait but incapable of waiting. My pillow smelled of her hair. I moved toward my glimmering darling, stopping or retreating every time I thought she stirred or was about to stir. A breeze from wonderland had begun to affect my thoughts, and now they seemed couched in italics, as if the surface reflecting them were wrinkled by the phantasm of that breeze. Time and again my consciousness folded the wrong way, my shuffling body entered the sphere of sleep, shuffled out again, and once or twice I caught myself drifting into a melancholy snore. Mists of tenderness enfolded mountains of longing. Now and then it seemed to me that the enchanted prey was about to meet halfway the enchanted hunter, that her haunch was working its way toward me under the soft sand of a remote and fabulous beach; and then her dimpled dimness would stir, and I would know she was farther away from me than ever.

If I dwell at some length on the tremors and gropings of that distant night, it is because I insist upon proving that I am not, and never was, and never could have been, a brutal scoundrel. The gentle and dreamy regions through which I crept were the patrimonies of poets—*not* crime's prowling ground. Had I reached my goal, my ecstasy would have been all softness, a case of internal combustion of which she would hardly have felt the heat, even if she were wide awake. But I still hoped she might gradually be engulfed in a completeness of stupor that would allow me to taste more than a glimmer of her. And so, in between tentative approximations, with a confusion of perception metamorphosing her into eyespots of moonlight or a fluffy flowering bush, I would dream I regained consciousness, dream I lay in wait.

In the first antemeridian hours there was a lull in the restless hotel night. Then around four the corridor toilet cascaded and its door banged. A little after five a reverberating monologue began to arrive, in several installments, from some courtyard or parking place. It was not really a monologue, since the speaker stopped every few seconds to listen (presumably) to another fellow, but that other voice did not reach me, and so no real meaning could be derived from the part heard. Its matter-of-fact intonations, however, helped to bring in the dawn, and the room was already suffused with lilac gray, when several industrious toilets went to work, one after the other, and the clattering and whining elevator began to rise and take down early risers and downers, and for some minutes I miserably dozed, and Charlotte was a mermaid in a greenish tank, and somewhere in the passage Dr. Boyd said "Good morning to you" in a fruity voice, and birds were busy in the trees, and then Lolita yawned.

Frigid gentlewomen of the jury! I had thought that months, perhaps years, would elapse before I dared to reveal myself to Dolores Haze; but by six she was wide awake, and by six fifteen we were technically lovers. I am going to tell you something very strange: it was she who seduced me.

Upon hearing her first morning yawn, I feigned handsome profiled sleep. I just did not know what to do. Would she be shocked at finding me by her side, and not in some spare bed? Would she collect her clothes and lock herself up in the bathroom? Would she demand to be taken at once to Ramsdale—to her mother's bedside—back to camp? But my Lo was a sportive lassie. I felt her eyes on me, and when she uttered at last that beloved chortling note of hers, I knew her eyes had been laughing. She rolled over to my side, and her warm brown hair came against my collarbone. I gave a mediocre imitation of waking up. We lay quietly. I gently caressed her hair, and we gently kissed. Her kiss, to my delirious embarrassment, had some rather comical refinements of flutter and probe which made me conclude she had been coached at an early age by a little Lesbian. No Charlie boy could have taught her *that*. As if to see whether I had my fill and learned the lesson, she drew away and surveyed me. Her cheekbones were flushed, her full underlip glistened, my dissolution was near. All at once, with a burst of rough glee (the sign of the nymphet!), she put her mouth to my ear—but for quite a while my mind could not separate into words the hot thunder of her whisper, and she laughed, and brushed the hair off her face, and tried again, and gradually the odd sense of living in a brand new, mad new dream world, where everything was permissible, came over me as I realized what she was suggesting. I answered I did not know what game she and Charlie had played. "You mean you have never—?"—her features twisted into a stare of disgusted incredulity. "You have never—" she started again. I took time out by nuzzling her a little. "Lay off, will you," she said with a twangy whine, hastily removing her brown shoulder from my lips. (It was very curious the way she considered—and kept doing so for a long time—all caresses except kisses on the mouth or the stark act of love either "romantic slosh" or "abnormal".)

"You mean," she persisted, now kneeling above me, "you never did it when you were a kid?"

"Never," I answered quite truthfully.

"Okay," said Lolita, "here is where we start."

However, I shall not bore my learned readers with a detailed account of Lolita's presumption. Suffice it to say that not a trace of modesty did I perceive in this beautiful hardly formed young girl whom modern co-education, juvenile mores, the campfire racket and so forth had utterly and hopelessly depraved. She saw the stark act merely as part of a youngster's furtive world, unknown to adults. What adults did for purposes of procreation was no business of hers. My life was handled by little Lo in an energetic, matter-of-fact manner as if it were an insensate gadget unconnected with me. While eager to impress me with the world of tough kids, she was not quite prepared for certain discrepancies between a kid's life and mine. Pride alone prevented her from giving up; for, in my strange predicament, I feigned supreme stupidity and had her have her way—at least while I could still bear it. But really these are irrelevant matters; I am not concerned with so-called "sex" at all. Anybody can imagine those elements of animality. A greater endeavor lures me on: to fix once for all the perilous magic of nymphets.

30

I have to tread carefully. I have to speak in a whisper. Oh you, veteran crime reporter, you grave old usher, you once popular policeman, now in solitary confinement after gracing that school crossing for years, you wretched emeritus read to by a boy! It would never do, would it, to have you fellows fall madly in love with my Lolita! Had I been a painter, had the management of The Enchanted Hunters lost its mind one summer day and commissioned me to redecorate their dining room with murals of my own making, this is what I might have thought up, let me list some fragments:

There would have been a lake. There would have been an arbor in flame-flower. There would have been nature studies— a tiger pursuing a bird of paradise, a choking snake sheathing whole the flayed trunk of a shoat. There would have been a sultan, his face expressing great agony (belied, as it were, by his molding caress), helping a callypygean slave child to climb a column of onyx. There would have been those luminous globules of gonadal glow that travel up the opalescent sides of juke boxes. There would have been all kinds of camp activities on the part of the intermediate group, Canoeing, Coranting, Combing Curls in the lakeside sun. There would have been poplars, apples, a suburban Sunday. There would have been a fire opal dissolving within a ripple-ringed pool, a last throb, a last dab of color, stinging red, smarting pink, a sigh, a wincing child.

31

I am trying to describe these things not to relive them in my present boundless misery, but to sort out the portion of hell and the portion of heaven in that strange, awful, maddening world—nymphet love. The beastly and beautiful merged at one point, and it is that borderline I would like to fix, and I feel I fail to do so utterly. Why?

The stipulation of the Roman law, according to which a girl may marry at twelve, was adopted by the Church, and is still preserved, rather tacitly, in some of the United States. And fifteen is lawful everywhere. There is nothing wrong, say both hemispheres, when a brute of forty, blessed by the local priest and bloated with drink, sheds his sweat-drenched finery and thrusts himself up to the hilt into his youthful bride. "In such stimulating temperate climates [says an old magazine in this prison library] as St. Louis, Chicago and Cincinnati, girls mature about the end of their twelfth year." Dolores Haze was born less than three hundred miles from stimulating Cincinnati. I have but followed nature. I am nature's faithful hound. Why then this horror that I cannot shake off? Did I deprive her of her flower? Sensitive gentlewomen of the jury, I was not even her first lover. [1,2] [3] [4]

32

She told me the way she had been debauched. We ate flavorless mealy bananas, bruised peaches and very palatable potato chips, and *die Kleine* told me everything. Her voluble but disjointed account was accompanied by many a droll *moue*. As I think I have already observed, I especially remember one wry [5] [6] face on an "ugh!" basis: jelly-mouth distended sideways and eyes rolled up in a routine blend of comic disgust, resignation and tolerance for young frailty.

Her astounding tale started with an introductory mention of her tent-mate of the previous summer, at another camp, a "very select" one as she put it. That tent-mate ("quite a derelict character," "half-crazy," but a "swell kid") instructed her in various manipulations. At first, loyal Lo refused to tell me her name.

"Was it Grace Angel?" I asked.

She shook her head. No, it wasn't, it was the daughter of a big shot. He—

"Was it perhaps Rose Carmine?"

"No, of course not. Her father—"

"Was it, then, Agnes Sheridan perchance?"

She swallowed and shook her head—and then did a double take.

"Say, how come you know all those kids?"

I explained.

"Well," she said. "They are pretty bad, some of that school bunch, but not that bad. If you have to know, her name was Elizabeth Talbot, she goes now to a swanky private school, her father is an executive."

I recalled with a funny pang the frequency with which poor Charlotte used to introduce into party chat such elegant tidbits as "when my daughter was out hiking last year with the Talbot girl."

I wanted to know if either mother learned of those sapphic
1   diversions?

"Gosh no," exhaled limp Lo mimicking dread and relief, pressing a falsely fluttering hand to her chest.

I was more interested, however, in heterosexual experience. She had entered the sixth grade at eleven, soon after moving to Ramsdale from the Middle West. What did she mean by "pretty bad"?

2   Well, the Miranda twins had shared the same bed for years, and Donald Scott, who was the dumbest boy in the school, had done it with Hazel Smith in his uncle's garage, and Kenneth

Knight—who was the brightest—used to exhibit himself wherever and whenever he had a chance, and—

"Let us switch to Camp Q," I said. And presently I got the whole story.

Barbara Burke, a sturdy blond, two years older than Lo and by far the camp's best swimmer, had a very special canoe which she shared with Lo "because I was the only other girl who could make Willow Island" (some swimming test, I imagine). Through July, every morning—mark, reader, every blessed morning—Barbara and Lo would be helped to carry the boat to Onyx or Eryx (two small lakes in the wood) by Charlie Holmes, the camp mistress' son, aged thirteen—and the only human male for a couple of miles around (excepting an old meek stone-deaf handyman, and a farmer in an old Ford who sometimes sold the campers eggs as farmers will); every morning, oh my reader, the three children would take a short cut through the beautiful innocent forest brimming with all the emblems of youth, dew, birdsongs, and at one point, among the luxuriant undergrowth, Lo would be left as sentinel, while Barbara and the boy copulated behind a bush.

At first, Lo had refused "to try what it was like," but curiosity and camaraderie prevailed, and soon she and Barbara were doing it by turns with the silent, coarse and surly but indefatigable Charlie, who had as much sex appeal as a raw carrot but sported a fascinating collection of contraceptives which he used to fish out of a third nearby lake, a considerably larger and more populous one, called Lake Climax, after the booming young factory town of that name. Although conceding it was "sort of fun" and "fine for the complexion," Lolita, I am glad to say, held Charlie's mind and manners in the greatest contempt. Nor had her temperament been roused by that filthy fiend. In fact, I think he had rather stunned it, despite the "fun."

By that time it was close to ten. With the ebb of lust, an ashen sense of awfulness, abetted by the realistic drabness of a gray neuralgic day, crept over me and hummed within my temples. Brown, naked, frail Lo, her narrow white buttocks to me, her sulky face to a door mirror, stood, arms akimbo, feet

1

(in new slippers with pussy-fur tops) wide apart, and through a forehanging lock tritely mugged at herself in the glass. From the corridor came the cooing voices of colored maids at work, and presently there was a mild attempt to open the door of our room. I had Lo go to the bathroom and take a much-needed soap shower. The bed was a frightful mess with overtones of potato chips. She tried on a two-piece navy wool, then a sleeveless blouse with a swirly clathrate skirt, but the first was too tight and the second too ample, and when I begged her to hurry up (the situation was beginning to frighten me), Lo viciously sent those nice presents of mine hurtling into a corner, and put on yesterday's dress. When she was ready at last, I gave her a lovely new purse of simulated calf (in which I had slipped quite a few pennies and two mint-bright dimes) and told her to buy herself a magazine in the lobby.

"I'll be down in a minute," I said. "And if I were you, my dear, I would not talk to strangers."

Except for my poor little gifts, there was not much to pack; but I was forced to devote a dangerous amount of time (was she up to something downstairs?) to arranging the bed in such a way as to suggest the abandoned nest of a restless father and his tomboy daughter, instead of an ex-convict's saturnalia with a couple of fat old whores. Then I finished dressing and had the hoary bellboy come up for the bags.

Everything was fine. There, in the lobby, she sat, deep in an overstuffed blood-red armchair, deep in a lurid movie magazine. A fellow of my age in tweeds (the genre of the place had changed overnight to a spurious country-squire atmosphere) was staring at my Lolita over his dead cigar and stale newspaper. She wore her professional white socks and saddle oxfords, and that bright print frock with the square throat; a splash of jaded lamplight brought out the golden down on her warm brown limbs. There she sat, her legs carelessly highcrossed, and her pale eyes skimming along the lines with every now and then a blink. Bill's wife had worshiped him from afar long before they ever met: in fact, she used to secretly admire the famous young actor as he ate sundaes in Schwab's drugstore. Nothing could have been

more childish than her snubbed nose, freckled face or the purplish spot on her naked neck where a fairytale vampire had 1
feasted, or the unconscious movement of her tongue exploring
a touch of rosy rash around her swollen lips; nothing could be
more harmless than to read about Jill, an energetic starlet who
made her own clothes and was a student of serious literature;
nothing could be more innocent than the part in that glossy
brown hair with that silky sheen on the temple; nothing could
be more naïve—But what sickening envy the lecherous fellow
whoever he was—come to think of it, he resembled a little my
Swiss uncle Gustave, also a great admirer of *le découvert*—would 2
have experienced had he known that every nerve in me was still
anointed and ringed with the feel of her body—the body of some
immortal daemon disguised as a female child. 3

Was pink pig Mr. Swoon absolutely sure my wife had not
telephoned? He was. If she did, would he tell her we had gone
on to Aunt Clare's place? He would, indeedie. I settled the bill 4
and roused Lo from her chair. She read to the car. Still reading,
she was driven to a so-called coffee shop a few blocks south.
Oh, she ate all right. She even laid aside her magazine to eat,
but a queer dullness had replaced her usual cheerfulness. I
knew little Lo could be very nasty, so I braced myself and
grinned, and waited for a squall. I was unbathed, unshaven, and
had had no bowel movement. My nerves were a-jangle. I did
not like the way my little mistress shrugged her shoulders and
distended her nostrils when I attempted casual small talk. Had
Phyllis been in the know before she joined her parents in Maine?
I asked with a smile. "Look," said Lo making a weeping grimace,
"let us get off the subject." I then tried—also unsuccessfully,
no matter how I smacked my lips—to interest her in the road
map. Our destination was, let me remind my patient reader
whose meek temper Lo ought to have copied, the gay town of
Lepingville, somewhere near a hypothetical hospital. That des- 5
tination was in itself a perfectly arbitrary one (as, alas, so many
were to be), and I shook in my shoes as I wondered how to
keep the whole arrangement plausible, and what other plausible
objectives to invent after we had taken in all the movies in

Lepingville. More and more uncomfortable did Humbert feel. It was something quite special, that feeling: an oppressive, hideous constraint as if I were sitting with the small ghost of somebody I had just killed.

As she was in the act of getting back into the car, an expression of pain flitted across Lo's face. It flitted again, more meaningfully, as she settled down beside me. No doubt, she reproduced it that second time for my benefit. Foolishly, I asked her what was the matter. "Nothing, you brute," she replied. "You what?" I asked. She was silent. Leaving Briceland. Loquacious Lo was silent. Cold spiders of panic crawled down my back. This was an orphan. This was a lone child, an absolute waif, with whom a heavy-limbed, foul-smelling adult had had strenuous intercourse three times that very morning. Whether or not the realization of a lifelong dream had surpassed all expectation, it had, in a sense, overshot its mark—and plunged into a nightmare. I had been careless, stupid, and ignoble. And let me be quite frank: somewhere at the bottom of that dark turmoil I felt the writhing of desire again, so monstrous was my appetite for that miserable nymphet. Mingled with the pangs of guilt was the agonizing thought that her mood might prevent me from making love to her again as soon as I found a nice country road where to park in peace. In other words, poor Humbert Humbert was dreadfully unhappy, and while steadily and inanely driving toward Lepingville, he kept racking his brains for some quip, under the bright wing of which he might dare turn to his seatmate. It was she, however, who broke the silence:

"Oh, a squashed squirrel," she said. "What a shame."

"Yes, isn't it?" (eager, hopeful Hum).

"Let us stop at the next gas station," Lo continued. "I want to go to the washroom."

"We shall stop wherever you want," I said. And then as a lovely, lonely, supercilious grove (oaks, I thought; American trees at that stage were beyond me) started to echo greenly the rush of our car, a red and ferny road on our right turned its head before slanting into the woodland, and I suggested we might perhaps—

"Drive on," my Lo cried shrilly.

"Righto. Take it easy." (Down, poor beast, down.)

I glanced at her. Thank God, the child was smiling.

"You chump," she said, sweetly smiling at me. "You revolting creature. I was a daisy-fresh girl, and look what you've done to me. I ought to call the police and tell them you raped me. Oh, you dirty, dirty old man."

Was she just joking? An ominous hysterical note rang through her silly words. Presently, making a sizzling sound with her lips, she started complaining of pains, said she could not sit, said I had torn something inside her. The sweat rolled down my neck, and we almost ran over some little animal or other that was crossing the road with tail erect, and again my vile-tempered companion called me an ugly name. When we stopped at the filling station, she scrambled out without a word and was a long time away. Slowly, lovingly, an elderly friend with a broken nose wiped my windshield—they do it differently at every place, from chamois cloth to soapy brush, this fellow used a pink sponge.

She appeared at last. "Look," she said in that neutral voice that hurt me so, "give me some dimes and nickels. I want to call mother in that hospital. What's the number?"

"Get in," I said. "You can't call that number."

"Why?"

"Get in and slam the door."

She got in and slammed the door. The old garage man beamed at her. I swung onto the highway.

"Why can't I call my mother if I want to?"

"Because," I answered, "your mother is dead."

33

In the gay town of Lepingville I bought her four books of comics, a box of candy, a box of sanitary pads, two cokes, a manicure set, a travel clock with a luminous dial, a ring with a real topaz, a tennis racket, roller skates with white high shoes, field glasses, a portable radio set, chewing gum, a transparent raincoat, sunglasses, some more garments—swooners, shorts, all kinds of summer frocks. At the hotel we had separate rooms, but in the middle of the night she came sobbing into mine, and we made it up very gently. You see, she had absolutely nowhere else to go.

PART TWO

1

It was then that began our extensive travels all over the States. To any other type of tourist accommodation I soon grew to prefer the Functional Motel—clean, neat, safe nooks, ideal places for sleep, argument, reconciliation, insatiable illicit love. At first, in my dread of arousing suspicion, I would eagerly pay for both sections of one double unit, each containing a double bed. I wondered what type of foursome this arrangement was ever intended for, since only a pharisaic parody of privacy could be attained by means of the incomplete partition dividing the cabin or room into two communicating love nests. By and by, the very possibilities that such honest promiscuity suggested (two young couples merrily swapping mates or a child shamming sleep to earwitness primal sonorities) made me bolder, and every now and then I would take a bed-and-cot or twin-bed cabin, a prison cell of paradise, with yellow window shades pulled down to create a morning illusion of Venice and sunshine when actually it was Pennsylvania and rain.

We came to know—*nous connûmes*, to use a Flaubertian intonation—the stone cottages under enormous Chateaubriandesque trees, the brick unit, the adobe unit, the stucco court, on what the Tour Book of the Automobile Association describes as "shaded" or "spacious" or "landscaped" grounds. The log kind, finished in knotty pine, reminded Lo, by its golden-brown glaze, of fried-chicken bones. We held in contempt the plain whitewashed clapboard Kabins, with their faint sewerish smell or some other gloomy self-conscious stench and nothing to boast of (except "good beds"), and an unsmiling landlady always prepared to have her gift ("...well, I could give you...") turned down.

Nous connûmes (this is royal fun) the would-be enticements of their repetitious names—all those Sunset Motels, U-Beam Cottages, Hillcrest Courts, Pine View Courts, Mountain View Courts, Skyline Courts, Park Plaza Courts, Green Acres, Mac's Courts. There was sometimes a special line in the write-up, such as "Children welcome, pets allowed" (*You* are welcome, *you* are allowed). The baths were mostly tiled showers, with an endless variety of spouting mechanisms, but with one definitely non-Laodicean characteristic in common, a propensity, while in use, to turn instantly beastly hot or blindingly cold upon you, depending on whether your neighbor turned on his cold or his hot to deprive you of a necessary complement in the shower you had so carefully blended. Some motels had instructions pasted above the toilet (on whose tank the towels were unhygienically heaped) asking guests not to throw into its bowl garbage, beer cans, cartons, stillborn babies; others had special notices under glass, such as Things to Do (Riding: *You will often see riders coming down Main Street on their way back from a romantic moonlight ride.* "Often at 3 A.M.," sneered unromantic Lo).

Nous connûmes the various types of motor court operators, the reformed criminal, the retired teacher and the business flop, among the males; and the motherly, pseudo-ladylike and madamic variants among the females. And sometimes trains would cry in the monstrously hot and humid night with heartrending and ominous plangency, mingling power and hysteria in one desperate scream.

We avoided Tourist Homes, country cousins of Funeral ones, old-fashioned, genteel and showerless, with elaborate dressing tables in depressingly white-and-pink little bedrooms, and photographs of the landlady's children in all their instars. But I did surrender, now and then, to Lo's predilection for "real" hotels. She would pick out in the book, while I petted her in the parked car in the silence of a dusk-mellowed, mysterious side-road, some highly recommended lake lodge which offered all sorts of things magnified by the flashlight she moved over them, such as congenial company, between-meals snacks, outdoor barbecues —but which in my mind conjured up odious visions of stinking high school boys in sweatshirts and an ember-red cheek pressing against hers, while poor Dr. Humbert, embracing nothing but two masculine knees, would cold-humor his piles on the damp turf. Most tempting to her, too, were those "Colonial" Inns, which apart from "gracious atmosphere" and picture windows, promised "unlimited quantities of M-m-m food." Treasured recollections of my father's palatial hotel sometimes led me to seek for its like in the strange country we traveled through. I was soon discouraged; but Lo kept following the scent of rich food ads, while I derived a not exclusively economic kick from such roadside signs as TIMBER HOTEL, *Children under 14 Free.* On the other hand, I shudder when recalling that *soi-disant* "high-class" resort in a Midwestern state, which advertised "raid-the-icebox" midnight snacks and, intrigued by my accent, wanted to know my dead wife's and dead mother's maiden names. A two-days' stay there cost me a hundred and twenty-four dollars! And do you remember, Miranda, that other "ultrasmart" robbers' den with complimentary morning coffee and circulating ice water, and no children under sixteen (no Lolitas, of course)?

Immediately upon arrival at one of the plainer motor courts which became our habitual haunts, she would set the electric fan a-whirr, or induce me to drop a quarter into the radio, or she would read all the signs and inquire with a whine why she could not go riding up some advertised trail or swimming in that local pool of warm mineral water. Most often, in the slouching, bored way she cultivated, Lo would fall prostrate and abominably desirable into a red springchair or a green chaise longue, or a steamer chair of striped canvas with footrest and canopy, or a sling chair, or any other lawn chair under a garden umbrella on the patio, and it would take hours of blandishments, threats and promises to make her lend me for a few seconds her brown limbs in the seclusion of the five-dollar room before undertaking anything she might prefer to my poor joy.

A combination of naïveté and deception, of charm and vulgarity, of blue sulks and rosy mirth, Lolita, when she chose, could be a most exasperating brat. I was not really quite prepared for her fits of disorganized boredom, intense and vehement griping, her sprawling, droopy, dopey-eyed style, and what is called goofing off—a kind of diffused clowning which she thought was tough in a boyish hoodlum way. Mentally, I found her to be a disgustingly conventional little girl. Sweet hot jazz, square dancing, gooey fudge sundaes, musicals, movie magazines and so forth—these were the obvious items in her list of beloved things. The Lord knows how many nickels I fed to the gorgeous music boxes that came with every meal we had! I still hear the nasal voices of those invisibles serenading her, people with names like Sammy and Jo and Eddy and Tony and Peggy and Guy and Patty and Rex, and sentimental song hits, all of them as similar to my ear as her various candies were to my palate. She believed, with a kind of celestial trust, any advertisement or advice that appeared in *Movie Love* or *Screen Land*—Starasil Starves Pimples, or "You better watch out if you're wearing your shirttails outside your jeans, gals, because Jill says you shouldn't." If a roadside sign said: VISIT OUR GIFT SHOP—we *had* to visit it, *had* to buy its Indian curios, dolls, copper jewelry, cactus candy. The words "novelties and souvenirs" simply entranced her by their trochaic lilt. If some café sign proclaimed Icecold Drinks, she was automatically stirred, although all drinks everywhere were ice-cold. She it was to whom ads were dedicated: the ideal consumer, the subject and object of every foul poster. And she attempted—unsuccessfully—to patronize only those restaurants where the holy spirit of Huncan Dines had descended upon the cute paper napkins and cottage-cheese-crested salads.

In those days, neither she nor I had thought up yet the system of monetary bribes which was to work such havoc with my nerves and her morals somewhat later. I relied on three other methods to keep my pubescent concubine in submission and passable temper. A few years before, she had spent a rainy summer under Miss Phalen's bleary eye in a dilapidated Appalachian farmhouse that had belonged to some gnarled Haze or other in the dead past. It still stood among its rank acres of golden rod on the edge of a flowerless forest, at the end of a permanently muddy road, twenty miles from the nearest hamlet. Lo recalled that scarecrow of a house, the solitude, the soggy old pastures, the wind, the bloated wilderness, with an energy of disgust that distorted her mouth and fattened her half-revealed tongue. And it was there that I warned her she would dwell with me in exile for months and years if need be, studying under me French and Latin, unless her "present attitude" changed. Charlotte, I began to understand you!

A simple child, Lo would scream no! and frantically clutch at my driving hand whenever I put a stop to her tornadoes of temper by turning in the middle of a highway with the implication that I was about to take her straight to that dark and dismal abode. The farther, however, we traveled away from it west, the less tangible that menace became, and I had to adopt other methods of persuasion.

Among these, the reformatory threat is the one I recall with the deepest moan of shame. From the very beginning of our concourse, I was clever enough to realize that I must secure her complete co-operation in keeping our relations secret, that it should become a second nature with her, no matter what grudge she might bear me, no matter what other pleasures she might seek.

"Come and kiss your old man," I would say, "and drop that moody nonsense. In former times, when I was still your dream male [the reader will notice what pains I took to speak Lo's tongue], you swooned to records of the number one throb-and-sob idol of your coevals [Lo: "Of my what? Speak English"]. That idol of your pals sounded, you thought, like friend Humbert. But now, I am just your *old man*, a dream dad protecting his dream daughter.

"My *chère Dolorès!* I want to protect you, dear, from all the horrors that happen to little girls in coal sheds and alley ways, and, alas, *comme vous le savez trop bien, ma gentille*, in the blueberry woods during the bluest of summers. Through thick and thin I will still stay your guardian, and if you are good, I hope a court may legalize that guardianship before long. Let us, however, forget, Dolores Haze, so-called legal terminology, terminology that accepts as rational the term 'lewd and lascivious cohabitation.' I am not a criminal sexual psychopath taking indecent liberties with a child. The rapist was Charlie Holmes;

1 I am the therapist—a matter of nice spacing in the way of distinction. I am your daddum, Lo. Look, I've a learned book here about young girls. Look, darling, what it says. I quote: the normal girl—normal, mark you—the normal girl is usually extremely anxious to please her father. She feels in him the forerunner of the desired elusive male ('elusive' is good, by

2 Polonius!). The wise mother (and your poor mother would have been wise, had she lived) will encourage a companionship between father and daughter, realizing—excuse the corny style —that the girl forms her ideals of romance and of men from her association with her father. Now, what association does this cheery book mean—and recommend? I quote again: Among Sicilians sexual relations between a father and his daughter are accepted as a matter of course, and the girl who participates in such relationship is not looked upon with disapproval by the society of which she is part. I'm a great admirer of Sicilians, fine athletes, fine musicians, fine upright people, Lo, and great lovers. But let's not digress. Only the other day we read in the newspapers some bunkum about a middle-aged morals offender who pleaded guilty to the violation of the Mann Act and to transporting a nine-year-old girl across state lines for immoral purposes, whatever these are. Dolores darling! You are not nine but almost thirteen, and I would not advise you to consider

3 yourself my cross-country slave, and I deplore the Mann Act as lending itself to a dreadful pun, the revenge that the Gods of Semantics take against tight-zippered Philistines. I am your father, and I *am* speaking English, and I love you.

"Finally, let us see what happens if you, a minor, accused of having impaired the morals of an adult in a respectable inn, what happens if you complain to the police of my having kidnaped and raped you? Let us suppose they believe you. A minor female, who allows a person over twenty-one to know her carnally, involves her victim into statutory rape, or second-degree sodomy, depending on the technique; and the maximum penalty is ten years. So I go to jail. Okay. I go to jail. But what happens to you, my orphan? Well, you are luckier. You become the ward of the Department of Public Welfare—which I am afraid sounds a little bleak. A nice grim matron of the Miss Phalen type, but more rigid and not a drinking woman, will take away your lipstick and fancy clothes. No more gadding about! I don't know if you have ever heard of the laws relating to dependent, neglected, incorrigible and delinquent children. While I stand gripping the bars, you, happy neglected child, will be given a choice of various dwelling places, all more or less the same, the correctional school, the reformatory, the juvenile detention home, or one of those admirable girls' protectories where you knit things, and sing hymns, and have rancid pancakes on Sundays. You will go there, Lolita—*my* Lolita, *this* Lolita will leave her Catullus and go there, as the wayward girl you are. In plainer words, if we two are found out, you will be analyzed and institutionalized, my pet, *c'est tout*. You will dwell, my Lolita will dwell (come here, my brown flower) with thirty-nine other dopes in a dirty dormitory (no, allow me, please) under the supervision of hideous matrons. This is the situation, this is the choice. Don't you think that under the circumstances Dolores Haze had better stick to her old man?"

By rubbing all this in, I succeeded in terrorizing Lo, who despite a certain brash alertness of manner and spurts of wit was not as intelligent a child as her I.Q. might suggest. But if I managed to establish that background of shared secrecy and shared guilt, I was much less successful in keeping her in good humor. Every morning during our yearlong travels I had to devise some expectation, some special point in space and time for her to look forward to, for her to survive till bedtime. Otherwise, deprived of a shaping and sustaining purpose, the skeleton of her day sagged and collapsed. The object in view might be anything—a lighthouse in Virginia, a natural cave in Arkansas converted to a café, a collection of guns and violins somewhere in Oklahoma, a replica of the Grotto of Lourdes in Louisiana, shabby photographs of the bonanza mining period in the local museum of a Rocky Mountains resort, anything whatsoever—but it had to be there, in front of us, like a fixed star, although as likely as not Lo would feign gagging as soon as we got to it.

By putting the geography of the United States into motion, I did my best for hours on end to give her the impression of "going places," of rolling on to some definite destination, to some unusual delight. I have never seen such smooth amiable roads as those that now radiated before us, across the crazy quilt of forty-eight states. Voraciously we consumed those long highways, in rapt silence we glided over their glossy black dance floors. Not only had Lo no eye for scenery but she furiously resented my calling her attention to this or that enchanting detail of landscape; which I myself learned to discern only after being exposed for quite a time to the delicate beauty ever present in the margin of our undeserving journey. By a paradox of pictorial thought, the average lowland North-American countryside had at first seemed to me something I accepted with a shock of amused recognition because of those painted oilcloths which were imported from America in the old days to be hung above washstands in Central-European nurseries, and which fascinated a drowsy child at bed time with the rustic green views they depicted—opaque curly trees, a barn, cattle, a brook, the dull white of vague orchards in bloom, and perhaps a stone fence or hills of greenish gouache. But gradually the models of those elementary rusticities became stranger and stranger to the eye, the nearer I came to know them. Beyond the tilled plain, beyond the toy roofs, there would be a slow suffusion of inutile loveliness, a low sun in a platinum haze with a warm, peeled-peach tinge pervading the upper edge of a two-dimensional, dove-gray cloud fusing with the distant amorous mist. There might be a line of spaced trees silhouetted against the horizon, and hot still noons above a wilderness of clover, and Claude Lorrain clouds inscribed remotely into misty azure with only their cumulus part conspicuous against the neutral swoon of the background. Or again, it might be a stern El Greco horizon, pregnant with inky rain, and a passing glimpse of some mummy-necked farmer, and all around alternating strips of quick-silverish water and harsh

green corn, the whole arrangement opening like a fan, somewhere in Kansas.

Now and then, in the vastness of those plains, huge trees
would advance toward us to cluster self-consciously by the roadside and provide a bit of humanitarian shade above a picnic
table, with sun flecks, flattened paper cups, samaras and dis- 1
carded ice-cream sticks littering the brown ground. A great user
of roadside facilities, my unfastidious Lo would be charmed by
toilet signs—Guys-Gals, John-Jane, Jack-Jill and even Buck's-
Doe's; while lost in an artist's dream, I would stare at the honest
brightness of the gasoline paraphernalia against the splendid
green of oaks, or at a distant hill scrambling out—scarred but still
untamed—from the wilderness of agriculture that was trying to
swallow it.

At night, tall trucks studded with colored lights, like dreadful
giant Christmas trees, loomed in the darkness and thundered by
the belated little sedan. And again next day a thinly populated
sky, losing its blue to the heat, would melt overhead, and Lo
would clamor for a drink, and her cheeks would hollow vigorously over the straw, and the car inside would be a furnace when
we got in again, and the road shimmered ahead, with a remote
car changing its shape mirage-like in the surface glare, and seeming to hang for a moment, old-fashionedly square and high, in
the hot haze. And as we pushed westward, patches of what the
garage-man called "sage brush" appeared, and then the mysterious outlines of table-like hills, and then red bluffs ink-blotted
with junipers, and then a mountain range, dun grading into blue,
and blue into dream, and the desert would meet us with a steady
gale, dust, gray thorn bushes, and hideous bits of tissue paper
mimicking pale flowers among the prickles of wind-tortured
withered stalks all along the highway; in the middle of which
there sometimes stood simple cows, immobilized in a position
(tail left, white eyelashes right) cutting across all human rules of
traffic.

My lawyer has suggested I give a clear, frank account of the
itinerary we followed, and I suppose I have reached here a point
where I cannot avoid that chore. Roughly, during that mad year

(August 1947 to August 1948), our route began with a series of
wiggles and whorls in New England, then meandered south, up
1 and down, east and west; dipped deep into *ce qu'on appelle*
Dixieland, avoided Florida because the Farlows were there,
veered west, zigzagged through corn belts and cotton belts (this
is not *too* clear I am afraid, Clarence, but I did not keep any
notes, and have at my disposal only an atrociously crippled tour
book in three volumes, almost a symbol of my torn and tattered
past, in which to check these recollections); crossed and re-
crossed the Rockies, straggled through southern deserts where
we wintered; reached the Pacific, turned north through the pale
lilac fluff of flowering shrubs along forest roads; almost reached
the Canadian border; and proceeded east, across good lands and
bad lands, back to agriculture on a grand scale, avoiding, despite
little Lo's strident remonstrations, little Lo's birthplace, in a
corn, coal and hog producing area; and finally returned to the
fold of the East, petering out in the college town of Beardsley.

2

Now, in perusing what follows, the reader should bear in mind
not only the general circuit as adumbrated above, with its many
sidetrips and tourist traps, secondary circles and skittish devia-
tions, but also the fact that far from being an indolent *partie de*
2 *plaisir,* our tour was a hard, twisted, teleological growth, whose
3 sole *raison d'être* (these French clichés are symptomatic) was
to keep my companion in passable humor from kiss to kiss.
    Thumbing through that battered tour book, I dimly evoke
that Magnolia Garden in a southern state which cost me four
bucks and which, according to the ad in the book, you must
4 visit for three reasons: because John Galsworthy (a stone-dead
writer of sorts) acclaimed it as the world's fairest garden; because in 1900 Baedeker's Guide had marked it with a star; and
finally, because... O, Reader, My Reader, guess! ... because
children (and by Jingo was not my Lolita a child!) will "walk

starry-eyed and reverently through this foretaste of Heaven, drinking in beauty that can influence a life." "Not mine," said grim Lo, and settled down on a bench with the fillings of two Sunday papers in her lovely lap.

We passed and re-passed through the whole gamut of American roadside restaurants, from the lowly Eat with its deer head (dark trace of long tear at inner canthus), "humorous" picture post cards of the posterior "Kurort" type, impaled guest checks, life savers, sunglasses, adman visions of celestial sundaes, one half of a chocolate cake under glass, and several horribly experienced flies zigzagging over the sticky sugar-pour on the ignoble counter; and all the way to the expensive place with the subdued lights, preposterously poor table linen, inept waiters (ex-convicts or college boys), the roan back of a screen actress, the sable eyebrows of her male of the moment, and an orchestra of zoot-suiters with trumpets.

We inspected the world's largest stalagmite in a cave where three southeastern states have a family reunion; admission by age; adults one dollar, pubescents sixty cents. A granite obelisk commemorating the Battle of Blue Licks, with old bones and Indian pottery in the museum nearby, Lo a dime, very reasonable. The present log cabin boldly simulating the past log cabin where Lincoln was born. A boulder, with a plaque, in memory of the author of "Trees" (by now we are in Poplar Cove, N.C., reached by what my kind, tolerant, usually so restrained tour book angrily calls "a very narrow road, poorly maintained," to which, though no Kilmerite, I subscribe). From a hired motorboat operated by an elderly, but still repulsively handsome White Russian, a baron they said (Lo's palms were damp, the little fool), who had known in California good old Maximovich and Valeria, we could distinguish the inaccessible "millionaires' colony" on an island, somewhere off the Georgia coast. We inspected further: a collection of European hotel picture post cards in a museum devoted to hobbies at a Mississippi resort, where with a hot wave of pride I discovered a colored photo of my father's Mirana, its striped awnings, its flag flying above the retouched palm trees. "So what?" said Lo, squinting at the

[157]

1   bronzed owner of an expensive car who had followed us into the
Hobby House. Relics of the cotton era. A forest in Arkansas
and, on her brown shoulder, a raised purple-pink swelling (the
work of some gnat) which I eased of its beautiful transparent
poison between my long thumbnails and then sucked till I was
gorged on her spicy blood. Bourbon Street (in a town named
New Orleans) whose sidewalks, said the tour book, "may [I
liked the "may"] feature entertainment by pickaninnies who
will [I liked the "will" even better] tap-dance for pennies" (what
fun), while "its numerous small and intimate night clubs are
thronged with visitors" (naughty). Collections of frontier lore.
Ante-bellum homes with iron-trellis balconies and hand-worked
stairs, the kind down which movie ladies with sun-kissed shoulders run in rich Technicolor, holding up the fronts of their
flounced skirts with both little hands in that special way, and
the devoted Negress shaking her head on the upper landing. The
Menninger Foundation, a psychiatric clinic, just for the heck of
it. A patch of beautifully eroded clay; and yucca blossoms, so
2   pure, so waxy, but lousy with creeping white flies. Independence,
Missouri, the starting point of the Old Oregon Trail; and
3   Abilene, Kansas, the home of the Wild Bill Something Rodeo.
Distant mountains. Near mountains. More mountains; bluish
beauties never attainable, or ever turning into inhabited hill after
hill; south-eastern ranges, altitudinal failures as alps go; heart
and sky-piercing snow-veined gray colossi of stone, relentless
peaks appearing from nowhere at a turn of the highway; timbered enormities, with a system of neatly overlapping dark firs,
interrupted in places by pale puffs of aspen; pink and lilac
4   formations, Pharaonic, phallic, "too prehistoric for words" (blasé
Lo); buttes of black lava; early spring mountains with young-
5   elephant lanugo along their spines; end-of-the-summer mountains, all hunched up, their heavy Egyptian limbs folded under
folds of tawny moth-eaten plush; oatmeal hills, flecked with
6   green round oaks; a last rufous mountain with a rich rug of
7   lucerne at its foot.
        Moreover, we inspected: Little Iceberg Lake, somewhere in
Colorado, and the snow banks, and the cushionets of tiny alpine

flowers, and more snow; down which Lo in red-peaked cap tried
to slide, and squealed, and was snowballed by some youngsters,
and retaliated in kind *comme on dit*. Skeletons of burned aspens,   1
patches of spired blue flowers. The various items of a scenic
drive. Hundreds of scenic drives, thousands of Bear Creeks, Soda
Springs, Painted Canyons. Texas, a drought-struck plain. Crystal
Chamber in the longest cave in the world, children under 12
free, Lo a young captive. A collection of a local lady's homemade
sculptures, closed on a miserable Monday morning, dust, wind,
witherland. Conception Park, in a town on the Mexican border
which I dared not cross. There and elsewhere, hundreds of gray
hummingbirds in the dusk, probing the throats of dim flowers.   2
Shakespeare, a ghost town in New Mexico, where bad man   3
Russian Bill was colorfully hanged seventy years ago. Fish
hatcheries. Cliff dwellings. The mummy of a child (Florentine
Bea's Indian contemporary). Our twentieth Hell's Canyon. Our   4, 5
fiftieth Gateway to something or other *fide* that tour book, the
cover of which had been lost by that time. A tick in my groin.
Always the same three old men, in hats and suspenders, idling
away the summer afternoon under the trees near the public
fountain. A hazy blue view beyond railings on a mountain pass,
and the backs of a family enjoying it (with Lo, in a hot, happy,
wild, intense, hopeful, hopeless whisper—"Look, the McCrystals,
please, let's talk to them, please"—let's talk to them, reader!—
"please! I'll do anything you want, oh, please..."). Indian
ceremonial dances, strictly commercial. ART: American Refrigerator Transit Company. Obvious Arizona, pueblo dwellings,
aboriginal pictographs, a dinosaur track in a desert canyon,
printed there thirty million years ago, when I was a child. A
lanky, six-foot, pale boy with an active Adam's apple, ogling Lo
and her orange-brown bare midriff, which I kissed five minutes
later, Jack. Winter in the desert, spring in the foothills, almonds
in bloom. Reno, a dreary town in Nevada, with a nightlife said
to be "cosmopolitan and mature." A winery in California, with
a church built in the shape of a wine barrel. Death Valley.   6
Scotty's Castle. Works of Art collected by one Rogers over a   7
period of years. The ugly villas of handsome actresses. R. L.

1   Stevenson's footprint on an extinct volcano. Mission Dolores:
2, 3 good title for book. Surf-carved sandstone festoons. A man having
4   a lavish epileptic fit on the ground in Russian Gulch State Park.
Blue, blue Crater Lake. A fish hatchery in Idaho and the State
Penitentiary. Somber Yellowstone Park and its colored hot
springs, baby geysers, rainbows of bubbling mud—symbols of
my passion. A herd of antelopes in a wildlife refuge. Our hun-
dredth cavern, adults one dollar, Lolita fifty cents. A chateau
built by a French marquess in N.D. The Corn Palace in S.D.;
and the huge heads of presidents carved in towering granite. The
Bearded Woman read our jingle and now she is no longer single.
A zoo in Indiana where a large troop of monkeys lived on concrete replica of Christopher Columbus' flagship. Billions of dead,
or halfdead, fish-smelling May flies in every window of every
eating place all along a dreary sandy shore. Fat gulls on big
stones as seen from the ferry *City of Cheboygan,* whose brown
woolly smoke arched and dipped over the green shadow it cast
on the aquamarine lake. A motel whose ventilator pipe passed
under the city sewer. Lincoln's home, largely spurious, with
parlor books and period furniture that most visitors reverently
accepted as personal belongings.

   We had rows, minor and major. The biggest ones we had took
place: at Lacework Cabins, Virginia; on Park Avenue, Little
5   Rock, near a school; on Milner Pass, 10,759 feet high, in Colorado; at the corner of Seventh Street and Central Avenue in
Phoenix, Arizona; on Third Street, Los Angeles, because the
tickets to some studio or other were sold out; at a motel called
Poplar Shade in Utah, where six pubescent trees were scarcely
6   taller than my Lolita, and where she asked, *à propos de rien,*
how long did I think we were going to live in stuffy cabins, doing
filthy things together and never behaving like ordinary people?
On N. Broadway, Burns, Oregon, corner of W. Washington,
facing Safeway, a grocery. In some little town in the Sun Valley
of Idaho, before a brick hotel, pale and flushed bricks nicely
mixed, with, opposite, a poplar playing its liquid shadows all
over the local Honor Roll. In a sage brush wilderness, between
Pinedale and Farson. Somewhere in Nebraska, on Main Street,

near the First National Bank, established 1889, with a view of a railway crossing in the vista of the street, and beyond that the white organ pipes of a multiple silo. And on McEwen St., corner of Wheaton Ave., in a Michigan town bearing his first name.   1

We came to know the curious roadside species, Hitchhiking Man, *Homo pollex* of science, with all its many sub-species and   2 forms: the modest soldier, spic and span, quietly waiting, quietly conscious of khaki's viatic appeal; the schoolboy wishing to go   3 two blocks; the killer wishing to go two thousand miles; the mysterious, nervous, elderly gent, with brand-new suitcase and clipped mustache; a trio of optimistic Mexicans; the college student displaying the grime of vacational outdoor work as proudly as the name of the famous college arching across the front of his sweatshirt; the desperate lady whose battery has just died on her; the clean-cut, glossy-haired, shifty-eyed, white-faced young beasts in loud shirts and coats, vigorously, almost priap-ically thrusting out tense thumbs to tempt lone women or sad-   4 sack salesmen with fancy cravings.

"Let's take him," Lo would often plead, rubbing her knees together in a way she had, as some particularly disgusting *pollex*, some man of my age and shoulder breadth, with the *face à claques* of an unemployed actor, walked backwards, practically   5 in the path of our car.

Oh, I had to keep a very sharp eye on Lo, little limp Lo! Owing perhaps to constant amorous exercise, she radiated, de-spite her very childish appearance, some special languorous glow which threw garage fellows, hotel pages, vacationists, goons in luxurious cars, maroon morons near blued pools, into fits of concupiscence which might have tickled my pride, had it not   6 incensed my jealousy. For little Lo was aware of that glow of hers, and I would often catch her *coulant un regard* in the direc-   7 tion of some amiable male, some grease monkey, with a sinewy golden-brown forearm and watch-braceleted wrist, and hardly had I turned my back to go and buy this very Lo a lollipop, than I would hear her and the fair mechanic burst into a perfect love song of wisecracks.

When, during our longer stops, I would relax after a particularly violent morning in bed, and out of the goodness of my lulled heart allow her—indulgent Hum!—to visit the rose garden or children's library across the street with a motor court neighbor's plain little Mary and Mary's eight-year-old brother, Lo would come back an hour late, with barefoot Mary trailing far behind, and the little boy metamorphosed into two gangling, golden-haired high school uglies, all muscles and gonorrhea. The reader may well imagine what I answered my pet when—rather uncertainly, I admit—she would ask me if she could go with Carl and Al here to the roller-skating rink.

I remember the first time, a dusty windy afternoon, I did let her go to one such rink. Cruelly she said it would be no fun if I accompanied her, since that time of day was reserved for teenagers. We wrangled out a compromise: I remained in the car, among other (empty) cars with their noses to the canvas-topped open-air rink, where some fifty young people, many in pairs, were endlessly rolling round and round to mechanical music, and the wind silvered the trees. Dolly wore blue jeans and white high shoes, as most of the other girls did. I kept counting the revolutions of the rolling crowd—and suddenly she was missing. When she rolled past again, she was together with three hoodlums whom I had heard analyze a moment before the girl skaters from the outside—and jeer at a lovely leggy young thing who had arrived clad in red shorts instead of those jeans or slacks.

At inspection stations on highways entering Arizona or California, a policeman's cousin would peer with such intensity at us that my poor heart wobbled. "Any honey?" he would inquire, and every time my sweet fool giggled. I still have, vibrating all along my optic nerve, visions of Lo on horseback, a link in the chain of a guided trip along a bridle trail: Lo bobbing at a walking pace, with an old woman rider in front and a lecherous rednecked dude-rancher behind; and I behind him, hating his fat flowery-shirted back even more fervently than a motorist does a slow truck on a mountain road. Or else, at a ski lodge, I would see her floating away from me, celestial and solitary, in an ethereal chairlift, up and up, to a glittering summit where laughing athletes stripped to the waist were waiting for her, for her.

In whatever town we stopped I would inquire, in my polite European way, anent the whereabouts of natatoriums, museums, local schools, the number of children in the nearest school and so forth; and at school bus time, smiling and twitching a little (I discovered this *tic nerveux* because cruel Lo was the first to mimic it), I would park at a strategic point, with my vagrant schoolgirl beside me in the car, to watch the children leave school—always a pretty sight. This sort of thing soon began to bore my so easily bored Lolita, and, having a childish lack of sympathy for other people's whims, she would insult me and my desire to have her caress me while blue-eyed little brunettes in blue shorts, copperheads in green boleros, and blurred boyish blondes in faded slacks passed by in the sun.

As a sort of compromise, I freely advocated whenever and wherever possible the use of swimming pools with other girl-children. She adored brilliant water and was a remarkably smart diver. Comfortably robed, I would settle down in the rich post-meridian shade after my own demure dip, and there I would sit, with a dummy book or a bag of bonbons, or both, or nothing but my tingling glands, and watch her gambol, rubber-capped, be-pearled, smoothly tanned, as glad as an ad, in her trim-fitted satin pants and shirred bra. Pubescent sweetheart! How smugly would I marvel that she was mine, mine, mine, and revise the recent matitudinal swoon to the moan of the mourning doves, and devise the late afternoon one, and slitting my sun-speared eyes, compare Lolita to whatever other nymphets parsimonious chance collected around her for my anthological delectation and judgment; and today, putting my hand on my ailing heart, I really do not think that any of them ever surpassed her in de-sirability, or if they did, it was so two or three times at the most, in a certain light, with certain perfumes blended in the air—once in the hopeless case of a pale Spanish child, the daughter of a heavy-jawed nobleman, and another time—*mais je divague.*

Naturally, I had to be always wary, fully realizing, in my lucid jealousy, the danger of those dazzling romps. I had only to turn away for a moment—to walk, say, a few steps in order to see if our cabin was at last ready after the morning change of linen—and

Lo and Behold, upon returning, I would find the former, *les*
1 *yeux perdus*, dipping and kicking her long-toed feet in the water
on the stone edge of which she lolled, while, on either side of
her, there crouched a *brun adolescent* whom her russet beauty
and the quicksilver in the baby folds of her stomach were sure
2 to cause to *se tordre*—oh Baudelaire!—in recurrent dreams for
months to come.

I tried to teach her to play tennis so we might have more
amusements in common; but although I had been a good player
in my prime, I proved to be hopeless as a teacher; and so, in
California, I got her to take a number of very expensive lessons
with a famous coach, a husky, wrinkled old-timer, with a harem
3 of ball boys; he looked an awful wreck off the court, but now
and then, when, in the course of a lesson, to keep up the exchange, he would put out as it were an exquisite spring blossom
of a stroke and twang the ball back to his pupil, that divine
delicacy of absolute power made me recall that, thirty years
4 before, I had seen *him* in Cannes demolish the great Gobbert!
Until she began taking those lessons, I thought she would never
learn the game. On this or that hotel court I would drill Lo, and
try to relive the days when in a hot gale, a daze of dust, and
queer lassitude, I fed ball after ball to gay, innocent, elegant
Annabel (gleam of bracelet, pleated white skirt, black velvet
hair band). With every word of persistent advice I would only
augment Lo's sullen fury. To our games, oddly enough, she preferred—at least, before we reached California—formless pat ball
approximations—more ball hunting than actual play—with a
5 wispy, weak, wonderfully pretty in an *ange gauche* way coeval.
A helpful spectator, I would go up to that other child, and inhale
her faint musky fragrance as I touched her forearm and held her
knobby wrist, and push this way or that her cool thigh to show
her the back-hand stance. In the meantime, Lo, bending forward, would let her sunny-brown curls hang forward as she stuck
her racket, like a cripple's stick, into the ground and emitted a
tremendous ugh of disgust at my intrusion. I would leave them
to their game and look on, comparing their bodies in motion, a
silk scarf round my throat; this was in south Arizona, I think—

and the days had a lazy lining of warmth, and awkward Lo would slash at the ball and miss it, and curse, and send a simulacrum of a serve into the net, and show the wet glistening young down of her armpit as she brandished her racket in despair, and her even more insipid partner would dutifully rush out after every ball, and retrieve none; but both were enjoying themselves beautifully, and in clear ringing tones kept the exact score of their ineptitudes all the time.

One day, I remember, I offered to bring them cold drinks from the hotel, and went up the gravel path, and came back with two tall glasses of pineapple juice, soda and ice; and then a sudden void within my chest made me stop as I saw that the tennis court was deserted. I stooped to set down the glasses on a bench and for some reason, with a kind of icy vividness, saw Charlotte's face in death, and I glanced around, and noticed Lo in white shorts receding through the speckled shadow of a garden path in the company of a tall man who carried two tennis rackets. I sprang after them, but as I was crashing through the shrubbery, I saw, in an alternate vision, as if life's course constantly branched, Lo, in slacks, and her companion, in shorts, trudging up and down a small weedy area, and beating bushes with their rackets in listless search for their last lost ball.

I itemize these sunny nothings mainly to prove to my judges that I did everything in my power to give my Lolita a really good time. How charming it was to see her, a child herself, showing another child some of her few accomplishments, such as for example a special way of jumping rope. With her right hand holding her left arm behind her untanned back, the lesser nymphet, a diaphanous darling, would be all eyes, as the pavonine sun was all eyes on the gravel under the flowering trees, while in the midst of that oculate paradise, my freckled and raffish lass skipped, repeating the movements of so many others I had gloated over on the sun-shot, watered, damp-smelling sidewalks and ramparts of ancient Europe. Presently, she would hand the rope back to her little Spanish friend, and watch in her turn the repeated lesson, and brush away the hair from her brow, and fold her arms, and step on one toe with the other, or drop her hands loosely upon her still unflared hips, and I would satisfy myself that the damned staff had at last finished cleaning up our cottage; whereupon, flashing a smile to the shy, dark-haired page girl of my princess and thrusting my fatherly fingers deep into Lo's hair from behind, and then gently but firmly clasping them around the nape of her neck, I would lead my reluctant pet to our small home for a quick connection before dinner.

"Whose cat has scratched poor you?" a full-blown fleshy handsome woman of the repulsive type to which I was particularly attractive might ask me at the "lodge," during a table d'hôte dinner followed by dancing promised to Lo. This was one of the reasons why I tried to keep as far away from people as possible, while Lo, on the other hand, would do her utmost to draw as many potential witnesses into her orbit as she could.

She would be, figuratively speaking, wagging her tiny tail, her whole behind in fact as little bitches do—while some grinning stranger accosted us and began a bright conversation with a comparative study of license plates. "Long way from home!" Inquisitive parents, in order to pump Lo about me, would suggest her going to a movie with their children. We had some close shaves. The waterfall nuisance pursued me of course in all our caravansaries. But I never realized how wafery their wall substance was until one evening, after I had loved too loudly, a neighbor's masculine cough filled the pause as clearly as mine would have done; and next morning as I was having breakfast at the milk bar (Lo was a late sleeper, and I liked to bring her a pot of hot coffee in bed), my neighbor of the eve, an elderly fool wearing plain glasses on his long virtuous nose and a convention badge on his lapel, somehow managed to rig up a conversation with me, in the course of which he inquired, if my missus was like his missus a rather reluctant get-upper when not on the farm; and had not the hideous danger I was skirting almost suffocated me, I might have enjoyed the odd look of surprise on his thin-lipped weather-beaten face when I drily answered, as I slithered off my stool, that I was thank God a widower.

How sweet it was to bring that coffee to her, and then deny it until she had done her morning duty. And I was such a thoughtful friend, such a passionate father, such a good pediatrician, attending to all the wants of my little auburn brunette's body! My only grudge against nature was that I could not turn my Lolita inside out and apply voracious lips to her young matrix, her unknown heart, her nacreous liver, the sea-grapes of her lungs, her comely twin kidneys. On especially tropical afternoons, in the sticky closeness of the siesta, I liked the cool feel of armchair leather against my massive nakedness as I held her in my lap. There she would be, a typical kid picking her nose while engrossed in the lighter sections of a newspaper, as indifferent to my ecstasy as if it were something she had sat upon, a shoe, a doll, the handle of a tennis racket, and was too indolent to remove. Her eyes would follow the adventures of her favorite strip characters: there was one well-drawn sloppy bobby-soxer, 1 with high cheekbones and angular gestures, that I was not above enjoying myself; she studied the photographic results of head-on collisions; she never doubted the reality of place, time and circumstance alleged to match the publicity pictures of naked-thighed beauties; and she was curiously fascinated by the photographs of local brides, some in full wedding apparel, holding bouquets and wearing glasses.

A fly would settle and walk in the vicinity of her navel or explore her tender pale areolas. She tried to catch it in her fist 2 (Charlotte's method) and then would turn to the column Let's Explore Your Mind.

"Let's explore your mind. Would sex crimes be reduced if children obeyed a few don'ts? Don't play around public toilets. Don't take candy or rides from strangers. If picked up, mark down the license of the car."

". . . and the brand of the candy," I volunteered.

She went on, her cheek (recedent) against mine (pursuant); 3 and this was a good day, mark, O reader!

"If you don't have a pencil, but are old enough to read—"

"We," I quip-quoted, "medieval mariners, have placed in this bottle—" 4

"If," she repeated, "you don't have a pencil, but are old

[167]

enough to read and write—this is what the guy means, isn't it, you dope—scratch the number somehow on the roadside."

"With your little claws, Lolita.'"

3

1 She had entered my world, umber and black Humberland, with rash curiosity; she surveyed it with a shrug of amused distaste; and it seemed to me now that she was ready to turn away from it with something akin to plain repulsion. Never did she vibrate under my touch, and a strident "what d'you think you are doing?" was all I got for my pains. To the wonderland I had to offer, my fool preferred the corniest movies, the most cloying fudge. To think that between a Hamburger and a Humburger, she would—invariably, with icy precision—plump for the former. There is nothing more atrociously cruel than an adored child. Did I mention the name of that milk bar I visited a moment ago? It was, of all things, The Frigid Queen. Smiling a little
2 sadly, I dubbed her My Frigid Princess. She did not see the wistful joke.

Oh, do not scowl at me, reader, I do not intend to convey the impression that I did not manage to be happy. Reader must understand that in the possession and thralldom of a nymphet the enchanted traveler stands, as it were, *beyond happiness*. For there is no other bliss on earth comparable to that of fondling a
3 nymphet. It is *hors concours*, that bliss, it belongs to another class, another plane of sensitivity. Despite our tiffs, despite her nastiness, despite all the fuss and faces she made, and the vulgarity, and the danger, and the horrible hopelessness of it all, I still dwelled deep in my elected paradise—a paradise whose skies were the color of hell-flames—but still a paradise.

The able psychiatrist who studies my case—and whom by now Dr. Humbert has plunged, I trust, into a state of leporine
4 fascination—is no doubt anxious to have me take my Lolita to the seaside and have me find there, at last, the "gratification" of

[168]

a lifetime urge, and release from the "subconscious" obsession of an incomplete childhood romance with the initial little Miss Lee.

Well, comrade, let me tell you that I *did* look for a beach, though I also have to confess that by the time we reached its mirage of gray water, so many delights had already been granted me by my traveling companion that the search for a Kingdom by the Sea, a Sublimated Riviera, or whatnot, far from being the impulse of the subconscious, had become the rational pursuit of a purely theoretical thrill. The angels knew it, and arranged things accordingly. A visit to a plausible cove on the Atlantic side was completely messed up by foul weather. A thick damp sky, muddy waves, a sense of boundless but somehow matter-of-fact mist—what could be further removed from the crisp charm, the sapphire occasion and rosy contingency of my Riviera romance? A couple of semitropical beaches on the Gulf, though bright enough, were starred and spattered by venomous beasties and swept by hurricane winds. Finally, on a Californian beach, facing the phantom of the Pacific, I hit upon some rather perverse privacy in a kind of cave whence you could hear the shrieks of a lot of girl scouts taking their first surf bath on a separate part of the beach, behind rotting trees; but the fog was like a wet blanket, and the sand was gritty and clammy, and Lo was all gooseflesh and grit, and for the first time in my life I had as little desire for her as for a manatee. Perhaps, my learned readers may perk up if I tell them that even had we discovered a piece of sympathetic seaside somewhere, it would have come too late, since my real liberation had occurred much earlier: at the moment, in point of fact, when Annabel Haze, alias Dolores Lee, alias Loleeta, had appeared to me, golden and brown, kneeling, looking up, on that shoddy veranda, in a kind of fictitious, dishonest, but eminently satisfactory seaside arrangement (although there was nothing but a second-rate lake in the neighborhood).

So much for those special sensations, influenced, if not actually brought about, by the tenets of modern psychiatry. Consequently, I turned away—I headed my Lolita away—from beaches which were either too bleak when lone, or too populous when ablaze. However, in recollection, I suppose, of my hopeless hauntings of public parks in Europe, I was still keenly interested in outdoor activities and desirous of finding suitable playgrounds in the open where I had suffered such shameful privations. Here, too, I was to be thwarted. The disappointment I must now register (as I gently grade my story into an expression of the continuous risk and dread that ran through my bliss) should in no wise reflect on the lyrical, epic, tragic but never Arcadian American wilds. They are beautiful, heart-rendingly beautiful, those wilds, with a quality of wide-eyed, unsung, innocent surrender that my lacquered, toy-bright Swiss villages and exhaustively lauded Alps no longer possess. Innumerable lovers have clipped and kissed on the trim turf of old-world mountainsides, on the innerspring moss, by a handy, hygienic rill, on rustic benches under the initialed oaks, and in so many *cabanes* in so many beech forests. But in the Wilds of America the open-air lover will not find it easy to indulge in the most ancient of all crimes and pastimes. Poisonous plants burn his sweetheart's buttocks, nameless insects sting his; sharp items of the forest floor prick his knees, insects hers; and all around there abides a sustained rustle of potential snakes—*que dis-je*, of semi-extinct dragons!—while the crablike seeds of ferocious flowers cling, in a hideous green crust, to gartered black sock and sloppy white sock alike.

I am exaggerating a little. One summer noon, just below timberline, where heavenly-hued blossoms that I would fain call larkspur crowded all along a purly mountain brook, we did find, Lolita and I, a secluded romantic spot, a hundred feet or so above the pass where we had left our car. The slope seemed untrodden. A last panting pine was taking a well-earned breather on the rock it had reached. A marmot whistled at us and withdrew. Beneath the lap-robe I had spread for Lo, dry flowers crepitated softly. Venus came and went. The jagged cliff crowning the upper talus and a tangle of shrubs growing below us seemed to offer us protection from sun and man alike. Alas, I had not reckoned with a faint side trail that curled up in cagey fashion among the shrubs and rocks a few feet from us.

It was then that we came closer to detection than ever before, and no wonder the experience curbed forever my yearning for rural amours.

I remember the operation was over, all over, and she was weeping in my arms;—a salutory storm of sobs after one of the fits of moodiness that had become so frequent with her in the course of that otherwise admirable year! I had just retracted some silly promise she had forced me to make in a moment of blind impatient passion, and there she was sprawling and sobbing, and pinching my caressing hand, and I was laughing happily, and the atrocious, unbelievable, unbearable, and, I suspect, eternal horror that I know *now* was still but a dot of blackness in the blue of my bliss; and so we lay, when with one of those jolts that have ended by knocking my poor heart out of its groove, I met the unblinking dark eyes of two strange and beautiful children, faunlet and nymphet, whom their identical flat dark hair and bloodless cheeks proclaimed siblings if not twins. They stood crouching and gaping at us, both in blue play-suits, blending with the mountain blossoms. I plucked at the lap-robe for desperate concealment—and within the same instant, something that looked like a polka-dotted pushball among the undergrowth a few paces away, went into a turning motion which was transformed into the gradually rising figure of a stout lady with a raven-black bob, who automatically added a wild lily to her bouquet, while staring over her shoulder at us from behind her lovely carved bluestone children.

Now that I have an altogether different mess on my conscience, I know that I am a courageous man, but in those days I was not aware of it, and I remember being surprised by my own coolness. With the quiet murmured order one gives a sweat-stained distracted cringing trained animal even in the worst of plights (what mad hope or hate makes the young beast's flanks pulsate, what black stars pierce the heart of the tamer!), I made Lo get up, and we decorously walked, and then indecorously scuttled down to the car. Behind it a nifty station wagon was parked, and a handsome Assyrian with a little blue-black beard, *un monsieur très bien*, in silk shirt and magenta slacks, presumably the corpulent botanist's husband, was gravely taking the picture of a signboard giving the altitude of the pass. It was well over 10,000 feet and I was quite out of breath; and with a scrunch and a skid we drove off, Lo still struggling with her clothes and swearing at me in language that I never dreamed little girls could know, let alone use.

There were other unpleasant incidents. There was the movie theatre once, for example. Lo at the time still had for the cinema a veritable passion (it was to decline into tepid condescension during her second high school year). We took in, voluptuously and indiscriminately, oh, I don't know, one hundred and fifty or two hundred programs during that one year, and during some of the denser periods of movie-going we saw many of the news-reels up to half-a-dozen times since the same weekly one went with different main pictures and pursued us from town to town. Her favorite kinds were, in this order: musicals, underworlders, westerners. In the first, real singers and dancers had unreal stage careers in an essentially grief-proof sphere of existence where-from death and truth were banned, and where, at the end, white-haired, dewy-eyed, technically deathless, the initially reluctant father of a show-crazy girl always finished by applauding her apotheosis on fabulous Broadway. The underworld was a world apart: there, heroic newspapermen were tortured, telephone bills ran to billions, and, in a robust atmosphere of incompetent marksmanship, villains were chased through sewers and store-houses by pathologically fearless cops (I was to give them less exercise). Finally there was the mahogany landscape, the florid-faced, blue-eyed roughriders, the prim pretty schoolteacher arriving in Roaring Gulch, the rearing horse, the spectacular stampede, the pistol thrust through the shivered windowpane, the stupendous fist fight, the crashing mountain of dusty old-fashioned furniture, the table used as a weapon, the timely somersault, the pinned hand still groping for the dropped bowie knife, the grunt, the sweet crash of fist against chin, the kick in the belly, the flying tackle; and immediately after a plethora of pain that would have hospitalized a Hercules (I should know by now), nothing to show but the rather becoming bruise on the

1

bronzed cheek of the warmed-up hero embracing his gorgeous frontier bride. I remember one matinee in a small airless theatre crammed with children and reeking with the hot breath of popcorn. The moon was yellow above the neckerchiefed crooner, and his finger was on his strumstring, and his foot was on a pine log, and I had innocently encircled Lo's shoulder and approached my jawbone to her temple, when two harpies behind us started muttering the queerest things—I do not know if I understood aright, but what I thought I did, made me withdraw my gentle hand, and of course the rest of the show was fog to me. 1

2

Another jolt I remember is connected with a little burg we were traversing at night, during our return journey. Some twenty miles earlier I had happened to tell her that the day school she would attend at Beardsley was a rather high-class, non-coeducational one, with no modern nonsense, whereupon Lo treated me to one of those furious harangues of hers where entreaty and insult, self-assertion and double talk, vicious vulgarity and childish despair, were interwoven in an exasperating semblance of logic which prompted a semblance of explanation from me. Enmeshed in her wild words (swell chance . . . I'd be a sap if I took your opinion seriously . . . Stinker . . . You can't boss me . . . I despise you . . . and so forth), I drove through the slumbering town at a fifty-mile-per-hour pace in continuance of my smooth highway swoosh, and a twosome of patrolmen put their spotlight on the car, and told me to pull over. I shushed Lo who was automatically raving on. The men peered at her and me with malevolent curiosity. Suddenly all dimples, she beamed sweetly at them, as she never did at my orchideous masculinity; for, in a 3 sense, my Lo was even more scared of the law than I—and when the kind officers pardoned us and servilely we crawled on, her eyelids closed and fluttered as she mimicked limp prostration.

At this point I have a curious confession to make. You will laugh—but really and truly I somehow never managed to find out quite exactly what the legal situation was. I do not know it yet. Oh, I have learned a few odds and ends. Alabama prohibits a guardian from changing the ward's residence without an order of the court; Minnesota, to whom I take off my hat, provides that when a relative assumes permanent care and custody of any child under fourteen, the authority of a court does not come into play. Query: is the stepfather of a gaspingly adorable pubescent pet, a stepfather of only one month's standing, a neurotic widower of mature years and small but independent means, with the parapets of Europe, a divorce and a few madhouses behind him, is he to be considered a relative, and thus a natural guardian? And if not, must I, and could I reasonably dare notify some Welfare Board and file a petition (how do you file a petition?), and have a court's agent investigate meek, fishy me and dangerous Dolores Haze? The many books on marriage, rape, adoption and so on, that I guiltily consulted at the public libraries of big and small towns, told me nothing beyond darkly insinuating that the state is the super-guardian of minor children. Pilvin and Zapel, if I remember their names right, in an impressive volume on the legal side of marriage, completely ignored stepfathers with motherless girls on their hands and knees. My best friend, a social service monograph (Chicago, 1936), which was dug out for me at great pains from a dusty storage recess by an innocent old spinster, said "There is no principle that every minor must have a guardian; the court is passive and enters the fray only when the child's situation becomes conspicuously perilous." A guardian, I concluded, was appointed only when he expressed his solemn and formal desire; but months might elapse before he was given notice to appear at a hearing and grow his pair of gray wings, and in the meantime the fair daemon child was legally left to her own devices which, after all, was the case of Dolores Haze. Then came the hearing. A few questions from the bench, a few reassuring answers from the attorney, a smile, a nod, a light drizzle outside, and the appointment was made. And still I dared not. Keep away, be a mouse, curl up in your hole. Courts became extravagantly active only when there was some monetary question involved: two greedy guardians, a robbed orphan, a third, still greedier, party. But here all was in perfect order, an inventory had been made, and her mother's small property was waiting untouched for Dolores Haze to grow up. The best policy seemed to be to refrain from any application. Or would some busybody, some Humane Society, butt in if I kept *too* quiet?

Friend Farlow, who was a lawyer of sorts and ought to have been able to give me some solid advice, was too much occupied with Jean's cancer to do anything more than what he had promised—namely, to look after Charlotte's meager estate while I recovered very gradually from the shock of her death. I had conditioned him into believing Dolores was my natural child, and so could not expect him to bother his head about the situation. I am, as the reader must have gathered by now, a poor businessman; but neither ignorance nor indolence should have prevented me from seeking professional advice elsewhere. What stopped me was the awful feeling that if I meddled with fate in any way and tried to rationalize her fantastic gift, that gift would be snatched away like that palace on the mountain top in the Oriental tale which vanished whenever a prospective owner 1
asked its custodian how come a strip of sunset sky was clearly visible from afar between black rock and foundation.

I decided that at Beardsley (the site of Beardsley College for 2
Women) I would have access to works of reference that I had not yet been able to study, such as Woerner's Treatise "On the American Law of Guardianship" and certain United States 3
Children's Bureau Publications. I also decided that anything was better for Lo than the demoralizing idleness in which she lived. I could persuade her to do so many things—their list might stupefy a professional educator; but no matter how I pleaded or stormed, I could never make her read any other book than the so-called comic books or stories in magazines for American females. Any literature a peg higher smacked to her of school, and though theoretically willing to enjoy *A Girl of the Limberlost* or the *Arabian Nights*, or *Little Women*, she was quite sure 4
she would not fritter away her "vacation" on such highbrow reading matter.

I now think it was a great mistake to move east again and have her go to that private school in Beardsley, instead of somehow scrambling across the Mexican border while the scrambling was good so as to lie low for a couple of years in subtropical bliss

until I could safely marry my little Creole for I must confess
that depending on the condition of my glands and ganglia, I
could switch in the course of the same day from one pole of
insanity to the other—from the thought that around 1950 I
would have to get rid somehow of a difficult adolescent whose
magic nymphage had evaporated—to the thought that with patience and luck I might have her produce eventually a nymphet
with my blood in her exquisite veins, a Lolita the Second, who
would be eight or nine around 1960, when I would still be *dans
la force de l'âge;* indeed, the telescopy of my mind, or un-mind,
was strong enough to distinguish in the remoteness of time a
vieillard encore vert—or was it green rot?—bizarre, tender, sali-
vating Dr. Humbert, practicing on supremely lovely Lolita the
Third the art of being a granddad.

In the days of that wild journey of ours, I doubted not that as
father to Lolita the First I was a ridiculous failure. I did my best;
I read and reread a book with the unintentionally biblical title
Know Your Own Daughter, which I got at the same store where
I bought Lo, for her thirteenth birthday, a de luxe volume with
commercially "beautiful" illustrations, of Andersen's *The Little
Mermaid.* But even at our very best moments, when we sat
reading on a rainy day (Lo's glance skipping from the window
to her wrist watch and back again), or had a quiet hearty meal
in a crowded diner, or played a childish game of cards, or went
shopping, or silently stared, with other motorists and their
children, at some smashed, blood-bespattered car with a young
woman's shoe in the ditch (Lo, as we drove on: "That was the
exact type of moccasin I was trying to describe to that jerk in
the store"); on all those random occasions, I seemed to myself
as implausible a father as she seemed to be a daughter. Was,
perhaps, guilty locomotion instrumental in vitiating our powers
of impersonation? Would improvement be forthcoming with a
fixed domicile and a routine schoolgirl's day?

In my choice of Beardsley I was guided not only by the fact
of there being a comparatively sedate school for girls located
there, but also by the presence of the women's college. In my
desire to get myself *casé,* to attach myself somehow to some

patterned surface which my stripes would blend with, I thought of a man I knew in the department of French at Beardsley College; he was good enough to use my textbook in his classes and had attempted to get me over once to deliver a lecture. I had no intention of doing so, since, as I have once remarked in the course of these confessions, there are few physiques I loathe more than the heavy low-slung pelvis, thick calves and deplorable complexion of the average coed (in whom I see, maybe, the coffin of coarse female flesh within which my nymphets are buried alive); but I did crave for a label, a background, and a simulacrum, and, as presently will become clear, there was a reason, a rather zany reason, why old Gaston Godin's company would be particularly safe.

Finally, there was the money question. My income was cracking under the strain of our joy-ride. True, I clung to the cheaper motor courts; but every now and then, there would be a loud hotel de luxe, or a pretentious dude ranch, to mutilate our budget; staggering sums, moreover, were expended on sightseeing and Lo's clothes, and the old Haze bus, although a still vigorous and very devoted machine, necessitated numerous minor and major repairs. In one of our strip maps that has happened to survive among the papers which the authorities have so kindly allowed me to use for the purpose of writing my statement, I find some jottings that help me compute the following. During that extravagant year 1947–1948, August to August, lodgings and food cost us around 5,500 dollars; gas, oil and repairs, 1,234, and various extras almost as much; so that during about 150 days of actual motion (we covered about 27,000 miles!) plus some 200 days of interpolated standstills, this modest *rentier* spent around 8,000 dollars, or better say 10,000 because, unpractical as I am, I have surely forgotten a number of items.

And so we rolled East, I more devastated than braced with the satisfaction of my passion, and she glowing with health, her bi-iliac garland still as brief as a lad's, although she had added two inches to her stature and eight pounds to her weight. We had been everywhere. We had really seen nothing. And I catch myself thinking today that our long journey had only defiled with a sinuous trail of slime the lovely, trustful, dreamy, enormous country that by then, in retrospect, was no more to us than a collection of dog-eared maps, ruined tour books, old tires, and her sobs in the night—every night, every night—the moment I feigned sleep.

4

When, through decorations of light and shade, we drove up to 14 Thayer Street, a grave little lad met us with the keys and a note from Gaston who had rented the house for us. My Lo, without granting her new surroundings one glance, unseeingly turned on the radio to which instinct led her and lay down on the living room sofa with a batch of old magazines which in the same precise and blind manner she landed by dipping her hand into the nether anatomy of a lamp table.

I really did not mind where to dwell provided I could lock my Lolita up somewhere; but I had, I suppose, in the course of my correspondence with vague Gaston, vaguely visualized a house of ivied brick. Actually the place bore a dejected resemblance to the Haze home (a mere 400 miles distant): it was the same sort of dull gray frame affair with a shingled roof and dull green drill awnings; and the rooms, though smaller and furnished in a more consistent plush-and-plate style, were arranged in much the same order. My study turned out to be, however, a much larger room, lined from floor to ceiling with some two thousand books on chemistry which my landlord (on sabbatical leave for the time being) taught at Beardsley College.

I had hoped Beardsley School for girls, an expensive day school, with lunch thrown in and a glamorous gymnasium, would, while cultivating all those young bodies, provide some formal education for their minds as well. Gaston Godin, who was seldom right in his judgment of American habitus, had warned me that the institution might turn out to be one of those where girls are taught, as he put it with a foreigner's love for such things: "not to spell very well, but to smell very well." I don't think they achieved even that.

At my first interview with headmistress Pratt, she approved of my child's "nice blue eyes" (blue! Lolita!) and of my own friendship with that "French genius" (a genius! Gaston!)—and then, having turned Dolly over to a Miss Cormorant, she wrinkled her brow in a kind of *recueillement* and said:

"We are not so much concerned, Mr. Humbird, with having our students become bookworms or be able to reel off all the capitals of Europe which nobody knows anyway, or learn by heart the dates of forgotten battles. What we are concerned with is the adjustment of the child to group life. This is why we stress the four D's: Dramatics, Dance, Debating and Dating. We are confronted by certain facts. Your delightful Dolly will presently enter an age group where dates, dating, date dress, date book, date etiquette, mean as much to her as, say, business, business connections, business success, mean to you, or as much as [smiling] the happiness of my girls means to me. Dorothy Humbird is already involved in a whole system of social life which consists, whether we like it or not, of hot-dog stands, corner drugstores, malts and cokes, movies, square-dancing, blanket parties on beaches, and even hair-fixing parties! Naturally at Beardsley School we disapprove of some of these activities; and we rechannel others into more constructive directions. But we do try to turn our backs on the fog and squarely face the sunshine. To put it briefly, while adopting certain teaching techniques, we are more interested in communication than in composition. That is, with due respect to Shakespeare and others, we want our girls to *communicate* freely with the live world around them rather than plunge into musty old books. We are still groping perhaps, but we grope intelligently, like a gynecologist feeling a tumor. We think, Dr. Humburg, in organismal and organizational terms. We have done away with the mass of irrelevant topics that have traditionally been presented to young girls, leaving no place, in former days, for the knowledges and the skills, and the attitudes they will need in managing their lives and—as the cynic might add—the lives of their husbands. Mr. Humberson, let us put it this way: the position of a star is important, but the most practical spot for an icebox in the kitchen may be even more important to the budding housewife. You say that all you expect a child to obtain from school is a sound education. But what do we mean by education? In the old days it was in the main a verbal phenomenon; I mean, you could have a child learn by heart a good encyclopedia and he or she would know as much as or more than a school could offer. Dr. Hummer, do you realize that for the modern pre-adolescent child, medieval dates are of less vital value than weekend ones [twinkle]?—to repeat a pun that I heard the Beardsley college psychoanalyst permit herself the other day. We live not only in a world of thoughts, but also in a world of things. Words without experience are meaningless. What on earth can Dorothy Hummerson care for Greece and the Orient with their harems and slaves?"

This program rather appalled me, but I spoke to two intelligent ladies who had been connected with the school, and they affirmed that the girls did quite a bit of sound reading and that the "communication" line was more or less ballyhoo aimed at giving old-fashioned Beardsley School a financially remunerative modern touch, though actually it remained as prim as a prawn.

Another reason attracting me to that particular school may seem funny to some readers, but it was very important to me, for that is the way I am made. Across our street, exactly in front of our house, there was, I noticed, a gap of weedy wasteland, with some colorful bushes and a pile of bricks and a few scattered planks, and the foam of shabby mauve and chrome autumn roadside flowers; and through that gap you could see a shimmery section of School Rd., running parallel to our Thayer St., and immediately beyond that, the playground of the school. Apart from the psychological comfort this general arrangement should afford me by keeping Dolly's day adjacent to mine, I immediately foresaw the pleasure I would have in distinguishing from my study-bedroom, by means of powerful binoculars, the statistically inevitable percentage of nymphets among the other girl-children playing around Dolly during recess; unfortunately, on the very first day of school, workmen arrived and put up a fence some way down the gap, and in no time a construction of tawny wood maliciously arose beyond that fence utterly blocking my magic vista; and as soon as they had erected a sufficient amount of material to spoil everything, those absurd builders suspended their work and never appeared again.

5

In a street called Thayer Street, in the residential green, fawn, and golden of a mellow academic townlet, one was bound to have a few amiable fine-dayers yelping at you. I prided myself on the exact temperature of my relations with them: never rude, always aloof. My west-door neighbor, who might have been a businessman or a college teacher, or both, would speak to me once in a while as he barbered some late garden blooms or watered his car, or, at a later date, defrosted his driveway (I don't mind if these verbs are all wrong), but my brief grunts, just sufficiently articulate to sound like conventional assents or interrogative pause-fillers, precluded any evolution toward chumminess. Of the two houses flanking the bit of scrubby waste opposite, one was closed, and the other contained two professors of English, tweedy and short-haired Miss Lester and fadedly feminine Miss Fabian, whose only subject of brief sidewalk conversation with me was (God bless their tact!) the young loveliness of my daughter and the naïve charm of Gaston Godin. My east-door neighbor was by far the most dangerous one, a sharp-nosed character whose late brother had been attached to the College as Superintendent of Buildings and Grounds. I remember her waylaying Dolly, while I stood at the living-room window, feverishly awaiting my darling's return from

school. The odious spinster, trying to conceal her morbid in-
quisitiveness under a mask of dulcet goodwill, stood leaning
on her slim umbrella (the sleet had just stopped, a cold wet sun
had sidled out), and Dolly, her brown coat open despite the
raw weather, her structural heap of books pressed against her
stomach, her knees showing pink above her clumsy wellingtons,
a sheepish frightened little smile flitting over and off her snub-
nosed face, which—owing perhaps to the pale wintry light—
looked almost plain, in a rustic, German, *Mägdlein*-like way,
as she stood there and dealt with Miss East's questions "And
where is your mother, my dear? And what is your poor father's
occupation? And where did you live before?" Another time the
loathsome creature accosted me with a welcoming whine—but I
evaded her; and a few days later there came from her a note in
a blue-margined envelope, a nice mixture of poison and treacle,
suggesting Dolly come over on a Sunday and curl up in a chair to
look through the "loads of beautiful books my dear mother gave
me when I was a child, instead of having the radio on at full
blast till all hours of the night."

I had also to be careful in regard to a Mrs. Holigan, a charwoman and cook of sorts whom I had inherited with the vacuum
cleaner from the previous tenants. Dolly got lunch at school,
so that this was no trouble, and I had become adept at providing her with a big breakfast and warming up the dinner that
Mrs. Holigan prepared before leaving. That kindly and harmless woman had, thank God, a rather bleary eye that missed
details, and I had become a great expert in bedmaking; but still
I was continuously obsessed by the feeling that some fatal stain
had been left somewhere, or that, on the rare occasions where
Holigan's presence happened to coincide with Lo's, simple Lo
might succumb to buxom sympathy in the course of a cozy
kitchen chat. I often felt we lived in a lighted house of glass,
and that any moment some thin-lipped parchment face would
peer through a carelessly unshaded window to obtain a free
glimpse of things that the most jaded *voyeur* would have paid a
small fortune to watch.

6

A word about Gaston Godin. The main reason why I enjoyed
—or at least tolerated with relief—his company was the spell of
absolute security that his. ample person cast on my secret. Not
that he knew it; I had no special reason to confide in him, and
he was much too self-centered and abstract to notice or suspect
anything that might lead to a frank question on his part and a
frank answer on mine. He spoke well of me to Beardsleyans,
he was my good herald. Had he discovered *mes goûts* and
Lolita's status, it would have interested him only insofar as
throwing some light on the simplicity of my attitude toward
him, which attitude was as free of polite strain as it was of
ribald allusions; for despite his colorless mind and dim memory,
he was perhaps aware that I knew more about him than the
burghers of Beardsley did. He was a flabby, dough-faced, melancholy bachelor tapering upward to a pair of narrow, not quite
level shoulders and a conical pear-head which had sleek black
hair on one side and only a few plastered wisps on the other.
But the lower part of his body was enormous, and he ambulated
with a curious elephantine stealth by means of phenomenally
stout legs. He always wore black, even his tie was black; he
seldom bathed; his English was a burlesque. And, nonetheless,
everybody considered him to be a supremely lovable, lovably
freakish fellow! Neighbors pampered him; he knew by name
all the small boys in our vicinity (he lived a few blocks away
from me) and had some of them clean his sidewalk and burn
leaves in his back yard, and bring wood from his shed, and
even perform simple chores about the house, and he would
feed them fancy chocolates, with *real* liqueurs inside—in the
privacy of an orientally furnished den in his basement, with
amusing daggers and pistols arrayed on the moldy, rug-adorned
walls among the camouflaged hot-water pipes. Upstairs he had
a studio—he painted a little, the old fraud. He had decorated its
sloping wall (it was really not more than a garret) with large
photographs of pensive André Gide, Tchaïkovsky, Norman
Douglas, two other well-known English writers, Nijinsky (all

thighs and fig leaves), Harold D. Doublename (a misty-eyed left-wing professor at a Midwestern university) and Marcel Proust. All these poor people seemed about to fall on you from their inclined plane. He had also an album with snapshots of all the Jackies and Dickies of the neighborhood, and when I happened to thumb through it and make some casual remark, Gaston would purse his fat lips and murmur with a wistful pout

1 *"Oui, ils sont gentils."* His brown eyes would roam around the various sentimental and artistic bric-a-brac present, and his own

2 banal *toiles* (the conventionally primitive eyes, sliced guitars, blue nipples and geometrical designs of the day), and with a vague gesture toward a painted wooden bowl or veined vase, he would say *"Prenez donc une de ces poires. La bonne dame d'en face*

3 *m'en offre plus que je n'en peux savourer."* Or: *"Missise Taille*

4 *Lore vient de me donner ces dahlias, belles fleurs que j'exècre."* (Somber, sad, full of world-weariness.)

For obvious reasons, I preferred my house to his for the games of chess we had two or three times weekly. He looked like some old battered idol as he sat with his pudgy hands in his lap and stared at the board as if it were a corpse. Wheezing he would meditate for ten minutes—then make a losing move. Or the

5 good man, after even more thought, might utter: *Au roi!* with a slow old-dog woof that had a gargling sound at the back of it which made his jowls wabble; and then he would lift his circumflex eyebrows with a deep sigh as I pointed out to him that he was in check himself.

Sometimes, from where we sat in my cold study I could hear Lo's bare feet practicing dance techniques in the living room downstairs; but Gaston's outgoing senses were comfortably dulled, and he remained unaware of those naked rhythms— and-one, and-two, and-one, and-two, weight transferred on a straight right leg, leg up and out to the side, and-one, and-two, and only when she started jumping, opening her legs at the height of the jump, and flexing one leg, and extending the other, and flying, and landing on her toes—only then did my pale, pompous, morose opponent rub his head or cheek as if confusing those distant thuds with the awful stabs of my formidable Queen.

Sometimes Lola would slouch in while we pondered the board —and it was every time a treat to see Gaston, his elephant eye still fixed on his pieces, ceremoniously rise to shake hands with her, and forthwith release her limp fingers, and without looking once at her, descend again into his chair to topple into the trap I had laid for him. One day around Christmas, after I had not seen him for a fortnight or so, he asked me *"Et toutes vos fillettes, elles vont bien?"* from which it became evident to me that he had multiplied my unique Lolita by the number of sartorial categories his downcast moody eye had glimpsed during a whole series of her appearances: blue jeans, a skirt, shorts, a quilted robe.

I am loath to dwell so long on the poor fellow (sadly enough, a year later, during a voyage to Europe, from which he did not return, he got involved in a *sale histoire*, in Naples of all places!). I would have hardly alluded to him at all had not his Beardsley existence had such a queer bearing on my case. I need him for my defense. There he was, devoid of any talent whatsoever, a mediocre teacher, a worthless scholar, a glum repulsive fat old invert, highly contemptuous of the American way of life, triumphantly ignorant of the English language—there he was in priggish New England, crooned over by the old and caressed by the young—oh, having a grand time and fooling everybody; and here was I.

7

I am now faced with the distasteful task of recording a definite drop in Lolita's morals. If her share in the ardors she kindled had never amounted to much, neither had pure lucre ever come to the fore. But I was weak, I was not wise, my school-girl nymphet had me in thrall. With the human element dwindling, the passion, the tenderness, and the torture only increased; and of this she took advantage.

Her weekly allowance, paid to her under condition she fulfill her basic obligations, was twenty-one cents at the start of the

Beardsley era—and went up to one dollar five before its end. This was a more than generous arrangement seeing she constantly received from me all kinds of small presents and had for the asking any sweetmeat or movie under the moon—although, of course, I might fondly demand an additional kiss, or even a whole collection of assorted caresses, when I knew she coveted very badly some item of juvenile amusement. She was, however, not easy to deal with. Only very listlessly did she earn her three pennies—or three nickels—per day; and she proved to be a cruel negotiator whenever it was in her power to deny me certain life-wrecking, strange, slow paradisal philters without which I could not live more than a few days in a row, and which, because of the very nature of love's languor, I could not obtain by force. Knowing the magic and might of her own soft mouth, she managed—during one schoolyear!—to raise the bonus price of a fancy embrace to three, and even four bucks. O Reader! Laugh not, as you imagine me, on the very rack of joy noisily emitting dimes and quarters, and great big silver dollars like some sonorous, jingly and wholly demented machine vomiting riches; and in the margin of that leaping epilepsy she would firmly clutch a handful of coins in her little fist, which, anyway, I used to pry open afterwards unless she gave me the slip, scrambling away to hide her loot. And just as every other day I would cruise all around the school area and on comatose feet visit drugstores, and peer into foggy lanes, and listen to receding girl laughter in between my heart throbs and the falling leaves, so every now and then I would burgle her room and scrutinize torn papers in the wastebasket with the painted roses, and look under the pillow of the virginal bed I had just made myself. Once I found eight one-dollar notes in one of her books (fittingly—*Treasure Island*), and once a hole in the wall behind Whistler's Mother yielded as much as twenty-four dollars and some change—say twenty-four sixty—which I quietly removed, upon which, next day, she accused, to my face, honest Mrs. Holigan of being a filthy thief. Eventually, she lived up to her I.Q. by finding a safer hoarding place which I never discovered; but by that time I had brought prices down drastically by having her earn the hard and nauseous way permission to participate in the school's theatrical program; because what I feared most was not that she might ruin me, but that she might accumulate sufficient cash to run away. I believe the poor fierce-eyed child had figured out that with a mere fifty dollars in her purse she might somehow reach Broadway or Hollywood—or the foul kitchen of a diner (Help Wanted) in a dismal ex-prairie state, with the wind blowing, and the stars blinking, and the cars, and the bars, and the barmen, and everything soiled, torn, dead.

1

8

I did my best, your Honor, to tackle the problem of boys. Oh, I used even to read in the Beardsley *Star* a so-called Column for Teens, to find out how to behave!

2

A word to fathers. Don't frighten away daughter's friend. Maybe it is a bit hard for you to realize that now the boys are finding her attractive. To you she is still a little girl. To the boys she's charming and fun, lovely and gay. They like her. Today you clinch big deals in an executive's office, but yesterday you were just highschool Jim carrying Jane's school books. Remember? Don't you want your daughter, now that her turn has come, to be happy in the admiration and company of boys she likes? Don't you want them to have wholesome fun together?

Wholesome fun? Good Lord!

Why not treat the young fellows as guests in your house? Why not make conversation with them? Draw them out, make them laugh and feel at ease?

Welcome, fellow, to this bordello.

If she breaks the rules don't explode out loud in front of her partner in crime. Let her take the brunt of your displeasure in private. And stop making the boys feel she's the daughter of an old ogre.

First of all the old ogre drew up a list under "absolutely for-bidden" and another under "reluctantly allowed." Absolutely forbidden were dates, single or double or triple—the next step being of course mass orgy. She might visit a candy bar with her girl friends, and there giggle-chat with occasional young males, while I waited in the car at a discreet distance; and I promised her that if her group were invited by a socially acceptable group in Butler's Academy for Boys for their annual ball (heavily chaperoned, of course), I might consider the question whether a girl of fourteen can don her first "formal" (a kind of gown that makes thin-armed teen-agers look like flamingoes). Moreover, I promised her to throw a party at our house to which she would be allowed to invite her prettier girl friends and the nicer boys she would have met by that time at the Butler dance. But I was quite positive that as long as my regime lasted she would never, never be permitted to go with a youngster in rut to a movie, or neck in a car, or go to boy-girl parties at the houses of schoolmates, or indulge out of my earshot in boy-girl telephone conversations, even if "only discussing his relations with a friend of mine."

Lo was enraged by all this—called me a lousy crook and worse—and I would probably have lost my temper had I not soon discovered, to my sweetest relief, that what really angered her was my depriving her not of a specific satisfaction but of a general right. I was impinging, you see, on the conventional program, the stock pastimes, the "things that are done," the routine of youth; for there is nothing more conservative than a child, especially a girl-child, be she the most auburn and russet, the most mythopoeic nymphet in October's orchard-haze.

Do not misunderstand me. I cannot be absolutely certain that in the course of the winter she did not manage to have, in a casual way, improper contacts with unknown young fellows; of course, no matter how closely I controlled her leisure, there would constantly occur unaccounted-for time leaks with over-elaborate explanations to stop them up in retrospect; of course, my jealousy would constantly catch its jagged claw in the fine fabrics of nymphet falsity; but I did definitely feel—and can now vouchsafe for the accuracy of my feeling—that there was no reason for serious alarm. I felt that way not because I never once discovered any palpable hard young throat to crush among the masculine mutes that flickered somewhere in the background; but because it was to me "overwhelmingly obvious" (a favorite expression with my aunt Sybil) that all varieties of high school boys—from the perspiring nincompoop whom "holding hands" thrills, to the self-sufficient rapist with pustules and a souped-up car—equally bored my sophisticated young mistress. "All this noise about boys gags me," she had scrawled on the inside of a schoolbook, and underneath, in Mona's hand (Mona is due any minute now), there was the sly quip: "What about Rigger?" 1 (due too).

Faceless, then, are the chappies I happened to see in her company. There was for instance Red Sweater who one day, the day we had the first snow—saw her home; from the parlor window I observed them talking near our porch. She wore her first cloth coat with a fur collar; there was a small brown cap on my favorite hairdo—the fringe in front and the swirl at the sides and the natural curls at the back—and her damp-dark moccasins and white socks were more sloppy than ever. She pressed as usual her books to her chest while speaking or listening, and her feet gestured all the time: she would stand on her left instep with her right toe, remove it backward, cross her feet, rock slightly, sketch a few steps, and then start the series all over again. There was Windbreaker who talked to her in front of a restaurant one Sunday afternoon while his mother and sister attempted to walk me away for a chat; I dragged along and looked back at my only love. She had developed more than one conventional mannerism, such as the polite adolescent way of showing one is literally "doubled up" with laughter by inclining one's head, and so (as she sensed my call), still feigning helpless merriment, she walked backward a couple of steps, and then faced about, and walked toward me with a fading smile. On the other hand, I greatly liked—perhaps because it reminded me of her first unforgettable confession—her trick of sighing "oh dear!" in humorous wistful submission to fate, or emitting a long "no-o" in a deep almost growling undertone when the blow of fate had actually fallen. Above all—since we are speaking of movement and youth—I liked to see her spinning up and down Thayer Street on her beautiful young bicycle: rising on the pedals to work on them lustily, then sinking back in a languid posture while the speed wore itself off; and then she would stop at our mailbox and, still astride, would flip through a magazine she found there, and put it back, and press her tongue to one side of her upperlip and push off with her foot, and again sprint through pale shade and sun.

On the whole she seemed to me better adapted to her surroundings than I had hoped she would be when considering my spoiled slave-child and the bangles of demeanor she naïvely affected the winter before in California. Although I could never get used to the constant state of anxiety in which the guilty, the great, the tenderhearted live, I felt I was doing my best in the way of mimicry. As I lay on my narrow studio bed after a session of adoration and despair in Lolita's cold bedroom, I used to review the concluded day by checking my own image as it prowled rather than passed before the mind's red eye. I watched dark-and-handsome, not un-Celtic, probably high-church, possibly very high-church, Dr. Humbert see his daughter off to school. I watched him greet with his slow smile and pleasantly arched thick black ad-eyebrows good Mrs. Holigan, who smelled of the plague (and would head, I knew, for master's gin at the first opportunity). With Mr. West, retired executioner or writer of religious tracts—who cared?—I saw neighbor what's his name, I think they are French or Swiss, meditate in his frank-windowed study over a typewriter, rather gaunt-profiled, an almost Hitlerian cowlick on his pale brow. Weekends, wearing a well-tailored overcoat and brown gloves, Professor H. might be seen with his daughter strolling to Walton Inn (famous for its violet-ribboned china bunnies and chocolate boxes among which you sit and wait for a "table for two" still filthy with your predecessor's crumbs). Seen on weekdays, around one P.M., saluting with dignity Argus-eyed East while maneuvering the car out of the garage and around the damned evergreens, and down onto the slippery road. Raising a cold eye from book to clock in the positively sultry Beardsley College library, among bulky young women caught and petrified in the overflow of human knowledge. Walking across the campus with the college clergyman, the Rev. Rigger (who also taught Bible in Beardsley School). "Somebody told me her mother was a celebrated actress killed in an airplane accident. Oh? My mistake, I presume. Is that so? I see. How sad." (Sublimating her mother, eh?) Slowly pushing my little pram through the labyrinth of the supermarket, in the wake of Professor W., also a slow-moving and gentle widower with the eyes of a goat. Shoveling the snow in my shirt-sleeves, a voluminous black and white muffler around my neck. Following with no show of rapacious haste (even taking time to wipe my feet on the mat) my schoolgirl daughter into the house. Taking Dolly to the dentist—pretty nurse beaming at her—old magazines—*ne montrez pas vos zhambes*. At dinner with Dolly in town, Mr. Edgar H. Humbert was seen eating his steak in the continental knife-and-fork manner. Enjoying, in duplicate, a concert: two marble-faced, becalmed Frenchmen sitting side by side, with Monsieur H. H.'s musical little girl on her father's right, and the musical little boy of Professor W. (father spending a hygienic evening in Providence) on Monsieur G. G.'s left. Opening the garage, a square of light that engulfs the car and is extinguished. Brightly pajamaed, jerking down the window shade in Dolly's bedroom. Saturday morning, unseen, solemnly weighing the winter-bleached lassie in the bathroom. Seen and heard Sunday morning, no churchgoer after all, saying don't be too late, to Dolly who is bound for the covered court. Letting in a queerly observant schoolmate of Dolly's: "First time I've seen a man wearing a smoking jacket, sir—except in movies, of course." 1

2, 3

4

9

Her girl friends, whom I had looked forward to meet, proved on the whole disappointing. There was Opal Something, and Linda Hall, and Avis Chapman, and Eva Rosen, and Mona Dahl 5

1   (save one, all these names are approximations, of course). Opal was a bashful, formless, bespectacled, bepimpled creature who doted on Dolly who bullied her. With Linda Hall the school tennis champion, Dolly played singles at least twice a week: I suspect Linda was a true nymphet, but for some unknown reason she did not come—was perhaps not allowed to come—to our house; so I recall her only as a flash of natural sunshine on an indoor court. Of the rest, none had any claims to nymphetry except Eva Rosen. Avis was a plump lateral child with hairy legs, while Mona, though handsome in a coarse sensual way and only a year older than my aging mistress, had obviously long ceased to be a nymphet, if she ever had been one. Eva Rosen, a displaced little person from France, was on the other hand a good example of a not strikingly beautiful child revealing to the perspicacious amateur some of the basic elements of nymphet charm, such as a perfect pubescent figure and lingering eyes and high cheek-bones. Her glossy copper hair had Lolita's silkiness, and the features of her delicate milky-white face with pink lips and silverfish eyelashes were less foxy than those of her likes—the great clan of intra-racial redheads; nor did she sport their green uniform but wore, as I remember her, a lot of black or cherry dark—a very smart black pullover, for instance, and high-heeled black shoes, and garnet-red fingernail polish. I spoke French to her (much to Lo's disgust). The child's tonalities were still admirably pure, but for school words and play words she resorted to current American and then a slight Brooklyn accent would crop up in her speech, which was amusing in a little Parisian who went to a select New England school with phoney British aspirations. Unfortunately, despite "that French kid's uncle" being "a millionaire," Lo dropped Eva for some reason before I had had time to enjoy in my modest way her fragrant presence in the Humbert open house. The reader knows what importance I attached to having a bevy of page girls, consolation prize nymphets, around my Lolita. For a while, I endeavored to interest my senses in Mona Dahl who was a good deal around, especially during the spring term when Lo and she got so enthusiastic about dramatics. I have often wondered what secrets outrageously treacherous

Dolores Haze had imparted to Mona while blurting out to me by urgent and well-paid request various really incredible details concerning an affair that Mona had had with a marine at the seaside. It was characteristic of Lo that she chose for her closest chum that elegant, cold, lascivious, experienced young female whom I once heard (misheard, Lo swore) cheerfully say in the hallway to Lo—who had remarked that her (Lo's) sweater was of virgin wool: "The only thing about you that is, kiddo..." She had a curiously husky voice, artificially waved dull dark hair, earrings, amber-brown prominent eyes and luscious lips. Lo said teachers had remonstrated with her on her loading herself with so much costume jewelry. Her hands trembled. She was burdened with a 150 I.Q. And I also know she had a tremendous chocolate-brown mole on her womanish back which I inspected the night Lo and she had worn low-cut pastel-colored, vaporous dresses for a dance at the Butler Academy.

I am anticipating a little, but I cannot help running my memory all over the keyboard of that school year. In meeting my attempts to find out what kind of boys Lo knew, Miss Dahl was elegantly evasive. Lo who had gone to play tennis at Linda's country club had telephoned she might be a full half hour late, and so, would I entertain Mona who was coming to practice with her a scene from *The Taming of the Shrew*. Using all the modulations, all the allure of manner and voice she was capable of and staring at me with perhaps—could I be mistaken?—a faint gleam of crystalline irony, beautiful Mona replied: "Well, sir, the fact is Dolly is not much concerned with mere boys. Fact is, we are rivals. She and I have a crush on the Reverend Rigger." (This was a joke—I have already mentioned that gloomy giant of a man, with the jaw of a horse: he was to bore me to near murder with his impressions of Switzerland at a tea party for parents that I am unable to place correctly in terms of time.)

How had the ball been? Oh, it had been a riot. A what? A panic. Terrific, in a word. Had Lo danced a lot? Oh, not a frightful lot, just as much as she could stand. What did she, languorous Mona, think of Lo? Sir? Did she think Lo was doing well at school? Gosh, she certainly was quite a kid. But her general behavior was—? Oh, she was a swell kid. But still? "Oh, she's a doll," concluded Mona, and sighed abruptly, and picked up a book that happened to lie at hand, and with a change of expression, falsely furrowing her brow, inquired: "Do tell me about Ball Zack, sir. Is he really that good?" She moved up so close to my chair that I made out through lotions and creams her uninteresting skin scent. A sudden odd thought stabbed me: was my Lo playing the pimp? If so, she had found the wrong substitute. Avoiding Mona's cool gaze, I talked literature for a minute. Then Dolly arrived—and slit her pale eyes at us. I left the two friends to their own devices. One of the latticed squares in a small cobwebby casement window at the turn of the staircase was glazed with ruby, and that raw wound among the unstained rectangles and its asymmetrical position—a knight's move from the top—always strangely disturbed me.

10

Sometimes ... Come on, how often exactly, Bert? Can you recall four, five, more such occasions? Or would no human heart have survived two or three? Sometimes (I have nothing to say in reply to your question), while Lolita would be haphazardly preparing her homework, sucking a pencil, lolling sideways in an easy chair with both legs over its arm, I would shed all my pedagogic restraint, dismiss all our quarrels, forget all my masculine pride—and literally crawl on my knees to your chair, my Lolita! You would give me one look—a gray furry question mark of a look: "Oh no, not again" (incredulity, exasperation); for you never deigned to believe that I could, without any specific designs, ever crave to bury my face in your plaid skirt, my darling! The fragility of those bare arms of yours—how I longed to enfold them, all your four limpid lovely limbs, a folded colt, and take your head between my unworthy hands, and pull the temple-skin back on both sides, and kiss your chinesed eyes, and— "Pulease, leave me alone, will you," you would say, "for Christ's sake leave me alone." And I would get up from the floor while you looked on, your face deliberately twitching in imitation of my *tic nerveux*. But never mind, never mind, I am only a brute, never mind, let us go on with my miserable story.

11

One Monday forenoon, in December I think, Pratt asked me to come over for a talk. Dolly's last report had been poor, I knew. But instead of contenting myself with some such plausible explanation of this summons, I imagined all sorts of horrors, and had to fortify myself with a pint of my "pin" before I could face the interview. Slowly, all Adam's apple and heart, I went up the steps of the scaffold.

A huge woman, gray-haired, frowsy, with a broad flat nose and small eyes behind black-rimmed glasses—"Sit down," she said, pointing to an informal and humiliating hassock, while she perched with ponderous spryness on the arm of an oak chair. For a moment or two, she peered at me with smiling curiosity. She had done it at our first meeting, I recalled, but I could afford then to scowl back. Her eye left me. She lapsed into thought—probably assumed. Making up her mind she rubbed, fold on fold, her dark gray flannel skirt at the knee, dispelling a trace of chalk or something. Then she said, still rubbing, not looking up:

"Let me ask a blunt question, Mr. Haze. You are an old-fashioned Continental father, aren't you?"

"Why, no," I said, "conservative, perhaps, but not what you would call old-fashioned."

She sighed, frowned, then clapped her big plump hands together in a let's-get-down-to-business manner, and again fixed her beady eyes upon me.

"Dolly Haze," she said, "is a lovely child, but the onset of sexual maturing seems to give her trouble."

I bowed slightly. What else could I do?

"She is still shuttling," said Miss Pratt, showing how with her liver-spotted hands, "between the anal and genital zones of development. Basically she is a lovely—"

"I beg your pardon," I said, "what zones?"

"That's the old-fashioned European in you!" cried Pratt delivering a slight tap on my wrist watch and suddenly disclosing her dentures. "All I mean is that biologic and psychologic drives —do you smoke?—are not fused in Dolly, do not fall so to speak into a—into a rounded pattern." Her hands held for a moment an invisible melon.

"She is attractive, bright though careless" (breathing heavily, without leaving her perch, the woman took time out to look at the lovely child's report sheet on the desk at her right). "Her marks are getting worse and worse. Now I wonder, Mr. Haze—" Again the false meditation.

"Well," she went on with zest, "as for me, I do smoke, and, as dear Dr. Pierce used to say: I'm not proud of it but I jeest love it." She lit up and the smoke she exhaled from her nostrils was like a pair of tusks.

"Let me give you a few details, it won't take a moment. Now let me see [rummaging among her papers]. She is defiant toward Miss Redcock and impossibly rude to Miss Cormorant. Now here is one of our special research reports: Enjoys singing with group in class though mind seems to wander. Crosses her knees and wags left leg to rhythm. Type of by-words: a two-hundred-forty-two word area of the commonest pubescent slang fenced in by a number of obviously European polysyllabics. Sighs a good deal in class. Let me see. Yes. Now comes the last week in November. Sighs a good deal in class. Chews gum vehemently. Does not bite her nails though if she did, this would conform better to her general pattern—scientifically speaking, of course. Menstruation, according to the subject, well established. Belongs at present to no church organization. By the way, Mr. Haze, her mother was—? Oh, I see. And you are—? Nobody's business is, I suppose, God's business. Something else we wanted to know. She has no regular home duties, I understand. Making a princess of your Dolly, Mr. Haze, eh? Well, what else have we got here? Handles books gracefully. Voice pleasant. Giggles rather often. A littly dreamy. Has private jokes of her own, transposing for instance the first letters of some of her teachers' names. Hair light and dark brown, lustrous—well [laughing] you are aware of *that*, I suppose. Nose unobstructed, feet high-arched, eyes—let me see, I had here somewhere a still more recent report. Aha, here we are. Miss Gold says Dolly's tennis form is excellent to superb, even better than Linda Hall's, but concentration and point-accumulation are just "poor to fair." Miss Cormorant cannot decide whether Dolly has exceptional emotional control or none at all. Miss Horn reports she—I mean, Dolly—cannot verbalize her emotions, while according to Miss Cole Dolly's metabolic efficiency is superfine. Miss Molar thinks Dolly is myopic and should see a good ophthalmologist, but Miss Redcock insists that the girl simulates eye-strain to get away with scholastic incompetence. And to conclude, Mr. Haze, our researchers are wondering about something really crucial. Now I want to ask you something. I want to know if your poor wife, or yourself, or anyone else in the family—I understand she has several aunts and a maternal grandfather in California?—oh, *had!*—I'm sorry—well, we all wonder if anybody in the family has instructed Dolly in the process of mammalian reproduction. The general impression is that fifteen-year-old Dolly remains morbidly uninterested in sexual matters, or to be exact, represses her curiosity in order to save her ignorance and self-dignity. All right—fourteen. You see, Mr. Haze, Beardsley School does not believe in bees and blossoms, and storks and love birds, but it does believe very strongly in preparing its students for mutually satisfactory mating and successful child rearing. We feel Dolly could make excellent progress if only she would put her mind to her work. Miss Cormorant's report is significant in that respect. Dolly is inclined to be, mildly speaking, impudent. But all feel that *primo*, you should have your family doctor tell her the facts of life and, *secundo*, that you allow her to enjoy the company of her schoolmates' brothers at the Junior Club or in Dr. Rigger's organization, or in the lovely homes of our parents."

"She may meet boys at her own lovely home," I said.

"I hope she will," said Pratt buoyantly. "'When we questioned her about her troubles, Dolly refused to discuss the home situation, but we have spoken to some of her friends and really—well, for example, we insist you un-veto her nonparticipation in the dramatic group. You just must allow her to take part in *The*
1 *Hunted Enchanters*. She was such a perfect little nymph in the try-out, and sometime in spring the author will stay for a few days at Beardsley College and may attend a rehearsal or two in our new auditorium. I mean it is all part of the fun of being young and alive and beautiful. You must understand—"

"I always thought of myself," I said, "as a very understanding father."

"Oh no doubt, no doubt, but Miss Cormorant thinks, and I am inclined to agree with her, that Dolly is obsessed by sexual thoughts for which she finds no outlet, and will tease and martyrize other girls, or even our younger instructors because *they* do have innocent dates with boys."

Shrugged my shoulders. A shabby *émigré.*

"Let us put our two heads together, Mr. Haze. What on earth is wrong with that child?"

"She seems quite normal and happy to me," I said (disaster coming at last? was I found out? had they got some hypnotist?).

"What worries me," said Miss Pratt looking at her watch and starting to go over the whole subject again, "is that both teachers and schoolmates find Dolly antagonistic, dissatisfied, cagey—and everybody wonders why you are so firmly opposed to all the natural recreations of a normal child."

"Do you mean sex play?" I asked jauntily, in despair, a cornered old rat.

"Well, I certainly welcome this civilized terminology," said Pratt with a grin. "But this is not quite the point. Under the auspices of Beardsley School, dramatics, dances and other natural activities are not technically sex play, though girls do meet boys, if that is what you object to."

"All right," I said, my hassock exhaling a weary sigh. "You win. She can take part in that play. Provided male parts are taken by female parts."

"I am always fascinated," said Pratt, "by the admirable way foreigners—or at least naturalized Americans—use our rich language. I'm sure Miss Gold, who conducts the play group, will be overjoyed. I notice she is one of the few teachers that seem to like—I mean who seem to find Dolly manageable. This takes care of general topics, I guess; now comes a special matter. We are in trouble again."

Pratt paused truculently, then rubbed her index finger under her nostrils with such vigor that her nose performed a kind of war dance.

"I'm a frank person," she said, "but conventions are conventions, and I find it difficult . . . Let me put it this way . . . The Walkers, who live in what we call around here the Duke's Manor, you know the great gray house on the hill—they send their two girls to our school, and we have the niece of President Moore with us, a really gracious child, not to speak of a number of other prominent children. Well, under the circumstances, it is rather a jolt when Dolly, who looks like a little lady, uses words which you as a foreigner probably simply do not know or do not understand. Perhaps it might be better—Would you like me to have Dolly come up here right away to discuss things? No? You see—oh well, let's have it out. Dolly has written a most obscene four-letter word which our Dr. Cutler tells me is low-Mexican for urinal with her lipstick on some health pamphlets which Miss Redcock, who is getting married in June, distributed among the girls, and we thought she should stay after hours—another half hour at least. But if you like—"

"No," I said, "I don't want to interfere with rules. I shall talk to her later. I shall thrash it out."

"Do," said the woman rising from her chair arm. "And perhaps we can get together again soon, and if things do not improve we might have Dr. Cutler analyze her."

Should I marry Pratt and strangle her?

". . . And perhaps your family doctor might like to examine her physically—just a routine check-up. She is in Mushroom—the last classroom along that passage."

Beardsley School, it may be explained, copied a famous girls' school in England by having "traditional" nicknames for its various classrooms: Mushroom, Room-In 8, B-room, Room-BA and so on. Mushroom was smelly, with a sepia print of Reynolds' "Age of Innocence" above the chalkboard, and several rows of clumsy-looking pupil desks. At one of these, my Lolita was reading the chapter on "Dialogue" in Baker's *Dramatic Technique*, and all was very quiet, and there was another girl with a very naked, porcelain-white neck and wonderful platinum hair, who sat in front reading too, absolutely lost to the world and interminably winding a soft curl around one finger, and I sat beside Dolly just behind that neck and that hair, and unbuttoned my overcoat and for sixty-five cents plus the permission to participate in the school play, had Dolly put her inky, chalky, red-knuckled hand under the desk. Oh, stupid and reckless of me, no doubt, but after the torture I had been subjected to, I simply had to take advantage of a combination that I knew would never occur again.

12

Around Christmas she caught a bad chill and was examined by a friend of Miss Lester, a Dr. Ilse Tristramson (hi, Ilse, you were a dear, uninquisitive soul, and you touched my dove very gently). She diagnosed bronchitis, patted Lo on the back (all its bloom erect because of the fever) and put her to bed for a week or longer. At first she "ran a temperature" in American parlance, and I could not resist the exquisite caloricity of unexpected delights—Venus febriculosa—though it was a very languid Lolita that moaned and coughed and shivered in my embrace. And as soon as she was well again, I threw a Party with Boys.

Perhaps I had drunk a little too much in preparation for the ordeal. Perhaps I made a fool of myself. The girls had decorated and plugged in a small fir tree—German custom, except that colored bulbs had superseded wax candles. Records were chosen and fed into my landlord's phonograph. Chic Dolly wore a nice gray dress with fitted bodice and flared skirt. Humming, I retired to my study upstairs—and then every ten or twenty minutes I would come down like an idiot just for a few seconds; to pick up ostensibly my pipe from the mantelpiece or hunt for the newspaper; and with every new visit these simple actions became harder to perform, and I was reminded of the dreadfully distant days when I used to brace myself to casually enter a room in the Ramsdale house where Little Carmen was on.

The party was not a success. Of the three girls invited, one did not come at all, and one of the boys brought his cousin Roy, so there was a superfluity of two boys, and the cousins knew all the steps, and the other fellows could hardly dance at all, and most of the evening was spent in messing up the kitchen, and then endlessly jabbering about what card game to play, and sometime later, two girls and four boys sat on the floor of the living room, with all windows open, and played a word game which Opal could not be made to understand, while Mona and Roy, a lean handsome lad, drank ginger ale in the kitchen, sitting on the table and dangling their legs, and hotly discussing Predestination and the Law of Averages. After they had all gone my Lo said ugh, closed her eyes, and dropped into a chair with all four limbs starfished to express the utmost disgust and exhaustion and swore it was the most revolting bunch of boys she had ever seen. I bought her a new tennis racket for that remark.

January was humid and warm, and February fooled the forsythia: none of the townspeople had ever *seen* such weather. Other presents came tumbling in. For her birthday I bought her a bicycle, the doe-like and altogether charming machine already mentioned—and added to this a *History of Modern American Painting:* her bicycle manner, I mean her approach to it, the hip movement in mounting, the grace and so on, afforded me supreme pleasure; but my attempt to refine her pictorial taste was a failure; she wanted to know if the guy noon-napping on Doris Lee's hay was the father of the pseudo-voluptuous hoyden in the foreground, and could not understand why I said Grant Wood or Peter Hurd was good, and Reginald Marsh or Frederick Waugh awful.

1

13

By the time spring had touched up Thayer Street with yellow and green and pink, Lolita was irrevocably stage-struck. Pratt, whom I chanced to notice one Sunday lunching with some people at Walton Inn, caught my eye from afar and went through the motion of sympathetically and discreetly clapping her hands while Lo was not looking. I detest the theatre as being a primitive and putrid form, historically speaking; a form that smacks of stone-age rites and communal nonsense despite those

1 individual injections of genius, such as, say, Elizabethan poetry which a closeted reader automatically pumps out of the stuff. Being much occupied at the time with my own literary labors, I did not bother to read the complete text of *The Enchanted Hunters*, the playlet in which Dolores Haze was assigned the part of a farmer's daughter who imagines herself to be a woodland

2 witch, or Diana, or something, and who, having got hold of a book on hypnotism, plunges a number of lost hunters into various entertaining trances before falling in her turn under the spell of a vagabond poet (Mona Dahl). That much I gleaned from bits of crumpled and poorly typed script that Lo sowed all over the house. The coincidence of the title with the name of an unforgettable inn was pleasant in a sad little way: I wearily thought I had better not bring it to my own enchantress's notice, lest a brazen accusation of mawkishness hurt me even more than her failure to notice it for herself had done. I assumed the playlet was just another, practically anonymous, version of some banal legend. Nothing prevented one, of course, from supposing that in quest of an attractive name the founder of the hotel had been immediately and solely influenced by the chance fantasy of the second-rate muralist he had hired, and that subsequently the

3 hotel's name had suggested the play's title. But in my credulous, simple, benevolent mind I happened to twist it the other way round, and without giving the whole matter much thought really, supposed that mural, name and title had all been derived from a common source, from some local tradition, which I, an alien unversed in New England lore, would not be supposed to know.

In consequence I was under the impression (all this quite casually, you understand, quite outside any orbit of importance) that the accursed playlet belonged to the type of whimsey for juvenile consumption, arranged and rearranged many times, such as *Hansel and Gretel* by Richard Roe, or *The Sleeping Beauty* 1, 2 by Dorothy Doe, or *The Emperor's New Clothes* by Maurice Vermont and Marion Rumpelmeyer—all this to be found in any 3 *Plays for School Actors* or *Let's Have a Play!* In other words, I did not know—and would not have cared, if I did—that actually *The Enchanted Hunters* was a quite recent and technically original composition which had been produced for the first time only three or four months ago by a highbrow group in New York. To me—inasmuch as I could judge from my charmer's part—it seemed to be a pretty dismal kind of fancy work, with echoes from Lenormand and Maeterlinck and various quiet 4, 5 British dreamers. The red-capped, uniformly attired hunters, of 6 which one was a banker, another a plumber, a third a policeman, a fourth an undertaker, a fifth an underwriter, a sixth an escaped convict (you see the possibilities!), went through a complete change of mind in Dolly's Dell, and remembered their real lives only as dreams or nightmares from which little Diana had aroused them; but a seventh Hunter (in a *green* cap, the fool) 7 was a Young Poet, and he insisted, much to Diana's annoyance, that she and the entertainment provided (dancing nymphs, and elves, and monsters) were his, the Poet's, invention. I under- 8 stand that finally, in utter disgust at this cocksureness, barefooted Dolores was to lead check-trousered Mona to the paternal farm behind the Perilous Forest to prove to the braggard she was not a poet's fancy, but a rustic, down-to-brown-earth lass—and a last-minute kiss was to enforce the play's profound message, namely, that mirage and reality merge in love. I considered it wiser not to criticize the thing in front of Lo: she was so healthily en-grossed in "problems of expression," and so charmingly did she put her narrow Florentine hands together, batting her eyelashes and pleading with me not to come to rehearsals as some ridicu-lous parents did because she wanted to dazzle me with a perfect First Night—and because I was, anyway, always butting in and saying the wrong thing, and cramping her style in the presence of other people.

There was one very special rehearsal... my heart, my heart... there was one day in May marked by a lot of gay flurry—it all rolled past, beyond my ken, immune to my memory, and when I saw Lo next, in the late afternoon, balancing on her bike, pressing the palm of her hand to the damp bark of a young birch tree on the edge of our lawn, I was so struck by the radiant tenderness of her smile that for an instant I believed all our troubles gone. "Can you remember," she said, "what was the name of that hotel, *you* know [nose puckered], come on, you know—with those white columns and the marble swan in the lobby? Oh, you know [noisy exhalation of breath]—the hotel where you raped me. Okay, skip it. I mean, was it [almost in a whisper] The Enchanted Hunters? Oh, it was? [musingly] Was it?"—and with a yelp of amorous vernal laughter she slapped the glossy bole and tore uphill, to the end of the street, and then rode back, feet at rest on stopped pedals, posture relaxed, one hand dreaming in her print-flowered lap.

14

Because it supposedly tied up with her interest in dance and dramatics, I had permitted Lo to take piano lessons with a Miss Emperor (as we French scholars may conveniently call her) to whose blue-shuttered little white house a mile or so beyond Beardsley Lo would spin off twice a week. One Friday night toward the end of May (and a week or so after the very special rehearsal Lo had not had me attend) the telephone in my study, where I was in the act of mopping up Gustave's—I mean Gaston's—king's side, rang and Miss Emperor asked if Lo was coming next Tuesday because she had missed last Tuesday's and today's lessons. I said she would by all means—and went on with the game. As the reader may well imagine, my faculties were now impaired, and a move or two later, with Gaston to play, I noticed through the film of my general distress that he could collect my queen; he noticed it too, but thinking it might be a trap on the part of his tricky opponent, he demurred for quite a minute, and puffed and wheezed, and shook his jowls, and even shot furtive glances at me, and made hesitating half-thrusts with his pudgily bunched fingers—dying to take that juicy queen and not daring—and all of a sudden he swooped down upon it (who knows if it did not teach him certain later audacities?), and I spent a dreary hour in achieving a draw. He finished his brandy and presently lumbered away, quite satisfied with this result (*mon pauvre ami, je ne vous ai jamais revu et quoiqu'il y ait bien peu de chance que vous voyiez mon livre, permettez-moi de vous dire que je vous serre la main bien cordialement, et que toutes mes fillettes vous saluent*). I found Dolores Haze at the kitchen table, consuming a wedge of pie, with her eyes fixed on her script. They rose to meet mine with a kind of celestial vapidity. She remained singularly unruffled when confronted with my discovery, and said *d'un petit air faussement contrit* that she knew she was a very wicked kid, but simply had not been able to resist the enchantment, and had used up those music hours—O Reader, My Reader!—in a nearby public park rehearsing the magic forest scene with Mona. I said "fine"—and stalked to the telephone. Mona's mother answered: "Oh yes, she's in" and re-treated with a mother's neutral laugh of polite pleasure to shout off stage "Roy calling!" and the very next moment Mona rustled up, and forthwith, in a low monotonous not untender voice started berating Roy for something he had said or done and I interrupted her, and presently Mona was saying in her humblest, sexiest contralto, "yes, sir," "surely, sir," "I am alone to blame, sir, in this unfortunate business," (what elocution! what poise!) "honest, I feel very bad about it"—and so on and so forth as those little harlots say.

So downstairs I went clearing my throat and holding my heart. Lo was now in the living room, in her favorite overstuffed chair. As she sprawled there, biting at a hangnail and mocking me with her heartless vaporous eyes, and all the time rocking a stool upon which she had placed the heel of an outstretched shoeless foot, I perceived all at once with a sickening qualm how much she had changed since I first met her two years ago. Or had this happened during those last two weeks? *Tendresse?* Surely that was an exploded myth. She sat right in the focus of my incandescent anger. The fog of all lust had been swept away leaving nothing but this dreadful lucidity. Oh, she had changed! Her complexion was now that of any vulgar untidy highschool girl who applies shared cosmetics with grubby fingers to an unwashed face and does not mind what soiled texture, what pustulate epidermis comes in contact with her skin. Its smooth tender bloom had been so lovely in former days, so bright with tears, when I used to roll, in play, her tousled head on my knee. A coarse flush had now replaced that innocent fluorescence. What was locally known as a "rabbit cold" had painted with flaming pink the edges of her contemptuous nostrils. As in terror I lowered my gaze, it mechanically slid along the underside of her tensely stretched bare thigh—how polished and muscular her legs had grown! She kept her wide-set eyes, clouded-glass gray and slightly bloodshot, fixed upon me, and I saw the stealthy thought showing through them that perhaps after all Mona was right, and she, orphan Lo, could expose me without getting penalized herself. How wrong I was. How mad I was! Everything about her was of the same exasperating impenetrable order —the strength of her shapely legs, the dirty sole of her white sock, the thick sweater she wore despite the closeness of the room, her wenchy smell, and especially the dead end of her face with its strange flush and freshly made-up lips. Some of the red had left stains on her front teeth, and I was struck by a ghastly recollection—the evoked image not of Monique, but of another young prostitute in a bell-house, ages ago, who had been snapped up by somebody else before I had time to decide whether her mere youth warranted my risking some appalling disease, and who had just such flushed prominent *pommettes* and a dead *maman*, and big front teeth, and a bit of dingy red ribbon in her country-brown hair.

"Well, speak," said Lo. "Was the corroboration satisfactory?"

"Oh, yes," I said. "Perfect. Yes. And I do not doubt you two made it up. As a matter of fact, I do not doubt you have told her everything about us."

"Oh, yah?"

I controlled my breath and said: "Dolores, this must stop right away. I am ready to yank you out of Beardsley and lock you up you know where, but this must stop. I am ready to take you away the time it takes to pack a suitcase. This must stop or else anything may happen."

"Anything may happen, huh?"

I snatched away the stool she was rocking with her heel and her foot fell with a thud on the floor.

"Hey," she cried, "take it easy."

"First of all you go upstairs," I cried in my turn,—and simultaneously grabbed at her and pulled her up. From that moment, I stopped restraining my voice, and we continued yelling at each other, and she said unprintable things. She said she loathed me. She made monstrous faces at me, inflating her cheeks and producing a diabolical plopping sound. She said I had attempted to violate her several times when I was her mother's roomer. She said she was sure I had murdered her mother. She said she would sleep with the very first fellow who asked her and I could do nothing about it. I said she was to go upstairs and show me all her hiding places. It was a strident and hateful scene. I held her by her knobby wrist and she kept turning and twisting it this way and that, surreptitiously trying to find a weak point so as to wrench herself free at a favorable moment, but I held her quite hard and in fact hurt her rather badly for which I hope my heart may rot, and once or twice she jerked her arm so violently that I feared her wrist might snap, and all the while she stared at me with those unforgettable eyes where cold anger and hot tears struggled, and our voices were drowning the telephone, and when I grew aware of its ringing she instantly escaped.

With people in movies I seem to share the services of the machina telephonica and its sudden god. This time it was an irate neighbor. The east window happened to be agape in the

living room, with the blind mercifully down, however; and behind it the damp black night of a sour New England spring had
been breathlessly listening to us. I had always thought that type
1   of haddocky spinster with the obscene mind was the result of
considerable literary inbreeding in modern fiction; but now I am
convinced that prude and prurient Miss East—or to explode her
incognito, Miss Fenton Lebone—had been probably protruding
three-quarter-way from her bedroom window as she strove to
catch the gist of our quarrel.

"... This racket ... lacks all sense of ..." quacked the receiver,
"we do not live in a tenement here. I must emphatically ..."

I apologized for my daughter's friends being so loud. Young
people, you know—and cradled the next quack and a half.

Downstairs the screen door banged. Lo? Escaped?

Through the casement on the stairs I saw a small impetuous
ghost slip through the shrubs; a silvery dot in the dark—hub of
bicycle wheel—moved, shivered, and she was gone.

It so happened that the car was spending the night in a repair
shop downtown. I had no other alternative than to pursue on
foot the winged fugitive. Even now, after more than three years
have heaved and elapsed, I cannot visualize that spring-night
street, that already so leafy street, without a gasp of panic. Before
their lighted porch Miss Lester was promenading Miss Fabian's
2, 3   dropsical dackel. Mr. Hyde almost knocked it over. Walk three
steps and run three. A tepid rain started to drum on the chestnut leaves. At the next corner, pressing Lolita against an iron
railing, a blurred youth held and kissed—no, not her, mistake.
My talons still tingling, I flew on.

Half a mile or so east of number fourteen, Thayer Street
tangles with a private lane and a cross street; the latter leads to
the town proper; in front of the first drugstore, I saw—with what
melody of relief!—Lolita's fair bicycle waiting for her. I pushed
instead of pulling, pulled, pushed, pulled, and entered. Look
out! Some ten paces away Lolita, through the glass of a telephone booth (membranous god still with us), cupping the tube,
confidentially hunched over it, slit her eyes at me, turned away

with her treasure, hurriedly hung up, and walked out with a   1
flourish.

"Tried to reach you at home," she said brightly. "A great
decision has been made. But first buy me a drink, dad."

She watched the listless pale fountain girl put in the ice, pour
in the coke, add the cherry syrup—and my heart was bursting
with love-ache. That childish wrist. My lovely child. You have a
lovely child, Mr. Humbert. We always admire her as she passes
by. Mr. Pim watched Pippa suck in the concoction.   2

J'ai toujours admiré l'œuvre ormonde du sublime Dublinois.   3
And in the meantime the rain had become a voluptuous shower.

"Look," she said as she rode the bike beside me, one foot
scraping the darkly glistening sidewalk, "look, I've decided something. I want to leave school. I hate that school. I hate the play,
I really do! Never go back. Find another. Leave at once. Go for
a long trip again. But *this* time we'll go wherever *I* want, won't
we?"

I nodded. My Lolita.

"I choose? *C'est entendu?*" she asked wobbling a little beside   4
me. Used French only when she was a very good little girl.

"Okay. *Entendu.* Now hop-hop-hop, Lenore, or you'll get   5
soaked." (A storm of sobs was filling my chest.)

She bared her teeth and after her adorable school-girl fashion,
leaned forward, and away she sped, my bird.

Miss Lester's finely groomed hand held a porch-door open for
a waddling old dog *qui prenait son temps.*   6

Lo was waiting for me near the ghostly birch tree.

"I am drenched," she declared at the top of her voice. "Are
you glad? To hell with the play! See what I mean?"

An invisible hag's claw slammed down an upper-floor window.

In our hallway, ablaze with welcoming lights, my Lolita
peeled off her sweater, shook her gemmed hair, stretched towards
me two bare arms, raised one knee:

"Carry me upstairs, please. I feel sort of romantic to-night."

It may interest physiologists to learn, at this point, that I have
the ability—a most singular case, I presume—of shedding torrents of tears throughout the other tempest.

15

The brakes were relined, the waterpipes unclogged, the valves ground, and a number of other repairs and improvements were paid for by not very mechanically-minded but prudent papa Humbert, so that the late Mrs. Humbert's car was in respectable shape when ready to undertake a new journey.

We had promised Beardsley School, good old Beardsley School, that we would be back as soon as my Hollywood engagement came to an end (inventive Humbert was to be, I hinted, chief consultant in the production of a film dealing with "existentialism," still a hot thing at the time). Actually I was toying with the idea of gently trickling across the Mexican border—I was braver now than last year—and there deciding what to do with my little concubine who was now sixty inches tall and weighed ninety pounds. We had dug out our tour books and maps. She had traced our route with immense zest. Was it thanks to those theatricals that she had now outgrown her juvenile jaded airs and was so adorably keen to explore rich reality? I experienced the queer lightness of dreams that pale but warm Sunday morning when we abandoned Professor Chem's puzzled house and sped along Main Street toward the four-lane highway. My Love's striped, black-and-white, cotton frock, jaunty blue cap, white socks and brown moccasins were not quite in keeping with the large beautifully cut aquamarine on a silver chainlet, which gemmed her throat: a spring rain gift from me. We passed the New Hotel, and she laughed. "A penny for your thoughts," I said and she stretched out her palm at once, but at that moment I had to apply the brakes rather abruptly at a red light. As we pulled up, another car came to a gliding stop alongside, and a very striking looking, athletically lean young woman (where had I seen her?) with a high complexion and shoulder-length brilliant bronze hair, greeted Lo with a ringing "Hi!"—and then, addressing me, effusively, edusively (placed!), stressing certain words, said: "What a *shame* it was to *tear* Dolly away from the play—you should have *heard* the author *raving* about her after that rehearsal—" "Green light, you dope," said Lo under her breath, and simultaneously, waving in bright adieu a bangled arm, Joan of Arc (in a performance we saw at the local theatre) violently outdistanced us to swerve into Campus Avenue.

"Who was it exactly? Vermont or Rumpelmeyer?"

"No—Edusa Gold—the gal who coaches us." 1

"I was not referring to her. Who exactly concocted that play?"

"Oh! Yes, of course. Some old woman, Clare Something, I 2 guess. There was quite a crowd of them there."

"So she complimented you?"

"Complimented my eye—she kissed me on my pure brow"— and my darling emitted that new yelp of merriment which— perhaps in connection with her theatrical mannerisms—she had lately begun to affect.

"You are a funny creature, Lolita," I said—or some such words. "Naturally, I am overjoyed you gave up that absurd stage business. But what is curious is that you dropped the whole thing only a week before its natural climax. Oh, Lolita, you should be 3 careful of those surrenders of yours. I remember you gave up Ramsdale for camp, and camp for a joyride, and I could list other abrupt changes in your disposition. You must be careful. There are things that should never be given up. You must persevere. You should try to be a little nicer to me, Lolita. You should also watch your diet. The tour of your thigh, you know, should not exceed seventeen and a half inches. More might be fatal (I was kidding, of course). We are now setting out on a long happy journey. I remember—"

16

I remember as a child in Europe gloating over a map of North America that had "Appalachian Mountains" boldly running from Alabama up to New Brunswick, so that the whole region they spanned—Tennessee, the Virginias, Pennsylvania, New York, Vermont, New Hampshire and Maine, appeared to my imagination as a gigantic Switzerland or even Tibet, all mountain, glorious diamond peak upon peak, giant conifers, *le*

1 *montagnard émigré* in his bear skin glory, and *Felis tigris gold-*

2, 3 *smithi*, and Red Indians under the catalpas. That it all boiled down to a measly suburban lawn and a smoking garbage incinerator, was appalling. Farewell, Appalachia! Leaving it, we crossed Ohio, the three states beginning with "I," and Nebraska—ah,

4 that first whiff of the West! We travelled very leisurely, having more than a week to reach Wace, Continental Divide, where she passionately desired to see the Ceremonial Dances marking the seasonal opening of Magic Cave, and at least three weeks to reach Elphinstone, gem of a western State where she yearned to

5 climb Red Rock from which a mature screen star had recently jumped to her death after a drunken row with her gigolo.

Again we were welcomed to wary motels by means of inscriptions that read:

"We wish you to feel at home while here. *All* equipment was carefully checked upon your arrival. Your license number is on record here. Use hot water sparingly. We reserve the right to eject without notice any objectionable person. Do not throw waste material of *any* kind in the toilet bowl. Thank you. Call again. The Management. P.S. We consider our guests the Finest People of the World."

In these frightening places we paid ten for twins, flies queued outside at the screenless door and successfully scrambled in, the ashes of our predecessors still lingered in the ashtrays, a woman's hair lay on the pillow, one heard one's neighbor hanging his coat in his closet, the hangers were ingeniously fixed to their bars by coils of wire so as to thwart theft, and, in crowning insult, the pictures above the twin beds were identical twins. I also noticed that commercial fashion was changing. There was a tendency

6 for cabins to fuse and gradually form the caravansary, and, lo (she was not interested but the reader may be), a second story was added, and a lobby grew in, and cars were removed to a communal garage, and the motel reverted to the good old hotel.

I now warn the reader not to mock me and my mental daze. It is easy for him and me to decipher *now* a past destiny; but a destiny in the making is, believe me, not one of those honest mystery stories where all you have to do is keep an eye on the clues. In my youth I once read a French detective tale where the clues were actually in italics; but that is not McFate's way— even if one does learn to recognize certain obscure indications.

For instance: I would not swear that there was not at least one occasion, prior to, or at the very beginning of, the Midwest lap of our journey, when she managed to convey some information to, or otherwise get into contact with, a person or persons unknown. We had stopped at a gas station, under the sign of Pegasus, and she had slipped out of her seat and escaped to the rear of the premises while the raised hood, under which I had bent to watch the mechanic's manipulations, hid her for a moment from my sight. Being inclined to be lenient, I only shook my benign head though strictly speaking such visits were taboo, since I felt instinctively that toilets—as also telephones— happened to be, for reasons unfathomable, the points where my destiny was liable to catch. We all have such fateful objects—it may be a recurrent landscape in one case, a number in another— carefully chosen by the gods to attract events of special significance for us: here shall John always stumble; there shall Jane's heart always break.

Well—my car had been attended to, and I had moved it away from the pumps to let a pickup truck be serviced—when the growing volume of her absence began to weigh upon me in the windy grayness. Not for the first time, and not for the last, had I stared in such dull discomfort of mind at those stationary trivialities that look almost surprised, like staring rustics, to find themselves in the stranded traveller's field of vision: that green garbage can, those very black, very whitewalled tires for sale, those bright cans of motor oil, that red icebox with assorted drinks, the four, five, seven discarded bottles within the incompleted crossword puzzle of their wooden cells, that bug patiently walking up the inside of the window of the office. Radio music was coming from its open door, and because the rhythm was not synchronized with the heave and flutter and other gestures of wind-animated vegetation, one had the impression of an old scenic film living its own life while piano or fiddle followed a line of music quite outside the shivering flower, the swaying branch. The sound of Charlotte's last sob incongruously vibrated through me as, with her dress fluttering athwart the rhythm, Lolita veered from a totally unexpected direction. She had found the toilet occupied and had crossed over to the sign of the Conche in the next block. They said there they were proud of their home-clean restrooms. These prepaid postcards, they said, had been provided for your comments. No postcards. No soap. Nothing. No comments.

That day or the next, after a tedious drive through a land of food crops, we reached a pleasant little burg and put up at Chestnut Court—nice cabins, damp green grounds, apple trees, an old swing—and a tremendous sunset which the tired child ignored. She had wanted to go through Kasbeam because it was only thirty miles north from her home town but on the following morning I found her quite listless, with no desire to see again the sidewalk where she had played hopscotch some five years before. For obvious reasons I had rather dreaded that side trip, even though we had agreed not to make ourselves conspicuous in any way—to remain in the car and not look up old friends. My relief at her abandoning the project was spoiled by the thought that had she felt I were totally against the nostalgic possibilities of Pisky, as I had been last year, she would not have given up so easily. On my mentioning this with a sigh, she sighed too and complained of being out of sorts. She wanted to remain in bed till teatime at least, with lots of magazines, and then if she felt better she suggested we just continue westward. I must say she was very sweet and languid, and craved for fresh fruits, and I decided to go and fetch her a toothsome picnic lunch in Kasbeam. Our cabin stood on the timbered crest of a hill, and from our window you could see the road winding down, and then running as straight as a hair parting between two rows of chestnut trees, towards the pretty town, which looked singularly distinct and toylike in the pure morning distance. One could make out an elf-like girl on an insect-like bicycle, and a dog, a bit too large proportionately, all as clear as those pilgrims and mules winding up wax-pale roads in old paintings with blue hills and red little people. I have the European urge to use my feet when a drive can be dispensed with, so I leisurely walked down, eventually meeting the cyclist—a plain plump girl with pigtails, followed by a huge St. Bernard dog with orbits like pansies. In Kasbeam a very old barber gave me a very mediocre haircut: he babbled of a baseball-playing son of his, and, at every explodent, spat into my neck, and every now and then wiped his glasses on my sheet-wrap, or interrupted his tremulous scissor work to produce faded newspaper clippings, and so inattentive was I that it came as a shock to realize as he pointed to an easeled photograph among the ancient gray lotions, that the mustached young ball player had been dead for the last thirty years.

I had a cup of hot flavorless coffee, bought a bunch of bananas for my monkey, and spent another ten minutes or so in a delicatessen store. At least an hour and a half must have elapsed when this homeward-bound little pilgrim appeared on the winding road leading to Chestnut Castle.   1

The girl I had seen on my way to town was now loaded with linen and engaged in helping a misshapen man whose big head and coarse features reminded me of the "Bertoldo" character in low Italian comedy. They were cleaning the cabins of which   2 there was a dozen or so on Chestnut Crest, all pleasantly spaced amid the copious verdure. It was noon, and most of them, with a final bang of their screen doors, had already got rid of their occupants. A very elderly, almost mummy-like couple in a very new model were in the act of creeping out of one of the contiguous garages; from another a red hood protruded in some-   3 what cod-piece fashion; and nearer to our cabin, a strong and   4 handsome young man with a shock of black hair and blue eyes was putting a portable refrigerator into a station wagon. For some reason he gave me a sheepish grin as I passed. On the grass expanse opposite, in the many-limbed shade of luxuriant trees, the familiar St. Bernard dog was guarding his mistress' bicycle, and nearby a young woman, far gone in the family way, had seated a rapt baby on a swing and was rocking it gently, while a jealous boy of two or three was making a nuisance of himself by trying to push or pull the swing board; he finally succeeded in getting himself knocked down by it, and bawled loudly as he lay supine on the grass while his mother continued to smile gently at neither of her present children. I recall so clearly these minutiae probably because I was to check my impressions so thoroughly only a few minutes later; and besides, something in me had been on guard ever since that awful night in Beardsley. I now refused to be diverted by the feeling of well-being that my walk had engendered—by the young summer breeze that enveloped the nape of my neck, the giving crunch of the damp gravel, the juicy tidbit I had sucked out at last from a hollow tooth, and even the comfortable weight of my provisions which the general condition of my heart should not have allowed me to carry; but even that miserable pump of mine seemed to be working sweetly, and I felt *adolori d'amoureuse langueur*, to quote dear old Ronsard, as I reached the cottage where I had left my Dolores.

To my surprise I found her dressed. She was sitting on the edge of the bed in slacks and T-shirt, and was looking at me as if she could not quite place me. The frank soft shape of her small breasts was brought out rather than blurred by the limpness of her thin shirt, and this frankness irritated me. She had not washed; yet her mouth was freshly though smudgily painted, and her broad teeth glistened like wine-tinged ivory, or pinkish poker chips. And there she sat, hands clasped in her lap, and dreamily brimmed with a diabolical glow that had no relation to me whatever.

I plumped down my heavy paper bag and stood staring at the bare ankles of her sandaled feet, then at her silly face, then again at her sinful feet. "You've been out," I said (the sandals were filthy with gravel).

"I just got up," she replied, and added upon intercepting my downward glance: "Went out for a sec. Wanted to see if you were coming back."

She became aware of the bananas and uncoiled herself tableward.

What special suspicion could I have? None indeed—but those muddy, moony eyes of hers, that singular warmth emanating from her! I said nothing. I looked at the road meandering so distinctly within the frame of the window . . . Anybody wishing to betray my trust would have found it a splendid lookout. With rising appetite, Lo applied herself to the fruit. All at once I remembered the ingratiating grin of the Johnny nextdoor. I stepped out quickly. All cars had disappeared except his station wagon; his pregnant young wife was now getting into it with her baby and the other, more or less cancelled, child.

"What's the matter, where are you going?" cried Lo from the porch.

I said nothing. I pushed her softness back into the room and went in after her. I ripped her shirt off. I unzipped the rest of her. I tore off her sandals. Wildly, I pursued the shadow of her infidelity; but the scent I travelled upon was so slight as to be practically undistinguishable from a madman's fancy.

17

Gros Gaston, in his prissy way, had liked to make presents— presents just a prissy wee bit out of the ordinary, or so he prissily thought. Noticing one night that my box of chessmen was broken, he sent me next morning, with a little lad of his, a copper case: it had an elaborate Oriental design over the lid and could be securely locked. One glance sufficed to assure me that it was one of those cheap money boxes called for some reason "luizet-tas" that you buy in Algiers and elsewhere, and wonder what to do with afterwards. It turned out to be much too flat for holding my bulky chessmen, but I kept it—using it for a totally different purpose.

In order to break some pattern of fate in which I obscurely felt myself being enmeshed, I had decided—despite Lo's visible annoyance—to spend another night at Chestnut Court; definitely waking up at four in the morning, I ascertained that Lo was still sound asleep (mouth open, in a kind of dull amazement at the curiously inane life we all had rigged up for her) and satisfied myself that the precious contents of the "luizetta" were safe. There, snugly wrapped in a white woollen scarf, lay a pocket automatic: caliber .32, capacity of magazine 8 cartridges, length a little under one ninth of Lolita's length, stock checked walnut, finish full blued. I had inherited it from the late Harold Haze, with a 1938 catalog which cheerily said in part: "Particularly well adapted for use in the home and car as well as on the person." There it lay, ready for instant service on the person or persons, loaded and fully cocked with the slide lock in safety position, thus precluding any accidental discharge. We must remember that a pistol is the Freudian symbol of the Ur-father's central forelimb.

I was now glad I had it with me—and even more glad that I had learned to use it two years before, in the pine forest around my and Charlotte's glass lake. Farlow, with whom I had roamed those remote woods, was an admirable marksman, and with his .38 actually managed to hit a hummingbird, though I must say not much of it could be retrieved for proof—only a little iridescent fluff. A burley ex-policeman called Krestovski, who in the twenties had shot and killed two escaped convicts, joined us and bagged a tiny woodpecker—completely out of season, incidentally. Between those two sportsmen I of course was a novice and kept missing everything, though I did wound a squirrel on a later occasion when I went out alone. "You lie here," I whispered to my light-weight compact little chum, and then toasted it with a dram of gin.

18

The reader must now forget Chestnuts and Colts, and accompany us further west. The following days were marked by a number of great thunderstorms—or perhaps, there was but one single storm which progressed across country in ponderous frog-leaps and which we could not shake off just as we could not shake off detective Trapp: for it was during those days that the problem

of the Aztec Red Convertible presented itself to me, and quite 1
overshadowed the theme of Lo's lovers.

Queer! I who was jealous of every male we met—queer, how I
misinterpreted the designations of doom. Perhaps I had been
lulled by Lo's modest behavior in winter, and anyway it would
have been too foolish even for a lunatic to suppose another
Humbert was avidly following Humbert and Humbert's nymphet
with Jovian fireworks, over the great and ugly plains. I surmised, 2
donc, that the Red Yak keeping behind us at a discreet distance 3
mile after mile was operated by a detective whom some busybody had hired to see what exactly Humbert Humbert was doing
with that minor stepdaughter of his. As happens with me at
periods of electrical disturbance and crepitating lightnings, I had 4
hallucinations. Maybe they were more than hallucinations. I
do not know what she or he, or both had put into my liquor but
one night I felt sure somebody was tapping on the door of our
cabin, and I flung it open, and noticed two things—that I was
stark naked and that, white-glistening in the rain-dripping darkness, there stood a man holding before his face the mask of Jutting Chin, a grotesque sleuth in the funnies. He emitted a muffled 5
guffaw and scurried away, and I reeled back into the room, and
fell asleep again, and am not sure even to this day that the visit
was not a drug-provoked dream: I have thoroughly studied
Trapp's type of humor, and this might have been a plausible
sample. Oh, crude and absolutely ruthless! Somebody, I imagined, was making money on those masks of popular monsters
and morons. Did I see next morning two urchins rummaging in
a garbage can and trying on Jutting Chin? I wonder. It may all
have been a coincidence—due to atmospheric conditions, I
suppose.

Being a murderer with a sensational but incomplete and un-
orthodox memory, I cannot tell you, ladies and gentlemen, the
exact day when I first knew with utter certainty that the red
convertible was following us. I do remember, however, the first
time I saw its driver quite clearly. I was proceeding slowly one
afternoon through torrents of rain and kept seeing that red ghost
swimming and shivering with lust in my mirror, when presently

the deluge dwindled to a patter, and then was suspended alto-gether. With a swishing sound a sunburst swept the highway, and needing a pair of new sunglasses, I pulled up at a filling station. What was happening was a sickness, a cancer, that could not be helped, so I simply ignored the fact that our quiet pur-suer, in his converted state, stopped a little behind us at a café or bar bearing the idiotic sign: The Bustle: A Deceitful Seatful. Having seen to the needs of my car, I walked into the office to get those glasses and pay for the gas. As I was in the act of signing a traveller's check and wondered about my exact whereabouts, I happened to glance through a side window, and saw a terrible thing. A broad-backed man, baldish, in an oatmeal coat and dark-brown trousers, was listening to Lo who was leaning out of the car and talking to him very rapidly, her hand with outspread fingers going up and down as it did when she was very serious and emphatic. What struck me with sickening force was—how should I put it?—the voluble familiarity of her way, as if they had known each other—oh, for weeks and weeks. I saw him scratch his cheek and nod, and turn, and walk back to his convertible, a broad and thickish man of my age, somewhat resembling Gustave Trapp, a cousin of my father's in Switzerland—same smoothly tanned face, fuller than mine, with a small dark mus-tache and a rosebud degenerate mouth. Lolita was studying a road map when I got back into the car.

"What did that man ask you, Lo?"

"Man? Oh, that man. Oh yes. Oh, I don't know. He won-dered if I had a map. Lost his way, I guess."

We drove on, and I said:

"Now listen, Lo. I do not know whether you are lying or not, and I do not know whether you are insane or not, and I do not care for the moment; but that person has been following us all day, and his car was at the motel yesterday, and I think he is a cop. You know perfectly well what will happen and where you will go if the police find out about things. Now I want to know exactly what he said to you and what you told him."

She laughed.

"If he's really a cop," she said shrilly but not illogically, "the worst thing we could do, would be to show him we are scared. Ignore him, *Dad*."

"Did he ask where we were going?"

"Oh, he knows *that*" (mocking me).

"Anyway," I said, giving up, "I have seen his face now. He is not pretty. He looks exactly like a relative of mine called Trapp."

"Perhaps he is Trapp. If I were you—Oh, look, all the nines are changing into the next thousand. When I was a little kid," she continued unexpectedly, "I used to think they'd stop and go back to nines, if only my mother agreed to put the car in reverse."

It was the first time, I think, she spoke spontaneously of her pre-Humbertian childhood; perhaps, the theatre had taught her that trick; and silently we travelled on, unpursued.

But next day, like pain in a fatal disease that comes back as the drug and hope wear off, there it was again behind us, that glossy red beast. The traffic on the highway was light that day; nobody passed anybody; and nobody attempted to get in between our humble blue car and its imperious red shadow—as if there were some spell cast on that interspace, a zone of evil mirth and magic, a zone whose very precision and stability had a glass-like virtue that was almost artistic. The driver behind me, with his stuffed shoulders and Trappish mustache, looked like a display dummy, and his convertible seemed to move only because an invisible rope of silent silk connected it with our shabby vehicle. We were many times weaker than his splendid, lacquered machine, so that I did not even attempt to outspeed him. *O lente currite noctis equi!* O softly run, nightmares! We climbed long grades and rolled downhill again, and heeded speed limits, and spared slow children, and reproduced in sweeping terms the black wiggles of curves on their yellow shields, and no matter how and where we drove, the enchanted interspace slid on intact, mathematical, mirage-like, the viatic counterpart of a magic carpet. And all the time I was aware of a private blaze on my right: her joyful eye, her flaming cheek.

A traffic policeman, deep in the nightmare of crisscross streets —at half-past-four P.M. in a factory town—was the hand of chance that interrupted the spell. He beckoned me on, and then with the same hand cut off my shadow. A score of cars were launched in between us, and I sped on, and deftly turned into a narrow lane. A sparrow alighted with a jumbo bread crumb, was tackled by another, and lost the crumb.

When after a few grim stoppages and a bit of deliberate meandering, I returned to the highway, our shadow had disappeared.

Lola snorted and said: "If he is what you think he is, how silly to give him the slip."

"I have other notions by now," I said.

"You should—ah—check them by—ah—keeping in touch with him, fahther deah," said Lo, writhing in the coils of her own sarcasm. "Gee, you *are* mean," she added in her ordinary voice.

We spent a grim night in a very foul cabin, under a sonorous amplitude of rain, and with a kind of prehistorically loud thunder incessantly rolling above us.

1   "I am not a lady and do not like lightning," said Lo, whose dread of electric storms gave me some pathetic solace.

2   We had breakfast in the township of Soda, pop. 1001.

"Judging by the terminal figure," I remarked, "Fatface is already here."

"Your humor," said Lo, "is sidesplitting, deah fahther."

We were in sage-brush country by that time, and there was a day or two of lovely release (I had been a fool, all was well, that 3   discomfort was merely a trapped flatus), and presently the mesas gave way to real mountains, and, on time, we drove into Wace.

Oh, disaster. Some confusion had occurred, she had misread a date in the Tour Book, and the Magic Cave ceremonies were over! She took it bravely, I must admit—and, when we dis-
4   covered there was in kurortish Wace a summer theatre in full swing, we naturally drifted toward it one fair mid-June evening. I really could not tell you the plot of the play we saw. A trivial affair, no doubt, with self-conscious light effects and a mediocre leading lady. The only detail that pleased me was a garland of seven little graces, more or less immobile, prettily painted, bare-limbed—seven bemused pubescent girls in colored gauze that had been recruited locally (judging by the partisan flurry here and

[222]

there among the audience) and were supposed to represent a living rainbow, which lingered throughout the last act, and rather teasingly faded behind a series of multiplied veils. I remember thinking that this idea of children-colors had been lifted by authors Clare Quilty and Vivian Darkbloom from a passage in James Joyce, and that two of the colors were quite exasperatingly lovely—Orange who kept fidgeting all the time, and Emerald who, when her eyes got used to the pitch-black pit where we all heavily sat, suddenly smiled at her mother or her protector.

As soon as the thing was over, and manual applause—a sound my nerves cannot stand—began to crash all around me, I started to pull and push Lo toward the exit, in my so natural amorous impatience to get her back to our neon-blue cottage in the stunned, starry night: I always say nature is stunned by the sights she sees. Dolly-Lo, however, lagged behind, in a rosy daze, her pleased eyes narrowed, her sense of vision swamping the rest of her senses to such an extent that her limp hands hardly came together at all in the mechanical action of clapping they still went through. I had seen that kind of thing in children before but, by God, this was a special child, myopically beaming at the already remote stage where I glimpsed something of the joint authors—a man's tuxedo and the bare shoulders of a hawklike, black-haired, strikingly tall woman.

"You've again hurt my wrist, you brute," said Lolita in a small voice as she slipped into her car seat.

"I am dreadfully sorry, my darling, my own ultraviolet darling," I said, unsuccessfully trying to catch her elbow, and I added, to change the conversation—to change the direction of fate, oh God, oh God: "Vivian is quite a woman. I am sure we saw her yesterday in that restaurant, in Soda pop."

"Sometimes," said Lo, "you are quite revoltingly dumb. First, Vivian is the male author, the gal author is Clare; and second, she is forty, married and has Negro blood."

"I thought," I said kidding her, "Quilty was an ancient flame of yours, in the days when you loved me, in sweet old Ramsdale."

"What?" countered Lo, her features working. "That fat dentist? You must be confusing me with some other fast little article."

And I thought to myself how those fast little articles forget everything, everything, while we, old lovers, treasure every inch of their nymphancy.

19

With Lo's knowledge and assent, the two post offices given to the Beardsley postmaster as forwarding addresses were P.O. Wace and P.O. Elphinstone. Next morning we visited the former and had to wait in a short but slow queue. Serene Lo studied the rogues' gallery. Handsome Bryan Bryanski, alias Anthony Bryan, alias Tony Brown, eyes hazel, complexion fair, was wanted for kidnaping. A sad-eyed old gentleman's faux-pas was mail fraud, and, as if that were not enough, he was cursed with deformed arches. Sullen Sullivan came with a caution: Is believed armed, and should be considered extremely dangerous. If you want to make a movie out of my book, have one of these faces gently melt into my own, while I look. And moreover there was a smudgy snapshot of a Missing Girl, age fourteen, wearing brown shoes when last seen, rhymes. Please notify Sheriff Buller.

I forget my letters; as to Dolly's, there was her report and a very special-looking envelope. This I deliberately opened and perused its contents. I concluded I was doing the foreseen since she did not seem to mind and drifted toward the newsstand near the exit.

"Dolly-Lo: Well, the play was a grand success. All three hounds lay quiet having been slightly drugged by Cutler, I suspect, and Linda knew all your lines. She was fine, she had alertness and control, but lacked somehow the *responsiveness*, the *relaxed vitality*, the charm of *my*—and the author's—Diana; but there was no author to applaud us as last time, and the terrific electric storm outside interfered with our own modest off-stage thunder. Oh dear, life does fly. Now that everything is over, school, play, the Roy mess, mother's confinement (our baby, alas, did not live!), it all seems such a long time ago, though practically I still bear traces of the paint.

"We are going to New York after to-morrow, and I guess I can't manage to wriggle out of accompanying my parents to Europe. I have even worse news for you. Dolly-Lo! I may not be back at Beardsley if and when you return. With one thing and another, one being you know who, and the other not being who you think you know, Dad wants me to go to school in Paris for one year while he and Fullbright are around.

"As expected, poor Poet stumbled in Scene III when arriving at the bit of French nonsense. Remember? *Ne manque pas de dire à ton amant, Chimène, comme le lac est beau car il faut qu'il t'y mène.* Lucky beau! *Qu'il t'y*—What a tongue-twister! Well, be good, Lollikins. Best love from your Poet, and best regards to the Governor. Your Mona. P.S. Because of one thing and another, my correspondence happens to be rigidly controlled. So better wait till I write you from Europe." (She never did as far as I know. The letter contained an element of mysterious nastiness that I am too tired to-day to analyze. I found it later preserved in one of the Tour Books, and give it here *à titre documentaire.* I read it twice.)

I looked up from the letter and was about to—There was no Lo to behold. While I was engrossed in Mona's witchery, Lo had shrugged her shoulders and vanished. "Did you happen to see—" I asked of a hunchback sweeping the floor near the entrance. He had, the old lecherer. He guessed she had seen a friend and had hurried out. I hurried out too. I stopped—she had not. I hurried on. I stopped again. It had happened at last. She had gone for ever.

In later years I have often wondered why she did *not* go for ever that day. Was it the retentive quality of her new summer clothes in my locked car? Was it some unripe particle in some general plan? Was it simply because, all things considered, I might as well be used to convey her to Elphinstone—the secret terminus, anyway? I only know I was quite certain she had left me for ever. The noncommittal mauve mountains half encircling the town seemed to me to swarm with panting, scrambling, laughing, panting Lolitas who dissolved in their haze. A big W made of white stones on a steep talus in the far vista of a cross street seemed the very initial of woe.

The new and beautiful post office I had just emerged from stood between a dormant movie house and a conspiracy of poplars. The time was 9 A.M. mountain time. The street was Main Street. I paced its blue side peering at the opposite one: charming it into beauty, was one of those fragile young summer mornings with flashes of glass here and there and a general air of faltering and almost fainting at the prospect of an intolerably torrid noon. Crossing over, I loafed and leafed, as it were, through one long block: Drugs, Real Estate, Fashions, Auto Parts, Cafe, Sporting Goods, Real Estate, Furniture, Appliances, Western Union, Cleaners, Grocery. Officer, officer, my daughter has run away. In collusion with a detective; in love with a black-mailer. Took advantage of my utter helplessness. I peered into all the stores. I deliberated inly if I should talk to any of the sparse foot-passengers. I did not. I sat for a while in the parked car. I inspected the public garden on the east side. I went back to Fashions and Auto Parts. I told myself with a burst of furious sarcasm—*un ricanement*—that I was crazy to suspect her, that she would turn up in a minute.

She did.

I wheeled around and shook off the hand she had placed on my sleeve with a timid and imbecile smile.

"Get into the car," I said.

She obeyed, and I went on pacing up and down, struggling with nameless thoughts, trying to plan some way of tackling her duplicity.

Presently she left the car and was at my side again. My sense of hearing gradually got tuned in to station Lo again, and I became aware she was telling me that she had met a former girl friend.

"Yes? Whom?"

"A Beardsley girl."

"Good. I know every name in your group. Alice Adams?"

"This girl was not in my group."

"Good. I have a complete student list with me. Her name please."

"She was not in my school. She is just a town girl in Beardsley."

"Good. I have the Beardsley directory with me too. We'll look up all the Browns."

"I only know her first name."

"Mary or Jane?"

"No—Dolly, like me."

"So that's the dead end" (the mirror you break your nose against). "Good. Let us try another angle. You have been absent twenty-eight minutes. What did the two Dollys do?"

"We went to a drugstore."

"And you had there—?"

"Oh, just a couple of Cokes."

"Careful, Dolly. We can check that, you know."

"At least, she had. I had a glass of water."

"Good. Was it that place there?"

"Sure."

"Good, come on, we'll grill the soda jerk."

"Wait a sec. Come to think it might have been further down —just around the corner."

"Come on all the same. Go in please. Well, let's see." (Opening a chained telephone book.) "Dignified Funeral Service. No, not yet. Here we are: Druggists-Retail. Hill Drug Store. Larkin's Pharmacy. And two more. That's all Wace seems to have in the way of soda fountains—at least in the business section. Well, we will check them all."

"Go to hell," she said.

"Lo, rudeness will get you nowhere."

"Okay," she said. "But you're not going to trap me. Okay, so we did not have a pop. We just talked and looked at dresses in show windows."

"Which? That window there for example?"

"Yes, that one there, for example."

"Oh Lo! Let's look closer at it."

It was indeed a pretty sight. A dapper young fellow was vacuum-cleaning a carpet of sorts upon which stood two figures that looked as if some blast had just worked havoc with them. One figure was stark naked, wigless and armless. Its comparatively small stature and smirking pose suggested that when clothed it had represented, and would represent when clothed again, a girl-child of Lolita's size. But in its present state it was sexless. Next to it, stood a much taller veiled bride, quite perfect and *intacta* except for the lack of one arm. On the floor, at the feet of these damsels, where the man crawled about laboriously with his cleaner, there lay a cluster of three slender arms, and a blond wig. Two of the arms happened to be twisted and seemed to suggest a clasping gesture of horror and supplication.

"Look, Lo," I said quietly. "Look well. Is not that a rather good symbol of something or other? However"—I went on as we got back into the car—"I have taken certain precautions. Here (delicately opening the glove compartment), on this pad, I have our boy friend's car number."

As the ass I was I had not memorized it. What remained of it in my mind were the initial letter and the closing figure as if the whole amphitheatre of six signs receded concavely behind a tinted glass too opaque to allow the central series to be deciphered, but just translucent enough to make out its extreme edges—a capital P and a 6. I have to go into those details (which in themselves can interest only a professional psychologue) because otherwise the reader (ah, if I could visualize him as a blond-bearded scholar with rosy lips sucking *la pomme de sa canne* as he quaffs my manuscript!) might not understand the quality of the shock I experienced upon noticing that the P had acquired the bustle of a B and that the 6 had been deleted altogether. The rest, with erasures revealing the hurried shuttle smear of a pencil's rubber end, and with parts of numbers obliterated or reconstructed in a child's hand, presented a tangle of barbed wire to any logical interpretation. All I knew was the state—one adjacent to the state Beardsley was in.

I said nothing. I put the pad back, closed the compartment, and drove out of Wace. Lo had grabbed some comics from the

[228]

back seat and, mobile-white-bloused, one brown elbow out of the window, was deep in the current adventure of some clout or clown. Three or four miles out of Wace, I turned into the shadow of a picnic ground where the morning had dumped its litter of light on an empty table; Lo looked up with a semi-smile of surprise and without a word I delivered a tremendous backhand cut that caught her smack on her hot hard little cheekbone.

And then the remorse, the poignant sweetness of sobbing atonement, groveling love, the hopelessness of sensual reconciliation. In the velvet night, at Mirana Motel (Mirana!) I kissed the yellowish soles of her long-toed feet, I immolated myself . . . But it was all of no avail. Both doomed were we. And soon I was to enter a new cycle of persecution.   1

In a street of Wace, on its outskirts . . . Oh, I am quite sure it was not a delusion. In a street of Wace, I had glimpsed the Aztec Red Convertible, or its identical twin. Instead of Trapp, it contained four or five loud young people of several sexes—but I said nothing. After Wace a totally new situation arose. For a day or two, I enjoyed the mental emphasis with which I told myself that we were not, and never had been followed; and then I became sickeningly conscious that Trapp had changed his tactics and was still with us, in this or that rented car.

A veritable Proteus of the highway, with bewildering ease he   2 switched from one vehicle to another. This technique implied the existence of garages specializing in "stage-automobile" operations, but I never could discover the remises he used. He seemed   3 to patronize at first the Chevrolet genus, beginning with a Campus Cream convertible, then going on to a small Horizon Blue sedan, and thenceforth fading into Surf Gray and Driftwood Gray. Then he turned to other makes and passed through a pale dull rainbow of paint shades, and one day I found myself attempting to cope with the subtle distinction between our own Dream Blue Melmoth and the Crest Blue Oldsmobile he had   4 rented; grays, however, remained his favorite cryptochromism,   5 and, in agonizing nightmares, I tried in vain to sort out properly such ghosts as Chrysler's Shell Gray, Chevrolet's Thistle Gray, Dodge's French Gray ...

The necessity of being constantly on the lookout for his little moustache and open shirt—or for his baldish pate and broad shoulders—led me to a profound study of all cars on the road—behind, before, alongside, coming, going, every vehicle under the dancing sun: the quiet vacationist's automobile with the box of Tender-Touch tissues in the back window; the recklessly speeding jalopy full of pale children with a shaggy dog's head protruding, and a crumpled mudguard; the bachelor's tudor sedan crowded with suits on hangers; the huge fat house trailer weaving in front, immune to the Indian file of fury boiling behind it; the car with the young female passenger politely perched in the middle of the front seat to be closer to the young male driver; the car carrying on its roof a red boat bottom up ... The gray car slowing up before us, the gray car catching up with us.

We were in mountain country, somewhere between Snow and Champion, and rolling down an almost imperceptible grade, when I had my next distinct view of Detective Paramour Trapp. The gray mist behind us had deepened and concentrated into the compactness of a Dominion Blue sedan. All of a sudden, as if the car I drove responded to my poor heart's pangs, we were slithering from side to side, with something making a helpless plap-plap-plap under us.

"You got a flat, mister," said cheerful Lo.

I pulled up—near a precipice. She folded her arms and put her foot on the dashboard. I got out and examined the right rear wheel. The base of its tire was sheepishly and hideously square. Trapp had stopped some fifty yards behind us. His distant face formed a grease spot of mirth. This was my chance. I started to walk towards him—with the brilliant idea of asking him for a jack though I had one. He backed a little. I stubbed my toe against a stone—and there was a sense of general laughter. Then a tremendous truck loomed from behind Trapp and thundered by me—and immediately after, I heard it utter a convulsive honk. Instinctively I looked back—and saw my own car gently creeping away. I could make out Lo ludicrously at the wheel,

[230]

and the engine was certainly running—though I remembered I had cut it but had not applied the emergency brake; and during the brief space of throb-time that it took me to reach the croaking machine which came to a standstill at last, it dawned upon me that during the last two years little Lo had had ample time to pick up the rudiments of driving. As I wrenched the door open, I was goddam sure she had started the car to prevent me from walking up to Trapp. Her trick proved useless, however, for even while I was pursuing her he had made an energetic U-turn and was gone. I rested for a while. Lo asked wasn't I going to thank her—the car had started to move by itself and— Getting no answer, she immersed herself in a study of the map. I got out again and commenced the "ordeal of the orb," as Charlotte used to say. Perhaps, I was losing my mind.

We continued our grotesque journey. After a forlorn and useless dip, we went up and up. On a steep grade I found myself behind the gigantic truck that had overtaken us. It was now groaning up a winding road and was impossible to pass. Out of its front part a small oblong of smooth silver—the inner wrapping of chewing gum—escaped and flew back into our windshield. It occurred to me that if I were really losing my mind, I might end by murdering somebody. In fact—said high-and-dry Humbert to floundering Humbert—it might be quite clever to prepare things—to transfer the weapon from box to pocket—so as to be ready to take advantage of the spell of insanity when it does come.

20

By permitting Lolita to study acting I had, fond fool, suffered her to cultivate deceit. It now appeared that it had not been merely a matter of learning the answers to such questions as what is the basic conflict in "Hedda Gabler," or where are the climaxes in "Love Under the Lindens," or analyze the prevailing mood of "Cherry Orchard"; it was really a matter of learning to betray me. How I deplored now the exercises in sensual simulation that I had so often seen her go through in our Beardsley parlor when I would observe her from some strategic point while she, like a hypnotic subject or a performer in a mystic rite, produced sophisticated versions of infantile make-believe by going through the mimetic actions of hearing a moan in the dark, seeing for the first time a brand new young stepmother, tasting something she hated, such as buttermilk, smelling crushed grass in a lush orchard, or touching mirages of objects with her sly, slender, girl-child hands. Among my papers I still have a mimeographed sheet suggesting:

Tactile drill. Imagine yourself picking up and holding: a pingpong ball, an apple, a sticky date, a new flannel-fluffed tennis ball, a hot potato, an ice cube, a kitten, a puppy, a horseshoe, a feather, a flashlight.

Knead with your fingers the following imaginary things: a piece of bread, india rubber, a friend's aching temple, a sample of velvet, a rose petal.

You are a blind girl. Palpate the face of: a Greek youth, Cyrano, Santa Claus, a baby, a laughing faun, a sleeping stranger, your father.

But she had been so pretty in the weaving of those delicate spells, in the dreamy performance of her enchantments and duties! On certain adventurous evenings, in Beardsley, I also had her dance for me with the promise of some treat or gift, and although these routine leg-parted leaps of hers were more like those of a football cheerleader than like the languorous and jerky motions of a Parisian *petit rat*, the rhythms of her not quite nubile limbs had given me pleasure. But all that was nothing, absolutely nothing, to the indescribable itch of rapture that her tennis game produced in me—the teasing delirious feeling of teetering on the very brink of unearthly order and splendor.

Despite her advanced age, she was more of a nymphet than ever, with her apricot-colored limbs, in her sub-teen tennis togs! Winged gentlemen! No hereafter is acceptable if it does not produce her as she was then, in that Colorado resort between Snow and Elphinstone, with everything right: the white wide little-boy shorts, the slender waist, the apricot midriff, the white breast-kerchief whose ribbons went up and encircled her neck to end behind in a dangling knot leaving bare her gaspingly young and adorable apricot shoulder blades with that pubescence and those lovely gentle bones, and the smooth, downward-tapering back. Her cap had a white peak. Her racket had cost me a small fortune. Idiot, triple idiot! I could have filmed her! I would have had her now with me, before my eyes, in the projection room of my pain and despair!

She would wait and relax for a bar or two of white-lined time before going into the act of serving, and often bounced the ball once or twice, or pawed the ground a little, always at ease, always rather vague about the score, always cheerful as she so seldom was in the dark life she led at home. Her tennis was the highest point to which I can imagine a young creature bringing the art of make-believe, although I daresay, for her it was the very geometry of basic reality.

The exquisite clarity of all her movements had its auditory counterpart in the pure ringing sound of her every stroke. The ball when it entered her aura of control became somehow whiter, its resilience somehow richer, and the instrument of precision she used upon it seemed inordinately prehensile and deliberate at the moment of clinging contact. Her form was, indeed, an absolutely perfect imitation of absolutely top-notch tennis— without any utilitarian results. As Edusa's sister, Electra Gold, a marvelous young coach, said to me once while I sat on a pulsating hard bench watching Dolores Haze toying with Linda Hall (and being beaten by her): "Dolly has a magnet in the center of her racket guts, but why the heck is she so polite?" Ah, Electra, what did it matter, with such grace! I remember at the very first game I watched being drenched with an almost painful convulsion of beauty assimilation. My Lolita had a way of raising her bent left knee at the ample and springy start of the service cycle when there would develop and hang in the sun for a second a vital web of balance between toed foot, pristine armpit, burnished arm and far back-flung racket, as she smiled up with gleaming teeth at the small globe suspended so high in the zenith of the powerful and graceful cosmos she had created for the express purpose of falling upon it with a clean resounding crack of her golden whip.

It had, that serve of hers, beauty, directness, youth, a classical purity of trajectory, and was, despite its spanking pace, fairly easy to return, having as it did no twist or sting to its long elegant hop.

That I could have had all her strokes, all her enchantments, immortalized in segments of celluloid, makes me moan to-day with frustration. They would have been so much more than the snapshots I burned! Her overhead volley was related to her service as the envoy is to the ballade; for she had been trained, my pet, to patter up at once to the net on her nimble, vivid, white-shod feet. There was nothing to choose between her forehand and backhand drives: they were mirror images of one another—my very loins still tingle with those pistol reports repeated by crisp echoes and Electra's cries. One of the pearls of Dolly's game was a short half-volley that Ned Litam had taught her in California.

She preferred acting to swimming, and swimming to tennis; yet I insist that had not something within her been broken by me—not that I realized it then!—she would have had on the top of her perfect form the will to win, and would have become a real girl champion. Dolores, with two rackets under her arm, in Wimbledon. Dolores endorsing a Dromedary. Dolores turning professional. Dolores acting a girl champion in a movie. Dolores and her gray, humble, hushed husband-coach, old Humbert.

There was nothing wrong or deceitful in the spirit of her game —unless one considered her cheerful indifference toward its outcome as the feint of a nymphet. She who was so cruel and crafty in everyday life, revealed an innocence, a frankness, a kindness of ball-placing, that permitted a second-rate but determined player, no matter how uncouth and incompetent, to poke and cut his way to victory. Despite her small stature, she covered the one thousand and fifty-three square feet of her half of the court with wonderful ease, once she had entered into the rhythm of a rally and as long as she could direct that rhythm; but any abrupt attack, or sudden change of tactics on her adversary's part, left her helpless. At match point, her second serve, which—rather typically—was even stronger and more stylish than her first (for she had none of the inhibitions that cautious winners have), would strike vibrantly the harp-cord of the net—and ricochet out of court. The polished gem of her dropshot was snapped up and put away by an opponent who seemed four-legged and wielded a crooked paddle. Her dramatic drives and lovely volleys would candidly fall at his feet. Over and over again she would land an easy one into the net—and merrily mimic dismay by drooping in a ballet attitude, with her forelocks hanging. So sterile were her grace and whipper that she could not even win from panting me and my old-fashioned lifting drive.

I suppose I am especially susceptible to the magic of games. In my chess sessions with Gaston I saw the board as a square pool of limpid water with rare shells and stratagems rosily visible upon the smooth tessellated bottom, which to my confused adversary was all ooze and squid-cloud. Similarly, the initial tennis coaching I had inflicted on Lolita—prior to the revelations that came to her through the great Californian's lessons—remained in my mind as oppressive and distressful memories—not only because she had been so hopelessly and irritatingly irritated by every suggestion of mine—but because the precious symmetry of the court instead of reflecting the harmonies latent in her was utterly jumbled by the clumsiness and lassitude of the resentful child I mistaught. Now things were different, and on that particular day, in the pure air of Champion, Colorado, on that admirable court at the foot of steep stone stairs leading up to Champion Hotel where we had spent the night, I felt I could rest from the nightmare of unknown betrayals within the innocence of her style, of her soul, of her essential grace.

She was hitting hard and flat, with her usual effortless sweep, feeding me deep skimming balls—all so rhythmically coordinated and overt as to reduce my footwork to, practically, a swinging stroll—crack players will understand what I mean. My rather heavily cut serve that I had been taught by my father who had learned it from Decugis or Borman, old friends of his and great champions, would have seriously troubled my Lo, had I really tried to trouble her. But who would upset such a lucid dear? Did I ever mention that her bare arm bore the 8 of vaccination? That I loved her hopelessly? That she was only fourteen?

An inquisitive butterfly passed, dipping, between us.

Two people in tennis shorts, a red-haired fellow only about eight years my junior, with sunburnt bright pink shins, and an indolent dark girl with a moody mouth and hard eyes, about two years Lolita's senior, appeared from nowhere. As is common with dutiful tyros, their rackets were sheathed and framed, and they carried them not as if they were the natural and comfortable extensions of certain specialized muscles, but hammers or blunderbusses or wimbles, or my own dreadful cumbersome sins. Rather unceremoniously seating themselves near my precious coat, on a bench adjacent to the court, they fell to admiring very vocally a rally of some fifty exchanges that Lo innocently helped me to foster and uphold—until there occurred a syncope in the series causing her to gasp as her overhead smash went out of court, whereupon she melted into winsome merriment, my golden pet.

I felt thirsty by then, and walked to the drinking fountain; there Red approached me and in all humility suggested a mixed double. "I am Bill Mead," he said. "And that's Fay Page, actress. Maffy On Say"—he added (pointing with his ridiculously hooded racket at polished Fay who was already talking to Dolly). I was about to reply "Sorry, but—" (for I hate to have my filly involved in the chops and jabs of cheap bunglers), when a remarkably melodious cry diverted my attention: a bellboy was tripping down the steps from the hotel to our court and making me signs. I was wanted, if you please, on an urgent long distance call—so urgent in fact that the line was being held for me. Certainly. I got into my coat (inside pocket heavy with pistol) and told Lo I would be back in a minute. She was picking up a ball —in the continental foot-racket way which was one of the few nice things I had taught her,—and smiled—she smiled at me!

An awful calm kept my heart afloat as I followed the boy up

to the hotel. This, to use an American term, in which discovery, retribution, torture, death, eternity appear in the shape of a singularly repulsive nutshell, was *it*. I had left her in mediocre hands, but it hardly mattered now. I would fight, of course. Oh, I would fight. Better destroy everything than surrender her. Yes, quite a climb.

At the desk, a dignified, Roman-nosed man, with, I suggest, a very obscure past that might reward investigation, handed me a message in his own hand. The line had not been held after all. The note said:

"Mr. Humbert. The head of Birdsley (sic!) School called. Summer residence—Birdsley 2-8282. Please call back immediately. Highly important."

I folded myself into a booth, took a little pill, and for about twenty minutes tussled with space-spooks. A quartet of propositions gradually became audible: soprano, there was no such number in Beardsley; alto, Miss Pratt was on her way to England; tenor, Beardsley School had not telephoned; bass, they could not have done so, since nobody knew I was, that particular day, in Champion, Colo. Upon my stinging him, the Roman took the trouble to find out if there had been a long distance call. There had been none. A fake call from some local dial was not excluded. I thanked him. He said: You bet. After a visit to the purling men's room and a stiff drink at the bar, I started on my return march. From the very first terrace I saw, far below, on the tennis court which seemed the size of a school child's ill-wiped slate, golden Lolita playing in a double. She moved like a fair angel among three horrible Boschian cripples. One of these, her partner, while changing sides, jocosely slapped her on her behind with his racket. He had a remarkably round head and wore incongruous brown trousers. There was a momentary flurry—he saw me, and throwing away his racket—mine!—scuttled up the slope. He waved his wrists and elbows in would-be comical imitation of rudimentary wings, as he climbed, bow-legged, to the street, where his gray car awaited him. Next moment he and the grayness were gone. When I came down, the remaining trio were collecting and sorting out the balls.

"Mr. Mead, who was that person?"

Bill and Fay, both looking very solemn, shook their heads.

That absurd intruder had butted in to make up a double, hadn't he, Dolly?

Dolly. The handle of my racket was still disgustingly warm. Before returning to the hotel, I ushered her into a little alley half-smothered in fragrant shrubs, with flowers like smoke, and was about to burst into ripe sobs and plead with her imperturbed dream in the most abject manner for clarification, no matter how meretricious, of the slow awfulness enveloping me, when we found ourselves behind the convulsed Mead twosome —assorted people, you know, meeting among idyllic settings in old comedies. Bill and Fay were both weak with laughter—we had come at the end of their private joke. It did not really matter.

Speaking as if it really did not really matter, and assuming, apparently, that life was automatically rolling on with all its routine pleasures, Lolita said she would like to change into her bathing things, and spend the rest of the afternoon at the swimming pool. It was a gorgeous day. Lolita!

21

"Lo! Lola! Lolita!" I hear myself crying from a doorway into the sun, with the acoustics of time, domed time, endowing my call and its tell-tale hoarseness with such a wealth of anxiety, passion and pain that really it would have been instrumental in wrenching open the zipper of her nylon shroud had she been dead. Lolita! In the middle of a trim turfed terrace I found her at last—she had run out before I was ready. Oh Lolita! There she was playing with a damned dog, not me. The animal, a terrier of sorts, was losing and snapping up again and adjusting between his jaws a wet little red ball; he took rapid chords with his front paws on the resilient turf, and then would bounce away. I had only wanted to see where she was, I could not swim with my heart in that state, but who cared—and there she was, and there was I, in my robe—and so I stopped calling; but suddenly something in the pattern of her motions, as she dashed this way and that in her Aztec Red bathing briefs and bra, struck me . . . there was an ecstasy, a madness about her frolics that was too much of a glad thing. Even the dog seemed puzzled by the extravagance of her reactions. I put a gentle hand to my chest as I surveyed the situation. The turquoise blue swimming pool some distance behind the lawn was no longer behind that lawn, but within my thorax, and my organs swam in it like excrements in the blue sea water in Nice. One of the bathers had left the pool and, half-concealed by the peacocked shade of trees, stood quite still, holding the ends of the towel around his neck and following Lolita with his amber eyes. There he stood, in the camouflage of sun and shade, disfigured by them and masked by his own nakedness, his damp black hair or what was left of it, glued to his round head, his little mustache a humid smear, the wool on his chest spread like a symmetrical trophy, his naval pulsating, his hirsute thighs dripping with bright droplets, his tight wet black bathing trunks bloated and bursting with vigor where his great fat bullybag was pulled up and back like a padded shield over his reversed beasthood. And as I looked at his oval nut-brown face, it dawned upon me that what I had recognized him by was the reflection of my daughter's countenance—the same beatitude and grimace but made hideous by his maleness. And I also knew that the child, my child, knew he was looking, enjoyed the lechery of his look and was putting on a show of gambol and glee, the vile and beloved slut. As she made for the ball and missed it, she fell on her back, with her obscene young legs madly pedalling in the air; I could sense the musk of her excitement from where I stood, and then I saw (petrified with a kind of sacred disgust) the man close his eyes and bare his small, horribly small and even, teeth as he leaned against a tree in which a multitude of dappled Priaps shivered. Immediately afterwards a marvelous transformation took place. He was no longer the satyr but a very good-natured and foolish Swiss cousin, the Gustave Trapp I have mentioned more than once, who used to counteract his "sprees" (he drank beer with milk, the good swine) by feats of weight-lifting—tottering and grunting on a lake beach with his otherwise very complete bathing suit jauntily stripped from one shoulder. *This* Trapp noticed me from afar and working the towel on his nape walked back with false insouciance to the pool. And as if the sun had gone out of the game, Lo slackened and slowly got up ignoring the ball that the terrier placed before her. Who can say what heartbreaks are caused in a dog by our discontinuing a romp? I started to say something, and then sat down on the grass with a quite monstrous pain in my chest and vomited a torrent of browns and greens that I had never remembered eating.

I saw Lolita's eyes, and they seemed to be more calculating than frightened. I heard her saying to a kind lady that her father was having a fit. Then for a long time I lay in a lounge chair swallowing pony upon pony of gin. And next morning I felt strong enough to drive on (which in later years no doctor believed).

22

The two-room cabin we had ordered at Silver Spur Court, Elphinstone, turned out to belong to the glossily browned pine-log kind that Lolita used to be so fond of in the days of our carefree first journey; oh, how different things were now! I am not referring to Trapp or Trapps. After all—well, really ... After all, gentlemen, it was becoming abundantly clear that all those identical detectives in prismatically changing cars were figments of my persecution mania, recurrent images based on coincidence and chance resemblance. *Soyons logiques*, crowed the cocky Gallic part of my brain—and proceeded to rout the notion of a Lolita-maddened salesman or comedy gangster, with stooges, persecuting me, and hoaxing me, and otherwise taking riotous advantage of my strange relations with the law. I remember humming my panic away. I remember evolving even an explanation of the "Birdsley" telephone call ... But if I could dismiss Trapp, as I had dismissed my convulsions on the lawn at

Champion, I could do nothing with the anguish of knowing Lolita to be so tantalizingly, so miserably unattainable and beloved on the very eve of a new era, when my alembics told me she should stop being a nymphet, stop torturing me.

An additional, abominable, and perfectly gratuitous worry was lovingly prepared for me in Elphinstone. Lo had been dull and silent during the last lap—two hundred mountainous miles uncontaminated by smoke-gray sleuths or zigzagging zanies. She hardly glanced at the famous, oddly shaped, splendidly flushed rock which jutted above the mountains and had been the take-off for nirvana on the part of a temperamental show girl. The town was newly built, or rebuilt, on the flat floor of a seven-thousand-foot-high valley; it would soon bore Lo, I hoped, and we would spin on to California, to the Mexican border, to mythical bays, saguaro deserts, fatamorganas. José Lizzarrabengoa, as you remember, planned to take his Carmen to the *Etats Unis*. I conjured up a Central American tennis competition in which Dolores Haze and various Californian schoolgirl champions would dazzlingly participate. Good-will tours on that smiling level eliminate the distinction between passport and sport. Why did I hope we would be happy abroad? A change of environment is the traditional fallacy upon which doomed loves, and lungs, rely.

Mrs. Hays, the brisk, brickly rouged, blue-eyed widow who ran the motor court, asked me if I were Swiss perchance, because her sister had married a Swiss ski instructor. I was, whereas my daughter happened to be half Irish. I registered, Hays gave me the key and a twinkling smile, and, still twinkling, showed me where to park the car; Lo crawled out and shivered a little: the luminous evening air was decidedly crisp. Upon entering the cabin, she sat down on a chair at a card table, buried her face in the crook of her arm and said she felt awful. Shamming, I thought, shamming, no doubt, to evade my caresses; I was passionately parched; but she began to whimper in an unusually dreary way when I attempted to fondle her. Lolita ill. Lolita dying. Her skin was scalding hot! I took her temperature, orally, then looked up a scribbled formula I fortunately had in a jotter

1, 2, 3
4

and after laboriously reducing the, meaningless to me, degrees Fahrenheit to the intimate centigrade of my childhood, found she had 40.4, which at least made sense. Hysterical little nymphs might, I knew, run up all kinds of temperature—even exceeding a fatal count. And I would have given her a sip of hot spiced wine, and two aspirins, and kissed the fever away, if, upon an examination of her lovely uvula, one of the gems of her body, I had not seen that it was a burning red. I undressed her. Her breath was bittersweet. Her brown rose tasted of blood. She was shaking from head to toe. She complained of a painful stiffness in the upper vertebrae—and I thought of poliomyelitis as any American parent would. Giving up all hope of intercourse, I wrapped her up in a laprobe and carried her into the car. Kind Mrs. Hays in the meantime had alerted the local doctor. "You are lucky it happened here," she said; for not only was Blue the best man in the district, but the Elphinstone hospital was as modern as modern could be, despite its limited capacity. With a heterosexual Erlkönig in pursuit, thither I drove, half-blinded by a royal sunset on the lowland side and guided by a little old woman, a portable witch, perhaps his daughter, whom Mrs. Hays had lent me, and whom I was never to see again. Dr. Blue, whose learning, no doubt, was infinitely inferior to his reputation, assured me it was a virus infection, and when I alluded to her comparatively recent flu, curtly said this was another bug, he had forty such cases on his hands; all of which sounded like the "ague" of the ancients. I wondered if I should mention, with a casual chuckle, that my fifteen-year-old daughter had had a minor accident while climbing an awkward fence with her boy friend, but knowing I was drunk, I decided to withhold the information till later if necessary. To an unsmiling blond bitch of a secretary I gave my daughter's age as "practically sixteen." While I was not looking, my child was taken away from me! In vain I insisted I be allowed to spend the night on a "welcome" mat in a corner of their damned hospital. I ran up constructivistic flights of stairs, I tried to trace my darling so as to tell her she had better not babble, especially if she felt as lightheaded as we all did. At one point, I was rather dreadfully rude to a very young and very cheeky nurse with overdeveloped gluteal parts and blazing black eyes —of Basque descent, as I learned. Her father was an imported shepherd, a trainer of sheep dogs. Finally, I returned to the car and remained in it for I do not know how many hours, hunched up in the dark, stunned by my new solitude, looking out open-mouthed now at the dimly illumed, very square and low hospital building squatting in the middle of its lawny block, now up at the wash of stars and the jagged silvery ramparts of the *haute montagne* where at the moment Mary's father, lonely Joseph Lore, was dreaming of Oloron, Lagore, Rolas—*que sais-je!* —or seducing a ewe. Such-like fragrant vagabond thoughts have been always a solace to me in times of unusual stress, and only when, despite liberal libations, I felt fairly numbed by the endless night, did I think of driving back to the motel. The old woman had disappeared, and I was not quite sure of my way. Wide gravel roads criss-crossed drowsy rectangular shadows. I made out what looked like the silhouette of gallows on what was probably a school playground; and in another wastelike block there rose in domed silence the pale temple of some local sect. I found the highway at last, and then the motel, where millions of so-called "millers," a kind of insect, were swarming around the neon contours of "No Vacancy"; and, when, at 3 A.M., after one of those untimely hot showers which like some mordant only help to fix a man's despair and weariness, I lay on her bed that smelled of chestnuts and roses, and peppermint, and the very delicate, very special French perfume I latterly allowed her to use, I found myself unable to assimilate the simple fact that for the first time in two years I was separated from my Lolita. All at once it occurred to me that her illness was somehow the development of a theme—that it had the same taste and tone as the series of linked impressions which had puzzled and tormented me during our journey; I imagined that secret agent, or secret lover, or prankster, or hallucination, or whatever he was, prowling around the hospital—and Aurora had hardly "warmed her hands," as the pickers of lavender say in the country of my birth, when I found myself trying to get into that dungeon again, knocking upon its green doors, breakfast-less, stool-less, in despair.

This was Tuesday, and Wednesday or Thursday, splendidly reacting like the darling she was to some "serum" (sparrow's sperm or dugong's dung), she was much better, and the doctor said that in a couple of days she would be "skipping" again.

Of the eight times I visited her, the last one alone remains sharply engraved on my mind. It had been a great feat to come for I felt all hollowed out by the infection that by then was at work on me too. None will know the strain it was to carry that bouquet, that load of love, those books that I had traveled sixty miles to buy: Browning's *Dramatic Works*, *The History of Dancing*, *Clowns and Columbines*, *The Russian Ballet*, *Flowers of the Rockies*, *The Theatre Guild Anthology*, *Tennis* by Helen Wills, who had won the National Junior Girl Singles at the age of fifteen. As I was staggering up to the door of my daughter's thirteen-dollar-a-day private room, Mary Lore, the beastly young part-time nurse who had taken an unconcealed dislike to me, emerged with a finished breakfast tray, placed it with a quick crash on a chair in the corridor, and, fundament jigging, shot back into the room—probably to warn her poor little Dolores that the tyrannic old father was creeping up on crepe soles, with books and bouquet: the latter I had composed of wild flowers and beautiful leaves gathered with my own gloved hands on a mountain pass at sunrise (I hardly slept at all that fateful week).

Feeding my Carmencita well? Idly I glanced at the tray. On a yolk-stained plate there was a crumpled envelope. It had contained something, since one edge was torn, but there was no address on it—nothing at all, save a phony armorial design with "Ponderosa Lodge" in green letters; thereupon I performed a *chassé-croisé* with Mary, who was in the act of bustling out again—wonderful how fast they move and how little they do, those rumpy young nurses. She glowered at the envelope I had put back, uncrumpled.

"You better not touch," she said, nodding directionally. "Could burn your fingers."

Below my dignity to rejoin. All I said was:

"*Je croyais que c'était un* bill—not a *billet doux.*" Then, 1
entering the sunny room, to Lolita: "*Bonjour, mon petit.*"

"Dolores," said Mary Lore, entering with me, past me,
through me, the plump whore, and blinking, and starting to
fold very rapidly a white flannel blanket as she blinked: "Dolores,
your pappy thinks you are getting letters from my boy friend.
It's me (smugly tapping herself on the small gilt cross she wore)
gets them. And my pappy can parlay-voo as well as yours."

She left the room. Dolores, so rosy and russet, lips freshly
painted, hair brilliantly brushed, bare arms straightened out on
neat coverlet, lay innocently beaming at me or nothing. On the
bed table, next to a paper napkin and a pencil, her topaz ring
burned in the sun.

"What gruesome funeral flowers," she said. "Thanks all the
same. But do you mind very much cutting out the French? It
annoys everybody."

Back at the usual rush came the ripe young hussy, reeking
of urine and garlic, with the *Deseret News*, which her fair 2
patient eagerly accepted, ignoring the sumptuously illustrated
volumes I had brought.

"My sister Ann," said Mary (topping information with after- 3
thought), "works at the Ponderosa place."

Poor Bluebeard. Those brutal brothers. *Est-ce que tu ne
m'aimes plus, ma Carmen?* She never had. At the moment I 4
knew my love was as hopeless as ever—and I also knew the two
girls were conspirators, plotting in Basque, or Zemfirian, against 5, 6
my hopeless love. I shall go further and say that Lo was playing
a double game since she was also fooling sentimental Mary 7
whom she had told, I suppose, that she wanted to dwell with
her fun-loving young uncle and not with cruel melancholy me.
And another nurse whom I never identified, and the village
idiot who carted cots and coffins into the elevator, and the
idiotic green love birds in a cage in the waiting room—all were
in the plot, the sordid plot. I suppose Mary thought comedy
father Professor Humbertoldi was interfering with the romance
between Dolores and her father-substitute, roly-poly Romeo (for 8

[245]

you *were* rather lardy, you know, Rom, despite all that "snow" and "joy juice").

My throat hurt. I stood, swallowing, at the window and stared at the mountains, at the romantic rock high up in the smiling plotting sky.

"My Carmen," I said (I used to call her that sometimes), "we shall leave this raw sore town as soon as you get out of bed."

"Incidentally, I want all my clothes," said the gitanilla, humping up her knees and turning to another page.

". . . Because, really," I continued, "there is no point in staying here."

"There is no point in staying anywhere," said Lolita.

I lowered myself into a cretonne chair and, opening the attractive botanical work, attempted, in the fever-humming hush of the room, to identify my flowers. This proved impossible. Presently a musical bell softly sounded somewhere in the passage.

I do not think they had more than a dozen patients (three or four were lunatics, as Lo had cheerfully informed me earlier) in that show place of a hospital, and the staff had too much leisure. However—likewise for reasons of show—regulations were rigid. It is also true that I kept coming at the wrong hours. Not without a secret flow of dreamy *malice*, visionary Mary (next time it will be *une belle dame toute en bleu* floating through Roaring Gulch) plucked me by the sleeve to lead me out. I looked at her hand; it dropped. As I was leaving, leaving voluntarily, Dolores Haze reminded me to bring her next morning . . . She did not remember where the various things she wanted were . . . "Bring me," she cried (out of sight already, door on the move, closing, closed), "the new gray suitcase and Mother's trunk"; but by next morning I was shivering, and boozing, and dying in the motel bed she had used for just a few minutes, and the best I could do under the circular and dilating circumstances was to send the two bags over with the widow's beau, a robust and kindly trucker. I imagined Lo displaying her treasures to Mary . . . No doubt, I was a little delirious—and on the following day I was still a vibration rather than a solid, for when I looked out of the bathroom window at the adjacent lawn, I saw Dolly's beautiful young bicycle propped up there on its support, the graceful front wheel looking away from me, as it always did, and a sparrow perched on the saddle—but it was the landlady's bike, and smiling a little, and shaking my poor head over my fond fancies, I tottered back to my bed, and lay as quiet as a saint—

1

> *Saint,* forsooth! While brown Dolores,
> On a patch of sunny green
> With Sanchicha reading stories
> In a movie magazine—

—which was represented by numerous specimens wherever Dolores landed, and there was some great national celebration in town judging by the firecrackers, veritable bombs, that exploded all the time, and at five minutes to two P.M. I heard the sound of whistling lips nearing the half-opened door of my cabin, and then a thump upon it.

It was big Frank. He remained framed in the opened door, one hand on its jamb, leaning forward a little.

Howdy. Nurse Lore was on the telephone. She wanted to know was I better and would I come today?

At twenty paces Frank used to look a mountain of health; at five, as now, he was a ruddy mosaic of scars—had been blown through a wall overseas; but despite nameless injuries he was able to man a tremendous truck, fish, hunt, drink, and buoyantly dally with roadside ladies. That day, either because it was such a great holiday, or simply because he wanted to divert a sick man, he had taken off the glove he usually wore on his left hand (the one pressing against the side of the door) and revealed to the fascinated sufferer not only an entire lack of fourth and fifth fingers, but also a naked girl, with cinnabar nipples and indigo delta, charmingly tattooed on the back of his crippled hand, its index and middle digit making her legs while his wrist bore her flower-crowned head. Oh, delicious . . . reclining against the woodwork, like some sly fairy.

I asked him to tell Mary Lore I would stay in bed all day

2

and would get into touch with my daughter sometime to-morrow if I felt probably Polynesian.

He noticed the direction of my gaze and made her right hip twitch amorously.

"Okey-dokey," big Frank sang out, slapped the jamb, and whistling, carried my message away, and I went on drinking, and by morning the fever was gone, and although I was as limp as a toad, I put on the purple dressing gown over my maize yellow pajamas, and walked over to the office telephone. Everything was fine. A bright voice informed me that yes, everything was fine, my daughter had checked out the day before, around two, her uncle, Mr. Gustave, had called for her with a cocker spaniel pup and a smile for everyone, and a black Caddy Lack, and had paid Dolly's bill in cash, and told them to tell me I should not worry, and keep warm, they were at Grandpa's ranch as agreed.

1, 2

Elphinstone was, and I hope still is, a very cute little town. It was spread like a maquette, you know, with its neat green-wool trees and red-roofed houses over the valley floor and I think I have alluded earlier to its model school and temple and spacious rectangular blocks, some of which were, curiously enough, just unconventional pastures with a mule or a unicorn grazing in the young July morning mist. Very amusing: at one gravel-groaning sharp turn I sideswiped a parked car but said to myself telestically—and, telephathically (I hoped), to its gesticulating owner—that I would return later, address Bird School, Bird, New Bird, the gin kept my heart alive but bemazed my brain, and after some lapses and losses common to dream sequences, I found myself in the reception room, trying to beat up the doctor, and roaring at people under chairs, and clamoring for Mary who luckily for her was not there; rough hands plucked at my dressing gown, ripping off a pocket, and somehow I seem to have been sitting on a bald brown-headed patient, whom I had mistaken for Dr. Blue, and who eventually stood up, remarking with a preposterous accent: "Now, who is nevrotic, I ask?"—and then a gaunt unsmiling nurse presented me with seven beautiful, *beautiful* books and the exquisitely

3

4

5

folded tartan lap robe, and demanded a receipt; and in the sudden silence I became aware of a policeman in the hallway, to whom my fellow motorist was pointing me out, and meekly I signed the very symbolic receipt, thus surrendering my Lolita to all those apes. But what else could I do? One simple and stark thought stood out and this was: "Freedom for the moment is everything." One false move—and I might have been made to explain a life of crime. So I simulated a coming out of a daze. To my fellow motorist I paid what he thought was fair. To Dr. Blue, who by then was stroking my hand, I spoke in tears of the liquor I bolstered too freely a tricky but not necessarily diseased heart with. To the hospital in general I apologized with a flourish that almost bowled me over, adding however that I was not on particularly good terms with the rest of the Humbert clan. To myself I whispered that I still had my gun, and was still a free man—free to trace the fugitive, free to destroy my brother.

23

A thousand-mile stretch of silk-smooth road separated Kasbeam, where, to the best of my belief, the red fiend had been scheduled to appear for the first time, and fateful Elphinstone which we had reached about a week before Independence Day. The journey had taken up most of June for we had seldom made more than a hundred and fifty miles per traveling day, spending the rest of the time, up to five days in one case, at various stopping places, all of them also prearranged, no doubt. It was that stretch, then, along which the fiend's spoor should be sought; and to this I devoted myself, after several unmentionable days of dashing up and down the relentlessly radiating roads in the vicinity of Elphinstone.

Imagine me, reader, with my shyness, my distaste for any ostentation, my inherent sense of the *comme il faut*, imagine me masking the frenzy of my grief with a trembling ingratiating smile while devising some casual pretext to flip through the hotel register: "Oh," I would say, "I am almost positive that I stayed here once—let me look up the entries for mid-June —no, I see I'm wrong after all—what a very quaint name for a home town, Kawtagain. Thanks very much." Or: "I had a customer staying here—I mislaid his address—may I...?" And every once in a while, especially if the operator of the place happened to be a certain type of gloomy male, personal inspection of the books was denied me.

I have a memo here: between July 5 and November 18, when I returned to Beardsley for a few days, I registered, if not actually stayed, at 342 hotels, motels and tourist homes. This figure includes a few registrations between Chestnut and Beardsley, one of which yielded a shadow of the fiend ("N. Petit, Larousse, Ill."); I had to space and time my inquiries carefully so as not to attract undue attention; and there must have been at least fifty places where I merely inquired at the desk—but that was a futile quest, and I preferred building up a foundation of verisimilitude and good will by first paying for an unneeded room. My survey showed that of the 300 or so books inspected, at least 20 provided me with a clue: the loitering fiend had stopped even more often than we, or else—he was quite capable of that—he had thrown in additional registrations in order to keep me well furnished with derisive hints. Only in one case had he actually stayed at the same motor court as we, a few paces from Lolita's pillow. In some instances he had taken up quarters in the same or in a neighboring block; not infrequently he had lain in wait at an intermediate spot between two bespoken points. How vividly I recalled Lolita, just before our departure from Beardsley, prone on the parlor rug, studying tour books and maps, and marking laps and stops with her lipstick!

I discovered at once that he had foreseen my investigations and had planted insulting pseudonyms for my special benefit. At the very first motel office I visited, Ponderosa Lodge, his entry, among a dozen obviously human ones, read: Dr. Gratiano Forbeson, Mirandola, NY. Its Italian Comedy connotations could not fail to strike me, of course. The landlady deigned to inform me that the gentleman had been laid up for five days with a bad cold, that he had left his car for repairs in some garage or other and that he had checked out on the 4th of July. Yes, a girl called Ann Lore had worked formerly at the Lodge, but was now married to a grocer in Cedar City. One moonlit night I waylaid white-shoed Mary on a solitary street; an automaton, she was about to shriek, but I managed to humanize her by the simple act of falling on my knees and with pious yelps imploring her to help. She did not know a thing, she swore. Who was this Gratiano Forbeson? She seemed to waver. I whipped out a hundred-dollar bill. She lifted it to the light of the moon. "He is your brother," she whispered at last. I plucked the bill out of her moon-cold hand, and spitting out a French curse turned and ran away. This taught me to rely on myself alone. No detective could discover the clues Trapp had tuned to my mind and manner. I could not hope, of course, he would ever leave his correct name and address; but I did hope he might slip on the glaze of his own subtlety, by daring, say, to introduce a richer and more personal shot of color than was strictly necessary, or by revealing too much through a qualitative sum of quantitative parts which revealed too little. In one thing he succeeded: he succeeded in thoroughly enmeshing me and my thrashing anguish in his demoniacal game. With infinite skill, he swayed and staggered, and regained an impossible balance, always leaving me with the sportive hope—if I may use such a term in speaking of betrayal, fury, desolation, horror and hate—that he might give himself away next time. He never did —though coming damn close to it. We all admire the spangled acrobat with classical grace meticulously walking his tight rope in the talcum light; but how much rarer art there is in the sagging rope expert wearing scarecrow clothes and impersonating a grotesque drunk! *I* should know.

The clues he left did not establish his identity but they reflected his personality, or at least a certain homogenous and striking personality; his genre, his type of humor—at its best at least—the tone of his brain, had affinities with my own. He mimed and mocked me. His allusions were definitely highbrow. He was well-read. He knew French. He was versed in logodaedaly

[251]

1 and logomancy. He was an amateur of sex lore. He had a feminine handwriting. He would change his name but he could not disguise, no matter how he slanted them, his very peculiar t's,
2 w's and l's. Quelquepart Island was one of his favorite residences. He did not use a fountain pen which fact, as any psychoanalyst will tell you, meant that the patient was a repressed undinist. One mercifully hopes there are water nymphs in the
3 Styx.

His main trait was his passion for tantalization. Goodness, what a tease the poor fellow was! He challenged my scholarship. I am sufficiently proud of my knowing something to be modest about my not knowing all; and I daresay I missed some
4 elements in that cryptogrammic paper chase. What a shiver of triumph and loathing shook my frail frame when, among the plain innocent names in the hotel recorder, his fiendish conundrum would ejaculate in my face! I noticed that whenever he felt his enigmas were becoming too recondite, even for such a solver as I, he would lure me back with an easy one. "Arsène
5 Lupin" was obvious to a Frenchman who remembered the detective stories of his youth; and one hardly had to be a Coleridg-
6 ian to appreciate the trite poke of "A. Person, Porlock, England." In horrible taste but basically suggestive of a cultured man—not a policeman, not a common goon, not a lewd salesman—were such assumed names as "Arthur Rainbow"—plainly the travestied author of *Le Bateau Bleu*—let me laugh a little too, gentlemen—and "Morris Schmetterling," of *L'Oiseau Ivre*
7 fame (*touché*, reader!). The silly but funny "D. Orgon, Elmira,
8 NY," was from Molière, of course, and because I had quite recently tried to interest Lolita in a famous 18th-century play,
9 I welcomed as an old friend "Harry Bumper, Sheridan, Wyo." An ordinary encyclopedia informed me who the peculiar look-
10 ing "Phineas Quimby, Lebanon, NH" was; and any good Freudian, with a German name and some interest in religious prostitution, should recognize at a glance the implication of
11 "Dr. Kitzler, Eryx, Miss." So far so good. That sort of fun was shoddy but on the whole impersonal and thus innocuous. Among entries that arrested my attention as undoubtable clues

per se but baffled me in respect to their finer points I do not care to mention many since I feel I am groping in a border-land mist with verbal phantoms turning, perhaps, into living vacationists. Who was "Johnny Randall, Ramble, Ohio"? Or was   1
he a real person who just happened to write a hand similar to "N.S. Aristoff, Catagela, NY"? What was the sting in "Cata-   2
gela"? And what about "James Mavor Morell, Hoaxton, Eng-   3
land"? "Aristophanes," "hoax"—fine, but what was I missing?

There was one strain running through all that pseudonymity which caused me especially painful palpitations when I came across it. Such things as "G. Trapp, Geneva, NY." was the sign   4
of treachery on Lolita's part. "Aubrey Beardsley, Quelquepart   5
Island" suggested more lucidly than the garbled telephone message had that the starting point of the affair should be looked for in the East. "Lucas Picador, Merrymay, Pa." insinuated that   6
my Carmen had betrayed my pathetic endearments to the im-   7
postor. Horribly cruel, forsooth, was "Will Brown, Dolores, Colo." The gruesome "Harold Haze, Tombstone, Arizona"   8, 9
(which at another time would have appealed to my sense of humor) implied a familiarity with the girl's past that in nightmare fashion suggested for a moment that my quarry was an old friend of the family, maybe an old flame of Charlotte's, maybe a redresser of wrongs ("Donald Quix, Sierra, Nev.").   10
But the most penetrating bodkin was the anagramtailed entry   11
in the register of Chestnut Lodge "Ted Hunter, Cane, NH.".   12, 1

The garbled license numbers left by all these Persons and Orgons and Morells and Trapps only told me that motel keepers omit to check if guests' cars are accurately listed. References— incompletely or incorrectly indicated—to the cars the fiend had hired for short laps between Wace and Elphinstone were of course useless; the license of the initial Aztec was a shimmer of shifting numerals, some transposed, others altered or omitted, but somehow forming interrelated combinations (such as "WS   14
1564" and "SH 1616," and "Q32888" or "CU 88322") which however were so cunningly contrived as to never reveal a common denominator.   15

It occurred to me that after he had turned that convertible over to accomplices at Wace and switched to the stage-motor car system, his successors might have been less careful and might have inscribed at some hotel office the archtype of those inter-related figures. But if looking for the fiend along a road I knew he had taken was such a complicated vague and unprofitable business, what could I expect from any attempt to trace unknown motorists traveling along unknown routes?

24

By the time I reached Beardsley, in the course of the har-rowing recapitulation I have now discussed at sufficient length, a complete image had formed in my mind; and through the—always risky—process of elimination I had reduced this image to the only concrete source that morbid cerebration and torpid memory could give it.

Except for the Rev. Rigor Mortis (as the girls called him), and an old gentleman who taught non-obligatory German and Latin, there were no regular male teachers at Beardsley School. But on two occasions an art instructor on the Beardsley College faculty had come over to show the schoolgirls magic lantern pictures of French castles and nineteenth-century paintings. I had wanted to attend those projections and talks, but Dolly, as was her wont, had asked me not to, period. I also remem-bered that Gaston had referred to that particular lecturer as a brilliant *garçon;* but that was all; memory refused to supply me with the name of the chateau-lover.

On the day fixed for the execution, I walked through the sleet across the campus to the information desk in Maker Hall, Beardsley College. There I learned that the fellow's name was Riggs (rather like that of the minister), that he was a bachelor, and that in ten minutes he would issue from the "Museum" where he was having a class. In the passage leading to the audi-torium I sat on a marble bench of sorts donated by Cecilia

Dalrymple Ramble. As I waited there, in prostatic discomfort, drunk, sleep-starved, with my gun in my fist in my raincoat pocket, it suddenly occurred to me that I was demented and was about to do something stupid. There was not one chance in a million that Albert Riggs, Ass. Prof., was hiding my Lolita at his Beardsley home, 24 Pritchard Road. He could not be the villain. It was absolutely preposterous. I was losing my time and my wits. He and she were in California and not here at all.

Presently, I noticed a vague commotion behind some white statues; a door—not the one I had been staring at—opened briskly, and amid a bevy of women students a baldish head and two bright brown eyes bobbed, advanced.

He was a total stranger to me but insisted we had met at a lawn party at Beardsley School. How was my delightful tennis-playing daughter? He had another class. He would be seeing me.

Another attempt at identification was less speedily resolved: through an advertisement in one of Lo's magazines I dared to get in touch with a private detective, an ex-pugilist, and merely to give him some idea of the *method* adopted by the fiend, I acquainted him with the kind of names and addresses I had collected. He demanded a goodish deposit and for two years— two years, reader!—that imbecile busied himself with checking those nonsense data. I had long severed all monetary relations with him when he turned up one day with the triumphant information that an eighty-year-old Indian by the name of Bill Brown lived near Dolores, Colo.   1

25

This book is about Lolita; and now that I have reached the part which (had I not been forestalled by another internal combustion martyr) might be called *"Dolorès Disparue,"* there   2 would be little sense in analyzing the three empty years that followed. While a few pertinent points have to be marked, the general impression I desire to convey is of a side door crashing open in life's full flight, and a rush of roaring black time drowning with its whipping wind the cry of lone disaster.

Singularly enough, I seldom if ever dreamed of Lolita as I remembered her—as I saw her constantly and obsessively in my conscious mind during my daymares and insomnias. More precisely: she did haunt my sleep but she appeared there in strange and ludicrous disguises as Valeria or Charlotte, or a cross between them. That complex ghost would come to me, shedding shift after shift, in an atmosphere of great melancholy and disgust, and would recline in dull invitation on some narrow board or hard settee, with flesh ajar like the rubber valve of a soccer ball's bladder. I would find myself, dentures fractured or hopelessly mislaid, in horrible *chambres garnies* where I would be entertained at tedious vivisecting parties that generally ended with Charlotte or Valeria weeping in my bleeding arms and being tenderly kissed by my brotherly lips in a dream disorder of auctioneered Viennese bric-à-brac, pity, impotence and the brown wigs of tragic old women who had just been gassed.

One day I removed from the car and destroyed an accumulation of teen-magazines. You know the sort. Stone age at heart; up to date, or at least Mycenaean, as to hygiene. A handsome, very ripe actress with huge lashes and a pulpy red underlip, endorsing a shampoo. Ads and fads. Young scholars dote on plenty of pleats—*que c'était loin, tout cela!* It is your hostess' duty to provide robes. Unattached details take all the sparkle out of your conversation. All of us have known "pickers"—one who picks her cuticle at the office party. Unless he is very elderly or very important, a man should remove his gloves before shaking hands with a woman. Invite Romance by wearing the Exciting New Tummy Flattener. Trims tums, nips hips. Tristram in Movielove. Yessir! The Joe-Roe marital enigma is making yaps flap. Glamourize yourself quickly and inexpensively. Comics. Bad girl dark hair fat father cigar; good girl red hair handsome daddums clipped mustache. Or that repulsive strip with the big gagoon and his wife, a kiddoid gnomide. *Et moi qui t'offrais mon génie* ... I recalled the rather charming nonsense verse I used to write her when she was a child: "nonsense," she used to say mockingly, "is correct."

> The Squirl and his Squirrel, the Rabs and their Rabbits
> Have certain obscure and peculiar habits.
> Male hummingbirds make the most exquisite rockets.
> The snake when he walks holds his hands in his pockets...

Other things of hers were harder to relinquish. Up to the end of 1949, I cherished and adored, and stained with my kisses and merman tears, a pair of old sneakers, a boy's shirt she had worn, some ancient blue jeans I found in the trunk compartment, a crumpled school cap, suchlike wanton treasures. Then, when I understood my mind was cracking, I collected these sundry belongings, added to them what had been stored in Beardsley—a box of books, her bicycle, old coats, galoshes—and on her fifteenth birthday mailed everything as an anonymous gift to a home for orphaned girls on a windy lake, on the Canadian border.

It is just possible that had I gone to a strong hypnotist he might have extracted from me and arrayed in a logical pattern certain chance memories that I have threaded through my book with considerably more ostentation than they present themselves with to my mind even now when I know what to seek in the past. At the time I felt I was merely losing contact with reality; and after spending the rest of the winter and most of the following spring in a Quebec sanatorium where I had stayed before, I resolved first to settle some affairs of mine in New York and then to proceed to California for a thorough search there.

Here is something I composed in my retreat:

> Wanted, wanted: Dolores Haze.
> Hair: brown. Lips: scarlet.
> Age: five thousand three hundred days.
> Profession: none, or "starlet."
>
> Where are you hiding, Dolores Haze?
> *Why* are you hiding, darling?
> (I talk in a daze, I walk in a maze,
> I cannot get out, said the starling).

Where are you riding, Dolores Haze?
What make is the magic carpet?
Is a Cream Cougar the present craze?
And where are you parked, my car pet?

Who is your hero, Dolores Haze?
Still one of those blue-caped star-men?
Oh the balmy days and the palmy bays,
And the cars, and the bars, my Carmen!

Oh Dolores, that juke-box hurts!
Are you still dancin', darlin'?
(Both in worn levis, both in torn T-shirts,
And I, in my corner, snarlin').

Happy, happy is gnarled McFate
Touring the States with a child wife,
Plowing his Molly in every State
Among the protected wild life.

1   My Dolly, my folly! Her eyes were *vair*,
And never closed when I kissed her.
2   Know an old perfume called *Soleil Vert*?
Are you from Paris, mister?

L'autre soir un air froid d'opéra m'alita:
Son fêlé—bien fol est qui s'y fie!
Il neige, le décor s'écroule, Lolita!
3   *Lolita, qu'ai-je fait de ta vie?*

Dying, dying, Lolita Haze,
Of hate and remorse, I'm dying.
And again my hairy fist I raise,
And again I hear you crying.

Officer, officer, there they go—
In the rain, where that lighted store is!
And her socks are white, and I love her so
And her name is Haze, Dolores.

Officer, officer, there they are—
Dolores Haze and her lover!
Whip out your gun and follow that car.
Now tumble out, and take cover.

Wanted, wanted: Dolores Haze.
Her dream-gray gaze never flinches.
Ninety pounds is all she weighs
With a height of sixty inches.

My car is limping, Dolores Haze,
And the last long lap is the hardest,
And I shall be dumped where the weed decays,
And the rest is rust and stardust.

By psychoanalyzing this poem, I notice it is really a maniac's masterpiece. The stark, stiff, lurid rhymes correspond very exactly to certain perspectiveless and terrible landscapes and figures, and magnified parts of landscapes and figures, as drawn by psychopaths in tests devised by their astute trainers. I wrote many more poems. I immersed myself in the poetry of others. But not for a second did I forget the load of revenge.

I would be a knave to say, and the reader a fool to believe, that the shock of losing Lolita cured me of pederosis. My accursed nature could not change, no matter how my love for her did. On playgrounds and beaches, my sullen and stealthy eye, against my will, still sought out the flash of a nymphet's limbs, the sly tokens of Lolita's handmaids and rosegirls. But one essential vision in me had withered: never did I dwell now on possibilities of bliss with a little maiden, specific or synthetic, in some out-of-the-way place; never did my fancy sink its fangs into Lolita's sisters, far far away, in the coves of evoked islands. *That* was all over, for the time being at least. On the other hand, alas, two years of monstrous indulgence had left me with certain habits of lust: I feared lest the void I lived in might drive me to plunge into the freedom of sudden insanity when confronted with a chance temptation in some lane between school and supper. Solitude was corrupting me. I needed company and care. My heart was a hysterical unreliable organ. This is how Rita enters the picture.

26

She was twice Lolita's age and three quarters of mine: a very slight, dark-haired, pale-skinned adult, weighing a hundred and five pounds, with charmingly asymmetrical eyes, an angular, rapidly sketched profile, and a most appealing *ensellure* to her supple back—I think she had some Spanish or Babylonian blood. I picked her up one depraved May evening somewhere between Montreal and New York, or more narrowly, between Toylestown and Blake, at a darkishly burning bar under the sign of the Tigermoth, where she was amiably drunk: she insisted we had gone to school together, and she placed her trembling little hand on my ape paw. My senses were very slightly stirred but I decided to give her a try; I did—and adopted her as a constant companion. She was so kind, was Rita, such a good sport, that I daresay she would have given herself to any pathetic creature or fallacy, an old broken tree or a bereaved porcupine, out of sheer chumminess and compassion.

When I first met her she had but recently divorced her third husband—and a little more recently had been abandoned by her seventh *cavalier servant*—the others, the mutables, were too numerous and mobile to tabulate. Her brother was—and no doubt still is—a prominent, pasty-faced, suspenders-and-painted-tie-wearing politician, mayor and booster of his ball-playing, Bible-reading, grain-handling home town. For the last eight years he had been paying his great little sister several hundred dollars per month under the stringent condition that she would never never enter great little Grainball City. She told me, with wails of wonder, that for some God-damn reason every new boy friend of hers would first of all take her Grainball-ward: it was a fatal attraction; and before she knew what was what, she would find herself sucked into the lunar orbit of the town, and would be following the flood-lit drive that encircled it—"going round and round," as she phrased it, "like a God-damn mulberry moth."

1

She had a natty little coupé; and in it we traveled to California so as to give my venerable vehicle a rest. Her natural speed was ninety. Dear Rita! We cruised together for two dim years, from summer 1950 to summer 1952, and she was the sweetest, simplest, gentlest, dumbest Rita imaginable. In comparison to her, Valechka was a Schlegel, and Charlotte a Hegel. There is no 2, 3 earthly reason why I should dally with her in the margin of this sinister memoir, but let me say (hi, Rita—wherever you are, drunk or hangoverish, Rita, hi!) that she was the most soothing, the most comprehending companion that I ever had, and certainly saved me from the madhouse. I told her I was trying to trace a girl and plug that girl's bully. Rita solemnly approved of the plan—and in the course of some investigation she undertook on her own (without really knowing a thing), around San Humbertino, got entangled with a pretty awful crook herself; I had the devil of a time retrieving her—used and bruised but still cocky. Then one day she proposed playing Russian roulette with my sacred automatic; I said you couldn't, it was not a revolver, and we struggled for it, until at last it went off, touching off a very thin and very comical spurt of hot water from the hole it made in the wall of the cabin room; I remember her shrieks of laughter.

The oddly prepubescent curve of her back, her ricey skin, her slow languorous columbine kisses kept me from mischief. It is not the artistic aptitudes that are secondary sexual characters as some shams and shamans have said; it is the other way around: 4 sex is but the ancilla of art. One rather mysterious spree that had 5 interesting repercussions I must notice. I had abandoned the search: the fiend was either in Tartary or burning away in my 6 cerebellum (the flames fanned by my fancy and grief) but certainly not having Dolores Haze play champion tennis on the Pacific Coast. One afternoon, on our way back East, in a hideous hotel, the kind where they hold conventions and where labeled, fat, pink men stagger around, all first names and business and booze—dear Rita and I awoke to find a third in our room, a blond, almost albino, young fellow with white eyelashes and large transparent ears, whom neither Rita nor I recalled having ever seen in our sad lives. Sweating in thick dirty underwear, and with old army boots on, he lay snoring on the double bed beyond my chaste Rita. One of his front teeth was gone, amber pustules grew on his forehead. Ritochka enveloped her sinuous nudity in my raincoat—the first thing at hand; I slipped on a pair of candy-striped drawers; and we took stock of the situation. Five glasses had been used, which, in the way of clues, was an embarrassment of riches. The door was not properly closed. A sweater and a pair of shapeless tan pants lay on the floor. We shook their owner into miserable consciousness. He was completely amnesic. In an accent that Rita recognized as pure Brooklynese, he peevishly insinuated that somehow we had purloined his (worthless) identity. We rushed him into his clothes and left him at the nearest hospital, realizing on the way that somehow or other after forgotten gyrations, we were in Grainball. Half a year later Rita wrote the doctor for news. Jack Humbertson as he had been tastelessly dubbed was still isolated from his personal past. Oh Mnemosyne, sweetest and most mischievous of muses!

1 I would not have mentioned this incident had it not started a chain of ideas that resulted in my publishing in the *Cantrip*
2 *Review* an essay on "Mimir and Memory," in which I suggested among other things that seemed original and important to that splendid review's benevolent readers, a theory of perceptual time based on the circulation of the blood and conceptually depending (to fill up this nutshell) on the mind's being conscious not only of matter but also of its own self, thus creating a continuous spanning of two points (the storable future and the stored past). In result of this venture—and in culmination of the impression
3 made by my previous *travaux*—I was called from New York, where Rita and I were living in a little flat with a view of gleaming children taking shower baths far below in a fountainous arbor of Central Park, to Cantrip College, four hundred miles away, for one year. I lodged there, in special apartments for poets and philosophers, from September 1951 to June 1952, while Rita

whom I preferred not to display vegetated—somewhat indecorously, I am afraid—in a roadside inn where I visited her twice
a week. Then she vanished—more humanly than her predecessor
had done: a month later I found her in the local jail. She was
très digne, had had her appendix removed, and managed to con- 1
vince me that the beautiful bluish furs she had been accused of
stealing from a Mrs. Roland MacCrum had really been a spontaneous, if somewhat alcoholic, gift from Roland himself. I
succeeded in getting her out without appealing to her touchy
brother, and soon afterwards we drove back to Central Park
West, by way of Briceland, where we had stopped for a few
hours the year before.

A curious urge to relive my stay there with Lolita had got hold
of me. I was entering a phase of existence where I had given up
all hope of tracing her kidnaper and her. I now attempted to fall
back on old settings in order to save what still could be saved in
the way of *souvenir, souvenir que me veux-tu?* Autumn was ring- 2
ing in the air. To a post card requesting twin beds Professor
Hamburg got a prompt expression of regret in reply. They were
full up. They had one bathless basement room with four beds
which they thought I would not want. Their note paper was
headed:

THE ENCHANTED HUNTERS

NEAR CHURCHES   NO DOGS
All legal beverages

I wondered if the last statement was true. All? Did they have
for instance sidewalk grenadine? I also wondered if a hunter,
enchanted or otherwise, would not need a pointer more than a
pew, and with a spasm of pain I recalled a scene worthy of a
great artist: *petite nymphe accroupie;* but that silky cocker 3
spaniel had perhaps been a baptized one. No—I felt I could not 4
endure the throes of revisiting that lobby. There was a much
better possibility of retrievable time elsewhere in soft, rich-
colored, autumnal Briceland. Leaving Rita in a bar, I made for
the town library. A twittering spinster was only too glad to help

me disinter mid-August 1947 from the bound *Briceland Gazette*, and presently, in a secluded nook under a naked light, I was turning the enormous and fragile pages of a coffin-black volume almost as big as Lolita.

1   Reader! *Bruder!* What a foolish Hamburg that Hamburg was! Since his supersensitive system was loath to face the actual scene, he thought he could at least enjoy a secret part of it—which reminds one of the tenth or twentieth soldier in the raping queue who throws the girl's black shawl over her white face so as not to see those impossible eyes while taking his military pleasure in the sad, sacked village. What *I* lusted to get was the printed picture that had chanced to absorb my trespassing image while the *Gazette's* photographer was concentrating on Dr. Braddock

2   and his group. Passionately I hoped to find preserved the portrait

3   of the artist as a younger brute. An innocent camera catching me on my dark way to Lolita's bed—what a magnet for Mnemosyne! I cannot well explain the true nature of that urge of mine. It was allied, I suppose, to that swooning curiosity which impels one to examine with a magnifying glass bleak little figures—still life practically, and everybody about to throw up—at an early morning execution, and the patient's expression impossible to make out in the print. Anyway, I was literally gasping for breath, and one corner of the book of doom kept stabbing me in the stomach

4   while I scanned and skimmed...*Brute Force* and *Possessed* were coming on Sunday, the 24th, to both theatres. Mr. Purdom, independent tobacco auctioneer, said that ever since 1925 he had

5   been an Omen Faustum smoker. Husky Hank and his petite bride were to be the guests of Mr. and Mrs. Reginald G. Gore,

6   58 Inchkeith Ave. The size of certain parasites is one sixth of the host. Dunkerque was fortified in the tenth century. Misses' socks, 39 c. Saddle Oxfords 3.98. Wine, wine, wine, quipped the

7   author of *Dark Age* who refused to be photographed, may suit a Persian bubble bird, but I say give me rain, rain, rain on the

8   shingle roof for roses and inspiration every time. Dimples are caused by the adherence of the skin to the deeper tissues. Greeks repulse a heavy guerilla assault—and, ah, at last, a little figure in white, and Dr. Braddock in black, but whatever spectral shoulder

was brushing against his ample form—nothing of myself could I make out.

I went to find Rita who introduced me with her *vin triste* smile to a pocket-sized wizened truculently tight old man saying this was—what was the name again, son?—a former schoolmate of hers. He tried to retain her, and in the slight scuffle that followed I hurt my thumb against his hard head. In the silent painted park where I walked her and aired her a little, she sobbed and said I would soon, soon leave her as everybody had, and I sang her a wistful French ballad, and strung together some fugitive rhymes to amuse her:

> The place was called *Enchanted Hunters*. Query:
> What Indian dyes, Diana, did thy dell
> endorse to make of Picture Lake a very
> blood bath of trees before the blue hotel?

She said: "Why blue when it is white, why blue for heaven's sake?" and started to cry again, and I marched her to the car, and we drove on to New York, and soon she was reasonably happy again high up in the haze on the little terrace of our flat. I notice I have somehow mixed up two events, my visit with Rita to Briceland on our way to Cantrip, and our passing through Briceland again on our way back to New York, but such suffusions of swimming colors are not to be disdained by the artist in recollection.

27

My letterbox in the entrance hall belonged to the type that allows one to glimpse something of its contents through a glassed slit. Several times already, a trick of harlequin light that fell through the glass upon an alien handwriting had twisted it into a semblance of Lolita's script causing me almost to collapse as I leant against an adjacent urn, almost my own. Whenever that happened—whenever her lovely, loopy, childish scrawl was horribly transformed into the dull hand of one of my few correspondents—I used to recollect, with anguished amusement, the times in my trustful, pre-dolorian past when I would be misled by a jewel-bright window opposite wherein my lurking eye, the ever alert periscope of my shameful vice, would make out from afar a half-naked nymphet stilled in the act of combing her

1 Alice-in-Wonderland hair. There was in the fiery phantasm a perfection which made my wild delight also perfect, just because the vision was out of reach, with no possibility of attainment to spoil it by the awareness of an appended taboo; indeed, it may well be that the very attraction immaturity has for me lies not so much in the limpidity of pure young forbidden fairy child beauty as in the security of a situation where infinite perfections fill the gap between the little given and the great promised—the great

2 rosegray never-to-be-had. *Mes fenêtres!* Hanging above blotched sunset and welling night, grinding my teeth, I would crowd all the demons of my desire against the railing of a throbbing balcony: it would be ready to take off in the apricot and black humid evening; did take off—whereupon the lighted image would move and Eve would revert to a rib, and there would be nothing in the window but an obese partly clad man reading the paper.

Since I sometimes won the race between my fancy and nature's reality, the deception was bearable. Unbearable pain began when chance entered the fray and deprived me of the smile meant for

3 me. "*Savez-vous qu'à dix ans ma petite était folle de vous?*" said a woman I talked to at a tea in Paris, and the *petite* had just married, miles away, and I could not even remember if I had ever noticed her in that garden, next to those tennis courts, a dozen years before. And now likewise, the radiant foreglimpse, the promise of reality, a promise not only to be simulated seductively but also to be nobly held—all this, chance denied me —chance and a change to smaller characters on the pale beloved writer's part. My fancy was both Proustianized and Procrus-

4, 5 teanized; for that particular morning, late in September 1952, as I had come down to grope for my mail, the dapper and bilious janitor with whom I was on execrable terms started to complain

[266]

that a man who had seen Rita home recently had been "sick like a dog" on the front steps. In the process of listening to him and tipping him, and then listening to a revised and politer version of the incident, I had the impression that one of the two letters which that blessed mail brought was from Rita's mother, a crazy little woman, whom we had once visited on Cape Cod and who kept writing me to my various addresses, saying how wonderfully well matched her daughter and I were, and how wonderful it would be if we married; the other letter which I opened and scanned rapidly in the elevator was from John Farlow.

I have often noticed that we are inclined to endow our friends with the stability of type that literary characters acquire in the reader's mind. No matter how many times we reopen "King Lear," never shall we find the good king banging his tankard in high revelry, all woes forgotten, at a jolly reunion with all three daughters and their lapdogs. Never will Emma rally, revived by the sympathetic salts in Flaubert's father's timely tear. Whatever evolution this or that popular character has gone through between the book covers, his fate is fixed in our minds, and, similarly, we expect our friends to follow this or that logical and conventional pattern we have fixed for them. Thus X will never compose the immortal music that would clash with the second-rate symphonies he has accustomed us to. Y will never commit murder. Under no circumstances can Z ever betray us. We have it all arranged in our minds, and the less often we see a particular person the more satisfying it is to check how obediently he conforms to our notion of him every time we hear of him. Any deviation in the fates we have ordained would strike us as not only anomalous but unethical. We would prefer not to have known at all our neighbor, the retired hot-dog stand operator, if it turns out he has just produced the greatest book of poetry his age has seen.

I am saying all this in order to explain how bewildered I was by Farlow's hysterical letter. I knew his wife had died but I certainly expected him to remain, throughout a devout widowhood, the dull, sedate and reliable person he had always been. Now he wrote that after a brief visit to the U.S. he had returned

1

2

to South America and had decided that whatever affairs he had controlled at Ramsdale he would hand over to Jack Windmuller of that town, a lawyer whom we both knew. He seemed particularly relieved to get rid of the Haze "complications." He had married a Spanish girl. He had stopped smoking and had gained thirty pounds. She was very young and a ski champion. They were going to India for their honeymonsoon. Since he was "building a family" as he put it, he would have no time henceforth for my affairs which he termed "very strange and very aggravating." Busybodies—a whole committee of them, it appeared—had informed him that the whereabouts of little Dolly Haze were unknown, and that I was living with a notorious divorcee in California. His father-in-law was a count, and exceedingly wealthy. The people who had been renting the Haze house for some years now wished to buy it. He suggested that I better produce Dolly quick. He had broken his leg. He enclosed a snapshot of himself and a brunette in white wool beaming at each other among the snows of Chile.

1

I remember letting myself into my flat and starting to say: Well, at least we shall now track them down—when the other letter began talking to me in a small matter-of-fact voice:

2

Dear Dad:

How's everything? I'm married. I'm going to have a baby. I guess he's going to be a big one. I guess he'll come right for Christmas. This is a hard letter to write. I'm going nuts because we don't have enough to pay our debts and get out of here. Dick is promised a big job in Alaska in his very specialized corner of the mechanical field, that's all I know about it but it's really grand. Pardon me for withholding our home address but you may still be mad at me, and Dick must not know. This town is something. You can't see the morons for the smog. Please do send us a check, Dad. We could manage with three or four hundred or even less, anything is welcome, you might sell my old things, because once we get there the dough will just start rolling in. Write, please. I have gone through much sadness and hardship.

Yours expecting,
Dolly (Mrs. Richard F. Schiller)

I was again on the road, again at the wheel of the old blue sedan, again alone. Rita had still been dead to the world when I read that letter and fought the mountains of agony it raised within me. I had glanced at her as she smiled in her sleep and had kissed her on her moist brow, and had left her forever, with a note of tender adieu which I taped to her navel—otherwise she might not have found it.

"Alone" did I say? *Pas tout à fait.* I had my little black chum with me, and as soon as I reached a secluded spot, I rehearsed Mr. Richard F. Schiller's violent death. I had found a very old and very dirty gray sweater of mine in the back of the car, and this I hung up on a branch, in a speechless glade, which I had reached by a wood road from the now remote highway. The carrying out of the sentence was a little marred by what seemed to me a certain stiffness in the play of the trigger, and I wondered if I should get some oil for the mysterious thing but decided I had no time to spare. Back into the car went the old dead sweater, now with additional perforations, and having reloaded warm Chum, I continued my journey.

The letter was dated September 18, 1952 (this was September 22), and the address she gave was "General Delivery, Coalmont" (not "Va.," not "Pa.," not "Tenn."—and not Coalmont, anyway—I have camouflaged everything, my love). Inquiries showed this to be a small industrial community some eight hundred miles from New York City. At first I planned to drive all day and all night, but then thought better of it and rested for a couple of hours around dawn in a motor court room, a few miles before reaching the town. I had made up my mind that the fiend, this Schiller, had been a car salesman who had perhaps got to know my Lolita by giving her a ride in Beardsley—the day her bike blew a tire on the way to Miss Emperor—and that he had got into some trouble since then. The corpse of the executed sweater, no matter how I changed its contours as it lay on the back seat of the car, had kept revealing various outlines pertaining to Trapp-Schiller—the grossness and obscene bonhommie of his body, and to counteract this taste of coarse corruption I resolved to make myself especially handsome and smart as I pressed home the nipple of my alarm clock before it exploded at the set hour of six A.M. Then, with the stern and romantic care of a gentleman about to fight a duel, I checked the arrangement of my papers, bathed and perfumed my delicate body, shaved my face and chest, selected a silk shirt and clean drawers, pulled on transparent taupe socks, and congratulated myself for having with me in my trunk some very exquisite clothes—a waistcoat with nacreous buttons, for instance, a pale cashmere tie and so on.

I was not able, alas, to hold my breakfast, but dismissed that physicality as a trivial contretemps, wiped my mouth with a gossamer handkerchief produced from my sleeve, and, with a blue block of ice for heart, a pill on my tongue and solid death in my hip pocket, I stepped neatly into a telephone booth in Coalmont (Ah-ah-ah, said its little door) and rang up the only Schiller—Paul, Furniture—to be found in the battered book. Hoarse Paul told me he did know a Richard, the son of a cousin of his, and his address was, let me see, 10 Killer Street (I am not going very far for my pseudonyms). Ah-ah-ah, said the little door.

At 10 Killer Street, a tenement house, I interviewed a number of dejected old people and two long-haired strawberry-blond incredibly grubby nymphets (rather abstractly, just for the heck of it, the ancient beast in me was casting about for some lightly clad child I might hold against me for a minute, after the killing was over and nothing mattered any more, and everything was allowed). Yes, Dick Skiller had lived there, but had moved when he married. Nobody knew his address. "They might know at the store," said a bass voice from an open manhole near which I happened to be standing with the two thin-armed, barefoot little girls and their dim grandmothers. I entered the wrong store and a wary old Negro shook his head even before I could ask anything. I crossed over to a bleak grocery and there, summoned by a customer at my request, a woman's voice from some wooden abyss in the floor, the manhole's counterpart, cried out: Hunter Road, last house.

[270]

Hunter Road was miles away, in an even more dismal district, all dump and ditch, and wormy vegetable garden, and shack, and gray drizzle, and red mud, and several smoking stacks in the distance. I stopped at the last "house"—a clapboard shack, with two or three similar ones farther away from the road and a waste of withered weeds all around. Sounds of hammering came from behind the house, and for several minutes I sat quite still in my old car, old and frail, at the end of my journey, at my gray goal, *finis*, my friends, *finis*, my fiends. The time was around two. My pulse was 40 one minute and 100 the next. The drizzle crepitated against the hood of the car. My gun had migrated to my right trouser pocket. A nondescript cur came out from behind the house, stopped in surprise, and started good-naturedly woof-woofing at me, his eyes slit, his shaggy belly all muddy, and then walked about a little and woofed once more.

29

I got out of the car and slammed its door. How matter-of-fact, how square that slam sounded in the void of the sunless day! *Woof*, commented the dog perfunctorily. I pressed the bell button, it vibrated through my whole system. *Personne. Je resonne. Repersonne.* From what depth this re-nonsense? Woof, said the dog. A rush and a shuffle, and woosh-woof went the door.

Couple of inches taller. Pink-rimmed glasses. New, heaped-up hairdo, new ears. How simple! The moment, the death I had kept conjuring up for three years was as simple as a bit of dry wood. She was frankly and hugely pregnant. Her head looked smaller (only two seconds had passed really, but let me give them as much wooden duration as life can stand), and her pale-freckled cheeks were hollowed, and her bare shins and arms had lost all their tan, so that the little hairs showed. She wore a brown, sleeveless cotton dress and sloppy felt slippers.

"We—e—ell!" she exhaled after a pause with all the emphasis of wonder and welcome.

"Husband at home?" I croaked, fist in pocket.

I could not kill *her*, of course, as some have thought. You see, I loved her. It was love at first sight, at last sight, at ever and ever sight.

"Come in," she said with a vehement cheerful note. Against the splintery deadwood of the door, Dolly Schiller flattened herself as best she could (even rising on tiptoe a little) to let me pass, and was crucified for a moment, looking down, smiling down at the threshold, hollow-cheeked with round *pommettes*, her watered-milk-white arms outspread on the wood. I passed without touching her bulging babe. Dolly-smell, with a faint fried addition. My teeth chattered like an idiot's. "No, you stay out" (to the dog). She closed the door and followed me and her belly into the dollhouse parlor.

"Dick's down there," she said pointing with an invisible tennis racket, inviting my gaze to travel from the drab parlor-bedroom where we stood, right across the kitchen, and through the back-doorway where, in a rather primitive vista, a dark-haired young stranger in overalls, instantaneously reprieved, was perched with his back to me on a ladder fixing something near or upon the shack of his neighbor, a plumper fellow with only one arm, who stood looking up.

This pattern she explained from afar, apologetically ("Men will be men"); should she call him in?

No.

Standing in the middle of the slanting room and emitting questioning "hm's," she made familiar Javanese gestures with her wrists and hands, offering me, in a brief display of humorous courtesy, to choose between a rocker and the divan (their bed after ten P.M.). I say "familiar" because one day she had welcomed me with the same wrist dance to her party in Beardsley. We both sat down on the divan. Curious: although actually her looks had faded, I definitely realized, so hopelessly late in the day, how much she looked—had always looked—like Botticelli's russet Venus—the same soft nose, the same blurred beauty. In my pocket my fingers gently let go and repacked a little at the tip, within the handkerchief it was nested in, my unused weapon.

"That's not the fellow I want," I said.

The diffuse look of welcome left her eyes. Her forehead puckered as in the old bitter days:

"Not *who?*"

"Where is he? Quick!"

"Look," she said, inclining her head to one side and shaking it in that position. "Look, you are not going to bring that up."

"I certainly am," I said, and for a moment—strangely enough the only merciful, endurable one in the whole interview—we were bristling at each other as if she were still mine.

A wise girl, she controlled herself.

Dick did not know a thing of the whole mess. He thought I was her father. He thought she had run away from an upper-class home just to wash dishes in a diner. He believed anything. Why should I want to make things harder than they were by raking up all that muck?

But, I said, she must be sensible, she must be a sensible girl (with her bare drum under that thin brown stuff), she must understand that if she expected the help I had come to give, I must have at least a clear comprehension of the situation.

"Come, his name!"

She thought I had guessed long ago. It was (with a mischievous and melancholy smile) such a sensational name. I would never believe it. She could hardly believe it herself.

His name, my fall nymph.

It was so unimportant, she said. She suggested I skip it. Would I like a cigarette?

No. His name.

She shook her head with great resolution. She guessed it was too late to raise hell and I would never believe the unbelievably unbelievable—

I said I had better go, regards, nice to have seen her.

She said really it was useless, she would never tell, but on the other hand, after all—"Do you really want to know who it was? Well, it was—"

And softly, confidentially, arching her thin eyebrows and puckering her parched lips, she emitted, a little mockingly, somewhat fastidiously, not untenderly, in a kind of muted whistle, the name that the astute reader has guessed long ago.

1 Waterproof. Why did a flash from Hourglass Lake cross my consciousness? I, too, had known it, without knowing it, all along. There was no shock, no surprise. Quietly the fusion took place, and everything fell into order, into the pattern of branches that I have woven throughout this memoir with the express purpose of having the ripe fruit fall at the right moment; yes, with the express and perverse purpose of rendering—she was talking but I sat melting in my golden peace—of rendering that golden and monstrous peace through the satisfaction of logical recogni-
2 tion, which my most inimical reader should experience now.

She was, as I say, talking. It now came in a relaxed flow. He was the only man she had ever been crazy about. What about Dick? Oh, Dick was a lamb, they were quite happy together, but she meant something different. And *I* had never counted, of course?

She considered me as if grasping all at once the incredible—and somehow tedious, confusing and unnecessary—fact that the
3 distant, elegant, slender, forty-year-old valetudinarian in velvet coat sitting beside her had known and adored every pore and follicle of her pubescent body. In her washed-out gray eyes, strangely spectacled, our poor romance was for a moment reflected, pondered upon, and dismissed like a dull party, like a rainy picnic to which only the dullest bores had come, like a humdrum exercise, like a bit of dry mud caking her childhood.

I just managed to jerk my knee out of the range of a sketchy tap—one of her acquired gestures.

She asked me not to be dense. The past was the past. I had been a good father, she guessed—granting me *that*. Proceed, Dolly Schiller.

Well, did I know that he had known her mother? That he was practically an old friend? That he had visited with his uncle in
4 Ramsdale?—oh, years ago—and spoken at Mother's club, and had tugged and pulled her, Dolly, by her bare arm onto his lap in front of everybody, and kissed her face, she was ten and furious with him? Did I know he had seen me and her at the inn

where he was writing the very play she was to rehearse in Beardsley, two years later? Did I know—It had been horrid of her to sidetrack me into believing that Clare was an old female, maybe a relative of his or a sometime lifemate—and oh, what a close shave it had been when the Wace *Journal* carried his picture.

The *Briceland Gazette* had not. Yes, very amusing.

Yes, she said, this world was just one gag after another, if somebody wrote up her life nobody would ever believe it.

At this point, there came brisk homey sounds from the kitchen into which Dick and Bill had lumbered in quest of beer. Through the doorway they noticed the visitor, and Dick entered the parlor.

"Dick, this is my Dad!" cried Dolly in a resounding violent voice that struck me as totally strange, and new, and cheerful, and old, and sad, because the young fellow, veteran of a remote war, was hard of hearing.

Arctic blue eyes, black hair, ruddy cheeks, unshaven chin. We shook hands. Discreet Bill, who evidently took pride in working wonders with one hand, brought in the beer cans he had opened. Wanted to withdraw. The exquisite courtesy of simple folks. Was made to stay. A beer ad. In point of fact, I preferred it that way, and so did the Schillers. I switched to the jittery rocker. Avidly munching, Dolly plied me with marshmallows and potato chips. The men looked at her fragile, *frileux*, diminutive, old-world, youngish but sickly, father in velvet coat and beige vest, maybe a viscount.

They were under the impression I had come to stay, and Dick with a great wrinkling of brows that denoted difficult thought, suggested Dolly and he might sleep in the kitchen on a spare mattress. I waved a light hand and told Dolly who transmitted it by means of a special shout to Dick that I had merely dropped in on my way to Readsburg where I was to be entertained by some friends and admirers. It was then noticed that one of the few thumbs remaining to Bill was bleeding (not such a wonder-worker after all). How womanish and somehow never seen that way before was the shadowy divison between her pale breasts when she bent down over the man's hand! She took him for repairs to the kitchen. For a few minutes, three or four little

eternities which positively welled with artificial warmth, Dick
and I remained alone. He sat on a hard chair rubbing his fore-
limbs and frowning. I had an idle urge to squeeze out the blackheads on the wings of his perspiring nose with my long agate
claws. He had nice sad eyes with beautiful lashes, and very
white teeth. His Adam's apple was large and hairy. Why don't
they shave better, those young brawny chaps? He and his Dolly
had had unrestrained intercourse on that couch there, at least a
hundred and eighty times, probably much more; and before that
—how long had she known him? No grudge. Funny—no grudge
at all, nothing except grief and nausea. He was now rubbing his
nose. I was sure that when finally he would open his mouth, he
would say (slightly shaking his head): "Aw, she's a swell kid,
Mr. Haze. She sure is. And she's going to make a swell mother."
He opened his mouth—and took a sip of beer. This gave him
countenance—and he went on sipping till he frothed at the
1   mouth. He was a lamb. He had cupped her Florentine breasts.
His fingernails were black and broken, but the phalanges, the
whole carpus, the strong shapely wrist were far, far finer than
mine: I have hurt too much too many bodies with my twisted
poor hands to be proud of them. French epithets, a Dorset
2   yokel's knuckles, an Austrian tailor's flat finger tips—that's
Humbert Humbert.

Good. If he was silent I could be silent too. Indeed, I could
very well do with a little rest in this subdued, frightened-to-death
3   rocking chair, before I drove to wherever the beast's lair was—
and then pulled the pistol's foreskin back, and then enjoyed the
orgasm of the crushed trigger: I was always a good little follower
4   of the Viennese medicine man. But presently I became sorry
5   for poor Dick whom, in some hypnotoid way, I was horribly
preventing from making the only remark he could think up
("She's a swell kid . . .").

"And so," I said, "you are going to Canada?"

In the kitchen, Dolly was laughing at something Bill had said
or done.

"And so," I shouted, "you are going to Canada? Not Canada"
—I re-shouted—"I mean Alaska, of course."

He nursed his glass and, nodding sagely, replied: "Well, he cut it on a jagger, I guess. Lost his right arm in Italy."

Lovely mauve almond trees in bloom. A blown-off surrealistic arm hanging up there in the pointillistic mauve. A flowergirl tattoo on the hand. Dolly and band-aided Bill reappeared. It occurred to me that her ambiguous, brown and pale beauty excited the cripple. Dick, with a grin of relief stood up. He guessed Bill and he would be going back to fix those wires. He guessed Mr. Haze and Dolly had loads of things to say to each other. He guessed he would be seeing me before I left. Why do those people guess so much and shave so little, and are so disdainful of hearing aids?

"Sit down," she said, audibly striking her flanks with her palms. I relapsed into the black rocker.

"So you betrayed me? Where did you go? Where is he now?"

She took from the mantelpiece a concave glossy snapshot. Old woman in white, stout, beaming, bowlegged, very short dress; old man in his shirtsleeves, drooping mustache, watch chain. Her in-laws. Living with Dick's brother's family in Juneau.

"Sure you don't want to smoke?"

She was smoking herself. First time I saw her doing it. *Streng verboten* under Humbert the Terrible. Gracefully, in a blue mist, Charlotte Haze rose from her grave. I would find him through Uncle Ivory if she refused.

"Betrayed you? No." She directed the dart of her cigarette, index rapidly tapping upon it, toward the hearth exactly as her mother used to do, and then, like her mother, oh my God, with her fingernail scratched and removed a fragment of cigarette paper from her underlip. No. She had not betrayed me. I was among friends. Edusa had warned her that Cue liked little girls, had been almost jailed once, in fact (nice fact), and he knew she knew. Yes...Elbow in palm, puff, smile, exhaled smoke, darting gesture. Waxing reminiscent. He saw—smiling—through everything and everybody, because he was not like me and her but a genius. A great guy. Full of fun. Had rocked with laughter when she confessed about me and her, and said he had thought so. It was quite safe, under the circumstances, to tell him...

Well, Cue—they all called him Cue—

1 Her camp five years ago. Curious coincidence— ... took her to a dude ranch about a day's drive from Elephant (Elphin-

2 stone). Named? Oh, some silly name—Duk Duk Ranch—*you* know just plain silly—but it did not matter now, anyway, because the place had vanished and disintegrated. Really, she meant, I could not imagine how utterly lush that ranch was, she meant it had everything but everything, even an indoor

3 waterfall. Did I remember the redhaired guy we ("we" was good) had once had some tennis with? Well, the place really belonged to Red's brother, but he had turned it over to Cue for the summer. When Cue and she came, the others had them actually go through a coronation ceremony and then—a terrific ducking, as when you cross the Equator. *You* know.

Her eyes rolled in synthetic resignation.

"Go on, please."

Well. The idea was he would take her in September to Hollywood and arrange a tryout for her, a bit part in the tennis-match scene of a movie picture based on a play of his—*Golden Guts*— and perhaps even have her double one of its sensational starlets on the Klieg-struck tennis court. Alas, it never came to that.

"Where is the hog now?"

He was not a hog. He was a great guy in many respects. But it was all drink and drugs. And, of course, he was a complete freak in sex matters, and his friends were his slaves. I just could not imagine (I, Humbert, could not imagine!) what they all did at Duk Duk Ranch. She refused to take part because she loved him, and he threw her out.

"What things?"

"Oh, weird, filthy, fancy things. I mean, he had two girls and two boys, and three or four men, and the idea was for all of us to tangle in the nude while an old woman took movie pictures."

4 (Sade's Justine was twelve at the start.)

"What things exactly?"

"Oh, things ... Oh, I—really I"—she uttered the "I" as a subdued cry while she listened to the source of the ache, and for lack of words spread the five fingers of her angularly up-and-down-moving hand. No, she gave it up, she refused to go into particulars with that baby inside her.

That made sense.

"It is of no importance now," she said pounding a gray cushion with her fist and then lying back, belly up, on the divan. "Crazy things, filthy things. I said no, I'm just not going to [she used, in all insouciance really, a disgusting slang term which, in a literal French translation, would be *souffler*] your beastly boys, because I want only you. Well, he kicked me out."

There was not much else to tell. That winter 1949, Fay and she had found jobs. For almost two years she had—oh, just drifted, oh, doing some restaurant work in small places, and then she had met Dick. No, she did not know where the other was. In New York, she guessed. Of course, he was so famous she would have found him at once if she had wanted. Fay had tried to get back to the Ranch—and it just was not there any more— it had burned to the ground, *nothing* remained, just a charred heap of rubbish. It was so *strange, so strange*—

She closed her eyes and opened her mouth, leaning back on the cushion, one felted foot on the floor. The wooden floor slanted, a little steel ball would have rolled into the kitchen. I knew all I wanted to know. I had no intention of torturing my darling. Somewhere beyond Bill's shack an afterwork radio had begun singing of folly and fate, and there she was with her ruined looks and her adult, rope-veined narrow hands and her goose-flesh white arms, and her shallow ears, and her unkempt armpits, there she was (my Lolita!), hopelessly worn at seventeen, with that baby, dreaming already in her of becoming a big shot and retiring around 2020 A.D.—and I looked and looked at her, and knew as clearly as I know I am to die, that I loved her more than anything I had ever seen or imagined on earth, or hoped for anywhere else. She was only the faint violet whiff and dead leaf echo of the nymphet I had rolled myself upon with such cries in the past; an echo on the brink of a russet ravine, with a far wood under a white sky, and brown leaves choking the brook, and one last cricket in the crisp weeds . . . but thank God it was not that echo alone that I worshiped. What I used to pamper among the tangled vines of my heart, *mon grand péché radieux*, had dwindled to its essence: sterile and selfish vice, all *that* I canceled and cursed. You may jeer at me, and threaten to clear the court, but until I am gagged and half-throttled, I will shout my poor truth. I insist the world know how much I loved my Lolita, *this* Lolita, pale and polluted, and big with another's child, but still gray-eyed, still sooty-lashed, still auburn and almond, still Carmencita, still mine; *Changeons de vie, ma Carmen, allons vivre quelque part où nous ne serons jamais séparés;* Ohio? The wilds of Massachusetts? No matter, even if those eyes of hers would fade to myopic fish, and her nipples swell and crack, and her lovely young velvety delicate delta be tainted and torn—even then I would go mad with tenderness at the mere sight of your dear wan face, at the mere sound of your raucous young voice, my Lolita.

"Lolita," I said, "this may be neither here nor there but I have to say it. Life is very short. From here to that old car you know so well there is a stretch of twenty, twenty-five paces. It is a very short walk. Make those twenty-five steps. Now. Right now. Come just as you are. And we shall live happily ever after."

Carmen, voulez-vous venir avec moi?

"You mean," she said opening her eyes and raising herself slightly, the snake that may strike, "you mean you will give us [us] that money only if I go with you to a motel. Is *that* what you mean?"

"No," I said, "you got it all wrong. I want you to leave your incidental Dick, and this awful hole, and come to live with me, and die with me, and everything with me" (words to that effect).

"You're crazy," she said, her features working.

"Think it over, Lolita. There are no strings attached. Except, perhaps—well, no matter." (A reprieve, I wanted to say but did not.) "Anyway, if you refuse you will still get your . . . *trousseau.*"

"No kidding?" asked Dolly.

I handed her an envelope with four hundred dollars in cash and a check for three thousand six hundred more.

Gingerly, uncertainly, she received *mon petit cadeau;* and
then her forehead became a beautiful pink. "You mean," she
said, with agonized emphasis, "you are giving us *four thousand
bucks?*" I covered my face with my hand and broke into the
hottest tears I had ever shed. I felt them winding through my
fingers and down my chin, and burning me, and my nose got
clogged, and I could not stop, and then she touched my wrist.

"I'll die if you touch me," I said. "You are sure you are not
coming with me? Is there no hope of your coming? Tell me only
this."

"No," she said. "No, honey, no."

She had never called me honey before.

"No," she said, "it is quite out of the question. I would sooner
go back to Cue. I mean—"

She groped for words. I supplied them mentally (*"He* broke
my heart. *You* merely broke my life").

"I think," she went on—"oops"—the envelope skidded to the
floor—she picked it up—"I think it's oh utterly *grand* of you to
give us all that dough. It settles everything, we can start next
week. Stop crying, please. You should understand. Let me get
you some more beer. Oh, don't cry, I'm so sorry I cheated so
much, but that's the way things are."

I wiped my face and my fingers. She smiled at the *cadeau.*
She exulted. She wanted to call Dick. I said I would have to leave
in a moment, did not want to see him at all, at all. We tried to
think of some subject of conversation. For some reason, I kept
seeing—it trembled and silkily glowed on my damp retina—a
radiant child of twelve, sitting on a threshold, "pinging" pebbles
at an empty can. I almost said—trying to find some casual remark
—"I wonder sometimes what has become of the little McCoo
girl, did she ever get better?"—but stopped in time lest she
rejoin: "I wonder sometimes what has become of the little Haze
girl . . ." Finally, I reverted to money matters. That sum, I said,
represented more or less the net rent from her mother's house;
she said: "Had it not been sold years ago?" No (I admit I *had*
told her this in order to sever all connections with R.); a lawyer

would send a full account of the financial situation later; it was rosy; some of the small securities her mother had owned had gone up and up. Yes, I was quite sure I had to go. I had to go, and find him, and destroy him.

Since I would not have survived the touch of her lips, I kept retreating in a mincing dance, at every step she and her belly made toward me.

She and the dog saw me off. I was surprised (this a rhetorical figure, I was not) that the sight of the old car in which she had ridden as a child and a nymphet, left her so very indifferent. All she remarked was it was getting sort of purplish about the gills. I said it was hers, I could go by bus. She said don't be silly, they would fly to Jupiter and buy a car there. I said I would buy this one from her for five hundred dollars.

"At this rate we'll be millionnaires next," she said to the ecstatic dog.

Carmencita, lui demandais-je ... "One last word," I said in my horrible careful English, "are you quite, quite sure that— well, not tomorrow, of course, and not after tomorrow, but— well—some day, any day, you will not come to live with me? I will create a brand new God and thank him with piercing cries, if you give me that microscopic hope" (to that effect).

"No," she said smiling, "no."

"It would have made all the difference," said Humbert Humbert.

Then I pulled out my automatic—I mean, this is the kind of fool thing a reader might suppose I did. It never even occurred to me to do it.

"Good by-aye!" she chanted, my American sweet immortal dead love; for she is dead and immortal if you are reading this. I mean, such is the formal agreement with the so-called authorities.

Then, as I drove away, I heard her shout in a vibrant voice to her Dick; and the dog started to lope alongside my car like a fat dolphin, but he was too heavy and old, and very soon gave up.

And presently I was driving through the drizzle of the dying day, with the windshield wipers in full action but unable to cope with my tears.

Leaving as I did Coalmont around four in the afternoon (by Route X—I do not remember the number), I might have made Ramsdale by dawn had not a short-cut tempted me. I had to get onto Highway Y. My map showed quite blandly that just beyond Woodbine, which I reached at nightfall, I could leave paved X and reach paved Y by means of a transverse dirt road. It was only some forty miles long according to my map. Otherwise I would have to follow X for another hundred miles and then use leisurely looping Z to get to Y and my destination. However, the short-cut in question got worse and worse, bumpier and bumpier, muddier and muddier, and when I attempted to turn back after some ten miles of purblind, tortuous and tortoise-slow progress, my old and weak Melmoth got stuck in deep clay. All was dark and muggy, and hopeless. My headlights hung over a broad ditch full of water. The surrounding country, if any, was a black wilderness. I sought to extricate myself but my rear wheels only whined in slosh and anguish. Cursing my plight, I took off my fancy clothes, changed into slacks, pulled on the bullet-riddled sweater, and waded four miles back to a roadside farm. It started to rain on the way but I had not the strength to go back for a mackintosh. Such incidents have convinced me that my heart is basically sound despite recent diagnoses. Around midnight, a wrecker dragged my car out. I navigated back to Highway X and traveled on. Utter weariness overtook me an hour later, in an anonymous little town. I pulled up at the curb and in darkness drank deep from a friendly flask.

The rain had been cancelled miles before. It was a black warm night, somewhere in Appalachia. Now and then cars passed me, red tail-lights receding, white headlights advancing, but the town was dead. Nobody strolled and laughed on the sidewalks as relaxing burghers would in sweet, mellow, rotting Europe. I was alone to enjoy the innocent night and my terrible thoughts. A wire receptacle on the curb was very particular about acceptable contents: Sweepings. Paper. No Garbage.

Sherry-red letters of light marked a Camera Shop. A large thermometer with the name of a laxative quietly dwelt on the front of a drugstore. Rubinov's Jewelry Company had a display of artificial diamonds reflected in a red mirror. A lighted green clock swam in the linenish depths of Jiffy Jeff Laundry. On the other side of the street a garage said in its sleep—genuflexion lubricity; and corrected itself to Gulflex Lubrication. An airplane, also gemmed by Rubinov, passed, droning, in the velvet heavens. How many small dead-of-night towns I had seen! This was not yet the last.

Let me dally a little, he is as good as destroyed. Some way further across the street, neon lights flickered twice slower than my heart: the outline of a restaurant sign, a large coffee-pot, kept bursting, every full second or so, into emerald life, and every time it went out, pink letters saying Fine Foods relayed it, but the pot could still be made out as a latent shadow teasing the eye before its next emerald resurrection. We made shadowgraphs. This furtive burg was not far from The Enchanted Hunters. I was weeping again, drunk on the impossible past.

31

At this solitary stop for refreshments between Coalmont and Ramsdale (between innocent Dolly Schiller and jovial Uncle Ivor), I reviewed my case. With the utmost simplicity and clarity I now saw myself and my love. Previous attempts seemed out of focus in comparison. A couple of years before, under the guidance of an intelligent French-speaking confessor, to whom, in a moment of metaphysical curiosity, I had turned over a Protestant's drab atheism for an old-fashioned popish cure, I had hoped to deduce from my sense of sin the existence of a Supreme Being. On those frosty mornings in rime-laced Quebec, the good priest worked on me with the finest tenderness and understanding. I am infinitely obliged to him and the great Institution he represented. Alas, I was unable to transcend the simple human fact that whatever spiritual solace I might find, whatever lithophanic eternities might be provided for me, nothing could make my Lólita forget the foul lust I had inflicted upon her. Unless it can be proven to me—to me as I am now, today, with my heart and my beard, and my putrefaction —that in the infinite run it does not matter a jot that a North American girl-child named Dolores Haze had been deprived of her childhood by a maniac, unless this can be proven (and if it can, then life is a joke), I see nothing for the treatment of my misery but the melancholy and very local palliative of articulate art. To quote an old poet:

> The moral sense in mortals is the duty
> We have to pay on mortal sense of beauty.

32

There was the day, during our first trip—our first circle of paradise—when in order to enjoy my phantasms in peace I firmly decided to ignore what I could not help perceiving, the fact that I was to her not a boy friend, not a glamour man, not a pal, not even a person at all, but just two eyes and a foot of engorged brawn—to mention only mentionable matters. There was the day when having withdrawn the functional promise I had made her on the eve (whatever she had set her funny little heart on—a roller rink with some special plastic floor or a movie matinee to which she wanted to go alone), I happened to glimpse from the bathroom, through a chance combination of mirror aslant and door ajar, a look on her face . . . that look I cannot exactly describe . . . an expression of helplessness so perfect that it seemed to grade into one of rather comfortable inanity just because this was the very limit of injustice and frustration—and every limit presupposes something beyond it— hence the neutral illumination. And when you bear in mind that these were the raised eyebrows and parted lips of a child, you may better appreciate what depths of calculated carnality, what reflected despair, restrained me from falling at her dear feet and dissolving in human tears, and sacrificing my jealousy to whatever pleasure Lolita might hope to derive from mixing with dirty and dangerous children in an outside world that was real to her.

And I have still other smothered memories, now unfolding themselves into limbless monsters of pain. Once, in a sunset-ending street of Beardsley, she turned to little Eva Rosen (I was taking both nymphets to a concert and walking behind them so close as almost to touch them with my person), she turned to Eva, and so very serenely and seriously, in answer to something the other had said about its being better to die than hear Milton Pinski, some local schoolboy she knew, talk about music, my Lolita remarked:

"You know, what's so dreadful about dying is that you are completely on your own"; and it struck me, as my automaton knees went up and down, that I simply did not know a thing about my darling's mind and that quite possibly, behind the awful juvenile clichés, there was in her a garden and a twi-
1   light, and a palace gate—dim and adorable regions which happened to be lucidly and absolutely forbidden to me, in my polluted rags and miserable convulsions; for I often noticed that living as we did, she and I, in a world of total evil, we would become strangely embarrassed whenever I tried to discuss something she and an older friend, she and a parent, she and a real healthy sweetheart, I and Annabel, Lolita and a sublime, puri-fied, analyzed, deified Harold Haze, might have discussed—an
2, 3   abstract idea, a painting, stippled Hopkins or shorn Baudelaire,
4   God or Shakespeare, anything of a genuine kind. Good will! She would mail her vulnerability in trite brashness and bore-dom, whereas I, using for my desperately detached comments an artificial tone of voice that set my own last teeth on edge, pro-voked my audience to such outbursts of rudeness as made any further conversation impossible, oh my poor, bruised child.
5   I loved you. I was a pentapod monster, but I loved you. I
6   was despicable and brutal, and turpid, and everything, *mais je*
7   *t'aimais, je t'aimais!* And there were times when I knew how

[286]

you felt, and it was hell to know it, my little one. Lolita girl, brave Dolly Schiller.

I recall certain moments, let us call them icebergs in paradise, when after having had my fill of her—after fabulous, insane exertions that left me limp and azure-barred—I would gather her in my arms with, at last, a mute moan of human tenderness (her skin glistening in the neon light coming from the paved court through the slits in the blind, her soot-black lashes matted, her grave gray eyes more vacant than ever—for all the world a little patient still in the confusion of a drug after a major operation)—and the tenderness would deepen to shame and despair, and I would lull and rock my lone light Lolita in my marble arms, and moan in her warm hair, and caress her at random and mutely ask her blessing, and at the peak of this human agonized selfless tenderness (with my soul actually hanging around her naked body and ready to repent), all at once, ironically, horribly, lust would swell again—and "oh, *no*," Lolita would say with a sigh to heaven, and the next moment the tenderness and the azure—all would be shattered.

Mid-twentieth century ideas concerning child-parent relationship have been considerably tainted by the scholastic rigmarole and standardized symbols of the psychoanalytic racket, but I hope I am addressing myself to unbiased readers. Once when Avis's father had honked outside to signal papa had come to take his pet home, I felt obliged to invite him into the parlor, and he sat down for a minute, and while we conversed, Avis, a heavy, unattractive, affectionate child, drew up to him and eventually perched plumply on his knee. Now, I do not remember if I have mentioned that Lolita always had an absolutely enchanting smile for strangers, a tender furry slitting of the eyes, a dreamy sweet radiance of all her features which did not mean a thing of course, but was so beautiful, so endearing that one found it hard to reduce such sweetness to but a magic gene automatically lighting up her face in atavistic token of some ancient rite of welcome—hospitable prostitution, the coarse reader may say. Well, there she stood while Mr. Byrd twirled his hat and talked, and—yes, look how stupid of me, I have left out the main characteristic of the famous Lolita smile, namely: while the tender, nectared, dimpled brightness played, it was never directed at the stranger in the room but hung in its own remote flowered void, so to speak, or wandered with myopic softness over chance objects—and this is what was happening now: while fat Avis sidled up to her papa, Lolita gently beamed at a fruit knife that she fingered on the edge of the table, whereon she leaned, many miles away from me. Suddenly, as Avis clung to her father's neck and ear while, with a casual arm, the man enveloped his lumpy and large offspring, I saw Lolita's smile lose all its light and become a frozen little shadow of itself, and the fruit knife slipped off the table and struck her with its silver handle a freak blow on the ankle which made her gasp, and crouch head forward, and then, jumping on one leg, her face awful with the preparatory grimace which children hold till the tears gush, she was gone—to be followed at once and consoled in the kitchen by Avis who had such a wonderful fat pink dad and a small chubby brother, and a brand-new baby sister, and a home, and two grinning dogs, and Lolita had nothing. And I have a neat pendant to that little scene—also in a Beardsley setting. Lolita, who had been reading near the fire, stretched herself, and then inquired, her elbow up, with a grunt: "Where is she buried anyway?" "Who?" "Oh, you know, my murdered mummy." "And *you* know where her grave is," I said controlling myself, whereupon I named the cemetery—just outside Ramsdale, between the railway tracks and Lakeview Hill. "Moreover," I added, "the tragedy of such an accident is somewhat cheapened by the epithet you saw fit to apply to it. If you really wish to triumph in your mind over the idea of death—" "Ray," said Lo for hurray, and languidly left the room, and for a long while I stared with smarting eyes into the fire. Then I picked up her book. It was some trash for young people. There was a gloomy girl Marion, and there was her stepmother who turned out to be, against all expectations, a young, gay, understanding redhead who explained to Marion that Marion's dead mother had really been a heroic woman since she had deliberately dissimulated her great love for Marion because she was dying, and did not want her child to miss her. I did not rush up to her room with cries. I always preferred the mental hygiene of noninterference. Now, squirming and pleading with my own memory, I recall that on this and similar occasions, it was always my habit and method to ignore Lolita's states of mind while comforting my own base self. When my mother, in a livid wet dress, under the tumbling mist (so I vividly imagined her), had run panting ecstatically up that ridge above Moulinet to be felled there by a thunderbolt, I was but an infant, and in retrospect no yearnings of the accepted kind could I ever graft upon any moment of my youth, no matter how savagely psychotherapists heckled me in my later periods of depression. But I admit that a man of my power of imagination cannot plead personal ignorance of universal emotions. I may also have relied too much on the abnormally chill relations between Charlotte and her daughter. But the awful point of the whole argument is this. It had become gradually clear to my conventional Lolita during our singular and bestial cohabitation that even the most miserable of family lives was better than the parody of incest, which, in the long run, was the best I could offer the waif.

33

Ramsdale revisited. I approached it from the side of the lake. The sunny noon was all eyes. As I rode by in my mud-flecked car, I could distinguish scintillas of diamond water between the far pines. I turned into the cemetery and walked among the long and short stone monuments. *Bonzhur*, Charlotte. On some of the graves there were pale, transparent little national flags slumped in the windless air under the evergreens. Gee, Ed, that was bad luck—referring to G. Edward Grammar, a thirty-five-year-old New York office manager who had just been arrayed on a charge of murdering his thirty-three-year-old wife, Dorothy. Bidding for the perfect crime, Ed had bludgeoned his wife and put her into a car. The case came to light when two county policemen on patrol saw Mrs. Grammar's new big blue Chrysler, an anniversary present from her husband, speeding crazily down a hill, just inside their jurisdiction (God bless our good cops!). The car sideswiped a pole, ran up an embankment covered with beard grass, wild strawberry and cinquefoil, and overturned. The wheels were still gently spinning in the mellow sunlight when the officers removed Mrs. G's body. It appeared to be a routine highway accident at first. Alas, the woman's battered body did not match up with only minor damage suffered by the car. I did better.

I rolled on. It was funny to see again the slender white church and the enormous elms. Forgetting that in an American sub-urban street a lone pedestrian is more conspicuous than a lone motorist, I left the car in the avenue to walk unobtrusively past 342 Lawn Street. Before the great bloodshed, I was entitled to a little relief, to a cathartic spasm of mental regurgitation. Closed were the white shutters of the Junk mansion, and some-body had attached a found black velvet hair ribbon to the white FOR SALE sign which was leaning toward the sidewalk. No dog barked. No gardener telephoned. No Miss Opposite sat on the vined porch—where to the lone pedestrian's annoyance two pony-tailed young women in identical polka-dotted pina-fores stopped doing whatever they were doing to stare at him: she was long dead, no doubt, these might be her twin nieces from Philadelphia.

1   Should I enter my old house? As in a Turgenev story, a tor-rent of Italian music came from an open window—that of the living room: what romantic soul was playing the piano where
2   no piano had plunged and plashed on that bewitched Sunday with the sun on her beloved legs? All at once I noticed that from the lawn I had mown a golden-skinned, brown-haired nymphet of nine or ten, in white shorts, was looking at me with wild fascination in her large blue-black eyes. I said something pleasant to her, meaning no harm, an old-world compliment, what nice eyes you have, but she retreated in haste and the music stopped abruptly, and a violent-looking dark man, glis-tening with sweat, came out and glared at me. I was on the

point of identifying myself when, with a pang of dream-embarrassment, I became aware of my mud-caked dungarees, my filthy and torn sweater, my bristly chin, my bum's bloodshot eyes. Without saying a word, I turned and plodded back the way I had come. An aster-like anemic flower grew out of a remembered chink in the sidewalk. Quietly resurrected, Miss Opposite was being wheeled out by her nieces, onto her porch, as if it were a stage and I the star performer. Praying she would not call to me, I hurried to my car. What a steep little street. What a profound avenue. A red ticket showed between wiper and windshield; I carefully tore it into two, four, eight pieces.

Feeling I was losing my time, I drove energetically to the downtown hotel where I had arrived with a new bag more than five years before. I took a room, made two appointments by telephone, shaved, bathed, put on black clothes and went down for a drink in the bar. Nothing had changed. The barroom was suffused with the same dim, impossible garnet-red light that in Europe years ago went with low haunts, but here meant a bit of atmosphere in a family hotel. I sat at the same little table where at the very start of my stay, immediately after becoming Charlotte's lodger, I had thought fit to celebrate the occasion by suavely sharing with her half a bottle of champagne, which had fatally conquered her poor brimming heart. As then, a moon-faced waiter was arranging with stellar care fifty sherries on a round tray for a wedding party. Murphy-Fantasia, this time. It   1
was eight minutes to three. As I walked through the lobby, I had to skirt a group of ladies who with *mille grâces* were   2
taking leave of each other after a luncheon party. With a harsh cry of recognition, one pounced upon me. She was a stout, short woman in pearl-gray, with a long, gray, slim plume to her small hat. It was Mrs. Chatfield. She attacked me with a fake smile, all aglow with evil curiosity. (Had I done to Dolly, perhaps, what Frank Lasalle, a fifty-year-old mechanic, had done to eleven-year-old Sally Horner in 1948?) Very soon I had that avid glee well under control. She thought I was in California. How was—? With exquisite pleasure I informed her that my stepdaughter had just married a brilliant young mining engineer

[291]

with a hush-hush job in the Northwest. She said she disapproved of such early marriages, she would never let her Phyllis, who was now eighteen—

"Oh yes, of course," I said quietly. "I remember Phyllis. Phyllis and Camp Q. Yes, of course. By the way, did she ever tell you how Charlie Holmes debauched there his mother's little charges?"

Mrs. Chatfield's already broken smile now disintegrated completely.

"For shame," she cried, "for shame, Mr. Humbert! The poor boy has just been killed in Korea."

1 I said didn't she think "*vient de*," with the infinitive, expressed recent events so much more neatly than the English "just," with the past? But I had to be trotting off, I said.

There were only two blocks to Windmuller's office. He greeted me with a very slow, very enveloping, strong, searching grip. He thought I was in California. Had I not lived at one time at Beardsley? His daughter had just entered Beardsley College. And how was—? I gave all necessary information about Mrs. Schiller. We had a pleasant business conference. I walked out into the hot September sunshine a contented pauper.

Now that everything had been put out of the way, I could dedicate myself freely to the main object of my visit to Ramsdale. In the methodical manner on which I have always prided myself, I had been keeping Clare Quilty's face masked in my dark dungeon, where he was waiting for me to come with barber

2 and priest: "*Réveillez-vous, Laqueue, il est temps de mourir!*" I have no time right now to discuss the mnemonics of physiognomization—I am on my way to his uncle and walking fast—but let me jot down this: I had preserved in the alcohol of a

3 clouded memory the toad of a face. In the course of a few glimpses, I had noticed its slight resemblance to a cheery and rather repulsive wine dealer, a relative of mine in Switzerland. With his dumbbells and stinking tricot, and fat hairy arms, and bald patch, and pig-faced servant-concubine, he was on the whole a harmless old rascal. Too harmless, in fact, to be confused with my prey. In the state of mind I now found myself,

[292]

I had lost contact with Trapp's image. It had become completely engulfed by the face of Clare Quilty—as represented, with artistic precision, by an easeled photograph of him that stood on his uncle's desk.

In Beardsley, at the hands of charming Dr. Molnar, I had 1 undergone a rather serious dental operation, retaining only a few upper and lower front teeth. The substitutes were dependent on a system of plates with an inconspicuous wire affair running along my upper gums. The whole arrangement was a masterpiece of comfort, and my canines were in perfect health. However, to garnish my secret purpose with a plausible pretext, I told Dr. Quilty that, in hope of alleviating facial neuralgia, I had decided to have all my teeth removed. What would a complete set of dentures cost? How long would the process take, assuming we fixed our first appointment for some time in November? Where was his famous nephew now? Would it be possible to have them all out in one dramatic session?

A white-smocked, gray-haired man, with a crew cut and the big flat cheeks of a politician, Dr. Quilty perched on the corner of his desk, one foot dreamily and seductively rocking as he launched on a glorious long-range plan. He would first provide me with provisional plates until the gums settled. Then he would make me a permanent set. He would like to have a look at that mouth of mine. He wore perforated pied shoes. He had not visited with the rascal since 1946, but supposed he could be found at his ancestral home, Grimm Road, not far from Parkington. It was a noble dream. His foot rocked, his gaze was inspired. It would cost me around six hundred. He suggested 2 he take measurements right away, and make the first set before starting operations. My mouth was to him a splendid cave full of priceless treasures, but I denied him entrance.

"No," I said. "On second thoughts, I shall have it all done by Dr. Molnar. His price is higher, but he is of course a much better dentist than you."

I do not know if any of my readers will ever have a chance to say that. It is a delicious dream feeling. Clare's uncle remained sitting on the desk, still looking dreamy, but his foot had stopped push-rocking the cradle of rosy anticipation. On the other hand, his nurse, a skeleton-thin, faded girl, with the tragic eyes of unsuccessful blondes, rushed after me so as to be able to slam the door in my wake.

Push the magazine into the butt. Press home until you hear or feel the magazine catch engage. Delightfully snug. Capacity: eight cartridges. Full Blued. Aching to be discharged.

34

A gas station attendant in Parkington explained to me very clearly how to get to Grimm Road. Wishing to be sure Quilty would be at home, I attempted to ring him up but learned that his private telephone had recently been disconnected. Did that mean he was gone? I started to drive to Grimm Road, twelve miles north of the town. By that time night had eliminated most of the landscape and as I followed the narrow winding highway, a series of short posts, ghostly white, with reflectors, borrowed my own lights to indicate this or that curve. I could make out a dark valley on one side of the road and wooded slopes on the other, and in front of me, like derelict snowflakes, moths drifted out of the blackness into my probing aura. At the twelfth mile, as foretold, a curiously hooded bridge sheathed me for a moment and, beyond it, a white-washed rock loomed on the right, and a few car lengths further, on the same side, I turned off the highway up gravelly Grimm Road. For a couple of minutes all was dank, dark, dense forest. Then, Pavor Manor, a wooden house with a turret, arose in a circular clearing. Its windows glowed yellow and red; its drive was cluttered with half a dozen cars. I stopped in the shelter of the trees and abolished my lights to ponder the next move quietly. He would be surrounded by his henchmen and whores. I could not help seeing the inside of that festive and ramshackle castle in terms of "Troubled Teens," a story in one of her magazines, vague "orgies," a sinister adult with penele cigar, drugs, bodyguards. At least, he was there. I would return in the torpid morning.

Gently I rolled back to town, in that old faithful car of mine which was serenely, almost cheerfully working for me. My Lolita! There was still a three-year-old bobby pin of hers in the depths of the glove compartment. There was still that stream of pale moths siphoned out of the night by my headlights. Dark barns still propped themselves up here and there by the roadside. People were still going to the movies. While searching for night lodgings, I passed a drive-in. In a selenian glow, truly mystical in its contrast with the moonless and massive night, on a gigantic screen slanting away among dark drowsy fields, a thin phantom raised a gun, both he and his arm reduced to tremulous dishwater by the oblique angle of that receding world,—and the next moment a row of trees shut off the gesticulation.

35

I left Insomnia Lodge next morning around eight and spent some time in Parkington. Visions of bungling the execution kept obsessing me. Thinking that perhaps the cartridges in the automatic had gone stale during a week of inactivity, I removed them and inserted a fresh batch. Such a thorough oil bath did I give Chum that now I could not get rid of the stuff. I bandaged him up with a rag, like a maimed limb, and used another rag to wrap up a handful of spare bullets.

A thunderstorm accompanied me most of the way back to Grimm Road, but when I reached Pavor Manor, the sun was visible again, burning like a man, and the birds screamed in the drenched and steaming trees. The elaborate and decrepit house seemed to stand in a kind of daze, reflecting as it were my own state, for I could not help realizing, as my feet touched the springy and insecure ground, that I had overdone the alcoholic stimulation business.

A guardedly ironic silence answered my bell. The garage, however, was loaded with his car, a black convertible for the nonce. I tried the knocker. Re-nobody. With a petulant snarl, I pushed the front door—and, how nice, it swung open as in a medieval

1 fairy tale. Having softly closed it behind me, I made my way across a spacious and very ugly hall; peered into an adjacent drawing room; noticed a number of used glasses growing out of the carpet; decided that master was still asleep in the master bedroom.

So I trudged upstairs. My right hand clutched muffled Chum in my pocket, my left patted the sticky banisters. Of the three bedrooms I inspected, one had obviously been slept in that night. There was a library full of flowers. There was a rather

2 bare room with ample and deep mirrors and a polar bear skin on the slippery floor. There were still other rooms. A happy thought struck me. If and when master returned from his constitutional in the woods, or emerged from some secret lair, it might be wise for an unsteady gunman with a long job before him to prevent his playmate from locking himself up in a room. Consequently, for at least five minutes I went about—lucidly insane, crazily calm, an enchanted and very tight hunter—turning whatever keys in whatever locks there were and pocketing

3 them with my free left hand. The house, being an old one, had more planned privacy than have modern glamour-boxes, where the bathroom, the only lockable locus, has to be used for the furtive needs of planned parenthood.

Speaking of bathrooms—I was about to visit a third one when

4 master came out of it, leaving a brief waterfall behind him. The corner of a passage did not quite conceal me. Gray-faced, baggy-eyed, fluffily disheveled in a scanty balding way, but still perfectly recognizable, he swept by me in a purple bathrobe, very like one I had. He either did not notice me, or else dismissed me as some familiar and innocuous hallucination—and, showing me his hairy calves, he proceeded, sleepwalker-wise, downstairs. I pocketed my last key and followed him into the entrance hall. He had half opened his mouth and the front door, to peer out through a sunny chink as one who thinks he has heard a half-hearted visitor ring and recede. Then, still ignoring

the raincoated phantasm that had stopped in midstairs, master walked into a cozy boudoir across the hall from the drawing room, through which—taking it easy, knowing he was safe—I now went away from him, and in a bar-adorned kitchen gingerly unwrapped dirty Chum, taking care not to leave any oil stains on the chrome—I think I got the wrong product, it was black and awfully messy. In my usual meticulous way, I transferred naked Chum to a clean recess about me and made for the little boudoir. My step, as I say, was springy—too springy perhaps for success. But my heart pounded with tiger joy, and I crunched a cocktail glass underfoot.

Master met me in the Oriental parlor.

"Now who are you?" he asked in a high hoarse voice, his hands thrust into his dressing-gown pockets, his eyes fixing a point to the northeast of my head. "Are you by any chance Brewster?"

By now it was evident to everybody that he was in a fog and completely at my so-called mercy. I could enjoy myself.

"That's right," I answered suavely. "*Je suis Monsieur Brustère.* 1 Let us chat for a moment before we start."

He looked pleased. His smudgy mustache twitched. I removed my raincoat. I was wearing a black suit, a black shirt, no tie. We sat down in two easy chairs.

"You know," he said, scratching loudly his fleshy and gritty gray cheek and showing his small pearly teeth in a crooked grin, "you don't *look* like Jack Brewster. I mean, the resemblance is not particularly striking. Somebody told me he had a brother with the same telephone company."

To have him trapped, after those years of repentance and rage...To look at the black hairs on the back of his pudgy hands...To wander with a hundred eyes over his purple silks and hirsute chest foreglimpsing the punctures, and mess, and music of pain...To know that this semi-animated, subhuman trickster who had sodomized my darling—oh, my darling, this was intolerable bliss!

"No, I am afraid I am neither of the Brewsters."

He cocked his head, looking more pleased than ever.

1   "Guess again, Punch."

"Ah," said Punch, "so you have not come to bother me about those long-distance calls?"

"You do make them once in a while, don't you?"

"Excuse me?"

I said I had said I thought he had said he had never—

"People," he said, "people in general, I'm not accusing you, Brewster, but you know it's absurd the way people invade this 2 damned house without even knocking. They use the *vaterre*, they use the kitchen, they use the telephone. Phil calls Phila- 3 delphia. Pat calls Patagonia. I refuse to pay. You have a funny accent, Captain."

"Quilty," I said, "do you recall a little girl called Dolores 4 Haze, Dolly Haze? Dolly called Dolores, Colo.?"

"Sure, she may have made those calls, sure. Any place. Para- 5 dise, Wash., Hell Canyon. Who cares?"

"I do, Quilty. You see, I am her father."

"Nonsense," he said. "You are not. You are some foreign liter-ary agent. A Frenchman once translated my *Proud Flesh* as *La* 6 *Fierté de la Chair*. Absurd."

"She was my child, Quilty."

In the state he was in he could not really be taken aback by anything, but his blustering manner was not quite convincing. A sort of wary inkling kindled his eyes into a semblance of life. They were immediately dulled again.

"I'm very fond of children myself," he said, "and fathers are among my best friends."

He turned his head away, looking for something. He beat his pockets. He attempted to rise from his seat.

"Down!" I said—apparently much louder than I intended.

"You need not roar at me," he complained in his strange feminine manner. "I just wanted a smoke. I'm dying for a smoke."

"You're dying anyway."

"Oh, chucks," he said. "You begin to bore me. What do you 7 want? Are you French, mister? Woolly-woo-boo-are? Let's go to the barroomette and have a stiff—"

He saw the little dark weapon lying in my palm as if I were offering it to him.

"Say!" he drawled (now imitating the underworld numbskull of movies), "that's a swell little gun you've got there. What d'you want for her?"

I slapped down his outstretched hand and he managed to knock over a box on a low table near him. It ejected a handful of cigarettes.

"Here they are," he said cheerfully. "You recall Kipling: *une femme est une femme, mais un Caporal est une cigarette?* Now we need matches." 1

"Quilty," I said. "I want you to concentrate. You are going to die in a moment. The hereafter for all we know may be an eternal state of excruciating insanity. You smoked your last cigarette yesterday. Concentrate. Try to understand what is happening to you."

He kept taking the Drome cigarette apart and munching bits of it.

"I am willing to try," he said. "You are either Australian, or a German refugee. Must you talk to me? This is a Gentile's house, you know. Maybe, you'd better run along. And do stop 2 demonstrating that gun. I've an old Stern-Luger in the music room."

I pointed Chum at his slippered foot and crushed the trigger. It clicked. He looked at his foot, at the pistol, again at his foot. I made another awful effort, and, with a ridiculously feeble and juvenile sound, it went off. The bullet entered the thick pink rug, and I had the paralyzing impression that it had merely trickled in and might come out again.

"See what I mean?" said Quilty. "You should be a little more careful. Give me that thing for Christ's sake."

He reached for it. I pushed him back into the chair. The rich joy was waning. It was high time I destroyed him, but he must understand why he was being destroyed. His condition infected me, the weapon felt limp and clumsy in my hand.

"Concentrate," I said, "on the thought of Dolly Haze whom you kidnaped—"

"I did not!" he cried. "You're all wet. I saved her from a beastly pervert. Show me your badge instead of shooting at my foot, you ape, you. Where is that badge? I'm not responsible for the rapes of others. Absurd! That joy ride, I grant you, was a silly stunt but you got her back, didn't you? Come, let's have a drink."

I asked him whether he wanted to be executed sitting or standing.

"Ah, let me think," he said. "It is not an easy question. Incidentally—I made a mistake. Which I sincerely regret. You see, I had no fun with your Dolly. I am practically impotent, to tell the melancholy truth. And I gave her a splendid vacation. She met some remarkable people. Do you happen to know—"

And with a tremendous lurch he fell all over me, sending the pistol hurtling under a chest of drawers. Fortunately he was more impetuous than vigorous, and I had little difficulty in shoving him back into his chair.

He puffed a little and folded his arms on his chest.

"Now you've done it," he said. "*Vous voilà dans de beaux draps, mon vieux.*"

His French was improving.

I looked around. Perhaps, if—Perhaps I could—On my hands and knees? Risk it?

"*Alors, que fait-on?*" he asked watching me closely.

I stooped. He did not move. I stooped lower.

"My dear sir," he said, "stop trifling with life and death. I am a playwright. I have written tragedies, comedies, fantasies. I have made private movies out of *Justine* and other eighteenth-century sexcapades. I'm the author of fifty-two successful scenarios. I know all the ropes. Let me handle this. There should be a poker somewhere, why don't I fetch it, and then we'll fish out your property."

Fussily, busybodily, cunningly, he had risen again while he talked. I groped under the chest trying at the same time to keep an eye on him. All of a sudden I noticed that he had noticed that I did not seem to have noticed Chum protruding from beneath the other corner of the chest. We fell to wrestling again.

We rolled all over the floor, in each other's arms, like two huge helpless children. He was naked and goatish under his robe, and I felt suffocated as he rolled over me. I rolled over him. We rolled over me. They rolled over him. We rolled over us.

In its published form, this book is being read, I assume, in the first years of 2000 A.D. (1935 plus eighty or ninety, live long, my love); and elderly readers will surely recall at this point the obligatory scene in the Westerns of their childhood. Our tussle, however, lacked the ox-stunning fisticuffs, the flying furniture. He and I were two large dummies, stuffed with dirty cotton and rags. It was a silent, soft, formless tussle on the part of two literati, one of whom was utterly disorganized by a drug while the other was handicapped by a heart condition and too much gin. When at last I had possessed myself of my precious weapon, and the scenario writer had been reinstalled in his low chair, both of us were panting as the cowman and the sheepman never do after their battle.

I decided to inspect the pistol—our sweat might have spoiled something—and regain my wind before proceeding to the main item in the program. To fill in the pause, I proposed he read his own sentence—in the poetical form I had given it. The term "poetical justice" is one that may be most happily used in this respect. I handed him a neat typescript.

"Yes," he said, "splendid idea. Let me fetch my reading glasses" (he attempted to rise).

"No."

"Just as you say. Shall I read out loud?"

"Yes."

"Here goes. I see it's in verse.

> Because you took advantage of a sinner
> because you took advantage
> because you took
> because you took advantage of my disadvantage . . .

1

"That's good, you know. That's damned good."

> . . . when I stood Adam-naked
> before a federal law and all its stinging stars

"Oh, grand stuff!"

> ...Because you took advantage of a sin
> when I was helpless moulting moist and tender
> hoping for the best
> dreaming of marriage in a mountain state
> aye of a litter of Lolitas...

1

"Didn't get that."

> Because you took advantage of my inner
> essential innocence
> because you cheated me—

"A little repetitious, what? Where was I?"

> Because you cheated me of my redemption
> because you took
> her at the age when lads
> play with erector sets

"Getting smutty, eh?"

> a little downy girl still wearing poppies
> still eating popcorn in the colored gloam
> where tawny Indians took paid croppers
> because you stole her
> from her wax-browed and dignified protector
> spitting into his heavy-lidded eye
> ripping his flavid toga and at dawn
> leaving the hog to roll upon his new discomfort
> the awfulness of love and violets
> remorse despair while you
> took a dull doll to pieces
> and threw its head away
> because of all you did
> because of all I did not
> you have to die

2

"Well, sir, this is certainly a fine poem. Your best as far as I am concerned."

He folded and handed it back to me.

[302]

I asked him if he had anything serious to say before dying.
The automatic was again ready for use on the person. He looked
at it and heaved a big sigh.

"Now look here, Mac," he said. "You are drunk and I am a
sick man. Let us postpone the matter. I need quiet. I have to
nurse my impotence. Friends are coming in the afternoon to
take me to a game. This pistol-packing farce is becoming a
frightful nuisance. We are men of the world, in everything—
sex, free verse, marksmanship. If you bear me a grudge, I am
ready to make unusual amends. Even an old-fashioned *rencontre*,   1
sword or pistol, in Rio or elsewhere—is not excluded. My memory and my eloquence are not at their best today but really,
my dear Mr. Humbert, you were not an ideal stepfather, and
I did not force your little protégée to join me. It was she made
me remove her to a happier home. This house is not as modern
as that ranch we shared with dear friends. But it is roomy, cool
in summer and winter, and in a word comfortable, so, since I
intend retiring to England or Florence forever, I suggest you
move in. It is yours, gratis. Under the condition you stop pointing at me that [he swore disgustingly] gun. By the way, I do
not know if you care for the bizarre, but if you do, I can offer
you, also gratis, as house pet, a rather exciting little freak, a
young lady with three breasts, one a dandy, this is a rare and
delightful marvel of nature. Now, *soyons raisonnables*. You will   2
only wound me hideously and then rot in jail while I recuper-
ate in a tropical setting. I promise you, Brewster, you will be
happy here, with a magnificent cellar, and all the royalties from
my next play—I have not much at the bank right now but I
propose to borrow—you know, as the Bard said, with that cold   3
in his head, to borrow and to borrow and to borrow. There
are other advantages. We have here a most reliable and bribable
charwoman, a Mrs. Vibrissa—curious name—who comes from   4
the village twice a week, alas not today, she has daughters,
granddaughters, a thing or two I know about the chief of police
makes him my slave. I am a playwright. I have been called
the American Maeterlinck. Maeterlinck-Schmetterling, says I.   5
Come on! All this is very humiliating, and I am not sure I am

doing the right thing. Never use herculanita with rum. Now drop that pistol like a good fellow. I knew your dear wife slightly. You may use my wardrobe. Oh, another thing—you are going to like this. I have an absolutely unique collection of erotica upstairs. Just to mention one item: the in folio de-luxe *Bagration Island* by the explorer and psychoanalyst Melanie Weiss, a remarkable lady, a remarkable work—drop that gun—with photographs of eight hundred and something male organs she examined and measured in 1932 on Bagration, in the Barda Sea, very illuminating graphs, plotted with love under pleasant skies—drop that gun—and moreover I can arrange for you to attend executions, not everybody knows that the chair is painted yellow—"

Feu. This time I hit something hard. I hit the back of a black rocking chair, not unlike Dolly Schiller's—my bullet hit the inside surface of its back whereupon it immediately went into a rocking act, so fast and with such zest that any one coming into the room might have been flabbergasted by the double miracle: that chair rocking in a panic all by itself, and the armchair, where my purple target had just been, now void of all live content. Wiggling his fingers in the air, with a rapid heave of his rump, he flashed into the music room and the next second we were tugging and gasping on both sides of the door which had a key I had overlooked. I won again, and with another abrupt movement Clare the Impredictable sat down before the piano and played several atrociously vigorous, fundamentally hysterical, plangent chords, his jowls quivering, his spread hands tensely plunging, and his nostrils emitting the soundtrack snorts which had been absent from our fight. Still singing those impossible sonorities, he made a futile attempt to open with his foot a kind of seaman's chest near the piano. My next bullet caught him somewhere in the side, and he rose from his chair higher and higher, like old, gray, mad Nijinski, like Old Faithful, like some old nightmare of mine, to a phenomenal altitude, or so it seemed, as he rent the air—still shaking with the rich black music—head thrown back in a howl, hand pressed to his brow, and with his other hand clutching his armpit as if stung by a hornet, down he came on his heels and, again a normal robed man, scurried out into the hall.

I see myself following him through the hall, with a kind of double, triple, kangaroo jump, remaining quite straight on straight legs while bouncing up twice in his wake, and then bouncing between him and the front door in a ballet-like stiff bounce, with the purpose of heading him off, since the door was not properly closed.

Suddenly dignified, and somewhat morose, he started to walk up the broad stairs, and, shifting my position, but not actually following him up the steps, I fired three or four times in quick succession, wounding him at every blaze; and every time I did it to him, that horrible thing to him, his face would twitch in an absurd clownish manner, as if he were exaggerating the pain; he slowed down, rolled his eyes half closing them and made a feminine "ah!" and he shivered every time a bullet hit him as if I were tickling him, and every time I got him with those slow, clumsy, blind bullets of mine, he would say under his breath, with a phoney British accent—all the while dreadfully twitching, shivering, smirking, but withal talking in a curiously detached and even amiable manner: "Ah, that hurts, sir, enough! Ah, that hurts atrociously, my dear fellow. I pray you, desist. Ah—very painful, very painful, indeed . . . God! Hah! This is abominable, you should really not—" His voice trailed off as he reached the landing, but he steadily walked on despite all the lead I had lodged in his bloated body—and in distress, in dismay, I understood that far from killing him I was injecting spurts of energy into the poor fellow, as if the bullets had been capsules wherein a heady elixir danced.

I reloaded the thing with hands that were black and bloody— I had touched something he had anointed with his thick gore. Then I rejoined him upstairs, the keys jangling in my pockets like gold.

He was trudging from room to room, bleeding majestically, trying to find an open window, shaking his head, and still trying to talk me out of murder. I took aim at his head, and he retired to the master bedroom with a burst of royal purple where his ear had been.

"Get out, get out of here," he said coughing and spitting; and in a nightmare of wonder, I saw this blood-spattered but still buoyant person get into his bed and wrap himself up in the chaotic bedclothes. I hit him at very close range through the blankets, and then he lay back, and a big pink bubble with juvenile connotations formed on his lips, grew to the size of a toy balloon, and vanished.

I may have lost contact with reality for a second or two—oh, nothing of the I-just-blacked-out sort that your common criminal enacts; on the contrary, I want to stress the fact that I was responsible for every shed drop of his bubbleblood; but a kind of momentary shift occurred as if I were in the connubial bedroom, and Charlotte were sick in bed. Quilty was a very sick man. I held one of his slippers instead of the pistol—I was sitting on the pistol. Then I made myself a little more comfortable in the chair near the bed, and consulted my wrist watch. The crystal was gone but it ticked. The whole sad business had taken more than an hour. He was quiet at last. Far from feeling any relief, a burden even weightier than the one I had hoped to get rid of was with me, upon me, over me. I could not bring myself to touch him in order to make sure he was really dead. He looked it: a quarter of his face gone, and two flies beside themselves with a dawning sense of unbelievable luck. My hands were hardly in better condition than his. I washed up as best I could in the adjacent bathroom. Now I could leave. As I emerged on the landing, I was amazed to discover that a vivacious buzz I had just been dismissing as a mere singing in my ears was really a medley of voices and radio music coming from the downstairs drawing room.

I found there a number of people who apparently had just arrived and were cheerfully drinking Quilty's liquor. There was a fat man in an easy chair; and two dark-haired pale young beauties, sisters no doubt, big one and small one (almost a child), demurely sat side by side on a davenport. A florid-faced fellow with sapphire-blue eyes was in the act of bringing two glasses out of the bar-like kitchen, where two or three women were chatting and chinking ice. I stopped in the doorway and said: "I have just killed Clare Quilty." "Good for you," said the florid fellow as he offered one of the drinks to the elder girl. "Somebody ought to have done it long ago," remarked the fat man. "What does he say, Tony?" asked a faded blonde from the bar. "He says," answered the florid fellow, "he has killed Cue." "Well," said another unidentified man rising in a corner where he had been crouching to inspect some records, "I guess we all should do it to him some day." "Anyway," said Tony, "he'd better come down. We can't wait for him much longer if we want to go to that game." "Give this man a drink somebody," said the fat person. "Want a beer?" said a woman in slacks, showing it to me from afar.

Only the two girls on the davenport, both wearing black, the younger fingering a bright something about her white neck, only they said nothing, but just smiled on, so young, so lewd. As the music paused for a moment, there was a sudden noise on the stairs. Tony and I stepped out into the hall. Quilty of all people had managed to crawl out onto the landing, and there we could see him, flapping and heaving, and then subsiding, forever this time, in a purple heap.

"Hurry up, Cue," said Tony with a laugh. "I believe, he's still—" He returned to the drawing room, music drowned the rest of the sentence.

This, I said to myself, was the end of the ingenious play staged for me by Quilty. With a heavy heart I left the house and walked through the spotted blaze of the sun to my car. Two other cars were parked on both sides of it, and I had some trouble squeezing out.

36

The rest is a little flattish and faded. Slowly I drove downhill, and presently found myself going at the same lazy pace in a direction opposite to Parkington. I had left my raincoat in the boudoir and Chum in the bathroom. No, it was not a house I would have liked to live in. I wondered idly if some surgeon of genius might not alter his own career, and perhaps the whole destiny of mankind, by reviving quilted Quilty, Clare Obscure. Not that I cared; on the whole I wished to forget the whole mess—and when I did learn he was dead, the only satisfaction it gave me, was the relief of knowing I need not mentally accompany for months a painful and disgusting convalescence interrupted by all kinds of unmentionable operations and relapses, and perhaps an actual visit from him, with trouble on my part to rationalize him as not being a ghost. Thomas had something. It is strange that the tactile sense, which is so infinitely less precious to men than sight, becomes at critical moments our main, if not only, handle to reality. I was all covered with Quilty —with the feel of that tumble before the bleeding.

The road now stretched across open country, and it occurred to me—not by way of protest, not as a symbol, or anything like that, but merely as a novel experience—that since I had disregarded all laws of humanity, I might as well disregard the rules of traffic. So I crossed to the left side of the highway and checked the feeling, and the feeling was good. It was a pleasant diaphragmal melting, with elements of diffused tactility, all this enhanced by the thought that nothing could be nearer to the elimination of basic physical laws than deliberately driving on the wrong side of the road. In a way, it was a very spiritual itch. Gently, dreamily, not exceeding twenty miles an hour, I drove on that queer mirror side. Traffic was light. Cars that now and then passed me on the side I had abandoned to them, honked at me brutally. Cars coming towards me wobbled, swerved, and cried out in fear. Presently I found myself approaching populated places. Passing through a red light was like a sip of forbidden Burgundy when I was a child. Meanwhile complications were arising. I was being followed and escorted. Then in front of me I saw two cars placing themselves in such a manner as to completely block my way. With a graceful movement I turned off the road, and after two or three big bounces, rode up a grassy slope, among surprised cows, and there I came to a gentle

rocking stop. A kind of thoughtful Hegelian synthesis linking 1
up two dead women.

I was soon to be taken out of the car (Hi, Melmoth, thanks
a lot, old fellow)—and was, indeed, looking forward to surrender myself to many hands, without doing anything to co-
operate, while they moved and carried me, relaxed, comfortable,
surrendering myself lazily, like a patient, and deriving an eerie
enjoyment from my limpness and the absolutely reliable support
given me by the police and the ambulance people. And while I
was waiting for them to run up to me on the high slope, I evoked
a last mirage of wonder and hopelessness. One day, soon after
her disappearance, an attack of abominable nausea forced me to
pull up on the ghost of an old mountain road that now accompanied, now traversed a brand new highway, with its population
of asters bathing in the detached warmth of a pale-blue afternoon in late summer. After coughing myself inside out, I rested
a while on a boulder, and then, thinking the sweet air might do
me good, walked a little way toward a low stone parapet on the
precipice side of the highway. Small grasshoppers spurted out of
the withered roadside weeds. A very light cloud was opening its
arms and moving toward a slightly more substantial one belonging to another, more sluggish, heavenlogged system. As I approached the friendly abyss, I grew aware of a melodious unity of
sounds rising like vapor from a small mining town that lay at my
feet, in a fold of the valley. One could make out the geometry of 2
the streets between blocks of red and gray roofs, and green puffs
of trees, and a serpentine stream, and the rich, ore-like glitter of
the city dump, and beyond the town, roads crisscrossing the crazy
quilt of dark and pale fields, and behind it all, great timbered
mountains. But even brighter than those quietly rejoicing colors
—for there are colors and shades that seem to enjoy themselves
in good company—both brighter and dreamier to the ear than
they were to the eye, was that vapory vibration of accumulated
sounds that never ceased for a moment, as it rose to the lip of
granite where I stood wiping my foul mouth. And soon I realized
that all these sounds were of one nature, that no other sounds
but these came from the streets of the transparent town, with the

women at home and the men away. Reader! What I heard was but the melody of children at play, nothing but that, and so limpid was the air that within this vapor of blended voices, majestic and minute, remote and magically near, frank and divinely enigmatic—one could hear now and then, as if released, an almost articulate spurt of vivid laughter, or the crack of a bat, or the clatter of a toy wagon, but it was all really too far for the eye to distinguish any movement in the lightly etched streets. I stood listening to that musical vibration from my lofty slope, to those flashes of separate cries with a kind of demure murmur for background, and then I knew that the hopelessly poignant thing was not Lolita's absence from my side, but the absence of her voice from that concord.

This then is my story. I have reread it. It has bits of marrow sticking to it, and blood, and beautiful bright-green flies. At this or that twist of it I feel my slippery self eluding me, gliding into deeper and darker waters than I care to probe. I have camouflaged what I could so as not to hurt people. And I have toyed with many pseudonyms for myself before I hit on a particularly

1   apt one. There are in my notes "Otto Otto" and "Mesmer
2,3 Mesmer" and "Lambert Lambert," but for some reason I think my choice expresses the nastiness best.

4   When I started, fifty-six days ago, to write *Lolita*, first in the psychopathic ward for observation, and then in this well-heated, albeit tombal, seclusion, I thought I would use these notes in toto at my trial, to save not my head, of course, but my soul. In mid-composition, however, I realized that I could not parade living Lolita. I still may use parts of this memoir in hermetic sessions, but publication is to be deferred.

For reasons that may appear more obvious than they really are, I am opposed to capital punishment; this attitude will be, I trust, shared by the sentencing judge. Had I come before myself, I would have given Humbert at least thirty-five years for rape, and dismissed the rest of the charges. But even so, Dolly Schiller will probably survive me by many years. The following decision I make with all the legal impact and support of a signed testament:

I wish this memoir to be published only when Lolita is no longer alive.

Thus, neither of us is alive when the reader opens this book. But while the blood still throbs through my writing hand, you are still as much part of blessed matter as I am, and I can still talk to you from here to Alaska. Be true to your Dick. Do not let other fellows touch you. Do not talk to strangers. I hope you 1 will love your baby. I hope it will be a boy. That husband of yours, I hope, will always treat you well, because otherwise my specter shall come at him, like black smoke, like a demented giant, and pull him apart nerve by nerve. And do not pity C. Q. One had to choose between him and H. H., and one wanted 2 H. H. to exist at least a couple of months longer, so as to have him make you live in the minds of later generations. I am thinking of aurochs and angels, the secret of durable pigments, prophetic sonnets, the refuge of art. And this is the only immortality you and I may share, my Lolita.

VLADIMIR NABOKOV

ON A BOOK ENTITLED *LOLITA*

After doing my impersonation of suave John Ray, the character in *Lolita* who pens the Foreword, any comments coming straight from me may strike one—may strike me, in fact—as an impersonation of Vladimir Nabokov talking about his own book. A few points, however, have to be discussed; and the autobiographic device may induce mimic and model to blend.

Teachers of Literature are apt to think up such problems as "What is the author's purpose?" or still worse "What is the guy trying to say?" Now, I happen to be the kind of author who in starting to work on a book has no other purpose than to get rid of that book and who, when asked to explain its origin and growth, has to rely on such ancient terms as Interreaction of Inspiration and Combination—which, I admit, sounds like a conjurer explaining one trick by performing another.

The first little throb of *Lolita* went through me late in 1939 or early in 1940, in Paris, at a time when I was laid up with a severe attack of intercostal neuralgia. As far as I can recall, the initial shiver of inspiration was somehow prompted by a newspaper story about an ape in the Jardin des Plantes, who, after months of coaxing by a scientist, produced the first drawing ever charcoaled by an animal: this sketch showed the bars of the poor creature's cage. The impulse I record had no textual connection with the ensuing train of thought, which resulted, however, in a prototype of my present novel, a short story some thirty pages long. I wrote it in Russian, the language in which I had been writing novels since 1924 (the best of these are not translated into English, and all are prohibited for political reasons in

Russia). The man was a Central European, the anonymous nymphet was French, and the loci were Paris and Provence. I had him marry the little girl's sick mother who soon died, and after a thwarted attempt to take advantage of the orphan in a hotel room, Arthur (for that was his name) threw himself under the wheels of a truck. I read the story one blue-papered wartime night to a group of friends—Mark Aldanov, two social revolutionaries, and a woman doctor; but I was not pleased with the thing and destroyed it sometime after moving to America in 1940.

Around 1949, in Ithaca, upstate New York, the throbbing, which had never quite ceased, began to plague me again. Combination joined inspiration with fresh zest and involved me in a new treatment of the theme, this time in English—the language of my first governess in St. Petersburg, circa 1903, a Miss Rachel Home. The nymphet, now with a dash of Irish blood, was really much the same lass, and the basic marrying-her-mother idea also subsisted; but otherwise the thing was new and had grown in secret the claws and wings of a novel.

The book developed slowly, with many interruptions and asides. It had taken me some forty years to invent Russia and Western Europe, and now I was faced by the task of inventing America. The obtaining of such local ingredients as would allow me to inject a modicum of average "reality" (one of the few words which mean nothing without quotes) into the brew of individual fancy, proved at fifty a much more difficult process than it had been in the Europe of my youth when receptiveness and retention were at their automatic best. Other books intervened. Once or twice I was on the point of burning the unfinished draft and had carried my Juanita Dark as far as the shadow of the leaning incinerator on the innocent lawn, when I was stopped by the thought that the ghost of the destroyed book would haunt my files for the rest of my life.

Every summer my wife and I go butterfly hunting. The specimens are deposited at scientific institutions, such as the Museum of Comparative Zoology at Harvard or the Cornell University collection. The locality labels pinned under these butterflies will be a boon to some twenty-first-century scholar with a taste for recondite biography. It was at such of our headquarters as Telluride, Colorado; Afton, Wyoming; Portal, Arizona; and Ashland, Oregon, that *Lolita* was energetically resumed in the evenings or on cloudy days. I finished copying the thing out in longhand in the spring of 1954, and at once began casting around for a publisher.

At first, on the advice of a wary old friend, I was meek enough to stipulate that the book be brought out anonymously. I doubt that I shall ever regret that soon afterwards, realizing how likely a mask was to betray my own cause, I decided to sign *Lolita*. The four American publishers, W, X, Y, Z, who in turn were offered the typescript and had their readers glance at it, were shocked by *Lolita* to a degree that even my wary old friend F.P. had not expected.

While it is true that in ancient Europe, and well into the eighteenth century (obvious examples come from France), deliberate lewdness was not inconsistent with flashes of comedy, or vigorous satire, or even the verve of a fine poet in a wanton mood, it is also true that in modern times the term "pornography" connotes mediocrity, commercialism, and certain strict rules of narration. Obscenity must be mated with banality because every kind of aesthetic enjoyment has to be entirely replaced by simple sexual stimulation which demands the traditional word for direct action upon the patient. Old rigid rules must be followed by the pornographer in order to have his patient feel the same security of satisfaction as, for example, fans of detective stories feel—stories where, if you do not watch out, the real murderer may turn out to be, to the fan's disgust, artistic originality (who for instance would want a detective story without a single dialogue in it?). Thus, in pornographic novels, action has to be limited to the copulation of clichés. Style, structure, imagery should never distract the reader from his tepid lust. The novel must consist of an alternation of sexual scenes. The passages in between must be reduced to sutures of sense, logical bridges of the simplest design, brief expositions and explanations, which the reader will probably skip but must know they exist in order not to feel cheated (a mentality stemming from the routine of "true" fairy tales in childhood). Moreover, the sexual scenes in the book must follow a crescendo line, with new variations, new combinations, new sexes, and a steady increase in the number of participants (in a Sade play they call the gardener in), and therefore the end of the book must be more replete with lewd lore than the first chapters.

Certain techniques in the beginning of *Lolita* (Humbert's Journal, for example) misled some of my first readers into assuming that this was going to be a lewd book. They expected the rising succession of erotic scenes; when these stopped, the readers stopped, too, and felt bored and let down. This, I suspect, is one of the reasons why not all the four firms read the typescript to the end. Whether they found it pornographic or not did not interest me. Their refusal to buy the book was based not on my treatment of the theme but on the theme itself, for there are at least three themes which are utterly taboo as far as most American publishers are concerned. The two others are: a Negro-White marriage which is a complete and glorious success resulting in lots of children and grandchildren; and the total atheist who lives a happy and useful life, and dies in his sleep at the age of 106.

Some of the reactions were very amusing: one reader suggested that his firm might consider publication if I turned my Lolita into a twelve-year-old lad and had him seduced by Humbert, a farmer, in a barn, amidst gaunt and arid surroundings, all this set forth in short, strong, "realistic" sentences ("He acts crazy. We all act crazy, I guess. I guess God acts crazy." Etc.). Although everybody should know that I detest symbols and allegories (which is due partly to my old feud with Freudian voodooism and partly to my loathing of generalizations devised by literary mythists and sociologists), an otherwise intelligent reader who flipped through the first part described Lolita as "Old Europe debauching young America," while another flipper saw in it "Young America debauching old Europe." Publisher X, whose advisers got so bored with Humbert that they never got beyond page 188, had the naïveté to write me that Part Two was too long. Publisher Y, on the other hand, regretted there were no good people in the book. Publisher Z said if he printed Lolita, he and I would go to jail.

No writer in a free country should be expected to bother about the exact demarcation between the sensuous and the sensual; this is preposterous; I can only admire but cannot emulate the accuracy of judgment of those who pose the fair young mammals photographed in magazines where the general neckline is just low enough to provoke a past master's chuckle and just high enough not to make a postmaster frown. I presume there exist readers who find titillating the display of mural words in those hopelessly banal and enormous novels which are typed out by the thumbs of tense mediocrities and called "powerful" and "stark" by the reviewing hack. There are gentle souls who would pronounce Lolita meaningless because it does not teach them anything. I am neither a reader nor a writer of didactic fiction, and, despite John Ray's assertion, Lolita has no moral in tow. For me a work of fiction exists only insofar as it affords me what I shall bluntly call aesthetic bliss, that is a sense of being somehow, somewhere, connected with other states of being where art (curiosity, tenderness, kindness, ecstasy) is the norm. There are not many such books. All the rest is either topical trash or what some call the Literature of Ideas, which very often is topical trash coming in huge blocks of plaster that are carefully transmitted from age to age until somebody comes along with a hammer and takes a good crack at Balzac, at Gorki, at Mann.

Another charge which some readers have made is that *Lolita* is anti-American. This is something that pains me considerably more than the idiotic accusation of immorality. Considerations of depth and perspective (a suburban lawn, a mountain meadow) led me to build a number of North American sets. I needed a certain exhilarating milieu. Nothing is more exhilarating than philistine vulgarity. But in regard to philistine vulgarity there is no intrinsic difference between Palearctic manners and Nearctic manners. Any proletarian from Chicago can be as bourgeois (in the Flaubertian sense) as a duke. I chose American motels instead of Swiss hotels or English inns only because I am trying to be an American writer and claim only the same rights that other American writers enjoy. On the other hand, my creature Humbert is a foreigner and an anarchist, and there are many things, besides nymphets, in which I disagree with him. And all my Russian readers know that my old worlds—Russian, British, German, French—are just as fantastic and personal as my new one is.

Lest the little statement I am making here seem an airing of grudges, I must hasten to add that besides the lambs who read the typescript of *Lolita* or its Olympia Press edition in a spirit of "Why did he have to write it?" or "Why should I read about maniacs?" there have been a number of wise, sensitive, and staunch people who understood my book much better than I can explain its mechanism here.

Every serious writer, I dare say, is aware of this or that published book of his as of a constant comforting presence. Its pilot light is steadily burning somewhere in the basement and a mere touch applied to one's private thermostat instantly results in a quiet little explosion of familiar warmth. This presence, this glow of the book in an ever accessible remoteness is a most companionable feeling, and the better the book has conformed to its prefigured contour and color the ampler and smoother it glows. But even so, there are certain points, byroads, favorite hollows that one evokes more eagerly and

enjoys more tenderly than the rest of one's book. I have not reread
1 *Lolita* since I went through the proofs in the spring of 1955 but I
find it to be a delightful presence now that it quietly hangs about the
house like a summer day which one knows to be bright behind the
haze. And when I thus think of *Lolita*, I seem always to pick out for
2 special delectation such images as Mr. Taxovich, or that class list
3, 4 of Ramsdale School, or Charlotte saying "waterproof," or Lolita in
5 slow motion advancing toward Humbert's gifts, or the pictures
6 decorating the stylized garret of Gaston Godin, or the Kasbeam
7, 8 barber (who cost me a month of work), or Lolita playing tennis, or
the hospital at Elphinstone, or pale, pregnant, beloved, irretrievable
9 Dolly Schiller dying in Gray Star (the capital town of the book), or
the tinkling sounds of the valley town coming up the mountain trail
(on which I caught the first known female of *Lycaeides sublivens*
10 Nabokov). These are the nerves of the novel. These are the secret
points, the subliminal co-ordinates by means of which the book is
plotted—although I realize very clearly that these and other scenes
will be skimmed over or not noticed, or never even reached, by those
who begin reading the book under the impression that it is something
on the lines of *Memoirs of a Woman of Pleasure* or *Les Amours de
Milord Grosvit*. That my novel does contain various allusions to the
physiological urges of a pervert is quite true. But after all we are not
children, not illiterate juvenile delinquents, not English public school
boys who after a night of homosexual romps have to endure the
paradox of reading the Ancients in expurgated versions.

It is childish to study a work of fiction in order to gain information
about a country or about a social class or about the author. And yet
one of my very few intimate friends, after reading *Lolita*, was sincerely
worried that I (I!) should be living "among such depressing people"
—when the only discomfort I really experienced was to live in my
workshop among discarded limbs and unfinished torsos.

After Olympia Press, in Paris, published the book, an American critic
suggested that *Lolita* was the record of my love affair with the romantic novel. The substitution "English language" for "romantic novel"
would make this elegant formula more correct. But here I feel my
voice rising to a much too strident pitch. None of my American
friends have read my Russian books and thus every appraisal on the
strength of my English ones is bound to be out of focus. My private
tragedy, which cannot, and indeed should not, be anybody's concern,
11 is that I had to abandon my natural idiom, my untrammeled, rich,

and infinitely docile Russian tongue for a second-rate brand of English, devoid of any of those apparatuses—the baffling mirror, the black velvet backdrop, the implied associations and traditions—which the native illusionist, frac-tails flying, can magically use to transcend 1 the heritage in his own way.

November 12, 1956

NOTES

The word or passage in the text to which each annotation refers is indicated by two numbers, the first giving the page and the second the number in the margin of the text. The numbering begins anew on each page, and disregards chapter divisions. All page references to other Nabokov books are to the first American editions (hardcover).

FOREWORD

5/1 *two titles:* the term "white widowed" occurs in the case histories of psychiatric works, while the entire subtitle parodies the titillating confessional novel, such as John Cleland's *Memoirs of a Woman of Pleasure* (1749), and the expectations of the reader who hopes *Lolita* will provide the pleasures of pornography (see 278/2). Although Nabokov could hardly have realized it at the time of writing, there is no small irony in the fact that the timidity of American publishers resulted in the novel's being first brought out by the Olympia Press, publishers of *The Sexual Life of Robinson Crusoe* and other "eighteenth-century sexcapades" (to use Clare Quilty's description of Sade's *Justine, ou, Les Infortunes de la vertu* [... *The Misfortunes of Virtue*]; see p. 300).

5/2 *preambulates:* to make a preamble, introduce.

5/3 *"Humbert Humbert":* in his *Playboy* interview (1964), Nabokov says, "The double rumble is, I think, very nasty, very suggestive. It is a hateful name for a hateful person. It is also a kingly name, but I did need a royal vibration for Humbert the Fierce and Humbert the Humble.

Lends itself also to a number of puns." Like James Joyce, Nabokov fashions his puns from literary sources, from any of the several languages available to him, from obsolete words, or the roots of arcane words. If the associations are rich enough, a pun succeeds in projecting a theme central to the fiction, in summarizing or commenting on the action. In both *The Gift* (1937) and the 1959 Foreword to the English translation of *Invitation to a Beheading* (1935–1936), Nabokov mentions *Discours sur les ombres*, by Pierre Delalande, "the only author whom I must gratefully recognize as an influence upon me at the time of writing this book...[and] whom I invented." Delalande's *Discours* provided the epigraph for *Invitation*—"*Comme un fou se croît Dieu, nous nous croyons mortels*" ["As a madman deems himself God, we deem ourselves mortal"]—and Nabokov's entire corpus might be described as a "Discourse on Shadows, or Shades." John Shade is the author of the poem *Pale Fire*. In a rejected draft of his poem, he writes, "I like my name: Shade, *Ombre*, almost 'man' / In Spanish..."—an accurate etymological pairing (hombre>ombre) and a resonant pun that figuratively places *hombre* in ombre—a card game popular in the seventeenth and eighteenth centuries—and sets man to playing in Nabokov's "game of worlds" (see 22/4). Humbert was brought up on the French Riviera; pronounced with a French accent, his name partakes of these shadows and shades. By "solipsizing" Lolita (p. 62), Humbert condemns her to the solitary confinement of his obsessional shadowland. "She had entered my world, umber and blank Humberland," says Humbert (p. 168), who, by choosing to chase the figurative shadows that play on the walls of his "cave," upends Plato's famous allegory. Although Humbert has had the benefit of a journey in the sunny "upper world"—a Riviera boyhood, in fact, and a full-sized wife or two—he nevertheless pursues the illusion that he can recapture what is inexorably lost. As Humbert demonstrates, illusions *are* realities in their ability to destroy us. "I was the shadow of the waxwing slain / By the false azure in the windowpane," writes John Shade in the opening lines of *Pale Fire*, while in Nabokov's poem "An Evening of Russian Poetry" (1945), the speaker says:

> My back is Argus-eyed. I live in danger.
> False shadows turn to track me as I pass
> and, wearing beards, disguised as secret agents,
> creep in to blot the freshly written page
> and read the blotter in the looking-glass.
> And in the dark, under my bedroom window,
> until, with a chill whirr and shiver, day
> presses its starter, warily they linger

> or silently approach the door and ring
> the bell of memory and run away.

Seventeen years later in *Pale Fire* the Shadows are the Zemblan "regicidal organization" who dispatch Gradus, one of whose aliases is d'Argus, to assassinate the exiled King Charles (Kinbote). But the Shadows' secret agent accidentally kills Shade instead. *Lolita* offers the converse, for "Shade" (Humbert) purposely kills his "shadow" (Clare Quilty). Thus the delusive nature of identity and perception, the constricting burdens of memory, and a haunting sense of mutability are all capsuled in a reverberating pun.

5/4 *solecism:* an irregularity or impropriety in speech and diction, grammar or syntax. Also in conduct, and therefore not an unwarranted definition in Humbert's instance.

5/5 *presented intact:* it is important to recognize how Nabokov belies the illusion of "realism" which both Ray and Humbert seem to create. See 11/1 and 34/7.

5/6 *cognomen:* its current definition, "a distinguishing nickname," is fundamental, and the humorous incongruity of using so high-toned a Latinate word is heightened by its original meaning: "The third or family name of a Roman citizen."

5/7 *this mask:* "Is 'mask' the keyword?" Humbert later asks (p. 55). In his Foreword to *Pale Fire*, Kinbote says of Shade: "His whole being constituted a mask."

5/8 *remain unlifted:* not quite; although the "real" name is never revealed, the mask does slip. See Chapter Twenty-six, the shortest in the book (p. 111).

6/1 *her first name:* Lolita's given name is "Dolores." See 11/5.

6/2 *"H.H." 's crime:* the murder of Clare Quilty (pp. 295–307), Humbert's grotesque alter ego and parodic Double. Humbert will henceforth be identified by his initials.

6/3 *1952:* a corrected author's error ("September-October 1952," instead of the 1958 edition's "September"). The following pages in the text contain corrections which are detailed in the Notes: pp. 6 (below), 8, 21, 25, 33, 34, 54, 62, 119, 123, 140, 152, 164, 187, 195, 197, 199, 201, 206, 227, 232, 234, 255, 261, 264, 266, 316, and 318. The 1958 Putnam's edition was set in type from the 1955 Olympia Press edition. The latter contains many minuscule mistakes (e.g., punctuation) which were carried over into the Putnam's edition and identified only when the present text was in page proof. Although these errors have been corrected, it was impossible to describe them separately in the Notes. However, since the present edition follows the Putnam's format exactly, assiduous students of such textual matters can easily identify these corrections by collating the two texts, as follows: p. 7, line sixteen; p. 33, line fourteen; p. 42, last line; p. 65, lines three and twenty-six; p. 75, line nineteen; p. 84, last line; p. 113, line seventeen; p. 138, line thirteen; p. 143, lines six and seven; p. 152, line twenty-five; p. 158, line six; p. 163, line fifteen; p. 166, line nine; p. 181, line three; p. 182, line nine; p. 220, line ten; p. 228, line seven; p. 241, line thirteen; p. 245, line twenty-three; p. 257, line five; p. 264, line twenty-five; p. 277, line four; and p. 278, line thirty-three.

6/4 *"real people"* ... *"true story"*: in the Afterword, Nabokov mentions his "impersonation of suave John Ray" (p. 313); but by mocking the conventional reader's desire for verisimilitude, as Nabokov does in the opening paragraphs of *Laughter in the Dark, Despair, Invitation to a Beheading,* and *The Gift,* Dr. Ray here expresses the concerns of a novelist rather than psychologist, suggesting that the mask has not remained totally in place. There are subtle oscillations between the shrill locutions and behavioristic homilies of Ray and the quite reasonable statements of an authorial voice projected, as it were, from the wings. Note 6/9 underlines this, while 7/1 and 7/3–7/5 suggest other instances of that presence.

6/5 *sophomore*: a corrected misprint (a period instead of the 1958 edition's semicolon after "sophomore").

6/6 Mrs. *"Richard F. Schiller"*: Lolita's married name, first revealed on p. 268. The covert disclosure of Lolita's death is significant, for the announcement that the three main characters are now dead challenges the "old-fashioned reader" 's idea of "story": to reveal the outcome before the story even begins is of course to ruin it. The heroine of "The Beauty" (1934), an untranslated Nabokov story, also dies in childbirth within a year after her marriage (noted by Andrew Field, *Nabokov: His Life in Act* [Boston, 1967], p. 330).

6/7 *1952*: for a hermetic allusion to this crucial year, see 253/14.

6/8 *Gray Star*: it is most remote, for there is no town by this name anywhere in the world. Nabokov calls it "the capital town of the book" (p. 318). A gray star is one veiled by haze (Lolita's surname), and H.H. recalls "the haze of stars" that has always "remained with me." See 17/1 and 282/1.

6/9 *"Vivian Darkbloom"* . . . *"My Cue"*: "Vivian Darkbloom" is Clare Quilty's mistress and an anagram of "Vladimir Nabokov" (see my 1967 *Wisconsin Studies* article, p. 216, and my 1968 *Denver Quarterly* article, p. 32 [see bibliography]). Among her alphabetical cousins are "Vivian Bloodmark, a philosophical friend of mine," who appears in *Speak, Memory* (p. 218), and "Mr. Vivian Badlook," a photographer and teacher of English in the 1968 translation of the 1928 novel *King, Queen, Knave* (p. 153)—and they all descend from "Vivian Calmbrood" (see Field, *op. cit.*, p. 73), the alleged author of *The Wanderers*, an uncompleted play written by Nabokov in Russian (the anagram is helped along by the fact that in Cyrillic, the *c* is a *k*). One act of it was published in the émigré almanac *Facets* (1923), as an English play written by Vivian Calmbrood in 1768 and translated by V. Sirin (the pen name under which all of Nabokov's Russian work appeared). In a discussion in *Ada* (1969) of Van Veen's first novel, *Letters from Terra*, mention is made of the influence "of an obscene ancient Arab, expounder of anagrammatic dreams, Ben Sirine" (p. 344).

As for H.H. and John Ray, unless characters in a novel can be said to have miraculously fashioned their creators, someone else must be responsible for an anagram of the author's name, and such phenomena undermine the narrative's realistic base by pointing beyond the book to Nabokov, the stage manager, ventriloquist, and puppeteer, who might simply state, "My cue." Because Nabokov considered publishing *Lolita* anonymously (see p. 315), there was also a purely utilitarian reason for anagrammatizing his name, as proof of authorship. "Cue" is also the cognomen of Clare Quilty, who pursues H.H. throughout the novel. But who *is* Quilty?—a question the reader will surely ask (see the Introduction, pp. xiii–lxviii, and 33/9). As with H.H. and Lolita (*née* Dolores Haze), Quilty's name lends itself to wordplay by turns jocose (see 225/1) and significant, since H.H. suggests that Clare Quilty is clearly guilty. Clare is also a town in Michigan (see 161/1), and, although Nabokov did not know it until this note came into being, Quilty is a town in County Clare, Ireland, appropriate to a verbally playful novel in which there are several apt references to James Joyce. See 6/11.

6/10 *etiolated:* to blanch or whiten a plant by exclusion of sunlight.

6/11 *outspoken book:* *Ulysses* (1922), by James Joyce (1882–1941), Irish novelist and poet. Judge Woolsey's historic decision paved the way for the 1934 American publication of *Ulysses,* and his decision, along with a statement by Morris Ernst, prefaces the Modern Library edition of the novel. Ray's parenthetical allusion echoes and compresses its complete title: "THE MONUMENTAL DECISION OF THE UNITED STATES DISTRICT COURT RENDERED DECEMBER 6, 1933, BY HON. JOHN M. WOOLSEY LIFTING THE BAN ON 'ULYSSES.' " Ray's Foreword in part burlesques the expert opinions which have inevitably prefaced subsequent "controversial" novels. For other allusions to Joyce, see 71/1, 122/4, 189/1, 200/3, 209/3, 223/1, 252/3, 264/3, and 286/4.

7/1 *moral apotheosis:* a just description of H.H.'s realization at the end of the novel: "the hopelessly poignant thing was not Lolita's absence from my side, but the absence of her voice from that concord" (p. 310).

7/2 *12%:* such "sextistics" (as H.H. or Quilty might call them) poke fun at the work of Alfred Kinsey (1894–1956) and his Indiana University Institute for Sex Research.

7/3 *Blanche Schwarzmann: schwarz* is German for "black"; her name is "White Blackman," because, to Nabokov, Freudians figuratively see no colors other than black and white (see 7/6). For a similarly hued lady, see p. 304 and "Melanie Weiss."

7/4 *a mixture of . . . supreme misery:* an accurate description of the pain at the center of H.H.'s playfulness.

7/5 *his singing violin:* another gap in the texture of Ray's rhetoric reveals the voice of his maker. In his Foreword to *Invitation to a Beheading,* Nabokov calls the novel a "violin in a void," and in *Speak, Memory* he calls the poet Boris Poplavski "a far violin among near balalaikas" (p. 287).

7/6 *a case history:* among other things, *Lolita* parodies such studies, and Nabokov's quarrel with psychoanalysis is well-known. No Foreword to his translated novels seems complete unless a few words are addressed to "the Viennese delegation," who are also invoked frequently throughout the works. Asked in a 1966 National Educational Television interview why he "detest[ed] Dr. Freud," Nabokov replied: "I think he's crude, I think he's medieval, and I don't want an elderly gentleman from Vienna with an umbrella inflicting his dreams upon me. *I* don't have the dreams that he discusses in his books. I don't see umbrellas in my dreams. Or balloons" (this half-hour interview may be rented for a nominal fee from the Audio-Visual Center, Indiana University, Bloomington, Indiana 47401; the film, notes their catalog, is "available to responsible individuals and groups both in and out of Indiana"). When I queried Nabokov about Freud (by now a trite question), just to see if he could rise to the occasion once more, he obliged me: "Oh, I am not up to discussing again that figure of fun. He is not worthy of more attention than I have granted him in my novels and in *Speak, Memory*. Let the credulous and the vulgar continue to believe that all mental woes can be cured by a daily application of old Greek myths to their private parts. I really do not care" (*Wisconsin Studies* interview).

In *Speak, Memory*, Nabokov recalls having seen from a Biarritz window "a huge custard-colored balloon...being inflated by Sigismond Lejoyeux, a local aeronaut" (p. 156); and "the police state of sexual myth" (p. 300) is in *Ada* called "psykitsch" (p. 29). The good doctor's paronomastic avatars are "Dr. Sig Heiler" (p. 28), and "A Dr. Froid...who may have been an émigré brother with a passport-changed name of the Dr. Froit of Signy-Mondieu-Mondieu" (p. 27). Since no parodist could improve on Erich Fromm's realization that "The little cap of red velvet in the German version of Little Red Riding Hood is a symbol of menstruation" (from *The Forgotten Language*, 1951, p. 240), or Dr. Oskar Pfister's felicitously expressed thought that "When a youth is all the time sticking his finger through his buttonhole...the analytic teacher knows that the appetite of the lustful one knows no limit in his phantasies" (from *The Psychoanalytical Method*, 1917, p. 79), Nabokov the literary anatomist simply includes these treasures in *Pale Fire* (p. 271). See *Lolita*, pp. 36, 169, 196–197, 252, and 287; and 37/1, 127/3, 256/3, and 276/4.

8/1 *John Ray, Jr.*: the first John Ray (1627–1705) was an English naturalist famous for his systems of natural classification. His system of plant classification greatly influenced the development of systematic botany (*Historia plantarium*, 1686–1704). He was the first to attempt a definition of what constitutes a species. His system of insects, as set forth in *Methodus insectorum* (1705) and *Historia insectorum* (1713), is based on the concept of metamorphosis (see 18/6). The reference to Ray is no coincidence (it was first pointed out by Diana Butler, in "Lolita Lepidoptera," *New World Writing 16* [1960], p. 63). Nabokov is a distinguished lepidopterist, worked in Lepidoptera as a Research Fellow in the Museum of Comparative Zoology at Harvard (1942–1948), and has published some twenty papers on the subject. While I was visiting him in 1966, he took from the shelf his copy of Alexander B. Klots's standard work, *A Field Guide to the Butterflies* (1951), and, opening it, pointed to the first sentence of the section on "*Genus* Lycæides *Scudder:* The Orange Margined Blues," which reads: "The recent work of Nabokov has entirely rearranged the classification of this genus" (p. 164). "That's real fame," said the author of *Lolita*. "That means more than anything a literary critic could say." In *Speak, Memory* (Chapter Six), he writes evocatively of his entomological forays, of the fleeting moments of ecstasy he experiences in catching exquisite and rare butterflies. These emotions are perhaps best summarized in his poem "A Discovery" (1943; from *Poems*, p. 15), its twentieth line echoing what he said to me more than two decades later:

> I found it in a legendary land
> all rocks and lavender and tufted grass,
> where it was settled on some sodden sand
> hard by the torrent of a mountain pass.
>
> The features it combines mark it as new
> to science: shape and shade—the special tinge,
> akin to moonlight, tempering its blue,
> the dingy underside, the checquered fringe.
>
> My needles have teased out its sculptured sex;
> corroded tissues could no longer hide
> that priceless mote now dimpling the convex
> and limpid teardrop on a lighted slide.
>
> Smoothly a screw is turned; out of the mist
> two ambered hooks symmetrically slope,
> or scales like battledores of amethyst
> cross the charmed circle of the microscope.
>
> I found it and I named it, being versed
> in taxonomic Latin; thus became
> godfather to an insect and its first
> describer—and I want no other fame.
>
> Wide open on its pin (though fast asleep),
> and safe from creeping relatives and rust,
> in the secluded stronghold where we keep
> type specimens it will transcend its dust.
>
> Dark pictures, thrones, the stones that pilgrims kiss,
> poems that take a thousand years to die
> but ape the immortality of this
> red label on a little butterfly.

There are many references to butterflies in *Lolita*, but it must be remembered that it is Nabokov, and not H.H., who is the expert. As Nabokov says, "H.H. knows nothing about Lepidoptera. In fact, I went out of my way to indicate [p. 112 and p. 159] that he confuses the hawk-moths visiting flowers at dusk with 'gray hummingbirds.' " The author has implored the unscientific annotator to omit references to Lepidoptera, "a tricky subject," and this is at least one instance when, in spite of Kinbote's ringing final phrase in the epigraph, the annotator has not had the last word. Only the most specific lepidopterological allusions will be noted, though even this modest trove will make it clear how the butterfly motif enables Nabokov to leave behind on H.H.'s pages a trail of his own phosphorescent fingerprints. For entomological allusions, see 11/5, 12/3, 14/1, 18/6, 44/5, 48/1, 58/2, 112/3, 114/1, 128/2, 143/1, 158/2, 159/2, 191/5, 211/1, 212/2, 213/4, 229/4, 233/1, 236/2, 260/5, 261/1, 264/6, 303/5, 317/1, and 318/10.

8/2 *1955:* a corrected author's error (the date was not included in the 1958 edition).

PART ONE

CHAPTER 1

11/1 *Lolita, light of my life:* her name is the first word in the Foreword, as well as the first and last words of the novel. Such symmetries and carefully effected alliterations and rhythms undermine the credibility of H.H.'s "point of view," since the narrative is presented as an unrevised first draft, mistakes intact, started in a psychiatric ward and completed in a prison cell, the product of the fifty-six frenzied final days of H.H.'s life (see his reminder, p. 310, and 34/7 and 36/3). When asked how her name occurred to him, Nabokov replied, "For my nymphet I needed a diminutive with a lyrical lilt to it. One of the most limpid and lumin-ous letters is 'L.' The suffix '-ita' has a lot of Latin tenderness, and this I required too. Hence: Lolita. However, it should not be pronounced as . . . most Americans pronounce it: Low-lee-ta, with a heavy, clammy 'L' and a long 'O.' No, the first syllable should be as in 'lollipop,' the 'L' liquid and delicate, the 'lee' not too sharp. Spaniards and Italians pronounce it, of course, with exactly the necessary note of archness and caress. Another consideration was the welcome murmur of its source name, the fountain name: those roses and tears in 'Dolores' [see 11/5]. My little girl's heart-rending fate had to be taken into account together with the cuteness and limpidity. Dolores also provided her with another, plainer, more familiar and infantile diminutive: Dolly, which went nicely

with the surname 'Haze,' where Irish mists blend with a German bunny
—I mean a small German hare [=*hase*]" (*Playboy* interview). Since most
everything is in a name, Nabokov both memorializes and instructs in
Ada: "For the big picnic on Ada's twelfth birthday...the child was
permitted to wear her lolita (thus dubbed after the little Andalusian
gipsy [see *Carmen* note, 246/1—A.A.] of that name in Osberg's novel
and pronounced, incidentally, with a Spanish 't,' not a thick English
one)..." (p. 77). Lolita's name is lovingly celebrated by Anthony Burgess in his poem, "To Vladimir Nabokov on His Seventieth Birthday,"
in *TriQuarterly*, No. 17 (Winter 1970):

> That nymphet's beauty lay less on her bones
> Than in her name's proclaimed two allophones.
> A boned veracity slow to be found
> In all the channels of recorded sound.

11/2 *Lo-lee-ta:* the middle syllable alludes to "Annabel Lee" (1849), by
Edgar Allan Poe (1809–1849). H.H. will lead one to believe that "Annabel Leigh" is the cause of his misery: "Annabel Haze, alias Dolores Lee,
alias Loleeta," he says on p. 169. References to Poe are noted in 33/5,
45/5, 77/5, 109/1, 120/2, 191/3, and 294/2; while "Annabel Lee" is variously invoked on pp. 42, 127, and 232, and otherwise as noted 11/7, 11/8,
14/1, 15/4, 41/1, 44/3, 49/4, 55/5, and 168/2. But rather than identify
every "Annabel Lee" echo occurring in the first chapter and elsewhere,
the text of the poem is provided:

> It was many and many a year ago,
> In a kingdom by the sea,
> That a maiden there lived whom you may know
> By the name of Annabel Lee;—
> And this maiden she lived with no other thought
> Than to love and be loved by me.
>
> *She* was a child and *I* was a child,
> In this kingdom by the sea,
> But we loved with a love that was more than love—
> I and my Annabel Lee—
> With a love that the winged seraphs of Heaven
> Coveted her and me.
>
> And this was the reason that, long ago,
> In this kingdom by the sea,
> A wind blew out of a cloud by night
> Chilling my Annabel Lee;

10

So that her high-born kinsmen came
   And bore her away from me,
To shut her up in a sepulchre
    In this kingdom by the sea.

The angels, not half so happy in Heaven,
   Went envying her and me:—
Yes! that was the reason (as all men know,
   In this kingdom by the sea)
That the wind came out of the cloud, chilling
   And killing my Annabel Lee.

But our love it was stronger by far than the love
   Of those who were older than we—
   Of many far wiser than we—
And neither the angels in Heaven above
    Nor the demons down under the sea
Can ever dissever my soul from the soul
   Of the beautiful Annabel Lee:—
For the moon never beams without bringing me dreams
   Of the beautiful Annabel Lee;

And the stars never rise but I see the bright eyes
   Of the beautiful Annabel Lee;
And so, all the night-tide, I lie down by the side
Of my darling, my darling, my life and my bride
    In her sepulchre there by the sea—
   In her tomb by the sounding sea.

Poe is referred to more than twenty times in *Lolita*, far more than any other writer (followed by Mérimée, Shakespeare, and Joyce, in that order). Not surprisingly, Poe allusions have been the most readily identifiable to readers and earlier commentators (I pointed out several in my 1967 *Wisconsin Studies* article, "*Lolita*: The Springboard of Parody" [see bibliography]). See also the earlier articles by Elizabeth Phillips ("The Hocus-Pocus of *Lolita*," *Literature and Psychology*, X [Summer 1960], 97–101) and Arthur F. DuBois ("Poe and *Lolita*," *CEA Critic*, XXVI [No. 6, 1963], 1, 7). Most recent is Carl R. Proffer's thorough compilation in *Keys to Lolita* (henceforth called *Keys*), pp. 34–45.

Although my Notes rarely discuss in any detail the significance of the literary allusions they limn, Poe's conspicuous presence surely calls for a few general remarks; subsequent Notes will establish the most specific—and obvious—links between H.H. and Poe (e.g., their "child brides"; see 45/5). Poe is appropriate for many reasons. He wrote the kind of *Doppelgänger* tale ("William Wilson") which the H.H.-Quilty relationship seemingly parallels but ultimately upends, and he of course "fathered" the detective tale. Although, as a reader, Nabokov today abhors the detective story, he is not alone in recognizing that the genre's properties are well-suited to the fictive treatment of metaphysical questions and problems of identity and perception. Thus—along with other contemporary writers such as Graham Greene (*Brighton Rock*, 1938), Raymond Queneau (*Pierrot mon ami* [*Pierrot*], 1942), Jorge Luis Borges ("Death and the Compass," "An Examination of the Work of Herbert Quain," "The Garden of Forking Paths" [first published in *Ellery Queen's Mystery Magazine*], and "The South"), Alain Robbe-Grillet (*Les Gommes* [*The Erasers*], 1953), Michel Butor (*L'Emploi du temps* [*Passing Time*], 1956), and Thomas Pynchon (*V.*, 1963)—Nabokov has often transmuted or parodied the forms, techniques, and themes of the detective story, as in *Despair, The Real Life of Sebastian Knight, Lolita,* and, less directly, in *The Eye,* where, Nabokov says, "The texture of the tale mimics that of detective fiction." The reader of *Lolita* is invited to wend his way through a labyrinth of clues in order to solve the mystery of Quilty's identity, which in part makes *Lolita* a "tale of ratiocination," to use Poe's phrase (see 33/9). Early in the novel one is told that H.H. is a murderer. Has he killed Charlotte? Or Lolita? (See also *Keys*, p. 39.) The reader is led to expect both possibilities, and his various attempts at ratiocination should ultimately tell the reader as much about his own mind as about the "crimes," "identities," or "psychological development" of fictional characters. For allusions to detective story writers other than Poe, see 33/2 (Agatha Christie), 66/1 (Conan Doyle), and 213/1 and 252/5 (Maurice Leblanc).

It is also in part through Poe that Nabokov manages to suggest some consistently held attitudes toward language and literature. H.H. says of his artistic labors, "The beastly and beautiful merged at one point, and it is that borderline I would like to fix, and I feel I fail to do so utterly. Why?" (p. 137). The rhetorical question is coy enough, because he has answered it at the beginning of his narrative; he hasn't failed, but neither can he ever be entirely successful, because "Oh, my Lolita, I have only words to play with!" (p. 34)—an admission many Romantic and Symbolist writers would not make. Nabokov's remark about Joyce's giving "too much verbal body to words" (*Playboy* interview) succinctly defines the burden the post-Romantics placed on the word, as though it were an endlessly resonant object rather than one component in a referential system of signs (see 122/4 for a parody of Joycean stream-of-consciousness writing). H.H.'s acknowledgment of the limitations of language leaves many writers open to criticism, especially Romantic poets such as Poe. "When I was young I liked Poe, and I still love Melville," says Nabokov; "I tore apart the fantasies of Poe," writes John Shade in *Pale Fire* (line 632 of the poem); the implications are clear enough. In *Lolita*, his choice of both subject matter and narrator parody Poe's designation, in "The Philosophy of Composition," of the "most poetical topic in the world": "the death of a beautiful woman... and equally is it beyond doubt that the lips best suited for such topic are those of a bereaved lover" (see also my 1967 *Wisconsin Studies* article, *op. cit.*, p. 236). Both Annabel Lee and Lolita "die," the latter figuratively as well as literally, in terms of her fading nymphic qualities and escape from H.H., who seems to invoke yet another of Poe's lost ladies when he calls Lolita "Lenore" (though the primary allusion is to Bürger's poem, says Nabokov; see 209/5).

The speaker in Poe's "Lenore" gropes for the right elegiac chord: "How *shall* the ritual, then, be read?—the requiem how be sung / By you—by yours, the evil eye,—by yours, the slanderous tongue / That did to death the innocence that died, and died so young?" How shall it be "sung" is also the main question in *Lolita*, and Nabokov found his answer in a parodic style that seems to parody *all* styles, including the novel's own. "You talk like a book, *Dad*," Lolita tells H.H.; and, in order to protect his own efforts to capture her essence, he tries to exhaust the "fictional gestures," such as Edgar Poe's, which would reduce the nymphet's ineffable qualities to a convention of language or literature. "Well-read Humbert" thus toys with one writer after another, as though only through parody and caricature can he rule out the possibility of his memoir's finally being nothing more than what the authorial voice in *Invitation to a Beheading* suggests to its captive creation: "Or is this all but obsolete romantic rot, Cincinnatus?" (p. 139).

11/3 *four feet ten*: see 264/6 for an involuted conversion to inches.

11/4 *Lola*: in addition to being a diminutive of "Dolores," it is the name of the young cabaret entertainer who enchants a middle-aged professor in the German film, *The Blue Angel* (1930), directed by Josef von Sternberg. Nabokov has never seen the film (though he has seen still photos from it) and doubts that he had the association in mind. Lola was played by Marlene Dietrich (1904–   ), and it is worth noting that H.H. describes Lolita's mother as having "features of a type that may be defined as a weak solution of Marlene Dietrich" (p. 39) and, after he reports her death, bids "Adieu, Marlene!" (p. 105). In *Ada*, Van Veen visits a don and his family, "a charming wife and a triplet of charming

twelve-year-old daughters, Ala, Lolá and Lalage—especially Lalage"
["the age"—twelve, a nymphet's prime (p. 353)].

11/5 *Dolores:* derived from the Latin, *dolor:* sorrow, pain (see 45/2).
Traditionally an allusion to the Virgin Mary, Our Lady of Sorrows,
and the Seven Sorrows concerning the life of Jesus. H.H. observes a
church, "Mission Dolores," and takes advantage of the ready-made pun:
"good title for book" (p. 160). Less spiritual are the sorrows detailed
in "Dolores" (1866), by Algernon Swinburne (1837–1909), English poet
(see also *Keys,* p. 28). "Our Lady of Pain" is its constant refrain, and
her father is Priap, whom H.H. mentions several times (see 44/4). The
name *Dolores* is in two ways "closely interwound with the inmost
fiber of the book," as John Ray says on p. 6. When in the Afterword
Nabokov defines the "nerves of the novel," he concludes with "the
tinkling sounds of the valley town coming up the mountain trail (on
which I caught the first known female of *Lycæides sublivens* Nabokov)"
(p. 318). Diana Butler, in "Lolita Lepidoptera," *op. cit.,* p. 62, notes that
this important capture was made at Telluride, Colorado (see p. 314),
and that in his paper on it, Nabokov identifies Telluride as a "cul-de-
sac . . . at the end of two converging roads, one from Placerville, the
other from Dolores" (*The Lepidopterists' News,* VI, 1952). Dolores is
in fact everywhere in that region: river, town, and county are so
named. When H.H. finally confronts Quilty, he asks, "do you recall a
little girl called Dolores Haze, Dolly Haze? Dolly called Dolores, Colo.?"
(p. 298). "Dolly" is an appropriate diminutive ("you / took a dull doll
to pieces / and threw its head away," writes H.H. of Quilty [p. 302]).
For the entomological allusions, see 8/1. On shipboard in *Ada,* Van
Veen sees a film of *Don Juan's Last Fling* in which Dolores the dancing girl turns out to be Ada (pp. 488–490). Ada later gives Van "a
sidelong 'Dolores' glance" (p. 513).

11/6 *in point of fact:* the childhood "trauma" which H.H. will soon offer
as the psychological explanation of his condition (see p. 15). H.H.'s
first chapter is so extraordinarily short in order to mock the traditional
novel's expository opening. How reassuring, by comparison, are the
initial paragraphs of those conventional novels—so anachronistic to Nabokov—which prepare the reader for the story about to unfold by supplying him with the complete psychological, social, and moral prehis-
tories of the characters. Anticipating such needs, H.H. poses the reader's
questions ("Did she have a precursor?"; "Oh when?"), and parodies
more than that kind of reader dependence on such exposition. It may
seem surprising in a supposedly "confessional" novel that this should
be the narrator's initial concern; but it is by way of a challenge to play,

like the good-humored cry of *"Avanti"* with which Luzhin greets Turati in *The Defense*, before they begin their great match game. H.H.'s "point of fact" mocks the "scientific" certitude of psychiatrists who have turned intensely private myths and symbols—in short, fictions—into hard fact. The H.H. who is the subject of a case study immediately undercuts the persuasiveness of his own specific "trauma" by projecting it in fragments of another man's verse; literary allusions, after all, point *away* from the unique, inviolable, formative "inner reality" of a neurotic or psychotic consciousness. Annabel Leigh, the object of H.H.'s unconsummated love, has no reality other than literary. See also *Keys*, p. 45.

11/7 *princedom by the sea:* a variant of the most famous line in "Annabel Lee." Poe's "kingdom" has been changed to accommodate the fact that H.H. is always an aspirant, never an absolute monarch. On p. 168 he calls Lolita "My Frigid Princess."

11/8 *noble-winged seraphs, envied:* a pastiche composed of a phrase from line 11 of "Annabel Lee" and a verb from line 22. "Seraphs" are the highest of the nine orders of angels; in the Bible they have six wings, as well as hands and feet, and a human voice (Isaiah, 6:2). "The seraph with his six flamingo wings" is invoked by John Shade in *Pale Fire* (line 225 of the poem).

11/9 *tangle of thorns:* another H.H., the penitent, confessor, and martyr to love, calls attention to his thorns, the immodest reference to so sacred an image suggesting that the reader would do well to judge H.H.'s tone rather than his deeds. When H.H. addresses the "Ladies and gentlemen of the jury," as he will do so often, he summarizes the judicial proclivities of those literal-minded and moralistic readers who, having soberly considered what John Ray, Jr., has said, already hate "Humbert the Horrible."

CHAPTER 2

12/1 *Jerome Dunn, the alpinist:* in a novel so allusive as *Lolita* it is only natural to be suspicious of the most innocuous references, and to search for allusions under every bush. Anticipating the efforts of future exegetes, I will occasionally offer non-notes—"anti-annotations" which simply state that Nabokov intends no allusion whatsoever. Thus, "Jerome Dunn" is non-allusive, as are "Clarence Choate Clark," H.H.'s lawyer (p. 5), and John Ray's residence of "Widworth, Mass." (p. 8). For important caveats in Nabokov's own words, see 58/1 and 223/2.

12/2 *paleopedology and Aeolian harps:* respectively, the branch of pedology concerned with the soils of past geological ages, and a box-shaped musical instrument on which the wind produces varying harmonies (after Aeolus, Greek god of the winds). A favorite Romantic metaphor for the poet's sensibility.

12/3 *midge:* a gnat-like insect. For entomological allusions, see 8/1.

12/4 *Sybil:* or *sibyl,* from the Greek; any of several prophetesses credited to widely separate parts of the ancient world. H.H.'s aunt is well-named, since she predicts her own death.

12/5 *Mirana:* a heat-shimmer blend of "mirage," "*se mirer*" (French; to look at oneself; admire oneself), "Mirabella," and "Fata Morgana" (a kind of mirage most frequently seen in the Strait of Messina, and formerly considered the work of fairies who would thus lure sailors aground). Bewitching Lolita is often characterized as a fairy (see 33/3); the latter word is derived from the Latin word *fatum* (fate, destiny), and H. H. is pursued by bedeviling "Aubrey McFate" (see 58/1).

12/6 *Mon... papa:* French; my dear little Daddy.

12/7 *Don Quixote:* the famous novel (1605, 1615) by Miguel Cervantes (1547–1616); see 253/10. *Les Misérables* (1862) is by Victor Hugo (1802–1885), French novelist, playwright, and poet; see 258/3.

13/1 *rose garden:* see 54/5 and 58/1.

13/2 *La Beauté Humaine:* French; "The Human Beauty." The book is invented, as is its author, whose name is a play on "*nichon,*" a French (slang) epithet for the female breast.

13/3 *lycée:* the basic institution of French secondary education; a student attends a Lycée for seven years (from age eleven to eighteen).

CHAPTER 3

14/1 *powdered Mrs. Leigh... Vanessa van Ness:* Poe's "Annabel Lee"; on p. 169 it is spelled *Lee*. The Red Admirable (or Admiral) butterfly, which figures throughout Nabokov, is *Vanessa atalanta,* family *Nymphalidae* (for more on "nymph," see 18/6); and butterflies, as well as women, are "powdered." H.H. is also alluding to Jonathan Swift's (1667–1745) "Vanessa," as he called the young woman whose passion he awakened (for the Swift allusion, see also *Keys,* p. 96). Nabokov expands the dual allusion in *Pale Fire.* John Shade addresses "My dark Vanessa, Crimson-barred, my blest / My Admirable butterfly! ..." (lines 270–271); and, in his note to these lines, Charles Kinbote quotes from Swift's "Cadenus and Vanessa," though he doesn't identify it by name: "When, lo! *Vanessa* in her bloom / Advanced like *Atalanta's* star." He also alludes to "Vanessa" 's actual name thusly: "*Van*homrigh, *Es*ther!" (p. 172) —thereby underscoring at least the alphabetical arrangement of Swift's anagramour (let me laugh a little, too, gentlemen, as H.H. says on p. 252). But in his succinct way, H.H. has already anticipated Kinbote ("van Ness"). A Red Admirable lands on Shade's arm the minute before he is killed (see lines 993–995 and Kinbote's note for them) and the insect appears in *King, Queen, Knave* just after Nabokov has withdrawn his omniscience (p. 44). In the final chapter of *Speak, Memory* Nabokov recalls having seen in a Paris park, just before the war, a live Red Admirable being promenaded on a leash of thread by a little girl; "there was some vaguely repulsive symbolism about her sullen sport," he writes (p. 306). When Van Veen casually mentions Ada's having pointed out "some accursed insect," the offended heroine parenthetically and angrily adds, "Accursed? *Accursed?* It was the newly described, fantastically rare vanessian, *Nymphalis danaus* Nab., orange-brown, with black-and-white foretips, mimicking, as its discoverer Professor Nabonidus of Babylon College, Nebraska, realized, not the Monarch butterfly directly, but the Monarch *through* the Viceroy, one of the Monarch's best known imitators" (p. 158). See 8/1.

14/2 *solipsism:* a central word in *Lolita.* An epistemological theory that the self knows only its present state and is the only existent thing, and that "reality" is subjective; concern with the self at the expense of social relationships. See 62/1.

14/3 *plage:* French; beach.

15/1 *chocolat glacé:* French; in those days, an iced chocolate drink with whipped cream (today it means "chocolate ice cream").

15/2 *red rocks:* see 41/3 and 58/1.

15/3 *lost pair of sunglasses:* the sunglasses image connects Annabel and Lolita. H.H. first perceives her as his "Riviera love peering at me over dark glasses" (see 41/1). See also *Keys,* p. 43 and p. 143n.

15/4 *point of possessing:* for a comment on the "traumatic" nature of this experience, see 211/3. "My darling" echoes line 39 of "Annabel Lee" (see 49/4 for the entire line, and 11/2 for the poem itself).

15/5 *Corfu:* Greek island.

CHAPTER 4

17/1 *haze of stars:* see 6/8. In one sense, the novel begins and ends in "Gray Star."

17/2 *her spell:* "spells" and "enchantments" are fundamental in *Lolita*. See 18/6, 47/3, and 262/2.

CHAPTER 5

17/3 *manqué:* French; unfulfilled.

18/1 *uranists:* H.H.'s own variant of the uncommon English word, *uranism*, derived from a Greek word for "spiritual" and meaning "homosexual." Havelock Ellis uses it in Chapter Five of *Psychology of Sex* (1938), and claims the term was invented by the nineteenth-century legal official Karl Ulrichs.

18/2 *Deux Magots:* the famous Left Bank café in Paris, where intellectuals congregate. *Magot* is a kind of monkey, but *"magots de Saxe"* means "statuettes of saxe [porcelain]" (eighteenth-century). Nabokov purposely seats his uranists in this particular café, because he wants to invoke the simian association and the image of the grotesque Chinese porcelain figures.

18/3 *pastiches:* the "quotation" is an assemblage including bits and pieces of "Gerontion" (1920), by T.S. Eliot, the Anglo-American poet (1888–1965): "...Fräulein von Kulp / Who turned in the hall, one hand on the door" (lines 27–28); "...De Bailhache, Fresca, Mrs. Cammel, whirled..." (line 66); "...Gull against the wind, in the windy straits / Of Belle Isle..." (lines 69–70). See 260/3 and 301/1 for other allusions to Eliot. Having small sympathy with some of Eliot's social prejudices, Nabokov ironically describes in *Ada* a "Mr. Eliot, a Jewish businessman" (p. 5), who later meets the late-blooming banker (Eliot's early vocation) Kithar Sween (=Eliot's "Sweeney"), author of *"The Waistline*, a satire in free verse on Anglo-American feeding habits, and *Cardinal Grishkin* [=Eliot's "Whispers of Immortality"], an overtly subtle yarn extolling the Roman faith" (p. 506). For *The Four Quartets*, see *Pale Fire*, lines 368–379. Nabokov says, "I was never exposed in the 'twenties and 'thirties, as so many of my coevals have been, to the poetry of Eliot and Pound. I read them late in the season, around 1945, in the guest room of an American friend's house, and not only remained completely indifferent to them, but could not understand why anybody should bother about them. But I suppose that they preserve some sentimental value for such readers as discovered them at an earlier age than I did" (*Playboy* interview).

18/4 *"Proustian theme ... Bailey"*: the letters of the English poet John Keats (1795-1821) to his close friend Benjamin Bailey (1791-1853) are among the important statements of Keats's poetic theory. In *Pale Fire*, Kinbote measures the progress of poetry "from the caveman to Keats" (p. 289). H.H.'s "Proustian theme" is no doubt on the nature of time and memory. Marcel Proust (1871-1922)—the great French novelist, the first half of whose *A la Recherche du temps perdu* (*Remembrance of Things Past*, 1913-1927) is to Nabokov one of the four "greatest masterpieces of twentieth century prose" (see 209/3)—is also mentioned on pp. 79 and 184, and as noted 255/2 and 266/4. He appears too in *Pale Fire*, pp. 87, 161-163, and 248, as well as in line 224 of Shade's poem (p. 41), where he envisions eternity, and "... talks / With Socrates and Proust in cypress walks." In *The Real Life of Sebastian Knight*, Knight's hack biographer, Mr. Goodman, mentions "the French author M. Proust, whom Knight consciously or subconsciously copied" (p. 116); and Knight himself parenthetically remarks in a letter, "I am [not] apologizing for that Proustian parenthesis" (p. 54)—a device H.H. consciously indulges, as when he parenthetically "prolong[s] these Proustian intonations" (p. 79). There are also many allusions to Proust in *Ada* (see pp. 9, 55-56, 66, 73, 168-169, 254, and 541).

18/5 *"Histoire ... anglaise"*: French; "A Short History of English Poetry."

18/6 *not human, but nymphic*: like Sinclair Lewis's "Babbitt" (*Babbitt*, 1922), Nabokov's "nymphet" has entered the language, though the latest dictionary entries which *Lolita* has inspired are as inelegant as they are inaccurate: *nymph*: "a woman of loose morals" (*Webster's Third New International*, echoed by the *Random House Dictionary*). The *Penguin English Dictionary*, G. N. Garmonsway, ed., gives under *nymphet*: "(coll.) very young but sexually attractive girl" (H.H., who strives so desperately to expropriate idiomatic English, would appreciate that "colloquial"). As for *nymph*, the mythological and zoological definitions are primary. In Greek and Roman mythology, a *nymph* is "One of the inferior divinities of nature represented as beautiful maidens dwelling in the mountains, waters, forests, etc." *Nympholepsy*, H.H.'s malady (hence, "nympholept" [p. 19]), is "a species of demoniac enthusiasm supposed to seize one bewitched by a nymph; a frenzy of emotion, as for some unattainable ideal" (more specifically, in *Blakiston's*

New Gould Medical Dictionary, it is defined as "ecstasy of an erotic type"). Under the entry for "The Nymphs" in *The Book of Imaginary Beings* (1969), Jorge Luis Borges notes that "Paracelsus limited their dominion to water, but the ancients thought the world was full of Nymphs . . . [some] Nymphs were held to be immortal or, as Plutarch obscurely intimates, lived for above 9,720 years . . . The exact number of the Nymphs is unknown; Hesiod gives us the figure three thousand . . . Glimpsing them could cause blindness and, if they were naked, death. A line of Propertius affirms this." H.H. echoes these definitions. Here and on the following pages he alludes to "spells," "magic," "fantastic powers," and "deadly demons" (for various enchantments, see 12/5 [Fata Morgana], 22/2 [Lilith], 33/3 [elves], 47/3 [*Carmen*], 73/1 [an incubus], and 242/2 [king of the elves]). Lolita's "inhuman" and "bewitching charms" suggest that she is Keats's "La Belle Dame Sans Merci" (1819) in bobby socks (Nabokov translated the poem into Russian in *The Empyrean Path*, 1923), and that the novel is in part a unique variant of the archetypal tale of a mortal destroyed by his love for a supernatural *femme fatale*, "The Lovely Lady Without Pity" of ballad, folk tale, and fairy tale. Nabokov has called *Lolita* a "fairy tale," and his nymph a "fairy princess" (p. 54); see 33/3.

One of Nabokov's lepidopterological finds is known as "Nabokov's Wood-Nymph" (belonging to the family *Nymphalidae*; see 14/1), and he is not unaware that a "nymph" is also defined as "a pupa," or "the young of an insect undergoing incomplete metamorphosis." Crucial to an understanding of *Lolita* is some sense of the various but simultaneous metamorphoses undergone by Lolita, H.H., the book, the author, and the reader, who is manipulated by the novel's game-element and illusionistic devices to such an extent that he too can be said to become, at certain moments, another of Vladimir Nabokov's creations—an experience which is bound to change him. The butterfly is thus a controlling metaphor that enriches *Lolita* in a more fundamental and organic manner than, say, the *Odyssey* does Joyce's *Ulysses*. Just as the nymph undergoes a metamorphosis in becoming the butterfly, so everything in *Lolita* is constantly in the process of metamorphosis, including the novel itself—a set of "notes" being compiled by an imprisoned man during a fifty-six-day period for possible use at his trial, emerging as a book after his death, and then only after it has passed through yet another stage, the nominal "editorship" of John Ray, Jr. As Lolita turns from a girl into a woman, so H.H.'s lust becomes love. His sense of a "safely solipsized" Lolita (p. 62) is replaced by his awareness that she was his "own creation" with "no will, no consciousness—indeed, no life of her own" (p. 64), that he did not know her (p. 286), and that their sexual intimacy only isolated him more completely from the helpless girl. These "metamorphoses" enable H.H. to transform a "crime" into a redeeming work of art, and the reader watches the chrysalis come to life. "And a metamorphosis is a thing always exciting to watch," says Nabokov in *Gogol* (p. 43), referring to etymological rather than entomological phenomena (see 120/3 and 214/2; also follow the multifarious permutations of "Humbert").

On his first night with Lolita at The Enchanted Hunters hotel, H.H. experiences "a confusion of perception metamorphosing her into eyespots of moonlight or a fluffy flowering bush" (p. 134), and, anticipating the design and progression of *Lolita*, the narrator of *The Real Life of Sebastian Knight* (1941) mentions the readers who "felt baffled by [*The Prismatic Bezel*'s] habit of metamorphosis" (p. 95; for the complete passage, see the epigraph to the Introduction). When Nabokov in his lectures at Cornell discussed "the theme of transformation" in R.L. Stevenson's *Dr. Jekyll and Mr. Hyde*, Gogol's *The Overcoat*, and Kafka's *The Metamorphosis*, he said that Stevenson's tale is a "thriller and mystery only in respect to artistic creativity. It is a phenomenon of style, a transformation through the art of writing." He likened the Jekyll-Hyde transformation to the metamorphosis of the larva into the pupa into the butterfly, and imagined Jekyll's final emergence from the melting and blackened features of the evil Hyde as "the rush of panic" which must accompany "the feeling of hatching." Once again, as in his book on Gogol, Nabokov has described his own performance by defining the art of another. As a metaphor for the artistic process, the nymph's cycle suggests a transcendent design. See Introduction, p. xxii. For entomological allusions, see 8/1.

19/1 *bubble of hot poison:* see 306/1; the bubble breaks.

19/2 *faunlet:* in mythology, the faun is a woodland deity represented as a man having the ears, horns, tail, and hind legs of a goat; a satyr. The diminutive form is H.H.'s coinage. See Nabokov's letter in *New Statesman*, Nov. 17, 1967, p. 680.

20/1 *fateful elf:* see 33/3.

20/2 *pollutive:* H.H.'s variant of *pollution;* the less common meaning, "emission of semen at other times than in coitus."

20/3 *pseudolibidoes:* H.H.'s usage (see p. 56 for "libidream") of *libido:* the sexual impulse; to Freud, the instinctual drive behind all human activities.

21/1 *Children ... 1933:* the Act actually reads: " 'Child' means a person under the age of fourteen years ... 'Young Person' means a person who has attained the age of fourteen years and is under the age of seventeen years." From *Children and Young Persons Act of 1933* 23 & 24 Geo. 5, c. 12, §107 (1). No specific definition of girl-child is given; but, even if H.H.'s quotation is wrong, he is a sound legal scholar, for a child must be eight years old to incur criminal liability. See p. 137.

21/2 *Massachusetts ... "a wayward child" ... immoral persons:* an accurate transcription; the parenthetical phrase is also a direct quotation from *Mass. Anno. Laws* ch. 119 §52 (1957).

21/3 *Hugh Broughton:* controversial Puritan divine and pamphleteer (1549–1612). The allusion is to his *A Consent of Scripture* (1588), an eccentric discourse on Biblical chronology.

21/4 *Rahab:* the Canaanite prostitute of Joshua 2: 1–21.

21/5 *Virgil ... perineum:* the Latin poet (70–19 B.C.). The *perineum* includes the urinogenital passages and the rectum. In the 1958 edition it read *peritonium* (the double serous membrane which lines the cavity of the abdomen). Although H.H.'s grotesque error is intentional on Nabokov's part, he decided to correct it here because the mistake, if discerned, might be taken for the author's, or remain ambiguous.

21/6 *King Akhnaten's ... Nile daughters:* Akhnaten of Egypt (reigned 1375–1358 B.C.) and Nefertiti had a total of seven daughters. On his monuments, the king is shown with six. H.H. also loses a "daughter."

21/7 *fascinum:* Latin; a penis of ivory used in certain ancient erotic rites.

21/8 *East Indian provinces:* the Lepchas are a Mongoloid people of Sikkim and the Darjeeling district of India. What H.H. says is true, and Nabokov thinks H.H. may have got it from somewhere in Havelock Ellis's monumental, many-volumed *Studies in the Psychology of Sex* (1891).

21/9 *Dante ... month of May:* Dante was born between May 15 and June 15, 1265. He was therefore nine years old when he met Beatrice in 1274, and she was supposedly eight. There was no romance.

21/10 *Petrarch ... Laureen:* Petrarch was born July 20, 1304. He was therefore twenty-three when he met Laura on April 6, 1327. She remains unknown to this day, and all attempts to identify her with historical persons are purely speculative. Her age therefore can not be determined.

21/11 *hills of Vaucluse:* an area in Southeastern France, the capital of which is Avignon. It was Petrarch's favorite home, but he found that natural beauty there only added to the sense of his loss of Laura.

22/1 *"enfant . . . fourbe":* French; "sly and lovely child."

22/2 *it was Lilith:* in Jewish legend, Lilith was Adam's wife before Eve. Also a female demon who attacked children and a famous witch in the demonology of the Middle Ages. In *Pale Fire,* a Zemblan "society sculptor" finds in Charles the Beloved's sister "what he sought and . . . used her breasts and feet for his *Lilith Calling Back Adam"* (p. 108). See 18/6 for more on enchantments.

22/3 *tiddles:* "trifles"; from *tiddle,* an obsolete verb except in dialect or slang; to fondle, to fuss or trifle.

22/4 *this is only a game:* in the *Wisconsin Studies* interview, Nabokov says "Satire is a lesson, parody is a game." The pun on H.H.'s name includes the game of ombre (see 5/3), which is played in Canto III of Alexander Pope's *The Rape of the Lock* (1714); see lines 87–100. Also see the games H.H. plays on pp. 184–185, 204–205, and 235.

22/5 *métro:* the Paris subway.

CHAPTER 6

23/1 *voluptas:* Latin; sensual pleasures.

23/2 *the Madeleine:* a church in Paris (a very prominent landmark).

23/3 *frétillement:* French; a wiggle.

23/4 *"Cent":* French; one hundred (francs).

23/5 *"Tant pis":* French; "Too bad!"

24/1 *petit cadeau:* French; small gift.

24/2 *"dix-huit":* French; "eighteen" (years old).

24/3 *"Oui, ce n'est pas bien":* French; "Yes, that is not nice."

24/4 *grues:* French; slang word for prostitutes.

24/5 *"Il était malin . . . truc-là":* French; "The man who invented this trick was a smart one."

24/6 *poser un lapin:* French; to stand someone up.

24/7 *"Tu es . . . de dire ça":* French; "You are very nice to say that."

24/8 *avant qu'on se couche:* French; before we go to bed.

25/1 *"Je vais m'acheter des bas":* French; "I am going to buy myself some stockings."

25/2 *"Regardez-moi ... brune":* French; "Take a look at this beautiful brunette." The 1958 edition omitted the period after the parenthesis.

25/3 *qui pourrait arranger la chose:* French; who could fix it.

26/1 *son argent:* French; her money.

26/2 *lui:* French; himself (pronoun which is redundant and serves to emphasize a noun).

26/3 *Marie ... stellar name:* derived from the Virgin's name; to Biblical commentators, it means *stellamaris,* star of the sea. H.H. has more fun with "stellar" later (see 291/1).

Chapter 7

27/1 *tachycardia:* a term from pathology; abnormal rapidity of the heart's action.

27/2 *mes malheurs:* French; my misfortunes.

27/3 *français moyen:* French; the average Frenchman, the man in the street.

Chapter 8

27/4 *pot-au-feu:* French; a common stew, containing meat, vegetables, and almost anything else.

27/5 *merkin:* an artificial female pudendum, or its false hair.

27/6 *à la gamine:* French; in imitation of a cute young girl.

28/1 *mairie:* French; town hall.

28/2 *melanic:* pigmented; hence, black or dark.

28/3 *baba:* although it is Franco-Russian for a ring-shaped pastry imbued with rum, Nabokov intends it otherwise: " 'Baba' colloquially means in Russian any female on the common side; a blousy, vulgar woman. It is also used metaphorically for certain thick, sturdy, columellar, menhir-like, compact things, such as the pastry *romovaya baba* (but this has nothing to do with its meaning here). Originally, *baba* meant a peasant woman."

28/4 *I felt like Marat ... stab me:* Jean Paul Marat (1743–1793), French revolutionist stabbed to death in his bath by Charlotte Corday; the subject of a famous painting by Jacques-Louis David, *Marat assassiné* (1793). The "original" tub can be seen at both Madame Tussaud's Wax Works in London and at Paris's wax museum, Musée Grevin. In *Pale Fire*, John Shade imagines how his biographer would describe him shaving in his bath: "... he'd / Sit like a king there, and like Marat bleed" (lines 893–894). On his travels, student Van Veen is shown "the peasant-bare footprint of Tolstoy preserved in the clay of a motor court in Utah where he had written the tale of Murat, the Navajo chieftain, a French general's bastard, shot by Cora Day in his swimming pool" (*Ada*, p. 171)—a combination of Murad (from Tolstoy's *Hadji Murad*), General Murat (Napoleon's brother-in-law and king of Naples), and Marat.

28/5 *Paris-Soir:* a sensationalistic daily newspaper; now *France-Soir*.

29/1 *mon oncle d'Amérique:* French; the proverbial rich American uncle who dies, leaving one a fortune; a curtain line in many old-fashioned melodramas.

29/2 *Nansen ... passport:* the special passport issued to émigrés in Europe before World War II; the document figures prominently in the story, " 'That in Aleppo Once ...' " in *Nabokov's Dozen* (1958).

29/3 *préfecture:* French; police headquarters.

30/1 *"Mais qui est-ce?":* French; "But who is it?"

30/2 *quite a scholar:* the ten-volume *Jean Christophe* (1904–1912), by the Frenchman Romain Rolland (1866–1944), is a panoramic novel of society, admired no more by Nabokov than by H.H. (see *Pnin*, p. 142).

31/1 *j'ai demannde pardonne:* French; "I beg your pardon." The tense is incorrect (should be "*je*"); and the wrong spelling—an extra *n* in both words—indicates a Russian accent.

31/2 *gredin:* French; scoundrel, villain.

32/1 *Maximovich ... taxies back to me:* see bottom of p. 30.

33/1 *fructuate:* rare; to bear fruit, to fructify.

33/2 *Agatha Christie: A Murder Is Announced* is the actual title of a 1950 novel by Agatha Christie (1891–   ), the well-known English mystery writer. A murder *is* announced on the next page (Clare Quilty's; see 34/5).

33/3 *Percy Elphinstone:* Elphinstone and his books are also genuine, according to Nabokov, though it has been impossible to document this. Nabokov recalls finding *A Vagabond in Italy* "in a hospital library, the nearest thing to a prison library." But the town of Elphinstone (pp. 240–249) is invented. H.H. calls Annabel "the initial fateful elf in my life" (p. 20); and Lolita's original home town in the Midwest was "Pisky," another form of *pixie* or *elf* (p. 48). When H.H. deposits Lolita in the Elphinstone Hospital, it is the last time he will see the nymphic incarnation of his initial "elf" (p. 248); for him, the "fairy tale" (and he imagines himself a "fairy-tale nurse" [p. 41]) ends in Elph's Stone just as it had begun in the town of "elf." Quilty in pursuit is seen as the "Erlkönig," the king of the elves in Goethe's poem of that name (see 242/2). At The Enchanted Hunters hotel, on the night that H.H. first possesses Lolita, he notes, "Nothing could have been more childish than . . . the purplish spot on her naked neck where a fairy tale vampire had feasted" (p. 141). Quilty's Pavor [Latin: fear, panic] Manor turns out to be on Grimm Road (p. 293), and when H.H. goes to kill him, the door "swung open as in a medieval fairy tale" (p. 296). As a birthday present, H.H. gives Lolita a de luxe edition of Hans Christian Andersen's *The Little Mermaid* (176/5); and allusions are made to *Hansel and Gretel, The Sleeping Beauty, The Emperor's New Clothes* (203/1), and *Bluebeard* (245/3). The simplicity of *Lolita*'s "story," such as it is—"plot," in the conventional sense, may be paraphrased in three sentences—and the themes of deception, enchantment, and metamorphosis are akin to the fairy tale (see 18/6); while the recurrence of places and motifs and the presence of three principal characters recall the formalistic design and symmetry of those archetypal tales (see 267/2). But the fate of Nabokov's "fairy princess" (p. 54) and the novel's denouement reverse the fairy-tale process, even though H.H. offers Lolita the opportunity of a formulaic fairy-tale ending: "we shall live happily ever after" (p. 280).

The fairy-tale element has a significance far greater than its local importance to *Lolita*. Several of Nabokov's novels, stories, and poems are "fairy tales" in the sense that they are set in imaginary lands. These lands extend from five of his untranslated Russian works (1924–1940), to *Bend Sinister*'s Padukgrad (1947), to *Pale Fire*'s kingdom of Zembla (1962), culminating in *Ada* (1969), where the entire universe has been reimagined. Held captive in his own Zemblan palace, King Charles helplessly looks down upon "lithe youths diving into the swimming pool of a fairy tale sport club" (p. 119); after making his escape, he stops at a warm farmhouse where he is "given a fairy-tale meal of bread and cheese" (p. 140). Because it is Nabokov's most extensive fantasia, *Ada* naturally abounds in fairy-tale references (see pp. 5 ["Lake Kitezh"], 87, 143, 164, 180, 191, 228 ["Cendrillon": Cinderella: "Ashette" on pp. 114 and 397], 281, and 287). God is called "Log" in *Ada*, and Hermann in *Despair* (1934) says that he cannot believe in God because "the fairy tale about him is not really mine, it belongs to strangers, to all men..." (p. 111). When in *Invitation to a Beheading* (1936) Cincinnatus extolls the powers of the imagination, M'sieur Pierre answers, "Only in fairy tales do people escape from prison" (p. 114). "The Fairy's Daughter," an untranslated fantasy in verse for children, is collected in *The Empyrean Path* (1923, the same year that Nabokov translated *Alice in Wonderland* into Russian [see 133/1]); and the untranslated story "A Fairytale" (1926) tells of a timid, erotically obsessed man who imagines a harem for himself. He makes an arrangement with a woman who turns out to be the devil. She offers him a choice of as many women as he desires, so long as the total number is odd. But his hopes are dashed when he chooses the same girl twice (a nymphet), for a total of twelve instead of thirteen (the story is summarized from Andrew Field, *op. cit.*, pp. 333–334). Before describing Hazel Shade's final poltergeist vigil, as imagined in his playlet *The Haunted Barn*, Kinbote notes "There are always 'three nights' in fairy tales, and in this sad fairy tale there was a third one too" (*Pale Fire*, p. 190). "Speaking of novels," Kinbote says to Sybil Shade, "you remember we decided once, you, your husband and I, that Proust's rough masterpiece was a huge, ghoulish fairy tale" (pp. 161–162); and mentioned in *Ada* are "the pretentious fairy tales" of "Osberg" (Borges; an anagram [p. 344]).

At Cornell (where the annotator was his student in 1953–1954), Nabokov would begin his first class by saying, "Great novels are above all great fairy tales.... Literature does not tell the truth but makes it up. It is said that literature was born with the fable of the boy crying, 'Wolf! Wolf!' as he was being chased by the animal. This was *not* the birth of literature; it happened instead the day the lad cried 'Wolf!' and the tricked hunters saw no wolf... the magic of art is manifested in the dream about the wolf, in the shadow of the invented wolf." As suggested in the Introduction, Nabokov goes to great lengths to show the reader that the boy has been crying "Wolf!" all along, and that the subject of Nabokov's art is in part the relationship between the old boy and the nonexistent wolf. See 34/7.

33/4 *dazzling coincidences...poets love:* evident everywhere in Nabokov's work is his "poet's love" of coincidence. The verbal figurations and "coincidences" limned in *Who's Who in the Limelight* are of great consequence, for H.H. alludes to "actors, producers, playwrights, and shots of static scenes" which prefigure the action of the novel. The three entries in this imaginary yearbook represent H.H., Lolita, and, obviously, Quilty. Although no "producer" is listed, it will shortly be seen that he reveals his name covertly (33/12), and shows his hand throughout. The importance of *Who's Who in the Limelight* is also discussed in Part Two of my 1967 *New Republic* article, *op. cit.*, p. 27, included in the Introduction, pp. xxvii–xxviii.

33/5 *Pym, Roland:* Pym is the title character in Edgar Allan Poe's *The Narrative of A. Gordon Pym* (1838); he is also mentioned in Nabokov's poem, "The Refrigerator Awakes" (1942), in *Poems* (p. 12). The name suits H.H. well, because, like Pym's, his is a first-person narrative that begins in the spirit of hoax but evolves into something very different. See 253/3 for "Hoaxton." As for "Roland," Nabokov intends no allusions to the medieval *Chanson de Roland*, to the character in Ariosto's *Orlando Furioso*, or to Browning's Childe Roland. For Poe, see 11/12.

33/6 *Elsinore Playhouse, Derby, N.Y.:* both exist. The former, invoking Hamlet's castle, is a common name for a theater. *Hamlet* is often referred to in Nabokov. In *Invitation to a Beheading*, M'sieur Pierre and Cincinnatus are "identically clad in Elsinore jackets" (p. 182); in *Ada*, a reviewer of Van Veen's first book is called "the First Clown in *Elsinore*, a distinguished London weekly" (p. 343); and in *Gogol*, "*Hamlet* is the wild dream of a neurotic scholar" (p. 140). Nabokov's own considerable Shakespearean scholarship is evident in Chapter Seven of *Bend Sinister*, which offers a totalitarian state version of the play. Nabokov himself has glossed this chapter in his valuable Introduction to the Time Reading Program edition (reprinted in *Nabokov's Congeries*, Page Stegner, ed. [New York, 1968], and in my own Twentieth Century Views edition, *Nabokov: A Collection of Critical Essays* [Englewood Cliffs, 1970]). The narrator of *The Real Life of Sebastian Knight*, who is Sebastian's half-brother, demolishes a biography of Knight by demonstrating that the biographer, Mr. Goodman, has incorporated several bogus stories into his book, simply because the leg-pulling Sebastian had said they were so: "Third story: Sebastian speaking of his very first novel (unpublished and destroyed) explained that it was about a fat young student who travels home to find his mother married to his uncle; this uncle, an ear-specialist, had murdered the student's father. Mr. Goodman misses the joke" (p. 64). Recognizing that Sebastian's trap telescopes Nabokov's methods, some readers will no doubt sympathize with hapless

Mr. Goodman. For another *Hamlet* allusion in *Lolita*, see 152/2. For further Shakespeare allusions, see pp. 179, 193 (*The Taming of the Shrew*), 245 (*Romeo and Juliet*), and 267 (*King Lear*), as well as 159/3, 253/14, 303/3 (*Macbeth*), and, for a summary note, 286/4.

33/7 *Made debut in Sunburst:* see p. 92, where H.H. refers to Charlotte Haze's impending death as "the ultimate sunburst," for it will indeed allow him to make his debut with her daughter. Unless they are annotated, the titles in the *Who's Who* entries are non-allusive and of no significance.

33/8 *The Strange Mushroom:* it is a "dazzling coincidence" that "Pym" should appear in a play authored by Quilty (see next entry). As for the specific origin of the "mushroom" image, literary history may be served by the strange fact related by Nabokov: "Somewhere, in a collection of 'cases,' I found a little girl who referred to her uncle's organ as 'his mushroom.'" The plant is in fact a sex symbol in many cultures.

33/9 *Quilty, Clare:* although alluded to by John Ray, Jr., in the "Foreword" (see 6/9), this is the first time that the omnipresent Quilty will be identified by his complete name (Quilty's role is discussed in the Introduction, p. lxiii ff.). H.H. withholds Quilty's identity until almost the end of *Lolita*, and adducing it by virtue of the trail of clues is one of the novel's special pleasures. His importance is most vividly demonstrated by gathering together all the Quilty references and hints as follows: pp. 6, 33, 34, 45, 65, 66, 71, 80, 91, 119, 123, 128–129, 132, 140, 141; [Part Two] 154, 161, 165, 172, 188, 198, 202–204, 205, 209–211, 213, 215, 217, 219–225, 226, 228–230, 234, 237, 238–240, 242, 243–245, 248–254, 264, 273–279, 281, 284, 292–294, 295–307, 308, and 311. Each appearance or allusion to Quilty will be duly noted below, but a reader armed only with this telescopic list should be able to identify Quilty whenever he appears or is evoked on a page. This compilation also appears in my 1967 *Wisconsin Studies* article, "*Lolita:* The Springboard of Parody" (p. 225), and there is more on Quilty in my 1968 *Denver Quarterly* article, "The Art of Nabokov's Artifice" (see bibliography). See also *Keys*, pp. 57–78. An excellent ancillary text is *Stories of the Double*, Albert J. Guerard, ed.

The killing of Quilty (pp. 295–307) was written well out of sequence, early in the composition of *Lolita*. "His death had to be clear in my mind in order to control his earlier appearances," says Nabokov. Nabokov removed from the final version of *Lolita* three scenes in which Quilty figured conspicuously: a talk before Charlotte Haze's club (see 80/1); a meeting with Lolita's friend Mona; and an appearance at a rehearsal of his own play, featuring Lolita. All three scenes were omitted because such foreground appearances interrupted the structure and rhythm of Quilty's pursuit of Lolita, and undermined the mystery surrounding his identity. Moreover, the latter two scenes created a most awkward narrative problem. Since H.H. couldn't narrate these scenes, Nabokov had to wait and let Lolita do it during their important confrontation scene (pp. 271 ff.), and that proved unwieldy. See 37/3 for mention of another omitted scene.

33/10 *The Little Nymph:* like *Fatherly Love* (in the same entry), this is an appropriate work for H.H.'s sinister alter ego to have authored.

33/11 *The Lady Who Loved Lightning:* Nabokov confirms the deduction that this is the unnamed play which H.H. and Lolita attend in Wace, pp. 222–223. See p. 222; Lolita says, "I am not a lady and do not like lightning" (see also my 1967 *Wisconsin Studies* article, *op. cit.*, p. 216). Although H.H.'s mother was killed by lightning (p. 12), Nabokov intends no cross reference; he grants, however, that "the connection is cozy and tempting." The *Who* in the play's title was not capitalized in the 1958 edition; the error has been corrected.

33/12 *in collaboration with Vivian Darkbloom:* at the very least she must be called Quilty's collaborator, since "she" is an anagram of "Vladimir Nabokov" (6/9).

33/13 *Dark Age:* see 264/7, where H.H. alludes to its author.

33/14 *The Strange Mushroom:* see above, 33/8.

33/15 *traveled 14,000 . . . New York:* H.H. "doubles" Quilty for a change, for he will travel some 27,000 miles with the little nymph (see p. 177), while Quilty's "play" of that name consumes virtually half of that distance.

33/16 *Hobbies . . . pets:* the three "hobbies" prefigure Quilty's pursuit of H.H. and Lolita ("fast cars"), his love of dogs (see 248/1), and the pornographic movies he will force his favorite "pet" to act in (see 278/2).

33/17 *Quine, Dolores:* "Dolores" is Lolita's given name (see 11/5), while "Quine" echoes Quilty, sets up an internal rhyme which condemns him (34/6), and is French for two fives at a game of tric-trac (a form of backgammon). Although Nabokov says he did not intend any allusion, "*Une quine à la lotérie*" is a bid prize, an advantage, which describes the way H.H. and Quilty variously bid for Lolita, and the way the book's game-element manipulates the reader (see p. 301); Quilty reads aloud from H.H.'s poem, "because you took advantage of my disadvantage".

34/1 *Never Talk to Strangers:* this is no idle title. See p. 140 ("I would not talk to strangers," H.H. advises Lolita) and 311/1, where he repeats and expands upon this excellent fatherly advice: "Be true to your [husband]. Do not let other fellows touch you. Do not talk to strangers."

34/2 *Has disappeared:* see next note, and p. 255, where H.H. says, "I have reached the part which ... might be called *'Dolorès Disparue'* " (a play on *Albertine disparue,* the title of the penultimate volume of the original French edition of Marcel Proust's *A la Recherche du temps perdu*). An error in the 1958 edition has been corrected (the transposing of the concluding bracket and period after "follows").

34/3 *I notice ... in the preceding paragraph:* the "slip" refers to "Has disappeared" instead of "Has appeared," another foreshadowing of his loss. Lolita will be cast in a play by Quilty, *The Enchanted Hunters.* See pp. 202–204. It is central to a full sense of the novel.

34/4 *Clarence:* H.H.'s lawyer, to whom the manuscript of this "unrevised" draft is entrusted. See p. 5.

34/5 *The Murdered Playwright:* the prefiguration of the murder announced above is completed here (33/2). H.H. now explicitly refers to his killing of Quilty (pp. 295–307), which is prefigured several more times (see 47/4 and 49/6). By strategically placing *Who's Who in the Limelight* early in *Lolita*—like Black Guinea's list of the avatars of the confidence man in Chapter Three of Herman Melville's *The Confidence-Man: His Masquerade* (1857)—Nabokov gives the reader an opportunity to make at least some of these connections as the novel unfolds.

34/6 *Quine the Swine ... my Lolita:* Quilty, and for "my Lolita," see 47/1 and 194/2.

34/7 *I have only words to play with:* even if H.H. has only words, the reader must consider the implications of his extraordinary control of them. The interlacements which lead in and out of this veritable nerve center reveal a capacity for design and order that, given the conditions under which his narrative has allegedly been composed, is only within the reach of the manipulative author above the book. By no accident is *Who's Who in the Limelight* a theatrical yearbook, for the involutions which spiral out of it demonstrate that playwright Quilty, H.H., and Lolita, as well as the actor and actress who serve as their stand-ins in *Who's Who,* are all performing in another of Nabokov's puppet shows. "Guess again, Punch," H.H. tells Quilty (p. 298); and, of their fight, H.H. says, "He and I were two large dummies, stuffed with dirty cotton and rags" (p. 301). The novel's first reference to Quilty thus offers a summary phrase (6/9); for the countless involuted verbal figurations

[351]

and cross references in *Lolita* all represent "Vivian Darkbloom" 's "cue," and suggest that the authorial consciousness is somehow profoundly involved in a tale that in every literal way is surely separate from it.

Having recognized the novel's verisimilar disguise, the reader is afforded a global view of the book *qua* book, whose dappled surface now reveals patterns that seem almost visual. In the Foreword to the 1966 version of *Speak, Memory*, Nabokov says that in looking for a title for the first edition, he "toyed with *The Anthemion* which is the name of a honeysuckle ornament, consisting of elaborate interlacements and expanding clusters, but nobody liked it"; it would be a fitting, if precious, subtitle for *Lolita* (as well as for several other Nabokov works). A grand anthemion entwines H.H.'s narrative, like some vast authorial watermark, and its outlines are traced by the elegantly ordered networks of alliteration, "coincidences," narrative "inconsistencies," lepidopterological references, "cryptocolors," and shadows and glimpses of Quilty.

Chapter 9

35/1 *charming . . . chap:* the cascade of alliterations in this paragraph, so carefully controlled, underscores the significance of *Who's Who*, as does a remark on the next page (36/3). Compare the often comic alliterations of *Lolita* with the stately and sonorous effects achieved in *Speak, Memory* (as in the opening and closing paragraphs of Chapter Six).

35/2 *Pierre Point in Melville Sound:* H.H.'s invention, from *Pierre* (1852) by Herman Melville (1819–1891).

36/1 *gremlin:* a mischievous little gnome reported by World War II airmen as causing mechanical trouble in airplanes. "Drumlins" (bottom of p. 35) is H.H.'s diminutive of *drum.*

36/2 *kremlin:* the name of the governing center of Russia completes this sequence of phonological pairings. The best example is found in *Pale Fire* (note to line 803). Nabokov continually manipulates the basic linguistic devices—auditory, morphological, and alphabetical, the latter most conspicuously. In *Pale Fire*, Zemblan is "the tongue of the mirror" (p. 242); and the fragmentation or total annihilation of the self reverberates in the verbal distortions in *Bend Sinister*'s police state, "where everybody is merely an anagram of everybody else," as well as in the alphabetical and psychic inversions and reversals of *Pale Fire*—such as Botkin-Kinbote and the Index references to Word Golf and "*Sudarg of Bokay*, a mirror maker of genius," the latter an anagrammatic reflection and poetic description of omnipresent death, represented in *Pale Fire* by the Zemblan assassin J[y]akob Gradus, who throws his shadow across the entire novel, its creations, creator, and readers.

36/3 *The reader will regret to learn ... I had another bout with insanity:* H.H. is right, readers *do* regret to hear this from a narrator; and H.H. virtually encloses his narrative within reminders of this "unreliability," for, toward the end (p. 257), he casually says he retired to another sanatorium ("I felt I was merely losing contact with reality" [*merely!*— A.A.]). Several of Nabokov's narrators are mad. Among other things, their madness functions as a parody of critical dogma about fiction, and a telling parody of the reader's own delusory "contact with reality." Of course H.H.'s is not a credible point of view in the terms laid down by Henry James, refined by Percy Lubbock, put into practice by Ford Madox Ford and Joseph Conrad, institutionalized by two generations of critics, and enforced by thousands of creative writing instructors—and the involuted, patterned surface of *Lolita* makes this even clearer. H.H.'s copy of *Who's Who* and Quilty's "cryptogrammic paper chase" (pp. 252–253), the two most important concentrations of authorial inlays, typical in method and effect, are thus symmetrically located at the beginning and near the end of the novel, almost next to those declarations of insanity which seem to frame it, though these symmetries cannot hope to be as exact as the one formed by the first and final words of the novel ("Lolita"). See Notes 53/1 through 54/3 for another concentration of involutions.

CHAPTER 10

37/1 *patients ... had witnessed their own conception:* Nabokov's attacks on Freud are consistent. Kinbote includes in his Commentary lines deleted in the draft of the poem *Pale Fire:*

> ... Your modern architect
> Is in collusion with psychanalysts:
> When planning parents' bedrooms, he insists
> On lockless doors so that, when looking back,
> The future patient of the future quack
> May find, all set for him, the Primal Scene. [p. 94]

In *Speak, Memory,* Nabokov similarly "reject[s] completely the vulgar, shabby, fundamentally medieval world of Freud, with its crankish quest for sexual symbols (something like searching for Baconian acrostics in Shakespeare's works) and its bitter little embryos spying, from their natural nooks, upon the love life of their parents" (p. 20); while in *Ada* he notes the "pale pencil which poor [public] speakers are obsessed with in familiar dreams (attributed by Dr. Froid of Signy-Mondieu-Mondieu to the dreamer's having read in infancy his adulterous parents' love letters)" (p. 549). For Freud, see 7/6.

37/2 *Humbertish:* H.H.'s coinage; after any language ending in the *-ish* suffix (Finnish, English, Lettish).

37/3 *house . . . burned down:* Nabokov omitted from the last draft of *Lolita* a hilarious scene describing H.H.'s arrival by taxi at the charred-out, bepuddled, roped-off ruins of the McCoo residence. A large crowd applauds H.H. as he grandly alights from the cab; only an encyclopedia has survived the holocaust. He recognizes that the lost opportunity to coach "the enigmatic [McCoo] nymphet" is no loss at all (see p. 43). Nabokov reinstated the scene in his screenplay of *Lolita*, but director Stanley Kubrick dropped it from the final version. It eventually will be seen when Nabokov publishes the complete original screenplay, a "project I have been nursing for some time," he says. "Although there are just enough borrowings from it in [Kubrick's] version to justify my legal position as author of the script, the final product is only a blurred skimpy glimpse of the marvelous picture I imagined and set down scene by scene during the six months I worked in a Los Angeles villa. I do not wish to imply that Kubrick's film is mediocre; in its own right, it is first-rate, but it is not what I wrote. A tinge of *poshlost* [see Introduction, pp. xlix–l] is often given by the cinema to the novel it distorts and coarsens in its crooked glass. Kubrick, I think, avoided this fault in his version, but I shall never understand why he did not follow my directions and dreams. It is a great pity; but at least I shall be able to have people read my *Lolita* play in its original form" (*Paris Review* interview, 1967). Speaking more positively three years earlier, Nabokov said, "The four main actors deserve the very highest praise. Sue Lyon bringing that breakfast tray or childishly pulling on her sweater in the car—these are moments of unforgettable acting and directing. The killing of Quilty [Peter Sellers] is a masterpiece, and so is the death of Mrs. Haze [Shelley Winters; James Mason was H.H.]. I must point out, though, that I had nothing to do with the actual production. If I had, I might have insisted on stressing certain things that were not stressed—for example, the different motels at which they stopped" (*Playboy* interview). The highways and motels were so little in evidence because the film, released in 1962, was shot in England.

37/4 *342:* for "coincidences," see 120/3 and 250/2.

38/1 *suburban dog:* a foreshadowing of Charlotte Haze's death, for Mr.

Beale will run over her when he swerves to avoid hitting what may well be this dog (see p. 104). See also *Keys*, p. 6.

38/2 *van Gogh:* the "Arlésienne" (1888) is a famous portrait of a woman from the town of Arles in Provence, by Vincent van Gogh (1853–1890). Mass-produced reproductions of it are quite popular in America. H.H.'s low opinion of van Gogh is shared by other Nabokov characters. In *Pnin*, the art teacher Lake thinks "That van Gogh is second-rate and Picasso supreme, despite his commercial foibles" (p. 96); and Victor Wind acknowledges "with a nod of ironic recognition" a framed reproduction of van Gogh's "La Berceuse" (p. 108).

39/1 *Marlene Dietrich:* see 11/4. Also pp. 53 and 103.

40/1 *René Prinet:* "The Kreutzer Sonata" was dedicated by Beethoven to Rodolphe Kreutzer in 1805 (Nabokov intends no allusion to Tolstoy's story of that name). Prinet's painting (1898) today illustrates the Tabu perfume advertisement, often found in *The New Yorker* and chic ladies' magazines. It shows, in Nabokov's words, an "ill-groomed girl pianist rising like a wave from her stool after completing the duo, and being kissed by a hirsute violinist. Very unappetizing and clammy, but has 'camp' charm."

41/1 *Riviera love ... over dark glasses:* the confluence of sunglasses and H.H.'s Riviera love suggest that H.H. has stumbled upon a veritable Lost-and-Found Department (see 15/3).

41/2 *fairy-tale:* see 18/6 and 33/3.

41/3 *"Roches Roses":* the "red rocks" of p. 15. See 58/1. Both H.H.'s and Poe's "Annabel Lee" are alluded to on this and the next page.

42/1 *nouvelle:* French; new one. For "this Lolita, *my* Lolita, see 47/1.

42/2 *mummery:* the performance of an actor in a dumb show; *mummer* is obsolete slang for a play-actor.

42/3 *fruit vert:* "green fruit"; French (dated) slang for " 'unripe' females attractive to ripe gentlemen," notes Nabokov.

42/4 *Au fond, ça m'est bien égal:* French; "Really, I don't care at all."

CHAPTER 11

42/5 *en escalier:* set-up in an oblique typography; French for "staircase style."

42/6 *Blank . . . Blankton, Mass.:* there is no such town. The "blanks" make fun of the "authenticity" of the pages of both the diary and the entire novel, H.H.'s "photographic memory" notwithstanding. Thus *Lolita's* parodic design also includes the literary journal or diary. Nabokov regards with profound skepticism the possibilities of complete autobiographical revelation. When Fyodor shaves himself in *The Gift,* "A pale self-portrait looked out of the mirror with the serious eyes of all self-portraits" (p. 120); Nabokov does not abide such portraits. "Manifold self-awareness" (as he calls it in *Speak, Memory*) is not to be achieved through solemn introspection, certainly not through the diarist's compulsive egotism, candid but totally self-conscious self-analysis, carefully created "honesty," willful irony, and studied self-deprecation. Nabokov has been burlesquing the literary diary since as far back as 1934. Near the end of *Despair,* Hermann's first-person narrative "degenerates into a diary"—"the lowest form of literature" (p. 218)—and this early parody is fully realized in *Lolita,* especially in the present chapter. For more on the confessional mode, see 72/3.

42/7 *phoenix:* a legendary bird represented by the ancient Egyptians as living for five or six centuries, being consumed in fire by its own act, and then rising from its ashes; an emblem of resurrection and immortality.

43/1 *sebum:* the material secreted by the sebaceous glands.

43/2 *Humbert le Bel:* Humbert the Fair; a kingly epithet (e.g., Charles le Bel of France).

44/1 *entrée:* appearance on a stage; grand entrance.

44/2 *favonian:* of or pertaining to the west wind; thus, gentle.

44/3 *phocine:* pertaining to the zoological sub-family which includes the common seal, the image against which H.H. measures "the seaside of [Lolita's] schoolgirl thighs"—an allusion to the lost "kingdom" of Annabel (see 11/2).

44/4 *Priap:* son of Dionysus and Aphrodite, Priapus was the Greco-Roman god of procreation and fertility, usually portrayed in a manly state. Also mentioned on pp. 161, 239, and less mythically, on p. 215. See 11/5.

44/5 *predator . . . prey:* H.H. often characterizes himself as a predator, most often as an ape or spider (prominent among the butterfly's natural enemies). For further discussion, see my 1967 *Wisconsin Studies* article, *op. cit.,* pp. 222 and 228.

45/1 *stippled:* engraved, by means of dots rather than lines; in painting, refers to the use of small touches which coalesce to produce gradations of light and shade. See 286/2.

45/2 *Delectatio morosa . . . dolors:* Latin; morose pleasure, a monastic term. In the next sentence, as on p. 55, H.H. toys with the Latin etymology of "Dolores" (see 11/5).

45/3 *Our Glass Lake:* see 83/2.

45/4 *nacreous:* having a pearly iridescence.

45/5 *Virginia . . . Edgar:* Poe was born January 19, 1809. He was therefore twenty-seven when in 1836 he married his thirteen-year-old cousin, Virginia Clemm, who died of a lingering disease in 1847. She was the inspiration for many of his poems. For his first conjugal night with Lolita, H.H. appropriately registers as "Edgar" (see 120/2). He also employs the name on pp. 77 and 191 (see also *Keys,* p. 37). For a summary of the Poe allusions, see 11/2.

45/6 *Je m'imagine cela:* French; I can imagine that.

45/7 *"Monsieur Poe-poe":* H.H. puns on "poet," but the schoolboy had in mind *"popo"* (or *"popotin"*), French slang for the posterior.

45/8 *resemble . . . actor chap:* Clare Quilty. They *do* resemble one another. For a summary of Quilty allusions, see 33/9.

45/9 *nictating: rare;* winking.

46/1 *"ne montrez pas vos zhambes":* French; "don't show your legs" (*jambes* is misspelled to indicate an American accent). See 191/2.

46/2 *à mes heures:* French; when in the right mood.

47/1 *the writer's ancient lust:* H.H. sees himself in a line descending from the great Roman love poets, and he frequently imitates their locutions. The intonational stresses of *"this Lolita, my Lolita"* are borrowed from a donnish English translation of a Latin poem (see pp. 42, 67–68, 153, 279, 280, 295). H.H.'s "ancient" models include Propertius (c. 50–16 B.C.) on Cynthia, Tibullus (c. 55–19 B.C.) on Delia, and Horace (65–8 B.C.) on any of the sixteen women to whom he wrote poems. See 194/2.

47/2 *Our Glass Lake:* a "mistake"; see 83/2.

47/3 *"Little Carmen":* a pun: little [train]men, or "Dwarf Conductors" (see also *Keys,* p. 144n). The allusions to *Carmen* have nothing to do with Bizet's opera. They refer only to the novella (1845) by Prosper Mérimée (1803–1870). For a pun on his name, see 253/7. Like H.H.,

José Lizzarrabengoa, Carmen's abandoned and ill-fated lover (see 241/3), tells his story from prison (but not until the third chapter, when the narrative frame is withdrawn). The story of love, loss, and revenge is appropriate. The *Carmen* allusions also serve as a trap for the sophisticated reader who is misled into believing that H.H., like José, will murder his treacherous Carmen; see p. 282, where H.H. springs the trap. H.H. quotes Mérimée (245/4, 280/2, 280/4) and frequently calls Lolita "Carmen," the traditional name of a bewitching woman (pp. 61, 62, 63, 244–245, 253, 258, 280, 282). Carl R. Proffer discusses the *Carmen* allusions in *Keys*, pp. 45–53. In Latin, *carmen* means song, poetry, and charm. "My charmin', my Carmen," says H.H. (p. 62), thus demonstrating that he knows its etymology and original English meaning: the chanting of a verse having magic power; "to bewitch, enchant, subdue by magic power." See 18/6. H.H. calls himself "an enchanted hunter," takes Lolita to the hotel of that name, speaks of an "enchanted island of time" (p. 20), and so forth. Nabokov told his lecture classes at Cornell that a great writer was at once a storyteller, a teacher, and, most supremely, an enchanter. See 110/2.

47/4 *I shot ... said: Ah!:* a prevision of Quilty's death; see 89/1 and 305/1.

48/1 *Pisky:* "Pixie"; see 33/3. The town is invented. Also means "moth" in rural England. For entomological allusions, see 8/1.

49/1 *le mot juste:* French; the right word; a phrase made famous by the French novelist Gustave Flaubert (1821–1880), who often took a week to find *le mot juste*. For other allusions to Flaubert, see 147/3, 204/2, and 267/2.

49/2 *Ronsard's "la vermeillette fente":* Pierre de Ronsard (1524–1585), the greatest poet of the French Renaissance. H.H. alludes to a sonnet entitled *L.M.F.*, and its first line, "*Je te salue, o vermeillette fante*" ("*fente*" is the modern spelling): "I salute [or hail] you, oh little red slit" ("*Blason du sexe feminin*," Edition Pléiade, II, 775). A "*blason*" is a short poem in praise or criticism of a certain subject. For another allusion to Ronsard, see 216/1. During his émigré period in Germany in the 'twenties and early 'thirties, Nabokov published Russian translations of many of the writers alluded to by H.H., including Ronsard, Verlaine, Byron, Keats, Baudelaire, Shakespeare, Rimbaud, Goethe, Pushkin, Carroll, and Romain Rolland.

49/3 *Remy Belleau's "un petit ... escarlatte":* Belleau (1528–1577), Ronsard's colleague in the Pléiade group, also writes a "*blason*" in praise of the external female genitalia; "the hillock velveted with delicate moss, / traced in the middle with a little scarlet thread [labia]." For obvious reasons, the poem is rarely anthologized and is difficult to find. It appears in the Leyden reprint (1865) of the rare anthology *Recueil de pièces choisies rassemblées par les soins du cosmopolite*, duc d'Aiguillon, ed. (1735). The Cornell Library owns a copy, notes Nabokov.

49/4 *of my darling … my bride:* line 39 of Poe's "Annabel Lee." See 11/2 for the poem.

49/5 *Mystery of the Menarche:* the menarche is the initial menstrual period. In Ireland it is called "The Curse of the Irish."

49/6 *kill in my dreams:* another prevision of Quilty's death scene; see p. 299.

50/1 *toothbrush mustache:* Quilty has one too; see p. 220. Poe also had one, but Nabokov says that no allusion is intended here.

50/2 *ape-ear:* H.H. several times characterizes himself this way. See p. 313 for a most resonant ape image.

51/1 *Ces matins gris si doux:* French; "Those gray mornings, so soft …"

52/1 *rumor, roomer:* a homophone. In *The Real Life of Sebastian Knight*, the narrator speaks of "mad Sebastian, struggling in a naughty world of Juggernauts, and aeronauts, and naughts, and what-nots" (p. 65).

52/2 *Is it Fate:* "McFate" is quietly introduced; see 54/3 and 58/1.

52/3 *"And behold":* Lolita completes her mother's "Lo," and H.H. later twists the epithet (225/4).

53/1 *her class at … school:* in *Pnin*, young Victor Wind sees in the glass headlight or chrome plating of a car "a view of the street and himself comparable to the microcosmic version of a room (with a dorsal view of diminutive people) in that very special and very magical small convex mirror that, half a millennium ago, Van Eyck and Petrus Christus and Memling used to paint into their detailed interiors, behind the sour merchant or the domestic madonna" (pp. 97–98). Like *Who's Who in the Limelight* (pp. 33–34) and the "cryptogrammic paper chase" (pp. 252–253), the "poetic" class list serves as a kind of magical mirror. The list is printed on the back of an unfinished map of the U.S., drawn by Lolita, suggesting the scale of the gameboard on which the action is played. The image of the map secreted in the *Young People's Encyclo-*

pedia prefigures their journeys (on which H.H. will "finish" the map by showing Lolita the country), just as the class list prefigures and mirrors an extraordinary number of other things.

53/2 *Beale:* the Beales' father kills Charlotte Haze (p. 100), and they are the first of no less than four sets of twins in Lolita's class (the Cowans, the Talbots, and the incestuous Mirandas [see p. 138]), a microscopic vision of the doubling (H.H. and Quilty) and mirroring that occurs in the roomy interior of the entire book (including Ray's Foreword), where even cars have their twins (p. 229); "the long hairy arm of coincidence" is said to have its unpredictable "twin limb" (p. 107); and obscure women of science mirror one another in spite of the almost 300 pages separating them (Blanche Schwarzmann: "White Blackman," and Melanie Weiss: "Black White"; see p. 304).

Double names, initials, and phonetic effects prevail throughout *Lolita*, whether the twinning is literal (Humbert Humbert, Vanessa van Ness, Quilty's Duk Duk Ranch, and H.H.'s alternate pseudonyms of "Otto Otto," "Mesmer Mesmer," and "Lambert Lambert"); or alliterative (Clare Quilty, Gaston Godin, Harold Haze, Bill Brown, and Clarence [Choate] Clark); or trickily alphabetical (John Ray, Jr.: J.R., Jr.). The double consonants of the almost infinite succession of humorously alliterative place names and points of interest H.H. visits are thus thematically consistent (Pierre Point, Hobby House, Hazy Hills, Kumfy Kabins, Raspberry Room, Chestnut Court, and so forth). Numbers even adhere to the pattern; H.H. imagines Lolita's unborn child "dreaming already in her of becoming a big shot and retiring around 2020 A.D." (p. 279). The name of "Harold D. Doublename" represents a summary phrase (p. 184), but the annotator's double initials are only a happy coincidence. For more on mirrors, see 121/2.

53/3 *Carmine, Rose:* see 58/1.

54/1 *Falter:* German; butterfly—and a companion of "Miss Phalen" (*phalène:* moth [58/2]) and the playwright "Schmetterling" (butterfly [303/5]). For a summary of the entomological allusions, see 8/1.

54/2 *Fantasia:* a corrected misprint (*s* instead of *z* in the 1958 edition). She is married on p. 291 (the "Murphy-Fantasia" wedding party).

54/3 *McFate, Aubrey:* a vagrant auditor, rather than a member of the class (see 58/1), though the reader may not realize it for four more pages. McFate's appearance in the middle of the class list undercuts the inviolable "reality" of much more than just the list. By placing the McFate allusions back-to-back on pp. 54 and 58, Nabokov gives the reader a fighting chance to make the association, and to realize its implications. It would be "easier" on the reader, of course, if the class list came *after* p. 58 (notes 253/1 and 255/1 limn similar effects). McFate's first name suggests Aubrey Beardsley (see 253/5), the "decadent" Art Nouveau artist (1872–1898) quite out of fashion when *Lolita* was written, and reveals another mother lode of verbal figurations: the invented town of "Beardsley," its school and college, and Gaston Godin (see 183/1).

54/4 *Windmuller:* Louise and her father appear on p. 6; he on p. 292.

54/5 *bodyguard of roses:* classmates "Rose" and "Rosaline" serve as Lolita's rosy page-girls. The rose is of course the flower traditionally associated with gems, decorations, wine, perfume, and women of great charm and / or virtue. Lolita is continually linked with the flower. See 58/1. See also *Keys*, p. 118.

55/1 *Is "mask" the keyword?:* yes, because the masked author has just been mirrored, as it were, in the class list; see the Introduction and Chapter Twenty-six (111/1).

55/2 *charshaf:* a veil worn by Turkish women.

55/3 *Irving:* the reader may wonder why H.H. is sorry for "Flashman, Irving" (p. 54). "Poor Irving," says Nabokov, "he is the only Jew among all those Gentiles." See 263/4.

55/4 *ullulations:* or *ululation;* a loud, mournful, rhythmical howl.

55/5 *ribald sea monsters:* the intrusive bearded bathers of p. 15. "Annabel" and H.H.'s seasickness refers to Poe's poem. See 11/2.

55/6 *"Mais allez-y, allez-y!":* French; "But go ahead, go!"

56/1 *Dr. Blanche Schwarzmann:* mentioned by John Ray. See 7/3.

56/2 *libidream:* H.H.'s portmanteau of "libido" and "dream."

56/3 *Dorsal:* belonging to, or situated on or near the back of an animal.

57/1 *manège:* French; tactics.

CHAPTER 12

57/2 *pederosis:* H.H.'s description of his condition. Although rare, the term exists; from the Greek *paid-*, meaning "child," plus *erōs*, "sexual love" (akin to *erasthai:* "to love, desire ardently"), plus Latin suffix, from Greek, *-ōsis*, an "abnormal or diseased condition" (e.g., *sclerosis*). *Pedophilia* is the more common word for H.H.'s malaise.

58/1 *Aubrey McFate...devil of mine*: the devilish "force" responsible for H.H.'s misfortunes is invoked on pp. 54, 109, 118, 212, 213, 258. When H.H. perceives Quilty—the worst aspect of his McFate—as a "red-beast" or "red fiend," Nabokov is parodying that archetypal Double, the Devil. Red is Quilty's color, just as rose is associated with Annabel (41/3) and Lolita; her classmate's name, "Rose Carmine" (p. 53), defines the two motifs nicely. Its significance, however, has nothing to do with "symbolism"; the red and rose stipplings are the work of the author, rather than McFate, and add some vivid touches of color to the anthemion (see 34/7). Once pointed out, the color motif need not be identified further; but the reader is reminded again that Nabokov is no "symbolist." After reading the first draft of these Notes, Nabokov thought that this point had not been made clear enough, and, moved too by the annotator's loose play with some "red" images, wrote the following for my information, under the heading "A Note about Symbols and Colors *re* 'Annotated *Lolita*.'" It is included here because I think it is one of the most significant statements Nabokov has made about his own art. He writes:

> There exist novelists and poets, and ecclesiastic writers, who deliberately use color terms, or numbers, in a strictly symbolic sense. The type of writer I am, half-painter, half-naturalist, finds the use of symbols hateful because it substitutes a dead general idea for a live specific impression. I am therefore puzzled and distressed by the significance you lend to the general idea of "red" in my book. When the intellect limits itself to the general notion, or primitive notion, of a certain color it deprives the senses of its shades. In different languages different colors were used in a general sense before shades were distinguished. (In French, for example, the "redness" of hair is now expressed by "*roux*" meaning rufous, or russet, or fulvous with a reddish cast.) For me the shades, or rather colors, of, say, a fox, a ruby, a carrot, a pink rose, a dark cherry, a flushed cheek, are as different as blue is from green or the royal purple of blood (Fr. "*pourpre*") from the English sense of violet blue. I think your students, your readers, should be taught to *see* things, to discriminate between visual shades as the author does, and not to lump them under such arbitrary labels as "red" (using it, moreover, as a sexual symbol, though actually the dominant shades in males are mauve—to bright blue, in certain monkeys)....Roses may be white, and even black-red. Only cartoonists, having three colors at their disposal, use red for hair, cheek and blood.

See 223/2 for further remarks on color.

58/2 *Miss Phalen:* from the French *phalène:* moth. For the entomological allusions, see 8/1.

CHAPTER 13

61/1 *friable:* easily crumbled or pulverized.

61/2 *parkled:* H.H.'s coinage.

62/1 *safely solipsized:* see 14/2. An important phrase (see second half of 18/6). The verbal form of *solipsist* is of course H.H.'s coinage—a most significant portmanteau suggesting that Lolita has been reduced in more than size, as H.H. comes to realize.

62/2 *corpuscles of Krause:* after the German anatomist: minute sensory particles occurring in the mucous membranes of the genitalia. An author's error has been corrected (*s* in Krause instead of *z* in the 1958 edition).

62/3 *seraglio:* the portion of a Moslem house reserved for the wives and harem.

64/1 *Drew his .32:* the revenge murder of Lolita which *doesn't* take place; see p. 282.

CHAPTER 14

64/2 *loan God:* from a cultural sequence (e.g., Greek-Roman, Hebrew-Christian); "lone" in the paperback edition, and thus an "existential image" to one critic.

65/1 *Dr. Quilty:* the "playwright" is his nephew (or cousin), Clare Quilty. For a summary of Quilty allusions, see 33/9.

66/1 *Shirley Holmes:* after Sir Arthur Conan Doyle's (1859–1930) famous detective hero, Sherlock Holmes (see 252/5). Between the ages of ten and fifteen, Nabokov was a Holmes devotee. That enthusiasm has faded, though traces remain. "I spent a poor night in a charming, airy, prettily furnished room where neither window nor door closed properly, and where an omnibus edition of Sherlock Holmes which had pursued me for years supported a bedside lamp," writes the narrator of *Pnin,* at the end of the novel (p. 190). The narrator of *The Real Life of Sebastian Knight* "use[s] an old Sherlock Holmes stratagem" (p. 153); and, in *Despair,* Hermann addresses Conan Doyle directly: "What an opportunity, what a subject you missed! For you could have written one last tale concluding the whole Sherlock Holmes epic; one last episode beautifully setting off the rest; the murderer in that tale should have turned out to be not the one-legged bookkeeper, not the Chinaman Ching and not the woman in crimson, but the very chronicler of the crime stories, Dr. Watson himself—Watson, who, so to speak, knew what was Whatson. A staggering surprise for the reader" (pp. 131–132)—and a figurative description of several of Nabokov's own narrative strategies. "Was he in *Sherlock Holmes,* the fellow whose / Tracks pointed back when he reversed his shoes?" wonders John Shade in Canto One of *Pale Fire* (lines 27–28). After identifying Holmes in the Commentary, Kinbote says he "suspect[s] that our poet simply made up this Case of the Reversed Footprints" (p. 78). Right or wrong, his suspicion summarizes the way that Nabokov frequently parodies and transmutes the methods and themes of that genre, just as "Shirley Holmes" is a jocular reminder that *Lolita* is, among other things, a kind of mystery story demanding a considerable amount of armchair detection. See the remarks on Poe and the detective story, 11/2. For the penultimate moment in this "tale of ratiocination," see 274/1; and for a telling allusion to Holmes, drawn from *The Defense,* see 274/2.

CHAPTER 15

66/2 *Camp Q:* "Cue" is Quilty's nickname. "The 'Q,' " notes Nabokov, "had to be changed to 'Kilt' in the French translation because of the awful pun, Q = *cul!*"

66/3 *Botticellian pink:* Sandro Botticelli (1444 or 1445–1510), master of the early Italian Renaissance, known for his tender renderings of sensual but melancholy femininity. That pink is most manifest in the vision of the three graces in his painting "Primavera," while the "wet, matted eyelashes" suggest his famous "The Birth of Venus," which H.H. invokes on pp. 272 and 276.

67/1 *her coccyx:* the end of the vertebral column.

67/2 *iliac:* anatomical word; pertaining to the *ilium,* "the dorsal and upper one of the three bones composing either lateral half of the pelvis."

68/1 *Catullus . . . forever:* Gaius Valerius Catullus (c. 84–54 B.C.), Roman lyric, erotic, and epigrammatic poet. H.H.'s *"that* Lolita, *my* Lolita" (p. 67) echoes Catullus' evocation of his enchanting Lesbia, as well as imitations such as "My sweetest Lesbia" (1601), by Thomas Campion (1567–1620), English poet. See 47/1 and 153/1.

68/2 *D.P.*: during and shortly after World War II, refugees were officially described as "Displaced Persons"; hence "D.P."s.

68/3 *Berthe au Grand Pied:* Bertha (or Bertrade) with the Big Feet (or Bigfoot Bertha); the epithet is not pejorative. A French historical figure (d. 783), she was Pépin le Bref's wife and Charlemagne's mother, and is alluded to by François Villon in his ballad with the refrain *"Mais où sont les neiges d'antan?"*

68/4 *mais rien:* French; but nothing.

CHAPTER 16

69/1 *mon cher, cher monsieur:* French; my dear, dear sir.

69/2 *Départez:* the wrong French for "leave!" Correct: *Partez!*

70/1 *chéri:* French; darling.

70/2 *mon très, très cher:* French; my very, very dear.

71/1 *Morell:* Thomas Morell (1703–1784), an English classical scholar, wrote the song "See the Conquering Hero Comes." George Frederick Handel (1685–1759) used it in his oratorios *Joshua* and *Judas Maccabeus.* Sung by a Chorus of Youths in *Joshua,* it begins, "See the conquering hero comes! Sound the trumpet, beat the drums" (Act III, scene 2). It was also used in later versions of Nathaniel Lee's (1653–1692) tragedy, *The Rival Queens* (1677), and is quoted in Joyce's *Ulysses* in reference to Molly's seducer, Blazes Boylan (1961 Random House edition, p. 264). It is apt that the "conquering hero" should be above Quilty's picture, since that motto predicts his victory. For Joyce, see 6/11.

71/2 *A distinguished playwright...Drome:* Quilty. A *dromedary* is a one-humped camel, and H.H. is both playing with the familiar brand name and correcting the manufacturer's error: the beast on the cigarette wrapper is not a camel, strictly speaking. H.H.'s aside, "The resemblance was slight," refers to 45/8, where he is said to resemble Quilty. Note, too, that "Lo's chaste bed" is under Quilty. See 33/9 for a summary of Quilty allusions.

CHAPTER 17

72/1 *pavor nocturnus:* Latin; night panic. Quilty lives in "Pavor Manor" (p. 295).

72/2 *peine forte et dure:* French; strong and hard torture.

72/3 *Dostoevskian grin:* Fyodor Dostoevsky (1821–1881), the famous Russian novelist, has long been one of Nabokov's primary targets. In the *Playboy* interview he says, "Non-Russian readers do not realize two things; that not all Russians love Dostoevsky as much as Americans do, and that most of those Russians who do, venerate him as a mystic and not as an artist. He was a prophet, a claptrap journalist and a slapdash comedian. I admit that some of his scenes, some of his tremendous, farcical rows are extraordinarily amusing. But his sensitive murderers and soulful prostitutes are not to be endured for one moment—by this reader anyway." "Heart-to-heart talks, confessions in the Dostoevskian manner are also not in my line," he writes in *Speak, Memory* (p. 284). But H.H. is the ultimate in "sensitive murderers," and by casting his tale as a "confession," Nabokov lets Dostoevsky lay down the rules and then beats "old Dusty" at his own game. See 42/6 for remarks on another convention allied with the confession—the literary diary.

72/4 *Well-read Humbert:* the lines he quotes are from Canto III, stanza 116 of *Childe Harold's Pilgrimage* (1812, 1816, 1818), by George Gordon, Lord Byron (1788–1824), English poet. These lines occur almost at the end of the Canto (lines 1080–1081), and are addressed to Ada, Harold's absent daughter. Byron was in Italy at this time, estranged from the wife he had married for the sake of tranquility and respectability—a gesture H.H. would no doubt appreciate, as he would sympathize with the difficulties occasioned by the amorous poet's incestuous relationship with his half sister. Dr. Byron is the Haze family physician, and he too has a daughter (see 96/2). But, as an unwitting accomplice to a seduction, he belies his name, for the sleeping pills he dispenses prove ineffective at The Enchanted Hunters hotel (see p. 130). Byron's works and Byron's Augusta Ada, a gifted girl in her own right, resonate in Nabokov's latest novel, as does the "Byronic" (and Chateaubriandesque) theme of incest; Ada Veen even has a bit part in a film called *Don Juan's Last Fling.* Nabokov's deep knowledge of Byron is made evident throughout his *Eugene Onegin* Commentary (see the "Byron" entry in the Index, Vol. IV).

72/5 *Charlotte:* the name of Werther's tragic love in *The Sorrows of Young Werther* (1774), by Johann Wolfgang von Goethe (1749–1832). The choice of a name is clearly ironic, since Goethe's Charlotte marries another. Weepy Werther, an artist of sorts, remains hopelessly in love with her and eventually takes his own life. "A faded charm still clings about this novel, which artistically is greatly inferior to Chateaubriand's *René* and even to Constant's *Adolphe,*" writes Nabokov in his *Eugene Onegin* Commentary (Vol. II, p. 345). See 78/1. Goethe is also invoked on 242/2. For Chateaubriand, see 147/4.

72/6 *quel mot:* French; what a word.

73/1 *incubus:* an evil spirit or demon, originally in personified representations of the nightmare, supposed to descend upon persons in their sleep, and especially to seek sexual intercourse with women. In the Middle Ages their existence was recognized by ecclesiastical and civil law. The epithet "Humbert the Cubus" is of course his own variant. For more on enchantments, see 18/6.

73/2 *mauvemail:* H.H.'s coinage; mauve is pale pinkish purple.

74/1 *"The orange ... grave":* a parody of a "poetic" quotation.

74/2 *raree-show:* a show carried about in a box; a peep show.

74/3 *Une petite attention:* a nice thought (a favor).

75/1 *Incarnadine:* flesh-colored or bright pink. This word appears in a stanza from *The Rubáiyát;* see 264/8.

75/2 *eructations:* violent belches.

75/3 *by Pan!:* H.H.'s "by God!" In Greek mythology, a god of forests, flocks, and shepherds, having the horns and hoofs of a goat.

CHAPTER 18

76/1 *soi-disant:* French; so-called (also used on p. 149).

77/1 *a Turk:* Charlotte is not quite sure of H.H.'s "racial purity." Neither is Jean Farlow, who intercepts an anti-Semitic remark (p. 81), nor The Enchanted Hunters' management (p. 120). See 260/2 and 263/4.

77/2 *contretemps:* French; an embarrassing or awkward occurrence.

77/3 *rattles:* the sound-producing organs on a rattlesnake's tail.

77/4 *rubrique:* a newspaper section.

77/5 *"Edgar" ... "writer and explorer":* Edgar A. Poe, whose *Narrative of A. Gordon Pym* was the product of an alleged polar expedition (see 33/5). For the Poe allusions, see 11/2.

77/6 *Peacock, Rainbow:* Thomas Love Peacock (1785–1866), English poet and novelist, whose name recalls the "Rainbow," or Arthur Rimbaud (1854–1891), French poet. After abandoning literature at the age of eighteen, Rimbaud traveled widely. In 1888 in Abyssinia, where he sold guns, the English called the ex-poet "trader Rainbow," as Nabokov notes in his *Eugene Onegin* Commentary (Vol. III, p. 412). For further allusions, see 165/6, 174/1, 252/7, and 280/1.

78/1 *Lottelita, Lolitchen:* H.H. toys with "Lotte," a diminutive of "Charlotte," and discerns *Lolita* in *Lotte* ("Lottelita"), which is also a phonetic transcription of American idiom and diction (*Lot of* [*Lo*]*lita*). *Lolitchen* is formed with the German diminutive ending -*chen*. H.H. no doubt recalls that Goethe's Werther calls his Charlotte "Lotte" and "Lottchen." See 72/5.

79/1 *ecru and ocher: ecru* is a grayish yellow that is greener and paler than chamois or old ivory. *Ocher* is a dark yellow color derived from or resembling ocher, a hydrated iron oxide.

80/1 *the jovial dentist:* Clare Quilty's Uncle Ivor. Much later H.H. will learn from Lolita herself that Quilty met her through this association. On p. 274, H.H. recapitulates their confrontation: "Well, did I know that he was practically an old friend? That he had visited with his uncle in Ramsdale?—oh, years ago—and spoken at Mother's club, and had tugged and pulled her, Dolly . . . onto his lap . . ." An earlier draft of the novel contained Quilty's appearance before the ladies. See 33/9 for a summary of his appearances.

80/2 *arrière-pensée:* French; hidden thoughts, ulterior motives.

81/1 *interrupted Jean:* John is about to say "Jews," and Jean, suspecting that H.H. may be Jewish, tactfully interrupts. See 263/4.

CHAPTER 19

83/1 *A Guide to . . . Development:* the titles H.H. mentions are by turns invented (*Who's Who in the Limelight* [p. 33]; *Clowns and Columbines* [244/1]), actual (the other titles on p. 244; *Brute Force* [264/4]), or close approximations of existing works, as in this instance. A plethora of actual titles circle about this "fool's book" (e.g., *Guide to Child Development through the Beginning School Years* [1946]), and Nabokov seems to have created a central, summary title (though the exact title may yet exist). See 176/4.

CHAPTER 20

83/2 *Hourglass Lake . . . spelled:* earlier it was "Our Glass Lake" (see 45/3 and 47/2). H.H. doesn't correct "errors" in his "unrevised" draft.

Whether right or wrong, both the names are significant, underscoring H.H.'s solipsism (the circumscribing mirror of "our glass") and obsession with time ("hourglass").

85/1 *the gesture:* it inspires the mock quotation, "look, Lord..." as if to demonstrate one's chains.

85/2 *c'est moi qui décide:* French; it is I who decide.

88/1 *acrosonic:* a noise reaching to or past the sonic barrier. It would seem to be H.H.'s own word.

89/1 *shooting her lover...making him say "akh!":* a preview of Quilty's death. See 47/4 and 305/1. He may indeed have been "her lover," however fleetingly; "I knew your dear wife slightly," Quilty later admits to H.H. (p. 304).

89/2 *at first wince:* H.H.'s variant of "at first glance."

90/1 *Krestovski:* to give them one kind of scare or another; see 218/1.

91/1 *Cavall and Melampus:* the Farlows' dogs. "Cavall" comes from *cavallo* (a horse), and "Melampus" from the seer in Greek mythology who understood the tongue of dogs and introduced the worship of Dionysus. More specifically, notes Nabokov, the dogs are named after those of a famous person, though he is not certain who owned them. He thinks it was Lord Byron, who had many bizarrely named dogs. In any event, these allusions are hardly within the cultural reach of the Farlows.

91/2 *Waterproof:* the wristwatch. See 274/1, where H.H. offers this interlude as a central clue to Quilty's identity.

91/3 *old Ivor...his nephew:* Clare Quilty. For a summary of allusions to Quilty, see 33/9.

CHAPTER 21

91/4 *"Ce qui...comme ça":* French; "What drives me crazy is the fact that I do not know what you are thinking about when you are like this."

92/1 *the ultimate sunburst:* in *Who's Who in the Limelight*, "Roland Pym" is said to have "Made debut in *Sunburst*" (see 33/7).

92/2 *Beaver Eaters:* a portmanteau of "Beefeaters" (the yeomen of the British royal guard) and their beaver hats.

CHAPTER 22

95/1 *Euphemia:* from the Greek *euphēmos;* auspicious, sounding good.

96/1 *olisbos:* the leather phallos worn by participants in the Greek Dionysia.

96/2 *child of Dolly's age:* "Byron, Marguerite" (see p. 53). For Dr. Byron's namesake, see 72/4.

CHAPTER 23

104/1 *savoir vivre:* French; good manners, good breeding.

105/1 *alembic:* anything used to distill or refine.

105/2 *Adieu, Marlene:* Dietrich; see 11/4.

CHAPTER 24

106/1 *simian:* monkey- or apelike.

CHAPTER 25

107/1 *Eh bien, pas du tout!:* French; Well, not at all!

107/2 *Climax:* however broad the joke may be, there happen to be seven towns in the United States by this name (as well as a Lolita, Texas). Demon Veen, the father of *Ada*'s hero, retreats to his "aunt's ranch near Lolita, Texas" (p. 16), a town which doubtless boasts no bookstore or library.

108/1 *stylized blood:* everything red is "stylized."

108/2 *argent: archaic;* silver, silvery, shining—as in French.

109/1 *Vee . . . and Bea:* see 45/5 and 21/9. For a summary of Poe allusions, see 11/2.

109/2 *glans:* anatomical word; the conical vascular body which forms the extremity of the penis.

109/3 *oolala black:* pseudo-French epithet for "sexy" black frills.

109/4 *anthropometric entry:* anthropometry is the science of measuring the human body and its parts.

110/1 *glaucous:* a pale yellowish-green hue.

110/2 *The Enchanted Hunters:* note the plural (H.H., Quilty, and, in another sense, the author). For "enchantment," see 47/3. Quilty names his play after the hotel (pp. 202–204) and adapts an anagram of it for one of his many pseudonyms (253/13); the married Lolita ends up living on "Hunter Road" (p. 270). See also my 1967 *Wisconsin Studies* article, *op. cit.,* p. 210.

CHAPTER 26

111/1 *Heart, head—everything:* "Is 'mask' the keyword?" H.H. asked on p. 55 (see 6/4). As his narrative approaches the first conjugal night with Lolita, H.H. is overcome by anguish, and in the bare six lines of Chapter Twenty-six—the shortest "chapter" in the book—he loses control, and for a moment the mask drops. Not until the very end of the passage does the voice again sound like our Hum the Hummer, when the desperation of "Heart, head—everything" suddenly gives way to the resiliently comic command to the printer. In that one instant H.H.'s masking takes place before the reader, who gets a fleeting look into those "two hypnotic eyes" (to quote John Ray [p. 5]) and sees the pain in them. *Lolita* is so deeply moving a novel because of our sharp awareness of the great tension sustained between H.H.'s mute despair and his compensatory jollity. "Crime and Pun" is one of the titles the murderous narrator of *Despair* considers for his manuscript, and it would serve H.H. just as well, for language is as much a defense to him as chess is to Grandmaster Luzhin. But even when H.H. lets the mask slip, one glimpses only his desperation, not the "real" H.H. or the manipulative author. As Nabokov says in Chapter Five of *Gogol,* analogously discussing Akaky Akakyevich and the "holes" and "gaps" in the narrative texture of *The Overcoat:* "We did not expect that, amid the whirling masks, one mask would turn out to be a real face, or *at least the place where that face ought to be*" [italics mine—A.A.].

CHAPTER 27

112/1 *redheaded . . . lad:* Charlie Holmes turns out to be Lolita's first lover (p. 139).

112/2 *moth or butterfly:* a reminder that H.H. is no entomologist. See 8/1. Nabokov stresses "Humbert's complete incapacity to differentiate between Rhopalocera and Heterocera."

113/1 *lentigo:* a freckly skin pigmentation.

113/2 *aux yeux battus:* French; with circles round one's eyes.

113/3 *plumbaceous umbrae:* Latin; leaden shadows.

113/4 *mägdlein:* German; little girl.

114/1 *Lepingville ... nineteenth century:* as to the "identity" of this poet, Nabokov responded, "That poet was evidently Leping who used to go lepping (i.e. lepidoptera hunting) but that's about all anybody knows about him." See 143/1.

115/1 *backfisch:* German; an immature, adolescent girl; a teenager.

115/2 *simulacrum:* a sham; an unreal semblance.

115/3 *psychotherapist ... rapist:* H.H. calls our attention to the rapist in the therapist. Nabokov similarly employs semantic constituents in *Despair,* when he poses a sensible question: "What is this jest in majesty? This ass in passion?" (p. 56).

115/4 *what shadow ... after?:* in traditional *Doppelgänger* fiction the reprehensible self is often imagined as a shadow, as in Hans Christian Andersen's "The Shadow." H.H. constantly toys with the convention.

116/1 *Ensuite?:* French; then?

116/2 *shadowgraphs:* amateur X-ray pictures. The girls made pictures of each other's bones; not invented, but actual "educational" recreation at "progressive" camps c. 1950.

117/1 *"C'est bien tout?":* "Is that all?" The answer *"C'est"* ("It is") is incorrect French, a direct translation from English syntax.

118/1 *carbuncles:* medical; "a painful local inflammation of the subcutaneous tissue, larger and more serious than a boil; a pimple or red spot, due to intemperance." Originally, a jewel such as a ruby. H.H. is of course referring to the truck's parking lights.

119/1 *magic ... rubious:* a corrected misprint ("rubous" in the 1958 edition). The ruby-like convertible is Quilty's, a dark red shining in the rain and the night. His appearances are summarized in 33/9.

119/2 *frock-fold ... Browning:* not a quotation, but an allusion to *Pippa Passes* (1842), a verse drama by Robert Browning, the English poet (1812–1889):

On every side occurred suggestive germs
Of that—the tree, the flower—or take the fruit—
Some rosy shape, continuing the peach,
Curved beewise o'er its bough; as rosy limbs,
Depending, nestled in the leaves; and just
From a cleft rose-peach the whole Dryad sprang. [lines 87–92]

See 209/2. A *Dryad* is a wood nymph (see 123/2). For nymph, see 18/6.

119/3 *cocker spaniel:* the old lady's dog (p. 120). See 248/1 and 263/4.

119/4 *porcine:* swinelike; the pig image is introduced in the first sentence of the previous paragraph.

120/1 *not Humberg:* H.H. corrects the desk clerk, who has coldly bestowed on him a Jewish-sounding name. The hotel is euphemistically restrictive (see 263/4). "Professor Hamburg" finds them "full up" (p. 263).

120/2 *Dr. Edgar H. Humbert and daughter:* H.H.'s *nom de registration* is in deference to Edgar A. Poe and *his* child bride (see 45/5). H.H. also uses the "Edgar" elsewhere (see 77/5 and 191/3). For the Poe allusions, see 11/2.

120/3 *A key (342!):* although H.H. is trying not to lose control of the language, as he did on p. 111, he (or *someone else*) is here managing to tell how H.H. was served by Mr. Swine, who is assisted by Mr. Potts, who can't find any cots, because Swine has dispatched them to the Swoons (see 214/2). A "key" to the meaning of this extraordinary verbal control is immediately provided by another "coincidence": the room number is the same as the Haze house number. H.H. will shortly offer a figurative key by placing the number within quotation marks, which is of course the only proper way to treat a fiction (p. 125). "McFate" produces "342" once more; see 250/2. Such coincidences serve a two-fold purpose: they at once point to the authorial consciousness that has plotted them, and can also be imagined as coordinates situated in time and space, marking the labyrinth from which a character cannot escape. The "342" confluence is also discussed in my article, "Nabokov's Puppet Show —Part II," *The New Republic*, CLVI (January 21, 1967), 27, included above; see Introduction, p. xxvii.

121/1 *Parody of a hotel corridor ... and death:* *parody* to H.H. because nothing seems "real" to him on this most crucial of nights; *parody* to Nabokov because the world within a work of art *is* "unreal" (see Introduction, *ibid.*). But to repeat Marianne Moore's well-known line, poetry

[373]

is "imaginary gardens with real toads in them," and Nabokov's novel is a parody of death with real suffering in it—H.H.'s and Lolita's.

121/2 *a mirror:* the room is a little prison of mirrors, a metaphor for his solipsism and circumscribing obsession. " 'So that's the dead end' (the mirror you break your nose against)," an overwrought H.H. tells Lolita after catching her in a lie (p. 227). See 53/2 and 296/2. "In our earthly house, windows are replaced by mirrors," writes Nabokov in *The Gift* (p. 322). His characters continually confront mirrors where they had hoped to find windows, and the attempt to transcend solipsism is one of Nabokov's major themes. As a literal image and overriding metaphor, the mirror is central to the form and content of Nabokov's novels; in *Ada,* it describes the universe, for Antiterra's sibling planet Terra is imagined as a "distortive glass of our distorted glebe" (p. 18). If one perceives *Pale Fire* spatially, with John Shade's poem on the "left" and Charles Kinbote's Commentary on the "right," the poem is seen as an object to be perceived, and the Commentary becomes the world seen through the distorting prism of a mind—a monstrous concave mirror held up to an objective "reality." The narrator of *Despair* loathes mirrors, avoids them, and comments on those "monsters of mirrors," the "crooked ones," in which a man is stripped, squashed, or "pulled out like dough and then torn in two" (p. 31). Nabokov has placed these crooked reflectors everywhere in his fiction: Doubles and mock-Doubles, parodies and self-parodies (literature trapped in a prison of amusement-park mirrors), works within works, worlds refracting worlds, and words distorting words—that is, translations (art's "crazy-mirror," says Nabokov) and language games (see 36/2). *Pale Fire's* invented language is "the tongue of the mirror," and the portmantoid pun is the principal mirror-language of *Lolita.* See 5/3.

121/3 *Enfin seuls:* French for "alone at last," the trite phrase of the honeymooner.

122/1 *lentor: archaic;* slowness.

122/2 *spoonerette:* a *spoonerism* is the accidental transposition of sounds in two or more words ("wight ray"). By acknowledging his spoonerisms, H.H. reminds us what a wordsmith he is (in *Pale Fire* John Shade teaches at Wordsmith University). The affectionate suffix *-ette* may recall *majorette,* as well as the slang meaning of *spooner,* one who "necks" (or, as one dictionary archly puts it, "act[s] with silly and demonstrative fondness"). The suffix also parodies a recognizable and overused *préciosité* of Ronsard's, who in fact employed *"nymphette"* in one of his poems. See *"vermeillette"* (49/2) and Quilty's "barroomette" (p. 298).

122/3 *kitzelans:* lusting; from the German *kitzel,* "inordinate desire," and *kitzler,* "clitoris." See 252/11.

122/4 *seva ascendes . . . quidquam:* the language of Horace, Catullus, et al. (see 47/1) is appropriate to this modern, if hysterical, elegiast, whose "Latin" here turns out to be a curious mishmash of Latin, English, French, German, and Italian: "The sap ascendeth, pulsates, burning [*brulans,* from the French *brûler,* "to burn"], itching, most insane, elevator clattering, pausing, clattering, people in the corridor. No one but death would take this one [Lolita] away from me! Slender little girl, I thought most fondly, observing nothing at all." At moments of extreme crisis, H.H. croaks incomprehensibly, losing more than his expropriated English; for his attempts "to fix once for all the perilous magic of nymphets" (p. 136) almost resist language altogether, carrying him close to the edge of non-language and a figurative silence. Thus H.H. significantly announces this scene as a "Parody of silence" (p. 121), and, far from being nonsensical, the ensuing "Latin" is a parodic stream-of-consciousness affording a brief critical comment on a technique Nabokov finds unsatisfactory, even in the novels of Joyce, whom he reveres ("poor Stream of Consciousness, *marée noire* by now," writes Nabokov toward the end of a similar parody in *Ada* [p. 300]). "We think not in words but in shadows of words," Nabokov says. "James Joyce's mistake in those otherwise marvelous mental soliloquies of his consists in that he gives too much verbal body to thoughts" (*Playboy* interview). To Nabokov, the unconnected impressions and associations that impinge on the mind are irrational until they are consciously ordered and to order them in art is to fulfill virtually a moral obligation, for without rational language man has "grown a very / landfish, languageless, / a monster," as Thersites says of Ajax in Shakespeare's *Troilus and Cressida.* Even the imprisoned Cincinnatus, under sentence of death, is "already thinking of how to set up an alphabet" which might humanize the dystopian world of *Invitation to a Beheading* (p. 139). See the second half of 11/2.

123/1 *nota bene:* Latin; mark well. The 1958 edition incorrectly ran the two words together.

123/2 *dryads and trees:* see 119/2.

123/3 *writer fellow . . . ad:* Clare Quilty (see 71/2). "Dromes" is a corrected misprint ("Droms" in the 1958 edition). For allusions to Quilty, see 33/9.

123/4 *Femina:* Latin; woman.

124/1 *Purpills:* a contraction of "Papa's Purple Pills" from the previous paragraph.

CHAPTER 28

125/1 *le grand moment:* French; the great moment.

125/2 *hot hairy fist:* Quilty also has conspicuously hairy hands (p. 297).

125/3 *sicher ist sicher:* German; sure is sure.

125/4 *my uncle Gustave:* Gustave Trapp, sometimes a "cousin," whom H.H. mistakes for Quilty (see p. 141). A cousin of one's mother is both one's cousin and, in a sense, uncle.

126/1 *Jean-Jacques Humbert:* after Jean-Jacques Rousseau (1712–1778), Swiss-born French philosopher and author of the famous *Confessions.*

127/1 *one's dungeon . . . some rival devil:* Quilty, H.H.'s "rival devil," is staying at The Enchanted Hunters, and appears on the next page. The lust figuratively emanating from H.H.'s "dungeon" is objectified much later: "I had been keeping Clare Quilty's face masked in my dark dungeon" (see 292/2).

127/2 *comme on dit:* French; as they say.

127/3 *King Sigmund:* Sigmund Freud (1856–1939), founder of psychoanalysis. See 7/6 and 37/1.

128/1 *antiphony:* a musical response; a musical piece alternately sung by a choir divided into two parts.

128/2 *powdered bugs:* Nabokov says "The 'powdered bugs' wheeling around the lamps are noctuids and other moths which look floury on the wing (hence 'millers,' which, however, may also come from the verb), as they mill in the electric light against the damp night's blackground. 'Bugs' is an Americanism for *any* insect. In England, it means generally bedbugs." For entomological allusions, see 8/1.

128/3 *somebody sitting . . . porch:* Quilty. Their verbal sparring on p. 129 telescopes their pursuit of one another and prefigures the physical struggle of pp. 295–307. The allusions to Quilty are summarized in 33/9.

129/1 *a rose, as the Persians say:* the fatidic flower and an allusion to *The Rubáiyát* (see 264/8).

129/2 *a blinding flash . . . can be deemed immortal:* for the photograph in question, see 265/1. H.H. was *not* immortalized.

CHAPTER 29

130/1 *entre nous soit dit:* French; just between you and me.

131/1 *grand Dieu:* French; good God!

131/2 *La Petite ... Ridicule: The Sleeping Maiden or the Ridiculous Lover.* There is no picture by this name. The mock-title and subject matter parody eighteenth-century genre engravings.

132/1 *someone ... beyond our bathroom:* Clare Quilty (see 250/4). Quilty also creates a "waterfall" on 296/4. For a summary of his appearances, see 33/9.

133/1 *A breeze from wonderland:* there are several references to *Alice in Wonderland* (1865) by Lewis Carroll, the pseudonym of Charles L. Dodgson (1832–1898), English writer, mathematician, and nympholept (see 266/1). "I always call him Lewis Carroll Carroll," says Nabokov, "because he was the first Humbert Humbert." Nabokov translated *Alice* into Russian (Berlin, 1923). "I got five dollars (quite a sum during the inflation in Germany)," he recalls (*Speak, Memory,* p. 283). In *The Real Life of Sebastian Knight,* a character speaks "in the elenctic tones of Lewis Carroll's caterpillar" (p. 123), while in Nabokov's latest novel, "Ada in Wonderland" (p. 129), "Ada's adventures in Adaland" (p. 568), and the "titles" *Palace in Wonderland* (p. 53) and *Alice in the Camera Obscura* (p. 547) are variously invoked (the latter a play on the original title of *Laughter in the Dark*). "In common with many other English children (I was an English child) I have been always very fond of Carroll," he says in the *Wisconsin Studies* interview. "No, I do not think his invented language shares any roots with mine [in *Bend Sinister* and *Pale Fire*]. He has a pathetic affinity with H.H. but some odd scruple prevented me from alluding in *Lolita* to his wretched perversion and to those ambiguous photographs he took in dim rooms. He got away with it, as so many other Victorians got away with pederasty and nympholepsy. His were sad scrawny little nymphets, bedraggled and half-undressed, or rather semi-undraped, as if participating in some dusty and dreadful charade." But it might seem as though Nabokov *did* allude to Carroll in *Lolita,* through what might be called "the photography theme": H.H. cherishes his worn old photograph of Annabel, has in a sense been living with this "still," tries to make Lolita conform to it, and often laments his failure to capture her on film. Quilty's hobby is announced as "photography," and the unspeakable films he produces at the Duk Duk

Ranch would seem to answer Carroll's wildest needs. Asked about this, Nabokov replied, "I did not consciously think of Carroll's hobby when I referred to the use of photography in *Lolita*."

"I have only words to play with," moans H.H. (p. 34), and several readers have been tempted to call the ensuing wordplay "Joycean"— loosely enough, since "Carrollian" might do almost as well, given Nabokov's fondness for auditory wordplay and portmanteau words, and the fact that the latter usage was coined by Carroll. The family line is nicely established on Sebastian Knight's neatest book shelf, where *Alice in Wonderland* and *Ulysses* stand side by side, along with works by some of Nabokov's other favorite writers (Stevenson, Chekhov, Flaubert, Proust, Wells, and Shakespeare, who encloses the shelf at either end with *Hamlet* and *King Lear* [p. 41]). For Shakespeare, see 286/4.

134/1 *metamorphosing:* see 18/6.

CHAPTER 30

136/1 *emeritus read to by a boy:* an echo of the opening of Eliot's "Gerontion": "Here I am, an old man in a dry month,/Being read to by a boy ..." See 18/3.

136/2 *shoat:* a young pig; a hog.

136/3 *callypygean slave ... onyx:* or *callipygian;* "having shapely buttocks." *Onyx* is a variety of agate, a semiprecious stone. H.H. is no doubt here referring to *onyx marble* (alabaster). See 139/1.

136/4 *gonadal glow:* a gonad is a sexual gland; an ovary or testis.

136/5 *canoeing, Coranting:* the latter is the participle of H.H.'s variant of *courant,* "a dance of Italian origin marked by quick running steps," and also dialectal English for "romping" and "carousing." H.H. is still in Volume C of the *Girls' Encyclopedia* (see p. 94).

CHAPTER 31

137/1 *Roman law ... girl may marry at twelve:* the legal opinions offered in this paragraph move from fact to fiction (see 21/1). The first is true, though the legal question and its history are far more complex than H.H. would suggest. See Corbett, *The Roman Law of Marriage* (1930), pp. 51–52.

137/2 *adopted by the Church:* also true; see Bouscaren and Ellis, *Canon Law: A Text and Commentary* (1957), p. 513.

137/3 *still preserved ... in some of the United States:* only in ten states (Colorado, Florida, Maine, Maryland, Massachusetts, Tennessee, Virginia, Idaho, Kansas, and Louisiana). See Vernier, *American Family Laws* (1931), pp. 115–117.

137/4 *fifteen is lawful everywhere:* not in Alaska, Arizona, California, Connecticut, Delaware, Illinois, Indiana, Michigan, Minnesota, Montana, Nebraska, Nevada, New Mexico, Ohio, Pennsylvania, West Virginia, or Wyoming, where the age is sixteen, or in New Hampshire or New Jersey, where it is eighteen. But there are exceptions granted if the girl is pregnant or if she is willing, over twelve, and the marriage has been consummated. Since none of these (save the consummation) apply to Lolita, it seems that H.H.'s confident legal scholarship has given way to dissembling. See Vernier, *ibid.*, pp. 116–118.

CHAPTER 32

137/5 *die Kleine:* German; the little one.

137/6 *moue:* grimace, facial contraction.

138/1 *sapphic diversions:* reference to the reputed lesbianism of the group associated with Sappho, Greek lyric poetess of Lesbos (c. 600 B.C.).

138/2 *Miranda twins:* in Lolita's class list, p. 54 (see 53/2).

139/1 *boat to Onyx or Eryx:* there are no such lakes. *Onyx* is often used for cameos, while *Eryx* refers to the ancient cult of Aphrodite (Venus) of Eryx, an Elymian settlement on a mountain above Drepana in western Sicily, built below their temple of Aphrodite (the goddess of love and beauty, to whom Lolita is often compared; "Venus came and went," says H.H. on p. 170; and the magazine picture of a surrealistic "plaster replica of the Venus di Milo, half-buried in sand" metaphorically projects Lolita's life with him [p. 60]). See 252/11, where scholarly H.H. obliquely informs the reader that the priestesses at the Temple of Eryx were prostitutes.

140/1 *I would not talk to strangers:* see 34/1 and 311/1.

140/2 *saturnalia:* the festival of Saturn in ancient Rome, celebrated with feasting and revelry; a licentious spectacle.

140/3 *A fellow of my age:* Quilty (see 33/9); the "blood-red armchair" should alert the reader. H.H. stresses their similar ages; see 220/1.

140/4 *Schwab's drugstore:* an author's error has been corrected (*a* instead of *o* in the 1958 edition). The Schwab's chain drugstores in Hollywood are a meeting place for film people and young aspirants. In the 'thirties and 'forties several subsequent stars were discovered there, some—according to folklore—while eating sundaes or drinking sodas.

141/1 *a fairytale vampire:* for the fairy tale theme, see 33/3.

141/2 *le découvert:* French; the nude.

141/3 *immortal daemon . . . child:* see 18/6.

141/4 *Aunt Clare's place:* by mentioning Quilty's first name, H.H., a sly teaser, throws the reader something more than a hint. See 33/9 for a summary of Quilty allusions.

141/5 *hypothetical hospital:* "hypothetical" is the best word to use, since its name would be whatever H.H. chose to make it.

CHAPTER 33

143/1 *gay . . . Lepingville:* see 114/1. H.H.'s "lepping" is over; the town's name and gaiety mark the fact that, as Part One ends, H.H. secures his capture.

144/1 *swooners:* H.H.'s variant of the noun, its meaning expanded to include some garment that evokes a swoon.

PART TWO

CHAPTER 1

147/1 *pharisaic:* self-righteous and censorious; resembling the Pharisees, a sect of the ancient Jews famed for its strict observance of ceremonies, rites, and traditions.

147/2 *earwitness:* H.H.'s coinage.

147/3 *nous connûmes:* Flaubert uses the verb *connaître* in the literary tense *passé simple* when in *Madame Bovary* (1857) he is describing her unhappy experiments with all kinds of diversions, especially her lovers and their activities together. For other allusions, see 49/1, 204/2 and 267/2. Nabokov intends no allusion to Frédéric Moreau's travels in *L'Education sentimentale* (1869); "Not the education of the senses," he says, "a poor novel which I only vaguely remember." *Bovary* is funned in *King,*

Queen, Knave and "Floeberg" burlesqued briefly in *Ada* (p. 128). Although Kinbote synchronizes Gradus' travels through space and time and the stages of Shade's composition of the poem *Pale Fire*, he nevertheless complains when Shade similarly alternates two themes: "the synchronization device has been already worked to death by Flaubert and Joyce" (p. 196).

147/4 *Chateaubriandesque trees:* the first European writers and painters who visited America were impressed by its great trees, and H.H. no doubt drew the image from *Atala* (1801), a separately published episode from *Le Génie du christianisme* (1802) by François-René de Chateaubriand (1768-1848), whose arrival in America is mentioned in *Pale Fire* (p. 274). In the *Eugene Onegin* Commentary, Nabokov calls *René*, another episode from *Le Génie*, "a work of genius by the greatest French writer of his time" (Vol. III, p. 98). See 72/5. Though unlabeled, there are many "Chateaubriandesque trees" in *Ada*'s Ardis Park, and by design, for Chateaubriand is to *Ada* what Poe and Mérimée are to *Lolita*. Van Veen reads Ada's copy of *Atala* (p. 89), and *René*, with its "subtle perfume of incest" (*Onegin* Commentary, Vol. III, p. 100), is alluded to directly (pp. 131 and 133). Mlle. Larivière, the Veens' grotesque governess, writes a novel and film scenario whose hero is named "René" (see pp. 198-199, 217, 249, and 424), and since "incest" and "insect" are anagrammatically linked (p. 85), a mosquito is named after Chateaubriand —Charles Chateaubriand, that is, "not related to the great poet and memoirist" (p. 106). For further discussion of Chateaubriand and *Ada*, see my article, *"Ada* described," *TriQuarterly*, No. 17 (Winter 1970). For another Chateaubriand allusion in *Lolita*, see 212/1.

148/1 *non-Laodicean:* in Revelation iii, 14-16, the Laodicean church is characterized as "lukewarm, and neither hot nor cold" in matters of religion.

148/2 *madamic:* H.H.'s coinage, referring to the madam, or proprietress, of a brothel.

148/3 *instars:* an insect or other anthropod in one of the forms assumed between molts. The pupa of a butterfly is an instar.

149/1 *do you remember, Miranda:* an echo of the opening lines and refrain of "Tarantella" (1923), a poem by Hilaire Belloc (1870-1953); "Do you remember an Inn, / Miranda? / Do you remember an Inn?" See p. 187.

150/1 *the nasal voices:* because "this book is being read, I assume, in the first years of 2000 A.D." (as H.H. says [p. 301]), readers not having had the benefit of a 1947-1952 adolescence may not be able to complete the names of the "invisibles" who serenaded Lolita. They include Jo Stafford (date of birth a secret), Edwin Jack "Eddie" Fisher (1928–   ), Tony Bennett (1926–   ), Peggy Lee (born Norma Egstrom: 1920–   ), Guy Mitchell (1925–   ), and Patti Page (1927–   ), whose most successful recording, "The Tennessee Waltz" (c. 1950), is commemorated in *Ada* with the mention of "a progressive poet in residence at Tennessee Waltz College" (p. 134). As Joyce says in *Finnegans Wake*, "Wipe your glosses with what you know."

150/2 *Starasil:* an actual ointment.

150/3 *trochaic lilt:* in prosody, a *trochee* is a foot of two syllables, the first stressed or half-stressed, and the second unstressed.

150/4 *Huncan Dines:* the spoonerism hardly conceals Duncan Hines (1880–1959), author of such guidebooks as *Adventures in Good Eating, Lodging for a Night,* and *Duncan Hines' Food Odyssey.*

151/1 *chère Dolorès:* French; dear Dolores.

151/2 *comme . . . gentille:* French; as you know too well, my sweet one.

152/1 *rapist . . . therapist:* a slight variation of earlier wordplay; see 115/3. In *Ada*, thinkers who speculate on the existence of Terra are called "ter-rapists" (p. 341).

152/2 *by Polonius:* the talkative and complacent old man of *Hamlet*. The reference is probably to the warnings he gives his daughter, Ophelia, about the slippery ways of men. See 33/6.

152/3 *Mann Act:* the obvious "dreadful pun" is Mann: man. "Act" was not capitalized in the 1958 edition; the error has been corrected here.

153/1 *my Lolita . . . her Catullus:* the Latin love-poem motif; see 68/1.

153/2 *c'est tout:* French; that is all.

154/1 *crazy quilt of forty-eight states:* it is appropriate that Part Two's first allusion to Quilty should be this geographic metaphor, since H.H. and his nemesis pursue each other back and forth across "the crazy quilt." When all the journeys are ended, he is "quilted Quilty" (p. 308).

154/2 *inutile:* French; useless, unprofitable.

154/3 *Lorrain clouds:* Claude Gelée, known as Claude Lorrain (1600–1682), French painter who settled in Rome and established landscape painting as a respectable form. His open vistas and lyrical evocations of light and atmosphere influenced Poussin, among others. A character in *King, Queen, Knave* (1928) points at something "with the air of Rembrandt indicating a Claude Lorrain" (p. 91), a reminder of the consistency of Nabokov's vision.

154/4 *El Greco horizon:* the famous painter (1541?–1614?), born in Greece, schooled in Italy, resident of Spain. H.H. discovers in Kansas the turbulent Toledo landscapes of Greco. Since many readers, especially the British and French, think *Lolita* is resolutely "anti-American," one should note the book's tender landscape details, and the tribute paid to "the lovely, trustful, enormous country" (p. 178).

155/1 *samara:* a dry, winged fruit, usually one-seeded, as in the ash or elm.

156/1 *ce qu'on appelle:* French; what one calls.

CHAPTER 2

156/2 *partie de plaisir:* French; outing, picnic.

156/3 *raison d'être:* French; the reason for being, the justification.

156/4 *John Galsworthy:* English novelist (1867–1933), author of *The Forsyte Saga* (1922).

157/1 *canthus:* the inner corner of the eye where the upper and lower eyelids meet.

157/2 *"Kurort" type:* German; health resort, watering place.

157/3 *roan back:* a color: chestnut interspersed with gray or white—said of a horse; also a low-grade sheepskin tanned and colored to imitate ungrained Morocco.

157/4 *author of "Trees":* Joyce Kilmer (1886–1918), American poet, best known for the sentimental poem which H.H. refers to here.

158/1 *bronzed owner of an expensive car:* although Quilty-hunters may find this man suspect, Nabokov says it is definitely not Quilty.

158/2 *lousy with ... flies:* notes Nabokov: "The insects that poor Humbert mistakes for 'creeping white flies' are the biologically fascinating little moths of the genus *Pronuba* whose amiable and indispensable females transport the pollen that fertilizes the yucca flowers (see, what Humbert failed to do, 'Yucca Moth' in any good encyclopedia)." For entomological allusions, see 8/1.

158/3 *Independence . . . Abilene:* also a juxtaposition of the "starting points" of successive American presidents: Harry S Truman (1884–   ) and Dwight D. Eisenhower (1890–1969).

158/4 *lilac . . . phallic:* H.H. continually reminds us that he has "only words to play with" (p. 34). His *phallic* is built on the semantic constituents of *lilac* and *Pharaonic* (of or pertaining to Pharaoh, the title of the sovereigns of ancient Egypt).

158/5 *lanugo:* anatomical word; in a restricted sense, the downy growth which covers the young of otherwise non-hairy animals.

158/6 *rufous:* a bright russet or brownish-orange hue.

158/7 *lucerne:* a deep-rooted European herb with bluish-purple flowers; in the U.S. usually called *alfalfa.*

159/1 *comme on dit:* French; as they say.

159/2 *hundreds of . . . hummingbirds:* these are not birds, notes Nabokov, "but hawkmoths which do move exactly like hummingbirds (which are neither gray nor nocturnal)." For entomological allusions, see 8/1.

159/3 *Shakespeare . . . New Mexico:* not invented; a mining town founded c. 1870 on property that had previously been involved in one of the largest unsuccessful mining speculations of the period in the Southwest. Now a "ghost town," it is no longer listed in any atlas.

159/4 *Florentine Bea's . . . contemporary:* Dante's Beatrice (see 21/9). A thirteenth-century mummy.

159/5 *Our twentieth Hell's Canyon:* see 298/5.

159/6 *winery in California . . . wine barrel:* it exists. Crossing over into Death Valley from Nevada, H.H. and Lolita travel down to Los Angeles and then wend their way northward up the California coast to Oregon (Crater Lake, p. 160). These Notes seldom comment on H.H.'s topographical observations; the field remains wide-open. A generous grant from the Guggenheim Foundation or the American Council of Learned Societies will no doubt one day enable some gentle don to retrace meticulously H.H.'s foul footsteps.

159/7 *Scotty's Castle:* an enormous and grotesque structure built in the 'twenties by Walter ("Death Valley") Scott, formerly with Buffalo Bill's Wild West Show.

160/1 *R.L. Stevenson's footprint on an extinct volcano:* the Scottish writer (1850–1895) followed the woman he loved to California, where he lived for a year (1879–1880). In *From Scotland to Silverado*, James D. Hart, ed. (1966), collects his writing about the state. Stevenson is buried on the volcanic Mount Vaea in Samoa; but H.H., who may or may not know that, is here referring to his honeymoon stay on Mount St. Helena, California, generally thought to be an extinct volcano (it is in fact not one). There is a Robert Louis Stevenson Memorial there, but he left no actual footprint. H.H., having just noted "The ugly villas of handsome actresses," was no doubt more impressed by the footprints and handprints of movie stars immortalized in the cement pavements outside Grauman's Chinese Theatre in Hollywood. For further Stevenson allusions, see 186/2 and 208/3.

160/2 *Mission Dolores: good title for book:* this book, of course. The mission observed by H.H. exists, in San Francisco.

160/3 *festoons:* in architecture, a molded or carved ornament representing a festoon (a garland or wreath hanging in a curve). H.H. is observing the coastline of Monterey.

160/4 *Russian Gulch State Park:* in Sonoma, California; named by Russian colonists.

160/5 *Little Rock, near a school:* rereading this passage in 1968, Nabokov called it "nicely prophetic" (the larger "row" over school desegregation, September 1957). For further "prophecy," see 228/3.

160/6 *à propos de rien:* French; not in relation to anything else; casually.

161/1 *town ... first name:* "his" refers to Quilty. Clare, Michigan; an actual town.

161/2 *species ... Homo pollex:* H.H. combines the familiar Latin *homo*, "the genus of mammals consisting of mankind," with *pollex*, or "thumb."

161/3 *viatic:* H.H. sustains his "scientific" vocabulary; a coinage from the Latin root *via*. *Viaticum* is English—an allowance for traveling expenses —but H.H. has gone back to the Latin word *viaticus*, which specifically refers to the road.

161/4 *priapically:* from Priapus, the god of procreation; see 44/4.

161/5 *man of my age ... face à claques:* Quilty, with a "face that deserves to be slapped; an ugly, mischievous face." For an index to his appearances, see 33/9.

161/6 *concupiscence:* lustfulness.

161/7 *coulant un regard:* French; casting a sly glance.

162/1 *slow truck...road:* see 231/2; after an encounter with "Trapp" (Quilty), H.H. finds himself behind such a truck.

163/1 *natatoriums:* swimming pools.

163/2 *matitudinal:* H.H.'s coinage, from matin, an ecclesiastical duty performed early in the morning; or, though its usage is rare, a morning call or song (of birds).

163/3 *mais je divague:* French; but I am wandering away from the point; rambling.

164/1 *les yeux perdus:* French; a lost look in the eyes.

164/2 *oh Baudelaire!:* Charles Baudelaire (1821–1867), French poet. The image of the dream and the French phrases, *"brun adolescent"* ("dark [brown-haired] adolescent") and *"se tordre"* ("to undergo contortions" [erotic]), are drawn from Baudelaire's *Le Crépuscule du matin,* or "Morning Twilight" (1852): *"C'était l'heure où l'essaim des rêves malfaisants / Tord sur leurs oreillers les bruns adolescents"* ("It was the hour when a swarm of evil dreams contorts [or twists] dark [or swarthy] adolescents on their pillows"). For other Baudelaire allusions, see 264/1 and 286/3. "Poor Baudelaire" is evoked in a variant from Shade's poem in *Pale Fire* (p. 167); and Kinbote's gardener aspires "to read in the original Baudelaire and Dumas" (p. 291). The title of *Invitation to a Beheading* is drawn from Baudelaire's *L'Invitation au voyage,* and the poem's opening lines are quoted and toyed with in *Ada* (p. 106).

164/3 *a famous coach...with a harem of ball boys:* a tennis star of the 'twenties (1893–1953), as famous in his sport as Red Grange and Babe Ruth were in theirs; winner of the American championship seven times, the Wimbledon title three times, and the U.S. doubles championship five times. In 1946 he was jailed on a morals charge, and H.H. and Lolita meet him after his tragic double life has become public knowledge, and only a few years before his death. Given the context, the prosaic phrase and vocation of "ball boy" becomes a pun. When asked if the deceased player should be identified by name, Nabokov imagined him now "consorting with ball boys...on Elysian turf. Shall we spare his shade?"

164/4 *Gobbert:* a corrected author's error (one *b* in the 1958 edition). André H. Gobbert was a French tennis champion c. World War I. "I saw him beaten by Patterson in 1919 or 1920 at Wimbledon," recalls Nabokov. "He had a tremendous (old-fashioned) serve, but would double fault up to four times in a game. Big dark fellow, doubled with Decugis against Brookes and Patterson, I think" (see 236/1).

164/5 *ange gauche:* French; awkward angel.

165/1 *simulacrum:* an unreal semblance (a favorite word of H.H.'s; see pp. 115 and 177).

165/2 *a tall man:* a mirage of Quilty. The subsequent teasing ambiguity as to whether H.H.'s pursuer is "real" or an autoscopic hallucination (see p. 219) parodies Golyadkin, Jr., and the central problem of Dostoevsky's *The Double* (the narrator of *Despair* considers *The Double* as a title for his book, "But Russian literature possessed one already," he says [p. 211]). For Quilty, see 33/9.

165/3 *diaphanous:* delicate to the extent of being transparent or translucent.

165/4 *pavonine:* like a peacock; iridescent.

165/5 *oculate:* eye-spotted.

165/6 *ramparts of ancient Europe:* translation and paraphrase of line 84 of Rimbaud's *Le Bâteau ivre* ("The Drunken Boat" [1871]): *"Je regrette l'Europe aux Anciens parapets"* ("I long for Europe with its ancient quays" [ramparts]). Rimbaud's use of *"parapets"* is shortly reinforced in an echo of the phrase (174/1). See 252/7 for another allusion to this poem. Nabokov translated it into Russian in *The Rudder*, December 16, 1928. Rimbaud's poem is transmuted, along with almost everything else, in *Ada's* antiworld; Van Veen receives a message "in the Louvre right in front of Bosch's *Bâteau Ivre*, the one with a jester drinking in the riggings (poor old Dan [Veen] thought that it had something to do with Brant's satirical poem!)" (p. 331). Ada and Van know by heart Rimbaud's *Mémoire*, and it is one of two texts they use for their coded letters (p. 161). For more on Rimbaud, see 77/6.

166/1 *caravansaries:* from a Persian word; in the East, an inn in the form of a bare building surrounding a court, where caravans stop for the night.

167/1 *well-drawn ... bobby-soxer: Penny,* the comic strip created by Harry Haenigsen in 1943. For other allusions to comic strips, see 219/5, 256/5, and 256/6. As responsive as he is scholarly, Nabokov the literary anatomist is also amused and delighted by "lower" forms of art, and is not above making selective use of such materials in his writing. No one, he laments in the Foreword to the revised *Speak, Memory,* "discovered the name [in the first edition] of a great cartoonist and a tribute to him in the last sentence of Section Two, Chapter Eleven. It is most embarrassing for a writer to have to point out such things himself" (p. 15). The tribute is to Otto Soglow, creator of *The Little King:* "The ranks of words I reviewed were again *so glow*ing, with their puffed-out little chests and trim uniforms ... [italics mine—A.A.]" (p. 219). "Who will bother to notice," wonders Nabokov in the Introduction to the *Time* Reading Program edition of *Bend Sinister,* "that the urchins in the yard (Chapter Seven) have been drawn by Saul Steinberg" (p. xvii). In *Ada,* an 1871 Sunday supplement of the *Kaluga Gazette* "feature[s] on its funnies page the now long defunct Goodnight Kids, Nicky and Pimpernella (sweet siblings who shared a narrow bed)"—based, in reality, on an old French comic strip (p. 6). At the end of *Ada,* ninety-seven-year-old Van Veen describes how he "look[s] forward with juvenile zest to the delightful effect of a spoonful of sodium bicarbonate dissolved in water that was sure to release three or four belches as big as the speech balloons in the 'funnies' of his boyhood" (p. 570).

167/2 *areolas:* the more-or-less shaded narrow areas around the nipples.

167/3 *recedent:* a heraldic term, to match *pursuant.*

167/4 *"We ... in this bottle":* the "quip" derives from the fact that the mariners could not possibly know they lived in the Middle Ages, just as the reader of this annotation has no idea what the twenty-sixth century will call our epoch.

CHAPTER 3

168/1 *umber ... Humberland:* the pun (see 5/3) turns on the not-uncommon place name of Northumberland (England; New Hampshire; Virginia; Pennsylvania).

168/2 *Frigid Queen ... Princess:* the actual name of a milk bar, recorded by Nabokov in a little black notebook. The "Princess" alludes to "Annabel Lee" (11/7), who, fused with Freud, is once more in the novel's foreground: "the search for a Kingdom by the Sea, a Sublimated Riviera, or whatnot" (p. 169).

168/3 *hors concours:* out of the competition: when something is exhibited at a show (e.g., livestock, tulips) but is so superior to the rest of the exhibition that it is barred from receiving the awards or prizes.

168/4 *leporine fascination:* like a hare. The "able psychiatrist" is being hypnotized as a rabbit is by a serpent (H.H.).

169/1 *manatee:* any of several aquatic mammals, such as the sea cow.

170/1 *Arcadian...wilds:* from Arcadia, the idyllic rural region of Greece and the classic image of pastoral simplicity. "Even in Arcady am I, says Death in the tombal scripture," notes Kinbote in *Pale Fire* (p. 174).

170/2 *rill:* a very small brook.

170/3 *cabanes:* huts; simple dwellings.

170/4 *que dis-je:* French; what am I saying?

170/5 *marmot:* any rodent of the genus Marmota, such as the woodchuck.

170/6 *Venus came and went:* H.H. is being verbally playful about a sexual climax.

171/1 *un monsieur très bien:* French; a proper gentleman (a very pompous and bourgeois expression).

172/1 *hospitalized...by now:* reference to H.H.'s Western-style fight with Quilty on p. 301.

173/1 *strumstring:* H.H.'s coinage; the crooner is Gene Autry (1907–   ).

173/2 *harpies:* from classical mythology; foul creatures, part woman, part bird, that stole the souls of the dead, or defiled or seized their victims' food.

173/3 *orchideous masculinity:* belonging to the natural order of plants akin to genus *Orchis.* Its Greek etymology adds a comic dimension, for *orchis* means "testicle" as well as the plant. The *hideous* increases the humor.

174/1 *parapets of Europe:* a Rimbaud echo; see 165/6.

175/1 *Oriental tale:* invented by Nabokov.

175/2 *Beardsley:* after Aubrey Beardsley; see 54/3.

175/3 *Woerner's Treatise:* it exists.

175/4 *A Girl of the Limberlost:* by Gene Stratton Porter (1863–1924), it was once a great favorite of schoolgirls (published 1914). *Little Women* (1869), by Louisa May Alcott (1832–1882), continues to be read.

176/1 *ganglia:* plural of *ganglion,* an anatomical and zoological word; "a mass of nerve tissue containing nerve cells, a nerve center"; a center of strength and energy.

176/2 *dans . . . l'âge:* French; in a mature age (when he is most robust).

176/3 *vieillard encore vert:* French; literally, "an old man still green"—that is, sexually potent.

176/4 *Know Your Own Daughter:* the "biblical title" is real, says Nabokov, although it has been impossible to document. Many similar titles exist, all lending themselves to *double-entendre:* Frances K. Martin, *Know Your Child* (1946); C. Lewis, *How Well Can We Know Our Children?* (1947); C.W. Young, *Know Your Pupil* (1945); and E.D. Adlerblum, *Know Your Child Through His Play* (1947). See 83/1.

176/5 *The Little Mermaid:* anyone familiar with this fairy tale by Hans Christian Andersen (1805–1875), the Danish fabulist, knows that H.H.'s gift has been carefully chosen, and that there are several ironies involved. The little mermaid longs to "enchant a mortal heart"—namely, the prince —and thus win an immortal soul. Lolita has succeeded all too well; but neither H.H., Quilty, nor her husband Dick Schiller, who will carry her off to Alaska, qualifies as prince in the fairy tale *Lolita*. At the end of Andersen's tale, the mermaid has been transposed into one of the freely circulating children of the air, who must float for three hundred years before they are admitted into the kingdom of heaven. But they can get in earlier, as one explains as the tale concludes: "Unseen we float into the houses of mortals where there are children, and for every day that we find a good child who makes his parents happy and deserves their love, God shortens our period of trial. The child does not know when we fly through the room, and when we smile over it with joy a year is taken from the three hundred. But if we see a naughty and wicked child, we must weep tears of sorrow, and each tear adds a day to our period of trial" (from *The Twelve Dancing Princesses and Other Fairy Tales*, Alfred and Mary Elizabeth David, eds., New York, 1964, p. 274). H.H., who later sheds "merman tears" (257/1), no doubt hopes that Lolita will take this to heart. See also *Keys*, p. 134n. For the fairy tale theme, see 33/3.

176/6 *casé:* settled.

177/1 *27,000 miles:* see 33/15.

177/2 *rentier:* a man who lives from the interest of his invested capital (generally applies to an old, retired man).

177/3 *bi-iliac:* the two most prominent points of the crests of the iliac bones.

CHAPTER 4

178/1 *habitus:* a not uncommon Latin noun meaning moral condition, state, disposition, character, etc.

179/1 *Miss Cormorant:* she is named after the voracious sea bird.

179/2 *recueillement:* self-communion, "collectedness."

180/1 *harems and slaves:* of course she can care, and H.H. has compared her lot to theirs.

CHAPTER 5

181/1 *Lester . . . Fabian:* their respective first and final syllables form "lesbian" (see also *Keys,* p. 96). See 197/2 for a similar effect.

CHAPTER 6

183/1 *Gaston Godin:* his "Beardsley existence" (p. 185) is also figurative, for he might well have been drawn by Aubrey Beardsley. H.H.'s caricature resembles the famous cover drawing of "Ali Baba" (for a projected edition of *The Forty Thieves,* never undertaken [1897]), as well as Oscar Wilde, whose post-prison alias is bestowed on H.H.'s car (see 229/4). Gaston is *fin de siècle* in many ways, as pp. 183–184 make clear.

183/2 *mes goûts:* French; my tastes.

183/3 *He always wore black:* H.H.'s attire; see p. 297.

183/4 *large photographs:* they constitute a veritable pantheon of homosexual artists: André Gide (1869–1951), French writer, author of *Les Faux-Monnayeurs (The Counterfeiters,* 1925), winner of the Nobel prize in 1947; Pëtr Ilich Tchaikovsky (1840–1893), Russian composer, whose "vile" and "silly" opera *Eugene Onegin* Nabokov cannot abide (*Gogol,* p. 145; *Onegin* Commentary, Vol. II, p. 333); Norman Douglas (1868–1952), English writer, author of *South Wind* (1917); Waslaw Nijinsky (1890–1950), Russian ballet dancer of Polish descent (see p. 304), afflicted with insanity, and an associate of Diaghilev (who in *Ada* is the ballet master Dangleleaf [p. 430]); and Marcel Proust (see 18/4).

183/5 *two other . . . writers:* one of whom, W. Somerset Maugham (1874–1965), author of *Of Human Bondage* (1915), would have been named had he not been still alive, says Nabokov.

184/1 *Oui, ils sont gentils:* French; Yes, they are nice.

184/2 *toiles:* French; canvasses (paintings).

184/3 *"Prenez...savourer":* "Please take one of these pears. The good lady who lives across the street gives me more than I can relish" (Gaston's French is pedantic and his prose properly decadent, especially in the following).

184/4 *"Mississe Taille Lore...j'exécre":* "Mrs. Taylor [phonetically rendered to indicate Gaston's foreign accent] has just given me these beautiful flowers which I abhor."

184/5 *au roi!:* check!

185/1 *"Et toutes...bien?":* "How about all your little girls? Are they all right?"

185/2 *sale histoire:* compromising episode (sexual in nature).

CHAPTER 7

186/1 *painted roses:* the smallest details cohere; see 54/5.

186/2 *Treasure Island:* the children's classic (published 1883) by Robert Louis Stevenson. See 160/1.

186/3 *Whistler:* James McNeill Whistler (1834–1903), Anglo-American painter and etcher. The famous painting of his mother is actually titled "Arrangement in Grey and Black."

187/1 *cars...bars...barmen:* the fripperous internal rhymes burlesque Belloc's "Tarantella" (149/1): "And the cheers and the jeers of the young muleteers..." H.H. is paraphrasing his own verse; a complete version appears, in all its majesty, on pp. 257-259.

CHAPTER 8

187/2 *Star:* the newspaper's name was not italicized in the 1958 edition; the error has been corrected.

188/1 *time leaks:* spent with Quilty. For an index to his appearances, see 33/9.

189/1 *sly quip...Rigger:* The Right Reverend Rigger (in some versions "Reverend MacTrigger") figures in an old limerick that begins, "There was a right royal old nigger." "His five hundred wives / Had the time of their lives," and the rest is too obscene to appear here. But see Joyce's *Ulysses*, where Bloom quotes it (1961 Random House ed., pp. 171–172). For a summary of Joyce allusions, see 6/11.

190/1 *Argus-eyed:* "observant"; from the hundred-eyed monster of Greek mythology, who was set to watch Io, a maiden loved by Zeus. In *Laughter in the Dark*, Albinus meets his fatal love in the Argus cinema, where she is an usher (p. 22). "My back is Argus-eyed," says the speaker in "An Evening of Russian Poetry" (see 5/3). In *Pale Fire*, one of the aliases of the assassin Gradus is "d'Argus"; Hermann in *Despair* envisions "argus-eyed angels" (p. 111); the title character in *The Real Life of Sebastian Knight* "seems argus-eyed" (p. 97); Ada and Van dread "traveling together to Argus-eyed destinations" (*Ada*, p. 425), and Van, in search of the nature and meaning of Time, drives an "Argus" car (p. 551).

191/1 *celebrated actress:* an allusion to her resemblance to Marlene Dietrich; p. 105.

191/2 *ne montrez pas vos zhambes:* French; do not show your legs (*jambes* phonetically spelled to indicate an American accent—a recollection of Charlotte; see 46/1).

191/3 *Edgar:* in honor of Poe; see 77/5 and 120/2. For a summary of Poe allusions, see 11/2.

191/4 *hygienic evening in Providence:* at that time Providence, R.I., possessed a large redlight district.

Chapter 9

191/5 *Avis Chapman:* "When naming incidental characters," says Nabokov, "I like to give them some mnemonic handle, a private tag: thus 'Avis Chapman' which I mentally attached to the South-European butterfly *Callophrys avis* Chapman (where Chapman, of course, is the name of that butterfly's original describer)." For entomological allusions, see 8/1.

192/1 *save one . . . names are approximations:* Mona Dahl. Because she was Lolita's accomplice in deceit, a cover (or quilt!) for Quilty, H.H. takes his vengeance by revealing Mona's name to the world.

194/1 *Ball Zack:* Honoré de Balzac (1799–1850), French novelist.

[393]

CHAPTER 10

194/2 *my Lolita:* this brief chapter sounds an urgent chord in what might be called the "true love" theme. The succinct "Latin" locution (see 47/1) is sounded on pp. 34, 46, 55, 68, 81, 82, 94, 113, 117, 130, 136, 156, 168, 169, 178, 192, 200, 201, 209, 233, 243, 249, 269, 279, 280, 286, 295, 311. "My lone light Lolita" (p. 287) and "my conventional Lolita" (p. 289) vary the pattern.

CHAPTER 11

195/1 *"Why, no,"* I *said:* the comma after *no* was omitted in the 1958 edition; the error has been corrected.

197/1 *teachers':* the apostrophe was omitted in the 1958 edition.

197/2 *Miss Horn . . . Miss Cole:* the first letters of the teachers' names have been transposed. "Corrected," the names combine to form an obscene verb. For their anagrammatic colleagues, see 181/1.

198/1 *The Hunted Enchanters:* "the author" is Quilty (see p. 202), though Pratt has the title wrong (*The Enchanted Hunters,* after the hotel and the nympholepts, common and uncommon varieties [see 110/2]). She is figuratively correct, however, since Quilty *is* hunting the enchanter (Lolita), and it is apt that Pratt, her keeper, should make this accurate "error." For a summary of Quilty allusions, see 33/9.

199/1 *She is in Mushroom:* the very astute reader of *Who's Who in the Limelight* knows this already; see 33/8.

199/2 *girls':* the apostrophe was omitted in the 1958 edition.

200/1 *Reynolds:* Joshua Reynolds (1723–1792), English painter. "The Age of Innocence" portrays a very young girl alone under a tree.

200/2 *Baker:* George Pierce Baker (1866–1935) gave a famous course in playwrighting at Harvard, and his *Dramatic Technique* (1919) was a popular text.

CHAPTER 12

200/3 *Dr. Ilse Tristramson:* Tristram[n] was the famous hero of Celtic legend, and the love of Tristram and Iseult has often been celebrated. The story of Tristram is in Sir Thomas Malory's *Morte Darthur* (1485), Books Ten through Twelve. Matthew Arnold treated the theme in "Tristram and Iseult" (1852), Swinburne in "Tristram of Lyonesse" (1871), and Tennyson in "The Last Tournament" (1871). "Tristram in movielove," notes H.H. (p. 256). The punning name of the physician who examines Lolita is in the spirit of a novel that is both a love story and a parody of love stories; but, more than that, it acknowledges Laurence Sterne, whose involuted and a-realistic *Tristram Shandy* (1767) might be called the first modern novel (for the *Shandy* reference, see also *Keys*, p. 96). The aesthetic kinship of Sterne and Joyce and Nabokov, which has nothing to do with "literary influence," is strong enough to call both *Ulysses* and *Lolita* "Tristram's sons." "I love Sterne but had not read him in my Russian period," says Nabokov (*Wisconsin Studies* interview). See 257/4 for another Sterne allusion.

200/4 *caloricity:* "the physiological ability to develop and maintain bodily heat."

200/5 *Venus febriculosa:* Latin; "slightly feverish Venus." Lolita's malady in mock medicalese. See 139/1 for other references to the Roman goddess of love and beauty. See pp. 272 and 276 for allusions to Botticelli's famous painting of her.

201/1 *Doris Lee...Frederick Waugh:* the Doris Lee (1905–   ) painting under discussion is called "Noon." It shows a man with his hat over his face, asleep on a haystack, while in the foreground a girl and another man are making love beside a haystack (reproduced in *Life*, III, September 20, 1937). All of these artists are realistic painters. Grant Wood (1892–1942) is well-known for his meticulous renderings of eminently American subjects, especially for "American Gothic" (1930)—"good title for book"—the coolly sardonic portrait of a Midwestern farm couple. The subject matter of Peter Hurd (1904–   ) is primarily Southwestern, including his portrait painting (his name became legend in 1967 when President Lyndon B. Johnson refused a Hurd portrait of him, calling it the "ugliest thing I ever saw"). Reginald Marsh (1898–1954) indefatigably chronicled the common (if not low) life of New York City, in a style more graphic than painterly (a misprint in his name has been corrected [*s* instead of *c* in the 1958 edition]). Frederick Waugh (1861–1940) concentrated on marine subjects. Like their maker (see 265/3), Nabokov's characters usually know a good deal about art and express their opinions freely (see *Pnin*, pp. 95–99).

CHAPTER 13

202/1 *Elizabethan:* that epoch's play-within-the-play is relevant here, for *The Enchanted Hunters* functions in the same manner (as do other "playlets" mentioned on p. 203, though the latter are of less significance). See 53/1 and the Introduction, pp. xxix–xxx.

202/2 *Diana:* Roman moon goddess, patroness of hunting and virginity; identified with the Greek Artemis.

202/3 *suggested the play's title:* the title was of course suggested by Lolita's enchantment of H.H. and Quilty; their conversation at the hotel is on pp. 128–129. As happens so often in the universe of Nabokov's fiction, the title reflects or refracts a motif distant in time but not in space, insofar as "the poet . . . is the nucleus" of everything (*Speak, Memory,* p. 218). The year of his death, Sebastian Knight "is said to have been three times to see the same film—a perfectly insipid one called *The Enchanted Garden*" (*The Real Life of Sebastian Knight* [1941], p. 184). See Introduction, p. xxviii, and, for typical examples, 5/3, 14/1, 190/1, and 242/1.

203/1 *Hansel and Gretel:* the three "playlets" are adaptations of fairy tales that have to do with deception or enchantment.

203/2 *Richard Roe:* a party to legal proceedings whose real name is unknown; the second party when two are unknown, just as "John Doe" is the first party. *Dorothy Doe* is an alliterative party of no legal significance.

203/3 *Maurice Vermont . . . Rumpelmeyer:* Nabokov says, "I vaguely but persistently feel that both Vermont and Rumpelmeyer exist!" (probably culled from a telephone directory). Whether "real" or not, these names were chosen because they are a play on (and with) the emperor's old clothes: *to rumple* (to form irregular folds) and the *Vermont,* a merino sheep having greatly exaggerated skin folds. *Maurice* points below to Maeterlinck, a purveyor of more pretentious fairy tales; while *Rumpelmeyer* also suggests Rumpelstiltskin, a fairy tale that is resolved only when the fair protagonist discovers the grotesque villain's name. For a similar moment in *Lolita,* see p. 274.

203/4 *Lenormand:* Henri René Lenormand (1882–1951). In the period between the two world wars, he was the center of those French dramatists concerned with subconscious motivation. He was regarded as a Freudian, but he claimed that his plays were based on emotional conflicts rather than on intellectual systems. Lenormand believed that all altruistic action was motivated by egoistic impulses. In his plays man is set in physical nature and climatic conditions are considered as a shaping force in human behavior. *Le Temps est un songe* (1919) and *À l'Ombre du mal* (1924) are among his best-known works. The allusion to Lenormand is generalized, says Nabokov. Although some of them are a parodist's delight, Nabokov had no specific Lenormand works in mind. Lenormand's play, *La Maison des Remparts*, features a girl named Lolita, but Nabokov has never seen or read it.

203/5 *Maeterlinck:* the reputation of Maurice Maeterlinck (1862–1949) was at its height in the last decade of the nineteenth and the first decade of this century, when the Belgian-born writer's anti-naturalistic symbolist plays exerted a wide influence. In an effort to communicate the mysteries of man's inner life and his relation to the universe, he created a theater of stasis, rich in atmosphere and short in action. He won the Nobel prize for literature in 1911. Among his most famous plays are *Pelléas et Mélisande* (1892) and *L'Oiseau bleu* (1909): see 252/7 and 303/5.

203/6 *British dreamers:* Nabokov has in mind Sir James M. Barrie (1860–1937), Scottish novelist and dramatist who wrote *Peter Pan* (1904) and *A Kiss for Cinderella* (1916), and Lewis Carroll (see 133/3 and 266/1).

203/7 *a seventh Hunter:* see 251/2 and the Introduction, p. xxx.

203/8 *elves:* for "elves" and the fairy tale theme, see 33/3, which underscores the fact that the entertainment is indeed "the poet's invention."

204/1 *Was it?:* her euphoria is caused by the realization that Quilty has named his play in her honor.

CHAPTER 14

204/2 *Miss Emperor:* Mlle. Lempereur is Emma Bovary's music teacher. By pretending to go to lessons Emma is able to meet Léon in Rouen and deceive her husband (Part III, Chapter 5). See also *Keys*, p. 25. See 147/3 for Flaubert.

204/3 *Gustave's:* because Lolita has followed Emma's example, Flaubert (not Trapp) is still on H.H.'s mind.

205/1 *mon pauvre ami ... saluent:* French; my poor fellow, I have never seen you again and although there is little likelihood of your seeing my book, allow me to tell you that I give you a very cordial handshake and that all my little girls send you greetings.

205/2 *d'un ... contrit:* French; a look of contrived mortification.

205/3 *rehearsing*...*with Mona:* she meets Quilty here. See 33/9 for a summary of his appearances.

206/1 *pommettes:* cheekbones. A corrected author's error (not italicized in 1958 edition).

208/1 *haddocky:* fishy (akin to the cod); the adjectival use is H.H.'s.

208/2 *dackel:* German; a dachshund.

208/3 *Mr. Hyde:* in Robert Louis Stevenson's *Dr. Jekyll and Mr. Hyde* (1886), Hyde similarly knocks over a little girl. Note that H.H. identifies himself with the evil self of Stevenson's *Doppelgänger* tale. For Stevenson, see 160/1 and the Introduction, pp. lxiv and lxvi.

209/1 *hurriedly hung up:* the conversation was with Quilty.

209/2 *Pim*...*Pippa:* an allusion to the play *Mr. Pim Passes By* (1919), by A.A. Milne (1882–1956), and to Browning's *Pippa Passes*. See also *Keys,* p. 20. See 119/2 for another reference to *Pippa Passes,* and *Pale Fire,* p. 186. For *My Last Duchess*'s Fra Pandolf, see *Pale Fire,* p. 246.

209/3 *J'ai toujours*...*Dublinois:* "I have always admired the [*ormonde*] work of the sublime Dubliner." The sublime one is James Joyce, but *ormonde* does not exist in French; it refers to Dublin's Hotel Ormond (no *e*), whose restaurant provides the setting for the so-called "Sirens" episode of *Ulysses,* and whose name is a most Joycean pun—*hors* [*de ce*] *monde* ("out-of-this-world," a further tribute). (See also *Keys,* p. 20.) The reverential allusion is delivered obliquely in the requisite Joycean manner. Also in the Dubliner's spirit is the "jolls-joyce" car in which the hero of *Ada* rides in one scene (p. 473). See 6/11. In a 1966 National Educational Television network interview, Nabokov said the "greatest masterpieces of twentieth-century prose are, in this order: Joyce's *Ulysses;* Kafka's *Transformation;* Bely's *St. Petersburg;* and the first half of Proust's fairy tale, *In Search of Lost Time.*" "*On fait son grand Joyce* after doing one's *petit Proust,*" reads a parenthetical statement in *Ada,* added to the "manuscript" by gently derisive Ada herself, "In [her] lovely hand" (p. 169). When Véra Nabokov saw some of the opened pages of the annotator's copy of *Lolita,* the typeface barely visible beneath an overlay of comments in several colors of pencil and ink, she turned to her husband and said, "Darling, it looks like your copy of *Ulysses.*" Although there are strong artistic affinities between Joyce and Nabokov, he dismisses the possibility of formal "influence": "My first real contact with *Ulysses,* after a leering glimpse in the early 'twenties, was in the 'thirties at a time when I was definitely formed as a writer and immune to any literary influence. I studied *Ulysses* seriously only much later, in the 'fifties, when preparing my Cornell courses. That was the best part of the education I received at Cornell" (*Wisconsin Studies* interview). See 223/1.

In addition to admiring Joyce, Nabokov also knew him. "I saw [Joyce] a few times in Paris in the late 'thirties," recalls Nabokov. "Paul and Lucie Léon, close friends of his, were also old friends of mine. One night they brought him to a French lecture I had been asked to deliver on Pushkin under the auspices of Gabriel Marcel (it was later published in the *Nouvelle Revue Française*). I had happened to replace at the very last moment a Hungarian woman writer, very famous that winter, author of a bestselling novel, I remember its title, *La Rue du Chat qui Pêche*, but not the lady's name. A number of personal friends of mine, fearing that the sudden illness of the lady and a sudden discourse on Pushkin might result in a suddenly empty house, had done their best to round up the kind of audience they knew I would like to have. The house had, however, a pied aspect since some confusion had occurred among the lady's fans. The Hungarian consul mistook me for her husband and, as I entered, dashed towards me with the froth of condolence on his lips. Some people left as soon as I started to speak. A source of unforgettable consolation was the sight of Joyce sitting, arms folded and glasses glinting, in the midst of the Hungarian football team. Another time my wife and I had dinner with him at the Léons' followed by a long friendly evening of talk. I do not recall one word of it but my wife remembers that Joyce asked about the exact ingredients of *myod*, the Russian 'mead,' and everybody gave him a different answer."

Nabokov makes a Joycean appearance in Gisèle Freund and V.B. Carleton's *James Joyce in Paris: His Final Years* (New York, 1965). Pictured on pp. 44–45 is a meeting of the editorial board of the Parisian journal *Mesures*. Nine literati are shown gathered around a garden table, and a caption identifies the group, which includes Sylvia Beach, Adrienne Monnier, Henri Michaux, Jean Paulhan—and Jacques Audiberti, a tall, thin man standing in the back, looking down, his face in shadows, a trace of a smile suggesting some miraculous foreknowledge of the caption that twenty-eight years later would mistakenly identify him as "Audiberti," and in thus denying the existence of the already pseudonymous V. Sirin, would summarize the vicissitudes and spectral qualities of Russian émigré life, and cast him as The Mystery Man in the Garden, a role based on the nameless man in the brown macintosh, the mystery man of *Ulysses*, the "lankylooking galoot" (as Bloom calls him) whose name is misunderstood by a newspaper reporter as "M'Intosh," under which name he is immortalized. The photo is also included in *TriQuarterly* 17 (Winter 1970).

209/4 *C'est entendu?:* French; that's agreed?

209/5 *Lenore:* although Poe wrote a poem thusly titled, the primary allusion is to the title character in one of the most popular dramatic ballads of Gottfried August Bürger (1747–1794), German poet of the *Sturm und Drang* period. H.H. echoes the best-known line, in which Lenore and her ghostly lover ride off: *"Und hurre, hurre, hop, hop, hop, hop! ..."* (line 149). See also *Keys*, p. 141n. The allusion is ironic, since Lenore grieves over her lover. Nabokov discusses the poem in the Commentary to his *Eugene Onegin* translation (Vol. III, pp. 153–154).

209/6 *qui ... temps:* French; who was taking his time.

CHAPTER 15

210/1 *Professor Chem:* for "Chemistry."

210/2 *edusively (placed!):* a portmanteau word; from *educible* (*educe:* "to draw forth; elicit"; see *Edusa*, p. 211), coined to rhyme with *effusively*. By punning on Edusa's name he manages to place her.

210/3 *the author:* Quilty. See 33/9.

211/1 *Edusa Gold:* named after the Clouded Yellow, a golden-orange European butterfly known at one time as *Colias edusa*. See 233/1. For entomological allusions, see 8/1.

211/2 *Some old woman:* Quilty; Lolita's diversionary ploy is successful; see 275/1.

211/3 *natural climax:* an echo of the "traumatic" experience; 15/3.

CHAPTER 16

212/1 *le montagnard émigré:* "the exiled mountaineer," the legend under a picture of Chateaubriand and the title of one of his *romances* (a sentimental ballad or song). An *émigré* is an expatriate; the word originally referred to Royalist fugitives from the French Revolution (such as Chateaubriand). *Le Montagnard émigré* was first published in 1806 and later included in Chateaubriand's story *Les Aventures du dernier Abencerage*, where the untitled verses are sung by a young French prisoner of war. Several of its lines are important in *Ada,* and appear literally at the center of the Ardis section; see pp. 138–139 and 141 (also see pp. 106, 192, 241, 342, 428, and 530). For more on Chateaubriand, see 147/4.

212/2 *Felis tigris goldsmithi:* taxonomic Latin: "Goldsmith's tiger" (*Felis:* genus; *tigris:* species; *goldsmithi:* subspecies), an allusion to line 356 of "The Deserted Village" (1770), by Oliver Goldsmith (c. 1730–1774): "where crouching tigers wait their hapless prey" (the animal is in fact a cougar rather than a tiger). "I found it and I named it, being versed / in taxonomic Latin," writes Nabokov in his poem "A Discovery" (8/1). Surely the same cannot be said of H.H., who is completely unversed in such matters (see Nabokov's remarks, 8/1).

212/3 *catalpas:* botanical term; "any of a small genus of American and Asiatic trees of the trumpet-creeper family."

212/4 *Nebraska...first whiff of the West:* a parody of the state's omnipresent pre-1960 slogan, "Nebraska—Where the West Begins!"

212/5 *Red Rock:* the initial rock is on p. 15.

212/6 *caravansary:* see 166/1.

213/1 *detective tale:* one of the works of Maurice Leblanc (1864–1941), who was a kind of French Conan Doyle. See 252/5.

213/2 *persons unknown:* Quilty. For a summary of allusions to him, see 33/9.

213/3 *sign of Pegasus:* trademark of Mobil Oil; in Greek mythology, Pegasus is the winged horse sprung from Medusa at her death. Because a blow of his hoof brought forth Hippocrene, the fountain of the Muses, he is an emblem of poetic inspiration.

213/4 *that bug:* according to Nabokov, "this 'patient bug' is not necessarily a moth—it could be some clumsy big fly or miserable beetle." For entomological allusions, see 8/1.

214/1 *the Conche:* Shell Oil's trademark; in Greek mythology, the sea demigod Triton, son of Poseidon and Amphitrite, played a trumpet made of a conch. See 229/2.

214/2 *Cheṣtnut Court:* throughout the novel, the smallest verbal units are undergoing a kind of metamorphosis (see 120/3). The chestnut trees below the motel are said to be "toylike," and H.H. is indeed toying with

"Chestnuts." On p. 215, "Chestnut Court" becomes "Chestnut Castle," five lines later turns into "Chestnut Crest," and on p. 217 it returns to its "Chestnut Court" form; given a new context on p. 218, it becomes a horse. See 253/12, by which time it has become "Chestnut Lodge." As happens so often, Nabokov himself has described the process best: "The names Gogol invents are really nicknames which we surprise in the very act of turning into family names—and a metamorphosis is a thing always exciting to watch" (*Gogol*, p. 43).

214/3 *an elf-like girl on an insect-like bicycle:* H.H. has just mentioned that they are near Lolita's home town of Pisky ("pixie"; see 48/1); elves are thus indigenous to the region, and Nabokov has blended the fairy-tale theme with the entomological motif.

215/1 *Chestnut Castle:* see 214/2.

215/2 *"Bertoldo" ... comedy:* the famous clown of Italian popular legend, who was the subject of a sixteenth-century collection of witty tales, *Vita di Bertoldo*, by Giulio Ceasare Croce. Bertoldo is planted here to show that H.H. could easily understand Quilty's later allusion to Italian comedy (p. 250).

215/3 *red hood:* Quilty; the devil's presence is more than fleeting; see 216/2. His appearances are summarized in 33/9.

215/4 *cod-piece fashion:* in the fifteenth and sixteenth centuries, a flap or bag, often ornamental, concealing an opening in the front of men's breeches; *cod-piece* is archaic for "penis" (often used by such writers as François Rabelais [c. 1490–1553], author of *Gargantua*).

216/1 *adolori ... langueur:* "affected by love's languor." The phrase *"d' amoureuse langueur"* appears several times, with slight variations, in Ronsard's *Amours*. *"Adolori,"* a punning tribute to Lolita (*à Dolores*), is of course H.H.'s addition. See also *Keys*, p. 137n. See 49/2 for another Ronsard allusion.

216/2 *diabolical glow:* Quilty. She was with him at about the time H.H. was having his hair cut by the grotesque barber (p. 215).

217/1 *the shadow:* Quilty is continually identified as such.

CHAPTER 17

217/2 *Gros:* French; fat.

[402]

217/3 *"luizetta"*: H.H.'s invention; from *louis d'or*, the French gold coin.

217/4 *the ... life we all had rigged*: that "we all" (= H.H., Quilty, McFate, and Nabokov) involutes the narrative once more. See 34/7.

218/1 *burley ... Krestovski*: see 90/1. The punning adjective summarizes his essence: *burly* (sturdy, stout) plus *burley* (an American tobacco, used in cigarettes and plugs).

CHAPTER 18

218/2 *Chestnuts and Colts*: freed from all modifiers (see 214/2), the trees, motels, and unstated brand names of the above pistols are here able to frolic together briefly as horses. "We are faced by the remarkable phenomenon of mere forms of speech directly giving rise to live creatures," as Nabokov says of *Dead Souls* (*Gogol*, p. 78).

219/1 *Aztec Red*: Quilty's "red shadow" and "red beast" (p. 221), characterized below as a "Red Yak."

219/2 *Jovian*: in Roman mythology, Jove (or Jupiter) is god of the sky.

219/3 *donc*: French; therefore.

219/4 *crepitating*: crackling.

219/5 *Jutting Chin ... funnies*: the comic strip *Dick Tracy*, created by Chester Gould (1900–) in 1931.

220/1 *of my age ... rosebud ... mouth*: Quilty; the fact and the motif are familiar. H.H. had thought of growing such a mustache (50/1), and they also own similar bathrobes (p. 296).

221/1 *O lente ... equi*: "O slowly run, horses of the night"; H.H.'s adjacent "translation" puns on the literal Latin (night mares). Less one *lente*, this line is from *The Tragical History of the Life and Death of Doctor Faustus* (V, ii, 140), by Christopher Marlowe (1564–1593). With only one hour left before eternal damnation, Faustus hopes for more time. H.H. does not try to "outspeed" Quilty, that latter-day Mephistopheles. See also *Keys*, pp. 31–32. For a similar pun—nightmares and stallions—see *Ada*, p. 214.

221/2 *viatic*: see 161/3.

222/1 *lady ... lightning*: see 33/11. The allusions to *The Lady Who Loved Lightning* and "Fatface" anticipate the next passage, in which H.H. and Lolita attend Quilty's play. He and his collaborator are mentioned by name on p. 223 and even appear on stage.

222/2 *Soda, pop. 1001:* there is in California a Lake Soda, pop. unknown. The magical "1001" is well chosen. It is simultaneously a numerical mirroring (see 53/2) and an allusion to the fairy-tale theme (see 33/3) via another vertiginously involuted work, *The Thousand and One Nights.*

222/3 *flatus:* gas generated in the bowels or stomach.

222/4 *kurortish: Kurort* is German for "health resort" (see p. 157); the usage is H.H.'s own.

223/1 *children-colors . . . a passage in James Joyce:* the colors of the spectrum; the "living rainbow" mimed by the "seven little graces" on p. 222. It is from *Finnegans Wake.* The theme of the diversity and unity of all things is central to the constantly metamorphosing dream world of *Finnegans Wake.* The seven colors of the spectrum represent diversity and are most frequently personified by seven "rainbow girls" who oppose the archetypal mother, Anna Livia Plurabelle. The book opens with a reversed rainbow; the seven clauses in the second paragraph each contain a color, shifting from violet to red. Although not wrong, H.H.'s mention of a single "passage" is misleading because the motif is sustained throughout the *Wake.* To have the hateful Quilty "lift" from *Finnegans Wake* rather than *Ulysses* constitutes a rather private and thus thoroughly Joycean joke, based on Nabokov's low opinion of the book he calls *Punnigans Wake,* or, in *Bend Sinister,* keeping its vast liquidity in mind, *"Winnipeg Lake,* ripple 585, Vico Press edition" (p. 103). *"Ulysses* towers over the rest of Joyce's writings," says Nabokov, "and in comparison to its noble originality and unique lucidity of thought and style the unfortunate *Finnegan's Wake* is nothing but a formless and dull mass of phony folklore, a cold pudding of a book, a persistent snore in the next room, most aggravating to the insomniac I am. . . . *Finnegans Wake*'s façade disguises a very conventional and drab tenement house, and only the infrequent snatches of heavenly intonations redeem it from utter insipidity. I know I am going to be excommunicated for this pronouncement" (*Wisconsin Studies* interview). Charles Kinbote sustains his maker's negative opinion: "it would have been unseemly for a monarch to appear in the robes of learning at a university lectern and present to rosy youths *Finnigan's* [*sic*—A.A.] *Wake* as a monstrous extension of Angus MacDiarmid's 'incoherent transactions' and of Southey's Lingo-Grande ('Dear Stumparumper,' etc.) . . ." (*Pale Fire,* p. 76).

Joyce himself helped to introduce Nabokov to *Finnegans Wake.* In Paris in 1937 or 1938, he gave Nabokov *Haveth Childers Everywhere* (1930), one of the fragments published before the *Wake* was completed. Future commentators will no doubt find several echoes of *Finnegans*

Wake in *Lolita;* but it could hardly be otherwise, since Joyce's book is so inclusive, so monstrously allusive (Phineas Quimby appears on p. 536 of the *Wake* [standard American edition], and on p. 252 of *Lolita*—but who *doesn't* appear in *Finnegans Wake?*). Moreover, Joyce's punning mutations anticipate and echo sentences which are yet to be written. The hero of *Finnegans Wake* is HCE—Here Comes Everybody, Humphrey Chimpden Earwicker, usually just Humphrey (with a humped back). Since he is "Everyman," there are some forty humming variations of his name, and, "influences" aside, there is statistically reason enough for some of Nabokov's humorously distorted forms of "Humbert" to coincide with a few of Joyce's punning phonetic variants. Thus Nabokov's sartorially splendid "Homburg" (p. 111) complements Joyce's "Humborg" (p. 72), and Joyce's "Humfries" (p. 97) should surely be served with Nabokov's "Hamburg[s]" (pp. 111 and 263)—but these are all coincidences, says Nabokov, for, "Generally speaking, *FW* is a very small and blurry smudge on the mirror of my memory." The only persistent "smudge" is a trace of Anna Livia Plurabelle. In *Bend Sinister,* Ophelia is imagined "wrestling—or, as another rivermaid's father would have said, 'wrustling'—with the willow" (p. 102); and in *Ada,* the title character alludes to the music of the self-contained A.L.P. section: "Did he know Joyce's poem about the two washerwomen?" she wonders (p. 54). The "children-colors," however, constitute the only intentional allusion to *Finnegans Wake* in *Lolita.* For a summary of Joyce allusions, see 6/11.

223/2 *Orange...and Emerald:* when I asked Nabokov if he chose these particular colors because they are also the common names of a butterfly and a moth, respectively, Nabokov responded: "The Dubliner's rainbow of children on p. 223 would have been a meaningless muddying of metaphors had I tried to smuggle in a Pierid of the Southern States and a European moth. My only purpose here was to render a prismatic effect. May I point out (at the risk of being pretentious) that I do not see the colors of lepidoptera as I do those of less familiar things—girls, gardens, garbage (similarly, a chessplayer does not see white and black as white and black), and that, for instance, if I use 'morpho blue' I am thinking not of one of the many species of variously blue *Morpho* butterflies of South America, but of the ornaments made of bits of the showy wings of the commoner species. When a lepidopterist uses 'Blues,' a slangy but handy term, for a certain group of Lycaenids, he does not see that word in any color connection because he knows that the diagnostic undersides of their wings are not blue but dun, tan, grayish, etc., and that many

Blues, especially in the female, are brown, not blue. In my case, the differentiation in artistic and scientific vision is particularly strong because I was really born a landscape painter, not a landless escape novelist as some think." For more on "blue," see 265/3; for a more generalized discussion of color, see 58/1.

CHAPTER 19

224/1 *P. O. Wace and P. O. Elphinstone:* = P.O.W. and Poe, and the imprisonment theme.

225/1 *Ne manque . . . Qu'il t'y:* an allusion to Quilty and a parody of the classical alexandrine verse of seventeenth-century France, specifically of *Le Cid* (1636), by Pierre Corneille (1606–1684): "Do not fail to tell your suitor, Chimène, how beautiful the lake is, because he should take you there." Chimène is from *Le Cid,* but the line itself is invented. See also *Keys,* p. 71. For an index to Quilty references, see 33/9.

225/2 *the mysterious nastiness:* Mona knew all about Quilty and injected his name. H.H. is not supposed to understand, at the time, the planted *"qu'il t'y,"* though he suspects some nasty trick.

225/3 *à titre documentaire:* French; just for the record.

225/4 *Lo to behold:* H.H. toys with the worn interjection, "Lo and behold," as Lolita did much earlier (52/3).

226/1 *detective:* Trapp (Quilty).

227/1 *Browns:* "Browns" reappear on pp. 247, 253, and 255.

227/2 *Cokes:* the 1958 edition did not capitalize the trademark; the error has been corrected.

228/1 *intacta:* H.H. uses the Latin form of the common word "intact," but invokes its less common meaning, "untouched virgin."

228/2 *boy friend:* Quilty.

228/3 *bearded scholar:* "Another little bit of prophecy" (see 160/5), says Nabokov. "Lots of bearded young scholars around these days."

228/4 *la pomme de sa canne:* French; the round knob of a cane.

229/1 *Mirana:* H.H.'s father had owned a Mirana hotel; see 12/5.

229/2 *Proteus of the highway:* Quilty; from Greek mythology; a prophetic sea-god in Poseidon's service, who would assume different shapes when seized.

229/3 *remises:* carriage houses.

229/4 *Melmoth:* a triple allusion. There is no such car; it is named after the four-volume Gothic novel *Melmoth the Wanderer* (1820), by Charles Robert Maturin (1782–1824), Irish clergyman and writer (also identified in *Keys*, p. 31). In his *Eugene Onegin* Commentary, Nabokov calls Maturin's Melmoth a "gloomy vagabond" (Vol. II, p. 352). "The book, although superior to [Monk] Lewis and Mrs. Radcliffe, is essentially second-rate, and Pushkin's high regard for it (in the French version) is the echo of a French fashion," writes Nabokov (*ibid.*, p. 353). Nabokov's paraphrase of the "action" of *Melmoth the Wanderer* (*ibid.*) underscores the humor of naming H.H.'s car after it:

> [John Melmoth] and his uncle are descendants of the diabolical Melmoth the Traveler ("Where he treads, the earth is parched! Where he breathes, the air is fire! Where he feeds, the food is poison! Where he turns his glance, is lightning.... His presence converts bread and wine into matter as viperous as the suicide foam of the dying Judas..."). John discovers a moldering manuscript. What follows is a long tale full of tales within tales—shipwrecks, madhouses, Spanish cloisters—and here I begin to nod.

> . . . .

> Melmoth's nature is marked by pride, intellectual glorying, "a boundless aspiration after forbidden knowledge," and a sarcastic levity that makes of him "a Harlequin of the infernal regions." Maturin used up all the platitudes of Satanism, while remaining on the side of the conventional angels. His hero enters into an agreement with a Certain Person who grants him power over time, space, and matter (that Lesser Trinity) under the condition that he tempt wretches in their hour of extremity with deliverance if they exchange situations with him.

Maturin's novel most likely supplied Oscar Wilde (1854–1900) with his post-prison pseudonym of "Sebastian Melmoth." In addition, adds Nabokov, "Melmoth may come from Mellonella Moth (which breeds in beehives) or, more likely, from Meal Moth (which breeds in grain)." For entomological allusions, see 8/1.

229/5 *grays ... his favorite cryptochromism:* a coinage; "secret colors." It is also an authorial favorite, in view of the puns on Haze, shadow, and ombre.

231/1 *"ordeal of the orb":* changing the tire.

231/2 *gigantic truck ... impossible to pass:* a fear confirmed; see 162/1.

CHAPTER 20

231/3 *"Love Under the Lindens":* planted between famous plays by Henrik Ibsen (1828–1906) and Anton Chekhov (1860–1904) is a combination of *Desire Under the Elms* (1924), by Eugene O'Neill (1888–1953), and *Unter den Linden* (a boulevard in Berlin). See also *Keys,* p. 150n. The portmanteau title, credited to "Eelmann" (O'Neill plus Thomas Mann), is mentioned in *Ada* (p. 403). Nabokov's low opinion of O'Neill's *Mourning Becomes Electra* is expressed in *Gogol* (p. 55).

232/1 *flashlight:* a corrected author's error (instead of "torchlight" in the 1958 edition). The quotation marks which enclosed this extract in the 1958 edition have also been corrected.

232/2 *Cyrano ... sleeping stranger:* after rereading this passage in 1968, Nabokov belatedly put words in H.H.'s mouth: "Cyrano's big nose. Cyranose. Sorry myself to have missed that portmantoid pun. 'A sleeping stranger,' " he added, "is enchanting and haunting." Edmond Rostand's famous play (1897) is based on the life of Cyrano de Bergerac (1619–1655), French writer and soldier. "Cyraniana" in *Ada* (p. 339) alludes to his most famous work, *Histoire comique des Etats et Empires de la Lune* (1656; modern edition: *A Voyage to the Moon*).

232/3 *petit rat:* a young ballet student at the Paris Opera (ages nine to fourteen).

233/1 *Electra:* "The name is based on that of a close ally of the Clouded Yellow butterfly," says Nabokov, "and has nothing to do with the Greek Electra." See 211/1. For entomological allusions, see 8/1.

234/1 *Ned Litam:* the anagrammatic (it reads backwards) pseudonym under which the great tennis player William T. (Bill) Tilden II wrote fiction. See 164/3.

234/2 *endorsing a Dromedary:* like Quilty; see 71/2. Note how H.H. is continually providing oblique clues; see 33/9 for a summary of Quilty allusions.

234/3 *fifty-three:* the 1958 edition omitted the hyphen; the error has been corrected.

235/1 *susceptible to the magic of games ... I saw the board:* H.H. is speaking for his maker, who would hope that the reader shares this limpid view of the gameboard that is *Lolita.*

235/2 *stratagems:* "beautiful word, stratagem—a treasure in a cave," writes Nabokov in *Gogol* (p. 59).

235/3 *tessellated:* laid with checkered work or adorned with mosaic.

236/1 *Decugis or Borman:* Max Decugis was a great European tennis player who often teamed with Gobbert (see 164/4). They were Wimbledon men's doubles champions in 1911. Paul de Borman was the Belgian champion in the first decade of this century. Nabokov recalls, "He was left-handed, and one of the first Europeans to use a sliced (or twist) service. There is a photograph of him in the Wallis Myers book on tennis (c. 1913)." I could not find the Myers book, but Decugis and Borman are discussed in George W. Beldman and P.A. Vaile's *Great Lawn Tennis Players* (New York, 1907). Beldman deplores Borman's lack of aggressiveness and poor position (resulting from the way he used his body to achieve his spins and cut shots), and writes of him, inimitably, "I do not know that he has a single perfect stroke, yet in every shot he made there was education for him who was able to take it" (pp. 350–351). Nabokov took it, and immortalized Borman in *Lolita*. At first wince (to quote H.H.), such minutiae may seem no better than Kinbotisms, but they are calmly offered as an example of the precise manner in which Nabokov's memory speaks to him and, as well, to suggest how he does indeed stock his "imaginary garden with real toads" (see 121/1).

236/2 *butterfly:* although Nabokov intends no "symbolism," it appears after H.H. has come as close to capturing Lolita's grace as he ever will. Nabokov only comments, "Butterflies are indeed inquisitive, and the dipping motion is characteristic of a number of genera." See 8/1.

236/3 *wimbles:* any of several instruments for boring holes.

236/4 *a syncope in the series:* an elision or loss of one or more letters or sounds from the middle of a word.

236/5 *Maffy On Say:* phonetic American pronunciation of *"ma fiancée."*

237/1 *purling:* gently murmuring, as a brook.

237/2 *three horrible Boschian cripples:* one of whom is Quilty. Hieronymous Bosch (c. 1450–1516), the great Flemish master of the grotesque, whose paintings abound in moral and physiological cripples. "And Flemish hells with porcupines and things" is a brief Boschian vision in the poem *Pale Fire* (line 226). On his deathbed, in *Ada*, Daniel Veen, an art collector and Bosch devotee, imagines that he is being put-upon by creatures from a Bosch painting, and dies "an odd Boschean death" (pp.

435–436). Nabokov then comments at length on the butterfly rendered at the center of Bosch's "Garden of Delights."

238/1 *That ... intruder ... a double:* Quilty; a pun: a double at tennis and a *Doppelgänger.* See 245/7.

CHAPTER 21

238/2 *red ball:* rolled by Quilty, who reappears on p. 239.

239/1 *Aztec Red:* H.H. remembers the color of Quilty's car. See 219/1.

239/2 *padded shield:* like the *olisbos* of 96/1; Quilty is seen as a grotesque Priapus who in this passage transforms nature into a veritable forest of phalli. *Priaps* (below) is H.H.'s usage.

CHAPTER 22

240/1 *Elphinstone:* where H.H. will lose his "elf"; see 33/3.

240/2 *Soyons logiques:* French; Let us be logical.

241/1 *saguaro:* a giant cactus with a thick stem and white flowers.

241/2 *fatamorganas:* mirages: see 12/5. A display in the fabulous department store in *King, Queen, Knave* offers "a Fata Morgana of coats" (p. 68).

241/3 *José Lizzarrabengoa:* Carmen's abandoned lover. See 47/3, 245/4, and 280/2.

241/4 *Etats Unis:* French; U.S.A.

241/5 *Mrs. Hays:* H.H. found Lo at Mrs. Haze's house, and will now lose her at the motor court of Mrs. Hays, also a widow.

242/1 *Blue:* from the common German name, "Blau." Dr. Starov, from the last chapter of *The Real Life of Sebastian Knight* (1941), and Dr. Blue combine in *Pale Fire* (1962) to form "The great Starover Blue [who] reviewed the role / Planets had played as landfalls of the soul" (lines 627–628). See 202/3.

242/2 *heterosexual Erlkönig in pursuit:* Quilty; an allusion to Goethe's poem *Erlkönig* ("Erlking"; king of the elves), in which spectral incarnations of the Erlking pursue a little boy who rides with his father through the dark and windy forest. Unable to possess the beloved boy, the Erlking wills his death. When the father arrives "safely" at the farmhouse, the child is dead in his arms. In *Pale Fire*, the Zemblan word *"alfear"* (Nabokov's coinage) is defined as "uncontrollable fear caused by elves" (p. 143); and a passage of John Shade's (lines 653–664) alludes to Goethe's poem, especially line 662, which Charles Kinbote likes enough to scan and then translate into Zemblan (p. 239). See the *Onegin* Commentary (Vol. II, p. 235). See also *Keys*, p. 138n. For "elf," see 33/3.

242/3 *"ague"*: a violent chill.

243/1 *haute montagne:* French; above-timberline pastures.

243/2 *Lore . . . Rolas:* the importation of Basques and their vicious sheep dogs, and the place names (Lore, etc.) are "real," Nabokov having encountered them both in the Pyrenees and the Rockies. *"Que sais-je!"* is a French cliché ("and so forth," "or whatever").

243/3 *French perfume:* the Soleil Vert of p. 258.

243/4 *secret agent . . . or hallucination:* Quilty.

243/5 *Aurora:* the dawn, as personified by the Romans (Eos for the Greeks). The image of the "warmed hands" means the sun had hardly risen high enough to warm the hillside.

243/6 *lavender:* a mint cultivated on hillsides in Southern France, used for its fragrant oil.

244/1 *Clowns and Columbines:* H.H.'s invention (the other titles exist). In the *commedia dell'arte* (see 215/2 and 250/6), the clown Pulcinella had a dual nature: witty, ironic, somewhat cruel, yet also silly, fawning, and timid. Columbine was the eternal coquette whose keen wit allows her to manipulate the most complex intrigues. She is the constant companion of Harlequin, the volatile, elusive character associated with Mercury as the patron of merchants, panderers, and thieves. The analogy with H.H., Lolita, and Quilty is clear.

244/2 *fundament jigging:* buttocks.

244/3 *a crumpled envelope:* the letter was from Quilty.

244/4 *chassé-croisé:* side stepping and re-side stepping each other.

245/1 *"Je croyais . . . doux":* "I thought that it was a *bill*—not a love-note" (a pun on *bill* and *billet doux*).

245/2 *Deseret News:* an actual newspaper in Utah.

245/3 *sister Ann:* it will be clear in a moment that H.H. is alluding to Charles Perrault's (1628–1703) fairy tale about Bluebeard, who murdered six wives. Hoping to be rescued by her two brothers, his seventh wife posts her sister Ann as sentinel; "Sister Ann, do you see anyone coming?"

is her constant refrain. She finally does, and the "brutal brothers" slay Bluebeard. See also *Keys*, p. 48. When I was writing this note, I called to my wife in the adjacent room, asking her if she remembered all the details in *Bluebeard*. "I know the story," replied Karen, my seven-year-old daughter, running into the room. I showed her the passage in *Lolita*, and, after helpfully identifying Sister Ann, she read H.H.'s dirge for Bluebeard. "Poor Bluebeard," she quoted. "*Poor* Bluebeard? He was *awful!* What kind of book *is* this?" For allusions to *Bluebeard* in *Ada*, see pp. 164 and 180, and in *King, Queen, Knave*, pp. 263–264. See 33/3.

245/4 *Est-ce que ... Carmen:* "Do you not love me any more, my Carmen?" José says this to Carmen in their penultimate confrontation (Chapter Three). José's very next beseechment is also quoted by H.H. (280/2). For Mérimée, see 47/3.

245/5 *plotting in Basque:* Carmen and José plot in Basque in the presence of her rich, uncomprehending English lover, whom José kills.

245/6 *Zemfirian:* "gypsy"; H.H.'s coinage, from the heroine of *The Gypsies* (1824, published 1827), the long poem by Russia's greatest poet, Aleksandr Pushkin (1799–1837). Another "Carmen" story, its hero Aleko kills both the treacherous Zemfira and her lover (also see *Keys*, p. 49). The poem is also an affirmation of a gypsy's freedom, which is another reason why H.H. says that the conspiratorial girls are speaking "Zemfirian," as well as Basque. Carmen is a gypsy too, and in her last moments proclaims this freedom; Ada is cast as Dolores, the fatal gypsy dancing girl in the film *Don Juan's Last Fling* (*Ada*, pp. 488–490).

245/7 *double game:* a pun; Nabokov is also playing it by leading the reader on with a *Doppelgänger* situation that parodies itself. See Introduction.

245/8 *father-substitute:* Quilty; a parody of the Freudian "transference" theory, whereby the daughter transfers her affections from her father to another, similar man, thus exorcising her Oedipal tension.

246/1 *gitanilla:* a diminutive of *gitana*, Spanish for "Gypsy girl," used often in Mérimée's *Carmen*. In *Ada*, "Osberg" (Borges) is the author of *The Gitanilla*, a novel reminiscent of *Lolita* (see 11/1), and several allusions to Osberg and his influence on Van Veen are jokes aimed at the critics who yoke Nabokov and Borges. A revolving paperback stand (p. 371) offers *The Gitanilla* along with several volumes no doubt as racy (*Our Laddies, Clichy Clichés*).

246/2 *une belle ... en bleu:* a beautiful lady all dressed in blue (a vision of the Virgin). "Visionary" nurse Mary is of Basque descent, and the Hautes-Pyrénées of her ancestors is in the same *département* (state) as

Lourdes, where many little French girls have experienced visions of the blue-garbed Virgin, phenomena duly celebrated in the press and popular literature. Nabokov mocks a best-selling romance on the subject in *Bend Sinister*, Chapter Three: "... that remarkable cross between a certain kind of wafer and a lollipop, Louis Sontag's *Annunciata*, which started so well in the Caves of St. Barthelemy and ended in the funnies" (the object of this parody is Franz Werfel's *Song of Bernadette*).

247/1 *a saint:* the lines which follow parody the first half of the fourth stanza of Robert Browning's "Soliloquy of the Spanish Cloister" (1842):

> *Saint*, forsooth! While brown Dolores
> Squats outside the Convent bank
> With Sanchicha, telling stories,
> Steeping tresses in the tank...

The lines describe the washing of linen. For more on this passage, see my 1968 *Denver Quarterly* article, p. 31. For Browning, see 119/2 and 209/2.

247/2 *a great holiday:* Fourth of July, 1949. "Independence Day—for Lolita," says Nabokov.

248/1 *Mr. Gustave ... spaniel pup:* Lolita has told Quilty that H.H. has mistaken him for his uncle (or cousin), Gustave Trapp; Quilty has known this for some time (see 253/4). Lolita liked the old lady's cocker spaniel at The Enchanted Hunters (pp. 119–120; commented upon by H.H., 263/4), which eavesdropper Quilty may have recalled and thus bought her this pup. But one of his three hobbies is "pets" (p. 33). For references to him, see 33/9.

248/2 *Caddy Lack:* an obvious pun, but young readers, especially in 2000 A.D., may not know that in the 1947–1952 period the Cadillac was by far the most luxurious American car, and a "status symbol," though H.H. uses its vulgar diminutive ("Caddy") to suggest otherwise.

248/3 *maquette:* a small, preliminary model of something planned, such as a stage set.

248/4 *telestically:* with the projection of a purpose, with a definite end in view, inwardly expressed.

248/5 *bemazed: archaic;* bewildered, stupefied.

249/1 *my brother:* Quilty; see 251/1 and 253/13.

CHAPTER 23

249/2 *fiend's spoor:* Quilty's trail; a "spoor" is the track of a wild animal.

249/3 *comme il faut:* French; good manners, decorum.

250/1 *Kawtagain:* "Caught again." Needless to say, there is no such town.

250/2 *342:* see 37/4 and 120/3.

250/3 *N. Petit ... Ill.:* abbreviated title of the illustrated French dictionary, *Nouveau Petit Larousse Illustré.* Lucette's "Little Larousse" in *Ada* is a pun on the French *rousse,* "red hair" (p. 368).

250/4 *a few paces from Lolita's pillow:* see 132/1.

250/5 *Ponderosa Lodge:* the return address on the letter received on p. 244.

250/6 *Dr. Gratiano ... Mirandola, N.Y.:* in the *commedia dell' arte,* Doctor Gratiano is a philosopher, astronomer, man of letters, cabalist, barrister, grammarian, diplomat, and physician. When the doctor speaks one cannot tell whether it is Latin or Low Breton, and he frequently delivers badly mangled quotations in Latin and Greek. His audiences usually must interrupt and thrash him in order to arrest the tide of "eloquence." The nonexistent "town" Mirandola has nothing to do with Pico, the Italian humanist, Nabokov says; like Forbeson, he was a minor character in Italian comedy. Nor, says Nabokov, does he intend any allusion to Mirandolina, the heroine of *Mine Hostess,* by Carlo Goldoni, Italian playwright. See 244/1.

251/1 *your brother:* H.H. has already said this of Quilty.

251/2 *an impossible balance:* a very important passage. The verbal figurations throughout *Lolita* demonstrate how Nabokov appears everywhere in the texture but never in the text, though the impersonator "come[s] damn close to it" (see 203/7), especially in the "cryptogrammic paper chase" on the next two pages. "Trapp" 's balancing act lucidly describes the performance of both the narrator and his creator, while the "thrashing anguish" also belongs to John Ray's "old-fashioned readers."

252/1 *logodaedaly* [p. 251] *and logomancy:* to prove that he is versed in *logodaedaly* (the arbitrary or capricious coining of words), H.H. the logomachist creates his own word from *logo* (word) plus the suffix *-mancy* ("divination in a [specified] manner").

252/2 *Quelquepart:* French; somewhere. Quilty must be there. See 253/5.

252/3 *fountain pen ... repressed undinist ... water nymphs in the Styx:* a most liquid passage. An *undine* is a female water spirit who could acquire a soul by marrying a mortal. "But," adds Nabokov, "the main point here is that 'undinist' is a person (generally male) who is erotically excited by another person's (generally female) making water (Havelock Ellis was an 'undinist,' or 'fountainist,' and so was Leopold Bloom)." Ellis was the first to use the word this way, and H.H.—like Quilty, "an amateur of sex lore"—no doubt has read the section on "Undinism" in *Studies in the Psychology of Sex*, Vol. VII. In Greek mythology, the Styx is the main river of the lower world.

252/4 *passion . . . cryptogrammic paper chase:* Quilty is indeed a tease, but so is H.H., who punningly alludes to the "melancholy truth" about Quilty's virtual impotence (p. 300). Thus H.H. refers to Cue's "teasing," his "passion for tantalization" (that is, his main passion), and the "ejaculat[ion]" of "his fiendish conundrum." The summary word "cryptogrammic" includes "cryptogamic" ("belonging or relating to the nonflowering plants"), which alludes to his sexuality, as well as his cryptogames. These games may be more gratifying than some, since Quilty's literary sources are so broadly hinted at in the text.

252/5 *Arsène Lupin:* the creation of Maurice Leblanc (see 213/1). See also *Keys,* p. 12. Most of the allusions in the two-page "paper chase" are also identified in *Keys,* pp. 12–19. *Arsène Lupin contre Sherlock Holmes* (1908) and *Les Confidences d'Arsène Lupin* (1914) are typical of the many Lupin volumes. For Conan Doyle, see 66/1. Hermann, the narrator of *Despair,* wonders, "But what are they—Doyle, Dostoevsky, Leblanc, Wallace—what are all the great novelists who wrote of nimble criminals . . . in comparison with me? Blundering fools!" (p. 132).

252/6 *A. Person, Porlock:* in the note which he affixed to "Kubla Khan" (1816), Samuel Taylor Coleridge (1772–1834), the English poet, explains how his dream was interrupted: "At this moment he was unfortunately called out by a person on business from Porlock. . . ." H.H.'s "dream" has been interrupted with equal finality by Quilty. In "The Vane Sisters" (1959; in *Nabokov's Quartet* and *Nabokov's Congeries*), a story about psychic phenomena, there is an eccentric librarian named Porlock, "who in the last years of his dusty life had been engaged in examining old books for miraculous misprints such as the substitution of 'l' for the second 'h' in the word 'hither.' "

252/7 *touché, reader!:* H.H. grants that the reader "got" these "easy" pokes; Rimbaud's poem *Le Bâteau ivre* (see 165/6 and 174/1) and Maurice Maeterlinck's play *L'Oiseau bleu* have been transposed (see 203/5). H.H. has written a book on "Rainbow" (see 77/6 for the garbled newspaper report, which Quilty has evidently read). *Schmetterling* is German for butterfly (see p. 303), and Maeterlinck was in fact an amateur entomologist.

252/8 *D. Orgon, Elmira, NY:* Orgon is the husband of Elmire in *Tartuffe*

(1664), by Molière (Jean Baptiste Poquelin [1622-1673]), French playwright and actor. The title character tries to seduce her. "Elmira" is of course an actual town, and the location of a college for women. Quilty was born in New Jersey and educated in New York (p. 33), and "D. Orgon" is an accurately transcribed phonetic rendering of the regional accent.

252/9 *Bumper, Sheridan:* Bumper is a character in *The School for Scandal* (1777), by Richard Sheridan (1751-1816), Irish playwright.

252/10 *Phineas Quimby, Lebanon, NH:* in mythology, Phineas provided Jason the directions to find the Golden Fleece; while Phineas Quimby (1802-1866) was an American pioneer in the field of mental healing, born in Lebanon, N.H. He initially specialized in mesmerism, and for several years gave public hypnotic exhibitions (1838-1847). H.H.'s coercion of both Lolita and the reader make him a latter-day specialist, and on p. 310 he says that "Mesmer Mesmer" was one of the possible pseudonyms he had considered for his narrative.

252/11 *Dr. Kitzler, Eryx, Miss.:* for *Kitzler*—H.H.'s tag, miraculously picked up by Quilty—see 122/3; for *Eryx*, the cult of Aphrodite, where "religious prostitution" was indeed practiced, see 139/1. The abbreviated form of Mississippi adds to the pun cluster an incongruous note of formality; "translated," it reads "Dr. Clitoris, Venus, Miss"—and "Miss Venus" is the archetypal if not the ultimate beauty contest winner.

253/1 *living vacationists:* "Johnny Randall of Ramble was a real person, I think (as was also Cecilia Dalrymple Ramble, p. 254)," says Nabokov, but the two are linked to form another verbal "coincidence."

253/2 *N. S. Aristoff...NY:* Catagela is the comic name of a town in the play *The Acharnians* (425 B.C.), by Aristophanes (445-385 B.C.). It is from a Greek word meaning "to deride."

253/3 *James...Hoaxton:* James Mavor Morell is one of the main characters in *Candida* (1894), a play by George Bernard Shaw (1856-1950). *Hoxton* (Shaw's spelling) is a place name therein. The additional *a* is well in the spirit of this "cryptogrammic paper chase," since Quilty is a permanent resident of "hoax town," and his maker has passed through that town more than once. Dreyer reads *Candida* in *King, Queen, Knave* (p. 263).

253/4 *G. Trapp, Geneva, NY.:* H.H.'s relative is Swiss, so nationalistic Quilty chooses a city found in America as well as in Switzerland.

253/5 *Aubrey Beardsley:* "Aubrey McFate" (58/1) and the Beardsleyan motif (54/3; 183/1) are finally united by Quilty in "Quelquepart"—that is, "somewhere."

253/6 *Lucas Picador:* in Mérimée's novella, Lucas the picador is Carmen's last lover; José, tired of killing her lovers, kills Carmen (see 47/3). In bullfighting, the picador is the member of the company who uses a lance to annoy and weaken the bull just prior to the kill. Although Quilty seems to cast himself as the picador, it is the tired bull who will ultimately make the kill.

253/7 *Merrymay, Pa....my Carmen:* a pun; Mérimée. The abbreviated *Pennsylvania* is a pun that nicely capsules Lolita's insulting, mock-familiar tone, as though she were saying, "the merry May festival is now being celebrated by Quilty, *Dad.*" H.H.'s betrayed "pathetic endearments" are his frequent epithets from *Carmen.*

253/8 *Will Brown, Dolores, Colo.:* Quilty echoes H.H., whose "forsooth" acknowledges the "coincidence"; see 247/1 (*"Saint,* forsooth! While brown Dolores") and 255/1 (for more on this see my 1968 *Denver Quarterly* article, p. 31). For "Dolores, Colo.," see 11/5 and 298/4.

253/9 *Harold Haze:* Lolita's deceased father.

253/10 *Donald Quix:* this pseudonym is appropriate to the Sierras, because they constitute so elevated a target for a windmill-tilter such as Quixote.

253/11 *bodkin:* a stiletto or dagger.

253/12 *Chestnut Lodge:* although H.H. is very sensitive to numerical and verbal "combinations," he is no match for Quilty, who is acute enough to have had miraculous access to H.H.'s previous pages: "Chestnut Lodge" completes H.H.'s cycle of changes on "Chestnut" (see 214/2 and 218/2); the key to the Lodge is held by Nabokov.

253/13 *Ted Hunter, Cane, NH.:* an anagram of "Enchanted Hunter" (see 110/2), it is as expertly done as "Vivian Darkbloom." Quilty's punning allusion to Cain is appropriate and indeed perceptive, since H.H. has just referred to him as his brother (see 249/1).

253/14 *interrelated combinations:* the letters and numerals on the first two license plates offer William Shakespeare's monograms and dates of birth and death (1564–1616). For Shakespeare, see 33/6 and 286/4. The letters on the second set of plates refer to Quilty and his nickname ("Cue"). Less obvious and most literally "cryptogrammic" are the numbers, which add up to a highly significant fifty-two. H.H. and Lolita spent a year on the road—that is, fifty-two weeks—and there are as many lines in the poem addressed to her on pp. 257–258. Ray's Foreword indicates that Lolita, H.H., and Quilty all die in 1952 (see p. 6). There are fifty-two cards in a deck, and the author of *King, Queen, Knave* still has a few up his sleeve, as he demonstrates here.

253/15 *cunningly contrived ... a common denominator:* cunning or not, it *is* revealed, for it is quite impossible that either H.H. or Quilty could realize the full significance of the number fifty-two; only one person can, and the "common denominator" points to the author. The "paper chase" is contrived in the same spirit as Ray's Foreword (see 6/4), the entomological motif (see 8/1), the opening chapter (see 11/1 and 11/6), *Who's Who in the Limelight* (see 34/7 and 36/3), and the Ramsdale class list (see 53/1 and 54/3)—to name only the main clusters and interlacements of Nabokov's grand anthemion. Of course, many of the allusions are within Quilty's reach, and there are plausible explanations for his knowing certain things. But other details are extraordinary, and it is not simply a matter of Quilty's brain having "affinities with my own," as H.H. says (p. 251). How could Quilty know that earlier in these pages H.H. had used *"Kitzler,"* identified *"Aubrey"* as his *"McFate,"* toyed with Chestnuts, alluded to Eryx (and Venus), and quoted "While brown Dolores"? Quilty knows all this—and everything else—because Nabokov wants him to know it, and because Quilty and H.H. can be said to "exist" only insofar as they have been created by the same man. In its concentrated effect, the "paper chase" is to the last part of the novel what *Who's Who* is to the first.

CHAPTER 24

254/1 *garçon:* French; fellow.

255/1 *Bill Brown ... Dolores:* see 247/1 and 253/8. The imbecilic detective has been hired for the benefit of the literal-minded reader, since H.H. himself plainly considers the material "nonsense data." The "information" provides a non-solution that parodies the reader's need for a solution and our belief that either literature or life will ever reveal one, in the largest sense. A hyphen, omitted in 1958, has been added to Bill's age.

CHAPTER 25

255/2 *Dolorès Disparue:* see 34/2. In the first French edition of Proust's great novel, *Albertine disparue* is the next-to-last volume. The definitive Pléiade edition (1954) has restored Proust's own title for it, *La Fugitive* (it is called *The Sweet Cheat Gone* in the Moncrieff translation). See 18/4.

256/1 *daymares:* H.H.'s coinage.

256/2 *chambres garnies:* French; furnished rooms.

256/3 *auctioneered Viennese bric-à-brac:* Freudian trappings, secondhand symbols. See 7/6 and 276/4.

256/4 *que . . . cela:* French; how far away all this was!

256/5 *Comics:* the first two are generalized and invented comic strips.

256/6 *gagoon . . . kiddoid gnomide:* on a visit to Montreux in 1968, I mentioned to Nabokov that I had been unable to identify that "repulsive strip" for this edition. Nabokov could not remember its name, but, expanding upon H.H.'s description, he dated it (the late nineteen-forties), noted that the strip "had science-fiction overtones," and vividly recalled "a big gangster, and his very small, big-eyed, lemur-like dwarf wife wearing a lot of jewelry." Because even that failed to awaken this annotator's memory, the author provided the following drawing:

The question remains unanswered, a challenge to future scholarship. For other comic strip allusions, see 166/1 and 219/5.

Gagoon is a portmanteau of *gag, goon,* and *baboon,* while *gnomide* draws on the common meaning of *gnome* (dwarf) and combines its original meaning (from the Greek: a general maxim, a saying) with the nearly synonymous *bromide* (a tiresome, commonplace person; a hackneyed expression). *Kiddoid* is also H.H.'s coinage. Because the *-oid* suffix (resembling, having the form of) is used in scientific terms formed on Greek words, its incongruous usage here becomes humorous (e.g., *anthropoid;* H.H.'s word is defined as "genus of kid"). See *hypnotoid,* p. 276.

256/7 *Et moi...génie:* "And I was offering you my genius!" A bogus quotation, echoing any French Romantic poet (e.g., Alfred de Musset [1810–1857]).

257/1 *merman:* a fabled marine male creature; the mermaid's counterpart. See 176/5. In *Pale Fire,* Odon, Zemblan actor and patriot, appears in *The Merman,* "a fine old melodrama" (p. 129).

257/2 *losing contact with reality:* for an earlier incarceration, see 36/3.

257/3 *something I composed:* H.H.'s "something" is generally light enough, especially in its humorously blatant rhymes, but its fifty-two lines are truly "composed" in the way they cohere with a larger pattern: the fifty-two weeks H.H. and Lo spend together on the road (August 1947–August 1948), the year of their deaths, and so forth (see 253/14).

257/4 *I cannot...starling:* a quotation from Laurence Sterne's *A Sentimental Journey through France and Italy* (1768). On a visit to Paris, Yorick the narrator takes lightly the infamous Bastille. But his attention is drawn to a caged talking starling: "'I can't get out,' said the starling." He is unable to free the bird, whose constant refrain moves him deeply. It becomes a symbol of all enslavement and confinement, and, returning to his room, he imagines at length a solitary captive in the Bastille. He next explains how the starling was given to him and subsequently changed hands countless times; the reader has perhaps seen the bird, suggests Yorick. From that time, he adds, he has borne the starling as the crest to his coat of arms, which he includes in the text. It bears an uncaged bird (see the Penguin English Library edition [1967], pp. 94–100). The starling that had learned only those "four simple words" is most important because it partakes of *Lolita*'s origin, and its lament is at the book's center. *Lolita*'s initial inspiration, writes Nabokov, was "prompted by a newspaper story about an ape [in the Paris zoo] who, after months of coaxing by a scientist, produced the first drawing ever charcoaled by an animal: this sketch showed the bars of the poor creature's cage" (p.

313). H.H., the "aging ape" writing from prison, whose impossible love metaphorically connects him with that imprisoned animal, learns the language, in his fashion, and records his "imprisonment." His narrative is the "picture" of the bars of the poor creature's cage—and an orchestration of the starling's four simple words.

258/1 *vair:* gray; the pale color of miniver fur.

258/2 *Soleil Vert:* French; Green Sun.

258/3 *L'autre soir ... de ta vie?:* "The other night, a cold *air* [italics mine —A.A.] from the opera forced me to take to my bed; / Broken note— he who puts his trust in it is quite foolish! / It is snowing, the decor collapses, Lolita! / Lolita, what have I done with your life?" The four lines are a splendid parody and pastiche of various kinds of French verse. The alexandrine verse of line one (see 225/1) scans perfectly in French. The *air froid* is an untranslatable pun (*air:* melody; draft or wind). Line two is a traditional saying, originating with Virgil, though it is in fact drawn here from *Le Roi s'amuse* (1832), a play by Victor Hugo:

> *Souvent femme varie,*
> *Bien fol est qui s'y fie!*
> *Une femme souvent*
> *N'est qu'une plume au vent.*

These lines are sung by the King, first in Act IV, scene ii, in a cabaret. The first two lines are repeated from off stage in Act V, scene iii, which informs Triboulet (or Rigoletto) that the King is still alive (he had planned to murder the King, but kills his daughter instead). The play was performed only once before being banned by royal decree. It is the source of Verdi's *Rigoletto* (1851); Piave adapted the words and Verdi was responsible only for the music. The French version, which H.H. undoubtedly knows, is *Rigoletto, ou Le Buffon du prince. Rigoletto* is appropriate, since, figuratively speaking, H.H. is in his own right a grotesque clown. For Hugo, see 12/7. Line three of H.H.'s pastiche is overly sonorous, but the burlesqued entreaty of line four manages to express both the "truth and a caricature of it" (the artistic intention of Fyodor in *The Gift,* p. 212).

259/1 *pederosis:* see 57/2.

CHAPTER 26

260/1 *ensellure:* French; the concave curve formed by the spine; in a woman, the lumbar incurvation.

260/2 *Babylonian blood:* H.H. is very coy in "racial" matters, and enjoys using euphemisms (e.g., "Turk," p. 77) in the manner of the Victorians, with their "Mediterranean types." See 263/4.

260/3 *depraved May:* echo of a well-known line in T.S. Eliot's "Gerontion": "In depraved May, dogwood and chestnut, flowering judas" (line 20). See 18/3.

260/4 *Blake:* after the English poet and engraver William Blake (1757–1827). The invented *Toylestown* is a pun commemorating his "London" (1794)—toil's town.

260/5 *burning . . . Tigermoth:* a play on Blake's "The Tiger" (1794)— "Tiger! Tiger! burning bright"—and a reference to the actual Tigermoth ("an Arctid," notes Nabokov). For entomological allusions, see 8/1.

260/6 *cavalier servant:* a knight who is vassal to his fair lady; a medieval archetype of courtly love.

261/1 *mulberry moth:* writes Nabokov: "Rita's phrase 'Going round and round like a mulberry moth' combines rather pleasingly the 'round and round the mulberry tree' of the maypole song and the silk moth of China which breeds on mulberry." See 8/1.

261/2 *Valechka:* like Ritochka (p. 262), a Russian diminutive.

261/3 *Schlegel . . . Hegel:* Friedrich Schlegel (1772–1829) and Georg Wilhelm Friedrich Hegel (1770–1831), the German philosophers, form a nonsense rhyme.

261/4 *shams and shamans:* H.H. enjoys the fact that while shamans (conjurers, witch doctors) may be shams, the semantic similarities are also illusory; the former is Anglo-Saxon in origin, the latter Tungusic and Sanskritic. *Columbine* (two lines above in the text) was misspelled in the 1958 edition (*o* instead of *u*); it has been corrected.

261/5 *ancilla:* accessory, aid; literally, in Latin, "maidservant."

261/6 *Tartary:* from *Tartarus,* the infernal regions of mythology; any region, usually in European Russia and Asia, inhabited by the violent Tatar (or Tartar) tribes or hordes, who are mostly Turkic. The Tartar empire is restored in *Ada's* Antiterra.

262/1 *Mnemosyne:* in Greek mythology, a Titaness, daughter of Uranus and Gaea. She is associated with memory or remembrance. The nine Muses resulted from her union with Zeus. In the Foreword to the revised *Speak, Memory*, Nabokov says, "I had planned to entitle the British edition *Speak, Mnemosyne* but was told that 'little old ladies would not want to ask for a book whose title they could not pronounce.' "

262/2 *Cantrip . . . Mimir:* a cantrip is a charm or spell, while Mimir is a giant in Norse mythology who lived by the well at the root of Yggdrasill, the great tree symbolizing the universe. By drinking its water, he knew the past and future.

262/3 *travaux:* French; works.

263/1 *très digne:* French; very dignified.

263/2 *souvenir . . . veux-tu?:* "memory, memory, what do you want of me?" The opening line (minus *"l'automne,"* the last word) of "Nevermore" (title in English), by Paul Verlaine (1844–1896). H.H. begins his next sentence with that last word. Memories awakened by The Enchanted Hunters bring this line to mind. Verlaine's poem ends with the poet telling his beloved that his most perfect day was when she charmingly murmured *"Le premier* oui"—her first yes (see also *Keys,* p. 33). For further Verlaine allusions, see 266/2 and 280/1. In *Pale Fire,* Kinbote recalls a visit to Nice, and "an old bearded bum . . . who stood like a statue of Verlaine with an unfastidious sea gull perched in profile on his matted hair" (p. 170). Ada and Van Veen are touched by "the long sobs of the violins," the opening lines of Verlaine's *Chanson d'automne* (1866), translated and quietly absorbed into the text of *Ada* (p. 411). Van's "assassin pun" (p. 541) puns on *"la Pointe assassine,"* line seventeen of Verlaine's *Art poétique* (1882). "Verlaine had been also a teacher somewhere / In England. And what about Baudelaire, / Alone in his Belgian hell?" writes Nabokov in "Exile," an uncollected poem (*The New Yorker,* October 24, 1942, p. 26). For Baudelaire, see 164/2.

263/3 *petite . . . accroupie:* nymphet crouching.

263/4 *spaniel . . . baptized:* the old lady's dog, with which Lolita had played (119/3). H.H. wonders if the hotel's policy of "NO DOGS" had been broken to accommodate Christian dogs, because "NEAR CHURCHES" was commonly used (c. 1940–1960) as a code sign, a discreet indication that only Gentiles were accepted. A similar *quid pro quo* occurs in the same hotel when "Humbert" is misunderstood and distorted into a Jewish-sounding "Humberg" (p. 120), just as "Professor Hamburg" now finds the hotel full. "Refugee" H.H. is often mistaken for a Jew; see p. 81, where John Farlow is on the point of making an anti-Semitic remark and is interrupted by sensitive Jean. Quilty thinks H.H. may be a "German refugee," and reminds him, "This is a Gentile's house, you know" (299/2).

Nabokov's father was an outspoken foe of anti-Semitism. He wrote "The Blood Bath of Kishinev," a famous protest against the 1903 pogrom, and was fined by the Tsarist government for the fiery articles he wrote about the Beiliss trial (Maurice Samuel mentions him several times in his book on the Beiliss case, *Blood Accusation* [1966]—coincidentally published at the same time as Bernard Malamud's novel based on it, *The Fixer*—and quotes from Nabokov's reportage). Nabokov *fils* is also outraged by anti-Semitism, and, because his wife is Jewish, is sensitive to it in a most acutely personal way (witness the empathy for "poor Irving" [55/3]). Nabokov recalls going into a New England inn several years ago, accompanied by his son and his son's friend. Opening the menu, Nabokov noticed therein the succinct stipulation "Gentiles Only." He called over the waitress and asked her what the management would do if there appeared at the door that very moment a bearded and berobed man, leading a mule bearing his pregnant wife, all of them dusty and tired from a long journey. "What . . . what are you talking about?" the waitress stammered. "I am talking about Jesus Christ!" exclaimed Nabokov, as he pointed to the phrase in question, rose from the table, and led his party from the restaurant. "My son was very proud of me," says Nabokov. In *Pale Fire*, Kinbote and Shade discuss prejudice at length (note to line 470; pp. 216–218).

264/1 *Reader! Bruder!:* German; "brother." An echo of the last line of *Au Lecteur*, the prefatory poem in Baudelaire's *Les Fleurs du mal* (1857): *"—Hypocrite lecteur,—mon semblable,—mon frère!"* ("Hypocrite reader—my fellow man—my brother."). See 164/2.

264/2 *the Gazette's . . . Dr. Braddock and his group:* see p. 129. *Gazette* was not italicized in the 1958 edition; the error has been corrected.

264/3 *portrait . . . as a . . . brute:* an obvious play on Joyce's *A Portrait of the Artist as a Young Man* (1916). In searching for a title for his manuscript, the narrator of *Despair* considers "Portrait of the Artist in a Mirror," but rejects it as "too jejune, too *à la mode*" (p. 211). For Joyce, see 6/11.

264/4 *Brute Force:* the actual title of a movie released by Universal Pictures in 1947, directed by Jules Dassin, and starring Burt Lancaster, Charles Bickford, and Yvonne De Carlo. *Possessed* was released in 1947 by Warner Brothers, directed by Curtis Bernhardt, and starring Joan Crawford, Van Heflin, and Raymond Massey.

264/5 *Omen Faustum:* Latin; Lucky Omen, or Lucky Strike cigarettes (pointed out to me by the philologist and Latinist, Professor F. Colson Robinson), a companion to "Dromes" (p. 71); related to *dies faustus,* "a day of favorable omen," or, specifically, "a day on which Roman religious law permitted secular activities."

264/6 *58 Inchkeith Ave.:* obsolete for "inchworm" (or Looper), the *last* thing that should be used for the name of an avenue, since inchworms (the larvae of certain moths) destroy shade trees. For entomological allusions, see 8/1. Fifty-eight inches was Lolita's height at the outset of the novel (see 11/3).

264/7 *Dark Age:* the author is Quilty; see 33/13. *Dark Age* was not italicized in the 1958 edition. The misprint has been corrected.

264/8 *Wine, wine . . . for roses:* see 129/1. Quilty is toying with lines from the sixth stanza of Edward FitzGerald's translation of *The Rubáiyát* (1879), by Omar Khayyám (d. 1123?), Persian poet and mathematician:

> And David's lips are locked; but in divine
> High-piping Pehlevi, with "Wine! Wine! Wine!
> Red Wine!"—the Nightingale cries to the Rose
> That sallow cheek of hers to incarnadine.

The latter word was used earlier by H.H. (see 75/1), demonstrating once more that "the tone of [Quilty's] brain had affinities with my own" (p. 251).

265/1 *nothing of myself:* see 129/2; but Quilty's "spectral shoulder" has been immortalized. For a summary of allusions to Quilty, see 33/9.

265/2 *vin triste:* French; melancholy intoxication.

265/3 *Why blue:* when I asked Nabokov "why blue?" and whether it had anything to do with the butterflies commonly known as the "Blues," he replied: "What Rita does not understand is that a white surface, the chalk of that hotel, does look blue in a wash of light and shade on a vivid fall day, amid red foliage. H.H. is merely paying a tribute to French impressionist painters. He notes an optical miracle as E.B. White does somewhere when referring to the divine combination of 'red barn and blue snow.' It is the shock of color, not an intellectual blueprint or the shadow of a hobby . . . I was really born a landscape painter." See 223/2.

CHAPTER 27

266/1 *Alice-in-Wonderland:* for Lewis Carroll, see 133/1.

266/2 *Mes fenêtres:* French; "My windows," a mock title that parallels *Mes Hôpitaux* ("My Hospitals" [1892]) by Paul Verlaine, and in general parodies the traditional use of the possessive in autobiographical writing. See 263/2.

266/3 *"Savez...de vous?":* French; "Do you know that, when she was ten, my little daughter was madly in love with you?"

266/4 *Proustianized and Procrusteanized:* from *Procrustean;* violently forced into conformity or inflexibly adapted to a system or idea. Procrustes was the legendary robber who made his victims fit a certain bed by stretching or cutting off their legs. Proust is also alluded to on pp. 18, 184, and 255. Similar wordplay occurs in *Ada* when Van Veen discusses Space and Time: "avoid the Proustian bed and the assassin pun" (p. 541); the latter phrase is also an allusion to Verlaine (see 263/2).

266/5 *late:* a corrected author's error (instead of "early" in the 1958 edition).

267/1 *tankard:* a tall, one-handled drinking vessel with a lid.

267/2 *Never will Emma rally...timely tear:* a reference to *Madame Bovary,* Part III, Chapter Eight, where Homais the pharmacist and Emma's two physicians, Bovary and Carnivet, frantically try to save her life. They summon the very distinguished Dr. Larivière, but he cannot do anything for her ("He was the Third Doctor," adds Nabokov, "but that fairy tale Third did not work" [see 33/3]). Old Roualt, Emma's father ("Flaubert's father," because the author said "Emma Bovary? *c'est moi!*"), arrives after she has died; his subsequent tears are not too "timely" (III, Chapter Nine). See 147/3.

268/1 *honeymonsoon:* a portmanteau; *honeymoon* plus *monsoon,* the periodic wind and rainy season of Southern Asia.

268/2 *them:* Lolita and her kidnaper.

CHAPTER 28

269/1 *Pas tout à fait:* French; not quite.

270/1 *handkerchief . . . from my sleeve:* an English fad of the 'twenties and 'thirties. Affected rarely today, even among the pseudo-sophisticated.

270/2 *Ah-ah-ah:* simply the sound of a three-folding "harmonica" door.

270/3 *Dick Skiller:* a phonetic rendering of the pronunciation of "Schiller," and a blending of "Dick's killer" and the street name.

270/4 *Hunter Road:* a streamlined Enchanted Hunters; see 110/2.

CHAPTER 29

271/1 *Personne . . . Repersonne:* French; a humorous alliteration; "Nobody. I re-rang the bell. Re-nobody."

272/1 *russet Venus:* "The Birth of Venus"; see 66/3 and 276/1.

274/1 *Waterproof:* see 91/2; Jean Farlow almost mentions Clare Quilty's name as the chapter concludes. For further discussion, see my 1967 *Wisconsin Studies* article, *op. cit.*, pp. 232–233, included in the Introduction, p. lxvii ff. For allusions to Quilty, see 33/9.

274/2 *everything fell into order . . . the pattern of branches . . . the satisfaction of logical recognition:* this passage, and the novel's crystalline progression, are prefigured in *The Defense* (1930) when Nabokov describes the two books with which chessplayer Luzhin

> had fallen in love for his whole life, holding them in his memory as if under a magnifying glass, and experiencing them so intensely that twenty years later, when he read them over again, he saw only a dryish paraphrase, an abridged edition, as if they had been outdistanced by the unrepeatable, immortal image that he had retained. But it was not a thirst for distant peregrinations that forced him to follow on the heels of Phileas Fogg, nor was it a boyish inclination for mysterious adventures that drew him to that house on Baker Street, where the lanky detective with the hawk profile, having given himself an injection of cocaine, would dreamily play the violin. Only much later did he clarify in his own mind what it was that had thrilled him so about these two books; it was that exact and relentlessly unfolding pattern: Phileas, the dummy in the top hat, wending his complex elegant way with its justifiable sacrifices, now on an elephant bought for a million, now on a ship of which half has to be burned for fuel; and Sherlock endowing logic with the glamour of a daydream, Sherlock composing a monograph on the ash of all known sorts of cigars and with this ash as with a talisman progress-

ing through a crystal labyrinth of possible deductions to the one radiant conclusion. [pp. 33–34]

For more on Holmes, see 66/1.

274/3 *valetudinarian:* a person having a sick or weakly constitution.

274/4 *visited with his uncle . . . Mother's club:* see 80/1.

275/1 *sidetrack . . . female:* see 211/2.

275/2 *frileux:* chilly; susceptible of cold.

276/1 *Florentine:* Botticelli's Venus (p. 272).

276/2 *French . . . Dorset yokel . . . Austrian tailor:* the "salad of racial genes" mentioned on pp. 11 and 12, where a Swiss and "Danubian" dash is added. "I have carefully kept Russians out if it," notes Nabokov, "though I think his first wife had some Russian blood mixed with Polish." Similarly, there are very few specific allusions to Russian writers in *Lolita.*

276/3 *beast's lair:* Quilty.

276/4 *Viennese medicine man:* Freud. See 7/6.

276/5 *hypnotoid:* a variant of "hypnoid," of or pertaining to hypnosis.

277/1 *Streng verboten:* German; strictly forbidden.

277/2 *like her mother:* "Lolita's smoking manners were those of her mother," emphasizes Nabokov. "I remember being very pleased with that little vision when composing it."

277/3 *Cue:* Quilty's nickname; see 6/9.

278/1 *Curious coincidence:* "Camp Q" (p. 66). It's no "coincidence" at all; someone in the know has planned it this way.

278/2 *Duk Duk:* an obscene Oriental word for copulation, sometimes rendered in English as *dak* or *dok,* from the Persian *dakk* (vice, evil condition) and *dokhtan* (to pierce). No less "an amateur of sex lore" (p. 252) than Quilty, H.H. gleaned this from a sixteenth-century work, *The Perfumed Garden of the Cheikh Nefzaoui, a Manual of Arabian Erotology* (1886), translated by Sir Richard Burton (1821–1890), the British explorer and Orientalist (the treatise is mentioned by name in *Ada,* pp. 351–352). Such recondite material reminds one of *Lolita's* reputation, among non-readers, as a "pornographic novel," and also underscores how Nabokov has had the last laugh, in more ways than one. In *Speak,*

Memory, Nabokov writes about the "delusive opening moves, false scents, [and] specious lines of play" which characterize the chess problem. The subject matter of *Lolita* is in itself a bravura and "delusive opening move"—a withdrawn promise of pornography (see 5/1). The first one hundred or so pages of *Lolita* are often erotic—Lolita on H.H.'s lap, for instance—but starting with the seduction scene, Nabokov withholds explicit sexual descriptions, while H.H., trying to draw the reader into the vortex of the parody, exhorts us to "Imagine me: I shall not exist if you do not imagine me" (p. 131). "I am not concerned with so-called 'sex' at all," H.H. says (p. 136); Nabokov, on the contrary, is very much concerned with it, but with the reader's expectations rather than H.H.'s machinations.

"Anybody can imagine those elements of animality," he says, and yet a great many readers wished that he had done it for them—enough to have kept *Lolita* at the top of the best-seller list for almost a year, although librarians reported that many readers never finished the novel. The critics and remedial readers who complain that the second half of *Lolita* is less interesting are not aware of the possible significance of their admission. Their desire for highbrow pornography is "doubled" in Clare Quilty, whose main hobby is making pornographic films. When Lolita tells H.H. that Quilty forced her to star in one of his unspeakable "sexcapades," more than one voyeuristic reader has unconsciously wished that Quilty had been the narrator, his unseen movie the novel. But the novel's "habit of metamorphosis" is consistent, for the erotica which seemed to be there and turned out not to be was in fact present all along, most modestly; and it is Nabokov's final joke on the subject, achieved at the expense of the very common reader. Although the requisite "copulation of clichés" (p. 314) doesn't occur in the novel proper, its substratum reveals some racy stuff indeed: "Duk Duk"; "Undinist" (252/3); "Dr. Kitzler, Eryx, Miss." (252/11); the quotations in French from Ronsard and Belleau (49/2 and 49/3); anagrammatic obscenities (197/2), and so forth—erotica under lock and key, buried deep in the library stacks. Until now, only a few furtive "amateur[s] of sex lore," law-abiding linguists, and quiet scholars—good family men, all—have had exclusive access to this realm.

278/3 *redhaired guy:* see p. 236.

278/4 *Sade's . . . start: Justine, or, The Misfortunes of Virtue* (1791), by the Marquis de Sade (1740–1814), "French soldier and pervert" (as *Webster's Second* defines him). Like *Lolita, Justine* is prefaced by a Foreword resolutely "moral" in tone (in some editions, however, these initial paragraphs are not formally identified as a "Foreword"). The title character is an extraordinarily resilient young girl who exists solely for the pleasures of an infinite succession of sadistic libertines. She undergoes an array of rapes, beatings, and tortures as monstrously imaginative as they are frequent. Quilty has done a screenplay of *Justine* (300/3).

279/1 *souffler:* to "blow."

279/2 *my Lolita:* the "Latin" tag (see 47/1 and 194/2) appropriately concludes this important paragraph (p. 280), as it will the entire novel (311/3).

279/3 *dreaming ... of ... 2020* A.D.: "2020" because he has perfect prevision; also a numerical reflection of the doubling that occurs throughout the novel (see 53/2).

280/1 *mon ... radieux:* "my great radiant sin," a line from Verlaine's *Lunes* ("Moons"), part of the sequence titled *Laeti et errabundi,* in which the poet celebrates his liaison and travels with Rimbaud. For Rimbaud, see 77/6, 165/6, and 252/7; for more on Verlaine, 263/2.

280/2 *Changeons ... séparés:* "Let's change [our] life, my Carmen, let us go live in some place where we shall never be separated"; from Mérimée (see 245/4)—José and Carmen's next-to-last interview. He has romantically offered America as the place where they will be able "to lead a quiet life." H.H. is more specific in matters of geography. For Mérimée, see 47/3.

280/3 *And we shall live happily ever after:* H.H. holds out to Lolita the possibility of a stereotyped fairy-tale ending, even though the tale seems already to have ended in "Elphinstone" (240/1). For more on the fairy tale, see 33/3.

280/4 *Carmen ... moi:* "Carmen, do you want to come with me?" A quotation from Mérimée; a most dramatic moment at the end of the novella (see also *Keys,* p. 51). Carmen *does* go with José, but after they ride off she says that she will never live with him again, and will only follow him to death. A tearful imploration fails, and he kills her.

281/1 *mon petit cadeau:* French; my little gift, the little something. His "4000 bucks" in 1952 meant a great deal more than in today's money. "For some odd reason," says Nabokov, "this paragraph, top of p. 281, is the most pathetic in the whole book; stings the canthus, or should sting it."

282/1 *fly to Jupiter:* they are going to Juneau, but to H.H. it might as well be the planet. Jupiter is veiled by haze, and Lolita dies in "Gray Star, a settlement in the remotest Northwest" (see 6/8).

282/2 *Carmencita . . . -je:* "my little Carmen [in Spanish], I asked her"; another quotation from Mérimée.

282/3 *fool thing a reader . . . suppose:* especially the learned reader who has kept *Carmen* in mind. The several *Carmen* allusions on nearby pages serve as very fresh bait. See 47/3. See also *Keys,* p. 52.

282/4 *my American . . . dead love:* "One of the few real, lyrical, heartfelt outbursts on H.H.'s part," says Nabokov.

CHAPTER 30

283/1 *pulled on . . . sweater:* H.H. dons Quilty's fate, as it were.

284/1 *genuflexion lubricity:* worshipful lasciviousness or lewdness.

284/2 *he:* Quilty. For allusions to him, see 33/9.

284/3 *shadowgraphs:* see 116/2.

CHAPTER 31

285/1 *lithophanic: lithophane* is porcelain impressed with figures made distinct by light (e.g., a lampshade).

285/2 *To quote an old poet:* he is invented.

CHAPTER 32

286/1 *a garden and . . . a palace gate:* one of those rare moments when H.H. is "so tired of being cynical" (p. 111). He contemplates the hidden beauties of Lolita's soul, and the mood prefigures his realization of Lolita's loss, expressed on p. 310.

286/2 *stippled Hopkins:* Gerard Manley Hopkins (1844–1889), English poet. *Stippled:* dotted (see 45/1). Its use refers to Hopkins' "Pied Beauty" (1877): "Glory be to God for dappled things— . . . / For rose-moles all in stipple upon trout that swim."

286/3 *shorn baudelaire:* H.H. is referring to what might be called the poet's dramatic baldness. In the self-portrait c. 1860 and in Carjat's photograph of 1863, his hair seems to have been torn from the head; and the sculpture by Raymond Duchamp Villon (1911) and the etched portrait by his brother Jacques Villon (1920) accentuate the great forehead and cranium. See 164/2.

286/4 *God or Shakespeare:* an echo of Stephen Dedalus' invocation of "God, the sun, Shakespeare," in the Nighttown section of *Ulysses* (1961 Random House edition, p. 505). For Joyce, see 6/11. "The verbal poetical texture of Shakespeare is the greatest the world has known, and is immensely superior to the structure of his plays as plays," says Nabokov. "With Shakespeare it is the metaphor that is the thing, not the play" (*Wisconsin Studies* interview). Although the problem has not yet been submitted to a computer, Shakespeare would seem to be the writer Nabokov invokes most frequently in his novels in English. Part of Chapter Ten of *The Real Life of Sebastian Knight* and all of Chapter Seven of *Bend Sinister* are devoted to Shakespeare; he informs the center of *Pale Fire,* where streets of the Zemblan capital city are named Coriolanus Lane and Timon Alley. "Help me, Will," calls John Shade, searching for a title for his poem—and he does help, providing a passage from *Timon of Athens.* Nabokov has translated into Russian Shakespeare's Sonnets XVII and XXVII (*The Rudder,* September 18, 1927), two excerpts from *Hamlet* (Act IV, scene vii, and Act V, scene i [*The Rudder,* October 19, 1930]), and Hamlet's most famous soliloquy (Act III, scene i [*The Rudder,* November 23, 1930]). Regarding *Hamlet,* see 33/6.

286/5 *pentapod:* counting as fifth the monster's "foot of engorged brawn" (p. 285).

286/6 *turpid: rare;* foul, disgraceful.

286/7 *mais...t'aimais:* French; but I loved you, I loved you!

287/1 *azure-barred:* the motel's neon lights reaching their bed from the window.

287/2 *Avis:* Avis Byrd: a pun, since "Avis" is Latin for *bird.*

289/1 *above Moulinet:* in the Alpes-Maritimes.

CHAPTER 33

289/2 *scintillas:* sparks.

289/3 *Bonzhur:* (*bonjour*) "good day," phonetically spelled to mimic Charlotte's poor French accent; see 46/1.

289/4 *Edward Grammar...had just been arrayed:* an actual crime, notes Nabokov, drawn from a newspaper, as was the case of Frank LaSalle on p. 291. By saying that Ed had been *arrayed,* instead of *arraigned,* H.H. punningly describes the imposing display.

290/1 *Turgenev:* Ivan Turgenev (1818–1883), Russian writer. H.H. is al-

luding to the sonata of love that pours out the window near the end of his novel *A Nest of Gentlefolk* (1859).

290/2 *plashed: to plash* is to form a wave so convex that it splashes over (maritime term).

291/1 *Murphy-Fantasia:* the marriage of Lolita's classmate Stella Fantasia (p. 54). Note the verbal play on "moon-faced" and "stellar [Stella] care" (see also *Keys,* p. 8). See 26/3 for more stellar play.

291/2 *mille grâces:* French; a thousand affectations.

292/1 *vient de:* French; just (for the immediate past).

292/2 *"Réveillez-vous ... mourir":* French; "Wake-up, Laqueue [*La Que:* Cue; Quilty], it is now time to die!" A fake quotation, significant only for its reference to Quilty. The image of his residence in H.H.'s "dark dungeon" was introduced, in a more generalized way, at The Enchanted Hunters hotel (see 127/1).

292/3 *toad of a face:* a favorite pejorative image in Nabokov (see also *Keys,* p. 153n). "Toad" is the boyhood nickname of the dictator in *Bend Sinister.*

293/1 *Dr. Molnar:* the dentist's name aptly contains a molar; it is not, says Nabokov, an allusion to Ferenc Molnár, Hungarian playwright.

293/2 *six hundred:* at that time $600 was a huge sum for dentures.

294/1 *Full Blued:* simply a reference to its finish (p. 218).

Chapter 34

294/2 *Pavor:* Latin; panic, terror. The Manor on Grimm Road burlesques the Gothic castles of fairy tales, Poe's mouldering House of Usher, and the medieval settings in Maeterlinck.

295/1 *penele:* a coined adjective; "penis-like" (*penes* is a plural form).

295/2 *My Lolita!:* the penultimate elegiac "Latin" intonation. See 47/1.

295/3 *selenian:* of or relating to the moon.

295/4 *raised a gun:* a foreshadowing of Quilty's death; an echo of the murder prefiguration in Chapter Two of *Laughter in the Dark.*

CHAPTER 35

295/5 *Insomnia Lodge:* Nabokov's bravura reading of this chapter is not to be missed (Spoken Arts LP 902; Side Two includes seven poems, one in Russian). The recording is especially recommended for classroom use. The nuances of Nabokov's accent—Cambridge by way of old St. Petersburg, the French in perfect pitch—are a striking aural equivalent to the theme of exile in his work and the international nature of that art; and the gusto of his reading communicates vividly a sense of the man, as well as underscoring the comic tone of the novel. Sad experience has suggested that the latter is not always sufficiently appreciated by solemn students who, though they learn quickly, are often not ready enough to laugh at a novel supposedly about perversion.

296/1 *fairy tale:* the fairy-tale opening is appropriate, for this is the most fantastic chapter in the novel, as witnessed by the uncommon velocities and trajectories of the bullets H.H. will fire, and the extraordinary behavior of their target. H.H. inspects three bedrooms because that is the fairy-tale number. For more on the fairy tale, see 18/6, 33/3, and 305/2.

296/2 *deep mirrors:* Quilty literally lives in a house of mirrors, just as H.H. is figuratively imprisoned in one; see 53/2, 121/2, and below, where the mirror is held up to him and he sees a familiar bathrobe. For an index to Quilty's appearances, see 33/9.

296/3 *keys...locks...left hand:* the keys don't work because magic and terror prevail in the special world of Pavor Manor. See 305/2.

296/4 *brief waterfall:* Quilty has once before flushed the toilet thusly; see 132/1.

297/1 *Je suis...Brustère:* "I am Mr. Brewster," spelled in phonetic French.

298/1 *Punch:* the hook-nosed and hunchbacked principal character in the traditional "Punch and Judy" show (see Introduction and 34/7). Used here in the sense of "clown."

298/2 *vaterre:* "water," with a phonetic French spelling; slang for "water closet" (lavatory).

298/3 *Patagonia:* an actual town in Arizona.

298/4 *Dolores, Colo.:* see 11/5 and 253/8.

298/5 *Hell Canyon:* see 159/5.

NOTES FOR PAGES 298–303

298/6 La ... Chair: The Pride of the Flesh, not a noteworthy translation of Proud Flesh, which in French would be Tissu bourgeonnant or Fongosité.

298/7 Wooly-....-are?: a phonetic burlesque of American pronunciation: "Voulez-vous boire?" (French; "Do you want a drink?").

299/1 une femme ... cigarette: "a woman is a woman but a Caporal is a cigarette." Quilty has made nonsense out of "The Betrothed," by Rudyard Kipling (1865–1936): "A million surplus Maggies are willing to bear the yoke / And a woman is only a woman, but a good cigar is a smoke" (see also Keys, p. 136n). The pun is on corporal (military rank) and Caporal (the brand name of a French cigarette).

299/2 a Gentile's house: for a summary of what could be termed "the anti-Semitism theme," see 263/4.

300/1 "Vous ... vieux": French; "You are in a fine mess, my friend."

300/2 "Alors ... -on?": French; "What do we do then?"

300/3 Justine: see 278/4.

301/1 Because ... a sinner: a parody of T.S. Eliot's "Ash Wednesday" (1930): "Because I do not hope to turn again / Because I do not hope / Because I do not hope to turn...." H.H.'s structural use of "Because" in the remainder of the poem echoes Eliot's. For Eliot, see 18/3.

302/1 moulting: animals and insects moult; to cast off hair, feathers, skin, etc., which is replaced by new growth.

302/2 flavid: yellowish or tawny-colored.

303/1 rencontre: French; meeting (duel).

303/2 soyons raisonnables: French; let us be reasonable.

303/3 as the Bard said: in Macbeth (V, vii, 19); and for this pun Quilty deserves to die.

303/4 Vibrissa: one of the stiff, bristly hairs which many animals have about their mouths (a cat's whiskers); also the similar feathers on a bird.

303/5 Schmetterling: German; butterfly. During a conversation with Nabokov, I singled out this moment in the H.H.-Quilty confrontation as a good example of the kind of humorous but telling detail whose significance critics often miss. Nabokov nodded and with complete seriousness said, "Yes. That's the most important phrase in the chapter." At first this may seem to be an extreme statement or leg-pull; but in the context of the involuted patterning it is perfectly just (see 34/7), for by mentioning the German word for *butterfly* Quilty has superimposed the author's watermark on the scene, and it is the sole butterfly reference in the chapter. For Maeterlinck, see 203/5. For the entomological allusions, see 8/1.

304/1 *herculanita:* a very potent South American variety of heroin.

304/2 *Melanie Weiss:* "Black White"; from *melanin* ("black [pigmented]") and the German for "white"—and she does measure reality in black-and-white terms. Her work burlesques the researches of a famous woman anthropologist who also favored far Pacific isles. See 7/3 for the sisterly mirror reversal "Blanche Schwarzmann" ("White Blackman"), a verbal relationship that once again reveals the author's hand.

304/3 *Bagration . . . Barda Sea:* many islands in the Pacific were discovered by Russians, and named by them, but neither of these places exists. The first is after Prince Pëtr Ivanovich Bagration (1765–1812), the Russian General who fought with distinction against Napoleon at Borodino, where he was fatally wounded, in 1812. *Barda* is a vodka-distilling sop given to cattle in Russia. The "geographic" names offer an ironic tribute to Miss Weiss's heroic efforts.

304/4 *Feu:* French; Fire.

304/5 *lmpredictable:* a portmanteau word; *unpredictable* plus *impredicable* (from *predicated*): "incapable of being categorized."

305/1 *a feminine "ah!":* see 47/4 and 89/1.

305/2 *trudging from room to room:* the keys jangling in H.H.'s pocket have not locked the rooms (see 296/3); a fairy tale and nightmare blended.

306/1 *pink bubble:* see 19/1 for the original, figurative bubble.

307/1 *purple heap:* the color of his bathrobe and his prose.

307/2 *staged for me by Quilty:* see 33/8.

CHAPTER 36

308/1 *Thomas had something:* Thomas the Apostle, the "doubting" disciple of John 20:24, who refused to believe in the resurrection of Christ until he himself had touched the nail wounds. Asked if an allusion to

Thomas Mann might also be intended here, Nabokov replied, "The other Tom had nothing."

309/1 *Hegelian synthesis:* the death of Charlotte is remembered here (the killer's car going up the slope; p. 99), blending with the whole story of Lolita, from the cows on the slope (p. 114) to her assumed death (if the reader reads the book, Lolita must be dead; see pp. 6, 282, and 311).

309/2 *fold of the valley:* see Nabokov's comment on this, p. 318.

310/1 *Otto Otto:* queried about this name, Nabokov answered, "a doubled neutrality with something owlish about it."

310/2 *Mesmer:* after Franz *or* Friedrich Mesmer (1734–1815), the Austrian physician who established hypnotism. See 252/10.

310/3 *Lambert:* a step away from Humbert. No literary allusions intended.

310/4 *fifty-six days ago:* in the concluding paragraphs of *Lolita,* H.H. reasserts the verisimilar basis that has been belied everywhere in the preceding pages, linking the last three paragraphs of his manuscript with the first three paragraphs of "editor" John Ray's Foreword, creating an elegant pairing and extraordinary equipoise for which neither H.H. nor Ray is responsible (see 6/4).

311/1 *Do not talk to strangers:* in *Who's Who in the Limelight,* "Quine, Dolores" is said to have made her debut in *Never Talk to Strangers,* and on p. 140 H.H. advises Lolita similarly (see 34/1).

311/2 *Aurochs:* The European bison, now virtually extinct, as is this definition, thanks to Webster's 3rd.

311/3 *do not pity C.Q. . . . my Lolita:* "C.Q." is Clare Quilty. H.H.'s tone turns an unfamiliar shade. Although the narrative surface is still intact, the masked narrator does speak in a newly impersonal way. When asked if one is now supposed to "hear" a different voice, as at "the end" of so many of his novels (see Introduction), Nabokov said, "No, I did not mean to introduce a different voice. I did want, however, to convey a constriction of the narrator's sick heart, a warning spasm causing him to abridge names and hasten to conclude his tale before it was too late. I am glad I managed to achieve this remoteness of tone at the end" (*Wisconsin Studies* interview). This "remoteness" is appropriate, for Humbert's love and Nabokov's labors have become one. The final phrase sounds the "Latin" locution that has echoed through the narrative (see 47/1 and 194/2), and the last word of the novel, that fatal constriction, repeats the first: "Lolita." It is a fitting and final symmetry for this Byzantine edifice.

ON A BOOK ENTITLED LOLITA

313/1 *ON . . . ENTITLED LOLITA:* this Afterword was written to accompany the generous excerpts from *Lolita* which appeared in the 1957 edition of *The Anchor Review*, the novel's American debut, made possible mainly by Jason Epstein and the review's editor, Melvin J. Lasky. It was appended to the Putnam's edition in 1958, and has since been included in the twenty-five or so translations.

313/2 *the poor creature's cage:* see 257/4. In *Pale Fire*, Kinbote tells John Shade, "with no Providence the soul must rely on the dust of its husk, on the experience gathered in the course of corporeal confinement, and cling childishly to small-town principles, local by-laws, and a personality consisting mainly of the shadows of its own prison bars" (pp. 226–227). Writing about Sirin—himself—in *Conclusive Evidence* (1951), in a sentence omitted from the second edition (*Speak, Memory*), Nabokov says, "His best works are those in which he condemns his people to the solitary confinement of their souls" (p. 217). Nabokov has employed the prison trope in many ways. See my Introduction, pp. xx–xxi and lii.

313/3 *best . . . are not translated:* this of course is no longer true.

314/1 *destroyed it . . . after . . . 1940:* nor is this true. The story, entitled "The Magician," unexpectedly turned up among his papers in 1964, a fifty-four-page typescript rather than the thirty pages of memory. Two passages were made available to Andrew Field for use in his study *Nabokov: His Life in Art* (Boston, 1967). They are quoted in the Introduction, p. xxxvii ff. Nabokov informs me that he will never publish this reclaimed story.

314/2 *The book developed slowly:* its design and order of events, however, were clearly in mind early in its composition, says Nabokov, although various sections were written well out of sequence, as is customary with him. See Introduction, p. xxxix.

314/3 *"reality" (one of the few words which mean nothing without quotes):* in *Ada*, Nabokov writes, "It would not be sufficient to say that in his love-making with Ada [Van] discovered the pang, the *ogon'*, the agony of supreme 'reality.' Reality, better say, lost the quotes it wore like claws . . ." (pp. 219–220).

316/1 *America:* a corrected misprint ("American" in the 1958 edition).

317/1 *Palearctic ... Nearctic:* one of the four world faunal regions, the *Holarctic* (arctic and temperate zones), is subdivided into *Palearctic* (Europe and Asia) and *Nearctic* (North America). The "suburban lawn" and "mountain meadow" above are open country for a lepidopterist, notes Diana Butler in "Lolita Lepidoptera," *New World Writing 16,* p. 61. See 8/1 for a summary of all the entomological allusions.

318/1 *spring of 1955:* a corrected author's error (instead of "winter of 1954" in the 1958 edition).

318/2 *Mr. Taxovich:* Maximovich, the ex–White Russian colonel reduced to driving a taxi, is totally infatuated with H.H.'s first wife, Valeria. H.H. graciously lets her go. See pp. 30–32.

318/3 *class list of Ramsdale School:* it is most notable for the way it mirrors the artist who created it (see 53/1 ff.), and for "Flashman, Irving," who suffers quietly, the only Jew in a class of Gentiles. (see 55/3).

318/4 *"waterproof":* When Jean Farlow notices that H.H. has gone swimming with his watch on, Charlotte reassures her, and dreamily relishes a miracle of modern technology: " 'Waterproof,' said Charlotte softly, making a fish mouth" (see p. 91). The word is also the clue H.H. uses to torment the reader who strains to learn the identity of Lolita's abductor (see 274/1), and one is thus reminded that *Lolita* is a very special kind of detective story (see 11/2).

318/5 *in slow motion ... Humbert's gifts:* Lolita is remembered as an illusory creature in a dream, rather than as the object of H.H.'s lust (see p. 122), and the allusion to his gifts recalls his desperate bribery as well as its results.

318/6 *the pictures ... of Gaston Godin:* furtive love is invoked; like the artists whose portraits dominate his garret, Gaston is clearly homosexual. See 183/4.

318/7 *the Kasbeam barber:* he talks of his son, dead for thirty years, as though he were still alive (see p. 215).

318/8 *Lolita playing tennis:* if ever H.H. succeeds in "fix[ing] once for all the perilous magic of nymphets" (p. 136), it is in this scene (see pp. 234–236).

318/9 *the hospital at Elphinstone ... irretrievable Dolly Schiller dying in Gray Star:* Nabokov is referring to Lolita by her married name (see p. 6). Twin deaths are recorded: Lolita "dies" for H.H. when Quilty steals her from the hospital (pp. 240–249) and "dies" for Nabokov when the book is completed, and her image is irretrievable. But Lolita does not die *in* the book; as H.H. says, "I wish this memoir to be published only when Lolita is no longer alive" (p. 310). Her creator points beyond the novel's fictive time into the future, for he would agree with H.H.'s closing statement that art "is the only immortality you and I may share, my Lolita." It is important to note that none of these "secret points" is exclusively sexual. Rather, the images and characters all formulate varying states of isolation, loss, obsession, and ecstasy which generalize H.H.'s consuming passion; the concluding "co-ordinate," after all, places in their midst the author, butterfly net firmly in hand.

318/10 *tinkling sounds...Lycaeides sublivens Nabokov:* the final "co-ordinates" form a most interesting progression. The last "nerve of the novel" is in fact outside the novel and extends from the lepidopterist to the nympholept, who almost seem to bypass one another on the same trail. H.H. also experiences a most pleasing unity of sounds coming from a valley town (pp. 309–310); and the butterfly in question was captured by Nabokov near Dolores, Colorado (see 11/5 and 298/4). Nabokov comments: "This Coloradian member of the subgenus *Lycaeides* (which I now place in the genus *Plebejus*, a grouping corresponding exactly in scope to my former concept of *Plebejinae*) was described by me as a subspecies of Tutt's '*argyrognomon*' (now known as *idas* L.), but is, in my present opinion, a distinct species." See 8/1.

318/11 *My private tragedy...my natural idiom:* the narrator of *The Real Life of Sebastian Knight* (Nabokov's first novel in English) says something very similar about Knight:

> I know, I know as definitely as I know we had the same father, I know Sebastian's Russian was better and more natural to him than his English. I quite believe that by not speaking Russian for five years he may have forced himself into thinking he had forgotten it. But a language is a live physical thing which cannot be so easily dismissed. It should moreover be remembered that five years before his first book—that is, at the time he left Russia,—his English was as thin as mine. I have improved mine artificially years later (by dint of hard study abroad); he tried to let his thrive naturally in its own surroundings. It did thrive wonderfully but still I maintain that had he started to write in Russian, those particular linguistic throes would have been spared him. Let me add that I have in my possession a letter written by him not long before his death. And that short letter is couched in a Russian purer and richer than his English ever was, no matter what beauty of expression he attained in his books. [pp. 84–85]

Nabokov's "private tragedy" *is* our concern, for in varying degrees it involves us all. Nabokov's search for the language adequate to *Lolita* is H.H.'s search for the language that will reach Lolita; and it is a representative search, a heightened emblem of all of our attempts to communicate. " 'A penny for your thoughts,' I said, and she stretched out her palm at once" (p. 210). It is the almost insuperable distance between those thoughts and that palm which Nabokov has measured so accurately and so movingly in *Lolita*: the distance between people, the distance separating love from love-making, mirage from reality—the desperate extent of all human need and desire. "I have only words to play with," says H.H., and only words can bridge the gulf suggested by Lolita's palm. H.H. has failed once—"She would mail her vulnerability in trite brashness and boredom, whereas I use[d] for my desperately detached comments an artificial tone of voice that set my own teeth on edge" (p. 286)—but it is a necessary act of love to try, and perhaps Nabokov succeeds with the reader where H.H. failed with Lolita.

319/1 *frac-tails:* Nabokov wittily demonstrates that the "native illusionist" is now an internationalist: *frac* is French for "dress coat." It is just that Nabokov (and this edition) should conclude with a joke, however small, for, from behind "the bars of the poor creature's cage" (p. 313), desperate Humbert also exults. In *Gogol*, Nabokov notes how "one likes to recall that the difference between the comic side of things, and their cosmic side, depends upon one sibilant" (p. 142), a juxtaposition implicit in the early title, *Laughter in the Dark*. The title goes two ways: it records the laughter of the cosmic joker who has made a pawn of Albinus, blinding and tormenting him, but it also summarizes Nabokov's response to life, his course for survival. Toward the end of *Lolita*, the sick and despairing Humbert has finally tracked down Lolita, who is now the pregnant Mrs. Richard Schiller. He recalls how he rang the doorbell, ready to kill Dick. The bell seems to vibrate through his whole exhausted system, but suddenly Humbert takes his automatic French response to the sound and playfully twists it into verbal nonsense: *"Personne. Je resonne. Repersonne.* From what depth this re-nonsense?" he wonders (p. 271). It sounds from the depths of Vladimir Nabokov's profoundly humane comic vision, and the gusto of Humbert's narration, his punning language, his abundant delight in digressions, parodies, and games all attest to a comic vision that overrides the circumscribing sadness, absurdity, and terror of everyday life.

War, Peace, and
All That Jazz

W9-BSM-968

A H I S T O R Y O F U S

BOOK ONE   The First Americans

BOOK TWO   Making Thirteen Colonies

BOOK THREE   From Colonies to Country

BOOK FOUR   The New Nation

BOOK FIVE   Liberty for All?

BOOK SIX   War, Terrible War

BOOK SEVEN   Reconstruction and Reform

BOOK EIGHT   An Age of Extremes

BOOK NINE   War, Peace, and All That Jazz

BOOK TEN   All the People

BOOK ELEVEN   Sourcebook

The picture on the cover is a watercolor by Dwight Shepler, called Fighter Scramble—Guadalcanal. *The battle of Guadalcanal was the turning point in the Allies' Pacific campaign against Japan during World War II. The scene shows the fight for Henderson Field, the battle's main objective. When the Japanese attacked from the air, American Marine and Navy pilots would return to the airfield's Fighter Strip One for fuel and ammunition. They often took off three abreast in great clouds of dust as they returned to the fighting. (For more about this great battle and the war in the Pacific, turn to chapter 34.)*

Dwight Shepler was born in 1905 in Massachusetts and studied at Williams College and the Boston Museum School. In 1942 he joined the U.S. Naval Reserve. He was one of the first artists assigned to the Navy's Combat Art Section. Guadalcanal was only one of many important battles Shepler witnessed. After Guadalcanal, he was transferred to Europe, where he painted the Normandy invasion. He then returned to the Pacific to document the battles for the Philippines and Okinawa. In 1971 he published An Artist's Horizons, *which tells the story of his life and career—you might find it in your local public library.*

Oxford University Press

In these books you will find explorers, farmers, cow-boys, heroes, villains, inventors, presidents, poets, pirates, artists, slaves, teachers, revolutionaries, priests, musicians— the girls and boys, men and women, who all became Americans....

A History of Us

BOOK NINE

War, Peace, and All That Jazz

Joy Hakim

Oxford University Press
New York

Oxford University Press

Oxford   New York

Athens Auckland Bangkok Bogotá Buenos Aires Calcutta
Cape Town Chennai Dar es Salaam Delhi Florence Hong Kong Istanbul
Karachi Kuala Lumpur Madrid Melbourne Mexico City Mumbai
Nairobi Paris São Paulo Singapore Taipei Tokyo Toronto Warsaw

and associated companies in
Berlin   Ibadan

Copyright © 1995, 1999 by Joy Hakim

Maps copyright © 1995, 1999 by Wendy Frost and Elspeth Leacock
Additional maps and illustrations for the second edition copyright © 1999 by Wendy Frost
First edition produced by American Historical Publications

Second Edition

Published by Oxford University Press, Inc.,
198 Madison Avenue, New York, New York 10016
Oxford is a registered trademark of Oxford University Press

*All rights reserved. No part of this publication may be reproduced, stored in a retrieval system, or transmitted,
in any form or by any means, electronic, mechanical, photocopying, recording, or otherwise,
without the prior permission of Oxford University Press.*

Library of Congress Cataloging-in-Publication Data

Hakim, Joy.
War, peace, and all that jazz / Joy Hakim—2nd ed.
p.   cm.—(A history of US; bk. 9)
Includes bibliographical references and index.
Summary: Covers the period of American history from 1917 to 1945.

ISBN 0-19-512773-0 (set hardcover)—ISBN 0-19-512774-9 (set paperback)
ISBN 0-19-512767-6 (book 9 hardcover; alk. paper)—ISBN 0-19-512768-4 (book 9 paperback; alk. paper)

1. United States—History—1901–1953—Juvenile literature.
[1. United States—History—1901–1953.]
I. Title. II. Series: Hakim, Joy. A History of US (1999); bk. 9.
E178.3.H22 1999 vol. 9   [E741]   973 s—dc21   [973.91]   98-40437   CIP   AC

*The illustrations used herein were drawn from many sources, including commercial photographic archives and the holdings of major museums and
cultural institutions. The publisher has made every effort to identify proprietors of copyright, to secure permission to reprint materials protected by
copyright, and to make appropriate acknowledgments of sources and proprietary rights. Sources of all illustrations and notices of copyright are
given in the picture credits at the end of the volume. Please notify the publisher if oversights or errors are discovered.*

EDITORIAL AND PRODUCTION STAFF

PRODUCT MANAGER: Kathleen De Boer
PROJECT EDITOR: Christopher Caines
LINE EDITOR: Tamara Glenny
PROOFREADER: S. P. de Terre
INDEXERS: Catherine Fox, Terry Cagle
EDITORIAL ASSISTANT: Sara Courtney
ILLUSTRATIONS EDITOR: Jody Sperling
ILLUSTRATIONS RESEARCHER: Mary Blair Dunton (first edition)
ILLUSTRATIONS DATABASE DESIGNER: Ursula Bollini
BOOK DESIGNERS: Mervyn E. Clay (first edition),
Paul Lavenhar and Louanne Stebor, The Horizon Group (second edition)
COVER DESIGNER: Greg Wozny
CARTOGRAPHER AND ILLUSTRATOR: Wendy Frost

5 7 9 8 6
Printed in the United States of America on acid-free paper

"What happens to a dream deferred?" (page 7) is by Langston Hughes. Copyright © 1951 by Alfred A. Knopf, Inc.. Reprinted by permission of Alfred A. Knopf, Inc. The poem
by Ogden Nash on page 7 is reprinted by permission of Little, Brown, Inc. The passage on page 15 is from *A Girl from Yamhill* by Beverly Cleary. Copyright © 1988 by Beverly
Cleary. Reprinted by permission of Morrow Junior Books, a division of William Morrow, Inc. The excerpt on page 56 from *Having Our Say: The Delany Sisters' First Hundred
Years* by Sarah and A. Elizabeth Delany with Amy Hill Hearth is reprinted with permission of Kodansha America, Inc. Copyright © 1993 by Amy Hill Hearth, Sarah Louise
Delany and Annie Elizabeth Delany. The passage on page 69 is reprinted with permission of Scribner's, an imprint of Simon & Schuster, from *The Spirit of St. Louis* by Charles
A. Lindbergh. Copyright © 1953 by Charles Scribner's Sons; copyright renewed © 1981 by Anne Morrow Lindbergh. The passage on page 116 is from *Night* by Elie Wiesel.
Copyright © 1960 by MacGibbon & Kee, renewed © 1988 by the Collins Publishing Group. Reprinted by permission of Hill & Wang, a division of Farrar, Straus & Giroux, Inc.
The passage on page 147 is from *Farewell to Manzanar* by James D. and Jeanne Wakatsuki Houston. Copyright © 1973 by James D. Houston. Reprinted by permission of
Houghton Mifflin Co. All rights reserved. Ernie Pyle's column "The Death of Captain Waskow" on page 158 is reprinted by permission of the Scripps Howard Foundation.

THIS BOOK IS FOR THE TWO BEST TEACHERS I'VE EVER KNOWN:
IDA GINSBURG FRISCH AND JOHN MICHAEL FRISCH

IDA GINSBURG FRISCH, who played on the first girls' basketball team in Glens Falls, New York, was a flapper who bobbed her long hair and wore a coat with a mink collar.

She was hardly beyond her teens when she won an automobile for selling more subscriptions to the GLENS FALLS POST-DISPATCH than anyone else in town. (Having a car was unusual when she was a girl.) She didn't know how to drive, but a license and instructions came with the car, so she convinced her sister, Libbie, to get in with her, and the two of them took off for Saratoga. Fifty years later, Libbie still remembered that drive. "I didn't think I'd live through it," she said.

When Ida died, in her eighties, she was the youngest person I knew. She never stopped surprising me with her wit and vitality and curiosity. "What will happen if we try this?" "Or that?" "And let's see for ourselves." I couldn't keep up with her. She was my mother.

JOHN MICHAEL FRISCH—"Jack" to those who knew him—was shy and courtly and had strawberry-blond hair. He came to this country at age three, from Zhitomir in Ukraine, the son of poor Jewish immigrants. Soon there were two sisters. Before Jack finished school, his father had died and Jack had to support the family.

Photographs from the Roaring Twenties show him as a dandy who went to Broadway openings and wore spats on his shoes. I knew him later, when he sat in a big chair, read newspapers and books, thought about things, and knew the answer to any question my schoolbooks asked.

He always said exactly what he meant, and everyone understood that he was a man who could never be unkind or untruthful.

He taught me to love ideas and words and to listen to the music in language. Besides that, he could do magic tricks and stand on his head. He was my father.

Contents

Babe Ruth in an eBULLient mood

	PREFACE: Time Travelers	9
1	War's End	13
2	Fourteen Points	16
3	Another Kind of War	21
4	The Prohibition Amendment	25
5	Mom, Did You Vote?	29
6	Red Scare	34
7	Soft-Hearted Harding	37
8	Silent Cal and the Roaring Twenties	41
	FEATURE: MONKEYS ON TRIAL	44
9	Everyone's Hero	47
10	Only the Ball Was White	51
11	American Music	55
	FEATURE: RHAPSODIES IN RED, WHITE, AND BLUE	60
	FEATURE: HOORAY FOR HOLLYWOOD!	62
12	Space's Pioneer	63
13	The Lone Eagle	67
14	The Prosperity Balloon	72
15	Getting Rich Quickly	74
16	Down and Out	79
17	Economic Disaster	84
18	A Boy Who Loved History	88
19	How About This?	90
20	A Lonely Little Girl	93
21	First Lady of the World	95
22	Handicap or Character Builder?	97
23	Candidate Roosevelt	100
24	President Roosevelt	102

25 Twentieth-Century Monsters   **107**

26 A Final Solution   **112**

    FEATURE: ARRIVAL IN AUSCHWITZ   **116**

27 War and the Scientists   **120**

28 Fighting Wolves   **122**

29 Pearl Harbor   **125**

30 Taking Sides   **130**

31 World War   **135**

32 A Two-Front War   **139**

33 Forgetting the Constitution   **144**

34 A Hot Island   **149**

35 Axing the Axis   **154**

    FEATURE: THE END OF THE ROAD   **158**

36 Going for D-Day   **159**

37 A Wartime Diary   **164**

38 April in Georgia   **167**

39 President HST   **170**

40 A Final Journey   **172**

41 Day by Day   **176**

42 A Little Boy   **180**

43 Peace   **184**

44 Picturing History   **186**

    CHRONOLOGY OF EVENTS   **198**

    MORE BOOKS TO READ   **200**

    PICTURE CREDITS   **202**

    INDEX   **204**

    A NOTE FROM THE AUTHOR   **208**

FDR reports to Congress following the Yalta Conference, March 1945.

We Americans today—all of us—we are characters in the living book of democracy. But we are also its author. It falls upon us now to say whether the chapters that are to come will tell a story of retreat or a story of continued advance.

—FRANKLIN DELANO ROOSEVELT, 1940

One thing about the past,
It is likely to last.
Some of it is horrid and some sublime,
And there is more of it all the time.

—OGDEN NASH

What happens to a
   dream deferred?
Does it dry up
   like a raisin in the sun?
Or fester like a sore—
And then run?
Does it stink like rotten
   meat?
Or crust and sugar over—
   like a syrupy sweet?
Maybe it just sags
   like a heavy load.
Or does it explode?

—LANGSTON HUGHES

"A shack for negroes only at Belle Glade, Florida," April 1945

My hair!! how the wind blows.

ROCKET LINE.

PREFACE
Time Travelers

Benjamin Franklin looking serious and scholarly when he was ambassador to France, around 1780

Thomas Jefferson

James Madison

George Washington

How about climbing into a time capsule with me? You can set the ship's dial back a bit more than two centuries—to 1789. We're on our way to pick up some old friends: Benjamin Franklin, Thomas Jefferson, James Madison, and George Washington. Let's show them what is happening to the government they worked so hard to found. They called that government an "experiment"; they'll be curious to know how the experiment turned out.

Do you see them there, looking just as they did when we were with them last? You might want to help Ben climb on board; his gout is bothering him. Now, set the dial at 1917, which is a good year to begin this trip in time. Do you wonder what the Founding Fathers will think of these United States? Will they be startled by what they see?

Well, we've put old Ben in Philadelphia, and there he is—right where you would expect him to be—trying out a telephone. We'll never get him away from the new gadgets. Look at him now! Ben's dancing a jig, he's so excited about electric lights. You can't blame him; after all, it was his experiments with electricity that helped that branch of science get started.

But what about George Washington, Thomas Jefferson, and James Madison? We set them down in Washington, D.C. What do they think of the American government? Are they pleased? Are they surprised?

Yes, they are pleased—and not too surprised. The government is running much as they planned it. Power is divided between the states and the federal government. That federal government (in

9

Jefferson lost the competition to design the U.S. Capitol (*above*). Washington laid its first stone in 1793.

By the 1930s the radio was an important piece of furniture.

Washington, D.C.) hardly seems to touch most people's lives. It is only through the post office that it reaches the average citizen. The Founders learn that a just-approved amendment to the Constitution will allow Congress to impose an income tax. James Madison says that will certainly make Americans more aware of the government in Washington.

Jefferson is pleased that most Americans still live on farms or in very small towns—it is the way he meant America to be. And he is delighted with the elegance and beauty of the capital city. (You remember that he helped with its planning.) He says that Pierre L'Enfant's plan for the city seems to have turned out splendidly.

George Washington likes the president, Woodrow Wilson. After all, Wilson is a Virginian, and dignified, and a scholarly man. They all sit down together and discuss politics and philosophy.

Now that our friends have started this journey through time, they can't wait to go on. So let's capsule on—to 1990.

Watch Ben Franklin! He may get run over. His head is in the sky looking at high buildings and airplanes. Wait until he hears a radio. And sees

TV! "Astounding how healthy everyone seems," says Ben when he finally looks down. "Doesn't anyone suffer from the gout?"

"Have you ever seen smiles like these?" asks George Washington, pointing at some boys and girls with nice white teeth.

But look at Thomas Jefferson. He's acting strangely. Someone is telling him about all the century's wars. Someone is telling him about the huge federal and state governments. About the giant American military forces—army, navy, air force, and marines. Someone is telling him that most Americans live in big cities, not on farms. Jefferson looks ill.

Someone is telling George Washington about presidents who have thousands of people working on their staffs. Washington says it sounds kinglike. He calls it "an imperial presidency." So do other people.

The Founding Fathers say this isn't what they intended for the United States. They didn't want standing armies. They didn't want big government. They hate bureaucracies. Ben groans. "It seems like the cumbersome government of George III," he says.

Someone explains that it was all those 20th-century wars—and a depression, too—that made big government necessary. Actually, it began with that man they liked so much, President Woodrow Wilson. He needed to fight a war; things had to be done quickly; so he asked Congress for special powers, war powers.

Well, once one president had started things, it got easier to ask again, and again. First the presidents, then Congress, then the Supreme Court—all got stronger and stronger. The governments closest to the people—the state and local governments—began to depend on the federal government more and more.

Besides, that big government does many good things. It makes sure our food is safe and pure. It regulates banks so people can leave their money and not worry. It enforces laws to

In the 20th century America became an urban nation—a nation of cities. Cities don't have lakes and creeks, so these children in 1930s Harlem, New York, cooled off the city way: under the sprinkler.

Monticello *(above)* is the only residence in the United States on the United Nations' World Heritage list. (The Taj Mahal is on the same list. Do you know what and where that is?) If you can, plan to visit Monticello—you can tour its rooms and gardens. And, while you're in the area, check out Mr. Jefferson's university, too.

see that working people get fair wages and fair opportunities. The federal government even provides money for hot lunches for schoolchildren.

Some experts are trying to explain that to Jefferson, Madison, and Washington. After all, this is a modern world. The United States is huge; it has many citizens; it has enormous cities. The Founders' ideas were fine in the 18th century, and the 19th, too, but things are different today. Wait a minute—some of those experts are arguing. Not everyone agrees. Watch out. The experts may start fighting.

Jefferson and Madison are looking better. They are getting very interested in the 20th century, although they are a bit homesick for their own times. Well, we can jet them home—to Philadelphia, Mount Vernon, Monticello, and Montpelier. That makes them feel just fine. Their houses are still there, much as they left them.

Back in the nation's capital, the Founding Fathers are curious about all the well-dressed people on the streets. A guide tells them that these people have come from places like China, Cuba, Ethiopia, Russia, Pakistan, and Chile—and that all are now American citizens. "What a country!" says George Washington. "What a century!" says Tom Jefferson. "A fascinating time," says Jemmy Madison.

"But how about our ideas and our Constitution? Can a political order fashioned for a nation of independent farmers work in a world of cities and high technology?" Jefferson is asking Ben Franklin. "That," says the old philosopher, "is the question this society must answer for itself."

1 War's End

Calamity Jane was one of the huge heavy-artillery guns that fired a final fusillade at 10:59 A.M. on November 11, 1918.

In Europe, in 1918, on the 11th hour of the 11th day of the 11th month, it suddenly became quiet. The cannons were still. For the first time since 1914, men could hear each other without shouting. The Great War—soon to be known as World War I—was over.

It had been a horrible war. Nine million men died. It was not fought soldier against soldier, like medieval battles of knights in armor. The new weapons of killing—machine guns, tanks, long-range artillery, grenades, and poison gas—led to mass slaughter. "War," wrote one soldier, "is nothing but murder."

But now the guns were silent; the dying was finished.

In Washington, D.C., even though it was six o'clock in the morning, America's 28th president, Woodrow Wilson, was up and at his desk. Because he was considerate, and feared his clackety typewriter would wake his wife and staff, he sat and wrote these words with a pen on White House stationery:

> *Everything for which America has fought has been accomplished. It will now be our fortunate duty to assist by example, by sober, friendly counsel, and by material aid, in the establishment of just democracy throughout the world.*

They were the words of a high-minded leader. The slim, frail, bookish man had proved to be a great war president. In amazingly fast order he had

No one could buy his way out of service in World War I (unlike the Civil War). And for the first time women served officially in the armed forces.

Stretcher bearers carry the wounded from the ruined French town of Vaux, which was captured by the U.S. Army's 2nd Division.

Left: officers of the 129th Field Artillery. Second row, third from right, is a captain named Harry S. Truman. (More about him at the end of this book.) *Right:* Company M, 6th Regiment, greets the Armistice.

turned a peaceful nation into a strong fighting force. The country's factories had gone from making corsets, bicycles, and brooms to production of guns, ships, and uniforms. In just over a year—beginning in April 1917—more than a million American men had been drafted into the army, trained, and sent overseas. And just in time. In Europe the fighting had been going on for three years; both sides were near collapse.

It had been a heartbreaker of a war—awful, dreary, bloody—begun in Europe for selfish reasons. It ended up making nations and people cruel, and bitter, and angry, and it led to another terrible war.

The Central Powers (Germany, Austria-Hungary, and the Turkish Ottoman Empire) were on one side, against the Allies (Britain, France, Russia, Japan, and Italy), with a few other nations involved, too.

The Germans had taken a gamble. Before the United States entered the war, Germany sank neutral American ships carrying food and supplies. American lives were lost. The Germans knew that might bring the United States into

Gee, How They Sang!

Lieutenant Harry G. Rennagel of the 101st Infantry wrote his family:

Nothing quite so electrical in effect as the sudden stop that came at 11 A.M. has ever occurred to me. It was 10:60 precisely and—the roar stopped like a motor car hitting a wall. The resulting quiet was uncanny in comparison. From somewhere far below ground, Germans began to appear. They clambered to parapets and began to shout wildly. They threw their rifles, hats, bandoliers, bayonets, and trench knives toward us. They began to sing. Came one bewhiskered Hun with a concertina and he began goose stepping along the parapet followed in close file by fifty others—all goose stepping.... We kept the boys under restraint as long as we could. Finally the strain was too great. A big Yank named Carter ran out into No Man's Land and planted the Stars and Stripes on a signal pole in the lip of a shell hole. Keasby, a bugler, got out in front and began playing "The Star-Spangled Banner" on a German trumpet he'd found in Thiaucourt. And they sang—Gee, how they sang!

the war. They weren't worried. They thought it would take several years for the United States to get ready to fight. By that time they expected the war in Europe to be over. Most German leaders believed that the American system of government was very slow.

The scholarly, honorable man who was president stunned them. He was stronger than they thought possible. He asked Congress for special war powers; he was able to act quickly.

Woodrow Wilson's greatest strength was his integrity. People trusted him because they knew he was trustworthy. He inspired others. He believed in the American dream—in Jefferson's words about how all people have a right to "life, liberty and the pursuit of happiness." Wilson wanted to see that dream spread around the world. He convinced the people of the United States to go to war without thought of gain for themselves. He made it clear to everyone that America's only goal was "to make the world safe for democracy." He made America's participation in the war seem noble and unselfish.

It was still dark, but on November 11, 1918, the news of war's end was too good to wait for daybreak. Whistles tooted, church bells rang, and sirens blared. Before long the streets across the nation were filled with people cheering, shouting, hugging, and kissing. America had gone to war and the world was going to be a better place because of it, or so it seemed on that Armistice Day.

The morning is chilly. Mother and I wear sweaters as I follow her around the big old house. Suddenly bells begin to ring, the bells of Yamhill [Oregon]'s three churches, and the fire bell. Mother seizes my hand and begins to run, out of the house, down the steps, across the muddy barnyard toward the barn where my father is working. My short legs cannot keep up. I trip, stumble, and fall, tearing holes in the knees of my long brown cotton stockings, skinning my knees.

"You must never, never forget this day as long as you live," Mother tells me as Father comes running out of the barn to meet us.

Years later, I asked Mother what was so important about that day when all the bells in Yamhill rang, the day I was never to forget. She looked at me in astonishment and said, "Why, that was the end of the First World War." I was two years old at the time.

—BEVERLY CLEARY,
A GIRL FROM YAMHILL

The New York Times.

"All the News That's Fit to Print"   THE WEATHER

VOL. LXVIII...NO. 22,266.   NEW YORK, MONDAY, NOVEMBER 11, 1918.—TWENTY-FOUR PAGES.   TWO CENTS

ARMISTICE SIGNED, END OF THE WAR! BERLIN SEIZED BY REVOLUTIONISTS; NEW CHANCELLOR BEGS FOR ORDER; OUSTED KAISER FLEES TO HOLLAND

Armistice Day, New York City. "The...crowds," said one observer, "rarely raised a cheer....It was enough to walk...with 10,000 strangers, and to realize in that moment of good news not one of them was really a stranger."

15

2 Fourteen Points

President Wilson in London with King George V. Wilson stayed in Buckingham Palace, which was freezing (due to wartime coal shortages). The king gave him a small electric heater—it didn't help much.

I can predict with absolute certainty that within another generation there will be another world war if the nations of the world do not concert the method by which to prevent it.

—WOODROW WILSON, ON A 1919 SPEAKING TOUR

Clemenceau thought that Wilson was going too far with his Fourteen Points. He said, "The good Lord had only ten" (meaning the Ten Commandments).

The innocent, optimistic, sure-of-itself 19th century didn't actually end in America until the First World War began. The real start of the 20th century came in 1917. No question about it, the war changed things. It changed people. They began to question old ideas that had never been questioned before. Hardly anyone seemed sure of anything.

Except Woodrow Wilson. He was like an old-time Puritan, convinced of God's grace and very sure of himself. Wilson would do everything possible to lead his nation and the world on a path of righteousness. His father had been a minister; he had the preacher's genes. He spoke eloquently and told the world how to behave. Unfortunately, some people don't like being told what to do—even if the teller is right.

Before the war ended Woodrow Wilson came up with "Fourteen Points" on which the peace was to be based. Wilson didn't believe in revenge; he believed in the power of kindness. He said he wanted "peace without victory." Now that was a startling statement in a nation that had cheered Ulysses Grant when he called for "unconditional surrender." But Woodrow Wilson had grown up in the defeated South. He knew about the hatreds that can come after a war. He didn't think an enemy needed to be shamed, or made poor. He intended to lead the world toward a generous and lasting peace.

Wilson's Fourteen Points may have been the most forgiving peace plan ever. Under the Fourteen Points, people all over the world were to determine their own fate—by vote. It was called "self-determination." Self-determination was to end the old imperialist system that let winning nations grasp foreign colonies. The Fourteen Points also called for:

- *free trade (that means no tariffs)*
- *an end to secret pacts between nations*
- *freedom of the seas*
- *arms reduction*
- *the forming of a world organization—a League of Nations*

Wilson expected that league to guarantee freedom to all the world's peoples and keep the peace between nations.

Leaflets describing the Fourteen Points were dropped over Germany from those new vehicles that had been used, for the first time, as instruments of war: wood-framed airplanes. The German people—who were tired of the war and close to rebellion—read the leaflets, hoped for peace, and soon forced their ruler, the Kaiser (KY-zer), to flee the country.

With the war over, Wilson set off for Europe, the first American president ever to do so while in office. He wanted America to lead the world to a just peace, and he wanted to be the peacemaker. The European people were wild with admiration for Woodrow Wilson. They greeted him with flowers and cheers. They called him the savior of the world.

Too bad he went, say some historians. Others say it would have been worse if he'd stayed at home. Everyone agrees: Wilson didn't get what he wanted. Perhaps because of that, the Great War, which was called the "war to end wars," didn't end anything. It turned out to be World War I. Another world war—which was much worse—followed 21 years later.

What went wrong? Why didn't Wilson get his just peace?

Was it because he was too sure of himself?

Wilson's Fourteen Points provided for self-determination of the peoples of Europe. But in fact many of the new national boundaries were decided by the Allied politicians in secret meetings where they drew lines and argued over huge maps.

17

At Versailles: *(above, left to right)* **the Big Four—Lloyd George of Britain, Orlando of Italy, Clemenceau of France, and Wilson;** *(below)* **inside the Hall of Mirrors during the signing of the peace terms, June 28, 1919. "England and France," wrote Wilson, "have not the same views with regard to the peace by any means."**

Or because he didn't worry enough about jealous politicians, at home and in Europe? Was it the tragedy of his health? (Before he left the presidency, he exhausted himself, lost contact with reality, and became unable to fight for his beliefs.) Maybe it was all of those things—and more, too. After four years of war, many Americans seemed to have stopped caring. Most just wanted to get on with their lives; some didn't want to be bothered by ideals; others were disappointed that we hadn't smashed the enemy. Besides, President Wilson's sermons were getting tiresome.

France's crafty old premier (prime minister), Georges Clemenceau (cleh-mon-SO)—who was called "the Tiger"—said, "God gave us his Ten Commandments and we broke them. Wilson gave us his Fourteen Points—we shall see."

What Clemenceau saw was that France did, indeed, want revenge. Germany had invaded France twice within his memory (in 1870 and 1914). Two generations of young Frenchmen were dead. The French countryside was devastated. The French wanted protection and repayment for what they had suffered. They, and England and Italy, wanted—and got—a hard peace. They were angry with Germany.

The peace treaty was signed at a gorgeous French royal palace called Versailles (vair-SY). Some of Wilson's most important points got thrown out of the window at Versailles. Germany was blamed for the whole war and given a huge bill for war costs. The Germans (who had surrendered, in part, because of their faith in the Fourteen Points) felt betrayed. But the idea that meant most to Wilson—the League of Nations—was saved. He believed that the League would right the wrongs of the Old World order.

And it might have done so, if the nation that was now the most important power in the world had joined the League. (What nation could that be?)

American treaties with foreign powers must be agreed to by two-thirds of the members of the Senate—a simple majority won't do. At first, most Americans believed in the League of Nations. But there were strong senators who hated Wilson. Some were Republicans who were anxious to win the next election; they thought that a triumph for Wilson would hurt their party's chances.

When Wilson went to Europe he brought many advisers with him; they were either professors or Democrats. None were prominent Republicans. That wasn't wise or generous on Wilson's part. Some Republican senators began to fight the idea of the League. Many Americans, Democrats as well as Republicans, worried about America getting involved in Europe's problems.

Woodrow Wilson knew that the problems of any one part of the globe were now the problems of all peoples. America could not hide from world responsibility. So the president decided to do what he did best: explain things to the American people. That had worked for him before. But, in those days before radio and TV, it meant getting on a train and giving speeches. Wilson crossed the country; he gave three or four speeches a day talking about the importance of the League of Nations.

Above: signing the peace treaty. Wilson wanted "open covenants of peace, openly arrived at." He did not get them.

Wilson underestimated Republican opposition to the League of Nations—and ordinary Americans' lack of interest in it. With Congress against him, he took his treaty to the people. But he failed to drum up enough enthusiasm.

Senator Henry Cabot Lodge of Massachusetts led Republican opposition to the League.

It was too much for his health. Wilson had been working hard. In Paris he had been ill and had acted strangely. In Pueblo, Colorado, he was so sick he could not finish his speech. Then he had a stroke. He was never the same again.

Those who opposed the League in the Senate were now able to defeat it. The United States did not join the League of Nations. You can imagine how Woodrow Wilson felt. He believed that without a strong league to enforce peace, there might be another war—and that it would be much worse than the Great War. "What the Germans used were toys compared to what would be used in the next war," he said.

But we didn't listen. The United States embarked on a period of "isolation." We tried to stay away from the rest of the world and its concerns. We would learn that could no longer be done. Like it or not, the United States was now a world leader.

Justice Oliver Wendell Holmes, Jr.

In 1917 Congress passed an Espionage Act. In 1918 it passed a Sedition Act. (*Espionage* is spying; *sedition* means "inciting others to rebel.") Those acts were meant to ban speech that might harm the war effort.

The First Amendment guarantees free speech. Were these acts unconstitutional? Or do things change in wartime? Clearly, war demands national unity.

No Clear and Present Danger

When some anarchists threw 5,000 anti-war leaflets from a New York hat factory, and were arrested and convicted, the case was appealed all the way to the Supreme Court. (The pamphlets called for a strike by weapons makers.)

The court upheld (agreed with) the convictions, but two justices—Louis D. Brandeis and Oliver Wendell Holmes, Jr.—disagreed. Justice Holmes's dissent has become more famous and more often cited than the majority opinion. He said that speech may be punished only if it presents "a clear and present danger" of producing evils that the Constitution tries to prevent. "Now nobody can suppose that the surreptitious publishing of a silly leaflet…would present any immediate danger." His opinion was that "the defendants were deprived of their rights under the Constitution of the United States." Today, the concept of

clear and present danger is used as a test of whether speech should be censored. Holmes became known as the "Great Dissenter" for this and other strong opinions that were contrary to the majority of the court.

The Supreme Court invites Brandeis to join her ranks while fat cats look on in horror.

3 Another Kind of War

INFLUENZA
FREQUENTLY COMPLICATED WITH
PNEUMONIA
IS PREVALENT AT THIS TIME THROUGHOUT AMERICA.

THIS THEATRE IS CO-OPERATING WITH THE DEPARTMENT OF HEALTH.

YOU MUST DO THE SAME
IF YOU HAVE A COLD AND ARE COUGHING AND
SNEEZING. DO NOT ENTER THIS THEATRE

GO HOME AND GO TO BED UNTIL YOU ARE WELL

Coughing, Sneezing or Spitting Will Not Be
Permitted In The Theatre. In case you
must cough or sneeze, do so in your own hand
kerchief, and if the Coughing or Sneezing
Persists Leave The Theatre At Once.

This Theatre has agreed to co-operate with
the Department Of Health in disseminating
the truth about Influenza, and thus serve
a great educational purpose.

**HELP US TO KEEP CHICAGO THE
HEALTHIEST CITY IN THE WORLD**

JOHN DILL ROBERTSON
COMMISSIONER OF HEALTH

The usual October death rate from influenza and pneumonia was 4,000. In 1918 it was about 194,000.

I had a little bird,
And his name was Enza;
I opened the window,
And in flew Enza.

In flew Enza—say it fast and it becomes "influenza." It was a catchy little rhyme, and boys and girls skipped rope to it. It was also an epidemic; no, it was worse than that. It was a *pandemic*, which means a disease that spreads across many nations. This one went around the globe. And it was deadly.

Diseases don't fly in the window, but the influenza of 1918 almost seemed to. It lasted about nine months, and, worldwide, killed 20 million people. That was more than the total of deaths during the four years of the Great War. Mysteriously, it struck at about the same time in India, and Russia, and China—no major nation escaped. In the United States there were more than half a million victims. On one terrible day in Philadelphia, almost 1,000 people died. Neither doctors, nor hospitals, nor cemeteries could handle the

Returning soldiers, and anybody who didn't wear a mask, could be fined $100 and jailed. *Obey the laws, and wear the gauze, protect your jaws from septic paws*, went one ditty. But the masks were useless.

The word ***influenza*** first appeared in 1743 after an epidemic in Italy. It is an Italian word, related to *influence,* and it means an "intangible visitation" (a visit by something you can't touch). ***Pandemic*** comes from the Greek words *pan* ("all") and *demos* ("people").

A public-health doctor in Washington, D.C., found that the only way he could be sure of having enough room in his emergency hospital was to keep undertakers always waiting outside the door so that the dead could be taken away immediately.

awful burdens put upon them. In those days before the discovery of modern medicines, there was little doctors could do.

In New York and Chicago, laws were passed making it illegal to sneeze or cough in public without using a handkerchief. Police dutifully hauled sneezers and coughers to court, where they were given stiff fines. The police had time to worry about influenza because the robbers and murderers were sick, too. In October 1918, Chicago's crime rate dropped almost by half.

The epidemic spread most rapidly in cities—where people are crowded together—but many in the countryside died, too. A prominent senator lost a son and daughter. Soldiers, fighting heroically against enemies they could see, fell to invisible germs. In America the flu took 10 times as many lives as the war. The last week of October in 1918, 2,700 American soldiers died fighting in Europe; that same week, 21,000 Americans died at home of the flu.

It was called Spanish influenza—because people

Today, scientists believe that the 1918 influenza epidemic may have stopped killing people because of the way the influenza virus behaves. Dr. Michèle Barry, an infectious-diseases specialist at Yale University Medical School, says: "Every year, the influenza virus changes the coat of protein that surrounds it. Some protein coats seem to make the virus weaker or stronger. We think that during the course of the 1918 epidemic, the virus changed its protein coat and became weaker." She adds that it's also possible that after the disease killed off the most vulnerable victims (especially old people), the people who were left were tougher and less likely to die.

New York City's phone company begged people to make only urgent calls—many switchboard operators were hit by flu, too.

22

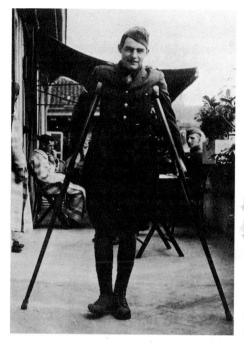

One of the wounded soldiers who came home to find things changing was a young man named Ernest Hemingway *(left),* who was soon writing novels and stories (of war and life between the wars).

If you were sick in 1920, you didn't go to the doctor's office. The doctor came to your house. He brought a black satchel with him. It was stuffed with medical supplies: pills, salves, bandages, and maybe a stethoscope and a thermometer. Those two pieces of equipment were about as high-tech as medicine got. The world of the modern hospital, and sophisticated equipment, was still decades away.

thought it had started in Spain. It hadn't. It may have begun in the United States, from a disease of hogs (it is sometimes called "swine flu," after the hogs). Some say it was the worst pandemic in history. It wasn't that it killed the most people, it was that it killed so rapidly. Someone figured, mathematically, that if it had continued spreading for another year, at the rate it was going, the world's population would have been wiped out.

By Armistice Day, November 11, the peak had passed. The disease soon departed as mysteriously as it had arrived. It left the country exhausted. Wasn't a war trouble enough? Everyone had worked hard supporting the war effort. Americans had done astonishing things in factories and on the farms. They'd fed Europe with an amazing harvest of grain; they'd armed the Allies. Citizens had given up luxuries and even some necessities to help others. That flu epidemic was the final straw. Someone needed to find something to cheer people up.

Soon a new word was being used. It was *normalcy.* That's what people wanted. They wanted to go back to the good old days before the war. But time won't march backward.

Those boys and girls who were skipping rope in 1918 had no idea what was ahead of them. They wouldn't have believed it if you had told them. Normalcy? No way. They were going to live in a world of radio, TV, computers, jets, and rockets. In 1918 that was the stuff of science fiction. Their

From Art to Science

Abraham Flexner, an educator who was asked (by the Carnegie Foundation) to study medical schools in America, inspected each of the country's 155 medical schools, and, in 1910, described them in a study that became very influential. Mostly, he thought American medical schools weren't very good and that they turned out poorly trained physicians. Flexner was especially critical of women's medical colleges (there were 16 of them) and black medical schools (there were 10). Doctors then earned little money and relied chiefly on experience and observation in treating patients. Flexner said that medicine needed to be a science. His report helped make it just that. It also drove most women and minorities from the practice.

world was slow-paced, and mostly powered by horses and mules.

Their older brothers—the soldiers who came home from Europe in 1919—had exciting things to tell them. They'd been to Paris and had seen fancy nightclubs, stunning buildings, and splendid boulevards. Some bragged about their heroism in battle, which was understandable; you had to be tough—or lucky—to be a survivor. A few came home without arms or legs. Some didn't want to talk about the war at all. They, too, were looking for normalcy.

The returning soldiers were surprised to find that America had changed in the year they'd been gone. They noticed two things right away. One had to do with beer and liquor. During the war it was considered unpatriotic to drink alcohol. Beer is made from grain, and grain was needed to feed soldiers. Now that the war was over, many people wanted to put an end to all liquor drinking. It would make the world a much better place, they said.

The other change gave some of the soldiers a chuckle. Imagine, women were demanding equal rights: they wanted to be full citizens. Why, soon they'd probably want to wear pants, too!

The Wild Beasts

Marcel Duchamp's Nude Descending a Staircase; *to some it was an outrage.*

It was a cold winter day in 1913 when the doors opened at an old, drafty armory on 25th Street and Lexington Avenue in New York City, and people got to see some new paintings and sculpture (including many from Europe). American art was never the same again. Some of the paintings in the Armory Show were done by Henri Matisse, Paul Cézanne, Pablo Picasso, Paul Gauguin, and Vincent van Gogh. Today we know them all as great artists, but in 1913 their work was unlike anything most people here had seen before. Matisse was part of a French group called Les Fauves, or "the wild beasts." Many viewers thought it a good title for all the artists.

One painting, by Marcel Duchamp, was called *Nude Descending a Staircase*. Classical paintings often showed naked figures reclining on couches. This painting showed what seemed to be a bunch of sticks—or maybe a figure; it was hard to tell—but something very active *was* happening on the canvas. It was worth a second, and even a third look. Many of the paintings included unrecognizable objects. Before, art had always more or less imitated reality. These paintings were completely different. In Chicago some art students burned effigies (stuffed figures) of Henri Matisse. But many Americans were profoundly changed by the new modernism. The artist Stuart Davis said that the Armory Show was "the greatest single experience…in all my work." He was not alone.

4 The Prohibition Amendment

You couldn't get drier than a camel—it became the symbol of Prohibition party supporters.

The Constitution does not give Congress the right to tell people what they may eat or drink. If someone wants to drink poison, only a state can make laws to try to keep him from doing so.

Many people say that alcohol can be a kind of poison. No one disagrees that drinking too much is harmful.

Drunkenness was a special problem in early America. Most drinking was done in saloons, where women were not admitted. Some men took their pay-

Women's Christian Temperance Union Parade, painted by Ben Shahn around 1934. The ladies of the WCTU campaigned "for God, for home, for native land." But lawmakers found that it was hard to make a crime out of drinking, which many had never seen as a crime before.

checks, went to a saloon, drank up, and then went home drunk, with no money left for their families. Reformers decided to attack the problem. Some of them believed in *temperance,* which means "moderation." Others believed in *prohibition,* which means "outlawing all drinking."

Some women's groups fought for prohibition. Several religious groups—especially Methodists and Baptists—joined the battle. Many states became *dry.* In a dry state it was against state law to buy or sell liquor. Some people wanted to go further. They wanted the whole nation to be dry. A constitutional amendment was needed.

It was the Progressive Era: people thought that laws could help make people perfect—or close to it. It took about 20 years to get the 18th Amendment passed, but finally it was done. The

Prohibition agents got to work disposing of booze. But there were only 1,500 agents, not really enough to enforce the law—especially when they were up against the ruthless gangsters who sold the liquor.

In this painting, *Bootleggers* (1934), Ben Shahn shows three ways to hide alcohol: tie a bottle to your leg, or tie it behind your back, or empty it into a hollow walking stick. In the background two men make whiskey in a homemade still.

Prohibition amendment became law in 1920. The amendment made it illegal to sell liquor anywhere in the United States. Most people thought it a very good idea. All but two states passed the Prohibition amendment.

It didn't work. Many people who wanted to drink kept drinking—although per capita (see page 28) alcohol consumption did fall during Prohibition years.

But some people, especially some

The Constitution of the United States, Article V

The Congress, whenever two thirds of both Houses shall deem it necessary, shall propose Amendments to this Constitution, or, on the Application of the Legislatures of two thirds of the several States, shall call a Convention for proposing Amendments, which, in either Case, shall be valid to all Intents and Purposes, as Part of this Constitution, when ratified by the Legislatures of three fourths of the several States, or by Conventions in three fourths thereof.

What does all that mean? Read it slowly and it isn't as difficult as it may seem. What it means is that the men who wrote the Constitution—James Madison, Gouverneur Morris, Ben Franklin, John Adams, and the others—understood that a constitution needs to be adaptable. The Founding Fathers wanted people in the future—you and me—to be able to change the Constitution. But they didn't want to make it too easy to change. If they did that the Constitution wouldn't have much lasting value: it would get changed all the time.

So they came up with the idea of amendments as a way to change the Constitution. It has been more than 200 years since the Constitution was written; hundreds of amendments have been proposed, but only 26 have been passed.

For an amendment to succeed, two-thirds of the Congress must pass it—that means two-thirds of both the Senate and the House of Representatives. Then three-fourths of the states must also approve the amendment. (The Constitution may also be amended if a constitutional convention is called by three-fourths of the states—that has never been done.)

Remember, we have a federal form of government. Power is shared among the national government in Washington, D.C., and the state governments. The Constitution lists all the things the president, Congress, and the courts can control. Any powers not listed in the Constitution belong to the states.

Per capita (pur-CAP-it-uh) is Latin, and means "by heads" or per person. In other words, the total amount of liquor consumed in the U.S., divided by the number of people in the U.S., showed there was less alcohol drunk during Prohibition than before. But many new kinds of people began drinking; that was the problem.

After the Prohibition amendment was passed, Congress needed to provide for its enforcement. That was done with a law called the Volstead Act. Prohibition didn't make it illegal to drink, or even to buy liquor; it just made it illegal to sell it.

women and young people, who had not drunk before, decided to try it. Prohibition wasn't supposed to do this, but in some crowds it made drinking fashionable. (Maybe it had to do with disillusionment after the war. Writers were calling this a "lost generation." People weren't really lost, but they were confused about right and wrong.)

Since selling liquor was now a crime, gangsters took over that activity. People who sold liquor were called "bootleggers." (Some of them stuck flasks inside high boots.) Ships running whiskey from foreign suppliers to coastal ports were called "rumrunners." Illegal bars, where drinks were sold, were called "speakeasies." (If people spoke loudly, and the police heard them, the bar would be raided. So they spoke "easy.")

No one expected it, but Prohibition made crime a big business in the United States. Americans learned that some kinds of prohibition must be done by persuasion and education. Laws and force don't always work.

Another amendment was needed to get rid of the Prohibition amendment. The 21st Amendment was passed in December 1933. It ended what was a well-meaning experiment. The experiment had failed.

But how do you get people to stop doing something that isn't good for them? Do the lessons of Prohibition apply to drugs? Some people say we should make it legal to buy drugs; then criminals could not earn big money selling drugs. Others say that would encourage people to use drugs. What do you think?

In 1933, the country had more than 200,000 illegal speakeasies. This painting, like those on pages 25, 27, and 35, was made by artist Ben Shahn, who put many of the social and political issues of his time on canvas.

5 Mom, Did You Vote?

In 1915, Alice Paul organized a women's suffrage motorcade that went from San Francisco to Washington, D.C., with a petition 18,000 feet long. It carried half a million names.

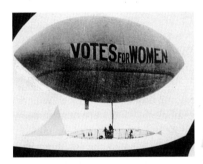

The suffragists had become experts at getting publicity for the cause.

We're heading back in time—just a bit. It is 1917, and some women are marching in front of the White House. They carry a big banner that says 20 MILLION AMERICAN WOMEN ARE NOT SELF-GOVERNED. In Europe, American soldiers are fighting for democracy; these women feel they should fight for it at home.

Day after day, for months, the women march in front of the president's house. They are peaceful and respectful, but persistent. Some people don't like it; they say the suffragists shouldn't annoy the president during wartime. The police tell the women to leave. "Has the law been changed?" asks Alice Paul, leader of the group. "No," says the police officer, "but you must stop."

"We have consulted our lawyers," says Alice Paul. "We have a legal right to picket."

The next day two women, Lucy Burns and Katherine Morey, are arrested. Other arrests soon follow.

On the Fourth of July a congressman speaks to a large crowd gathered behind the White House. "Governments derive their just powers from the consent of the governed," he says. Police keep the crowd orderly and protect the congressman's right to free speech.

Alice Paul went to England and learned tough tactics—chaining oneself to railings, disrupting public meetings—from British suffragists.

This is what we are doing with our banners before the White House, petitioning the most powerful representative of the government, the President of the United States, for a redress of grievances; we are asking him to use his great power to secure the passage of the national suffrage amendment.

—ANNE MARTIN

Dr. W. W. Parker of Richmond, Virginia, wrote an essay that he read to the Medical Society of Virginia. Women, he said, were "superior morally, inferior mentally, to man—not qualified for medicine or law." Then he continued, "God having finished this splendid world, placed at its grand arched gateway imperial man, stately and stalwart, with will and wisdom stamped upon his lofty brow."

At one demonstration outside the White House, men from the crowd tore the suffragists' banners down and pelted the women with eggs, tomatoes, and apples. Twenty-two banners and 14 party flags were destroyed.

Many Americans—men and women—don't bother to be active citizens. Many don't vote. The whole point of a democracy is that it gives everyone power. Those who don't vote give up their power.

Utter Nonsense

When Susan B. Anthony was a girl she asked the schoolmaster one day if she could learn long division with the boys. "Nonsense! Utter nonsense!" he told her. "A girl needs to know how to read her Bible and count her egg money, nothing more." But Susan Anthony was determined. So, slyly, she sat on a bench behind the boys and listened and worked problems and learned long division. Anthony never did what others did, unless she thought it right.

In front of the White House a group of 13 women silently holds a banner with those very same words from the Declaration of Independence. Some are young women, some white-haired grandmothers; all are arrested. The women are taken to court and fined. They refuse to pay their fines—to do so would mean to admit they are guilty. They do not believe themselves guilty of any crime. The police take them to jail. More women are arrested. Anne Martin speaks out in court:

As long as the government and the representatives of the government prefer to send women to jail on petty and technical charges we will go to jail. Persecution has always advanced the cause of justice. The right of American women to work for democracy must be maintained.

More women go to jail. They are separated from each other. Prison conditions are awful. For 17 days Ada Davenport Kendall is given nothing to eat but bread and water. Some women are held in solitary confinement. Some, who go on hunger strikes, are held down and fed against their will. Anne Martin, Lucy Burns, and Elizabeth McShane are force-fed. Burns is bruised on her lips and face; McShane throws up. Now the women have become interested in prison reform, as well as in women's suffrage. One woman writes that it is "necessary to make a stand for the ordinary rights of human beings for all the inmates."

In the White House, Woodrow Wilson has other concerns. He is fighting a war—that war for democracy. Wilson says he isn't against women's suffrage—in fact he is for it—but, like many men, he thinks that most other issues are more important.

The women keep marching. All kinds of women. Rich and poor. Could it be that they understand democracy in a way the president doesn't?

Mrs. John Rogers, Jr., is arrested. She is a descendant of Roger Sherman (a signer of the Declaration of Independence). Like her plain-speaking ancestor, Mrs. Rogers says what she thinks. She tells the judge:

We are not guilty of any offense...we know full well that we stand here because the president of the United States refuses to give liber-

Suffragists parade through New York City in 1913.

The right of citizens of the United States to vote shall not be denied or abridged by the United States or by any state on account of sex.

—19TH AMENDMENT
TO THE CONSTITUTION

31

Mass Meeting
TONIGHT
Ryman Auditorium
8 O'CLOCK
TO SAVE THE SOUTH
FROM THE SUSAN B. ANTHONY AMENDMENT
AND FEDERAL SUFFRAGE FORCE BILLS
Senator Oscar W. Underwood, of Alabama, and Ex-Gov. Ruffin G. Pleasant,
of Louisiana, Have Been Invited to Speak

Many people—women as well as men—fought desperately to block the 19th Amendment. At right, an antisuffrage propaganda poster implies that "emancipated" women abandoned their suffering families to pursue the vote.

Jeanette Rankin

Montana's Jeanette Rankin was the first woman elected to Congress. She served two terms in the House (1917–1919; 1941–1943). Rebecca Latimer Felton, age 87, was the first woman in the Senate. She didn't do much. After a Georgia senator died, she was appointed to fill the vacancy for two days in November 1922.

Rebecca
Latimer Felton

ty to American women. We believe, your honor, that the wrong persons are before the bar in this court....We believe the president is the guilty one and that we are innocent.

Now, isn't that what America is all about? The right of every citizen to speak out—even against the president.

Mrs. Rogers's cause is just, but her comments aren't quite fair. It is Congress that is holding things up, not Woodrow Wilson. But the president hasn't helped. Finally, he does. He urges Congress to pass the 19th Amendment. It is known as the Susan B. Anthony amendment. This battle for women's suffrage is not something new. Susan Anthony and her friend Elizabeth Cady Stanton began the fight in the mid-19th century. They spent their lives fighting for women's rights. So did Carrie Chapman Catt, the head of the National American Woman Suffrage Association.

Many men and women have worked hard for this cause. Most are people you have never even heard

Female Takeover

The perpetrators of Yoncalla's conspiracy of women after their takeover of the town council, with Mayor Mary Burt in the middle.

In 1920, the women of Yoncalla, Oregon, got together and made plans to take over the town government. They didn't tell anyone, not even their brothers or husbands. Men outnumbered women two to one in this community of fewer than 350 persons, but the women all voted. According to *Literary Digest,* they were "stirred by the alleged inefficiency of the municipal officials, and swept every masculine office-holder out of his job." When they went to the polls they elected an all-women's slate of town officials. Mrs. Mary Burt became the new mayor. The out-of-a-job former mayor, a Mr. Laswell, was said to be "much surprised."

Said Mr. Jones in Nineteen-Ten:
"Women, subject yourselves to men."
Nineteen-Eleven heard him quote:
"They rule the world without the vote."
By Nineteen-Twelve, he would submit
"When all the women wanted it."
By Nineteen-Thirteen, looking glum,
He said that it was bound to come.
This year I heard him say with pride:
"No reasons on the other side!"
By Nineteen-Fifteen, he'll insist
He's always been a suffragist.
And what is really stranger, too,
He'll think that what he says is true.

—ALICE DUERR MILLER, "EVOLUTION," IN *ARE WOMEN PEOPLE? A BOOK OF RHYMES FOR SUFFRAGE TIMES,* 1915

Carrie Chapman Catt campaigned all over Tennessee to get the amendment ratified. "The summer heat was endless, and many legislators lived in remote villages," she said. "Yet the women trailed these legislators, by train, by motor, by wagons, on foot...no woman faltered."

about. (See if you can find a history of the women's suffrage movement in your community.) In Tennessee, Harry Burn was 24 and the youngest representative in the legislature when he got a letter from his mother. "Don't forget to be a good boy," wrote his mother, "and help Mrs. Catt put the 'Rat' in ratification."

The Tennessee legislators were trying to decide whether to approve the 19th Amendment or not. Half were for women's suffrage, half were not. Burn held the deciding vote. He followed his mother's advice. It was 1919, and Tennessee was the last state needed to ratify. The next year, 1920, America's women finally went to the polls.

33

6 Red Scare

"Whose country is it anyway?" Uncle Sam takes care of "reds."

Communists were called **reds** after the red flag of the International, which was the worldwide communist organization.

Some people in America were scared by Russia's ideas. They were afraid of *communism*. Others were attracted to those ideas. Under communism, most property and goods belong to the state. People are expected to share. That sounds noble; it just never seems to work unless forced upon people. Communist nations have not been free nations.

After the world war, some people were scared that communists wanted to take over in the United States. There were a few communists in this country—but they were not success-

Russia Revolts

Russia fought with the Allies in World War I until the Russian people decided they'd had enough of the war. It was more important, as far as they were concerned, to solve their own problems. They wanted to get rid of their ruler—the tsar (ZAR). They wanted to end the big gap between rich and poor in Russia. They wanted what Americans had wanted in 1776. They wanted freedom. So they had a freedom revolution.

At first, it looked as if they might get freedom. The people who overthrew the tsar (in 1917) were trying to create a demo-cratic government. Then a revolutionary named Vladimir Lenin, who was living in Europe in exile, came back to Russia. That man changed the fate of Russia and the world. He became dictator of Russia. He didn't believe in democracy.

Things had been bad in Russia when the tsar was ruler. They got much worse under Lenin and the ruler who followed, Joseph Stalin. Lenin and Stalin brought totalitarianism to Russia. They brought repression, murder, state control, and misery. They brought an economic system called communism.

Lenin took Russia out of the war. That let Germany move troops from eastern Europe to France. It made the Great War tougher for the Allies.

What does all this have to do with U.S. history? A lot. You see, the world had become smaller. Not smaller in size, but in accessibility. At the beginning of the 19th century, it took at least two years for a ship to go from Salem, Massachusetts, to China and back. Now, with the telephone, communication was almost instantaneous. Modern technology meant that the ideas of one nation could spread quickly to others.

Left: In September 1920, a bomb exploded on Wall Street, killing 38 people and fueling fears that communists threatened the nation's existence. *Right:* A. Mitchell Palmer, President Wilson's attorney general.

ful. Most American people were not attracted to communism.

In that same postwar time, there were also some *anarchists* in America. Anarchists don't believe in government at all. You don't have to be very smart to realize that anarchy doesn't work. But, when the anarchists looked around and saw poverty, war, and evil, they thought that this was the fault of governments. Some may have really believed that the answer was to do away with all governments. A few tried to do that by setting off bombs intended to kill government leaders. That, of course, was criminal behavior. Newspapers made big headlines of the bombs. Many Americans were frightened. But what A. Mitchell Palmer, President Wilson's attorney general, did was irresponsible and criminal. (He got away with it—but not in the history books.)

Palmer went on a witch hunt. The witches he went after were communists and anarchists. He took the law in his hands, and, in two days of raids in major cities (in 1920), agents invaded homes, clubs, union halls, pool halls, and coffee shops, rounding up nearly 5,000 people, who were held in jail, not allowed to call anyone, and treated terribly. Those without citizenship papers were sent out of the country— to Russia. Most weren't guilty of anything.

Sacco and Vanzetti

Nicola Sacco and Bartolomeo Vanzetti were accused of murdering a paymaster and his guard at a shoe factory in South Braintree, Massachusetts. Did they do it? Even today, no one is sure. But they were convicted and executed. Sacco and Vanzetti were anarchists, and many said it was radical beliefs that were on trial. The trial was a *cause célèbre* (which, in French, means "a famous happening").

Ben Shahn made 23 paintings of the Sacco and Vanzetti case in 1931–1932, including this portrait from their trial.

In 1789, Congress passed an Alien law. It kept certain people from emigrating to the United States. A sedition law made it a crime to speak against the government. People were jailed for their ideas. The people who supported those laws said they wanted to keep "dangerous foreigners" out of the country. At the time, the foreigners they feared were French.

Behind the red scare was a fear of foreigners. These men being taken to prison are all immigrant aliens.

Communists are sometimes called "reds." Mitchell Palmer took advantage of America's fear of communism. He helped create a "red scare." He hoped it would make him president. During the red scare, Americans were not free to speak out about communism. They weren't free to criticize the government. Some people's lives were ruined.

Witch-hunting turns up every once in a while in American history. (It happened at Salem, Massachusetts, in colonial days; it happened after World War II with a senator named Joe McCarthy.) The good thing is, it never seems to last long. Persecution for ideas is not the American way.

The 1st Amendment (part of our Bill of Rights) says: *Congress shall make no law…abridging the freedom of speech.* Does that mean that communists and anarchists are free to speak out here—as long as they do not engage in criminal activity or plot to overthrow the government?

Everywhere reds were under the bed—or, as in this cartoon, slithering under cover of the Stars and Stripes.

Thomas Jefferson wrote: *Truth is great and will prevail if left to herself,* and *errors cease to be dangerous when it is permitted freely to contradict them.* He believed that when everyone's ideas are heard, people will make wise choices. Do you agree with him?

The Ku Klux Klan grew hugely in the 1920s. The Klan no longer limited its hatred and bigotry to blacks; it was anti-foreign, anti-communist, anti-Catholic, anti-Jewish.

7 Soft-Hearted Harding

Harding in 1882, aged 16, when he graduated from college and taught school for a year

The two presidents sat together in the elegant Pierce-Arrow touring car. The car had running boards on its sides, the presidential seal on its door, and no roof.

Both men wore tall black silk hats and fashionable coats with black velvet collars. Woodrow Wilson's face was ash white. He had always been slim; now he seemed shrunken, like a dry reed. It had taken all his energy to walk from the White House door to the automobile. Just two years earlier, Wilson had been the world's hero. Now he was ill and ignored. His country seemed to have no use for him or his ideas, and he knew it.

Sitting next to him was the president-elect. The candidate the people had chosen—enthusiastically—as 29th president: Warren Gamaliel (guh-MAY-lee-ul) Harding. If a movie director were casting a president's part, he might pick Harding. The man *looked* presidential. His hair was silver, his eyebrows black, his skin tanned bronze, his voice golden. He was handsome, well groomed, and distinguished looking. He was also a good-natured, pleasant man.

The Pierce-Arrow pulled up to the Capitol, where Woodrow Wilson signed his last official papers as president. The new vice president, Calvin Coolidge, was sworn into office in the Senate chambers. Then Warren Harding took his place at the center of the grandstand built for his inauguration in front of the Capitol. He put his hand on the Bible and swore to execute the office of president to the best of his ability. He had chosen a line from the Old Testament book of Micah, and he read it in a clear voice amplified by loudspeakers:

A ***running board*** was a long entry step that ran along the side of an automobile.

Florence Harding managed a lot of firsts along with being First Lady. She was the first president's wife to fly in an airplane and the first to hold press conferences for women reporters. She worked, successfully, to found the first rehabilitation penitentiary for women (that's a jail where prisoners are helped to change their criminal behavior rather than just punished for it). And she spoke out for women's equality in sports, schools, employment, and politics.

The scandal in the Harding administration centered on some naval oil reserves, including one at Teapot Dome, near Casper, Wyoming. (Geologists call a swollen upward curve in the earth's surface a "dome.") Congress was concerned that the military services have enough oil in case of emergencies, so it had set aside certain oil-rich areas for government use. Harding had appointed men who gave secret rights to those government oil lands to individuals and private companies that got rich on oil meant for public use.

What doth the Lord require of thee, but to do justly, and to love mercy, and to walk humbly with thy God.

Thanks to Thomas Nast (see *A History of US,* book 8) cartoonists often represent the Republican, or "Grand Old" Party (GOP), as an elephant (and the Democratic party as a donkey). The Teapot Dome scandal got the Republican party elephant into some very hot water.

The Marine band played "America."

After the stormy war years, this low-key, modest inaugural seemed just right. "We must strive for normalcy," said Warren Harding, and the public applauded.

Two years and five months later, Harding was dead, and the nation wept as it had not done since the death of Abraham Lincoln. In his lifetime, Warren Harding was one of the most popular presidents ever.

He is said to have died of heart failure, but perhaps it was of a broken heart. For he knew, before he died, that his friends, whom he trusted with important government jobs, had betrayed him and

The mustachioed men are Interior Secretary Albert Fall *(left)* and Edward Doheny. Doheny bribed Fall to lease the Teapot Dome oil fields.

the nation. They had stolen and plundered. They had given away priceless oil reserves, laughed at the conservationists, and taken bribes from business and criminal interests. They had become very rich.

And what did the American people think when they heard the news? At first they were angry at the senators and journalists who told them. Later, they became angry when they thought about Harding. Before long, historians were calling him the worst of all presidents.

He wasn't the worst. He created the Bureau of the Budget, reduced the national debt, cut taxes, and appointed black men to public office. It's a myth that he didn't work hard (although he did play a lot of poker and golf). But he may not have been tough enough, or smart enough, to handle the presidency. A president has to make hard decisions.

If you are president you need to appoint good people to the cabinet and to thousands of administrative jobs. You need to be a leader of the armed forces. You need to make a huge budget to run the country. You need to come up with ideas for domestic policies that will make the country prosperous and happy. You need to make foreign policies to guide the nation in its relations with other nations. You need to get along with Congress. You need to get along with the states and their governors. You need to be a role model for millions of citizens with differing ideas and desires. Being president is an enormous, complicated job.

Warren Harding, as I said, was a pleasant man, always gracious and considerate. Maybe it was because he was so good-hearted that he wanted to help his old friends. Maybe that's why he put some

Montana Senator Thomas Walsh investigated Teapot Dome. He was harassed by the FBI, which tapped his phones, opened his mail, and made anonymous threats on his life.

Loudspeakers were used at Harding's inauguration for the first time in the event's history.

Lord, Lord, man!" said one of Harding's aides to reporter William Allen White of the *Emporia Gazette.* "You can't know what the president is going through. You see he doesn't understand it; he just doesn't know a thousand things he ought to know. And he realizes his ignorance, and he is afraid. He has no idea where to turn."

Political Advice: Don't Say Yes—or No

Harding was the first president to address the nation over the radio.

Warren Harding, 29th president, was the owner and editor of a newspaper in Marion, Ohio, when he entered politics. He became a senator. In 1920, the Republican National Convention couldn't decide on a candidate—the delegates were deadlocked—so on the 10th ballot the party turned to well-liked, easygoing Senator Harding, and nominated him. During his campaign, Harding wouldn't say if he was for the League of Nations or against it. His opponent, Democrat James M. Cox (also of Ohio), said he was for the League. Cox lost the election.

Under Harding, a cartoonist said, the government had put the whole country up for sale.

of those friends in important jobs. Most weren't qualified for those jobs. Some were crooks who stole a whole lot of money from the nation.

Harding didn't realize it. But he should have. That was his job. A more able president might have saved the country a lot of grief.

Chicken-Bone Specials

Between 1910 and 1920, more than 1 million black people headed north. Working conditions in the South were awful; schools were worse; and most blacks couldn't vote. The North held the hope of better jobs, better schooling, and a chance to get ahead. For a while, the Pennsylvania Railroad offered free passage to blacks who could recruit others to come north. The trains came to be called "chicken-bone specials"; blacks weren't allowed to eat in the dining cars, so they had to bring their own food—usually fried chicken. New York's black population (centered in Harlem) increased by 66 percent in that 10-year period. Chicago's black population (centered in the South Side) increased by 50 percent. That black migration—from field to factory, from rural to urban—continued through most of the century. Jacob Lawrence painted the migration in a series of paintings that are small in size but powerful in impact.

Jacob Lawrence's The Migration of the Negro, Panel No. 1 *(1940–41). "There is absolutely nothing before them on the farm," said a government report on Southern labor, "no prospect...but to continue until they die." Instead, they fled.*

8 Silent Cal and the Roaring Twenties

Coolidge was happy to play the tunes big business wanted to hear—and it was music to the fat cats' ears.

Thrifty, Vermont-born Calvin Coolidge became president when Harding died. He had been an active governor of Massachusetts and, like most Vermonters, he didn't waste words, but he did get a lot done. So most people thought he would be an energetic and decisive chief executive. And he started that way. In his first message to Congress he called for federal laws to punish "the hideous act of lynching," and for more attention to education, minimum wages for women workers, and other progressive measures.

But then something terrible happened. Coolidge's son, 16-year-old Calvin Jr., died of blood poisoning, which developed from a toe blister he had gotten playing tennis. Coolidge was overwhelmed with grief. He couldn't concentrate. He developed an assortment of illnesses, including severe depression. His work suffered.

Still, the times were prosperous, he was popular, and almost no one, besides his wife and close friends, knew what was happening to him. Today, he is mostly remembered as a president who didn't say or do much—but he held more than seven press conferences a month, which was more than Theodore Roosevelt or Woodrow Wilson did before him or Franklin Roosevelt did after him. As for not doing much, that was part of his philosophy. He was against ac-

The first motion picture with synchronized sound, *Don Juan,* opens in 1926 and stars heartthrob John Barrymore. The sound comes from a phonograph record. (Until now, theaters have usually hired a piano player to play along with the films.) The first talking picture, *The Jazz Singer,* starring Al Jolson, opens in 1927.

1927: The United States Supreme Court in *Nixon* v. *Herndon* rules unanimously that a Texas law forbidding blacks to vote in primary elections violates the 14th Amendment and is unconstitutional.

1925: A Caviar Year

It is 1925 and the '20s are roaring! Wyoming elects the first woman governor in U.S. history, Nellie Taylor Ross; *The New Yorker* is introduced as a magazine for "caviar sophisticates... not for the old lady in Dubuque." The first issue costs 15 cents. At Nome, Alaska, dog-team relays bring serum to combat a serious diphtheria epidemic. Born in 1925: Robert F. Kennedy, Rod Steiger, and Malcolm X.

41

The '20s were the age of fad contests. People tried to set records for doing something—anything—the most, the fastest, or the longest. Dance marathons went to extremes. Resting only 15 minutes an hour, couples danced for days, even weeks. The last couple left won a little bit of money and a moment of fame.

"Teaching an old dog new tricks"—won't you Charleston, Charleston with me?

Women wearing bathing suits were measured to see if they were showing too much leg. Here, Chicago police make an arrest for "indecent exposure" in 1922.

tive government. "Perhaps one of the most important accomplishments of my administration has been minding my own business," he said. The argument between active government and stand-aside government continues today. Most Americans at the time thought Coolidge a splendid president.

He had a wry wit—typical of Vermonters. When a woman told him she had bet someone that she could get him to say more than three words to her, he responded, "You lose."

It was the 1920s. Some called the decade the "Roaring Twenties," some called it the "Jazz Age," and some the "Dance Age." Whichever you chose, it seemed like a time of fun and change.

More people had more money than ever before. And, mostly, they were intent on having a good time. Hardly anyone seemed to worry that some people were left out of the prosperity boom.

In 1919, before the '20s began their roar, women's ankles sometimes could be glimpsed beneath long skirts. Those ankles, however, were modestly hidden beneath high-topped shoes. Then skirts started going up, and up, and up.

That made it a tough time to be the parent of a girl. It wasn't easy to be a girl then either. Most young women were cutting their hair—short. They called it "bobbing." Some parents wouldn't allow it. Short hair seemed indecent to the older generation, but up to the minute to those who did it. The girls who weren't allowed to cut their hair felt old-fashioned.

Some daring women were wearing bathing suits that left their legs uncovered. Police arrested women on the beaches for doing that. And makeup! "Nice" women started wearing lipstick, rouge, and powder. The older generation worried. "What is the world coming to?"

Those girls who bobbed their hair and wore short skirts and lipstick were called "flappers." They did other things, too. They drove automobiles, got jobs, went to the movies, read romantic novels, played Ping-Pong, and danced. My, did they dance! It was the big thing in the '20s. And the big dance was the Charleston. (In New York City, Gimbel's department store advertised special Charleston dresses that swung loose on the body. The price was $1.58.) When you danced the Charleston you swung your arms, kicked up your heels, knocked your knees together, and moved frantically.

Frantic is a good word to describe the '20s. The idealism of the Wilson years seemed to have come to nothing. After the war, everything was supposed to be better. But anyone could see that it wasn't. And there was the Prohibition idea. Americans wanted to have a good nation—where all people behaved themselves and didn't get drunk—but that wasn't working either. If you read the newspapers you could see that criminals were becoming rich and powerful selling liquor. So maybe the best thing to do was to forget about ideals and have a good time—frantically—which was what a

In 1927, sculptor Gutzon Borglum, using a steam shovel and dynamite as chisel and mallet, begins carving four gigantic heads (60 feet high) on Mount Rushmore in South Dakota. (Whose heads are they?)

President Coolidge had a dog named Prudence Prim.

By the time Henry Ford brought out his Model A, in 1927, there were 21 million cars in America—and the traffic jam was beginning to be a familiar phenomenon.

lot of Americans did in the '20s.

It was a materialistic age. People concentrated on making money and buying things for themselves. Successful businesspeople became national heroes. There were more rich people than ever before in American history. No one seemed to notice, however, that there were also growing numbers of unemployed people—people who were desperately poor. And many farmers were in terrible trouble.

But for most Americans, the times seemed good. The stock market—like women's hems—went up and up and up. Land values boomed. People were able to buy things they never could buy before. In 1920 the car was a novelty. Ten years later, almost every family had a car. Many Americans who didn't have indoor toilets in their homes had motorcars in their yards. The automobile was becoming a necessity.

Before the war, life had been slow-paced; now change was coming with cyclone speed. Ordinary people owned radios and listened to comedy shows and the nightly news. In Florida, in 1924, a schoolboy named Red Barber heard radio for the first time at a friend's house. Barber was so excited he stayed up most of the night listening to news from around the nation. It was a new experience. "A man...in Pittsburgh said it was snowing there...someone sang in New York...a banjo plunked in Chicago...it was sleeting in New Orleans." (Red Barber later became a radio sports broadcaster.)

Monkeys on Trial

Jesus said, "Ye shall know the truth, and the truth shall make you free." Think about that quote for a minute.

Now here's another one, this from Thomas Jefferson, who helped separate church and state in the United States when he wrote *Truth is great and will prevail if left to herself.* Separating church and state means that the government can't pick a belief for you, make you go to church, or make you pay taxes to support a certain church. (Governments used to do that; some still do.) Put Jefferson's words in your head and then take yourself to the town of Dayton, Tennessee (population about 1,600). It is 1925.

Mule-drawn wagons and old Model Ts are rolling down the dusty roads into Dayton. Hot-dog and soft-drink vendors seem to be on every street corner. More than 100 reporters have arrived in town. So have photographers and motion-picture makers. A telegraph office—with 22 operators—is set up in a grocery store. A bookseller hawks biology texts. Another sells Bibles. Everywhere there are monkeys: monkey postcards, stuffed toy monkeys, and souvenir buttons that say *Your old man is a monkey.* Dayton has never seen so many people. What's going on?

It's a sensational court case; the best-known trial of the decade. Newspaper headlines are calling it the "monkey trial," and readers and radio listeners all over the country (and in other countries, too) can't seem to get enough of it.

A young schoolteacher is on trial because of what he is teaching in his classroom. Actually, it is modern science that is on trial, and separation of church and state. In Tennessee it is illegal to teach the science of evolution. Evolution traces life on earth through millions of years of development from simple one-celled creatures to increasingly complex plants and animals to humans. (Since apes and monkeys are a stage below us on the evolutionary ladder, jokesters have come up with the monkey label for the trial.)

Most fundamentalist Christians have a problem with evolution. They believe in the exact words of the Bible, and the Bible says that the world was created in six days and that Adam and Eve—humans—were part of the Creation from the very beginning. This is a disturbing issue, and very serious to many people. Can you be both a Christian and a believer in evolution? Most Christians (but not fundamentalists) say you can. The theory of evolution is accepted as fact at all of our major universities.

But, in 1925, Tennessee fundamentalist Christians have gotten a law passed that says it is *unlawful for any teacher...to teach any theory that denies the story of the divine creation of man as taught in the Bible, and to teach instead that man has descended from a lower order of animals.*

Now that state law is telling citizens what they should believe. The doctrine of a church is being imposed on public schools. It is the opposite of separation of church and state. The 1st Amendment to the Constitution protects that separation when it says, *Congress shall make no law respecting an establishment of religion, or prohibiting the free exercise thereof.* Because of the new law, Tennessee's citizens are no longer free to study evolution in public school. (Private schools may teach as they wish.)

Many schoolteachers ignore the law and keep teaching what is in their textbooks and what most believe in—evolutionary science. The American Civil Liberties Union believes the law is unconstitutional. The ACLU, a private organization, was founded in 1920 to protect civil rights in America. The ACLU says it will pay the legal expenses of anyone who wants to test the Tennessee law. In Dayton, some citizens sitting around in Robinson's drugstore decide to test the law. They ask 24-year-old John Scopes if he would mind being arrested—Scopes teaches evolution in high school. They joke that a trial might put Dayton on the map. It turns out to be no joke.

When William Jennings Bryan learns of the trial, he volunteers to be the prosecutor (in favor of the Tennessee law). Bryan has run for president three times; everyone knows him. He is kind, well liked, and a fundamentalist. Clarence Darrow volunteers to defend Scopes. Darrow is a brilliant lawyer, a friend of the underdog, and an agnostic (someone who is not sure if there is a God or not).

When the trial begins, it is hot, and the old courthouse is so crowded it acts as if it might collapse; the judge moves everyone outdoors. Darrow is in shirtsleeves and wears lavender suspenders to hold up his pants. Bryan turns his collar inside his shirt, ties a handkerchief around his neck, and cools himself with a palm-leaf fan.

Bryan accuses Darrow of wanting to "slur the Bible."

Darrow says he wants "to prevent bigots and ignoramuses from controlling the educational system of the

Clarence Darrow (left), *famous Chicago lawyer, and William Jennings Bryan* (right), *defender of fundamentalism, share a friendly moment at the Scopes trial in 1925.*

United States." Darrow puts Bryan on the stand (that isn't usually done to the other lawyer), and asks questions that Bryan admits he hasn't thought much about. When Darrow forces Bryan to say that six days might not be six actual days, Bryan's fundamentalist friends are aghast. The great Populist orator is made to look foolish. (He dies in his sleep five days after the trial ends.)

It is an angry trial, full of bad feelings, and it doesn't settle much of anything. Bryan does win the case: the local court and the state supreme court agree that Scopes broke the law. (Because of a technicality, the case cannot be appealed to the U.S. Supreme Court; the law stays on the books until 1967.) But, in most of the nation, people laugh about monkeys and don't take it seriously. Which is too bad. It is an issue that will keep popping up. In the 1980s, Arkansas and Louisiana pass laws that say that public schools teaching evolution must use "equal time" to teach creationism (the Bible's story of Creation). In 1987, the Supreme Court finds those laws in conflict with the First Amendment's guarantee of religious freedom. Do you understand why? Do you believe that guarantee is important?

A Writer for the Jazz Age

Francis Scott Fitzgerald, a young Minnesotan (named for an ancestor, Francis Scott Key), had a tough time in school—but he loved to write: *When I lived in St. Paul and was about 12, I wrote all through every class in school in the back of my geography book and first-year Latin book and in the margins of themes and mathematics problems. Two years later my family decided that the only way to force me to study was to send me to boarding school. That was a mistake. It took my mind off my writing.*

But not for long. In a short life (he died at age 44), Fitzgerald wrote five novels, more than 150 short stories, and many essays. Hardly anyone described America of the 1920s and '30s as well as he did. It was he who labeled the times the "Jazz Age." His characters tried to turn life into a glittering party, and then couldn't understand why they weren't happy. Something was wrong, Fitzgerald said. His generation had "grown up to find all Gods dead, all wars fought, all faiths in man shaken."

Young people were flocking to the movies and, in 1927, movies began to talk. Talk about fun!

The following year, in Hollywood, California, a young filmmaker named Walt Disney produced the first animated sound film, *Steamboat Willie,* and introduced a little mouse named Mickey to the American public.

Suddenly, America seemed filled with artistic geniuses: musicians George Gershwin and Aaron Copland; writers Ernest Hemingway, William Faulkner, and F. Scott Fitzgerald; and artists Mary Cassatt, Grant Wood, and Thomas Hart Benton. And those are just a few of the names.

Harlem (a part of New York City with a rapidly growing black population) began vibrating with artistry. It was contagious. Playwrights, poets, musicians, artists, and actors, all living within a few blocks of each other, were sharing ideas. Langston Hughes, Claude McKay, and Countee Cullen began writing poetry. Zora Neale Hurston and Jean Toomer wrote novels. Jacob Lawrence and Romare Bearden painted pictures. And Duke Ellington and a whole lot of other people made music. Artistic excellence was something that the segregationists couldn't suppress. And Harlem, during this time known as the "Harlem Renaissance," exploded with creativity.

While this was going on, sad, grieving Calvin Coolidge sat in the White House and did little. His campaign slogan, "Keep Cool with Coolidge," seemed right for the times. The country was thriving, so when he said, "The chief business of America is business," many agreed, without ever hearing the rest of his speech. "The accumulation of wealth cannot be justified as the chief end of existence....So long as wealth is made the means and not the end, we need not greatly fear it." He added, "I cannot repeat too often that America is a nation of idealists. That [idealism] is the only motive to which they [Americans] ever give any strong and lasting reaction."

Do you think he was right?

Coolidge was uncomfortable in front of the camera—in this down-home photo opportunity he looks as if he's never been on a farm in his life.

9 Everyone's Hero

Ruth the rookie found even riding an elevator exciting. "Why, he's just a babe in the woods," his teammates said.

George Ruth, Jr. *(right),* age seven, at St. Mary's with his baseball buddy John DeTullio

George Herman Ruth certainly didn't look like a hero. His body was shaped like a barrel with spindly legs sticking out of its bottom. His face wasn't much to look at either. In the middle was a mashed-in nose.

But none of that mattered, because Ruth—who was known as "the Babe"—turned beautiful when he stepped onto a baseball field. He was the most famous ballplayer of all time.

He had an awful childhood. He wasn't an orphan, as some books say, but his parents, who ran a tavern, didn't care for him much. So he spent most of his time on the streets of Baltimore, got in trouble, and, at age eight, was sent to a Catholic boys' home (where he played a lot of baseball). He was tough—he had to be—but not bitter or angry. Actually, he was funny and friendly, and had all the instincts of a natural ham actor. He loved playing baseball, he broke all its records, and he was always himself, which means no one could predict what he would do or say next. The crowds adored him.

Ruth was a lefty—a southpaw—and he started out as a pitcher (in 1914) with the Boston Red Sox. He was sensational. But he could also hit—harder and farther than anyone. So Boston had him pitch some days and sometimes had him play first base. In 1918 he was about the best left-handed pitcher in the game, and that year he also led the American League in home runs.

But Boston needed money, so they traded him to the New York Yankees. The Yankees put him in the outfield. Pitchers play only every three or four days. An outfielder plays every day. The Yankees were

Black Sox

Babe Ruth was a godsend for a national game deep in scandal. In 1919, members of the Chicago White Sox (forever after known as the "Black Sox") took money from gamblers and lost the World Series on purpose. Only a larger-than-life figure like Ruth could distract the millions of baseball fans from the ugly scandal and restore the game's innocence. Ruth, with his prodigious hitting, flamboyant behavior, and childlike enthusiasm, was just what the country needed.

Ruth *(second from right)* as a Red Sox rookie in 1914. His first professional baseball experience was with the Baltimore Orioles, who were down on their luck and in the minors. The owner was short of cash and sold Ruth to Boston after five months. By 1916 the Babe was the best left-handed pitcher in baseball.

America fell in love with organized sports during the Roaring Twenties. Sports stars became American heroes. Working hours were changing, and more Americans had more leisure time. They could go to ballparks or listen to games on radio. (Red Barber was now one of their favorite sportscasters.) They could also play sports themselves. When the Great War ended there were very few tennis courts or golf courses in the nation. Some states didn't have any at all. Those sports were mainly played by rich folks. By the end of the '20s, golf courses and tennis courts were popping up everywhere. Americans were hard at play.

counting on Babe Ruth's hitting.

Were they ever right! Before Ruth, baseball had been a low-scoring game. Pitchers were the stars, and batters did a lot of bunting and base-stealing. Ruth made it a hitter's game.

The all-time home-run record—set in 1884—was 27 home runs in one season. In 1920, Ruth hit 54 home runs. People came to the ballpark just to see those homers. Other ballplayers began holding the bat the way he did and swinging with all their might. Scores began going up. High-scoring games are a lot more exciting than pitchers' duels. The fans went wild. Baseball teams agreed to switch to a lively ball that went farther than the ball they had been using. The game got really exciting.

In 1921, Babe Ruth hit 59 home runs and scored a total of 177 runs. Yankee baseball attendance doubled. In 1923, the New York Yankees built big, beautiful Yankee Stadium. They used the money that came from increased attendance. It was called "the house that Ruth built."

Those who couldn't get to Yankee Stadium could still enjoy the game. The first radio station, KDKA in Pittsburgh, began broadcasting in October of 1920. Four years later there were 576 licensed stations and five million radio sets in use. People in Kansas could hear the Yankees play baseball. Radio announcers went to the ball games and described what was happening, play by play. At home, families clustered around their wood-covered radio sets, and, if the static wasn't too bad, listened for the swat of Babe Ruth's bat.

He was trying to beat his own home-run record. But when a reporter asked, "Which one was that, Babe?" the slugger was cool. "I'll hit 'em, you count 'em," he said.

In 1927, the Babe hit 60 home runs. That record stood for

34 years, until 1961, when Roger Maris hit 61. (There were 154 games in the 1927 season and 162 games in 1961.) It took 13 more years for someone to top his career home-run total—714 of them. (Atlanta Brave Hank Aaron did that.)

Babe Ruth loved kids. Someone told him that one of his young fans was dying in the hospital. Ruth went to see the boy, gave him an auto-graphed ball, and promised to hit a home run for him that very afternoon. He did it. The boy recov-ered and Babe Ruth said, "A home run is the best medicine in the world." At least, that was the story the publicity agents told. It was hard to sep-arate the truth about Ruth from the legend. Eleven-year-old Johnny Sylvester was badly hurt when he fell off a horse—but he wasn't dying.

Above, left: the house that Ruth built—Yankee Stadium. *Right:* the most famous swing in the history of baseball. At Ruth's funeral in 1948, an old newsman said, "I stopped talking about the Babe for the simple reason that I realized that those who had never seen him didn't believe me."

The End of a Streak

The first great baseball game—at least, the first that wowed the press and public—was played in Brooklyn, New York, on June 14, 1870. Some 12,000 fans tried to squeeze into a park built for 5,000 people to see the Cincinnati Red Stockings (the first professional team) play the Brooklyn Atlantics. The Red Stockings had an undefeated 91-game streak; the Atlantics had a lot of grit. They went nose to nose for nine in-nings until the game ended in a 5–5 tie. How about extra innings? The rules weren't exactly the same as they are today. The game was supposed to be over. But the crowd wouldn't go home—they want-ed a winner. So the teams got back on the field, and the pitchers held on, with the tension shift-ing back and forth, back and forth, until dusk came and the players could barely see. Top of the 12th and Cincinnati got two runs. Things looked desper-ate for the Atlantics until Joe Start (known as "Old Reliable") came to bat, hit a line drive (with a man on third), and a Brooklyn fan climbed on the back of a Cincinnati fielder (which did slow his throw a bit, just enough to let the runner score). Then right-handed Brooklyn captain Bob Ferguson surprised everyone by batting left-handed (being thus the first recorded switch hitter) and getting a hit. When Cincinnati's first baseman flubbed a grounder, the Red Stockings' winning streak was over.

49

The Other Babe

When Mildred Didrikson was growing up in Beaumont, Texas, she played baseball with the neighborhood boys. When she began hitting homers the boys couldn't catch, they gave her a nickname. What do you think it was? Why, Babe, of course. When it came to athletics, Babe Didrikson seemed to do it all. She was an all-American basketball player. She was a softball star and pitched in baseball exhibition games against major-league teams. She competed in swimming and diving events and played competitive tennis. She did some boxing. She became a national heroine when she earned three medals in track and field at the 1932 Olympic Games at Los Angeles, California. But she is best known as one of America's outstanding women golfers. Once she won 17 golf tournaments in a row. Babe became Babe Didrikson Zaharias (zuh-HAIR-ee-us) in 1938 when she married wrestler George Zaharias. She has been called the outstanding woman athlete of the first half of the 20th century. No American woman before or since has been a champion in so many sports.

"Is there anything you don't play?" a reporter asked Babe. "Yes," she said. "Dolls."

Babe Ruth was a photographer's dream; he loved to clown for the camera (*below,* in a movie publicity still). Said one of his friends: "There was only one Babe Ruth."

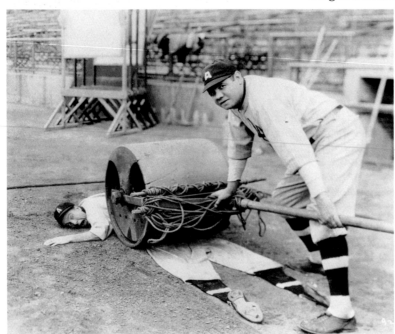

Still, the public couldn't get enough stories about Ruth, and he did spend a lot of time visiting children in orphanages and hospitals.

Babe did everything in a big way—including eating and drinking. So, when he got sick, with a fever and stomach cramps, reporters said it was because he ate 12 hot dogs and drank eight bottles of soda pop. That wasn't true. He ate like that regularly. But this time he was really sick. It was called "the bellyache heard round the world."

In 1935 Ruth was fat from eating too much. He was 40 years old. Still, there was no stopping him. He was now playing for the Boston Braves, and, in his last professional game, hit three home runs! His final home run was said to be the longest ever hit in Forbes Field.

10 Only the Ball Was White

Josh Gibson *(above)* "can do everything. He hits the ball a mile....Throws like a rifle," said pitching whiz Walter Johnson.

"Don't look back," said Satchel Paige *(left)*. "Something might be gaining on you." James Bell *(right)* was pitching for the St. Louis Stars and struck out some tough players. "That kid's cool," said a teammate. So they called him "Cool." But that didn't seem enough of a name, until someone added "Papa." It was 1922; he was 19.

Some people said that Josh Gibson once hit a ball over the roof at Yankee Stadium—which was farther than the Babe ever did. As for the unbelievable Satchel Paige, his pitching was so accurate they say he could have stayed in the strike zone pitching to Tom Thumb. Did he have a fast ball? Why, Satchel practically invented the fast ball. Someone who batted against him said that you never saw his pitched balls—just heard the thump in the catcher's mitt and knew they'd gone by. And Cool Papa Bell? Well, Paige himself swore that Bell ran so fast he could turn off the light switch and make it to bed before the light went out.

That lights-out story got repeated as a tall tale and a joke, although it happened to be true. Bell explained that he bet Paige he could do it one night when he learned a light switch was faulty. He won the bet. But usually he didn't need trickery. Cool Papa Bell was fast as Mercury (maybe faster), and Paige and everyone else knew it.

Paige and Bell and Gibson were stars of the Negro Leagues. These were Jim Crow times, when, in much of the United States, schools and ball teams and other things for blacks and whites were separate and unequal. Baseball didn't start that way. The brothers Fleet and

Two Cuban teams, the Cuban Stars and the New York Cubans, added a cosmopolitan touch to the Negro Leagues. Martin Dihigo, who played with the Cubans and with the Vera Cruz (Mexico) Eagles, ended up in baseball halls of fame in Cuba, Mexico, *and* the United States. In a league where everyone seemed versatile, he still managed to be outstanding. As one player said, "I seen them all for the past fifty years and I still think Dihigo was in a class by himself. He'd pitch one day, play center field the next, and the next day he'd be at first base. Sometimes he even played two or three positions in a single game."

Playing for the Cuban Giants, 1905

51

Moses (Fleet) Walker played 42 games for the Toledo Blue Stockings in 1884. That was the major-league record for a black player until 1947. A black man, he said, could never become "a full man ...of this Republic."

Welday Walker had played in the old American Association. But when the association died in 1892, Cap Anson (who was a big hitter and a big bigot) made sure that the new leagues fielded whites-only teams. So men of color formed their own leagues.

The Negro Leagues were filled with talented players who played hard and seemed to have a whole lot of fun, too. Not that it was an easy life. Money was usually short, the equipment shabby, the travel brutal, and, in segregated times, blacks almost always had trouble finding hotel rooms or restaurants to eat in. Sometimes they played 200 or 300 games in a six-month season. (Figure the math on that one.) Since they had no ballparks of their own, they had to rent, and the managers wanted to get their money's worth—so, when lights got put in ballfields, they'd often play a doubleheader, and then a night game, too.

What they did best, besides the regular league games, was barnstorm around the country bringing entertainment and fancy ballplaying to blacks (and some whites) in a whole lot of American towns. They were to baseball what

Cap Anson (back row, second from right) and the Chicago White Stockings in 1888, the year Anson started purging baseball of black players. He seemed to think it was okay to have a black mascot (in front of Anson).

Satchel Paige and his All Stars on a barnstorming tour against white pitcher Bob Feller's All Stars (Paige is in the doorway on the left). "This was a gravy train," said one of the team members. "My share was $7,500 for 17 days' work....Each team had a private plane. Segregated luxury."

the Harlem Globetrotters later became to basketball: wizards. Sometimes they played in formal attire, sometimes in clown costumes, sometimes in uniforms. They did comic routines, they juggled, they did ball tricks. Sometimes they came with a band and a midway. It was carnival, it was fun, and it was skilled ball, too. You had to love baseball to keep up the pace. Josh Gibson and Ted Page remembered playing a twilight game in Pittsburgh, driving to St. Louis for a day game, and then on to scorching Kansas City for a doubleheader. That evening the two of them made it to a hotel porch, where they sat, dog-tired, until they heard some kids playing sandlot ball. Naturally, they couldn't resist that, so they joined the game.

Except for the traveling, most of the ballplayers had a good time, although a few hated having to clown around. They just wanted to play ball. But,

Were the Men Scared?

It was 1931, and the Yankees were playing an exhibition game against the Chattanooga (Tennessee) Look-outs. Chattanooga's owner, Joe Engle (who once traded a ballplayer for a Thanksgiving turkey), had just signed a 17-year-old pitcher, Jackie Mitchell. When the great Babe came to the plate, the new pitcher was called to the mound—and SURPRISE: Mitchell was a *she*.

Her first pitch was low and a ball. The Sultan of Swat swung at the next—and missed. Ditto the next. Babe Ruth didn't like missing anyone's pitch—and a woman's! Babe demanded to see the ball. There was nothing wrong with it. Mitchell wound up, let go, and the Babe watched the pitch fly by. "Stee-rike!" The Bambino threw his bat, stalked off, and the crowd roared. The next batter was big hitter Lou Gehrig. Jackie threw three times. Gehrig swung three times. And that was that.

Some said that Ruth and Gehrig were just being polite to a woman, but no one who was there believed it. Years later, Jackie Mitchell said, "I had a drop pitch and when I was throwing it right, you couldn't touch it." Baseball's commissioner, Judge Kenesaw Mountain Landis, didn't care. He was a misogynist (miss-SODGE-ih-nist—someone who dislikes women). Landis said Mitchell's contract was void, and baseball lost out.

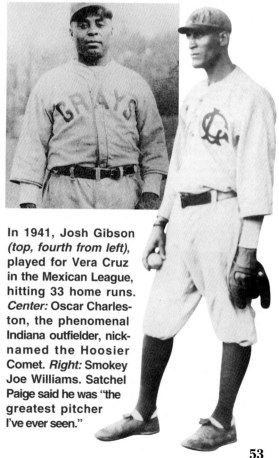

In 1941, Josh Gibson *(top, fourth from left)*, played for Vera Cruz in the Mexican League, hitting 33 home runs. *Center:* Oscar Charleston, the phenomenal Indiana outfielder, nicknamed the Hoosier Comet. *Right:* Smokey Joe Williams. Satchel Paige said he was "the greatest pitcher I've ever seen."

53

World Beater

Sometimes Jesse Owens joined the barnstorming Toledo Crawfords. Then the team had a big track star to help draw the crowds. Owens won four gold medals at the 1936 Olympics in Berlin, Germany (no one had ever won four at once before). That displeased the German leader, Adolf Hitler, who believed in Aryan (white northern European) supremacy and thought Negroes were inferior. Owens would race anyone who wanted to run against him (fans got a 10-yard lead). The only person he ever refused to race was Cool Papa Bell, who said he wanted to race around the bases. Owens even raced a horse—and won!

Owens flies past 26 feet, 5 inches for a gold medal in the long jump and an Olympic record in Berlin, 1936.

being black, or dark-skinned Cuban, or Mexican, they couldn't join the major leagues. It was crazy. One excuse was that blacks and whites wouldn't play together. But that wasn't so. White all-star teams often barnstormed with the blacks, playing exhibition games. (Black teams won more than they lost.) Everyone knew that players like Oscar Charleston, Smokey Joe Williams, and Buck Leonard were major talents.

"I have played against a Negro all-star team that was so good we didn't think we had even a chance," admitted white Dizzy Dean, who pitched for the St. Louis Cardinals and the Chicago Cubs. "There is no room in baseball for discrimination," said Lou Gehrig (one of the best first basemen ever). White catcher Gabby Hartnett (whose three sisters barnstormed in a women's league) said, "If managers were given permission there'd be a mad rush to sign up Negroes." Which is what finally happened (see book 10 of *A History of US* for that story). "Democracy is killing Negro baseball," lamented one black sportswriter. But it was a death most people welcomed.

Joe Louis—Making Mom Feel Proud

If [Joe Louis] is not the best boxer that ever lived, he is as near to it as we are ever likely to know. He was born in 1914 on a sharecropper's cotton patch in Alabama and was as country-poor as it is possible to be. In theory the farm was —it had been rented as—a cotton and vegetable farm. But the vegetables did not feed the family, not by the time Joe, the seventh child, came along. His father broke, as sharecroppers do, from the daily strain of not making enough in crops either to feed his children or to put shoes on them. They had no money to send him to a hospital. So he was carried off to a state institution, where he died. A widower came to help out and soon married Joe's mother. And his five children moved in with the eight Louises. Joe got a little more food and went to a one-room school. Then the family moved to Detroit, where the stepfather worked in an automobile factory. Joe went to trade school and worked in the evening doing the rounds with an ice wagon. Then came the Depression, and the family went on relief. This, said Joe, made his mother feel very bad. Years later Joe wrote out a careful check, for two hundred and sixty-nine dollars, which was the amount of relief checks they had had from the government. That, said Joe, made Mrs. Brooks, as she now was, feel better.

—ALISTAIR COOKE, *JOE LOUIS*

The Brown Bomber KO's Max Schmeling in one round in 1938.

11 American Music

Trumpeter Louis Armstrong in 1931. He started as a street kid and learned to play cornet at the Waifs' Home.

Do you ever stop and listen to the sounds around you? Have you noticed that indoor sounds are different from outdoor sounds?

Concentrate for a minute. It doesn't matter if it seems noisy or quiet; concentrate hard. You will hear sounds you were unaware of before. What you are hearing is the music of your world. Imagine what the music is like—that natural-sound music—if you are sitting on a California beach near the Pacific Ocean. Then pretend you are skiing in Colorado's Rocky Mountains and listen to the sounds around you. And then open your ears and take an imaginary walk down Broadway in New York City. Think of the differences between city sounds and country sounds, between sea sounds and mountain sounds. Some places, of course, have more sounds than other places.

New Orleans is one of those places with a lot of music in the air. If you look at a map, you'll find New Orleans down in Louisiana at the mouth of the Mississippi River. You can understand that New Orleans has water sounds: sounds from shrimp boats and tankers in the Gulf of Mexico,

There were once about 30 different tribes of Native Americans in the Louisiana region, including the Attakapa, Caddo, Chitimacha, and Tunica.

New Orleans kids made music with whatever they could find. This street band includes homemade drum set, trombone, harmonica, and dancers.

The great riverboats that plied up and down the Mississippi were a home for jazz bands—Louis Armstrong played on them—and often the place where people outside New Orleans heard jazz for the first time.

At the Back of the Bus

Sarah and Bessie Delany grew up in segregated North Carolina, and describe what life under Jim Crow was like in their book Having Our Say: The Delany Sisters' First 100 Years *(written with Amy Hill Hearth).*

We encountered Jim Crow laws for the first time on a summer Sunday afternoon. We were about five and seven years old at the time. Mama and Papa used to take us to Pullen Park in Raleigh [N.C.] for picnics, and that particular day, the trolley driver told us to go to the back. We children objected loudly, because we always liked to sit in front where the breeze would blow your hair. But Mama and Papa just gently told us to hush and took us to the back without making a fuss. When we got to Pullen Park, we found changes there, too. The spring where you got water now had a big wooden sign across the middle. On one side, the word "white" was painted, and on the other, the word "colored." Why, what in the world was all this about? We may have been little children, but, honey, we got the message loud and clear. But when nobody was looking, Bessie took the dipper from the white side and drank from it.

sounds of water lapping the shores of the city's Lake Pontchartrain, and dock and riverboat sounds from the great Mississippi.

Because New Orleans has a warm climate, people are out of doors most of the time. So there are people-on-the-street sounds. Today in New Orleans, you can also hear cars, trucks, motorcycles, and airplanes.

Back in 1900, the music of the streets was different. Oh, there were many of the same people sounds—but there were also chickens and pigs in the city, and they scratched and squealed. There was the clippety-clop of horses' hoofs, and the rolling sounds of wooden-wheeled wagons, the hoots of trains, and the sad notes of riverboat foghorns.

Some of the people sounds were different then, too. There were no big supermarkets, so people bought ice, milk, bread, fresh fruit, vegetables, meat, and other things from the backs of the clippety-cloppety wagons. The wagon drivers had to tell people what they were selling. Usually they sang their message. It was the same idea as a TV-commercial jingle, but it might go like this: *I got tomatoes big and fine, I got watermelons red to the rind.* Or like this: *My mule is white, the coal is black; I sell my coal two bits a sack.* Imagine a whole lot of street peddlers all singing their wares at the same time.

Now, on top of all this, New Orleans had, and has, an unusual mixture of peoples. The city was settled by the French in 1718. (In 1803, President Thomas Jefferson bought New Orleans as part of the Louisiana Purchase.) The French language stuck. Some of the sounds and words of that language can be heard in New Orleans even today.

Many of the French and Spanish men who came to New Orleans in the 18th century married African-American women. Their biracial children, called Creoles, often spoke French or Spanish as well as English.

Out of the sounds of New Orleans, and the mixed heritage of its people, a new music arose. It was American music—unlike anything heard in the world before. It combined the rhythm and drum beat of Africa with the instruments and heritage of Europe. It added a dash from the spirituals of the black Protestant churches, and much from the talents of some black musical geniuses who could be heard in street bands and nightclubs. It was called "jazz." It was unique (you-NEEK)—which means totally unlike anything before it. Have you ever mixed red paint with yellow? The color you get is not red, or yellow. It is orange. It is unique. Jazz is like that. It is not African music, or European music. It is uniquely American.

In 1900 nobody much outside of New Orleans had ever heard of it. But in the 1920s jazz began to spread: first to Chicago, then across the country, and then around the whole world.

The best way to learn about jazz is to listen to it. You could start with one of the greatest jazz performers: Louis Armstrong.

Louis was one of those boys who sold coal in New Orleans for two bits a sack. He was very poor. Then someone gave him a trumpet. It

By the mid-1920s, dance halls and speakeasies, like this club scene painted in 1929 by Archibald Motley, Jr., were booming in New York and Chicago. Jazz musicians went north, and soon Chicago had replaced New Orleans as the home of jazz and swing.

The first jazz is said to have been played by funeral bands that wailed music full of soul and sadness as they followed horsedrawn hearses down the streets of New Orleans. It was blues music.

Talking Without Drums

Willie Ruff plays the French horn. He knows a lot about jazz. He has taught about it at Yale University. Here is what Mr. Ruff says of the origins of jazz:

In Africa the drum is the most important musical instrument...people use their drums to talk. Please imagine that the drum method of speech is so exquisite that Africans can, without recourse to words, recite proverbs, record history, and send long messages. The drum is to West African society what the book is to literate society.

"In the seventeenth century," Ruff continues, "when West Africans were captured and brought to America as slaves, they brought their drums with them. But the slave owners were afraid of the drum because it was so potent; it could be used to incite the slaves to revolt. So they outlawed the drum. This very shrewd law had a tremendous effect on the development of black people's music. Our ancestors had to develop a variety of drum substitutes. One of them, for example, was tap dancing....By the time jazz started to develop, all African instruments in America had disappeared. So jazz borrowed the instruments of Western music."

Jazz is not African music, but it is mainly the creation of American blacks. But, from the beginning, white musicians also played jazz, and some made important contributions to the music. While the roots of jazz can be found in Africa, the fruit is a hybrid. (Willie Ruff is wrong to say all African instruments died out in America. The banjo is based on an African instrument.)

Above: Bessie Smith, one of the pioneer female jazz singers, in 1936. *Right:* Many of the early jazz leaders—such as Joe "King" Oliver (back row, on cornet, with his Creole Jazz Band)—were trumpeters, probably because the trumpet could be played while marching, and because its sweet, high sound carried over the street noise. Kneeling, front, is Louis Armstrong.

must have been a good angel. Louis Armstrong was born to play the trumpet. People began calling him "satchelmouth," because his cheeks seemed to hold a suitcase full of air. "Satchmo" was soon playing on riverboats that went up and down the Mississippi. Then he went to Chicago and began making history.

Satchmo had a big grin, but when he played the trumpet he closed his eyes and blew clear, heavenly tones. Listen to some of his recordings, and see what you think.

As soon as you start listening you will learn something: no two jazz performances are exactly alike. Composers who compose European-style music write down notes and expect musicians to play those notes just as

they are written. That isn't so in true jazz. You see, an important part of jazz is *improvisation*. Improvising means doing your own thing. Jazz musicians talk to each other with their instruments. It is something like African drum talk. One musician leads with a theme. Then someone answers that theme. He plays the theme his own way. Then maybe the first musician improvises with another variation on the theme. Soon the whole band is playing with it. Does that sound wild? It isn't easy to do it well.

People in the 1920s were crazy about jazz. The 1920s were called the "Jazz Age." When the Jazz Age '20s ended—with a big thud called the "Depression"—jazz continued to grow in popularity. Today, many people call it America's most original art form.

The Duke Roars with the Twenties

He wore dandy suits, ruffled shirts, top hats, and slicked-back hair. His high-school friends called him "The Duke," because he dressed like royalty. "He was wearing velvet slippers!" remembers one adoring fan. "No man I knew would have dared wear velvet slippers!" The Duke was a man of supreme grace—taking to heart his father's credo that "pretty can only get prettier, but beauty compounds itself."

But beneath the elegance and flash was music. Wild music. Some people called it *jazz,* but not Duke Ellington—that was too small a category. By the late '20s, his music was taking off. It was a time when everyone was desperately trying to be young again. The Great War was over; it had exhausted the world and killed much of its youth. Now that world was ready to party.

Painters came to New York to paint in bold new styles that forsook form altogether. Novelist F. Scott Fitzgerald sketched portraits of the fast life—decadent dreams where characters had such pressing observations as "I like big parties...at small parties there isn't any privacy." Duke Ellington, himself a painter turned composer, created music in colors with songs like "Mood

Duke Ellington

Indigo," "Magenta Haze," and "Blue Cellophane."

The sound of the '20s was jazz, originated by blacks but embraced by whites. Innovative jazzmen appeared all over the country. Louis Armstrong showcased his individual talent—many credit him with inventing the jazz solo. Duke's music borrowed from his African heritage, from European atonal theory, and from Western classical tradition—but the music he created was completely his own. It was deeply thoughtful music, sometimes achingly sad, and it reflected the romanticism and gentleness of its creator.

Duke had experienced a comfortable, middle-class childhood in Washington, D.C.—in his own words, he was "pampered and spoiled rotten." He was a man of infinite mystery; as his sister said, "There was just veil after veil after veil." We know that he never liked to argue, that, when confronted with racism, he "took the energy it takes to pout and wrote some blues." His music remains hard to classify; some people still wonder exactly what jazz is. "If you gotta ask," said Louis Armstrong, "you'll never know."

—DANNY HAKIM
(COURTESY OF *TLC MONTHLY*)

Rhapsodies in Red, White, and Blue

Americans have always made music—in the fields, in wagons heading west, on whaling boats, and in church. But it wasn't until the beginning of the 20th century that composers took that singing and fiddling and stomping and turned it into music that could hold its own in concert halls around the world. Here are three who led the way.

CHARLES IVES (1874–1954)

When Charles Ives was born—in Connecticut, toward the end of the 19th century—everyone who composed or played or listened to symphonies understood that serious music had rules and forms that had been established by the great European composers.

By the time Ives died—in the middle of the 20th century—many of those rules had been blown away. It was Charles Ives, as much as any other American, who set the dynamite charges.

He heard music everywhere: in revival hymns, in off-key singing, in children's shouts, in fire-engine whistles, in factory bells, and in the cacophony of city street noise. He took all those kinds of sounds, which were often discordant, and composed with them.

Before Ives, American composers tried to make their music sound like Beethoven or Mozart. Ives used some ideas from the European masters, but, since he talked like an American, he thought he should compose like an American. And he did. He quoted bits of barn-dance tunes, hymns, speeches, and songs in his music

Charles Ives

long before others began doing that. Most composers start with a simple theme and make it more complex. Ives often did just the opposite. He anticipated much of the "new" music of the 20th century.

As a boy, Ives had two special loves: music and baseball. When he was 12 he was playing drums in his father's band. At the same age, he was captain of his school baseball team. "He plays coolly and is quick at catching men napping at bases," his school newspaper reported. His father, who had been the youngest bandmaster in the Union Army in the Civil War, taught him Bach, and church music, and popular songs.

But when he began composing, his music wasn't taken seriously. It was too unusual. It took time for others to catch up. His Third Symphony (called *Camp Meeting*), which was completed in 1904, was first performed in 1946, awarded a Pulitzer Prize in 1947, and finally recorded in 1950.

Much of Ives's music is descriptive. It tells stories—stories of America. His beautiful Second Piano Sonata is about the writ-

ers who lived in Concord, Massachusetts, in the mid-19th century. Its four sections are titled "Emerson," "Hawthorne," "The Alcotts," and "Thoreau." Henry David Thoreau once said he wished to hear a flute at Walden Pond. Charles Ives added a flute passage to his piano sonata to make it happen.

When Ives began using quarter tones in his compositions, hardly anyone understood that he was giving the orchestra a whole extra set of notes to use. It was like putting new colors on an artist's palette. Today, several composers use quarter tones. That was just one of the innovative things Ives did. (See if you can find out what quarter tones are.)

Being way ahead of your time isn't easy. Ives needed to earn a living, so he became an insurance man and, eventually, president of the largest insurance company in the world. Few people have been creators in both the world of business and the world of the arts. Charles Ives was exceptional.

The best way to understand a composer is to listen to his music. You might start with "Putnam's Camp," which is part of a composition called *Three Places in New England*. It is narrative music that tells the story of a Fourth of July celebration during the Revolutionary War.

AARON COPLAND (1900–1990)

Aaron Copland was born right as the century began, to a Jewish family living in Brooklyn, New York, on a street that he described as "drab." It was an unlikely environment for an aspiring musician. "Music was the last thing anyone would have connected with it," he said. Copland went to public school and his older sister taught him to play piano. He soon knew that he wanted to be a composer, and he sent for a through-the-mail course in musical harmony.

Aaron Copland

Then he set out to learn from the best teachers he could find in New York. But when he heard a piece by Charles Ives, a teacher told him not to be "contaminated" by it. After that, at age 20, he went off to Paris and found a great music teacher, Nadia Boulanger, who polished his talents as she did those of some other American musicians. In Paris Copland met important European composers and musicians: Prokofiev, Milhaud, Koussevitzky. He realized that their music reflected their origins. He decided that his music should reflect America.

When Copland returned to America, in 1924, he was ready to take America's indigenous (in-DIDGE-in-uss—it means "native") music—especially jazz and folk songs—and make it symphonic. Eight years later he was recognized as an important composer, so when he played music by Charles Ives at a summer festival, people listened. He helped introduce Ives's music to a generation of young musicians. (Some were gladly "contaminated.")

Aaron Copland wrote symphonies and chamber music and film scores. His ballets *Billy the Kid* (1938) and *Rodeo* (1942) are all-American compositions and favorites of mine. Listen to one; I think you will like it.

Copland brought a youthful exuberance to all his endeavors; it gladdened his colleagues and inspired his music. He was a gentle man, and gracious, and he became a great teacher as well as a musician. To learn more, read Aaron Copland, *What to Listen for in Music* (McGraw-Hill, 1988).

GEORGE GERSHWIN (1898–1937)

George Gershwin heard a live jazz performance when he was six, and that hooked him for life. He was a poor boy, but he managed to get some piano lessons and, at 14, got his first song published. It was a good thing he started early and worked quickly, because he died at age 39. In that short lifetime, he became one of the most important of America's composers. He took jazz and popular music and blended them with elements of classical music to create works that are original and wonderful. (Gershwin never stopped studying. One of his teachers was a Russian composer known for his mathematical approach to music.)

It was in Broadway's musical theater that Gershwin came to fame. But he also wrote film scores and compositions for orchestra and piano. *Rhapsody in Blue, An American in Paris,* and *Lady Be Good* are among his best-known works. His brother Ira wrote lyrics for many of his songs.

If you've never heard Gershwin's opera *Porgy and Bess,* see if you can find a video to watch, or listen to a recording, or, if you're lucky, find a live performance. Gershwin began it after he read a novel by DuBose Heyward called *Porgy.* It was about African-Americans who lived on the coastal islands near Charleston, South Carolina. Gershwin went to the islands, lived there for a summer, heard the rhythms and sounds of the region, and composed a masterpiece.

George Gershwin

Hooray for Hollywood!

Hollywood, which was the name of a suburb of Los Angeles, was the capital of a make-believe world: nothing was quite real, although everything was made to seem real.

In its golden age, which was the 1930s, Hollywood was a movietown filled with studios where makeup artists, costumers, carpenters, writers, directors, and camera crews created scenes and characters that put dreams and laughter and exotic settings onto a big screen. It was pure enchantment, and it possessed the nation. In later years, the cameras would leave the studios and go "on location" to real places. Then computer technology would make astonishing effects possible; but none of it came close to capturing people the way those Hollywood films did.

Maybe it was the Depression that made people love going to the movies. Maybe cute Shirley Temple, dashing Clark Gable, the comical Marx Brothers, and glamorous Greta Garbo made people forget their troubles. Whatever the reason, some 80 million movie tickets sold each week in 1938—that equaled 65 percent of the U.S. population (although some people went more than once a week, which skewed the figures a bit). Compare it to this: in 1990 about 20 million tickets sold every week, representing less than 10 percent of the population. In the 1930s, movies mattered; now they entertain.

Tyrone Power and Gene Tierney (foreground) in a passionate embrace while filming The Razor's Edge *for Twentieth Century Fox before an intimate audience of at least 50 enthralled grips, continuity girls, lighting designers, cameramen, director, and producers.*

Miss Shirley Temple and Bill "Bojangles" Robinson tap dance down the stairs to fame.

TO HOLLYWOOD IN STYLE
In 1931, it took five days on two trains to get to Hollywood [from New York], but what a deluxe five days! Because that traffic was supported by the film industry, the Twentieth Century *to Chicago and the* Santa Fe Super Chief *[trains] to Los Angeles glittered with polished mahogany, shiny brass, and red brocade; the seats flaunted antimacassars of heavy lace.* —ANITA LOOS, *CAST OF THOUSANDS*

12 Space's Pioneer

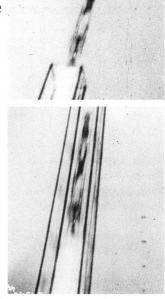

Robert Goddard in his lab in 1935, the year he became the first to shoot a liquid-fuel rocket at supersonic speed.

It was cold in Auburn, Massachusetts, on March 16, 1926. The three men and the woman who stood in an open field wore warm coats, and, as they talked, their breath turned into misty clouds of frost.

That didn't seem to concern them. They were concentrating on a tall structure. It was built of metal pipes. Actually, there was nothing special about the structure. What was attached to it was special. It was a small rocket.

The woman was Esther Kisk Goddard, and she held a motion-picture camera. She would film what was about to occur. Her husband, Robert Hutchings Goddard, a college professor, was in charge. The two other men were his assistants. They were standing in Goddard's Aunt Effie's field.

The rocket had a two-foot-long motor. Pipes ran from the base of the motor to two attached tanks: one tank held gasoline, the other oxygen. Goddard touched a blowtorch to an opening at the top of the rocket. The rocket let out a roar. Slowly it lifted off the launch pad—that is what the metal-pipe structure was—and rose into the air, speeding upward at 60 miles an hour. Then it crashed into the snowy field. The flight lasted three seconds. The space age had begun.

Robert Goddard and his assistants went back to their laboratory. They were physicists, and New England Yankees, and they understood the value of hard work. They knew they had much yet to do.

They also knew that what they had done that day was as important as what had been done by two brothers from Dayton, Ohio, at Kitty Hawk, North Carolina, in December of 1903. But almost no one

Esther Goddard's 1929 film of one of Robert's successful liftoffs. Even when the rockets worked, people laughed and called him "Moony" Goddard.

It took astronomer Percival Lowell 25 years of searching, but in 1930 he found a ninth planet and named it Pluto. It was mathematical investigation of the planet Uranus that made him believe another planet existed in our solar system.

Right: The launch pad in Aunt Effie's Auburn, Massachusetts, meadow. Goddard's liquid fuels were the same ones that would be used for Germany's V-2 rockets in World War II (more on them later).

else knew that. In 1926, most people would have laughed at a scientist who took the idea of space travel seriously. It would be a long time before the world understood about rockets and rocket travel. Few people ever knew about Robert Goddard.

Maybe that was because he was shy. No, it wasn't just his shyness. It was more than that. He was a loner, and a dedicated scientist. He didn't have much use for publicity. He wanted to get on with his work. He wanted to realize his dream.

He had dreamed of space and interplanetary travel from the time he was a boy. It all began with two books. One was *The War of the Worlds,* which was written by an Englishman, H. G. Wells. The other was *From the Earth to the Moon,* written by a Frenchman, Jules Verne. They are two of the earliest, and best, of the modern science-fiction novels. Goddard read them, reread them, and then read them again.

They made him believe that space travel was possible. In Jules Verne's book, astronauts catapult into space inside a capsule shot from a gigantic cannon. That didn't sound plausible to Robert Goddard. He decided that rockets were the way space would be conquered.

Rocket Science

In 1232, at the battle of Kai-Keng, the Chinese had gunpowder-filled tubes attached to long arrows. When the end of the tube was lit, the burning powder made fire, smoke, and a gas that produced a thrust and sent the blazing arrow through the air. Those early rockets were probably not very destructive, but they must have terrified the Mongols who saw them coming.

The Mongols soon produced their own rockets and brought them to Europe; Europeans began experimenting with them. In England, a monk named Roger Bacon improved them. In France, Jean Froissart launched rockets from inside a tube (like a modern bazooka). Joannes de Fontana of Italy designed a rocket-powered torpedo that zoomed across the surface of the water and set ships on fire. The English sometimes shot rockets to scare enemies. Otherwise they did little damage. It was in "the rockets' red glare" that Francis Scott Key composed a famous poem. (During which war?)

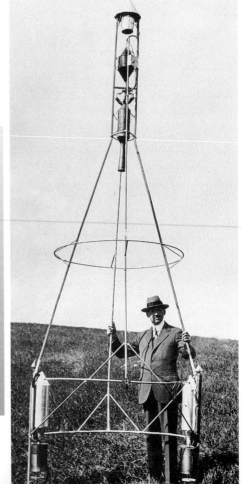

Automobile age meets space age. At 17, Goddard had a dream about building a space-flight machine. "I imagined how wonderful it would be to make some device which had even the *possibility* of ascending to Mars," he wrote.

He had three good reasons for that belief. Rockets have more push, or "thrust," than other engines of the same weight. Rockets can be designed to hold within themselves all that is needed to make them operate. Since rockets lose weight as they use up their fuel, their highest speeds can come at the end of a flight.

Rockets were nothing new. The Chinese had designed rockets way back in the 11th century. The Chinese rockets were powered by explosive powders. You lit the powder and, whammo, the rocket lifted off and the fuel was all used up. Chinese rockets were mostly used for fireworks.

Goddard realized that if a rocket was to soar out of Earth's atmosphere and beyond, it would need a fuel that provided steady power, a fuel that wouldn't burn up all at once. A liquid seemed the answer, but liquid fuels demand oxygen in order to burn. There is no oxygen in space. Now, it doesn't sound terribly complicated to figure all that out and build a rocket that carries its own fuel and oxygen tanks. It doesn't seem difficult because we now know it can be done. The first person to come up with an idea isn't sure it can be done. Or how to do it. It took Robert Goddard 10 years of experimenting to build the little rocket that climbed into the sky on that icy-cold March day in 1926.

A few other scientists—in Germany and Russia—were working on the same problem. They worked with theories. Theories are ideas. Goddard was different. He started with theories, but then he tested them. That is the true scientific way.

When he was 38 (six years before the 1926 test flight), Goddard wrote a paper for the Smithsonian Institution in which he theorized that a rocket of 10 tons might be made

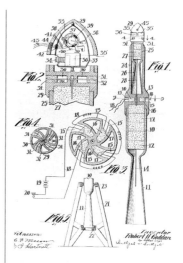

Goddard drew these plans for a patent application on a "rocket apparatus" in 1914.

Sir Isaac Newton (1643–1727), England's great scientific genius, came up with three laws of motion that explain how rockets work and why they can fly in space's vacuum. If you are interested in rocketry, study those laws.

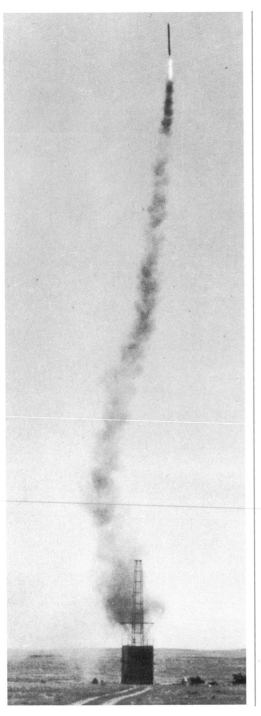

By the 1930s, a Goddard rocket *(left)* had gone as high as a mile above earth. At right, Goddard *(center)* with Harry Guggenheim *(left)*, and Charles Lindbergh, who asked Guggenheim's millionaire father, Daniel, to help Goddard; more about Lindbergh on the next page.

powerful enough to reach the moon. He spent much of the rest of his life working to make that possible.

New England isn't a good place to test rockets: too many trees and people. Goddard decided to do his testing in New Mexico, over the desert. Soon his rockets were traveling at 700 miles an hour; some were rising as much as a mile and a half high. He worked out ways to guide and control rockets. He developed the idea of a series of rockets as a means of reaching the moon. He devised parachutes to allow rockets to return to earth smoothly. He patented more than 200 of his ideas.

He didn't live to see his dream fulfilled. Robert Goddard died in 1945, 24 years before Apollo 11 landed on the moon. But his spirit must have been riding with the astronauts on that voyage, probably with Jules Verne and H. G. Wells tucked under its arms.

There is an old Chinese story of a low-ranking but inventive Chinese official named Wan Hu who is said to have designed a rocket-powered flying chair. Two large kites were attached to the chair; attached to the kites were 47 fire-arrow rockets. On the day that Wan Hu decided to test his invention, he sat in the chair and his assistants rushed forward with torches and lit the 47 rockets. According to the story, when the smoke cleared, Wan Hu and the chair were gone—never to be seen again. Today, no one knows what actually happened, but rockets are as likely to explode as to fly.

13 The Lone Eagle

Lindbergh quit college in his second year to go to flying school and buy a World War I biplane.

Robert Goddard might never have gone farther than that field in Auburn, Massachusetts, if a young man hadn't come to visit him. The young man was Charles A. Lindbergh, Jr., and he was famous. Newspapers were saying he was the most famous man on the planet. He may have been.

Lindbergh was wise enough not to be too impressed with himself. He was also wise enough to know the importance of Goddard's work. Lindbergh talked to a philanthropist (fil-AN-thro-pist) named Daniel Guggenheim. (A philanthropist is a person who gives money to good causes.) The Guggenheim Foundation gave Goddard money to build a laboratory in New Mexico.

Why was Lindbergh so famous? Well, back in 1919, a wealthy hotel man offered a prize of $25,000 to anyone who could fly from New York to Paris (or Paris to New York). Several pilots tried for the prize. None made it. Then, in 1927, the competition got fierce. Besides the money, everyone knew there would be much glory for the pilot who first crossed the Atlantic.

In April, Richard E. Byrd took off, crashed, and broke his wrist. (The Byrd family had been well known in America since the days of George Washington and even before.) That same April, two pilots set out from Virginia, crashed, and were killed. In early May, two French aces (top pilots) left Paris, headed out over the Atlantic, and were never heard of again.

In mid-May, three planes were being made ready. Newspapers were full of their stories. The competition had captured the imagination of people on both sides of the Atlantic. Most of the newspaper attention focused on Byrd, who was famous and eager to try again. His plane had three engines and a well-trained crew. The second plane,

Byrd Man

Richard Evelyn Byrd was the most renowned American explorer of his generation. In May 1926, he and co-pilot Floyd Bennett flew over the North Pole. (Much later, scientists discovered his calculations were off and he had missed the North Pole—but not by much.) Byrd was a superb leader and a naval officer who took polar exploration from dog-sled individualism to the discipline of government-sponsored science.

Naturally, one pole led to the other. In 1928, he headed an Antarctic expedition, set up a scientific base there named Little America, and, in 1929, flew over the South Pole. Byrd's radio reports of his adventures were listened to eagerly at home. He wrote books, made lecture tours, and opened Antarctica to scientific research.

While Lindbergh was an airmail pilot flying out of St. Louis he met the businessman who paid for the plane he would later fly to Paris. *Above:* Lindbergh loads the world's first sack of airmail. *Inset:* Lindbergh with the *Spirit of St. Louis.*

In 1922, Bessie Coleman becomes America's first licensed black pilot. Because of prejudice, she has to learn to fly in France.

with two engines, was to be flown by two experienced pilots. The third plane, a small single-engine craft, could hold only one person. It was called the *Spirit of St. Louis,* because a group of St. Louis businessmen had helped pay for it. The pilot, Charles Lindbergh, was little known. He'd been a barnstormer, a pilot who went around doing trick flying: circles and loops and daredevil things, and then taking people on plane rides for $5 a spin. That was the kind of thing most pilots did in those days. People didn't use airplanes for transportation. Trains were used to get places. Airplanes? No one was quite sure where the future of aviation lay. But if planes could fly across the ocean safely, they might have an important future.

Lindbergh was a good pilot. He was the first man to fly the U.S. mail

FLIGHT of the SPIRIT of ST. LOUIS

CANADA

UNITED STATES

① NEW YORK
8:00 AM
FRIDAY

② 4:00 PM.

③ 7:00 PM
FRIDAY

3,600 miles

④ 1:30PM
SATURDAY

ICELAND

ENGLAND
IRELAND

FRANCE
PARIS
⑤ 5:24 N.Y. TIME
10:24 PARIS TIME
SAT.

Atlantic Ocean

from St. Louis to Chicago. And the first to survive four forced parachute jumps. (Forced because his planes developed troubles.) There was a bold, daring side to him, and another side that was careful and methodical. It was a rare combination. In a crisis he would not panic.

Something about him attracted people. Partly it was his looks. He was tall—six-foot-two—skinny, with light, curly hair and a boyish grin. He looked younger than his 25 years. He was quiet, and was always more at ease with machines, or nature, than with people. He'd grown up in Minnesota, where his father was a congressman. He never did well in school—maybe because he went to a different school almost every year. But he was smart enough to do a lot of reading. He wrote well.

It was 8 A.M. on May 20 when he took off. The weather wasn't good, but he was anxious to

I slip Massachusetts into the map pocket, and pull out my Mercator's projection of the North Atlantic. What endless hours I worked over this chart in California, measuring, drawing, rechecking each 100-mile segment of its great-circle route, each theoretical hour of my flight. But only now, as I lay it on my knees, do I realize its full significance. A few lines and figures on a strip of paper, a few ounces of weight, this strip is my key to Europe. With it, I can fly the ocean. With it, that black dot at the other end marked "Paris" will turn into a famous French city with an aerodrome where I can land. But without this chart, all my years of training, all that went into preparing for this flight, no matter how perfectly the engine runs or how long the fuel lasts, all would be as directionless as those columns of smoke in the New England valleys behind me.

—CHARLES LINDBERGH,
THE SPIRIT OF ST. LOUIS

In 1929, Lieutenant James Doolittle, of the Army Air Corps, makes the first blind airplane landing, using instruments only.

In 1939, 12 years after Lucky Lindy's flight (that became Lindbergh's nickname), 22 passengers leave New York on the first commercial transatlantic flight. Their Pan American Airways Clipper has passenger compartments, sleeping berths, a dining room, and a bridal suite. The passengers each pay $375, and, with stops in the Azores and Portugal, it takes them 42 hours and 22 minutes to get to their destination: Marseilles, France.

Lindbergh was a genuine hero as long as he stuck to his specialty—flying. When he got involved with politics he was out of his league. More on that to come in this book.

beat the others, and he was used to flying the mail in all kinds of weather.

His little plane carried so much gasoline that some people thought it would never get into the air. But Lindbergh had planned carefully. There wasn't an extra ounce on the plane. He sat in a light wicker chair and carried little besides the fuel, a quart of water, a paper sack full of sandwiches, and a rubber raft. There was no parachute—it would be of no use over the ocean—and there was no radio. He would be on his own once he left the East Coast.

He headed out to sea, and people around the world learned of it on their radios. And then there was nothing to hear. That evening, during a boxing match at Yankee Stadium, the spectators rose and said a prayer for Charles Lindbergh, somewhere over the Atlantic Ocean. Boxing fans are not usually the prayingest people, but that night they were.

Lindbergh, meanwhile, was having a hard time. He had to stay awake or crash. After eight or ten hours of sitting in one place he began to doze. The night before the flight he had been so excited, and had had so much to do, that he had not slept at all. So he was tired before he got into the air. He got more tired, much more tired.

Luckily the plane was frail. It banged about in the wind, and each time he started to nod it went careening down toward the water. That woke him. Then, miraculously, the fatigue ended, he looked down, and there was Ireland. He was exactly where the charts—the charts he had drawn —said he should be. Lindbergh, like Columbus, was a superb navigator.

He didn't know that his plane was spotted over Ireland and the news radioed to America and France. People cheered and wept with relief. He was seen over London, and then over the English Channel. Thirty-three and a half hours after he left the United States, he circled the Eiffel Tower in Paris. It had taken less time than he expected, so he was worried that no one would be at the airport to meet him. Since he didn't speak French, he wondered how he would find his way from the airport into Paris. Then he looked down and saw a mob of people. They were waving and screaming.

The young flyer, who had brought nothing with him but the paper bag (which still had some sandwiches), was carried about on shoulders and hugged and kissed and cheered. He was rescued from the crowd only after his helmet was put on another American and the mob thought he was Lindbergh. Then the real Charles Lindbergh was taken to the American ambassador's house, where a butler ran his bath and put him to bed. Soon he was meeting kings and princes and more crowds of admirers. He wanted to stay in Europe and see the sights, but Calvin Coolidge sent a naval cruiser to Europe just to carry him and the *Spirit of St. Louis* back to America. He was a world hero.

People lost their heads over Charles Lindbergh. All over America there were parades and dinners and celebrations for the man they called the "Lone Eagle." It was wild. Nothing quite like it had ever happened before. Why did people go so crazy over Lindbergh?

What he did was daring and brave. But others did daring things. What he did was important. But if he hadn't flown the ocean, someone else would have soon enough. There was more to it than that. The frantic, roaring world of the '20s needed a hero. Lindbergh turned out to be just what was wanted.

You see, he was decent. He didn't drink and he didn't smoke. He was modest. He had good manners. He was offered a great deal of money to pretend to smoke for an advertisement. He wouldn't do it. He wouldn't do anything he didn't believe in.

New York City greets Charles Lindbergh in a blizzard of confetti and ticker tape. Later, Lindbergh flew all over the world and pioneered many commercial airline routes.

A publisher offered to hire a ghost writer to help him write a book about his flight. He said he'd write it himself. And he did. He turned down many money-making opportunities. He had values and standards, and he stuck to them.

In the Roaring Twenties, when many people thought only of having fun, or making money, or showing off, Lindbergh reminded people that courage, determination, and modesty were perhaps more satisfying. The American people had found a pretty good hero.

14 The Prosperity Balloon

Al Smith *(left)* lost the 1928 presidential election to Herbert Hoover *(right).* As secretary of commerce, Hoover had tried to restrain big business and the stock market—and failed. That led to big trouble during his presidency.

At its peak, in the mid-'20s, the Ku Klux Klan had 4 million members and political clout in the Midwest as well as the South.

Nineteen twenty-eight was an election year. Two good men were running for president. One was Herbert Hoover, an engineer and businessman, who had a reputation for accomplishing things. As a young college graduate, Hoover had managed a gold mine in the Australian desert and then gone to China as a mining expert. After that he got involved (successfully) with Burmese tin and Russian oil. He became known as a very capable man. When Woodrow Wilson needed someone to help feed Europe's starving people (during and after the First World War), he chose Herbert Hoover. He couldn't have found a better man for that job.

The other presidential candidate was the governor of New York. His name was Al Smith, and he was called the "Happy Warrior." Smith was colorful, full of fun, and honest and efficient, too. The governor introduced progressive reforms into New York State, appointed women and minorities to state jobs, and was fiscally responsible. (That means he did a good job with New York's budget.) The Happy Warrior was Catholic, Irish, and a New York City boy.

One of the reasons for reading history is to learn from past mistakes. That campaign was a mistake. Hoover didn't do bad things, but some of his supporters did.

They ran an anti-Catholic hate campaign. It was anti-city and anti-immigrant, too. The miserable Ku Klux Klan was still a powerful

force in parts of America. Those are the people who put sheets over their heads and minds. They, and other hate groups, said that the only real Americans were those whose backgrounds were Protestant, English, and white. They said that Catholics, Jews, Asians, Arabs, Germans, Irish, Italians, blacks, and American Indians—of all people—were not real Americans. And then, on top of that, they said they didn't like city people. They said that if Al Smith got elected, the Catholic pope would be ruling America from Rome. Would you believe that nonsense?

Well, sadly, a whole lot of people did.

Hoover was elected by an enormous majority. Perhaps Americans would have chosen him anyway, but the mean-spiritedness of that election should not have happened.

What kind of president was Herbert Hoover? Poor President Hoover. He wore stiff collars and he had a kind of stiff personality, but he didn't deserve the bad luck he had. He worked hard, yet his presidency was a disaster. But anyone elected in 1928 would have been in trouble.

No one understood that then. In 1928 most Americans were rejoicing. America seemed to have acquired King Midas's golden touch. (Although hardly anyone thought to remember what happened to Midas in the end.)

By 1928 the balloon of prosperity had been pumped so full of hot air that no one had ever seen anything quite like it. Many people were saying that something new had been found: an economic balloon that would just keep expanding. A few others were saying: "Stand back, cover your ears, and watch out."

The president goes fishin'. "There is no cause for worry," said Hoover's treasury secretary, Andrew Mellon. "The high tide of prosperity will continue."

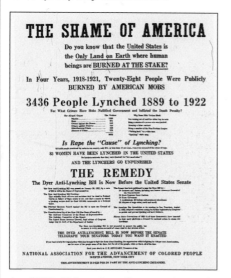

In 1922 this advertisement ran in support of an anti-lynching bill. The bill passed in the House but was defeated in the Senate.

Back to Africa

Marcus Garvey came to the United States from Jamaica in 1916 to launch his Universal Negro Improvement Association. Garvey, the most influential black leader of the 1920s, promoted self-help and race pride and urged blacks to return to their African heritage.

Marcus Garvey in 1922

15 Getting Rich Quickly

*Oh hush thee, my babe, granny's bought some
    more shares,
Daddy's gone out to play with the bulls and the bears,
Mother's buying on tips and she simply can't lose,
And baby shall have some expensive new shoes.*
—SATURDAY EVENING POST

In 1929 the stock market crashed, and some stockholders committed suicide.

October 24, 1929 was the stock market's day of reckoning— "Black Thursday."

The number of stockholders of American Telephone and Telegraph (AT&T) increased from 139,000 in 1920 to 567,000 in 1930. (That's *stockholders*, not shares of stock.)

Some companies issue millions of shares of stock. In 1997, IBM had 982,261,000 shares outstanding; Coca-Cola, 2,480,344,000. (Yes, that is more than 2 billion!)

In 1927, '28, and '29 it was easy to get rich. All you had to do was put a little money in the stock market. Then you could watch it turn into a whole lot of money. Here is how it worked.

Imagine that you are the owner of a large company: the ABC Automobile Company. You manufacture cars—good cars—and now you want to expand. You want to add new models. You need to build a new plant and buy a lot of equipment. You need money. So you decide to look for investors. You *go public*. You sell *shares* in your company. You sell 10,000 shares at $100 each. The shares are called "stock." Anyone who buys that stock becomes a part owner of the ABC Auto Company.

The new automobile models are a big success. The company earns a great deal of money. The stockholders get a percentage of the profits. The money they get is called a "dividend." The future of your company looks very good; many people want to buy stock in the ABC Company. Here is where a rule of economics, called *the law of supply and demand,* comes in. There are only 10,000 shares available. (That may sound like a lot, but it really isn't.) There is a big demand for ABC stock. People will pay $110 a share for it. Then they will pay $120 a share. Before long, ABC stock is selling for $200.

One stockholder, Mr. Jones, bought 10 shares at $100 each. (How much money did he spend?) Now he will sell them at $200 each. How much money will he have now? What is his profit? (You can do some problem-solving math here!)

Easy to make money that way, isn't it? Well, hold on. In the '20s it was even easier than that. People bought stocks on *margin*. (That means they borrowed most of the money. Today, laws restrict margin buying.) Margin means you don't have to pay $100 for $100 worth of stock. In 1927, you could pay $10, and borrow the other $90 from the stockbroker. (The person who buys and sells stock for you is called a "stockbroker.")

Now, if Mr. Jones puts $100 into ABC stock and buys on margin at 10 percent, he can have 10 shares instead of one. For $1,000, he will get 100 shares. If he sells the shares for $200 each, how much money will he have? He has to pay back the money he borrowed—$90 per share—but he still makes a whole lot of money. See if you can figure out how much. The good idea that many people soon had was to buy a lot of stock for very little money and get rich quickly.

The business of buying and selling stocks is called the "stock market." The place where stocks are bought and sold is called a "stock exchange." The most important stock exchange is in New York City, on Wall Street. Brokers from all over the world call Wall Street with orders to buy and sell.

The stock market usually reflects the business world. If things

The Securities and Exchange Commission (SEC), an independent government agency, was formed in 1934 to regulate securities (stocks and bonds) markets and investment businesses in the United States. Joseph P. Kennedy was its first chairman. Kennedy had a 17-year-old son, John Fitzgerald, with a big job in his future.

Conducting business at the New York Stock Exchange. A newspaper columnist wrote in 1928, "If buying and selling stocks is wrong, the government should close the Stock Exchange. If not, [it] should mind its own business."

Plans for New York City's Empire State Building (for many years the world's tallest) began at the height of the stock-market boom. By the time it was built, in 1931, half the office floors had to be closed because there were no businesses to occupy them.

Acumen (ACK-yoo-min) is "smarts."

In 1928 everyone was singing Eddie Cantor's hit, "Makin' Whoopee." A year later, there wasn't much whoopee around. Depression songs included: "I Got Plenty o' Nuthin'," "Shanty in an Old Shanty Town," the ironic "Life Is Just a Bowl of Cherries," and Eddie Cantor's new hit— "Potatoes are cheaper, Tomatoes are cheaper, Now's the time to fall in love."

Before he left office, President Coolidge said the stock market was "absolutely sound." Seven months later, this *New York Times* headline told a different story.

are going well, stocks go up. If business is poor, stocks go down. Brokers have a nickname for an "up" market. They call it a "bull" market. A down market is a "bear" market. The '20s were a prosperous time. Around 1924, the stock market started rising. At first it was a slow, moderate rise. Then the bulls got frisky.

In 1927, the market began to rise like fury. Almost overnight, stocks doubled and sometimes tripled in value. Everyone was talking about it. Newspapers wrote about it. The country's political leaders were all smiling. They felt it was their good leadership that was causing it. The business leaders were happy, too. Of course they thought it was their business acumen that was causing the stock-market boom. Many politicians and business leaders were saying that something new was happening. They said that the boom would just go on and on. That there was not going to be an end to it. And it wasn't just the business and political leaders who were saying all this. Professors from the nation's great universities were saying the same thing.

Now, suppose you are living in 1927. All your friends are getting rich and you aren't. You feel like a dummy, don't you? Why don't you take all your savings and buy as many stocks as you can? Buy them on margin so you can get lots of shares for your money. That's the smart thing to do, say many business experts.

TWO CENTS

STOCK PRICES SLUMP $14,000,000,000 IN NATION-WIDE STAMPEDE TO UNLOAD; BANKERS TO SUPPORT MARKET TODAY

Sixteen Leading Issues Down $2,893,520,108; Tel. & Tel. and Steel Among Heaviest Losers

A shrinkage of $2,893,520,108 in the open market value of the shares of sixteen representative companies resulted from yesterday's sweeping decline on the New York Stock Exchange. American Telephone and Telegraph was the heaviest loser.

PREMIER ISSUES HARD HIT

Unexpected Torrent of Liquidation Again

The broker has to sell when the stock price falls unless you come up with more money to pay for the drop in value—immediately.

So that is just what you do—in July of 1929. And some of your friends do it, too. The stock boom is phenomenal before July. That summer it is fantastic. Some people are buying stock in anything. It doesn't matter if the company has any real worth or not. No one seems to care. Just give me stock and more stock, I want to get rich. The stock balloon grows bigger and bigger and bigger.

And then guess what happens?

Picture a balloon being pumped up. Now watch that pin. You thought the balloon went up fast? Well, *whoosh*, it will come down much faster.

It happens in October of 1929. It is called the "panic." People go wild trying to sell. But now almost no one wants to buy.

Remember that $100 stock you bought on margin for $10? Well, when the price drops, your broker sells it. Too bad—you lose your $10. No. It's worse than that.

You see, you owe $90 on that stock. Deduct from the $90 the price your broker gets when he sells the stock. You owe the rest.

What was the pin that brought down the stock-market balloon in 1929?

After the Wall Street Crash, some people who once had good jobs were now selling apples on street corners. A popular comic strip of the times was called *Apple Mary*. Later, after the Depression, it was renamed *Mary Worth*.

77

OCT 29 ... DIES IRAE

Some Stock Prices

Company	SEPTEMBER 3, 1929	NOVEMBER 13, 1929
Radio Corporation of America (RCA)	505	28
Montgomery Ward	466½	49¼
General Motors	73	36

When the stock market crashed, artist James Rosenberg drew this picture of Wall Street with a panicked crowd, people jumping from collapsing buildings, thunderclouds and lightning, and flocks of black birds flying overhead. He called it Oct. 29 Dies Irae—Latin for "Day of Wrath," the name of a hymn sung in the mass for the dead.

New York hotel clerks were said to ask if guests wanted a room for jumping or for sleeping. Two business partners jumped from a high window at the Ritz Hotel, holding hands.

As fall the leaves by Autumn blown,
So fell those lovely shares I own.
Forlorn, disconsolate I sing,
Goodbye, goodbye to everything!

To car and plane and gleaming yacht
And rather ducal country cot
That all seemed surely mine by Spring,
Goodbye, goodbye to everything!

—NEW YORK TIMES,
NOVEMBER 3, 1929

But you bought 100 shares of stock—or was it 1,000, or 10,000? You put all your savings into the stock market. The experts said that was the smart thing to do.

Sorry, you owe the money. You don't have any money? You can sell your house, or your car, or both.

You just lost your job, too? You worked at the ABC Auto Company. Oh, that's too bad. Most people have stopped buying cars. Now the company is losing money. It has to sell that beautiful new plant. Why doesn't it sell stock to try to raise money? Are you kidding? No one is buying stock now.

And you know about the banks, don't you? The banks are all in trouble, too. You see, the banks lent money to the brokers and all those people who were buying stocks. Now they have no money. They are closing their doors.

What is happening in America?

We're having a depression, that's what. It will go on for 10 years. People will be out of work. The country will be in terrible shape.

Years later, economic historians will look at the wild stock-market boom and the awful depression and say that they didn't have to happen. If there had been good leadership and sensible regulations, they could have been prevented. That's where greed gets you, they'll say. That's where out-of-date thinking gets you, they'll say.

But where were those economists when they were needed?

And wasn't it fun while it lasted? (For some of us, anyway.) Those roaring, prosperous '20s are great to remember. Didn't we think we were smart that summer of 1929! Will you ever forget what it was like to be rich?

16 Down and Out

The Depression is an embarrassing thing. It is a shame to the system: the American Way that seemed so successful. All of a sudden, things broke down and didn't work. It's a difficult thing to understand today. To imagine this system, all of a sudden—for reasons having to do with paper, money, abstract things—breaking down.

—STUDS TERKEL,
HARD TIMES: AN ORAL HISTORY OF THE GREAT DEPRESSION

There were no jobs for 12 million. Many more had their hours and pay cut.

By 1932, at least 12 million people were out of work. That was one in four of all those who normally would work. Count your friends: pretend that the parents of every fourth person are unemployed. Start with yourself. Suddenly, your family has no income. What are you going to do?

America had had depressions before. They were supposed to be a kind of self-regulating part of capitalism. All the early depressions had something in common: it was the poorest workers who were hurt. They lost their jobs. They went hungry. The wealthy and the middle class suffered only slightly.

The Great Depression (which is what it came to be called) was different. It hurt more people—rich and poor—than any previous depression. And it went on, and on, and on.

To begin, the census of 1920 had shown that for the first time more than half the nation was urban. (Cities in the 1920s were small by today's measures; still, they were a

A depression is a time of decline in business activity accompanied by falling prices and high unemployment. The Great Depression was a time of severe decline in business activity. Today, the government tries to regulate such drastic ups and downs.

U.S. Steel's payroll of full-time workers fell from 225,000 in 1929 to zero on April 1, 1933; even the hands employed part-time in 1933 numbered only half as many as the full-time force of 1929. In Seattle, jobless families whose lights had been cut off spent every evening in darkness, some even without candles to light the blackened room. In December 1932, a New York couple moved to a cave in Central Park, where they lived for the next year.

—WILLIAM E. LEUCHTENBURG

79

In William Gropper's *Migration* a desperate farm family heads west, carrying their belongings. More than 3 million people left the Great Plains during the 1930s. They were called "Okies" and "Arkies." Why? Read John Steinbeck's novel *The Grapes of Wrath* for a great story about their plight.

In 1932, a wagon full of oats didn't pay for a pair of shoes. In Illinois in 1933, a bushel of corn sold for 10 cents. If there are 56 pounds in a bushel, how much does 25 cents' worth of corn weigh? Can you see why farmers had problems? Can you see why some talked about the failure of democracy and capitalism?

big change for people used to farm life.) This was the first major *urban* depression. City people have a terrible time without jobs or income.

Farmers don't have an easy time of it either, but at least they can usually feed themselves. America's farmers, as you remember, had not done well during the '20s. They didn't prosper with the rest of the nation. Crop prices stayed low. So the farmer's income was low, too. In 1929, most farms still didn't have electricity or indoor toilets. During the '30s, things got worse. The price of wheat and other grains dropped so low that it was sometimes below what it cost to grow it. Dairy farmers dumped thousands of gallons of milk onto the land to protest the low price of milk. Other farmers destroyed their own crops. All this waste was happening at a time when city children were hungry. Clearly, something was terribly wrong with our economic system.

Some public relief money for the destitute was organized under Hoover—but how did a family of four manage on $5.50 a week?

Photographer Dorothea Lange took this picture in Elm Grove, Oklahoma, in 1936 (see page 196 for another of her images). It was originally captioned: "People living in miserable poverty."

Farmers' income

in 1932 was one-third what it had been in 1929. Even farmers who could feed themselves were often unable to pay their mortages, loans, or taxes. So tens of thousands lost their farms. How would they feed themselves now? By 1932 a million people roamed the country, walking, hitchhiking, or riding boxcars. Starvation was rare, but hunger wasn't. Nor was shame and despair.

To **abuse** means to "hurt or to treat carelessly."

Many bankers, brokers, and investors had been wild and irresponsible in the '20s. That irresponsibility caused great hardship in the decade that followed. The American farmer had been irresponsible for generations. Mostly, he hadn't known better, although he should have: European farmers had been practicing crop rotation for over a century.

But, beginning in Jamestown, American farmers had abused land. Farmers used up the fertile land and moved on. They cut down trees and cut up the sod. It didn't have to happen. With careful farming, land can be preserved

Dust Bowl Days

The Dust Bowl is the name given to the region that was devastated by drought during the Depression years. It went from western Arkansas to the Oklahoma and Texas panhandles to New Mexico, Kansas, Colorado, and into Missouri. That area has little rainfall, light soil, and high winds. During World War I (when grain prices were high), farmers had plowed up thousands of acres of natural grassland to plant wheat. When drought struck (from 1934 to 1937), the soil lacked a grassy root system to hold it. Winds picked up the topsoil and turned it into black blizzards. Cattle choked and people fled. The government formed the Soil Conservation Service (in 1935) to teach farmers to terrace the land (to hold rainwater) and to plant trees and grass (to anchor the soil). Artists and writers such as Dorothea Lange, John Steinbeck, and Woody Guthrie photographed, wrote, and sang of the tragedy.

Alexander Hogue saw the awful effects of drought combined with dust and painted *Drought Stricken Area (above)*. Woody Guthrie walked the highways of the Dust Bowl and wrote a song called "So Long, It's Been Good to Know Yuh." Here's one stanza: *A dust storm hit, and it hit like thunder/ It dusted us over, and it covered us under/ Blocked out the traffic and blocked out the sun/ Straight for home all the people did run.*

and enriched. For generations, however, there had seemed to be so much land that few people in America worried. They weren't prepared for nature's tricks: for the droughts and wind storms that came, dried up the land, and turned it to desert. Soil—good, rich topsoil—became dust. Much of the Great Plains just blew away. It was so bad that sailors at sea, 20 miles off the Atlantic coast, swept Oklahoma dust from the decks of their ships. For drought-stricken farmers, there was nothing to do but leave the land, head for a city, and hope to find a job.

But there were no jobs to be found in the cities. City people were moving in with relatives on family farms. It was a time of national calamity.

Now, back to you. Remember, everyone in your family is out of work. How are you going to pay the rent? If you don't have any money, you can't do it. That means you're going to get evicted—thrown out—from your apartment. (If you live in a house and can't pay the mortgage, the bank will take your house.)

What are you going to do? Well, you're lucky: you happen to have a nice aunt and uncle, and they have jobs. So you move in with them. Things are crowded, and everyone gets a bit irritable, but you'll make it.

The family of your best friend—the girl who lives next door—isn't as lucky. They have no relatives to take them in and no place to go. The only thing they can think to do is to build a shack of old boxes and boards on some land near a garbage dump. They are not alone; hundreds of others are camped in that same unhealthy place. Those shanty towns—where people keep warm around open fires—spring up all over the nation. People call them "Hoovervilles," after the president, who says he is trying hard to solve the problem of the homeless and hungry. But nothing he does seems to help. By 1933, a million people in America are living in Hoovervilles.

Above: a glimpse of the fate of the American dream during the Depression. *Below:* This Hooverville in Seattle was home to thousands of "forgotten" men, women, and children.

17 Economic Disaster

We have now passed the worst and with continued unity of effort shall rapidly recover. (Herbert Hoover, 1930)
I do not believe that the power and duty of the general government ought to be extended to the relief of individual suffering. (Herbert Hoover, 1930)
We shall soon with the help of God be within sight of the day when poverty will be banished from the nation. (Herbert Hoover, 1932)

When Herbert Hoover is inaugurated, he says, "We in America today are nearer to the final triumph over poverty than ever before in the history of the land."

Herbert and Lou Henry Hoover in 1929.

Mellon pulled the whistle
Hoover rang the bell,
Wall Street gave the signal,
And the country went to hell. —ANONYMOUS DITTY

President Hoover thought the Depression was over. At least that is what he said, and he seems to have believed it. He said the economy was "fundamentally sound." And he said no one was starving in America.

Well, he was wrong about all those things. All he had to do was look out the windows of the White House and he would have seen hungry people. Thousands of veterans of the First World War were camped in the center of Washington, D.C. They were without jobs. Congress had voted them a bonus for their war service. The bonus was not due to be paid until 1945, but these were difficult times. The men needed the bonus now.

So they marched to Washington to see the president. Some brought their families. They built a Hooverville in Washington, D.C. They had no jobs or money, so they slept in tents, in empty buildings, in shacks on public grass. There were said to be 20,000 of

General MacArthur was helped in his breakup of the Bonus Army by another war hero to be, a Major Eisenhower. Hoover's public image got even worse.

them. They were called the "Bonus Army." Most carried American flags. Some were Medal of Honor winners; some had lost arms or legs in the services. Hoover wouldn't see any of them.

The police asked them to leave. They wouldn't go. So President Hoover sent the army. When the former soldiers first saw the army patrols and tanks and cavalry, they cheered. They thought the troops were parading for them. That was a mistake. The troops came with tear gas, guns, and bayonets. Their leader, General Douglas MacArthur, went farther than the president wished. His troops tore down the shacks; they used tear gas and billy clubs. People were hurt; a baby died. When it was over, Hoover said he saved the country from mob action. But many Americans hung their heads in shame.

What do popular songs tell you about a country? During the Depression people sang a song called "Brother, Can You Spare a Dime?" But the next presidential candidate campaigned with a song called "Happy Days Are Here Again."

The Bonus Marchers' shantytown burns down within sight of the Capitol. Millions watched it on movie newsreels.

In many cities, public employees such as teachers had to give up part of their already lean salaries to help pay for soup kitchens.

Mrs. Hoover *(right)* gives Christmas presents to poor families at the Central Union Mission in Washington, in 1932, to illustrate the virtue of private charity.

Hoover never understood. Each night he and Mrs. Hoover dressed formally for dinner—in tuxedo and long gown—and were served seven-course dinners by a large staff. Soldiers stood at attention around the table. Hoover thought about cutting down on White House expenditures, he said, but then decided that it would not be good for the people's morale. (Do you think the people agreed?)

Hoover was scared, and so were many other leaders. Democracy and capitalism seemed to be failing. Some people—who were considered to be sound thinkers—were saying that our system was finished. A new day was dawning, they said, and American democracy was out of date. All over the world the disruptions of war and depression were making people turn to dictators. Mussolini had taken control in Italy; Adolf Hitler was gaining power in Germany; and Joseph Stalin was in control in Soviet Russia. Some people in the United States thought those leaders were great men. We now know that they were terrible, bloodthirsty tyrants, but we are historians. We have the advantage of hindsight. We know how things came out. People in 1932 didn't know that.

Charles Lindbergh went to Germany and reported that Hitler was a fine leader. Wisconsin's governor, Philip LaFollette, was an admirer of Mussolini. Many intellectuals were fascinated with communism. They weren't the only ones. Senator Theodore Bilbo of Mississippi said, "I'm getting a little pink [communist] myself." The nation's favorite humorist, Will Rogers, said, "Those rascals in Russia...have got mighty good ideas... just think of everybody in a country going to work."

Could capitalism be saved? Were the democratic ideals of George Washington, Thomas Jefferson, and Abraham Lincoln old-fashioned? Mussolini said, "Democracy is sand driven by the wind." The writer William Manchester said that if Hoover had been re-elected, "the United States would have followed seven Latin American countries whose governments had been overthrown by Depression victims." That may be going a bit far. You don't have to agree with every historian. We in the United States have a strong Constitution and we value it. Still, this was a revolutionary age. Hoover, who was a brilliant engineer, was not the man for the times. He didn't understand the needs of ordinary people.

In 1930, when many Americans were going to bed hungry, he said: "The lesson should be constantly enforced that though the people support the government, the government should not support the people."

What Hoover meant was that no government money should be spent on relief programs. He thought people could help themselves. If government money was spent it should go to business. That would strengthen the economy, he said, and business money would "trickle down" to the people. Many economists believed as he did.

Of course WE CAN DO IT!

But how could we do it? We couldn't roll up our sleeves and get down to work when there was no work to be had.

Hoover didn't realize there was a need for new thinking. People were starving in the land of plenty. The gap between rich and poor had grown big as a chasm. Hoover believed in *voluntarism;* he thought individuals should help each other. It was a good idea, and there was a lot of neighborliness during the Depression, but it wasn't enough. More needed to be done, much more, or there might be a revolution.

Henry Ford, who was a pacifist (he didn't believe in fighting wars), bought a gun.

The poet Stephen Spender (who came from England for a visit) wrote about our country:

> *Despite its...amazing civilization, the social organization is right back in the Victorian Age....She has no pensions for her old people; no medical benefits for her workers; no unemployment insurance for any trade.*

We Americans had clung to the wrong parts of our economic past. No major industrial nation was so unprepared for calamity.

The United States needed a strong leader, someone who would be open to new ideas. Someone who would take charge. And that was just what we got. Fortunately, that strong leader loved America's democracy. He had been taught that being a good citizen means serving your country.

His name was Franklin Delano Roosevelt, and he became the most loved president since Abraham Lincoln—and also the most hated president since Abraham Lincoln. He was one of the most dynamic, active men in all of American history. And that is amazing, because he could hardly stand up by himself.

The Depression was a terrible spiral. Many people were so poor that they stopped buying goods altogether. If people didn't buy goods, manufacturers couldn't make them. So workers couldn't get work, and they, too, couldn't buy anything. So more and more people became poorer and poorer.

When Franklin Delano Roosevelt campaigned for the presidency he traveled all over the country to talk to people.

18 A Boy Who Loved History

James Roosevelt and his son, Franklin. Baby boys wore dresses in the 19th century.

As a boy he was called Frank. As an adult he was Franklin or FDR.

All of our people all over the country—except the pure-blooded Indians—are immigrants or descendants of immigrants, including even those who came over on the *Mayflower*.

—FRANKLIN DELANO ROOSEVELT, IN A SPEECH GIVEN IN BOSTON, 1944

"I think families are the most interesting things in the world," said Franklin Delano Roosevelt. His wife agreed. She said, "In the story of every family is the stuff from which both novels and eventually history is written."

They were right. Every family—rich or poor, famous or little known—has stories. If you don't know your family stories, start asking questions. You are sure to hear some interesting things.

Franklin Roosevelt's family was full of stories, and all his life he listened to them. His father, James Roosevelt, could remember the Civil War. He told Frank stories of Abraham Lincoln and of the general who gave Lincoln a hard time, James's friend General George B. McClellan.

Franklin Delano Roosevelt loved history. He loved the way history can connect you to past times. His own family connections went way back into early American history. The first American Roosevelt was a Dutch farmer named Claes. He arrived in New York about 1650. One of Claes's grandsons started the branch of the family that led to Franklin. Another grandson had descendants who included Theodore Roosevelt and Eleanor Roosevelt (we'll get to her soon).

When Franklin was growing up, his father liked to show him a teapot that

Franklin aged three with his dog Budgy and his pet donkey

Hyde Park, where FDR grew up, is a big, comfortable house, but it is homey, not a palace like the neighboring Vanderbilt mansion.

had belonged to Franklin's great-great-grandfather, Isaac Roosevelt. Isaac was a banker and a Patriot during the Revolutionary War and a friend of Alexander Hamilton. But it was Hamilton's rival, Thomas Jefferson, whom young Roosevelt really admired. He tried to find some connection between Isaac and Jefferson, but he never could. (Years later, when Franklin Roosevelt became president, he tried to be like Jefferson and concern himself with the average citizen, whom he called "the forgotten man." However, he also believed, like Alexander Hamilton, in the importance of a strong federal government.)

Franklin's father wasn't the only one with stories to tell. His mother talked of her family, the Delanos. The first American Delano was French, and a Huguenot, and he arrived at the Plymouth Colony in 1621. (He missed the *Mayflower* by a year.) It was love that brought him to America. He was in love with Priscilla Mullins. She must have been special; Myles Standish and John Alden loved her, too. She married Alden and rejected the Frenchman, Philippe de la Noye, who, some years later, married an Englishwoman named Hester. Then he dropped the *ye* from his name and became Delano.

The Roosevelts and Delanos prospered in America. Most of them, like Theodore Roosevelt, became Republicans. But James Roosevelt, Franklin's father, was a Democrat.

When Frank was five years old, in 1887, his father took him to meet President Grover Cleveland. Cleveland was the first Democrat to be president in 28 years. James Roosevelt had contributed money to help get him elected. But being president is no easy job; the day young FDR visited, the chief executive was tired. "My little man," said the huge president to the small boy dressed in a sailor suit standing in front of him, "I am making a strange wish for you. It is that you may never be president of the United States."

Well, you know how kids are. Just tell them what you don't want them to do, and that is what they will go for. So it may have been that day that Franklin Delano Roosevelt first got the idea that he would like to be president.

Franklin aged 11, with his mother, Sara. She smothered him with love, advice, and overprotection.

I am interested in and have respect for whatever people believe, even if I cannot understand their beliefs or share their experiences.

—FRANKLIN DELANO ROOSEVELT

89

19 How About This?

Franklin with the family dog, Monk. He did not go to school until he was 14. Instead he was tutored with the children of other local estate owners.

How would you like this: a house in New York City, a country house overlooking the Hudson River at Hyde Park, New York, and a summer house in Campobello, New Brunswick, by the sea? Now, just for variety you'll take plenty of trips: Paris this year, England the next. You'll be surrounded by servants: cooks, drivers, gardeners, a laundress, and your own private teachers. You'll have a pony and dogs and just about everything you want. In addition, you'll have loving parents who adore you and see that children come to play with you. When you finally go off to school—at age 14—your parents will take you in their own railroad car; it has a bedroom and living room.

Sounds pretty terrific? Well, it wasn't bad—and that was what Franklin Delano Roosevelt's childhood was like. No, he wasn't a prince; he just lived like one. So did other children of the wealthy American upper class in the late 19th century. That was at a time when 11 million of the 12 million families in America had an average income of $380 a year. Only a few thousand families could be called rich. And, compared with the really wealthy Vanderbilts or Astors, the Roosevelts were no big deal.

How do you think you would turn out if you had everything you wanted? Do you think you might be vain, arrogant, spoiled, and worth-

The Roosevelt house at Campobello in New Brunswick, Canada, near the coast of Maine

less? Well, that is just how some of those rich kids turned out. (Some poor kids probably turned out that way, too.) But not Frank Roosevelt.

His parents gave him good values. They expected him to behave like a gentleman: to be kind, considerate, and honest. They gave him a strong religious faith. (He was an Episcopalian.) That faith gave him courage when he needed it.

He needed courage many times in his life. First, when he went away to Groton. Groton was a rich boys' school (and still is, mostly), but the headmaster didn't believe in pampering. Every boy was expected to take a cold shower each morning. That wasn't really hard, if you gritted your teeth and showered fast; it was much harder trying to be just one of the group when you had always been the center of attention. Franklin was handsome, charming, and friendly—but he never got along with people his age as well as he did with those older and younger. At Groton, he didn't get picked for awards and teams he really wanted, and that hurt; but he had been taught not to complain.

It became a part of his character, not complaining. He would be enthusiastic and act as if everything was fine, even if it wasn't. It made him pleasant to be around, but it also made some of his friends uneasy. They never knew how he really felt.

Franklin went to Harvard, as his parents expected him to do, and to Columbia Law School. His mother intended him to live the comfortable life of a country squire, as his father had before him. After all, with the family money, he had no need to work hard. He didn't have to concern himself with others, but he did. When he was a student himself he wrote to segregated southern colleges appealing to them to do as Harvard did and accept black students.

He may have been concerned with those who were less fortunate than himself because of an important influence in his life, a man he admired more than anyone else. A man who cared about people and wanted to make the world better than he had found it. It was the president of the United States, his cousin Theodore.

When Frank was a child he loved to visit Sagamore Hill, TR's Long Island home in Oyster Bay. There he could romp and run with energetic, fun-loving Teddy and his five children. Frank decided that someday he, too, would have a big family and play with his family as TR did.

Franklin in a school play. He loved to have fun and play practical jokes.

Franklin, aged 20, now a big man on campus at Harvard

One day early that first term [at Groton] a group of older boys... trapped him in a corner of the corridor and ordered him to dance, jabbing hard at his ankles with hockey sticks to make sure he stepped fast enough....Refusing ever to seem a victim, even to himself, he pirouetted and toe-danced in apparent high spirits as if he were part of the fun instead of its object. No one sensed his fear. "He did what he was told," one eyewitness recalled, "with such good grace that the class soon let him go."

—GEOFFREY C. WARD,
BEFORE THE TRUMPET

The Vanderbilts had a huge king's palace of a mansion in Hyde Park just down the road from the Roosevelts' house. Maybe that was why Franklin Roosevelt never thought of himself as rich. Today, both houses are museums, and you can walk from one to the other on a special hiking trail that meanders alongside, affording a spectacular view of the Hudson River.

He also decided he would serve his country—and he set out to do it. First he became a New York state senator. Then Woodrow Wilson made him assistant secretary of the navy. (TR had held that job.) In 1920, he ran for vice president with James Cox against Warren Harding and Calvin Coolidge. He lost, but people began to talk of him as a politician to watch.

He soon had a fine family: a busy wife, a daughter, and four sons. He was an energetic father, full of good spirits, who loved to sail and hike. Yale's football coach watched him exercise and said, "Mr. Roosevelt is a beautifully built man with the long muscles of an athlete."

But what he wanted most of all was to be president. He told that to a classmate while he was still in college. And it looked as if he had a good chance to fulfill his ambition.

Then tragedy struck. He went to bed one night, not feeling well; the next morning, he couldn't move. He was 39 and he had a dreaded disease: *poliomyelitis* (PO-lee-o-my-uh-LY-tiss). Usually it struck children: its common name was *infantile paralysis*. It was especially hard on adult victims. (Later, Jonas Salk and Albert Sabin developed vaccines to prevent polio; but that was still 20 years in the future.)

Imagine you're an active man, father of five children, with big ideas. Then, overnight, you're crippled. At first Roosevelt couldn't move at all. Slowly, with painful therapy and concentration, he regained the use of his upper body. He would never run again. When he walked it was in heavy braces with agonizing steps. Would you have the courage to go on with your plans? Would you feel sorry for yourself? Would you take it easy and let people wait on you?

At first, everyone was sure his career was finished. Franklin's mother expected him to live the life of a wealthy invalid. But Franklin was determined to live normally. He was a cheerful man, and an optimist. Where others saw problems, he saw challenges.

His parents had trained him not to complain, and, even when he was in great pain, he didn't. As it turned out, he gained something from his terrible illness. It taught him patience and made him more determined. It made him know frustration, and sorrow, and anguish. He—the boy who had had everything—learned to understand those who had troubles.

On top of all that, he was married to a very unusual woman. She, too, was determined that he should not change his goals. Her name was Eleanor.

FDR held his job as assistant navy secretary for seven years. He loved the work, and was disappointed that the navy didn't see much action in the First World War.

20 A Lonely Little Girl

Elliott and Anna Hall Roosevelt, Eleanor's father and mother. Her mother was a great society beauty, but cold to her daughter. When she died Eleanor seemed hardly to feel the loss. But when Elliott died, two years later, she refused to believe it. After that he was always alive for her.

I knew a child once who adored her father. She was an ugly little thing, keenly conscious of her deficiencies, and her father, the only person who really cared for her, was away much of the time; but he never criticized her or blamed her, instead he wrote her letters and stories, telling her how much he dreamed of her growing up and what they would do together in the future, but she must be truthful, loyal, brave, well-educated, or the woman he dreamed of would not be there when the wonderful day came for them to fare forth together. The child was full of fears and because of them lying was easy; she had no intellectual stimulus at that time and yet she made herself as the years went on into a fairly good copy of the picture he had painted.

Even at three Eleanor was lonely. Her mother called her "Granny," because she was "old-fashioned" and not pretty.

Eleanor Roosevelt was writing about herself. She wasn't ugly, but she thought she was, perhaps because her mother was a great beauty. Eleanor had long blond hair, blue eyes, a plain face, and teeth that seemed too big for her mouth. She was shy, easily frightened, and serious. Sometimes she told little lies because she was afraid people would not want to hear the truth.

Her father, Theodore Roosevelt's handsome brother Elliott, was a daredevil horseman and a man-about-town. Everyone who knew Elliott loved him. He was sweet-natured and charming. He became an alcoholic. It ruined his life, and his family's life, too.

But he loved his sad-eyed daughter. He called her "little Nell," and told her that he wanted her to grow up to be good, brave, kind,

Eleanor at her grandmother's. She loved her horse and hated the childish short dresses her grandmother made her wear.

Eleanor's Other Mother

Marie Souvestre was the principal of the school that Eleanor attended in England. She was a strong, proud Frenchwoman, and the girls at Allenswood had to speak French. She taught Eleanor to think for herself, and she taught her that women could become something without the help of men.

and honest. And she did. She always remembered those things that were fine in Elliott Roosevelt and forgave him his shortcomings. All her life she kept his letters, read them and reread them, and tried to be the kind of woman who would have made him proud. That wasn't easy.

She had a dreadful childhood. Not an ordinary unhappy childhood; a horrible, awful, terribly lonely one.

She adored her father, but most of the time he wasn't there. She lived for his visits. Sometimes there were wonderful carriage rides with her father driving the horses fast and little Eleanor holding him tightly. Sometimes he promised to see her and then, perhaps because he was drunk, he disappointed his child. Once he took her and his prize terriers for a walk. They stopped at his men's club and he left Eleanor and the dogs with the doorkeeper while he went inside "for just a minute." Hours later he was carried out—drunk; the little girl was sent home in a taxi.

When she was eight her mother died. When she was nine her brother died. When she was ten her father died.

Is this too sad to read? It is all true. Eleanor and her younger brother, Hall, went to live with their grandmother. The grandmother didn't know anything about bringing up children. She lived in a big, spooky house. The noise of children playing bothered her. A governess took care of Eleanor and Hall. The governess didn't like Eleanor. She was mean to her.

Then Eleanor was sent away to school in England. Finally, her life took a happy turn. The principal of the school realized that Eleanor had a good mind and a generous, kind nature. Eleanor became her favorite student. Eleanor soon became everyone's favorite. She had a talent for leadership. She was able to inspire others to do their best.

The child who had not always told the truth, who had struggled against the demons that make people lie, was becoming the kind of person her father had wished her to be. For the rest of her life, Eleanor Roosevelt would be known for her truthfulness.

Eleanor smartly dressed for European travel on a school vacation.

21 First Lady of the World

Eleanor in her wedding dress. FDR's mother made them wait a year to announce the engagement.

Eleanor and Franklin at a friend's house in Scotland on their European honeymoon

When Eleanor came home from England she was tall and willowy. She still thought she was ugly, but other people didn't. Especially her cousin, Franklin, the most dashing of the young Roosevelts. Like Eleanor's uncle Theodore, Franklin had energy and ambition. Like Elliott Roosevelt, he had charm. He and Eleanor fell deeply in love.

They were soon married. Before long, Eleanor found herself with five children, three houses that needed managing, and a husband with a busy political career.

Then her husband fell ill with polio. She'd had experience with tragedy. Maybe that was why she handled it so well. Her husband's legs would never carry him again. She said that needn't stop him. There was no reason to change his goals. She could become his legs—and his eyes and ears, too.

They were a team, one of the greatest political teams in history. He became president, but she was his link to the people. He stayed in the White House; she went to coal mines and factories and workers' meetings. Then she told the president what people were thinking.

The first time she spoke before an audience her knees shook. Soon she was one of the most successful speakers of her day. She wrote a newspaper column and a magazine column and books. She was the first First Lady to hold regular press conferences. She served food to needy people, read stories to poor children, visited hospitals, and spoke out for minority rights

Eleanor as First Lady was usually out and about. Here she is visiting an Ohio coal mine.

95

Eleanor fought against racial discrimination. Here, she talks to Aubrey Williams, executive director of the National Youth Administration, and Mary McLeod Bethune, the NYA's Director of Negro Activities, at a conference.

The Bonus Army returned to Washington when Roosevelt was president. It was called the "Second Bonus Army." He offered the veterans the use of an army camp, sent food, coffee, a convention tent, and doctors, and then added a navy band to entertain them. Mrs. Roosevelt came to visit. "Hoover sent the army," said one Bonus Army man. "Roosevelt sent his wife." Roosevelt did not pay the bonuses, but he did offer the veterans jobs in the Civilian Conservation Corps (CCC), planting trees, creating parks, and so forth. Many went to work.

when few others did.

It is hard for a president—any president—to take time to check out government projects. Besides, everyone knows when a president is coming to visit, so things can be made to look good beforehand. But no one ever knew where Eleanor Roosevelt would pop up. The Secret Service had a code name for her: they called her "Rover." She checked up on government projects and told the president the truth about what was happening. If someone wrote to the president complaining about a problem, Eleanor made sure the letter got answered. Sometimes she invited the letter writer to dinner at the White House. She invited all kinds of people to White House meals: young and old, rich and poor, people of every race and religion.

Always, she fought for the underdog—for those who were persecuted, or treated unfairly. She wanted to see that all people were given an equal opportunity. She worked for women's rights. She worked for minority rights. She stood on the side of truth and justice.

When a women's organization refused to let Marian Anderson, a renowned black singer, use its auditorium, Mrs. Roosevelt resigned from the organization. She encouraged Marian Anderson to sing on the steps of the Lincoln Memorial in Washington, D.C. Marian Anderson sang "America," and more people heard her than could have fit in any auditorium.

Shy, insecure, ugly-duckling Eleanor had grown up to be a strong, sensitive, capable person. She had a kind of no-nonsense wisdom that made her admired around the world. She has been called the outstanding woman of the 20th century. Eleanor Roosevelt became everything her father wanted her to be—and more.

Eleanor's press conferences were generally only for women writers. That got newspapers to hire more female journalists.

Marian Anderson sings "America" on the steps of the Lincoln Memorial.

96

22 Handicap or Character Builder?

FDR's wheelchair, built from an ordinary kitchen chair

When Franklin Roosevelt first entered politics he was wealthy, charming, astoundingly good-natured, ambitious, and optimistic—but not very serious. Perhaps everything had come to him too easily. In his boyhood and youth and early manhood he had not known suffering. Now he knew. Now there were steel braces on his legs and a current of steel in his veins.

He had gone through a testing time of great pain when he could hardly move at all. He would never stand by himself again—he always had to call on others for help. Sometimes he crawled to the bathroom. For a proud man it must have been very hard. But if he felt sorry for himself he didn't show it. Even at first, when he was very sick, he made those who came to see him feel good. Everyone remarked on his good spirits, his lighthearted manner, and his great courage.

He was determined to conquer polio, so he worked hard exercising and swimming and learning to manipulate the seven-pound leg braces. His slim, boyish torso became strong, muscular, and powerful. For seven years he

"How marvelous it feels!" Roosevelt said, the first time he slid into the pool at Warm Springs. "I don't think I'll ever get out!"

He was brave, that Roosevelt. O Lordy he was brave. He must have known that he would never be whole, but he was brave. A clear-cut nothing-from-the-waist-down case, and yet he forced himself to walk. With steel and fire, he forced his arms to take him across the room, across the lawn, down the steps. He knew, some part of him knew he would never be walking at the head of the Labor Day Parade again, but he kept on pouring his will into what was left of his muscles, trying to walk that walk again.

—LORENZO MILAM,
THE CRIPPLE LIBERATION FRONT MARCHING BAND BLUES

Exuberance is "joyful enthusiasm."

Keeping It Simple

Roosevelt knew that good writing is clear and direct. In 1942, during the Second World War, there was fear that we might be attacked by air. It was important that lights not show at night and help enemy pilots spot targets. So a government official wrote this blackout order for Washington, D.C.:

Such preparations shall be made as will completely obscure all Federal buildings and non-Federal buildings occupied by the Federal government during an air raid for any period of time from visibility by reason of internal or external illumination.

Roosevelt rewrote the blackout order. "Tell them," he said, "that in buildings where they have to keep the work going to put something across the windows."

An aide wrote: "We are trying to construct a more inclusive society." Roosevelt changed that to: "We are going to make a country where no one is left out."

Roosevelt had to work tremendously hard to learn to walk with leg braces and crutches. But, said Eleanor, "It gave him strength and courage he had not had before."

stayed away from active political life, trying to learn to walk again, but his weak legs would not respond. If he despaired, if he was sorrowful, he didn't let anyone see it.

He refused to act like an invalid. And so he sailed and went to dances and did everything anyone else would have done. Only he did it with more energy and exuberance than most people. At a square dance—where he called the dances—others remarked at what a good time he seemed to be having. This was a man who had always loved to dance. How do you think he really felt?

Perhaps, by not showing his inner feelings, he convinced himself, as he convinced others, that he wasn't hurting.

A man whose office was next door to Roosevelt's mother's house in New York wrote this:

Our staff used to watch him from the windows as he got out of his car, clicking the brace on one leg into place, then the other. Pulling himself erect by his powerful arms, he would then make his way slowly up the inclined board-walk which covered one side of the steps. He never failed to pause, grin and wave a greeting to the girls in our windows…as always, every move was a test of courage, met as a matter of course with dignity; he simply would not allow bodily disability to defeat his will.

FDR had a Model A Ford built with hand controls. He loved to go out driving; in a car he could feel as physically independent as the next man.

It would have been easier to become president if he had not had polio. And it probably would have happened. After all, he had the Roosevelt name, that incredible energy, and determination. But his disease changed everything. It made the goal harder to achieve; it made the victory sweeter.

And it made the man different. He had been called a political *dilettante* (DILL-uh-tont), which means an "amateur": someone who dabbles, who plays the game for sport, as just one of many interests. There was something to the accusation.

William Phillips, a friend who knew him when he first entered politics, described him as "brilliant, lovable, and somewhat happy-go-lucky…always amusing, always the life of the party." But serious, or focused in his beliefs? No one thought that. "He was not a heavyweight…not particularly steady in his views."

Did his crippling disease make him a stronger, more sensitive, more serious person? There are many who believe it did.

Roosevelt collected and built model boats and ships. For a very busy man, he had a lot of hobbies.

23 Candidate Roosevelt

Hunger marchers in Washington, D.C. In 1932, the year FDR was elected president, one out of four Americans belonged to a family in which no one had full-time work.

The little plane tossed about in the heavy wind. The pilot, looking down, followed the path of the old Erie Canal; he was flying from Albany to Chicago. Twice he landed for more fuel. In the backseat, the plane's violent swaying was too much for young John Roosevelt. He threw up.

But John didn't even tell his parents. They were busy. His father was polishing a speech he was soon to deliver. FDR was on his way to the Democratic National Convention to personally accept that party's nomination for president of the United States. No candidate had done that before.

In the old horse-and-buggy days, before telephones, it sometimes took a week or more for a messenger to tell a candidate he had been chosen by his party to run for president. Only then was the candidate expected to make an acceptance

A New Deal—Deal Us In!

When Roosevelt accepted the Democratic Party's nomination for president, he pledged a "new deal for the American people." A cartoonist picked up the phrase, and *New Deal* was the name soon given to President Roosevelt's domestic (home) policies. The ideas of the New Deal were firmly in the American tradition. They were based on Progressive ideas: on opposition to mo- nopoly; on a belief that government should help regulate the economy; and on the conviction that no one wants to be poor and that most poverty is the result of social problems. The New Deal's methods were experimental; some worked, some didn't. The Progressive Party was important at the end of the 19th and beginning of the 20th century. Theodore Roosevelt was a Progressive.

speech. That time gap had been continued for tradition's sake. Roosevelt saw
no reason to stick with the old ways.

Besides, Roosevelt wanted people to
know he would be an active candidate
and president. If anyone was worried
that his weak legs would slow him down,
he would show them: they would not. So
he flew to Chicago, locked the braces on
his legs, and stood before the delegates.

Hyde Park's front porch on election night: left to right, daughter
Anna, son John, mother Sara, FDR, son Franklin Jr., and Eleanor.

"I pledge you, I pledge myself, to a new
deal for the American people," said FDR in his captivating, mellifluous voice. To a nation that had suffered three years of devastating depression, the words *new deal* sounded very good. The
Republican candidate, Herbert Hoover, didn't have a chance.

Whether he deserved it or not, Hoover was blamed for the
Depression. Roosevelt campaigned hard, but he didn't have to.
People wanted a change. The election was a landslide. Forty-two
of forty-eight states went Democratic.

Today, because of the 20th Amendment (adopted in 1933), a
candidate elected in November becomes president in January.

Mellifluous (muh-LIFF-floo-
us) means "flowing and sweet
as honey." It is from the same
roots as *mellow* and *fluid*.

In 1932, the delay was longer.
Roosevelt did not take office until
March. Between Election Day in
November 1932 and Inauguration
Day in March 1933, the economic
situation got worse and worse.

By March, the U.S. economy
seemed close to collapse. Every
day more and more banks closed.
Those who had gold were hoarding it. There was even a question
as to whether the government
had enough money to meet its
payroll. A newspaper reporter described the mood of the people in
Washington, D.C., as like "a beleaguered capital in wartime."
General Douglas MacArthur prepared his troops for a possible
riot. Capitalism, said many experts, was too sick to recover.

It wasn't only speculators who
lost money in the Great Crash.
A lot of banks failed, and many
people lost all their savings; there
was no banking insurance then.

As the black crows of hard times
come flying over the horizon, this
cartoon mocks Hoover's attempts
to scare them off with a straw man.

Beleaguered means "under siege."

101

24 President Roosevelt

Over the airwaves, FDR sounded warm, not like a speechmaking politician. He always began a radio talk with the words "My friends."

The patient seems to be dying. Dr. Leave Alone is in the sickroom. Leave Alone is a distinguished man. He wears a dark suit and a dark manner. He has been telling the patient that there is nothing wrong. But the patient is gasping for breath. He screams in pain. The doctor attempts to be calm. "Pull down the shades, keep your voices low, and don't disturb the patient," he tells the family. "Medical science has never encountered an illness like this. We will hope for a miracle." The family weeps, the patient groans. Dr. Leave Alone says, "We have done everything we can," and departs.

Desperate, the family turns to another doctor. A big, hearty man, he comes into the sickroom, pulls up the shades, lets in the sunshine, and in a booming voice tells the patient, "You're going to get well." Then he adds, "The

Let me first assert my firm belief that the only thing we have to fear is fear itself," said the new president in his inaugural address. "I shall ask the Congress for...broad executive power to wage a war against the emergency, as great as the power that would be given to me if we were invaded by a foreign foe," he said, and the people cheered.

Dr. New Deal brings an alphabet soup of medicines for sick Uncle Sam. If a remedy didn't work, he would try another.

only thing you have to fear is fear itself."

"Medical science may not know how to treat this illness," says confident Dr. New Deal, "but that won't stop us. We'll find a way. First we'll try one method, then another, then another. We'll throw out what doesn't work, we'll keep what does. Start smiling, everybody—you're going to see some action—we'll lick this disease!"

Dr. New Deal, of course, was Franklin D. Roosevelt. The sick patient was the economy of the United States. Almost everyone thought it was dying and would have to be replaced. But not FDR. He was a man of action. Besides that, he was a *pragmatist*. That means someone who believes in whatever will work. Someone who has practical intelligence. That was FDR. He also had energy and enthusiasm, and that gave people confidence. They believed in him. Here are some words to describe FDR:

FORCEFUL
DYNAMIC
RESOURCEFUL
OPTIMISTIC
OUTGOING
SENSITIVE
ENERGETIC
VIVACIOUS
ENTHUSIASTIC
LIKABLE
TIRELESS

When former president Calvin Coolidge was asked for his ideas on how to lick the Depression, he said:

> In other periods of depression it has always been possible to see some things which were solid and upon which you could base hope, but as I look about me I see nothing to give ground for hope—nothing of man.

A group of prominent bankers was called to Washington to see what suggestions they had for solving the banking crisis. They had none.

President Herbert Hoover said, "We are at the end of our string. There is nothing more we can do."

That gives you an idea of the gloom and pessimism

At the Democratic convention in 1932, comedian Will Rogers *(right)* introduced FDR *(far left)*. He certainly managed to make the candidate laugh uproariously.

Inauguration Day 1933. "America hasn't been as happy in three years as they are today," said Will Rogers (ungrammatically but cheerfully). "They know they got a man in there who is wise to Congress....If he burned down the Capitol, we would cheer and say, 'Well, at least we got a fire started anyhow.'"

Thomas Corcoran, a New Deal official, said, "Without bloodshed, the New Deal defanged our most dangerous internal crisis since the crisis of 1861." What did he mean? Do you agree?

"THE ONLY THING WE HAVE TO FEAR IS FEAR ITSELF--

This seems to be a photograph, but look closely: it's really a collage (a paste-up) put together from several photos by an anonymous artist to honor FDR.

One senator said, "The admirable trait about Roosevelt is that he has the guts to try." His opponents said programs such as Social Security *(right)* could be paid for only by raising taxes and spending too much money.

A Woman in the Cabinet

In 1933 President Roosevelt appoints Frances Perkins as his secretary of labor. She serves for 12 years, in all his administrations, and is the first woman cabinet member.

in Washington the day Hoover packed his bags and left the White House.

The next day, March 4, 1933, Franklin Roosevelt stood, bareheaded, in front of the Capitol, holding tightly to a lectern. It was his inauguration day. Some small boys perched in nearby tree limbs; dignitaries sat in special seats; but most of the crowd stood and shivered in the cold wind. When the new president spoke, his strong voice cut through the gloom. All across the land, people clustered around radios to hear what he had to say.

"This nation asks for action, and action now," said President Roosevelt. "We must act quickly."

And that was exactly what he did: act quickly. The first 100 days of his presidency are famous for all the things that got done. Congress was on vacation when Roosevelt took office. He called Congress back into session. He began to act. Soon new programs and laws were pouring out of Washington. "It is common sense to take a method and try it," said Roosevelt. "If it fails, admit it frankly and try another. But above all, try something."

And he also said, "The only thing we have to fear is fear itself."

FDR put together a group of advisers. Newspaper reporters called them "the brain trust." Many were college professors. They were new to government, but they had ideas, intelligence, and a desire to help their country. They worked hard. Washington became an exciting place for idealistic, energetic citizen workers.

Roosevelt's ideas really were a "New Deal." He changed America profoundly. He probably saved American capitalism, but he changed some of its habits. The New Deal did away with most child labor, regulated the stock market, made bank deposits safe, helped make employers pay fair wages to employees, encouraged workers' unions, limited hours of work, helped farmers, brought electricity into rural areas, and gave Americans an old-age pension policy called "Social Security." The New Deal made the government an active participant in citizens' lives. Yet most of the ideas of the New Deal were not really new. They were the old Progressive ideas in a new package. They had already been tried in Europe. America was behind the times when it came to social welfare.

In order to put people to work, the New Deal sent young people out of doors and paid them to plant trees, build parks, and fight fires. It paid painters to paint murals, writers to write books, and musicians to play and create music. Needy people were given money for food and shelter.

Civilian Conservation Corps members planting seedlings in Oregon. Young men aged between 18 and 25 whose families were on relief got room and board for a year and were paid $30 a month, $25 of which went straight to their families.

New Ideas for a New Deal

Here are some of the best-known New Deal programs (a star means the program still exists today):

• * The SECURITIES AND EXCHANGE COMMISSION (SEC) was formed to regulate the stock market.

• * The FEDERAL DEPOSIT INSURANCE CORPORATION (FDIC) insured bank deposits. We no longer had to fear bank failures.

• The CIVILIAN CONSERVATION CORPS (CCC) gave jobs to more than 2 million out-of-work young men in the nation's parklands: building roads, trails, cabins, and campgrounds. Many are still in use today. "Of all the forest planting, public and private, in the history of the nation, more than half was done by the CCC," says historian William Leuchtenburg.

• The PUBLIC WORKS ADMINISTRATION (PWA) built New York's Triborough Bridge and Lincoln Tunnel; Oregon's Coastal Highway; Texas's port of Brownsville; the road between Key West and mainland Florida; and the University of New Mexico's library.

• The CIVILIAN WORKS ADMINISTRATION (CWA) lasted less than a year, but employed more than 4 million men and women. Opera singers were sent to the Ozark mountains (where none had ever sung before); teachers kept rural schools open; Native Americans restocked the Kodiak Islands with snowshoe rabbits.

• * The TENNESSEE VALLEY AUTHORITY (TVA) began as an experiment in regional planning; it became a model corporation producing electric power and fertilizer.

• * The SOCIAL SECURITY ACT established old-age pensions, unemployment benefits, and welfare benefits for the elderly, children, and the handicapped.

• The WORKS PROGRESS ADMINISTRATION (WPA) was a huge program that put people to work building highways, clearing slums, and doing construction work in rural areas. Writers produced regional guidebooks and did oral histories and other research. Artists decorated hundreds of post offices and other public buildings with paintings and sculptures. Musicians organized orchestras and choruses. Actors toured plays to communities that had never seen live theater before. In five years (1935–1939), the WPA gave jobs to 8.5 million people at a cost of $11 billion.

This cartoon caption says, "Come along. We're going to the Trans-Lux to hiss Roosevelt." The Trans-Lux was a newsreel theater (this was before TV). Who are those people, and why are they going to hiss Roosevelt?

Critics of the New Deal saw the government diving gaily into an ocean of spending and debt and taking the drowning taxpayer with it.

Roosevelt did something else. Something that was really new and innovative. Something that people in power almost never do without a battle. He shared power with those who had never held it before.

From the country's earliest days, the leaders of the United States had mostly been drawn from one group: white Protestant men of northern European descent. (That wasn't fair; nor did it reflect the true spirit of the men, like Jefferson, Madison, and Washington, who were responsible for the Declaration of Independence and the Constitution.)

Franklin Roosevelt was part of that white-Protestant-male traditional aristocracy of privilege. But he opened its doors. He included in positions of government power those who had been excluded: women, blacks, eastern Europeans, southern Europeans, American Indians, Catholics, and Jews. He began a process that soon added Muslims, Buddhists, Hindus, and all who are citizens. He rejected the idea of an aristocracy of birth and replaced it with the goal of an aristocracy of talent.

There were those who hated him for doing it. It is hard for us today to imagine how much some people hated him. He was called "a traitor to his class." Some who had gone to school with him refused to speak his name.

Some, in the business world, hated him, too. Business leaders had been the heroes of the Roaring Twenties. Calvin Coolidge had said, "The business of America is business." The Depression changed all that. Now Roosevelt was the popular hero, and the American people were demanding that business be regulated for the public good.

Before the New Deal, government had been expected to provide conditions that would help business grow and be profitable. But government was expected to do nothing for the people—the workers—who made business profits possible. When Roosevelt was president, many laws were passed to help workers, farmers and ordinary citizens. Government money was spent on the poor. Some people didn't like that idea. But others understood that, if it was done wisely, the nation would be stronger and better for it.

25 Twentieth-Century Monsters

A magazine portrayed Hitler as the strongman come to deliver the German damsel in distress.

In the Weimar Republic in Germany, the chancellor was chosen (like the prime minister in Great Britain) by his party's leaders—not by direct election. The head of the party with the most seats in the Reichstag became chancellor. Hitler's party was the National Socialist (Nazi) Party.

On the very day of Franklin Delano Roosevelt's first inauguration, the day he told America that "the only thing we have to fear is fear itself," something fearful was happening in Germany. It would change the fate of the world. The Reichstag (RIKES-tahg)—Germany's congress—was deciding to give absolute government power to the German chancellor, Adolf Hitler.

Imagine a country letting its meanest, worst people take charge. Imagine giving those kinds of people the power of life and death over the whole nation. Imagine a nation where children are taught to be tattletales and tell the secret police about anyone who protests—even their parents. Imagine a nation that burns the books of its greatest writers because it fears and hates ideas and truth. Imagine a nation that kills people because it doesn't like their religion or their ideas, or because they are handicapped. That's what happened in Germany in the 1930s.

Germany no longer even attempted to be a democracy. It willingly became a dictatorship—the most evil dictatorship in recorded history. (Although the dictatorship in Soviet Russia was almost as bad.) The Germans used their intelligence and skill to create factories of death. They allowed their government to do unspeakable deeds. Some Germans did not approve, but few spoke out. To do so meant risking their lives.

But in that March of 1933, most people in America paid no attention to what was happening in Germany.

German industry and transportation collapsed after the Great War. In 1922, these women and children, desperate for fuel, were gleaning coal scraps on a mine dump heap.

In October 1922, 4,500 German marks bought one U.S. dollar. In November 1923, the exchange rate was 4.2 *trillion* marks to the dollar. One woman lit the fire with marks; children played blocks with bundles of bills.

During the Great War, the German leaders kept telling their people that Germany was winning. So it was a real shock when those same leaders surrendered. Somehow the Germans couldn't believe they had really lost. They felt betrayed.

The Versailles Treaty was harsh; but in 1918, the Germans had forced their own harsh peace treaty on Russia at a place in Poland called Brest-Litovsk.

The Depression seemed more important. Adolf Hitler? He was a little man with a black brush mustache and dark straight hair that fell into his face. He strutted about raising his arm in a straight salute and shrieking his speeches. He didn't seem evil; he seemed silly.

The German people didn't find him silly. They were still angry about the war they had lost. Their leaders and historians had misled them about the causes of the Great War. They had been told that Germany was no more to blame for the start of the First World War than any other nation. That wasn't true. But the Germans believed it; they thought the rest of the world had picked on them. They thought the Versailles Treaty—the treaty that had ended the Great War—was unfair. They were humiliated by the terms of peace. Germany was not allowed to have a large army, navy, or air force. Germany was to make large cash payments—called "reparations" (rep-uh-RAY-shuns)—to the winners to help pay back the costs of the war. Germany was made to say that it was totally to blame for the war.

Since most Germans thought they were no more to blame for the war than others, they were furious, especially about those payments. As it turned out, we lent Germany much more than they ever paid. But most German citizens didn't know that.

Germany's citizens were angry and unhappy. Their country was in awful shape economically. Soon after the war, Germany suffered a time of incredible inflation. The government began printing lots of money (partly to pay those reparations). Printing presses ran day and night. When you print a lot of currency, soon none of it is worth much. Prices in Germany rose beyond belief. In 1923, a Hershey chocolate bar cost 150,000 German marks (in the United States the same chocolate bar cost a nickel). German money was almost worthless. Buying a loaf of bread might take a bucketful of bills. People lost all their savings. They had to use up everything they had just to pay the rent. Then, after they had finally got the inflation under control, the Great Depression set in worldwide. Unemployment became a big problem.

What the German people wanted was a leader: someone who could lead them out of the economic mess, someone who could make them feel good about themselves. During this Depression era people in other countries were looking for strong leaders, too. The Americans chose Franklin Delano Roosevelt. The Germans turned to Adolf Hitler.

They made a big mistake. That mistake would cost them and the rest of the world grief beyond imagining. Their leader was an evil genius who captured his countrymen and women in a web of words and convinced them that he could solve all their problems. He told them that others were to blame for Germany's troubles. He told them that Germany was greater than any other nation and meant to rule the world. He told them that other peoples should be their slaves. He told them that they must love their "fatherland"—Germany—before all else. He told them that they must not worry about right and wrong, because anything Germany did would be right. He told them that *might makes right*—and most believed him.

Hitler wasn't the only one who preached the gospel of nationalism—that loving your nation was more important than loving truth and right actions. Militant nationalism was a 20th-century disease.

In Japan, a military dictatorship took control of the nation and began stomping on its neighbors. The Japanese, too, were suffering from economic depression. They thought they needed more room for their growing population.

They began by attacking China

Japanese troops keep captured guerrillas at bayonet point in 1932, during the first Japanese assault on the Asian continent, the invasion of Manchuria.

A mass roll call of Nazi troops at the third annual Nuremberg rally, November 1935. The rallies featured legions of soldiers and artillery, blaring music, torchlight parades, and speeches by Hitler that drove his listeners into a frenzy.

Summer camp for Hitler Youth, the Nazi children's organization. The pressure to join was very strong.

109

GERMAN AGGRESSION *by* 1941

NORWAY 1940

FINLAND

SWEDEN

ESTONIA

LATVIA

LITHUANIA

GER.

U.S.S.R.

IRELAND

DENMARK 1940

GREAT BRITAIN

NETHERLANDS 1940

1940 BELGIUM

1939

GERMANY

POLAND

1936 RHINELAND

1938-39 CZECHOSLOVAKIA

ATLANTIC OCEAN

FRANCE 1940

SWITZ. 1938 AUSTRIA

HUNGARY

ROMANIA

PORTUGAL

SPAIN

ITALY

YUGOSLAVIA 1941

ALBANIA

GREECE 1940

BULGARIA

TURKEY

Mediterranean Sea

After the Bolshevik Revolution in 1917, the old Russian empire became a collection of republics called the Union of Soviet Socialist Republics—the U.S.S.R., or Soviet Union. The republics were not all Russian—they included Central Asian Muslim peoples such as the Uzbeks, the Tadjiks, and the Azerbaijanis; Caucasian peoples such as the Georgians and Armenians; and Baltic peoples such as Latvians and Estonians. These countries were supposed to be independent, but they were not. They were controlled by Russia, the Soviet Union's largest and most powerful republic. Many in America referred to the U.S.S.R. as Russia, or Soviet Russia.

with a ferocity that is still hard to believe. In a massive campaign of terror, millions of civilians were tortured and killed. Just as in Germany, the Japanese rulers told the people they were a superior race and destined to rule others.

In Spain, a strongman named Francisco Franco muscled his way to power, although many Spaniards (and other Europeans, and some Americans, too) fought against him.

In Italy, a pompous dictator named Benito Mussolini took control of the government. Mussolini was a bully, and, like all bullies, he picked on those who were weak. He sent Italian forces to Ethiopia. There, Italian tanks, machine guns, and airplanes attacked brave

Francisco Franco

Benito Mussolini

Ethiopians, who fought back with spears and lances.

Russia's dictator, Joseph Stalin, killed millions of his own people—anyone who he believed might threaten his rule. His kind of government, he said, would soon conquer the world.

Joseph Stalin

Mussolini called his political movement *Fascism*. Hitler named his *Nazism,* for National Socialism. In Russia, the forces of evil took charge in the name of *communism*. These were all *totalitarian* forms of government. They were the opposite of democracy. In a totalitarian state, individual people don't matter—only the state is important.

Why did good people listen to these terrible leaders? Why did some modern nations become gangster nations? Those are questions that are hard to answer. It didn't happen here; it didn't happen in England. Were we just lucky, or did our democratic tradition give us the strength to resist the evil thinkers?

The Depression brought grave problems to the people of the United States. In 1933, hogs were selling for only 2½ cents a pound in the Midwest. One farmer had to sell all his hogs to pay his rent for a month. Another farmer sold a wagonload of oats to buy a pair of shoes. Hunger and malnutrition were serious problems in the '30s. Many Americans were angry and desperate. It is not surprising that some of them, too, listened to horrid voices. They needed to blame someone for their problems, so they paid attention to: the Ku Klux Klan; the German-American Bund (BOONT), which was inspired by the Nazis; a radio preacher, Father Coughlin, who spewed out a message of hate; and others. A few Americans no longer believed that "all men are created equal." A few wanted to throw out the Bill of Rights. But most Americans rejected the philosophies of wickedness.

Why did we escape the 20th-century virus of totalitarianism? Was it New Deal leadership? Was it our tradition of liberty and democracy? What do you think? Could it happen here?

Father Coughlin

The Bund combined Hitler worship—its salutes, rallies, and brown shirts—with perverted patriotism: Washington was the "first Fascist."

Charles Lindbergh urged Americans not to fight Hitler. He let his antiwar feelings make him do and say things he would later regret. He allowed himself to be used by the Nazis. The America First Committee that he supported got financial aid from Nazi Germany.

Communism is an economic system, and as such it is not evil. It just doesn't seem to work efficiently. When combined with a harsh political system, as it was in Soviet Russia, it was evil.

26 A Final Solution

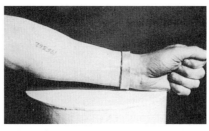

On arrival in a Nazi camp, new inmates' clothes and belongings were taken away, their heads shaved, and identification numbers tattooed on their arms.

He who permits evil, commits evil. This is what makes for the haunting sense of guilt in our culture. Many a member of the dominant group will earnestly aver that he never intended that Negroes should be insulted and maltreated: that his heart is sore and ashamed when he reads of the defiling of the Jewish synagogues by hoodlums. He did not intend these things, but he created the social sanction for these things.

—HENRY A. OVERSTREET

In Germany, as soon as the Nazis came to power, Jews were persecuted for no reason except their religion. Jews who weren't even religious were persecuted. A Jewish grandparent was enough to get you into trouble.

There was an evil disease in the world that had been around for a very long time. It was called "anti-Semitism." It was hatred of Jews. No one was quite sure where it came from—although the subject was studied endlessly.

No question about it, Jews have been troublesome to some kings and priests. Jews believe that every person is equal before God, which, if you think about it, means that a king is no different from a peasant. Now that is a nonconforming idea. It must have been maddening to some authorities. Imagine where it might lead if everyone thought that way. (Just where might it lead? To democracy, eventually?)

The Jews are people with a powerful book. It is a freedom document, written in Hebrew, and called a "bible." It tells stories that make people think and ask questions. It tells how, a long time ago, the Jews escaped from Egypt, where they were slaves of the pharaoh. It tells of Queen Esther and how she saved the Jews when they refused to bow to the king's agent, wicked Haman (HAY-mun).

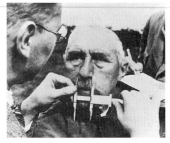

Using principles based on "scientific" ideas, Nazis subjected people to absurd tests of their ethnic origins, such as measuring the size of a nose.

Berlin, the morning after *Kristall-nacht*, November 10, 1938—the "Night of Broken Glass," when the windows of Jewish businesses were shattered by yelling mobs.

That Bible became the starting point for a new religion called Christianity, and for another, called Islam.

At first, Christians were persecuted. Then, in the 4th century C.E., the Roman emperor Constantine became a Christian. Before long, most Europeans were Christians. But not the Jews. The Jews stayed with their beliefs. They wouldn't change their religion even for the emperor or the pope. It was frustrating to those in charge. Others might catch their independent ideas. So some of those in power hated them, and blamed them for whatever was wrong at the time. If there was a plague, it was the Jews' fault; if there was an economic disaster, it was the Jews' fault. Finally, many of Europe's Christians went on religious wars called "Crusades." The crusaders' aim was to recapture Jerusalem from the Muslims; but anyone not a Christian was considered an *infidel*—a heretic—and was liable to be murdered. Thousands of Jews died, and Jewish property was up for grabs among the crusaders.

In Spain, in 1492, Jews were told they had to leave the country (Jews had already been expelled from many other parts of Europe). They couldn't take their possessions with them. It was a windfall for the rest of the Spaniards. Jews who converted to Christianity were able to stay in Spain, but some were tried by a religious court called the "Inquisition," and, if they were found guilty of not being sincere Christians, they were burned alive. That was the opposite of what real Christianity stands for, but most people didn't question the rulers and priests who were in command.

So anti-Semitism stayed in the air. It was still mainly about that nonconformism. Then, in 1517, Martin Luther came into conflict with the Catholic Church and things got complicated. The Catholics, and each of the new Protestant sects, seemed to believe that they alone had the only true religion; that led to centuries of religious wars. Christians were killing Christians—as well as Jews. Hatred and killing in the name of God shouldn't make sense, but it seemed to to some

Freedom of Conscience

In Virginia's Statute for Religious Freedom, Thomas Jefferson wrote: *Be it enacted by the General Assembly, that no man shall...suffer on account of his religious opinions or belief.*

John Adams, discussing the subject of religion and government was, as usual, blunt: *Congress shall never meddle with religion other than to say their own prayers.*

And James Madison said: *Religion and government will both exist in greater purity, the less they are mixed together.*

The Founding Fathers were clear: ours was to be a nation founded on the idea of separation of church and state. There are no religious restrictions on citizenship in the Constitution.

In the Name of Science

That pseudo-science of race led to another "science" called "eugenics," based on the idea that races should keep their blood pure by getting rid of problems. In the 1880s, Pennsylvania began sterilizing children who were said to be "feeble-minded." (*Sterilizing* means they were "made unable to have children themselves.") Indiana was the first state to pass a law forcing the sterilization of certain people who were thought undesirable. (That usually meant the retarded, or criminals, or, often, sexually active teenagers.) Another 31 states followed with sterilization laws. In California, some 17,000 people were sterilized, most of them immigrants. In Virginia, a 1924 sterilization law was challenged, taken to the U.S. Supreme Court—and upheld. In that case, *Buck* v. *Bell,* Carrie Buck had been sterilized because she was said to be retarded. Recent evidence suggests that was not even true. The Nazis used Virginia's law as a model. Under their sterilization act, thousands were made unable to have children.

GERMANS! DEFEND YOURSELVES! DO NOT BUY FROM JEWS! says the sign on this Jewish-owned store in Berlin. The Nazi boycott of Jewish businesses began on April 1, 1933. Shops were marked with a yellow Star of David. After 1939, German Jews had to wear the yellow star sewn onto their clothes, too.

Troops force Polish Jews out of the Warsaw ghetto.

people (who couldn't have been thinking deeply).

There was another factor that produced anti-Semitism. It was economic. Jews were often successful and provided competition. That may have made some people jealous or annoyed.

Then, toward the end of the 18th century, things began to change. After the French Revolution (in 1789), Jews, in one nation after another, were emancipated. They entered Europe's mainstream. People who had been locked in ghettoes were suddenly let out and began a period of great achievement. Especially in Germany, Austria, and Hungary, Jews flocked to the universities, and soon many of them were doctors, lawyers, bankers, store owners, newspaper writers, musicians, teachers, and political leaders. Although Jews made up only about 1 percent of the German population, they won one-quarter of all Germany's Nobel prizes in the first third of the 20th century. Some Germans were proud of that achievement, but others saw it as a problem.

There was something else. It had to do with a science—at least, some people thought it was a science. It was racism, and today we think of it as a false, or pseudo- (SU-doe) science. But, in the 19th century, some thinkers (who believed in what they were doing) divided the world's peoples into races and then said that some races were better than others. They even said that race determines blood, and character, and brain size. They said that the Jews were an evil race that was polluting Aryan (white northern European) blood. They said that people of color were inferior to whites. Since this theory was supposed to be scientific, there were many who believed them.

Hitler used that idea of racism, and bad blood, and the old anti-Semitic virus to explain Germany's problems. It was convenient. Whatever was wrong must be the fault of the Jews. Inflation? Depression? The Treaty of Versailles? It was all because of the Jews, said Hitler. He was an astonishing speaker. People were swept up by his words; they believed

The start of the journey for most eastern European Jews, like these people from Cracow in Poland, was a filthy, crowded train journey in a boxcar. The luckier ones ended up in camps where they had to work for the German war effort, such as at this airfield.

him. It was easier than blaming themselves.

Besides, many Jews had good jobs and nice homes. All their property was inviting. Hitler was soon giving it away.

Germany went farther down the road of wickedness than any nation in history. The Nazis used the technology of the modern world for purposes of murder. They built factories for killing. Then they hunted down the Jews of Europe, packed them in railroad cars, and sent them to be slaughtered. They didn't just kill Jews. Hitler hated Slavs (who lived in eastern Europe), gypsies, people who were crippled, and anyone who didn't agree with him. The Nazis killed as many of those people as they could. They enslaved others. It made Hitler and his terror troops feel powerful (and it set an example for other dictators in the future). Because of what was happening to the Jews and Hitler's other victims, all of Europe shivered. People knew that after the Jews were gone it could happen to them.

"The removal and transportation of Europe's Jews was a fact known to every inhabitant of the continent," says John Keegan, a historian of the Second World War. "Their disappearance defined the barbaric ruthlessness of Nazi rule...and warned that what had been done to one people might be done to another."

Guests or Prisoners?

After 1943 (until war's end), no Jews entered the United States except for 874 "guests of the president" who were denied visas, sent to an internment camp in Oswego, New York, kept behind barbed wire, and told they would have to leave the country as soon as the war was over. Some had close relatives in the U.S. One refugee, whose paralyzed wife lived on Long Island, could not visit her even at holiday time.

More than 55,000 immigrant quota spots for eastern Europeans went unfilled in 1944. During the war years, about 100,000 German prisoners of war—mostly Nazi soldiers—were safe in the United States.

Visiting through the barbed wire at Oswego.

Arrival in Auschwitz

Auschwitz (OWSH-vits) had been a Polish military barracks, but in 1940 it was turned into a concentration camp. Two years later, gas chambers and furnaces (for killing purposes) were added at a section of the camp called Birkenau. By this time Hitler was frantically rounding up Jews from across Europe; Auschwitz, because it was on a major railroad line between Cracow (in Poland) and Vienna (in Austria), was where most were sent. Day and night, sealed trains arrived from Holland, France, Austria, Czechoslovakia, Yugoslavia, Italy, and other European countries. Auschwitz grew to encompass 40 square miles.

The Wiesels arrived in 1944 on a train from Hungary. One of the family survived: a son named Elie. He wrote a book called Night *that tells what happened to him. Here is some of it.*

The cherished objects we had brought with us thus far were left behind in the train, and with them, at last, our illusions.

Every two yards or so an SS man held his tommy gun trained on us. Hand in hand we followed the crowd.

An SS noncommissioned officer came to meet us, a truncheon in his hand. He gave the order:

"Men to the left! Women to the right!"

Eight words spoken quietly, indifferently, without emotion. Eight short, simple words. Yet that was the moment when I parted from my mother. I had not had time to think, but already I felt the pressure of my father's hand: we were alone. For a part of a second I glimpsed my mother and my sisters moving away to the right. Tzipora held Mother's hand. I saw them disappear into my distance; my mother was stroking my sister's fair hair, as though to protect her, while I walked on with my father and the other men. And I did not know that in that place, at that moment, I was parting from my mother and Tzipora forever. I went on walking. My father held on to my hand.

Children at the camps were photographed in prison uniform so they could be identified if they escaped. Few lived long enough to try.

Behind me, an old man fell to the ground. Near him was an SS man, putting his revolver back in its holster.

My hand shifted to my father's arm. I had one thought—not to lose him. Not to be left alone.

The SS officers gave the order: "Form fives!"

Commotion. At all costs we must keep together.

"Here, kid, how old are you?"

It was one of the prisoners who asked me this. I could not see his face, but his voice was tense and weary.

"I'm not quite fifteen yet."

"No. Eighteen."

"But I'm not," I said. "Fifteen."

"Fool. Listen to what *I* say."

Then he questioned my father, who replied: "Fifty."

The other grew more furious than ever.

"No, not fifty. Forty. Do you understand? Eighteen and forty."

He disappeared into the night shadows. A second man came up, spitting oaths at us.

"What have you come here for, you sons of bitches? What are you doing here, eh?"

Someone dared to answer him. "What do you think? Do you suppose we've come here for our pleasure? Do you think we asked to come?"

A little more, and the man would have killed him.

"You shut your trap, you filthy swine, or I'll squash you right now! You'd have done better to have hanged yourselves where you were than to come here. Didn't you know what was in store for you at Auschwitz? Haven't you heard about it? In 1944?"

No, we had not heard. No one had told us.

Did all this have anything to do with the United States?

That is a good question.

Suppose you see someone beating up someone else. Really beating her up. She is going to end up in the hospital, or maybe dead.

What do you do? This isn't your fight. If you try to break it up you almost certainly will get slugged. Should you call the police? Should you stay out of it? If someone is killed it won't be your fault. Or will it?

Are we responsible for others? Do you agree that "He who permits evil, commits evil"?

In 1939, 20,000 children—all under 14—were in danger in Germany. Hitler wished to get rid of them. He was willing to let them leave the country. Many were Jewish; some were not. Quakers, Jews, Catholics, and members of other American church

Top left: laborers at the camp at Buchenwald. Many starved to death or were killed when too weak to work. *Top right:* inmates in an Austrian camp where the Nazis were said to perform "scientific" experiments on human beings. *Center:* a gas chamber at Maidanek, in Poland. New arrivals were told to undress for showers; poison gas came out of the showerheads. *Left:* a box full of the wedding rings that all were made to remove.

groups agreed to take responsibility for them. It would not cost the government any money. Surely America would accept them.

This is the land of promise. The land built on a spirit of generosity. The land that, from the days of the Pilgrims, has been a place of refuge for the persecuted of other nations.

Many Jews and opponents of the Nazis did escape, some to the United States. Among them were pianist Rudolf Serkin *(below)* and philosopher and writer Hannah Arendt *(above),* who wrote an important book about Hitler and fascism called *The Banality of Evil.*

The League of Nations had given Jews the right to buy land in Palestine, but the British put pressure on European nations not to let them emigrate to Palestine. In 1942, the ship *Struma,* with 769 refugees aboard, was turned away from Palestine by the British. The ship sank in the Bosphorus; one passenger survived.

Those who had founded this nation, and written its Constitution, had been clear about it. Although they were much alike—white, male, Protestant, and of English descent—the Founders didn't limit the nation to people like themselves. For they were unselfish in spirit and very wise. They believed they were creating something new on earth, a generous nation that would find strength in diversity. A nation that would take peoples from all over the world and allow them to become a new people—an American people—more varied in its roots than any before it.

The Founders offered the gift of citizenship, not just to their kinsmen, not just to the strong, or the handsome, or the rich, but fully and equally to all who came here to live.

The nation grew, and its citizens understood what was intended. Under the Statue of Liberty they carved the words *Give me your tired, your poor, your huddled masses yearning to breathe free.* Men, women, and children—from all over the world—came to this "promised land." Many were *refugees*—people fleeing tyranny and persecution.

Of course the children Hitler was threatening with death would be welcome in America. Or would they?

There was another tradition here. It was not the tradition of Jefferson, Washington, and Madison. It was a spirit of greed and selfishness.

It was that selfish spirit that had caused Alien and Sedition acts to be passed soon after the nation was founded. It was that spirit that had caused men to rise in Congress and say that slavery was a "positive good." It was the spirit behind the Know-Nothing Party and the nativists. It was the spirit of the Ku Klux Klan and the only-one-race-allowed country club. It was mean-spirited. It was anti-American, but it was there.

Here is what Abraham Lincoln wrote in 1855:

> As a nation we began by declaring that "all men are created equal." We now practically read it, "all men are created equal except Negroes." When the Know-Nothings get control, it will read "all men are created equal except Negroes and foreigners and Catholics." When it comes to this, I shall prefer emigrating to some country where they make no pretense of loving liberty.

The Imperial Wizard of the Ku Klux Klan, in 1923, said: *Negroes, Catholics, and Jews are the undesirable elements in America.* The Imperial Wizard was a bigot, but some people listened to him. They didn't know their history. Maybe they hadn't read the famous letter George Washington wrote the Jews of Newport, Rhode Island. In it, he said: *The government of the United States…gives to bigotry no sanction, to persecution no assistance.*

In 1924, Congress passed a racist immigration bill. Its aim was to keep Asians, Jews, blacks, and people who can't speak English out of America.

Anti-Semitism and xenophobia (zen-uh-FO-bee-ya—"anti-foreignism") had infected some Americans. Some of the people with the disease were in Congress, the State Department, and other government offices. Did they realize they were being un-American?

Most Americans are hospitable. Eighty-five newspapers wrote editorials urging Congress to pass a bill letting in those 20,000 children from Germany. Citizens offered their homes to the young refugees. Leaders of church, labor, and social organizations spoke out. But not loudly enough.

The head of a powerful group, the American Coalition of Patriotic Societies, told Congress to "protect the youth of America from this foreign invasion." He shouted the message of the racists. There was fear in the world, and a depression, and Congress listened.

Does this have anything to do with you? Isn't anti-Semitism a Jewish problem? No. It is a human problem. People who hate become hateful. A nation that allows bigotry and persecution is diminished by it. In 1939, the U.S. government gave sanction to bigotry and assistance to persecution. Those children were not allowed into the United States.

Hitler now knew that no one would rescue the children. He felt free to build death camps. That is where most of those 20,000 children—and a girl named Anne Frank—ended their lives.

The *St. Louis* Is Turned Back

Liane Reif-Lehrer, pictured here *(left)* in 1938 with her mother and brother, was born in Vienna, Austria, in 1934. These are her words:

I should have been a normal little girl, happy with my special doll, my big brother (who thought me a noisy nuisance but loved me anyway), and my doting parents. But the world around me was going mad, and the life I should have had was not to be.

Liane's father was a dentist, but the Nazis would not let him or other Jews work. One day he was found dead at the bottom of a stairwell. Did he commit suicide or was he murdered? Liane has never been quite sure.

She was not yet five when she, her mother, her brother, and 934 other Jewish passengers set sail for Cuba from the port of Hamburg, Germany, on the luxury liner *St. Louis*. The passengers all had Cuban entry permits, and most had quota numbers that would have let them into the United States eventually. But while they were at sea, Cuba changed its immigration policy. Most of the passengers were not allowed off the ship.

After days of frantic negotiations, the *St. Louis* was forced to leave Cuba. The captain didn't want to take the Jewish passengers back to Germany; he knew what would happen to them there. He headed for Miami. Telegrams were sent to President Roosevelt asking him to grant asylum to the refugees. The telegrams were not answered. A U.S. Coast Guard boat stayed close to the *St. Louis* to make sure no passengers jumped overboard and tried to swim ashore. Finally, the captain could do nothing; he headed back to Europe. Here are Liane's words again:

My mother and brother and I were among the passengers who survived—about a fourth of those on the ship. We were sent back to Europe and given haven in France, only to find the Nazis at our doorstep again a few months later. But somehow we managed to get to the U.S. in 1941. I was seven, a wide-eyed, bewildered girl, greeted by New York children playing street games to wartime hate ditties. I remember a particularly popular one: "Whistle while you work, Hitler is a jerk, Mussolini is a meanie, and the Japs are worse."

I tried to explain that some Germans were good and some bad. On more than one occasion my "non-groupy" response earned me the wrath of the parents, who did not hesitate to suggest that I "go back to where I came from." It hurts even now when I remember the tone with which those words were delivered.

Dr. Liane Reif-Lehrer moved to Massachusetts and became a research scientist, a mother, and an American.

27 War and the Scientists

Albert Einstein was a mathematical physicist who ranks with Galileo and Newton as one of the great thinkers who have helped us understand the universe. He published his theories of relativity in 1905 and 1916. In 1921 he won a Nobel prize. In 1933 he wrote *Why War?* with Sigmund Freud (the father of psychology, and also a Jew).

Einstein sought U.S. citizenship in 1935; immigration laws forced him to leave the country and then reenter it. So Einstein spent nine days in Bermuda with his family. He used this photo on his new immigration visa.

A.D. 1939

AMERICAN

HA

Immigrant identification card No. 831234 issued

Einstein *(left)* with American scientist Charles Steinmetz, on a visit to the U.S. in 1921, shortly before he won a Nobel prize.

There were some people who felt they had to see Roosevelt. But the president couldn't see everyone who wanted to see him—especially with a war on.

It was a group of scientists. They had something very important to tell the president. How could they get to him? If they had gone to Mrs. Roosevelt they might have had no problem. But they didn't think of that. They met and planned and worried.

Then someone got a bright idea. There was one scientist whom Roosevelt would listen to. Almost anyone in the world would listen to him. He was Albert Einstein, and he was the greatest scientist of the 20th century and one of the greatest scientists of all time. He had discovered the theory of relativity. That theory changed the way science looks at the world.

Einstein was born in Germany. Because he was Jewish he had to escape from that country, and he did. He became a fellow of the Institute for Advanced Study in Princeton, New Jersey, and an American citizen. Other scientists fled the evil regimes in Germany and Italy, too. Hitler lost their fine minds and talents. Britain and the United States gained them.

Some of those scientists knew that the Germans were working on a secret weapon. It was more powerful than anything the world had ever known. If the Germans developed it, they would probably win the war and rule the world. Roosevelt had to be told.

Italian physicist Enrico Fermi *(right)* meets Maria Martinez, the great potter of San Ildefonso in New Mexico, near Los Alamos, where the secret research was carried out.

Left: Hungarian John von Neumann helped create the first big computers; he also worked on the Manhattan project, as the secret weapon research was called. *Right:* Hans Bethe, from Germany, who had the ability to find simple ways to deal with complex problems.

But back then no one paid much attention to scientists who talked of secret weapons. They sounded like dreamers. Roosevelt was busy with important practical matters. He needed to strengthen the army and navy. He needed warships and carriers and tanks and planes. He had a depression to fight, too. Secret weapons? Super bombs? Wasn't that the stuff of science fiction?

The scientists got Einstein to write a letter to the president. Then they got Alexander Sachs, a businessman and an economist (he had advised the government about the New Deal), to deliver it to him. Sachs told the president about the Germans' secret weapon. The president didn't seem to be paying attention. He must have had all those other things on his mind. Sachs was desperate. How could he get the president to pay attention?

Finally, he remembered that Roosevelt loved history. He used that knowledge. He told Roosevelt that when the French emperor Napoleon was fighting the British, the American scientist Robert Fulton had gone to Napoleon with his steamship invention. Fulton told Napoleon that troops could be carried in steamships. Napoleon didn't pay attention. Roosevelt knew that if Napoleon had listened he might have been able to invade England and win his war.

Roosevelt didn't want to make the mistake Napoleon had made. He was ready to listen to the scientists. He was ready to read Einstein's letter. He decided that the United States should work on the secret weapon and try to develop it before the Germans did.

It was an enormous decision. It would be very costly. It was a race against time. The scientists told Roosevelt that they intended to split tiny particles of matter—atoms—and that would release vast amounts of energy. They could use that energy to make the most powerful weapon the world had ever seen. Roosevelt was convinced. The president made the decision to let the scientists go ahead with their plans. The project was top secret. Not even the vice president knew about it.

Hungarian-born physicist Edward Teller *(center)* was one of the key physicists in the field of atomic fission.

Einstein regretted forever his part in the atom bomb's development. "I made one great mistake in my life," he said, "when I signed the letter to President Roosevelt recommending that atom bombs be made...but there was some justification—the danger that the Germans would make them." Why do you think he felt like that? (Chapter 42 has some clues.)

1942: Enrico Fermi, Eugene Wigner, and other top scientists get together in a squash court under the stands of a University of Chicago football field to create the world's first controlled nuclear reaction from 50 tons of uranium and 500 tons of carbon. No football game has produced that kind of power!

28 Fighting Wolves

In an illustration for an anti-Axis propaganda film, *The Fruits of Aggression,* Hitler, Mussolini, and Tojo lick their lips and slice up a juicy watermelon world.

You are probably wondering how three nations—Germany, Italy, and Japan—could be a threat to the whole world. Have you ever thought about how a wolf terrorizes a flock of sheep? A lone wolf doesn't attack a big flock. He picks them off one by one. Give him enough time and he can kill them all.

Germany, Italy, and Japan were wolves. They were powerful. They thought they could devour the world's nations, one by one. They believed most other countries—especially the democracies—were weaklings.

They had good reason to believe that. In a democracy, everyone's ideas are heard. Sometimes democracies have a hard time acting quickly, because so many individuals and groups are debating each other. In the 1930s there were strong *isolationist* voices in America. They said that the oceans—the Pacific and the Atlantic—protected us from danger. They said we didn't

Isolate means to "separate from others." Isolationists believe a nation should stay out of world affairs. Some of the World War II isolationists were the same people who prevented the United States from joining the League of Nations after the Great War.

War in Europe suddenly made the Atlantic seem narrower. When the Germans invaded Poland, FDR said, "It has come at last. God help us all."

need to pay attention to what was going on in the rest of the world. Some of the isolationists were selfish. They didn't even want to help victims of the war.

Others who were *pacifists* didn't think it right to fight any war. They believed that if we behaved peacefully others might do the same.

American mothers protest Lend-Lease, a program to lend equipment and raw materials to help the Allies fight the war in Europe. The mothers feared a war that might include their sons. But there was no escape from this war.

Still others—in the military—were attached to old ways of thinking. They thought that battleships could protect us. Our battleships were huge. Some were 800 feet long. Imagine three football fields. (A football field is 300 feet long, so chop off a bit.) Float that picture, and add a crew of about 2,800 men, and guns that fire shells 20 miles or more, which was farther than any other weapon of the time. Battleships were much feared.

A few voices disagreed. They said that air power had changed all the rules of war. The oceans were no longer enough protection. Colonel William ("Billy") Mitchell of the U.S. Army said we needed to build up our air force. He said we needed to build aircraft carriers for our navy. An aircraft carrier is a floating airfield that carries its own airplanes. It is really big. (A bit longer than a battleship, and much wider.)

Mitchell pestered everyone: congressmen, army officers, naval officers, newspapermen. They got annoyed. Only a few people thought air power was important. Because he criticized his superiors in public, Mitchell was finally court-martialed and thrown out of the army. Some people said his ideas were laughable.

The official program of the Army–Navy football game, in November of 1941, showed a picture of the battleship *Arizona* with this caption: *Despite the claims of air enthusiasts no battleship has yet been sunk by bombs.* (That was meant as a slap at Billy Mitchell and those who agreed with him.)

Top: Billy Mitchell as General Pershing's chief of air services in the Great War. He tried to prove the effects of air power by bombing obsolete warships (*right*, the *Alabama* in 1921), but no one was interested. They said it would cost too much.

In 1942, a young architect named Albert Speer took control of German industry. Arms and munitions production, until then feeble and inefficient, increased hugely.

The United States had become weak militarily. We listened to the isolationists. It was partly for a good reason: we hated war. In 1941, our military force ranked 19th in the world, smaller than that of Belgium. At the same time, the armies and navies of Germany, Italy, and Japan had become strong.

Once its economy had recovered from the terrible effects of the Great War, Germany ignored the Versailles Treaty. It built a powerful army and air force. It turned out hundreds of submarines. Japan's naval fleet was awesome. Only a few people seemed concerned. "War could have been prevented," said a British statesman named Winston Churchill. "The malice of the wicked was reinforced by the weakness of the virtuous."

Roosevelt understood that the totalitarian powers were dangerous. He knew they hoped to rule the world. He took them seriously. The president wanted to build up our armed forces. It wasn't easy to fight the isolationists in Congress. He began by sending war supplies to England. That got our factories going. But we were still behind most other nations, and way behind Germany, Italy, and Japan, who were making plans to divide the world among themselves, and were known collectively as the *Axis*.

Militarily, we were weaklings. However, we had an advantage that the Axis powers didn't consider. It was the very thing they thought gave us a disadvantage. We were a democracy—a nation of free people. When free people set their minds to something, they become a powerful force. It took some time, but we became astonishingly strong.

Whether we wanted it or not, war was coming. We would win this war in our science laboratories and factories as well as on battlefields. The American people had been through a testing period that toughened them for a fight. The testing period was the Depression. We were used to tightening our belts and working hard. All of that, and more, was going to be necessary to win this war. It would be the most awful war in all of history.

29 Pearl Harbor

German tanks enter Czechoslovakia. Having to salute the invader was only the start of a conquered people's humiliation.

German troops arrive in Prague, March 15, 1939, the day Hitler announced, "Czechoslovakia has ceased to exist."

It is Sunday, December 7, 1941, and the sun is shining in Washington, D.C. To the morning churchgoers it seems just another bright winter day. At the White House, 31 guests are expected for lunch. There will be guests for dinner, too. None of that is unusual. The White House has become an informal, busy place since the Roosevelts moved in. That was more than eight years ago. FDR was reelected in 1936 and again in 1940. No other president has served more than two terms.

The American people (or most of them, anyway) have great faith in their president. These are dangerous times, and alarming things are happening all around the world. It is important to have a leader who can be trusted.

Hitler has steamrollered his way to some astounding victories. He has taken Austria, and Czechoslovakia, and Poland, and Denmark, and Norway, and Holland, and Belgium. One by one he picked off all those countries. The democracies let him do it. The democratic nations are so sick of war that they are willing to do anything to try to avoid it. What they have actually done is to make the war much worse than it would have been if they had stopped Hitler earlier.

It was when the Nazis marched into Poland that Britain and France finally responded. (Both nations had pledged their help to Poland if it was attacked.) Britain and France went to war.

The Polish army was hopelessly under-equipped and outdated; what could cavalry with lances do against a tank?

125

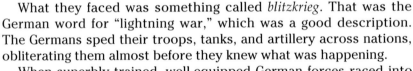

The Germans swept into Belgium and Holland at the same time. The Dutch city of Rotterdam resisted so strongly that Hitler bombed it to pieces out of spite. *Below:* a Belgian family stumbles through air-raid rubble. *Above:* the incredible sea rescue on the beaches of Dunkirk.

What they faced was something called *blitzkrieg*. That was the German word for "lightning war," which was a good description. The Germans sped their troops, tanks, and artillery across nations, obliterating them almost before they knew what was happening.

When superbly trained, well-equipped German forces raced into France, the country was overwhelmed. A large British–French army was trapped at Dunkirk, on the English Channel. It looked as if the soldiers were doomed. Then the British government sent out an appeal for boats. Soon fishermen, dentists, grocers, tugboat captains—anyone with a boat that could make it across the Channel—were sailing, back and forth, back and forth, ferrying soldiers to England. They saved an army, but they couldn't save France. On June 14, 1940, German tanks rolled into Paris.

Now almost the only European democracy left is Britain. And Britain is under attack. German bombers are pounding that small island. It looks as if it will go next. Everyone knows that the Nazis plan to invade England. Hitler's goal is world conquest. Americans have plenty of reason to worry.

In Asia, Japan has earlier occupied Manchuria (in 1931) and other parts of China (in 1937), and has just invaded French Indochina (now Vietnam, Laos, and Kampuchea) in July 1941. Japan is also threatening Thailand, the Philippines, and other Pacific nations. The United States sends letters to Japan objecting to this aggressive behavior, and finally imposes a total trade embargo and freezes Japanese funds in U.S. banks. Inside Japan there is a power struggle between civilian and military leaders. In the summer Prime Minister Prince Fumimaro Konoe offers to meet with Roosevelt. The president doesn't understand the importance of the request. He refuses the meeting. Konoe resigns, and is replaced by army minister General Hideki Tojo. In Japan, the military is now supreme.

This very day, December 7, Secretary of State Cordell Hull receives a call from two Japanese diplomats. They ask for an emergency meeting. Hull expects to be given the Japanese government's answer to an American peace letter. At the White House, after lunch, the president works on his stamp collection (he began collecting stamps as a boy). His good friend Harry Hopkins is with him; so is his Scottie dog, Fala. They are relaxing. The phone rings. It is close to 2 P.M., Eastern time.

Secretary of the Navy Frank Knox is on the line. His voice is quivering. A message has just been received from Hawaii. This is what it says: AIR RAID ON PEARL HARBOR—THIS IS NOT A DRILL.

Pearl Harbor, in the Hawaiian Islands, is where the Pacific Fleet is headquartered! On Sunday morning ships were lined up in the harbor; their crews were having breakfast, or relaxing, or sleeping. At 7:02 A.M. Hawaiian time, a radar operator saw some blips on his screen. The operator didn't pay attention to them. He thought they were bombers he was expecting from the West Coast.

By 7:55 A.M. he knew better. That was when the first dive bombers—with the red Japanese sun painted on their sides—let their bombs

One week after France surrendered, Hitler was in Paris.

Japan's prime minister, General Hideki Tojo, called the attack on Pearl Harbor "a blow for the liberation of Asia."

The U.S.S. *Shaw* explodes during the Japanese raid on Pearl Harbor.

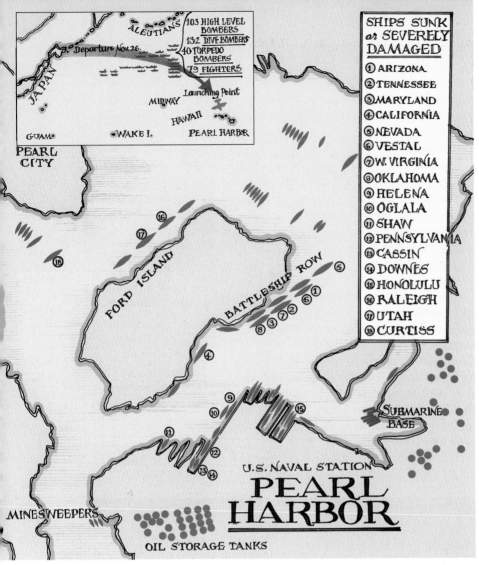

ALEUTIANS

103 HIGH LEVEL BOMBERS
132 DIVE BOMBERS
40 TORPEDO BOMBERS
79 FIGHTERS

Departure Nov. 26

JAPAN

MIDWAY

Launching Point

HAWAII

GUAM

WAKE I.

PEARL HARBOR

PEARL CITY

FORD ISLAND

BATTLESHIP ROW

SUBMARINE BASE

MINESWEEPERS

U.S. NAVAL STATION

PEARL HARBOR

OIL STORAGE TANKS

SHIPS SUNK or SEVERELY DAMAGED

① ARIZONA
② TENNESSEE
③ MARYLAND
④ CALIFORNIA
⑤ NEVADA
⑥ VESTAL
⑦ W. VIRGINIA
⑧ OKLAHOMA
⑨ HELENA
⑩ OGLALA
⑪ SHAW
⑫ PENNSYLVANIA
⑬ CASSIN
⑭ DOWNES
⑮ HONOLULU
⑯ RALEIGH
⑰ UTAH
⑱ CURTISS

loose on Battleship Row. The battleship *Arizona* gave off a tremendous roar, split in two, and slipped to the bottom of the harbor. That was just the beginning. All the American planes on the island were damaged or destroyed. Most of the warships were crippled or sunk. And more than 2,000 soldiers, sailors, and civilians were killed.

At 2:05 P.M. Washington time (which is 8:05 A.M. Hawaiian time), the Japanese envoys arrive at Secretary of State Cordell Hull's door. They are part of an elaborate Japanese plan of deception, but their timing is off. Before the secretary can see them, his phone rings. It is the president, with the awful news of the Japanese attack. Now, Hull is from Tennessee, and he claims he has a Tennessee temper. The stories of what he says to those envoys will differ, but it is known that they leave quickly, with their heads down.

Hull is soon at the White House. So are many government and military officials. Newspaper reporters begin arriving. At 2:25 P.M. the story goes out on news wires to the American people. The reports from Pearl Harbor are humiliating, but that isn't the only bad news. This same day, the Japanese have attacked American and British bases at Midway, Wake Island, Guam, Hong Kong, Singapore, and the Philippines.

It is an astonishing act of aggression. But this president is at his best in a crisis. His advisers are angry, fearful, and frustrated. The president remains calm. He came into office during the nation's worst economic crisis. This is worse: the free world is fighting for survival.

Nationalist China's old walled capital city, Nanking, was captured by the Japanese in December of 1937. What happened is told in a book by an American writer, Iris Chang, called *The Rape of Nanking.* It's a story of the unspeakable horrors of war and of heroism, too.

Pearl Harbor is a disaster, but it may also be a lucky break. It unites the nation. There are no more isolationists. Everyone joins the war effort. Pearl Harbor shows the damage that air power can do. It changes people's thinking on that subject.

The next day the president goes before Congress. The Japanese have launched an "unprovoked and dastardly attack," he says. December 7 is "a date which will live in infamy." He asks Congress to declare war on Japan. Three days later, Japan's allies—Germany and Italy—declare war on the United States. It is World War II. It will make the awful First World War seem like a fire drill. The United States will fight this war against the wolves, maintain its democracy (as it did during the terrible Depression), and remain, as Abraham Lincoln said, the last best hope of earth.

Infamy (IN-fuh-me): it means "evil reputation."

Secretary Hull with Japanese ambassador Nomura *(left)* and special envoy Kurusu on their way to the White House, three weeks before the bombs fall on Pearl Harbor.

The True Goal We Seek

Franklin Delano Roosevelt knew how to talk to people. He knew how to explain complicated things in simple language. As soon as he became president, he decided to use the radio to explain what the government was going to do about the Depression. He was as relaxed and informal as a friend sitting in the living room. He called his radio broadcast a "fireside chat." Soon those fireside chats became a regular thing. Americans liked listening to their president, especially since he had a good sense of humor. But on February 9, 1942, he didn't have anything funny to say. This is part of his speech to the American people that day:

We are now in this war. We are all in it—all the way. Every single man, woman, and child is a partner in the most tremendous undertaking of our American history....On the road ahead there lies hard work—grueling work—day and night, every hour and every minute. I was about to add that ahead there lies sacrifice for all of us. But it is not correct to use that word. The United States does not consider it a sacrifice to do all one can, to give one's best to our nation, when the nation is fighting for its existence and its future life....There is no such thing as security for any nation—or any individual—in a world ruled by the principles of gangsterism. There is no such thing as impregnable defense against powerful aggressors who sneak up in the dark and strike without warning. We have learned that our ocean-girt hemisphere is not immune from severe attack—that we cannot measure our safety in terms of miles on any map anymore....

The true goal we seek is far above and beyond the ugly field of battle. When we resort to force, as now we must, we are determined that this force shall be directed toward the ultimate good as well as against immediate evil. *We Americans are not destroyers; we are builders.*

We are now in the midst of a war, not for conquest, not for vengeance, but for a world in which this nation, and all that this nation represents, will be safe for our children....We are going to win the war and we are going to win the peace that follows.

And in the dark hours of this day—and through dark days that may be yet to come—we will know that the vast majority of the members of the human race are on our side. Many of them are fighting with us. All of them are praying for us. For, in representing our case, we represent theirs as well—our hope and their hope for liberty under God.

30 Taking Sides

After their first meeting, Churchill got a cable from FDR: "It is fun to be in the same decade with you."

FDR smoked cigarettes through an extra-long cigarette holder, and Winston Churchill puffed on an ever-present cigar. Few people then knew that smoking shortens lives and increases the risk of disease.

Berlin, Rome, and Tokyo are the capitals of which nations?

This is how the war was fought:

On one side was the Berlin–Rome–Tokyo Axis led by Adolf Hitler, Benito Mussolini, and Japan's premier, General Hideki Tojo.

On the other side were three major Allied forces. Who were they? Who were their leaders?

President Franklin Delano Roosevelt represented the United States. His was already a voice of freedom respected all over the world.

Britain, the second Allied power, was led by a man with a pudgy baby face. His name was Winston Churchill, and, like Roosevelt, he had a powerful voice and was inspiring when he spoke. Churchill had an American mother and a father who was a British lord. When he was young he was a poor student, but he got better. He went to Sandhurst—the British West Point—and became an army officer, a good one. He got medals for bravery. Then he became a newspaper reporter, learned to pilot a plane, wrote history books, entered politics, and became a member of Britain's Parliament. He was one of the first Englishmen to see the danger of Hitler's Nazi Party and to speak against it. That was when most people in England and America were

The Russians were stunned when Hitler invaded. The Nazi–Soviet Pact was dead, and they had a new role as Allies.

130

A cartoon sums up the Allied view of Stalin—cozying up to Hitler and his chief aide, Göring—before Germany turned the tables, double-crossed Stalin, and changed the whole course of the war.

acting like ostriches. They buried their heads in the sand, closed their ears, and didn't want to hear anything about war.

The third Allied power? Was it France? No. France was under German control. (However, as you know, a free French army was saved at Dunkirk. It was led by General Charles de Gaulle, and it did fight with the Allies.) How about China? Was China the third power? No. China was fighting Japan. And China was in turmoil. Civil war between the Communists and the Nationalists had broken out in China in the 1930s. That war wouldn't be finally decided until 1949: the Communists would win.

You may have a hard time believing who the third Allied power was, but here it is: Soviet Russia (the U.S.S.R.). Russia's leader, in 1941, was dictator Joseph Stalin. He was head of the Soviet Communist Party. He ruled Russia using secret police and terror. Many of his own people hated him. But others were fooled by Stalin. Roosevelt may have been one of them. Dictators often have charm, and Joe Stalin had a lot of charm—when he wanted. But what mattered was that he was fighting Hitler and so were we. As Winston Churchill said, "If Hitler invaded Hell I would make at least a favorable reference to the Devil in the House of Commons."

Russia, however, didn't start out on the Allied team. Here is some background.

In 1939, Hitler and Stalin signed a friendship pact. They said they would not fight each other. They made plans together to march into Poland—one from the east, the other from the west—and to gobble up that nation. They did it. Poland was squashed and divided.

Before the Nazi army marched into Poland, Hitler told his generals:

The victor will not be asked afterward whether or not he told the truth. In starting and waging war it is not right that matters but victory. Close your hearts to pity! Act brutally!…The stronger is in the right.

His generals did as they were told.

That was when France and England finally realized that they couldn't avoid war—although now it would be a difficult one. They had let Germany build a huge military force. At the same time, the free nations had cut their armies and navies. There wasn't a lot anyone could do when Germany marched armies into Belgium, Holland, Luxembourg, and France. The Nazis were winning everywhere.

The German air force—the Luftwaffe (LOOFT-vah-fuh)—soon began dropping bombs on England—tons and tons of bombs.

It is hard to lead a country in exile, and many said Charles de Gaulle was arrogant—including FDR, who couldn't stand him and said he was "a nut." But he was a good general and kept underground resistance going in France throughout the German occupation.

131

In August 1940, the first German bombs fell on London. Night bombing of London—"the Blitz"—began in September and went on until June. The Londoners stuck it out.

Then Hitler made some stupid moves. First, he went into Greece and Yugoslavia, where his forces faced some heroic fighters. That stopped Germany for a while. Then Hitler double-crossed Stalin. He decided to invade Russia. That had been his plan all along. He had even written a book, called *Mein Kampf* (it means "my struggle" in German), that told all about his goal of world domination. "No human being has ever declared or recorded what he wanted to do more often than me," he said.

Anyone who read Hitler's writings knew what he had planned. He said that Germans were the "master race," and that they needed more room, and other nations to serve them as slaves. Churchill and Roosevelt paid attention. They knew Hitler was capable and effective, as well as evil. For a long time, most other politicians just didn't take him seriously.

But Hitler didn't intend to share power. The Russians were a threat to his goal of world domination. So, when some of his generals told him not to go into Russia, he didn't listen. He needed oil and wheat and other resources from Russia. Besides, he thought Russia would be an easy victim. So did experts everywhere. The American secretary of war predicted that it would take Germany three months to conquer Russia.

Look at the map at the back of this book. The Germans prepared the most massive army ever assembled. Their

The damage done in London by the fires the bombs caused was as bad as their explosive effect. The great cathedral of St. Paul's, seen here during the worst raid of the Blitz, survived intact.

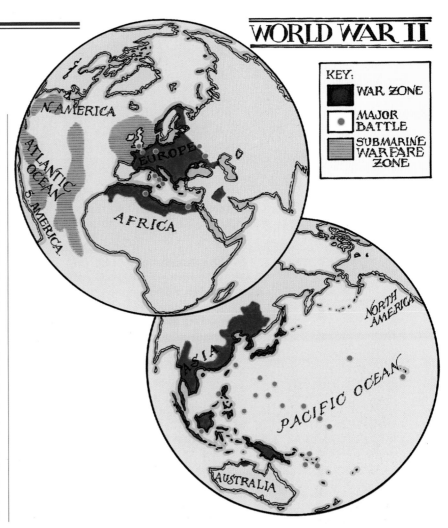

KEY:

■ WAR ZONE

▣ MAJOR BATTLE

▦ SUBMARINE WARFARE ZONE

forces stretched from Finland to the Black Sea. They attacked with the latest in military equipment: tanks, bombs, and artillery.

At first, the Germans had an easy time of it. The Russians weren't prepared; much of their military equipment was out of date. Hitler instructed the German army to turn Russia into a slave nation. The Nazis murdered millions of Russians.

Now look at the map again. Notice the size of Russia. Look at Moscow and Leningrad (which today is called by its old name, St. Petersburg). Those cities are very far north. They are cold places. Winter came early in the fall of 1941. The first snow fell in Moscow on October 2. The Germans weren't prepared for the cold. They got stuck in a Russian

Left: children outside what is left of their London home. Many city kids like these were "evacuated"—taken in by families in the country. Their white bags hold gas masks.

The Second World War was a truly global conflict, involving several continents and many nations and peoples (unlike World War I, which was fought largely in Europe and around the Mediterranean Sea).

Russia's winter had stopped Napoleon, too. Hitler should have remembered that.

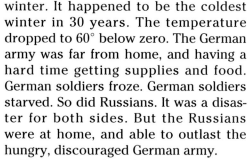

Even the cleated caterpillar tracks of the German tanks *(above)* bogged down in the snow. One of the victors in Russia was winter.

The Russian city of Leningrad was almost totally cut off from September 1941 until January 1943. People had no electricity or heat; water was contaminated because mains burst *(below, collecting water from a broken main)*. Leningraders ate dogs and rats and Vaseline and made soup from the glue in furniture or wallpaper. Many died of hunger anyway.

winter. It happened to be the coldest winter in 30 years. The temperature dropped to 60° below zero. The German army was far from home, and having a hard time getting supplies and food. German soldiers froze. German soldiers starved. So did Russians. It was a disaster for both sides. But the Russians were at home, and able to outlast the hungry, discouraged German army.

FDR sent his friend Harry Hopkins to Russia. "Give us anti-aircraft guns and aluminum and we can fight for three or four years," said Stalin. He was right. We sent guns, aluminum, food, tanks, planes, and more. The Russians gave their lives.

The Russians went all out in their fight against Nazi Germany. No nation fought harder.

No one knows how many Russians died in World War II. Some say 15 million. Some say more. No other country has ever suffered such war losses. Russia was our ally and friend during the world war. But Russia under Soviet communism was a dreadful place. Stalin was a vicious dictator. Stalin expected something for fighting Hitler. What he expected, and got, was domination over the other countries of eastern Europe. Could Hitler have been destroyed without Stalin's help? Perhaps not. Certainly it would have taken many, many more American and British lives.

31 World War

On officer mans the periscope in the control room of a U.S. submarine, about 1942.

The United States drafted black men, but segregated them—and often assigned them to service jobs instead of combat units. These Negro Seabees were members of the Navy's construction battalions, volunteers chosen for their skill in building or engineering. They are shown here in training near Norfolk, Virginia, practicing landing tactics, around 1942.

Sailors load machine-gun cartridge belts for dive bombers at Norfolk, Virginia.

Billy Mitchell was right: air power changed war. In World War II more people were killed by bombs or pieces of shells (called "shrapnel") than by bullets. In World War II cities were bombed; huge civilian populations were massacred.

There was something else about air war: it made killing a mechanical act. Imagine being in the infantry. You see the enemy eye to eye; it makes you realize the enemy is just like you—human. Officers know that some soldiers are never able to pull their triggers. They are never able to murder—even to save themselves. But a bomber pilot doesn't see his victims. A bomb can't tell the difference between an enemy soldier and a child on her way to school. It will kill them both.

An enormous number of bombs were dropped—by both sides—during World War II. Billy Mitchell thought air power would eliminate the need for foot soldiers. He was wrong about that. There was still plenty of old-fashioned infantry fighting.

Look at the world map on page 133. World War II was truly a world war. Here are just a few of the places where American troops fought; see if you can find them in an atlas.

France, Germany, Tunisia, Sicily, Italy, Morocco, Burma, Guam, Malaysia, Philippine Islands, Wake Island

Now imagine you are a general and you are

Above left: parachutes fill the sky as waves of paratroopers land in Holland during operations by the 1st Allied Airborne in September 1944. *Right:* one method of getting soldiers—along with their trucks and all their ammunition and supplies—across a river is with a kind of barge. This one in Burma is powered by ordinary outboard motors.

U-boat is the abbreviation for the German word *Unterseeboot*—"undersea boat."

A *torpedo* is like a giant bullet with a propeller that travels through water and can sink a ship.

planning a battle on a Pacific island. Suppose you want to get 15,000 men onto the island and surprise the enemy. How are you going to do it?

A parachute drop?

Maybe, but remember, parachutes make great targets. You'd be better off bringing them in by boat. Many of those islands don't have deep harbors, though. Big ships can't come in close.

Can the soldiers swim in?

Not with their guns and artillery and trucks and tanks and food and ammunition and medical supplies.

We're going to have to invent and develop new kinds of landing equipment and war gear. And we're going to have to do it very fast. We'll design huge landing craft that have big rooms—called "holds"— that can be flooded to form miniature lakes so that boats can zoom out. We'll design other landing ships that will carry tanks and trucks as well as men. We'll design *amphibious* (am-FIB-ee-us) vehicles that will go on land or water. One of the most useful—a truck that swims— will be called a "duck." Another new, tough vehicle—which can handle rough roads, mountain passes, and rutted fields—we'll call a "jeep."

We'll design superb submarines that can stay under water for months at a time. Then we'll design torpedoes and depth charges to destroy submarines. The Axis nations will be doing the same thing. Submarine warfare will be very important in this war. German subs are called "U-boats," and the Atlantic Ocean is full of them.

We're going to do amazing things in medical science so that disease and infection will no longer be the major causes of wartime deaths. The lives of many badly wounded men will be saved.

All through the war we will keep improving our weapons, planes, tanks, and armored vehicles. The Germans and Japanese have a head

start on us. They have fine scientists and technicians. This war will become a race to see who can produce the best weapons fastest. The Germans are working on rockets—called V-1s and V-2s—that are devastating. Luckily, it will take most of the war to get them perfected. When they start shooting rockets at England there will be many, many deaths. (The V-2 rockets are being designed to hit the United States.) We are behind on rocket development. After the war, German rocket engineers will tell us they got many of their ideas by studying the work of our rocket expert Robert Goddard.

We know something that they don't suspect we know. They think they are smarter than we are. They are wrong. We have learned to read their most difficult codes. That will prove more valuable than almost anything else we do.

Have you ever tried writing in code? It's easy. Just put numbers in place of letters and you have a code. Armies have always needed codes. Suppose a general wants to tell a faraway commander to attack. He sends a messenger. But he wants his orders in code in case the messenger is caught. He certainly doesn't want the enemy to know his plans.

In George Washington's day, a screen was sometimes put over a piece of paper. There were holes in the screen. The secret message was the words that showed through the holes. Everything else was there to fool you.

During World War II, both sides moved huge armies and navies and tried to do it secretly. Most orders were sent by telegraph.

Getting from A to B. *Top left:* lowering a jeep from a Coast Guard assault transport into a landing craft. *Top right:* each of these tiny cars carries a real bomb. *Above:* an aerial photo of U.S. troops wading ashore from landing craft onto Morotai Island, between New Guinea and the Philippines

137

A V-2 rocket prepared for launching. Nazi Germany's V-1 and V-2 rockets were the first long-range missiles—deadly and terrifying.

Germany's racial policies have caused many of its best scientists to flee the country. That helps the Allies and slows Germany's progress.

When American naval forces capture a German submarine off the coast of West Africa, they find a newly developed torpedo and a secret radio code on board. They pretend they have sunk the sub, so the Germans won't change the code.

Anyone could listen. So codes were vital. They became very complicated. The Germans and Japanese thought no one could possibly figure out their complex codes.

We cracked the Japanese secret code even before the war began. Solving the German military code was much harder. German coded messages were sent and received on special machines. Then a German tank was captured in Poland. It had a code machine inside. The machine was smuggled out of Poland to England. When it got to England no one could figure out how to work it. The English called the code machine "Enigma." An *enigma* is a puzzle. They put some of their best scientific and mathematical minds on the job of solving the puzzle. It was incredibly difficult. How they did it is a fascinating story. Several books have been written about it. You can find them in the library.

Once the code was broken, we knew almost everything the Axis powers were planning to do. Now we Allies had to pretend that we didn't know some things. We didn't want the codes to be changed.

Cryptography Means Code Making

In World War II, code makers (who all seemed to be geniuses) created extraordinary code machines in order to write secret languages that would baffle the enemy. But code breakers were, if anything, even smarter than the code makers. Just about all the codes did get broken—except for one that stumped all the geniuses. No one could figure it out. Maybe that's because it happened to be a real language, spoken by real people, who were faster than any of the fancy machines.

The language was Navajo, and it was spoken by 420 marines who called themselves *Dineh*—the People. In western movies, Indians are usually known for their silence. These Native Americans did plenty of talking. They made up their own code using their own words: Hitler was *Daghailchiih* (mustache smeller), bombers were *jaysho* (buzzards), and bombs, *ayeshi* (eggs). Navajos landed on every major island in the Pacific. Major Howard Conner said, "Without the Navajos the marines would never have taken Iwo Jima." They were a secret weapon in the Pacific.

Enigma. The possible number of encoding positions for each letter was unbelievably huge: 5,000 billion trillion trillion trillion trillion.

32 A Two-Front War

Tarawa, in the Gilbert Islands, where marines put up this lonely signpost, was a tiny spot in the Pacific. Yet it took bitter fighting to capture it.

Western Europe and the Far East (East Asia) were named by people who considered Jerusalem to be the center of the world. Western Europe is indeed west of Israel, and East Asia east of Israel—but to us they are the opposite. That is because the earth is a ball—which does make things confusing. As Robert Frost said of Christopher Columbus:

Remember he had made the test
Finding the East by sailing West.

Did you ever hear of Janus, the two-faced god of Roman mythology? *January* was named for Janus; he was the god of doorways and gates who looked in two directions at the same time.

During World War II the United States was like Janus. We had to look in two directions at the same time. We were fighting a two-ocean war. That was a terrible problem for our generals and admirals. How do you divide your forces? How do you protect two huge coasts from attack?

Looking west (to East Asia), the view was frightening. In the Pacific theater the Japanese moved like lightning. (Military officers call a war region a "theater." Strange, but that's the way it is.) Their forces were well trained and well equipped. At the start, Japan's aggressive strategy seemed to work. Remember, on December 7 they didn't just bomb Pearl Harbor—they attacked a whole string of strategic spots, almost simultaneously! In just a few months the Japanese captured Thailand, the Philippine Islands, the Malay peninsula, Java, Burma,

Simultaneously (sy-mul-TAY-nee-us-lee) means "at the same time."

In the first six months of war, under General Tojo *(left)*, Japanese forces such as this machine-gun crew *(right)* overran more territory than any army since Napoleon's.

139

In May 1942, in the battle of the Coral Sea, both the U.S. and Japan suffered heavy losses: here the crew of the sinking aircraft carrier U.S.S. *Lexington* bail out frantically. But the Japanese lost two of their carriers and had to retreat.

Black and White Blood

Charles R. Drew was uncommonly gifted. He was a star athlete (in football, basketball, baseball, and track!), a brilliant student at Amherst College, an outstanding doctor (he was a professor of medicine at Howard University), and the man who developed the idea of a blood bank for storing blood plasma (during World War II). In 1942, he organized the blood-bank programs for both the U.S. and Britain, and supervised the Red Cross's blood-donor program. Besides all that, he had an amiable personality—people liked him.

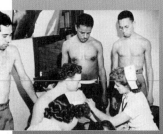

Home-front blood donors, 1944. The black men's blood will be segregated.

But he was enraged that black blood and white blood were segregated in blood banks, and he spoke out against that absurdity. He was killed in a car accident. A myth has grown that because of his color, he was refused treatment at an all-white hospital. That is not true. What is true is that his talents were often frustrated by the idiocy of prejudice.

Guam, Wake Island, the Gilbert Islands, Singapore, and Hong Kong. Check those places on a map and you'll see: the Japanese controlled East Asia. People in India and Australia were trembling. They thought they were next.

The Western theater—Europe— wasn't any better. As you know, the Nazis controlled most of Europe. They even had troops in North Africa; the Mediterranean was a kind of Nazi sea.

So was the Atlantic Ocean. That was because of the German U-boats. England and Russia were desperate for help. The United States had to ship weapons, tanks, oil, and men across the Atlantic to Europe. But the U-boats seemed to be everywhere. In the first four months of 1942, almost 200 of our ships were sunk. One summer day, people in Virginia Beach, Virginia, watched in horror as a ship was torpedoed and

sunk in sight of the beach. Ships were being sunk faster than they could be built. Each time a ship was torpedoed, American men drowned.

Somehow, people in this country didn't get discouraged. We were convinced we could win this war and we set about doing it. Dr. New Deal turned into Dr. Win the War. He became a great war president. No matter how gloomy things seemed, President Roosevelt remained confident and optimistic. He gave courage to the nation.

He had good people to work with. General George C. Marshall, his chief of staff, was a superb general, and modest. Someone said he had the wisdom of George Washington and the strategic sense of Robert E. Lee.

Before and after a U-boat sneak attack: targets sighted through the periscope (right); an Allied freighter, split in two by a torpedo (above).

Dwight D. Eisenhower

Tough and experienced Admiral Ernest J. King, chief of naval operations, did his job well. So did admirals Nimitz and Spruance and generals Dwight D. Eisenhower, H. H. "Hap" Arnold, Douglas MacArthur, and others. Remember all the trouble Abraham Lincoln had with his generals? Roosevelt was lucky; the nation was lucky, too.

Douglas MacArthur

But the first battles were grim. Admiral King warned, "The way to victory is long; the going will be hard." He was right. We started out as losers. Then things began to change. Maybe it was

Above: a water buffalo assault vessel near Guam. *Right:* the 165th Infantry reaches Makin atoll in 1943 (Tarawa was captured at the same time). The coral bottom makes for very hard wading.

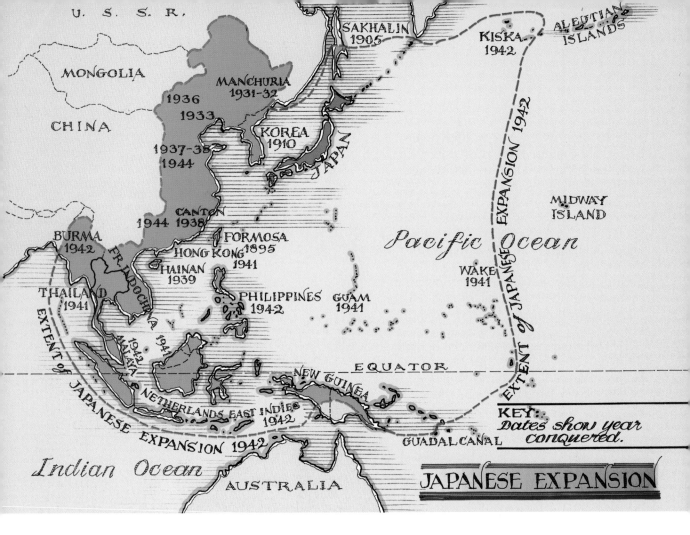

MONGOLIA

U. S. S. R.

CHINA

MANCHURIA
1931-32

1936

1933

1937-38
1944

KOREA
1910

JAPAN

SAKHALIN
1905

KISKA
1942

ALEUTIAN
ISLANDS

Pacific Ocean

CANTON
1944 1938

FORMOSA
1895

HONG KONG
1941

HAINAN
1939

BURMA
1942

FR. INDOCHINA

THAILAND
1941

PHILIPPINES
1942

GUAM
1941

MALAYA 1941
1942

NETHERLANDS EAST INDIES
1942

NEW GUINEA

EQUATOR

MIDWAY
ISLAND

WAKE
1941

EXTENT of JAPANESE EXPANSION 1942

EXTENT of

JAPANESE

EXPANSION 1942

GUADALCANAL

KEY:
Dates show year conquered.

Indian Ocean

AUSTRALIA

JAPANESE EXPANSION

1943: An American PT (propeller-torpedo) boat (like the one above) is rammed by a Japanese destroyer. Two Americans are killed. Eleven others cling to the boat and then swim to a nearby island. Their commander carves a message in a coconut and gives it to friendly islanders, who bring help. The commander's name is John F. Kennedy.

because the Japanese got greedy. They didn't know when to stop. They thought they were invincible—which means "unbeatable." Nobody is unbeatable. We had been taking a pounding in the Pacific. But when we won three big victories, the Japanese learned to respect our fighting ability. The victories were in the Coral Sea, at Midway Island, and at Guadalcanal.

The Coral Sea battle wasn't exactly a victory. There was a series of mistakes on both sides—big mistakes. Our losses were heavier than the enemy's. But we prevented them from capturing a strategic base in New Guinea, and that may have saved Australia from invasion.

The Japanese expected an easy win at tiny Midway Island. If they controlled that island they would control the air over Hawaii. Then, perhaps, they could attack our West Coast. In addition, they intended to destroy the ships in our fleet that had escaped Pearl Harbor—especially our aircraft carriers. Their plan was to lure us into a trap and surprise us. What they didn't know was that we could decode their secret messages. We knew of their plans. Still, they almost won. The battle over Midway was ferocious.

At first, things were awful for us. Forty-one of our torpedo bombers took off after the Japanese ships, and most were shot down. Then our dive bombers arrived, and destroyed four massive Japanese aircraft carriers. It was the first defeat the Japanese navy had suffered. And it was a battle that proved that air power would be the key to this war.

The battle for Guadalcanal was something else. If you hold on for a chapter I'll tell you about it. But before that you need to learn about something going on at home.

The battle of Midway took two days. U.S. Navy bombers such as the one below—the Japanese called them "hell divers"—caught the Japanese in the process of refueling and sank a number of ships, including the cruiser *Mikuma (bottom)*.

33 Forgetting the Constitution

The American citizen who owned this store put up the sign the day after Pearl Harbor was bombed. Like so many others, he had to sell his business at a sacrifice price and go to a camp.

Haruko Obata lived in a house in lovely, tree-shaded Berkeley, California. Her father was a professor at the University of California. Haruko was an American citizen. Like most Japanese Americans, she was proud of her Asian heritage, but she didn't approve of the ways of the warlords who ruled the Japanese empire. In school she studied the Constitution and its guarantees. She was happy to live in the land of liberty.

Then, one day, Haruko's world changed. Her father came home and told the family they were moving. They had just a few days to get ready. They could take only as much as they could carry. They might never again see the things they would leave behind. They were going to live—against their wishes—in a prisonlike camp.

What had they done? Just a minute, and I'll get to that. But first, imagine that you are Haruko. You have some hard decisions to make, and you need to make them quickly. What will you choose to take with you? Sorry, your dog can't go. You'll have to give her away. Books? Games? Toys? Not if

All four of the photographs on pages 144 and 145 are by Dorothea Lange, as are those on pages 81 and 196. What do you think Lange is saying in her work?

The Japanese internment camps on the West Coast, and the internment camp for Jews in Oswego, New York, were run by the same government agency. Even the food was the same.

One girl was seven when her family was taken to a camp in the California desert. "Someone tied a numbered tag to my collar and to the duffel bag," she wrote. Nobody explained why they suddenly had to move.

The only places with enough room to house so many people are cold, hot, or windy —places no one wants to live in, like Manzanar *(left)*.

they are heavy. No one knows exactly where this camp is. It may be very cold. Or hot. You won't be able to take much besides clothes. Your parents must sell the car, the house, and almost all their possessions; because they do it so quickly, they will get hardly anything for them.

You and your family are going to a camp that is surrounded by a barbed-wire fence. Armed guards stand in watchtowers. If someone tries to walk out into the desert he will be shot. What have you done that is so terrible? Why are you and your family in this prison camp?

You have not done anything wrong. Yes, you read that right. The Obatas have done nothing at all. They have been fine citizens.

But they are of Japanese descent, and the United States is at war with Japan. There is anti-Japanese hysteria in America, especially in California. Some of it is understandable. War is terrible. The Japanese government is horrible. But the Japanese in America have nothing to do with that. Some people don't understand that. Many authorities

The whole evacuation operation was so rushed that very few camps were ready when families arrived. Haruko Obata was sent to Tanforan *(below)*, where, at first, people had to line up just to get fed.

expect the Japanese to attack the West Coast. A Japanese submarine fires shells that land—harmlessly—near Los Angeles. People are terrified. There are rumors that Japanese-American fishermen are sending signals to Japanese ships and planes. There is no evidence for this, but in wartime, how can anyone be sure?

Reports of Japanese atrocities in Nanking, China, and elsewhere are horrible (and turn out to be true). But Japanese Americans have nothing to

A young woman named Miné Okubo was interned at Tanforan and then in Topaz, Utah. She drew pictures for a book about her life called *Citizen 13660.* The clothes the camps supplied never fit; the Utah mosquitoes were fierce; and the walls were so thin and badly built that quiet and privacy were impossible.

do with that, just as German Americans have nothing to do with the savagery in Nazi Germany.

Most Japanese Americans feel anguish. They love the United States, its opportunities and its inspiring vision. But they also take pride in their ancient Japanese heritage. For them, World War II is like a civil war.

In addition, the Japanese in America face a special problem. It is an old problem. It is racism. A racist law prevents Japanese immigrants from becoming citizens. However, anyone born here is automatically an American citizen. Two-thirds of the Japanese Americans are *Nisei*—the Japanese word for those born in America—and they are citizens. Racism has been part of America's history from the time of the first contact of Europeans and Native Americans. But so has the fight against racism. That clash—between bigotry and decency—is found in the human drama in every culture (and perhaps in every human heart).

Now the racists have something important on their side: it is the very real fear that war brings. There is something else here, too. It is greed. Japanese Americans have been industrious; their property is valuable. If they are put behind barbed wire, their property will have to be sold, and quickly, for much less than it is worth. Some people will profit mightily.

The first calls for internment (putting the Japanese in camps) come from newspaper columnists. Then a group of West Coast politicians join in. They include Earl Warren, who will later become chief justice of the Supreme Court. J. Edgar Hoover, head of the FBI, says quietly that internment is unnecessary; the FBI can handle surveillance of suspects. But Norman Thomas, leader of the American Socialist Party, is a lonely political figure when he speaks out forcefully, opposing internment.

The attorney general reminds the secretary of war that the Fourth Amendment protects citizens from "unreasonable searches and seizures." The 14th Amendment says "nor shall any State deprive any person of life, liberty or property without the due process of law." But we are at war, and the War Department is worried about "national security." The right of habeas corpus has been shelved in wartime before.

President Roosevelt issues Executive Order 9102. One hundred and twenty thousand Japanese Americans have a few days to get ready. They will be sent to 10 different internment camps.

Here is how Haruko Obata described her arrival at the Tanforan camp:

When we arrived at Tanforan it was raining; it was so sad and depressing. The roadway was all mud, thick mud and our shoes would get stuck in mud when you walked outside. They gave us a horse stable the size of our dining room with a divided door where the horse put his head out—that was our sleeping quarters. There were two twin beds made of wood, bunk beds, and another bed on the opposite wall. It was supposed to be a couch but it was made of wood too. There was nothing else. Nothing. That one time I cried so much. That was the only time I cried; it was awful.

There is much more to this story, much, much more. Mostly it is of a people who—as soon as they got settled—didn't cry. They did their best in a bad situation. They planted seeds and grew crops. They raised farm animals. They fed themselves and sent their surplus to support the war effort. They fixed up their sleeping quarters. They established schools, churches, recreational centers, newspapers, scout troops, baseball teams, and their own camp governments.

Some were let out of the camps to work in war factories. Many became soldiers. A Nisei regiment fighting in Europe won more commendations than any other regiment in the whole United States Army. Infantryman Harry Takagi explained:

We were fighting for the rights of all Japanese-Americans. We set out to break every record in the army. If we failed, it would reflect discredit on all Japanese-Americans. We could not let that happen.

More than 16,000 Nisei served in the Pacific, most in military intelligence work as interpreters. Some went behind enemy lines as American spies. Japanese-American women volunteered and served in the Woman's Army Corps, as army nurses, and in the Red Cross.

Japanese-American soldiers take cover from a German shell in Italy, 1945.

At first, people in the War Department objected to the idea of Nisei serving in the army. But, finally, President Roosevelt spoke up. He said:

The principle on which this country was founded and by which it has always been governed is that Americanism is a matter of the mind and heart; Americanism is not, and never was, a matter of race or ancestry.

If you don't know what habeas corpus *is, see book 3 of* A History of US.

They issued us army mess kits, the round metal kind that fold over, and plopped in scoops of canned Vienna sausage, canned string beans, steamed rice that had been cooked too long, and on top of the rice a serving of canned apricots.... Among the Japanese, of course, rice is never eaten with sweet foods, only with salty or savory foods. Few of us could eat such a mixture. But at this point no one dared protest. It would have been impolite. I was horrified when I saw the apricot syrup seeping through my little mound of rice. I opened my mouth to complain. My mother jabbed me in the back to keep quiet. We moved on through the line and joined the others squatting in the lee of half-raised walls, dabbing courteously at what was, for almost everyone there, an inedible concoction.

—JEANNE WAKATSUKI HOUSTON,
FAREWELL TO MANZANAR

The Hirano family with a photo of their other son in uniform. They were sent to Arizona.

Photographer Toyo Miyatake and his family were sent to Manzanar. He wasn't allowed a camera, so he made one and took secret pictures of life behind the barbed wire.

In the course of the war, 10 people were convicted of spying for Japan. All were white. Only one Japanese American was convicted of treason; she was Iva Ikuda Toguri, a graduate of UCLA, who was in Tokyo when the war began and couldn't get home. Toguri, known as Tokyo Rose, agreed to do propaganda broadcasting to avoid work in a munitions factory. She was paid $6.60 a month.

Eventually, the camps were closed and people went out and did their best to build new lives. It wasn't easy; they had lost all their possessions. Many still faced racism when they tried to find jobs and new homes.

Now, you may be thinking that racism is terrible, but that, really, it is only a problem for the people who are made to suffer. Don't be fooled. Hatred is a contagious disease; it spreads quickly. It is like the poison gas that both sides used during the First World War; when the wind changed, it blew back on the gassers.

No people is immune to the virus of hate. It is how they handle it that decides the kind of people they are. This nation was founded on the idea that *all men are created equal*. A group of women at Seneca Falls, New York, changed that to *all men and women are created equal*. That is what we believe. That is what this nation is all about.

We the People of the United States, in Order to form a more perfect Union, establish Justice, insure domestic Tranquillity, provide for the common defense, promote the general Welfare, and secure the Blessings of Liberty to ourselves and our Posterity, do ordain and establish this Constitution for the United States of America.

Remember George Washington's words:

The government of the United States...gives to bigotry no sanction, to persecution no assistance.

The more you read history, the more you will realize that the haters never win. Eventually, they get found out and put down. Often, unfortunately, it takes time.

Forty years after the end of the war, the American government officially apologized to the Japanese Americans for the terrible injustice done to them during World War II. Those who had been in the camps were given money in partial payment for their suffering. Today, when we Americans think back on the internment camps, we feel shame.

34 A Hot Island

Admiral Ernest King was a stern, opinionated man who was hardly ever known to smile.

General Eisenhower, who was a likable fellow, wrote in his diary in March of 1942: "One thing that might help win this war is to get someone to shoot King."

He was kidding. The King he was talking about was Admiral King. They disagreed on strategy. Do you think wars are easy to plan? Do you think the leaders all agree on how to go about it? Not often.

Most of our military leaders believed we should fight the war in Europe first and then the war in the Pacific. That made sense. Splitting your fighting forces is never a good idea. Besides, we didn't yet have enough supplies for two regions. But Admiral King said we couldn't just sit back and let the Japanese take over the Pacific. If we did, they would become so powerful that it would be almost impossible to win the war against them.

When the Japanese started building an airfield on an obscure island in the Solomon Island chain, Admiral King said that the United States needed to go on the

Do you remember when Thomas Jefferson wrote to James Madison about Patrick Henry? He said, "What we have to do, I think, is devotedly pray for his death." Patrick Henry was fighting some of Jefferson's ideas. Do you think Jefferson really wanted him dead?

U.S. troops of the 160th Infantry Regiment going ashore from a landing boat at Guadalcanal. It seemed a paradise—until they got past the beach.

149

Jungle warfare can be as much of a fight with the jungle as with the enemy. Some men's clothing was damp so long, it rotted on their bodies.

U.S. Marine Raiders and their dogs, which were used for scouting and sending messages. One platoon had specially trained dogs that tracked down Japanese hiding deep in the jungle.

offensive. So far—in Europe and the Pacific—we had been defensive fighters. King insisted that we take that island from the Japanese. It was an important decision. Not everyone agreed with it. It would cost many lives—American and Japanese. It turned out to be a decision that helped win the war.

The obscure island was named Guadalcanal, and it was such an out-of-the-way place that no one even had a map of it. But it was the right spot for a war base.

Find Australia on a map. Then look north, to New Guinea. To the east of New Guinea are the Solomon Islands. Guadalcanal is one of the southernmost of the Solomons. Anyone who has an airbase on Guadalcanal can make big trouble for ships and airplanes going to Australia, New Zealand, or even Japan (which was where the American military planned to go eventually). We couldn't let the Japanese put planes on that island.

From the air, Guadalcanal looks like a heavenly place: very green, with high mountains, thick forests, and jungles filled with wild orchids and bright-feathered and beaked tropical birds. To that picture, add sandy beaches, coconut palms, and banana trees. Does it sound like a place you'd like to visit? Well, the men who fought there called it "a bloody, stinking hole."

Guadalcanal is intensely hot (note the nearness of the Equator). Its jungles are filled with monster leeches, huge scorpions, poisonous centipedes, giant ants, writhing snakes, skulking rats, snapping crocodiles, and hungry anopheles (uh-NOF-fuh-lees) mosquitoes (whose bites bring malaria).

During the Spanish–American War, Walter Reed, an American doctor, discovered that quinine (KWY-nine) cures malaria. Quinine comes from a plant found in Java. The Japanese had captured Java. Doctors were working on synthetic quinine, but not fast enough for the troops who fought on Guadalcanal.

Most of Guadalcanal is tropical rainforest—which means steamy, thick jungle, a whole lot of rain, and black, squishy mud that comes up to a man's knees. Where there isn't rainforest there is kunai (KOON-i) grass. Kunai grass blades are saw-toothed, stiff as

I remember exactly the way it looked the day we came up on deck to go ashore: the delicious sparkling tropic sea, the long beautiful beach, the minute palms of the copra plantation waving in the sea breeze, the dark green band of jungle, and the dun mass and power of the mountains rising behind it to rocky peaks.

—NOVELIST JAMES JONES,
WHO FOUGHT AT GUADALCANAL

wood, and often seven feet high. Walk through kunai grass and your arms and legs will be a mess of cuts. Do you get the picture? Does Guadalcanal sound like a great place to fight? Watch out, you can't even see the enemy hiding in the grass or behind those jungle trees.

The 1st Marine Division landed in August of 1942. Marines are trained to fight on land or sea. The 1st Marine Division was a proud division—specially trained, and tough. They needed that toughness. Guadalcanal was one of the hardest-fought battles in history. Remember the back-and-forth slugfest at Gettysburg? This one was worse. It went on for six months. It combined jungle fighting with terrible sea and air battles.

At first, things seemed easy. The marines surprised the Japanese on the island, who were mostly construction crews building an airfield. The marines captured the airfield. They named it Henderson Field, after a pilot who had been killed at Midway Island. At last, said President Roosevelt, we have a

Above: Machine gunners in the jungle. *Below:* The fight for Henderson Field, the main objective of the entire battle of Guadalcanal. By the end, Japan had lost 600 aircraft and 24 warships.

Words made up from initial letters, like SNAFU, are called "acronyms." Some other acronyms are WASP ("white Anglo-Saxon Protestant") and NOW (National Organization for Women). Do you know other acronyms?

First Lt. Thomas J. "Stumpy" Stanley became a company commander in the 1st Marine Division. "We thought highly of Stumpy and respected him greatly," wrote E. B. Sledge in a book about the Pacific war called *With the Old Breed*. Tom Stanley was my brother-in-law (and a real hero).

toehold in the Pacific."

The Japanese were determined to knock that toe into the sea. We wanted to plant both feet on the island. To tell the story of what happened next would take a whole book. Here is some of it:

Let's begin with the military word for a mistake. It is SNAFU, a combination of letters for *Situation Normal, All Fouled Up*. It means that someone goofed.

Who goofed on Guadalcanal? Both sides. It happens all the time in warfare. The pressure and fear of battle often lead to mistakes. Most of our soldiers and even our officers were amateurs. They had not fought in a war before. They had to learn on the job.

One captain, unloading marines onto the beach, didn't want to risk a Japanese attack on his ships. So he pulled out before the loading was finished, taking supplies and marines with him. He stranded the marines already on the island. That was just one of the goofs.

The Japanese officers matched our snafus. They were too sure of themselves. An old Chinese proverb says, "A lion uses all his strength to fight a rabbit." The Japanese were lions in 1942, but they must not have heard of that proverb. They kept sending small forces to Guadalcanal. They thought Japanese fighters were unbeatable. They thought Americans were not good fighters. They were wrong.

When the marines wiped out the first group of Japanese soldiers, their leader was so ashamed he committed suicide. The next Japanese commander arrived on the island with a starched white uniform in his trunk. It was for the surrender ceremony he expected to conduct. After he and his men were destroyed, a marine found the trunk and dressed up in his uniform.

In six months, the marines, and the army units that came to fight with them, lost 1,598 men on Guadalcanal. Japanese war records show an incredible 23,800 deaths. Many Japanese deaths came in suicidal charges. Surrender was considered shameful. The Japanese also suffered many deaths from tropical disease. Our medical care was much better.

Most of the battle for Guadalcanal was fought at sea. There the statistics were more even. Each side lost 24 big ships and many smaller ones. The water near Guadalcanal was so full of sunken ships that it was called "Ironbottom Sound." It should have been called Graveyard Sound. About 20,000 American and Japanese sailors went down there with their ships.

The first of the sea fights—off nearby Savo Island—was the worst disaster in United States naval history. We were whipped. After that it was a seesaw of a conflict. It was bizarre: control

The battles at Guadalcanal, at Bougainville, Tarawa, and in Papua and New Guinea turned marines into seasoned jungle fighters. These Raiders posed in front of a Japanese dugout on Bougainville, near Guadalcanal in the Solomon Islands.

switched every 12 hours. The Japanese were skilled fighters in the dark; at night they were masters of water and air. During the night Japanese planes dropped bombs on Henderson Field; Japanese ships lobbed shells at the field.

In the mornings the Americans took over. Seabees (construction crews) repaired the holes in the airfield. Then our planes took off after Japanese ships and troops. Our pilots were superb during the daytime.

The battles on the island were ferocious. The Japanese were a brave foe. They had not lost a war in 400 years. But the marines outfought them. When it was all over, a doctor examining the marines wrote:

> *The weight loss averaged about 20 pounds per man....Many of these patients reported being buried in foxholes, blown out of trees, blown through the air, or knocked out.*

Of 36,000 Japanese soldiers on Guadalcanal when the battle began, only 12,000 got home alive.

The important thing was that they didn't give up. They held Guadalcanal. The marines ended the myth that the Japanese were invincible.

Guadalcanal was a turning point in the war. We went from defense to offense. The Japanese went from offense to defense. A captured Japanese document said, "Guadalcanal Island...is the fork in the road which leads to victory for them or us." We took the right road. It would lead to Japan.

35 Axing the Axis

We Can Do It!

Rosie the Riveter became the war's can-do symbol, and women took over many jobs usually done by men.

"We have reached the end of the beginning," said Churchill, early in 1943. He was right.

The beginning was horrible. The Germans had perfected their *blitzkrieg* (that lightning attack with planes, tanks, and armies all charging together). The Japanese used the same tactic, and mowed down everyone in their way. The Allies were losing the war. The Axis seemed invincible. Then things began to change. This is what happened:

• In February 1943, Japan pulled out of Guadalcanal.

• That same month, we cracked the Nazi naval code, *Triton*. Now we knew where their submarines were. The Atlantic was full of U-boats,

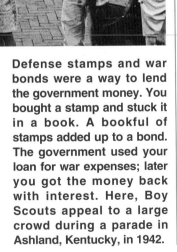

Defense stamps and war bonds were a way to lend the government money. You bought a stamp and stuck it in a book. A bookful of stamps added up to a bond. The government used your loan for war expenses; later you got the money back with interest. Here, Boy Scouts appeal to a large crowd during a parade in Ashland, Kentucky, in 1942.

Russian troops, in winter camouflage, advance. The Red Army pushed the Germans back from Moscow through the winter snows of 1941–1942.

154

American women threw themselves into the war effort. *Left:* polishing airplane nose cones at Willow Run. *Above:* Eastine Cowner, a former waitress, works as a scaler on the construction of the Liberty Ship S.S. *George Washington Carver* at the Kaiser shipyards in Richmond, California, 1943. Her job was to "scale," or clean and scrape off excess metal from the welded joints. Women also did many other non-military jobs usually held by men in peacetime—delivering mail, driving buses, and so on.

but we began sinking them. The German U-boat admiral couldn't figure out what was happening.

• We realized that the Germans must have broken our naval code. That would explain why they always seemed to know where our convoys were going. We changed our code. More ships made it to Europe. We began winning the war of the Atlantic.

• The Russians trapped a German army at Stalingrad. Then they laid siege to that army. They starved them. Finally, the German army surrendered. Then the Russians went on the offensive. They headed for Germany. Hitler hadn't planned on that.

• America's factories reached high gear. We began turning out guns, ships, tanks, planes, and other military equipment at an incredible rate—faster than anyone had believed possible. Picture this: a flat, sandy, empty field at a place called Willow Run (in Michigan). Now picture the same field, six months after Pearl Harbor. What you see is a vast building, half a mile long and a quarter of a mile wide. Someone described it as the "most enormous room in the history of man." Steel, rubber, and other raw materials are fed into one end of the room; airplanes emerge from the other end—almost 9,000 airplanes the first year. It is not surprising that many historians say the Second World War was won in America's factories and laboratories.

• In 1943, the Russians were fighting the Axis alone on the European continent. Stalin was crying for help. He asked his allies to land forces in Europe and take some pressure off his troops. He asked for a second front. American and British leaders agreed, and made plans for a joint landing. Its code

A *front* is a "battle line." Stalin's front was in Russia and eastern Europe. He wanted the Allies to launch a western front, so that the Germans would have to fight on two sides at once.

Convoys were "groups of ships." Ships carrying troops or supplies traveled together with destroyers for protection against submarines.

"The venture [in North Africa] was new," said General Eisenhower *(above, right,* with General Patton). "Up to that moment no government had ever attempted to carry out an overseas expedition involving a journey of thousands of miles from its bases and terminating in a major attack." *Right:* U.S. troops in North Africa.

In 1942, when Rommel (on the right, in Tripoli) reported to Hitler and Hermann Göring that Britain was dropping American shells on his men, Göring said, "Impossible. All the Americans can make are razor blades and refrigerators." Rommel replied, "I wish, *Herr Reichsmarschall,* that we had similar razor blades!"

name was *Operation Torch*.

But when the landing came, it was in North Africa, not Europe. That wasn't exactly what Stalin wanted, but it did help. North Africa was a good place to begin our offensive. It had been 23 years since we fought in World War I, and our troops needed combat experience. North Africa became a war school for us, with General Dwight D. Eisenhower in charge.

The Nazi forces there were led by General Erwin Rommel, who was known as the "desert fox." Rommel was intelligent, wily, and tough. His Afrika Korps had been destroying British troops. Then the British went on the offensive, heading west from Egypt. (Massive supplies helped.) Combined Allied forces headed east from Morocco and Algiers. A small French force came north from Chad. Rommel was caught in a pincer. We had managed to outfox the fox. We drove the Axis from North Africa. The Germans no longer controlled the Mediterranean Sea.

• We were now bombing Germany from the air day and night, but we needed to do more than that. We had to invade and help destroy Hitler's forces. Should we land in France and push east to Germany? Should we land in Italy and move north? Should we go through Greece? Finally, it was decided. We would start on the Mediterranean island of Sicily and go on to Italy. Look at the map at the back of this book and you'll see why Sicily was important.

• The invasion of Sicily was given the code name *Husky*. We landed by sea and air and captured the island. Amphibious ducks were used for the first time. But there was a snafu: we let an Axis army escape to Italy.

• The Italian people were now fed up with war. Our bombs were blasting Rome. Things hadn't worked out as some Italians thought they would. Their morale collapsed. They kicked Mussolini out of power. Their army went home. They got out of the war. Because of that, we thought Italy would be easy to capture. It wasn't. More snafus. The German army moved into the mountainous Italian peninsula and captured the mountaintops. Picture the enemy shooting down at you as you attempt to climb. That's what happened. The Germans were on the heights. Our soldiers faced ferocious fire. Italy was a bloody standoff.

• Planning began for *Operation Overlord*—code name for the invasion of France. It was to be the largest amphibious invasion in all of history. The Nazis knew it was coming, so they began planning to defeat it. We assembled men and materials in England. The Germans readied their defenses. They laid explosive mines all along the coast, layers and layers of mines. Then they put steel and concrete barriers in the water and on the beaches. They added barbed wire, huge steel spikes, and more mines on the beaches. They built rooms of thick concrete—called "bunkers"—and filled them with heavy antitank guns, versatile medium-size guns, deadly flamethrowers, and machine guns. They called all this the *Atlantic Wall*.

They fortified the whole coastline—from the Netherlands to the west coast of France—although they were sure they knew the exact spot where the landing would be made. Everyone knew. Look at the map on page 162, and see if you can figure it out, too.

The best route is obvious: from Dover, England, to the Pas de Calais (pah-duh-KAL-ay) in France. It is the shortest distance across the treacherous English Channel, it has gentle beaches, and it is the best place to land if you are heading for Germany's heartland. German intelligence officers decoded Allied messages that told of invasion plans for Calais. German pilots bombing England brought back photographs of tanks and trucks lined up near Dover. Spies reported on plans for a second invasion, on the same day, into Norway.

The messages were all fakes. The tanks and trucks were big balloons, designed to look real from aerial photographs. We weren't going to land at Pas de Calais. We weren't planning a Norway invasion. The German spies were double agents working secretly for us.

June 1944: Italian civilians cheer wildly as U.S. 5th Army troops and armored vehicles begin their triumphal march into Rome. Behind them looms one of Rome's great sights, the Victor Emmanuel monument, spared by Allied bombing.

Below: Rommel's ferocious Atlantic Wall on the beach at Pas de Calais.

The End of the Road

Ernie Pyle was a war correspondent. In this excerpt from his book Brave Men, *he is writing about the war in Italy.*

Ernie Pyle (center, *balding) on Iwo Jima early in 1945. He died the same year, shot on the island of Ie Shima.*

Captain Waskow was a company commander....He was very young, only in his middle twenties, but he carried in him a sincerity and gentleness that made people want to be guided by him.

"After my father, he came next," a sergeant told me.

"He always looked after us," a soldier said. "He'd go to bat for us every time."

"I've never known him to do anything unfair," another said.

I was at the foot of the mule trail the night they brought Captain Waskow down. The moon was nearly full and you could see far up the trail....Dead men had been coming down the mountain all evening, lashed onto the backs of mules. They came lying belly-down across the wooden packsaddles, their heads hanging down on one side, their stiffened legs sticking out awkwardly from the other, bobbing up and down as the mules walked.

I don't know who the first one was. You feel small in the presence of dead men, and you don't ask silly questions....We left him there beside the road, that first one, and we all went back into the cowshed and sat on water cans or lay on the straw, waiting for the next batch of mules....We talked soldier talk for an hour or more....Then a soldier came into the cowshed and said there were some more bodies outside. We went out into the road. Four mules stood there in the moonlight, in the road where the trail came down off the mountain. The soldiers who led them stood there waiting.

"This one is Captain Waskow," one of them said quietly.

Two men unlashed his body from the mule and lifted it off and laid it in the shadow beside the stone wall. Other men took the other bodies off. Finally, there were five lying end to end in a long row....The unburdened mules moved off to their olive grove. The men in the road seemed reluctant to leave. They stood around, and gradually I could sense them moving, one by one, close to Captain Waskow's body. Not so much to look, I think, as to say something in finality to him and to themselves. I stood close by and I could hear.

One soldier came and looked down, and he said out loud, "God damn it!" That's all he said, and then he walked away.....

Another man came. I think he was an officer. It was hard to tell officers from men in the dim light, for everybody was bearded and grimy. The man looked down into the dead captain's face and then spoke directly to him, as though he were alive, "I'm sorry, old man."

Then a soldier came and stood beside the officer and bent over, and he too spoke to his dead captain, not in a whisper but awfully tenderly, and he said, "I sure am sorry, sir."

Then the first man squatted down, and he reached down and took the captain's hand, and he sat there for a full five minutes holding the dead hand in his own and looking intently into the dead face. And he never uttered a sound all the time he sat there.

Finally he put the hand down. He reached over and gently straightened the points of the captain's shirt collar, and then he sort of rearranged the tattered edges of the uniform around the wound, and then he got up and walked away down the road in the moonlight, all alone.

The rest of us went back into the cowshed, leaving the five dead men lying in a line end to end in the shadow of the low stone wall. We lay down on the straw in the cowshed, and pretty soon we were all asleep.

36 Going for D-Day

June 6, 1944, England: Eisenhower gives paratroopers leaving for Normandy the orders for D-Day—to go all-out for a full victory.

General Erwin Rommel, Germany's brilliant desert warrior, looked at the skies and decided to take a two-day trip home to Germany. It was his wife Lucie's 50th birthday (he had bought her a gift—shoes from Paris); he also wanted to see the Führer and ask for more troops. The weather was too rough for an invasion, he said.

Hitler was known in Germany as *Der Führer* (FEW-rur), which means "the leader" in German.

General Eisenhower looked at the same skies and decided to go for it. The English Channel was in turmoil, but the moon was full and the tides were low.

The invasion began at night, when paratroopers dropped behind enemy lines. They captured bridges and lit flares to guide the gliders that followed. With all the sophisticated equipment available, it was a tiny child's toy—a snapper that made a sound like a cricket—that the paratroopers used as a signal during the night so they could find each other.

Then, at daybreak, the sky filled with airplanes—wingtip to wingtip—9,000 of them. Two submarines raised flags to mark a landing area. The largest armada ever assembled appeared off the French coast: landing vehicles, minesweepers, attack transports, tankers, cruisers, battleships, ocean liners, yachts, hospital ships and puffing tugs—all the

Troops plunge down their Coast Guard landing barge ramp and wade for the beach. Behind the clouds loom the Normandy cliffs they will climb.

General Rommel had good reasons for taking time off. He intended to see Hitler and ask for more men to beef up the beach defenses. He also wanted to see Manfred, his 14-year-old son, who had been drafted into the army. Some of the other officers who took time off got together to practice war games.

Anti-aircraft barrage balloons over Omaha Beach. Among the arrivals on June 7, D-Day-plus-1, are a group of hulks that will be sunk off the beach as the foundations for temporary artificial harbors. The Allies need a base from which their invading troops can be easily landed and their equipment and supplies handled.

The rains are ferocious, but General Eisenhower's weatherman—tall, serious-faced Captain James Stagg—gets reports from five weather stations in the Atlantic. They indicate that there will be a 16-hour "window" in the bad weather. Ike entered Europe through that window.

boats and ships that could be found. They made an awesome fleet 20 miles wide. Giant military barrage balloons floated above, to interfere with enemy planes.

It was June 6, 1944, and forever it would be known as *D-Day*. The Allies were heading for the treacherous, mine-strewn beaches of Normandy in France, 100 miles from the nearest English port across the turbulent Channel. Enemy soldiers, in bunkers on top of the Normandy cliffs, some of them 150 feet high, waited behind formidable heavy guns. But most were asleep. No one was expecting an attack in this weather. Rommel wasn't the only officer on vacation. Most of the German leaders had taken the weekend off.

Soldiers are supplied with assault equipment suited to their landing area. Those on the cliffs have ropes and ladders; these men have bikes.

General Omar Bradley *(right),* U.S. 1st Army commander, and British General Bernard Montgomery discussing maneuvers in a field near Omaha Beach.

What happened next? The landing had been planned with the precision of a ballet. Everyone had a place and time in the drama. And, at four of the five landing beaches, things went more or less on schedule. But on Omaha Beach (one of two beaches where Americans landed), everything seemed snafued. The first men ashore couldn't secure the beach. What was supposed to take minutes took hours. Of 32 tanks, with collars that were supposed to keep them afloat, 27 sank in the choppy water with men inside. Allied planes, sent to bomb the enemy's gun-filled bunkers, went too far, missed the guns, and dropped their bombs on French cows. Immense traffic jams of men and supplies backed up in the water and on the beaches. Mines and shells were exploding everywhere. Gliders dropped men and supplies behind the beaches into swampland, where many sank. "Our men simply could not get past the beach. They were pinned down right on the water's edge by an inhuman wall of fire....Our first waves were on the beach for hours, instead of a few minutes, before they could begin working inland," wrote war correspondent Ernie Pyle, who was there.

General Omar Bradley, on the command ship *Augusta,* thought about calling off the landing. Then a destroyer came up into the shallow water and lobbed a shell right inside a main bunker. When other ships added their firepower, the Nazi gunners in the concrete emplacements were in big trouble. The Navy had opened a crack in the German defenses and the Yanks were on their way.

American troops injured while storming Omaha Beach wait below the chalk cliffs for transport to a field hospital.

A Great War Photographer

Most of Robert Capa's Normandy photographs were never published; they were accidentally ruined by a Life *magazine darkroom technician.*

Robert Capa was one of the war's great photographers. He took part in the D-Day invasion:

The sea was rough and we were wet before our barge pushed away from the mother ship. It was already clear that General Eisenhower would not lead his people across the Channel with dry feet or dry anything else. In no time, the men started to puke. But this was a polite as well as a carefully prepared invasion, and little paper bags had been provided for the purpose. [There weren't enough of the bags; most men used their helmets.]

Emplacements are the areas where heavy artillery (guns) are positioned.

161

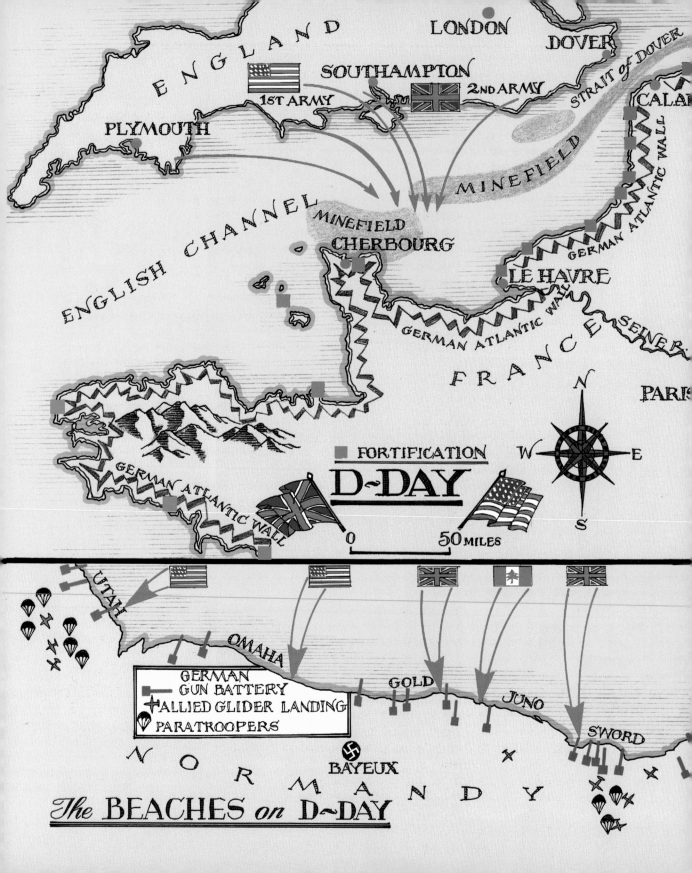

LONDON
DOVER

ENGLAND

PLYMOUTH

1ST ARMY   SOUTHAMPTON   2ND ARMY

STRAIT of DOVER

CALAIS

ENGLISH CHANNEL

MINEFIELD

MINEFIELD
CHERBOURG

LE HAVRE

GERMAN ATLANTIC WALL

GERMAN ATLANTIC WALL

SEINE R.

FRANCE

PARIS

GERMAN ATLANTIC WALL

■ FORTIFICATION

D~DAY

N
W   E
S

0   50 MILES

UTAH

OMAHA

GERMAN
GUN BATTERY
ALLIED GLIDER LANDING
PARATROOPERS

GOLD

JUNO

SWORD

N O R M A N D Y

BAYEUX

The BEACHES *on* D~DAY

Slowly at first, but then steadily, soldiers and medical personnel began to land and head inland, into the fierce guns on top of the bluffs. No word is big enough to describe their effort. *Heroic* will have to do.

The operation had been brilliantly planned. Troops and officers had trained for a year; it paid off. Equipment specially designed for this invasion worked superbly. Tanks unrolled reels of steel matting that made roadways across the sand. Other tanks, with flailing chain arms, detonated mines and began to make the beach safe. Some tanks carried small bridges. Naval engineers had built huge floating harbors; they were towed into place.

In the midst of the fighting, over the noise of battle, a British major shouted out words from Shakespeare's play *Henry V,* about another invasion of France.

> *We few, we happy few, we band of brothers;*
> *For he today that sheds his blood with me*
> *Shall be my brother; be he ne'er so vile,*
> *This day shall gentle his condition.*
> *And gentlemen in England now a-bed,*
> *Shall think themselves accursed they were not here;*
> *And hold their manhoods cheap whiles any speaks*
> *That fought with us upon Saint Crispin's day.*

It was D-Day, not St. Crispin's, but poets would write of this day, too: of heroism, of achievement, and of the waste of war. It was there to see on the beaches. They were littered with tanks and bodies and the leftovers of men's lives: socks, Bibles, toothbrushes, diaries, mirrors, letters, first-aid kits, photographs, and food rations. From Ernie Pyle:

> *There was a dog...on the water's edge, near a boat that lay twisted and half sunk at the waterline. He barked appealingly to every soldier who approached, trotted eagerly along with him for a few feet, and then, sensing himself unwanted in all the haste, he would run back to wait in vain for his own people at his own empty boat.*

By nightfall, Allied troops—American, British, Canadian, Free French, Polish—were holding French soil. We had made it. We were on our way to Berlin.

For the Axis, it was the beginning of the end.

The Allies liberate France. *Above:* U.S. infantrymen march through a town in Normandy past a wrecked German truck still in its camouflage. *Below:* An American tank rolls through the Arc de Triomphe in Paris, August 1944. "We couldn't stick around long though," said one soldier. "The Jerries were on the run and we wanted to keep them that way."

37 A Wartime Diary

At his fourth inaugural, FDR says:

Our constitution of 1787 was not a perfect instrument, it is not perfect yet. But it provided a firm base upon which all manner of men, of all races and colors and creeds, could build our solid structure of democracy.

The Battle of the Bulge was Hitler's last gamble on the western front. Much of it was fought in bad, snowy conditions. *Above:* GIs in a chow line

Find the Black Sea—above Turkey and below Russia— and you'll find the Crimean peninsula and Yalta.

You are a newspaper writer, a war correspondent, covering this world war. When it ends you will write a book about the times you have lived through, so you have been keeping a diary to record events. It is 1945. Here are some excerpts from your journal, and some notes from this author:

JANUARY 1: Allied forces are beginning to turn back a powerful German army in Belgium. Soldiers are calling this the Battle of the Bulge. *A strong German offensive created a bulge in the Allied defensive line.* Whatever you want to call this battle, it is fierce. Still, it looks as if this will be a good year for the Allies. Germany's armies are being battered on the ground, its cities pounded from the air.

JANUARY 20: FDR is inaugurated for a fourth term as president. No other president has served more than twice.

JANUARY 24: Russian soldiers have crossed the Oder River and, for the first time, are on German soil.

JANUARY 27: Today, in Poland, Soviet forces liberated a German concentration camp. It is named Auschwitz. People in the camp were used as slaves by a German industrial chemical company. The company has left charts of the costs and profits of slave labor. But the camp was built primarily for another purpose. It was built to kill people. The horror and evil of it all are

Christmas Eve, 1944: an 82nd Airborne Division infantryman on a one-man sortie through the lines during the Battle of the Bulge. The bump on the horizon is the head of the sniper covering him.

Left: the Big Three at Yalta. But their unity did not go far beyond beating Hitler, as this cartoon, showing Stalin with "secret plans," suggested.

more than anyone wants to believe. *Three million people were murdered at Auschwitz, most of them Jews.*

FEBRUARY 1: The sky is thick with planes—an incredible sight! One thousand airplanes are flying over Europe on their way to bomb Berlin.

FEBRUARY 4–11: President Roosevelt has flown to Yalta, in the Crimea, to meet with England's Winston Churchill and Russia's Joseph Stalin. They are said to be planning for the final battles of the war. They agree to call a meeting of the world's nations in San Francisco in April, to form a peacekeeping organization called the United Nations.

FEBRUARY 14: John D. Rockefeller, Jr., donates $8.5 million to buy land in New York City as a permanent home for the United Nations. Woodrow Wilson's idea of a league of nations may finally be achieved.

Above: Two days before the German army surrenders, U.S. troops force German citizens to inspect the bodies of victims of a Nazi concentration camp near their town.

January 1945: Red Army soldiers, now only 50 miles from Berlin, struggle to get a field gun across the river Oder.

165

Above: In this carefully staged photograph MacArthur wades ashore during initial landings at Leyte in the Philippines, October 1944. MacArthur liked wading, rather than having himself rowed in, because it looked grander. He sometimes had a photographer shoot the same picture many times, until he got it just right.

FEBRUARY 19: American marines have landed on Iwo Jima, an island in the Pacific. Reports tell of incredibly hard fighting and great losses on both sides.

FEBRUARY 24: General Douglas MacArthur promised to return to the Philippines—and he has done it.

MARCH 7: The U.S. 1st Army has crossed the river Rhine and is inside Germany. All German armies have been pushed back into the Fatherland.

MARCH 9: Today, 325 low-flying bombers dropped incendiary bombs on Tokyo. The bombs are filled with jellied gasoline meant to set fires. The Japanese capital became so hot that the water in its canals boiled. Still the Japanese refuse to surrender. *Later reports list 267,000 Tokyo buildings burned to the ground; 89,000 persons dead.*

MARCH 21: Today we watched an enormous air armada fly overhead on its way to Germany. *There were 7,000 Allied planes.* Until now, most bombing raids have been at night, to make it difficult for the anti-aircraft guns and fighter planes to see the bombers. Now Germany has little firepower left; the bombers fly at will. Bomb damage there is said to be devastating.

The Axis powers now have no hope of winning and yet neither Germany nor Japan will give up. Those who began this insane engine of war have cut out the brakes. They can't seem to stop. It is their own people who are suffering most. Do the warlords care?

Above: U.S. firebombs fall on Kobe, Japan. *Right:* In the war's most famous photograph, G.I.s raise the flag on Mt. Suribachi after the capture of the island of Iwo Jima. This photo was actually a posed shot taken after the battle. A small flag had been raised during the fighting, hours earlier.

38 April in Georgia

Much wartime propaganda, like this American postcard, was meant to reassure the troops, and the folks at home, that their efforts were succeeding and the war was worth fighting.

Where is Tokyo? Where is Dresden?

This statue seems to be contemplating the firestorm set off in Dresden, Germany, by Allied bombing in February 1945.

The madmen who run Japan and Germany refuse to give up. They talk of leading their nations in a fight to the death. Terrible firebombs are dropping on Tokyo and Dresden. Hundreds of thousands of people are dying. Just as a fist squeezes its contents, so British, American, and Russian troops are squeezing Germany. In the Pacific theater we are making plans to invade Japan. Everyone expects that invasion to be bloodier than the one in Normandy.

The Allies will win this war—that now seems clear—but the German and Japanese leaders are making it very difficult. Like ancient rulers who had their followers killed and buried in their tombs, these leaders seem determined to kill their own people.

The president knows of something that might end the war quickly. It is that secret weapon that almost no one else knows about. Partly because of this, he feels he can relax and catch up on some paperwork. He is exhausted. He has just turned 63, but he looks much older. The war has been a terrible strain: he has traveled around the world, he has run for a fourth term

167

The exhaustion brought on by the war years shows plainly in FDR's face as he arrives in the Crimea for the Yalta conference. He was a sick man.

On the island
of Okinawa, the U.S. Army suffers some 80,000 casualties. Japanese losses total 120,000.

Roosevelt is planning to attend a Jefferson's birthday celebration. Do you remember another famous party for that occasion? It was attended by Andrew Jackson and John Calhoun. (See book 6 of *A History of US* for details.)

as president, he has been active as commander in chief of the armed services, he has been an inspiring leader. He needs to take it easy for a few days. He makes plans to go to Warm Springs, Georgia. He first visited Warm Springs years earlier, when he was recovering from polio. The waters are healing. He has been back many times, and has grown to love the slow-paced gentleness of the South.

In Georgia, wild violets are blooming; so are purple-blue wisteria and sweet-smelling honeysuckle. It is springtime—April 12, 1945—and, at Warm Springs, cooks are preparing a picnic. The smells of barbecued beef and chicken fill the air. As the president works, an artist sits nearby, making sketches for a watercolor portrait.

Almost exactly 80 years earlier, another American president had decided to relax and go to the theater, knowing that a terrible war was coming to an end.

Like that other president, Roosevelt is concerned about the peace that is to come. He wants this war to have meaning. Soon after the war began, he met with Winston Churchill and signed a document called the *Atlantic Charter*. It says that after the war, nations will be free to choose their own forms of government. That is called "self-determination." Roosevelt wants to end the old, before-the-war imperialist ways. Then, a few European nations ruled much of the world. Sometimes they ruled well; sometimes not well. To Roosevelt, that doesn't matter now. People should be free to govern themselves. Great Britain still controls India and Burma. France expects to regain control of Indochina (which includes Vietnam). Japan has attempted to become an empire. The United States rules the Philippine Islands.

Roosevelt thinks imperialism—even well-meaning imperialism—is wrong. He will show the world: America has no desire for other lands. We will begin by granting independence to the Philippines. He is planning to go to the independence ceremonies himself.

Russia is a worry. The Russian people have fought magnificently. They have been brave allies. But they aren't a free people. Stalin is a dictator. Winston Churchill believes that Stalin cannot be trusted.

The president on the porch of his home in Warm Springs, known as the Little White House. It is still there.

Roosevelt is beginning to have worries about Stalin, too.

At Warm Springs he works on a speech to be given at the dinner to honor Jefferson's memory. This is part of what Roosevelt writes:

> *The once powerful, malignant Nazi state is crumbling. The Japanese war lords are receiving, in their own homeland, the retribution for which they asked when they attacked Pearl Harbor.*
>
> *But the mere conquest of our enemies is not enough.*
>
> *We must go on to do all in our power to conquer the doubts and the fears, the ignorance and the greed, which made this horror possible....If civilization is to survive, we must cultivate the science of human relationships—the ability of all peoples, of all kinds, to live together and work together, in the same world, at peace....*
>
> *The work, my friends, is peace. More than an end of this war—an end to the beginnings of all wars. Yes, an end, forever, to this impractical, unrealistic settlement of the differences between governments by the mass killing of peoples.*

The president is sitting in a leather armchair; he turns to the artist. "We've got just 15 minutes more," he says. Some cousins of his and a friend are in the room. They are quiet. The president is studying papers. The 15 minutes are almost up when he raises a hand to his temple. "I have a terrific headache," he says. They are the last words he will ever speak.

The **August 1941 meeting** between Roosevelt and Churchill aboard the U.S.S. *Augusta* that paved the way for America's entry into World War II.

Malignant means "harmful."
Retribution is "punishment."

Our only hope will lie in the frail web of understanding of one person for the pain of another.
—JOHN DOS PASSOS, DECEMBER 1940

What do you think Dos Passos means by that? Do you agree?

The last family photo taken before Roosevelt's death: FDR, Eleanor, and their 13 grandchildren at the White House on Inauguration Day, 1945.

39 President HST

In 1918 Captain Harry Truman commanded a field-artillery battery in France, where he saw active combat.

The solidly built, gray-haired man with metal-rimmed glasses sat at a high desk facing the Senate floor. A gold-bordered blue velvet drape hung behind him and made a frame for his chair. Vice President Harry S. Truman was presiding over the Senate. At least that was what he seemed to be doing. Actually, he was bored and was writing a letter to his mother and sister, who were back in his hometown of Independence, Missouri. This is part of what he wrote:

Dear Mama & Mary: I am trying to write you a letter today from the desk of the President of the Senate while a windy Senator…is making a speech on a subject with which he is in no way familiar.…Turn on your radio tomorrow night at 9:30 your time.…I think I'll be on all the networks.…I'll be followed by the President, whom I'll introduce.

It had amazed almost everyone—including Truman—when he was asked to be vice president. He hardly knew FDR. Some said it was the Democratic National Committee that selected Harry Truman; that the other candidates considered were all controversial.

Truman was asked to be vice president by Democratic National Chairman Robert Hannegan, but he refused—said he wasn't a candidate. Just then the phone rang. It was FDR. He asked Hannegan if he had "got that fellow lined up yet."

"He is the contrariest Missouri mule I've ever dealt with," said Hannegan.

"Well, you tell him," FDR shouted, and Truman could hear him, "that if he wants to break up the Democratic Party in the middle of a war, that's his responsibility."

Truman with friends in his Kansas City, Missouri, men's clothing and haberdashery store, around 1920

THE SPOKESMAN-REVIEW

ROOSEVELT IS DEAD, TRUMAN SWORN IN

President Dies Without Pain; Had Complained of Bad Headache

Truman didn't seem to have any enemies. But he didn't have many enthusiasts either. He had become a senator at age 50. He'd fought in the Great War, and had tried a number of jobs—he'd even owned a men's clothing store—but the store had failed, and he wasn't very successful at anything until he got into politics, first as a postmaster and then as a judge. He was a bookish sort, with an astounding knowledge of history: quiet, honest, likable, and fair-minded, although he sometimes lost his temper. It was as head of a Senate committee investigating military contracts that he had impressed people—including Roosevelt. His committee probably saved the government billions of dollars.

When the windy senator finally finished, Truman went to visit his old friend, the speaker of the House of Representatives, Texan Sam Rayburn. Rayburn's office was a gathering place where congressmen relaxed and gossiped. It was called—in jest—the Board of Education. It was there that Truman got a call from the president's press secretary, Steve Early. He was to come to the White House at once. Early's voice had an urgent tone.

Truman headed through the underground passage to the Senate Office building—there his Secret Service agents lost track of him. But his car and driver were waiting. As he drove the 15 long blocks to the White House, he guessed that the president had flown in from Georgia and wanted him for something ceremonial.

Upstairs at the White House, he learned differently. Eleanor Roosevelt put her hand on his shoulder and said softly, "Harry, the president is dead." For a moment he could say nothing. Then he asked if there was anything he could do for her.

"Is there anything we can do for you?" she answered. "You are the one in trouble now."

Election night in 1944. *Above left:* FDR *(left),* returning for a fourth term as president, with Henry Wallace *(right,* bareheaded), and the man taking over Wallace's job, vice president–elect Harry Truman *(center).* Truman would serve as vice president for only four months. *Below:* Truman, in his trademark round glasses and bow tie, is sworn in as the country's 33rd president. Truman's wife, Bess, and their daughter, Margaret, look on.

40 A Final Journey

In his fire-side chats, [Roosevelt] talked like a father discussing public affairs with his family in the living room.

—WILLIAM E. LEUCHTENBURG

"Mr. Roosevelt was great," a Harvard professor said to his students, "because he, like Lincoln, restored men's faith."

The poem Eleanor Roosevelt remembered was written by Millard Lampell.

It was as if a member of the family had died. He had been a world-dominating figure for 12 years—strong, witty, compassionate, able. Young people could remember no other president. The nation was in a state of shock.

Those who had felt left out by government before—the poor and disadvantaged—were especially grieved. This was a president who had done more than talk about fairness and opportunity; he had acted to begin to make them reality. And, while he had broken precedent by running for office four times, he had not forgotten that as president he was the servant of the people. He had never assumed kingly trappings. He had never lost his sense of humor or his easy informality.

In Warm Springs, the flag-draped coffin began its long, sad train journey—to Washington first, and then to Hyde Park, where the president was to be buried. Sitting inside the train, Eleanor Roosevelt kept remembering a poem about Lincoln's death. It wouldn't leave her mind:

> *A lonesome train on a lonesome track*
> *Seven coaches painted black,*
> *A slow train, a quiet train*
> *Carrying Lincoln home again.*

On April 13, 1945, a hearse rolled into Warm Springs train station. Franklin Delano Roosevelt, 32nd president of the United States, was going home to Hyde Park for the last time.

At night, unable to sleep, she said:

> *I lay in my berth...with the window shade up, looking out at the countryside he had loved and watching the faces of the people at stations, and even at the crossroads, who had come to pay their last tribute all through the night....I was truly surprised by the people along the way; not only at the stops but at every crossing.*

In the train's press car, reporters looking out the window saw black sharecroppers on their knees, hands outstretched in prayer. As the train slowed in a South Carolina city, members of a Boy Scout troop began singing "Onward, Christian Soldiers"; then others joined in, and soon, according to one who was there, "eight or ten thousand voices were singing like an organ." Everywhere people cried. The sobs continued as the coffin was carried, by horse-drawn caisson, through Washington to the White House. Then, during the memorial service, the whole grieving nation came to a halt and paid its respects.

Airplanes sat on runways; radios were silent; telephone service was cut off—there was not even a dial tone; news-service teletypes typed the word *silence* and went dead; movie theaters closed; cars and buses pulled to the curb; 505 New York subway trains stopped; stores shut their doors; and everywhere—in other countries, too—people put hands on hearts, or fell to their knees, or just stayed quiet. That day newspapers carried no advertisements.

Clearly he had been a great president. But how great? What would history say of him?

A poll of 50 leading historians soon ranked him just behind Lincoln and Washington as one of the three greatest presidents. Winston Churchill said that in world importance, Roosevelt was first.

And yet, as much as some loved and respected him, others hated and vilified him.

Later historians would look at him through two lenses. As an effective president, they agreed, he was like a magnificent symphony conductor who knows all the notes and just what to do with them. No question about it, they still agreed, he was a great president. But there was something that bothered many. As a human being, he was sometimes less than great. His personality was flawed. It was too bad to have to acknowledge it, but he could be devious. He could tell a person something and not mean it. He could tell a story that made him look good but wasn't quite true.

Perhaps it was that tendency to always act as if everything was fine, even when it wasn't, that some found disturbing. He was used to pretending. It was both a strength and a weakness.

His wife said:

Thousands lined the streets of Washington to watch FDR's funeral procession pass by.

After the president's death, Eleanor Roosevelt said that people often told her how "they missed the way the president used to talk to them...[in his radio fireside chats]. There was a real dialogue between Franklin and the people," she reflected. "That dialogue seems to have disappeared from the government since he died."

He was in a very special sense the people's president, because he made them feel that with him in the White House they shared the presidency. The sense of sharing the presidency gave even the most humble citizen a lively sense of belonging.

—JUSTICE WILLIAM O. DOUGLAS

173

More faces along the route of the president's funeral cortège *(below)*. "I felt as if I knew him," said one young man. "I felt as if he knew me—and I felt as if he liked me."

Because he disliked being disagreeable, he made an effort to give each person who came in contact with him the feeling that he understood what his particular interest was….Often people have told me that they were misled by Franklin….This misunderstanding not only arose from his dislike of being disagreeable, but from the interest that he always had in somebody else's point of view and his willingness to listen to it.

He listened intently, and that was flattering. People thought it meant that he agreed with them. He didn't tell them differently.

So some felt he couldn't be trusted.

But no one could take his achievements as president from him. They changed the nation. Here are the most important of them:

• He was a peerless crisis manager. He led the nation through two of its worst times—a depression and a world war—with gusto, courage, and an unfailing confidence.

The only thing we have to fear is fear itself.

• He was inspiring. He made people believe in their country and want to do their best for it. Perhaps only during that time when the Constitution was written were more brilliant thinkers attracted to government service.

This generation has a rendezvous with destiny.

• He believed in government for the people. During the Roosevelt administrations, Social Security, farm programs, aid for home buyers, aid for dependent children, and other caring programs were begun. He paid attention to laboring people and their needs. Some called it a "revolution." Perhaps it was. It was in line with a tradition of revolution that could be traced to the ideas of Thomas Jefferson, Andrew Jackson, the Populists, and the Progressives.

As we have recaptured and rekindled our pioneering spirit, we have insisted that it shall always be a spirit of justice, a spirit of teamwork, a spirit of sacrifice, and, above all, a spirit of neighborliness.

• He strengthened the two-party system.

The war casualty announcement, which listed daily those who had died in the military services, was headed on April 13 by the name of Franklin D. Roosevelt.

Since before the Civil War, only two Democrats —Grover Cleveland and Woodrow Wilson—had been elected president. (And Woodrow Wilson made it because the Republican Party was split.) After Roosevelt there was a better balance between the parties.

Here in the United States we have been a long time at the business of self-government. The longer we are at it the more certain we become that we can continue to govern ourselves; that progress is on the side of majority rule; that if mistakes are to be made we prefer to make them ourselves and to do our own correcting.

He brought new people into government. He named a woman, Frances Perkins, to his cabinet. He began the process to "include the excluded." (Wartime America was a land that accepted much discrimination.)

We are going to make a country where no one is left out.

• He cared about the environment. He sent young people from the inner cities out to plant trees, and he worked to protect our nation's natural heritage.

The conservation of our natural resources and their proper use constitute the fundamental problem which underlies almost every other problem of our national life....The government has been endeavoring to get our people to look ahead and to substitute a planned and orderly development of our resources in place of a haphazard striving for immediate profit....We are prone to think of the resources of this country as inexhaustible; this is not so.

• By his personal example he showed that—for people with energy and intelligence—there need not be any such thing as a handicap.

If you have spent two years in bed trying to wiggle your big toe, everything else seems easy.

• He won the war and set the stage for the prosperity that was to follow. It might not have happened with another leader.

In the future days, which we seek to make secure, we look forward to a world founded upon four essential freedoms.

The first is freedom of speech and expression—everywhere in the world.

The second is freedom of every person to worship God in his own way—everywhere in the world.

The third is freedom from want....The fourth is freedom from fear.

"We have learned," President Roosevelt said at his fourth inauguration, "to be citizens of the world, members of the human community. We have learned the simple truth, as Emerson said, that 'the only way to have a friend is to be one.'"

41 Day by Day

April 29: U.S. troops reach Dachau concentration camp in southern Germany. An inmate writes, "First American comes through the entrance. Dachau free!!! Indescribable happiness. Insane howling."

The Camps

In 1945, Leon Bass was a 19-year-old soldier attached to the American 3rd Army when his unit was sent to Weimar, Germany.

Immediately about five or six of us took off with an officer to a place called Buchenwald....Buchenwald was a concentration camp. I had no idea what kind of camp this was. I thought it might have been a prisoner-of-war camp where they kept soldiers who were captured. But on this day...I was to discover what human suffering was...about. I was going to take off the blinders that caused me to have tunnel vision. I was going to see clearly that, yes, I suffered and I was hurting because I was black in a white society, but I had also begun to understand that suffering is universal. It is not just relegated to me and mine; it touches us all.

More from the diary that you, the newspaper reporter, are keeping.

APRIL 12, 1945: American soldiers enter the Nazi concentration camp at Buchenwald and find death everywhere. Germans interviewed say they didn't know anything about the concentration camps. *As camp after camp is discovered, the Allies react with cold fury. More than 10 million human beings have died in the concentration camps. In one camp American soldiers discover bins with thousands of pairs of babies' shoes.*

APRIL 13: Everywhere there is shock and disbelief. The president is dead! It is hard to imagine the United States without FDR. The bombing of Germany continues—day and night. Germany's cities are in ruins. Mostly the bombs kill civilians. Are they to blame for this war?

This bombing of cities is called "strategic bombing." There is something about it that is strange. The tougher the bombing, the more it makes people want to work hard and fight back. When the German Luftwaffe was bombing England, it seemed to inspire the English to fight and produce. All selfishness was forgotten. Military production went up. The same thing happened in Germany and Japan. After last year's fierce raids on Germany, there was a short lull and then aircraft production great-

Anne Frank

ly increased. *The military experts don't want to believe it, but it seems to be true. The military experts say the purpose of the bombing is to destroy morale.*

APRIL **14:** The British liberate the Bergen-Belsen concentration camp. *On March 12, in this camp, a 14-year-old Dutch girl died. Her name was Anne Frank. After the war her diary is found and published.*

APRIL **20:** Hitler is 56 today. Is there anyone left who wishes him a happy birthday? *Probably. His strongman ideas had wide appeal. Democracy is difficult; it asks people to think and take part in their government. The totalitarian governments treat people like sheep—or is it dogs?*

APRIL **21:** Russian troops have entered the suburbs of Berlin, Germany's capital. The fighting is said to be fierce, although the Nazis have no hope of victory. *In less than one month, between April 16 and May 8, the Russians lose 304,887 men—killed, wounded, and missing—capturing Berlin. The total number of American deaths in the whole war, in Europe and the Pacific, is about 325,000.*

APRIL **24:** If only there were a way to end this war quickly. The deaths now seem so unnecessary. *On this day President Truman gets his first detailed briefing on the top-secret superweapon.*

APRIL **26:** Italy's dictator, Benito Mussolini, has been hanged by Italians fighting on the side of the Allies.

APRIL **30:** Hitler is dead. He has killed himself. He was living like a mole underground in a concrete bunker in Berlin.

At war's end, many German cities had been bombed to ash and rubble. Here, Germans search for usable bricks to begin to rebuild Dresden.

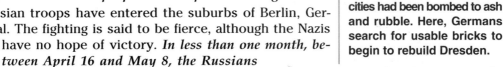

Left, top: Mussolini in death. *Bottom:* The mayor of Leipzig, Germany, and his wife and daughter have committed suicide as U.S. infantry close in on the city. *Above:* Russian soldiers approach the ruined Reichstag in Berlin. "Wherever we looked we saw desolation," said an American general.

177

Left: General Alfred Jodl signs the German surrender at Rheims, France. The war in Europe is over. None of Eisenhower's staff has a great idea for a victory statement, so the general writes his own: "The mission of this Allied force was fulfilled at 0241 local time May 7, 1945." *Right:* VE ("Victory in Europe") Day in New York.

All over Europe, in countries that had fought for the Allies and countries that had fought for the Axis, mothers like this woman in Austria wept for joy when their sons came home or for sorrow when they did not.

The aircraft carrier *Bunker Hill* blazes up after a Japanese kamikaze (suicide) pilot has crashed into it.

Hitler boasted that his creation—the German Third Reich—would live forever. Many believed him. It lasted 12 years.

MAY 7: German military leaders have surrendered to General Dwight D. Eisenhower at a school in Rheims, France. It is unconditional surrender. The war in Europe is over. It is hard to believe.

MAY 8: President Harry Truman proclaims this VE ("Victory in Europe") Day. It is his 61st birthday. People are cheering and hugging and crying and partying. *Maybe they should wait—the war isn't over in the Pacific.*

MAY 11: A Japanese pilot, trained for a suicide mission, crashes into

At the Potsdam conference, Stalin *(right)* talks of making Germany pay huge reparations to the Allied powers. When the Americans, headed by President Truman *(center;* Churchill is on the left*)*, hear that, they threaten to leave the conference. Do you remember how Germany felt about reparations after World War I—and what came of those feelings?

the aircraft carrier *Bunker Hill.* 373 Americans are killed.

JUNE: The cities of Nagoya, Kobe, Osaka, Yokohama, and Kawasaki have been firebombed. The destruction in Japan is said to be staggering. Japan's cities are built of wood. They burn quickly. Two million buildings have been destroyed; perhaps 10 million people made homeless; hundreds of thousands are dead or injured. The Japanese warlords still won't surrender.

JULY: Japan's 60 largest cities have been burned. There is almost no food in Japan; people are starving. Four hundred Japanese have been arrested because they talked of surrender.

In the New Mexican desert, scientists prepare to test an atomic device. No one knows if it will work. No one knows how powerful it is. They learn on July 16: it is more powerful than anything ever before devised by humans. It was "as though the earth had opened and the skies had split," said one who was there. You, and America's other citizens, are not told of the test.

JULY 26: Truman, Churchill, and China's leader, Chiang Kai-shek, broadcasting from a peace conference at Potsdam, Germany, demand the unconditional surrender of Japan but assure the Japanese of a "new order of peace, security, and justice." Otherwise, they warn, there will be "prompt and utter destruction of the Japanese homeland." The Japanese premier Baron Suzuki says the proposal is "unworthy of public notice."

At Potsdam, Harry Truman tells Joseph Stalin that the United States has a new and powerful weapon. The Soviet leader shows little interest. Plans for the secret weapon, stolen by spies, sit inside the Kremlin, Russia's government center. Stalin, a dictator admired by Hitler, knows all about the bomb.

Writer Paul Fussell, "a badly wounded former infantry lieutenant," warns about glamorizing war. *The truth is that very few people know anything about war. In an infantry division, for example, fewer than half the troops actually fight, that is fight with rifles, mortars, machine guns, grenades and trench knives. The others, thousands upon thousands of them, are occupied with truck driving, photocopying, cooking and baking, ammunition and ration supplying and similar housekeeping tasks....For most soldiers participating in World War II, the war meant inconvenience rising sometimes to hardship....For those unlucky enough to be in the forward combat units, the war meant death or maiming, usually in extraordinarily dirty and undignified circumstances.*

42 A Little Boy

Almost no structures could withstand the two atomic bombs dropped on Japanese cities, except the shells of a few western-style buildings (made of concrete and brick). But in Nagasaki, this *torii*, the wooden gateway to a Shinto shrine, somehow survived both the blast and the firestorm that followed it.

The U.S.S. *Indianapolis* brings key components of Little Boy to Tinian. Three days later, the ship is torpedoed and sunk in the Indian Ocean.

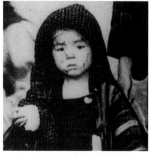

The face of Nagasaki, Japan, 24 hours after the bomb drops. This little boy is holding his emergency ration—a ball of boiled rice.

The men of the 509th Composite Group of the 313th Wing of the 21st Bombing Command of the 20th Air Force have been carefully chosen from a group of ace pilots. All have volunteered for a special mission. No one tells them what the mission will be. But whatever it is, they know they will be flying B-29s, the big workhorse bombers that are known as superfortresses.

Right away, there is something strange about the training they get at an airfield in Utah. Instead of flying planes loaded with huge bombs, they train with a single bomb of moderate size. And they are trained to worry about storms, especially electrical storms. Then, when they are sent to the Pacific, to the island of Tinian in the Marianas group of islands, they just sit around. It is frustrating. From Tinian it is an easy flight to Japan. The other airmen on the island are flying B-29s and dropping big bomb loads on Japan's cities. The 509th is sent on training flights—over and over again. Sometimes they are allowed to drop one bomb. It isn't long before the other pilots on Tinian begin making fun of the 509th. Someone even writes a poem about them. Its last lines are:

> *Take it from one who knows the score,*
> *The 509th is winning the war.*

That is cruel. Everyone knows the 509th isn't winning the war; it isn't doing anything.

Meanwhile, in Washington, President Truman has come to a decision. He has called on two teams of experts: a team of scientists and a team of civilians and soldiers. They are to help him decide about

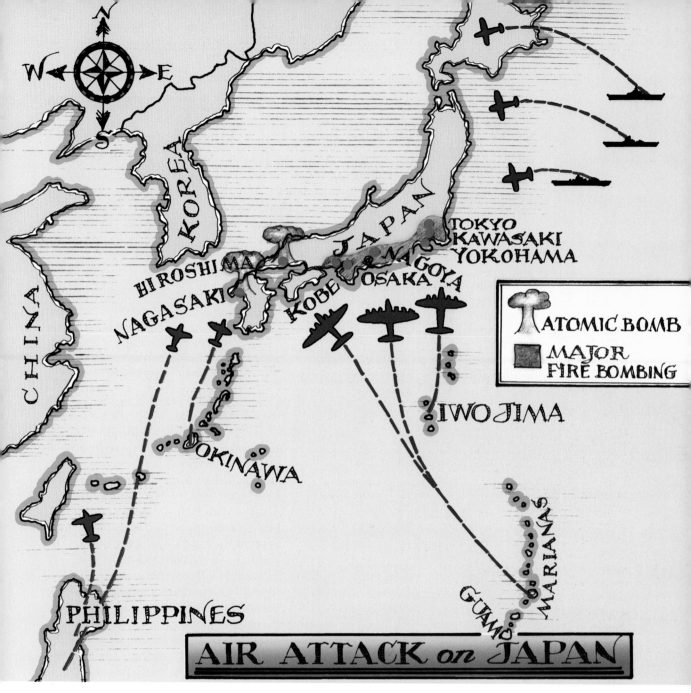

AIR ATTACK on JAPAN

the new superweapon. Will it be used? Can anything be used in its place? Both teams agree: the weapon should be used. They believe it will bring the war to an end. Without it, the war could continue for 10 or more years. Military chiefs, who don't know about the secret weapon, are pressing Truman to let them invade Japan. If that happens, America can expect a million casualties; Japan might have 10 times that number.

Above: Little Boy in person. The bomb was originally named Thin Man, after FDR; the Nagasaki bomb was Fat Man, after Churchill. The crew just called it "the gimmick." *Below:* the mushroom cloud over Nagasaki

Colonel Paul W. Tibbets, Jr., is commander of the 509th. He has named his plane the *Enola Gay*, after his mother. In early August, a single bomb 28 inches in diameter and 10 feet long is loaded onto the *Enola Gay*. The bomb weighs four metric tons, and is nicknamed Little Boy. A similar device was exploded in the New Mexican desert, but no one knows exactly what will happen when one is dropped from an airplane. Colonel Tibbets and the others now realize that this is dangerous stuff they are about to handle. If the *Enola Gay* crashes on takeoff, as some B-29s have done, Tinian could disappear.

Above: Colonel Tibbets waves from the cockpit of the *Enola Gay*, shortly before takeoff from Tinian on August 6, 1945.

The plan is to drop Little Boy on the Japanese city of Hiroshima. Hiroshima has been selected because of its war-making industries and because it is the headquarters of the 2nd Japanese Army. On August 4, more than 700,000 leaflets are dropped on Hiroshima warning that the city will be demolished. The warning is not taken seriously.

Captain William S. Parsons, of the U.S. Navy, is a surprise passenger on the *Enola Gay*. He has decided he will put the detonating parts of the bomb together after the plane is in the air. It will be safer. He doesn't know how to do that, but he has a day to learn. He learns.

At 1:45 A.M. on August 6, 1945, three B-29s take off for Japan. They will check on weather and on aircraft in the target area. The *Enola Gay* and two other B-29s follow an hour later. The night is perfect, with shining stars and a picture-book moon. As they fly, Captain Robert A. Lewis, co-pilot on the *Enola Gay*, writes a letter to his mother and father.

I think everyone will feel relieved when we have left our bomb, he writes. Later, he adds: *It is 5:52 and we are only a few miles from Iwo Jima. We are beginning to climb to a new altitude.* When they are over Honshu, Japan's central island, he writes, *Captain Parsons has put the final touches on this assembly job. We are now loaded. The bomb is alive. It is a funny feeling knowing it is right in back of you.*

For most people in Hiroshima the workday begins at 8 A.M. By 8:10, factories and shops are beginning to buzz. On August 6, the entire 2nd Japanese Army is on a parade field doing calisthenics. It is a bright, sunny morning and some children can be seen outdoors playing. (Many of Hiroshima's children have been evacuated to the suburbs.) A group of middle-school students has gotten up early and already put in more than an hour's work on a fire-control project. As clocks near 8:15 A.M., the Chuo Broadcasting Station reports that three B-29s have been spotted heading for Hiroshima.

At 8:15 the bomb bay opens; Little Boy is on his way. *There will be a short intermission while we bomb our target,* Captain Lewis writes. Then he adds, in letters that scrawl wildly on the page, *My God!*

He has not been prepared for what happens. The size and fury of the explosion are greater than anything ever before created by humans. The airmen are still able to see the inferno clearly when they have put 270 miles between themselves and the target. It is a sight they will never forget.

The atomic bomb (for that is what it is) has created a fireball whose center reaches 4,000° Celsius. (Iron melts at 1,550° Celsius.) The fireball gives birth to a shock wave and then a high-speed wind. Buildings are smashed by wave and wind and burned by fire. Dust from destroyed buildings makes the city night-dark within minutes of the bombing. The wind tosses people about. Thermal rays burn their bodies. As the fireball fades, a vacuum at the blast's center pulls up dust, air, and bomb debris, creating an enormous mushroom cloud that rises into the atmosphere. Liquid rain alternates with downpours of sparks and fire. The rain is ink-black and oily. Within minutes, the 2nd Japanese Army no longer exists. Seventy-eight thousand people are dead. One hundred thousand are injured.

The atomic age has begun.

This woman's skin burned in a pattern corresponding to parts of the kimono she was wearing when the bomb went off.

Survivors in Nagasaki, the day after the explosion there. By December, the city's estimated death count was 70,000.

The destruction at Hiroshima. "It seemed impossible," said one eyewitness, "that such a scene could have been created by human means."

43 Peace

VE Day had been a rehearsal. On VJ ("Victory in Japan") Day, Americans everywhere went wild (though this famous spontaneous-looking shot was, in fact, posed).

The Americans demand surrender—otherwise, they tell the Japanese, "they may expect a rain of ruin from the air." The Japanese do not respond.

On August 8 Russia enters the war against Japan. Russian forces attack Japanese armies in Manchuria and Korea. For some Japanese leaders this is more threatening than the bomb.

On August 9 a second atomic bomb is dropped. This one hits the port of Nagasaki. The nightmare of fire, wind, rain, and radiation is repeated. Has this war driven sane people to act insanely?

In Japan, the warlords and government ministers meet in stormy sessions to decide the fate of their people. They are split down the middle; most of the warriors vote to continue the fight, although everyone knows that may mean the destruction of the Japanese people. As Emperor Hirohito described it:

> There was no prospect of agreement no matter how many discussions they had....I was given the opportunity to express my own free will for the first time.

The emperor decides for his people.

From Tokyo, cables are sent to Washington, London, Moscow, and Chungking. Japan will accept the terms of the Potsdam Declaration, with one request: that the emperor remain as head of state.

"The time has come," said Emperor Hirohito (*center*, with General Tojo, *right*), "when we must bear the unbearable."

As soon as Harry Truman hears the news he calls Eleanor Roosevelt. Mrs. Roosevelt is now America's ambassador to the United Nations. President Truman tells her that he wishes her husband were alive to accept the peace proposal.

In Japan, some army officers break into the imperial palace, set fire to the home of the prime minister, and attempt to stop a broadcast of the emperor's words. They fail, and, along with the war minister, commit suicide in the public square.

The emperor, who wants to be sure that his words are exactly right, has recorded them in advance. The actual broadcast is taking place elsewhere.

It is August 15, 1945, and Hirohito's voice is heard in the first public speech an emperor has ever made. He asks the Japanese people to accept the coming of peace.

Above: Japanese officials arrive aboard the U.S.S. *Missouri* in Tokyo Bay to sign the surrender, September 2, 1945. *Below:* In New York City, Times Square is closed to traffic on VJ Day (August 14) as 2 million people crowd the streets, hugging and cheering.

44 Picturing History

George Bellows (1882–1925) called his painting of tenement-dwelling New Yorkers on a hot summer day *The Cliff Dwellers* (1913).

Derisively means "mockingly, scornfully, insultingly"; it comes from the verb *to deride*, which means "to ridicule."

The Ashcan of History

I decided to end this book with some works of art for two reasons: one, I like them; and two, I want to be sure that you don't think history is just about famous people and big events. History is everything that happened yesterday and the day before. It's science and poetry; it's sporting events and fashions; it's classroom life and museum shows; it's the songs people sing and the lives they lead, rich, poor, and in between.

At the beginning of the 20th century, most American artists were painting elegant, refined portraits and scenes and showing their best work at exhibitions at the National Academy of Design. Then along came some artists who broke the rules. They painted working people. They made pictures from real life: down-to-earth, open-hearted paintings. They were following the lead of some boldly realistic 19th-century painters—especially Thomas Eakins (AY-kinz) and Winslow Homer—except that this new group concentrated on urban scenes.

Finding vitality in shabby streets and down-on-their-luck people, they were called, derisively, the "Ashcan artists." The art establishment wanted nothing to do with them. Their paintings weren't "pretty"; it was "new" art, and a threat to the old. Sir Caspar Purdon Clarke, director of the eminent Metropolitan Museum of Art in New York, made his feelings clear. "There is a state of unrest all over the world in art as in all other things. It is the same in literature, as in music, in painting, and in sculpture. And I dislike unrest."

When John Sloan sent some of his etchings to be exhibited at the National Academy, they were rejected as "vulgar." So was most of the Ashcan art. (Today it's in museums.)

The group's leader was Robert Henri (HEN-rye)—a superb teacher as well as a fine painter. Edward Hopper was one of his students. Over and over, Hopper painted the loneliness of city life with scenes of people who don't seem to be doing anything—and yet they haunt your mind. George Bellows was another of Henri's students. He, too, painted city life, but look at the difference in his vision. Do you think some of those people are lonely?

Since they couldn't exhibit at the National Academy, Robert Henri arranged for the Ashcan artists to have their own show. That revolt against the art establishment (in 1910) began a tradition of independent exhibitions. Artist Stuart Davis (1894–1964) described what happened:

> The ordinary art student in the days of the Henri school wouldn't think of having a show in a gallery because there weren't any galleries that would admit this kind of work....So the Independent Show idea developed, and this was Henri's idea, where everyone could show who had done some-thing...then it was an amazing thing....They just hired an office build-ing...hung up all those paintings and charged admission.
>
> [Henri] was a man with an impulse to see and know things, and was able to put that impulse into execution...and that's why instead of just an art school, it was an opening-up type of instruction....There was nothing like that in any art school in New York, in Europe, or anywhere else as far as I know.

The artist John Sloan said:

> He was a catalyst, an enthusiast....His teaching was strong stuff in an era that put "art for art's sake" on a pedestal....Henri won us with his robust love for life.

But another catalyst was also challenging the traditionalists and gath-ering followers around himself. He was a modernist, in contrast to the Henri realists. Both art leaders lived in New York, and, between the two of them, they dominated the avant-garde world of American art in their time.

Edward Hopper (1882–1967) sold his first painting at the Armory Show (see page 24); he didn't sell another one for 10 years. This, one of his most famous, is called *Nighthawks* (1942).

A **catalyst** is a person or thing that makes something happen, or makes some-thing happen faster.

Avant-garde is a French word; it literally means "the vanguard"—the troops who move at the front of an army. In modern times, avant-garde artists are those who are in the forefront of a movement, at the cutting edge, ahead of their time.

In this 1903 portrait of New York's first skyscraper, the Flatiron building, Alfred Stieglitz used a snowy day and his camera to create a mood.

Two Ninety-One

Robert Henri's bold realism, his strong brushstrokes, and his sensitivity to the environment seemed innovative and daring until you looked at the art that was being done in Paris. Artists there were breaking *all* the old rules. Alfred Stieglitz (STEEG-lits) brought European art to his small New York gallery at 291 Fifth Avenue even before the Armory Show scandalized the nation (see page 24 of this book to read about the shocking Armory Show). That gallery, called "291," became a center for the best in new art.

Stieglitz—a small-framed, elegant man born in fashionable Hoboken, New Jersey—had superb artistic taste, tremendous talent, and the passion to fight for his ideas. He was a photographer at a time when photography was making huge technological leaps. Stieglitz studied in Berlin and was as skilled in photographic chemistry as anyone in the world. In addition, he had the sensitivities of an artist and fierce determination. And he was determined to make people aware that great photographs can be great art.

Besides that, he cared about art in general. When he found an artist whose work he liked, he would do everything he could to be of help. And artists often need help—especially if they are breaking new ground. Modern artists were looking at the world through unusual lenses. They distorted line and shape and color playfully and didn't worry about realistic conventions. They looked for inspiration everywhere. Stieglitz's 291 gallery showed the best of their work. It held the first serious exhibition of children's art in the United States. It exhibited African-American art. And it showed some startling new paintings from Europe. Both Stieglitz and Henri helped make the Armory Show happen.

Stieglitz believed American artists were creating major works of art, and he said so in an arts magazine he published. He encouraged and exhibited works by John Marin, Marsden Hartley, Arthur Dove, Elie Nadelman, and Max Weber (never charging them a fee or profiting from any of their work). The most important of all the artists he guided and helped became his wife. She was Georgia O'Keeffe.

Have you ever known a baker who could take ordinary ingredients, mix them together, and come up with a cake that is unforgettably delicious? Georgia O'Keeffe did something like that with art. She took a single flower, or an old bone, or a mountain, used it

Alfred Stieglitz created a series of more than 400 photographs of Georgia O'Keeffe *(below):* her hands, eyes, hair, body, and face—working, resting, thinking. No other portrait record of an artist compares with it. This 1922 portrait hangs in the National Gallery of Art in Washington, D.C.

for her subject, put a rainbow of colors on her artist's palette, and created paintings that are, in their own way, as luscious as a fresh-baked cake.

O'Keeffe grew up in prairie Wisconsin, went to high school in traditional Virginia, studied art in Chicago, arrived in New York in 1914, married Stieglitz, and eventually moved to New Mexico (and fell in love with its earth and sky and mountains). "I found I could say things with color and shapes that I couldn't say in any other way—things I had no words for," wrote O'Keeffe. She was right. Check out a book of her paintings from your public library to see more of her work.

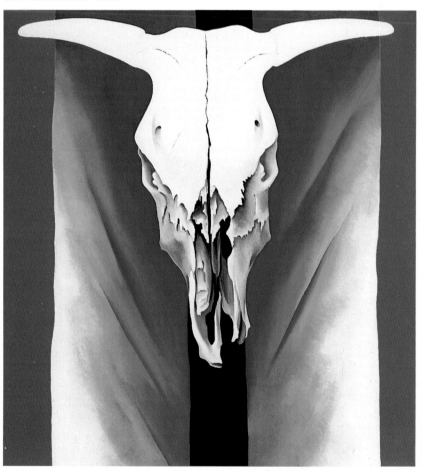

Imogen Cunningham was born in Oregon and grew up in Seattle. But to study photographic chemistry she had to go to Germany. On her way home, in 1910, she met Alfred Stieglitz. A few years later she married and had a family, and that kept her at home in San Francisco. So she went into her garden for inspiration and produced some photographs that have seldom been surpassed. She shot this photograph, *Magnolia Blossom*, in 1925.

Georgia O'Keeffe called this painting *Cow's Skull: Red, White and Blue*. She painted it in 1931. Today it is in the Metropolitan Museum in New York City.

189

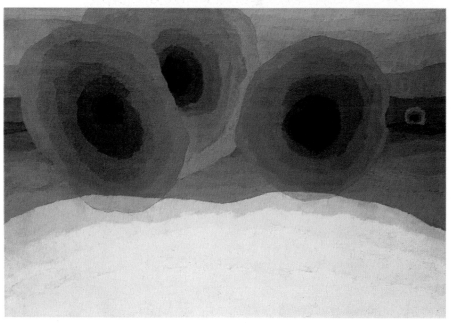

In this abstract painting, called *Foghorns* (1929), artist Arthur Dove said the circles represent the sound of sirens in the mist. You can see this picture at the Colorado Springs Fine Arts Center. "I would like to make something that is real in itself, that does not remind anyone of any other thing, and that does not have to be explained—like the letter A, for instance," wrote Dove.

Polish-born Elie Nadelman came to America from Paris in 1914. He and his wife became major collectors of American barnyard art. They saw beauty in what many thought was junk. Do you think barnyard art influenced Nadelman's work? This wood sculpture, made around 1917, is called *Woman at the Piano*. You can see it at the Museum of Modern Art in New York City.

Americans in Paris

In the western hemisphere, Europe was the center of the art world, and Paris was the center of Europe. After 1945, New York would take over. But in the early part of the century, Paris was the place to be if you were an artist, a writer, or a musician. Marc Chagall came from Russia, Pablo Picasso from Spain, Amadeo Modigliani from Italy, sculptor Elie Nadelman from Poland. Writer Ernest Hemingway was there, and composer Aaron Copland. Almost every American artist of significance (including Henri and Stieglitz) came, even if only for a short time. Some artists, like Henri Matisse and Paul Cézanne, didn't have to travel; they were French. If you ever find a magic wand and can put yourself in any time or place, you might consider Paris before World War I. It was as multicultural and creative as any society anywhere—ever.

Many of the Americans who went to Paris clustered around Gertrude Stein. She was a writer, but she had an eye for art, and she seemed to know everyone famous—like Picasso, who painted her portrait.

Marguerite Thompson arrived in Paris from Fresno, California, expecting to paint traditional canvases. Then she met Stein and Picasso, put pure color on her brushes, and painted boldly. Thompson was introduced to painter-sculptor William Zorach, who had come from Cleveland to Paris. They got married and became very popular

figures on the art scene.

It was a learning place, but fun, too. Paris was filled with music and dance, as well as the other arts. The "modern" painters didn't attempt to copy life; they seemed to be reinventing it with color and imagination. No one could quite explain why all this was happening, but some thought it related to the new science. The ideas of James Clerk Maxwell, Charles Darwin, and Albert Einstein had turned the world upside down. Time and space were no longer what they seemed. Einstein said that what we see depends on where we are and how fast we're traveling. Everything's relative.

Some of the modern paintings were abstractions—the artist started with something real and stretched and changed and made it his own. Some paintings—called "nonobjective"—were pure color and design. They didn't try to represent anything real. Some artists looked at people and structures and painted them as if they were made of building blocks—or cubes—of color. They were called "Cubists." The Fauves (it means "wild beasts" in French) used wild, imaginative colors. The Futurists were an Italian group who said, "There is with us…chaos and the clashing of rhythms, totally opposed to one another, which we nevertheless assemble into a new harmony."

Arthur Dove was in Paris in 1910 when he painted what is said to to be the first abstract painting by an American. When he went home, he joined the Stieglitz artists at 291.

But after the Armory Show, in 1913, modernism wasn't just a European thing. It invaded America.

Stuart Davis enrolled in Robert Henri's art school at age 15. Henri had his students tramp downtown city streets and sit in saloons listening to jazz. "The big point with us was that in all of these places you could hear the blues, or tin-pan-alley tunes turned into real music, for the cost of a five-cent beer. It seems fantastic that today I can…hear this kind of music [on the radio] without taking a bus to Newark or Harlem." Davis's exposure to jazz influenced his painting. So did the Armory Show (where he exhibited some of his work). In *Landscape with Garage Lights* (1932) you can tell what he was painting, but it is an abstraction. It hangs at the University of Rochester in Rochester, New York.

Joseph Stella's *Battle of Lights, Coney Island, Mardi Gras* (1913–1914). You can see this painting at the Yale University Art Gallery in New Haven, Connecticut. It's big (about 6 x 7 feet)—a bold, exciting oil on canvas.

Mighty Machines

In 1876, which was the year Joseph Stella (1876–1946) was born, Thomas Edison opened his "invention factory" in Menlo Park, New Jersey. Three years later he made a light bulb that shone for 45 hours. Have you ever had the power go out in your house? Can you picture a world without electric lights? Imagine how exciting lights were to people who had never had them. Now think of their reaction to an amusement park filled with lights. Coney Island, in Brooklyn (across the East River from Manhattan), was more than just an amusement park—it was a spectacular place, outlined with pulsating colored lights. How would you paint it if you were an artist? You can see how Joseph Stella did it in *Battle of Lights, Coney Island, Mardi Gras*. He was using the urban real-life subject matter of the Henri school and the futurist vision of some Italian poets and artists who wanted to do away with all traditional forms of art. (Stella studied art in Italy, Paris, and New York.)

Coney Island was painted in 1914, before World War I. Afterwards, things

Charles Sheeler, *American Landscape* (1930). It's in the Museum of Modern Art in New York. Can you find the man in the picture? He is just there to provide a sense of scale.

The Great Figure

Among the rain
and lights
I saw the figure 5
in gold
on a red
firetruck
moving
tense
unheeded
to gong clangs
siren howls
and wheels rumbling
through the dark city.

—WILLIAM CARLOS WILLIAMS

were different. Paris was never quite the same for the art community; New York began its climb as an arts center. There seemed to be less light on most artists' palettes, and more cynicism. There was also more prosperity.

It was the Roaring Twenties and the judgments of the marketplace dominated. Back in 1914 (the first year of assembly-line production), Henry Ford had sold 248,000 Model Ts. By 1929, American auto makers were selling 4.8 million vehicles a year. Henry Ford and Frederick Taylor were apostles of industry. (Read Robert Kanigel's *The One Best Way* to learn about Taylor.) Their production ideas were transforming the nation's values. "The man who builds a factory builds a temple. The man who works there, worships there," said Ford.

"Our factories are our substitute for religious expression," wrote Charles Sheeler, who was hired to photograph the Ford automobile plant. He soon went from taking photographs of factories to painting them—in a style that is hard, precise, and often exquisite. Rarely did he put anything living in his paintings—no trees, no people, no animals. Those paintings are hymns to a machine-age world—a world away from the nature-inspired paintings of earlier American artists.

Sheeler described himself as a "Precisionist," thereby coining a name that other artists used, too. In 1928, Charles Demuth, from Lancaster, Pennsylvania, painted the best-known Precisionist painting—*The Figure 5 in Gold*. It has been called an

Charles Demuth, *The Figure 5 in Gold* (1928). Note the initials *W.C.W.*, and the names *Bill*, and *Carlo[s]*. This painting is at the Metropolitan Museum in New York.

An *icon* is a symbolic image (originally the word meant a religious image, such as the portrait of a saint, painted on a wood panel).

icon of American modernism. (What do you think that means?) Demuth's friend, poet William Carlos Williams, was looking out a window from an artist's studio when a big red fire truck—with the number 5 in glossy paint on its rear—roared by. Williams described it in a poem full of clear images. Demuth (who was rich, brilliant, and often ill) took the poem and painted its images. (The poem and the painting are both on the previous page.)

Real American Art

Tom and Martha Smith, living in Kansas City, had a fine landscape hanging in the entrance hallway, and, in the parlor, Aunt Tillie gazed sternly from a portrait over the couch. What did the Smiths think of Joseph Stella or George Bellows? They'd never heard of them. But they had heard of the Armory Show and of modern art, and they associated both with the dangerous ideas that seemed to be coming from foreign lands and, sometimes, from New York. They knew of James Joyce, an Irishman whose book *Ulysses* was published in Paris and banned in the United States (that means you couldn't buy or sell it here) until 1933, when New York Federal District Judge John W. Woolsey decided in its favor in a landmark case against literary censorship.

Grant Wood, *American Gothic* (1930). Wood got his sister Nan to pose with a dentist from Cedar Rapids. Why do you think he is holding a pitchfork? The painting hangs in the Art Institute of Chicago.

To lose caste means "to lose social status or position."

Today many readers and critics consider *Ulysses* one of the greatest novels of the 20th century written in English. (It is not easy reading.) Joyce would influence other writers, but not be read by the Smiths, or their friends. They were bothered by the lack of tradition—and what they saw as vulgarity—in much modern art. Like many Americans, they were slow to embrace any of the new art, in books, music, or painting. But there were three contemporary artists whose work they did like: Thomas Hart Benton, John Steuart Curry, and Grant Wood. The Smiths first saw their paintings in 1933 in a show at the Kansas City Art Institute. They were presented as participants in a new regional art movement.

The three men barely knew each other, but a publicist for the museum wrote in the show's catalogue that "the shiploads of rubbish that had just been imported from the School of Paris were found to be just rubbish. The freaks…have lost caste." The artists in this show, he said, painted "real American art…which really springs from American soil and seeks to interpret American life."

When a *Time* magazine reporter saw the museum catalogue, he showed it to his boss, Henry Luce. Luce loved anything he thought was genuinely American. So he put Thomas Hart Benton on *Time*'s cover. Overnight, the three artists became stars. *Time* called them "earthy Midwesterners."

Only Iowa-born Grant Wood actually lived in the Midwest. Curry lived in

Connecticut and Benton had a studio in New York. But they all did have Midwestern roots. And they painted an idyllic America. They became known as "Regionalists." Benton (who was kin to a famous Missouri senator—see book 5 of *A History of US*) wrote of the acclaim they received, "A play was written and a stage erected for us. Grant Wood became the typical Iowa small-towner, John Curry the typical Kansas farmer, and I just an Ozark hillbilly. We accepted our roles."

So what kind of artists were they? Critic Robert Hughes says of Benton, "He was a dreadful artist most of the time." Of Curry he writes, "he was a semicompetent illustrator but an inept and formally incoherent painter." He describes Wood's "diligent and painstaking craftwork." But the Smiths loved the Regionalists. So do many Americans. And so do I.

Above: John Steuart Curry, *Tornado Over Kansas* (1929), Muskegon Museum of Art, Muskegon, Michigan.

Semicompetent means "only half-able to do something"; **inept** means "clumsy, awkward, bungling"; **incoherent** means "not sticking together; falling apart."

Left: Thomas Hart Benton, *Cradling Wheat* (1938), St. Louis Art Museum.

Dorothea Lange's *Migrant Mother, Nipomo, California,* (1936). The woman is Florence Thompson; she was 32 years old and had 10 children. Lange wrote: "In a squatter camp at the edge of the pea fields. The crop froze this year and the family is destitute [penniless]. On this morning they had sold the tires from their car to pay for food."

On the facing page is Aaron Douglas's painting *Aspects of Negro Life: From Slavery Through Reconstruction* (1934). This is part of a four-panel mural in the New York Public Library's Schomburg Center for Research in Black Culture. Note the blues musician and the migrant worker. Music and religion—and the power of the Negro spiritual—inform Douglas's art.

The Art of the Depression

In 1929, after the twenties finished roaring, another sound could be heard. Actually, it was more like a groan. The groan of hard times. Life was no longer a lark. It was grimy. The dreamy quality that characterized much of Stieglitz's fine work was replaced by stark reality in Depression-era photographs. The photographers who grappled with the Depression and the industrial era were called "social photographers." Walker Evans and Dorothea Lange were among the best of them.

Lange had polio as a child growing up in a poor section of New York City. She believed that gave her understanding of people with problems. As an adult, she lived in San Francisco with her sociologist husband and photographed city and farm life. When the Farm Security Administration went looking for photographers to document the effects of the Depression on farmers, Lange was one of six hired. Their photographs, intended for government records, turned out to be works of art as well.

William H. Johnson arrived in New York in 1918 from South Carolina and, like many African Americans, he headed for Harlem, which is north of the city's Central Park. Harlem was an exciting place to be, especially for writers and musicians who were creating important works during the Harlem Renaissance in the 1920s. Johnson studied at the National Academy and became skilled as a traditional artist. But Europe still lured Americans. So in 1926, Johnson went to Paris. From there he moved on to Denmark, where he married a potter. They went to Africa to study African art. By this time Johnson had developed his own style of painting, highly sophisticated, though it looked simple. It was based on primitive art and the work of some European artists called "Expressionists."

When Johnson returned to America, it was to the bleakness of the Depression. Like many other artists, he found work with the Works Progress Administration.

The WPA may have been the most creative idea our government has ever put into practice. Artists were especially hard hit by the Depression. When people are having difficulty finding enough money for food, they don't have any left for the arts. Franklin Roosevelt supported a program that put writers, painters, actors, sculptors, and musicians to work. This wasn't welfare. The artists had to produce work that the government then owned. They weren't paid much, but they earned respect, and they and others knew their government believed in their importance. In the eight years the program existed, 5,000 visual artists created 108,000 paintings, 18,000 pieces of sculpture, and

2,500 murals. Those works were placed in schools, libraries, post offices, and other government buildings (where you can see many of them today). They weren't all good—no one expected them to be—but many were. And the experiment of having the government value the arts was enormously encouraging to those who believe that a society without art would be a cold, sterile place. Besides, it kept a lot of artists eating.

Aaron Douglas, with a degree from the University of Nebraska, was one of the WPA muralists. His passionate work *Aspects of Negro Life* was painted for the 135th Street branch of the New York Public Library. He had been slated to be a high-school principal in Kansas City, but his friends insisted that his artistic gifts were too good to be denied. He headed for Harlem, and hard times.

But the greatest of the black artists who worked under WPA was Jacob Lawrence. He was too young, he said, for "a wall." So he didn't paint a mural. What he did paint were 60 small paintings that tell the story of black migration from South to North, from field to factory. They are among the most powerful social statements in American art (see page 40).

Sculptor Louise Nevelson said, "I got on the WPA. Now that gave me a certain kind of freedom....Our great artists like Rothko, de Kooning, Franz Kline...had that moment of peace...to continue with their work. I think it's a highlight of our American history." Jackson Pollock, from Cody, Wyoming, was a WPA artist. So was Ben Shahn (see chapter 4 and page 35), who said, "I was totally involved. It was a total commitment." Another painter wrote, "There's something that's unforgettable about that period. There was a sense of belonging to something, even if was an underprivileged and down-hearted time. It was exciting."

Above: William H. Johnson said he would try to "tell the story of the Negro as he existed." His dignified, graceful works do just that. This painting of a child, *Li'l Sis* (1944), is in the National Museum of American Art in Washington, D.C.

Chronology of Events

1905: President Theodore Roosevelt's niece Eleanor marries her fifth cousin Franklin D. Roosevelt

1907: Oklahoma becomes the 46th state

1912: New Mexico and Arizona become the 47th and 48th states

1914: War breaks out in Europe between the Entente countries (Britain, France, Italy, Russia) and the Central Powers (Germany, Austria-Hungary, Turkey)

1916: Woodrow Wilson is reelected president

Apr. 1917: The U.S. enters the war on the side of the Entente powers

Nov. 1917: In Russia, the revolutionary communist Bolshevik Party overthrows a more moderate regime and takes Russia out of the war

1918: A worldwide influenza epidemic kills nearly 500,000 Americans

1918: Armistice Day, November 11: the war is over; Germany accepts Wilson's Fourteen Points as the basis for peace negotiations

1919: Babe Ruth joins the New York Yankees and helps restore baseball's popularity after the Chicago Black Sox World Series scandal the same year

1919: At the Paris peace conference, Germany is humiliated and must pay punitive reparations; the Allies write a charter for a League of Nations

1919: Wilson asks Americans to support the League, but a stroke makes him hardly able to function

1919: The 18th Amendment to the Constitution prohibits making or selling alcohol in the U.S.

1920: The 19th Amendment gives women the vote

1920: Republican Warren G. Harding, advocating a "return to normalcy," becomes 29th president

1920: In a "red scare," thousands of immigrants are arrested on suspicion of being communist

1920: KDKA, the nation's first commercial radio station, begins broadcasting out of Pittsburgh

1920: The Census shows that for the first time more than half the United States population is urban

1921: Franklin D. Roosevelt is crippled by polio

1922: Harding ignores government corruption, which culminates in the Teapot Dome scandal

1922: Louis Armstrong leaves New Orleans to play for King Oliver's Creole Jazz Band in Chicago

1922: The era of the Harlem Renaissance in the arts among black Americans begins with the publication of Claude McKay's *Harlem Shadows*

1923: When Harding dies suddenly, Vice President Calvin Coolidge becomes 30th president; he is reelected the following year

1925: F. Scott Fitzgerald publishes *The Great Gatsby*

1925: A high-school teacher, John Scopes, is tried and convicted in Tennessee for teaching evolution

1926: Scientist Robert Goddard launches the first successful rocket powered by liquid fuel

1927: Charles Lindbergh makes the first solo flight across the Atlantic in the *Spirit of St. Louis*

1927: The first talking motion picture, *The Jazz Singer*

1927: In *Nixon* v. *Herndon*, the Supreme Court rules that a Texas law preventing blacks from voting in primary elections is unconstitutional

1927: Babe Ruth hits 60 home runs

1928: Walt Disney's Mickey Mouse makes his first appearance in *Steamboat Willie*

1928: Herbert Hoover becomes 31st president, defeating Democrat Al Smith in a landslide

1928: FDR is elected governor of New York

1929: The stock market crashes in October and hastens a worldwide economic depression

1931: Japan invades Manchuria

1932: The Bonus Army of war veterans marches to Washington, asking for early payment of war benefits

1932: Mildred "Babe" Didrikson wins three track-and-field medals at the Olympic Games

1932: Depression: one in four workers in America—12 million people—are unemployed

1932: Democrat Franklin D. Roosevelt pledges to beat the Depression and becomes 32nd president

1933: Adolf Hitler, leader of the Nazi Party, becomes chancellor of Germany

1933: Frances Perkins becomes secretary of labor and the first woman cabinet member

1933: The first "100 Days" of FDR's presidency: Congress creates more agencies and passes more laws to relieve poverty than ever before

1933: The 21st Amendment repeals Prohibition

1934–37: After three years of drought, the farms of the Plains have become the Dust Bowl; 3 million victims migrate west in search of work and land

1935: Social Security Act introduces taxes to pay for unemployment insurance and old-age pensions

1936: Jesse Owens wins four gold medals in track events at the Olympic Games in Berlin

1937: Marco Polo Bridge incident in China

1938: Germany annexes Austria

1939: All German Jews made to wear yellow stars of David sewn onto their clothes for identification

1939: Germany occupies Czechoslovakia

1939: Stalin signs a nonaggression pact with Hitler

1939: Germany invades Poland; Allies declare war

1939: Physicist Albert Einstein helps convince FDR to fund the Manhattan Project to build atom bomb

1940: Germany rapidly overwhelms Norway, Finland, Denmark, Holland, Belgium, and France

1940: FDR is first president elected to three terms

1940: Germany tries to bomb Britain into submission

June 1941: Hitler ignores the Nazi–Soviet Pact, invading the Soviet Union; Russia joins the Allies

Sep. 1941: The siege of Leningrad begins

1941: FDR creates the Lend-Lease program to supply the Allies with weapons and raw materials

1941: Germany pushes deep into Russia and Ukraine

Dec. 1941: Japan bombs the U.S. fleet in Pearl Harbor, Hawaii; America enters the war

Dec. 1941–Jan. 1942: Japan invades Thailand, Malaya, Borneo, Burma, the Philippines, Hong Kong, Indonesia; captures Midway and Wake islands

1942: FDR orders 112,000 Japanese Americans into internment camps for the war's duration

May 1942: Heavy losses for both U.S. and Japan in battle of Coral Sea; first setback for Japan

May 1942: U.S. surrenders in Philippines

June 1942: U.S. defeats Japan at battle of Midway

Aug. 1942: U.S. defeats Japan at Guadalcanal

1942: U.S. forces join British and French to fight Germany and Italy in North Africa

1942: The Nazis begin systematic murder of Jews and others in concentration camps

1942: The Allies capture Enigma, a code machine, and begin to crack German secret codes

Feb. 1943: The Soviet Red Army defeats Germany at Stalingrad and begins to push Germany back

June 1943: Allies win battle of Atlantic

July 1943: Allied forces invade Sicily

Sep. 1943: Italian army surrenders

Nov. 1943–Feb. 1944: U.S. takes back numerous Pacific islands from Japanese

June 1944: Allied forces enter Rome

June 1944: Combined U.S., British, and Canadian forces invade Normandy, France, on D-Day, June 6

Nov. 1944: FDR wins fourth term!

Jan. 1945: The U.S. returns to the Philippines

Jan. 1945: The Allies defeat Germany in Battle of the Bulge in the Ardennes mountains in Belgium

Feb. 1945: Roosevelt, Churchill, and Stalin meet at Yalta in the Crimea

Feb. 1945: Allies firebomb Dresden, Germany

Feb. 1945: U.S. troops land on island of Iwo Jima

Apr. 1945: Hitler commits suicide in Berlin

Apr. 1945: President Roosevelt dies; Harry S. Truman sworn in as 33rd president

Apr. 1945: Soviet troops enter Berlin

Apr. 1945: U.S. troops liberate 32,000 prisoners in Dachau concentration camp, Germany

May 1945: Germany surrenders; VE Day, May 8

June 1945: Charter established for United Nations

July 1945: Truman, Churchill, and Stalin meet at Potsdam in Germany to plan for peace in Europe

Aug. 1945: Atomic bombs dropped on Japanese cities of Hiroshima and Nagasaki

Aug. 1945: Japan surrenders; VJ Day, August 15

More Books to Read

Here are some books that tell about life during the period discussed in this book. Some were written for grown-ups—but they are not too hard to read, they tell wonderful stories, and they are the kind of books you will always remember. Besides these books, there is something else you should search out if you don't know about it: Cobblestone, which is a history magazine for young people. Each issue focuses on a subject in history, and back issues can be found in most libraries or ordered from Cobblestone Publishing, 30 Grove Street, Peterborough, NH 03458.

F. Scott Fitzgerald, *The Great Gatsby,* Scribner's, 1925. The best American novel of the 1920s. This story of crazy pleasure seekers and unrequited love is not very long, and it will make you laugh and cry at the same time. Then try some of Fitzgerald's short stories, which are quite easy to read.

Anne Frank, *The Diary of a Young Girl,* Modern Library, 1958. In Dutch, the language Anne Frank wrote in, her diary is called *The House Behind,* because she and her family, who were Jews, hid from the Nazis in a few secret rooms inside a Dutch family's Amsterdam home. This book may make you cry, but you will love Anne and be amazed at what a marvelous writer she was at the age of 14.

Ernest Hemingway, *A Farewell to Arms,* Scribner's, 1929. An enthralling novel that draws on the author's own experience as a soldier in the Great War.

John Hersey, *Hiroshima,* Knopf, 1946. This little book—it was originally an article in *The New Yorker* magazine—is a clear, sympathetic telling of the dropping of the first atomic bomb and its devastating effect on Hiroshima and its people. You should also try another very good book by John Hersey about the war called *A Bell for Adano* (Knopf, 1944).

Gloria Houston, *Littlejim,* Philomel, 1990. Littlejim Houston lives in the Appalachian mountains in North Carolina during the Great War. He's the best student at his school and works hard on the farm—but Littlejim's father wants his son to be a logger and hunter like him, and he thinks being good at studying is sissy. Then Littlejim en-

ters a big essay contest on "What it means to be an American"; what will his father think if he wins?

Jeanne Wakatsuki Houston and James D. Houston, *Farewell to Manzanar,* Houghton Mifflin, 1973. In 1942, when the author was seven years old, she and all her family, along with thousands of other Japanese-Americans, were sent suddenly to Manzanar internment camp in the desert of California's Owens Valley. Her father was sent even farther away; it was nine months before he was allowed to rejoin them. This book describes vividly the Wakatsukis' humiliations and hardships.

Zora Neale Hurston, *Their Eyes Were Watching God,* 1937 (several editions available). A terrific and very influential story about growing up poor and black in the South early in this century.

Jerome Lawrence and Robert E. Lee, *Inherit the Wind,* Bantam, 1969. This is a thrilling play (also made into a good movie that you might be able to find on video) which is a fictionalized dramatization of the Scopes "monkey trial" of 1925.

Lois Lenski, *Strawberry Girl,* Lippincott, 1945. Birdie Boyer is 10 when her family moves to the Florida backwoods to grow sugarcane, oranges, and strawberries. She finds out that it's hard dealing with drought and frost, but it's much harder to cope with unfriendly neighbors: the Slaters. This excellent story is all about how the Boyers farm, play, go to school—and deal with the Slaters.

Sonia Levitin, *Journey to America; Silver Days,* Atheneum, 1970, 1989. In 1938 Lisa Platt's father left Berlin for America in the middle of the night. Lisa, her sisters, and her mother have to wait until he has made enough money to send for them. But life for Jews in Hitler's Germany becomes more and more scary; finally the Platts escape to Switzerland—where they wait and wait, with no money and not enough to eat, for a letter to arrive from America. It wasn't easy even when they got here. In *Silver Days,* the sequel, the author tells about the difficulties of being poor Jewish refugees in wartime California.

Cornelius Ryan, *The Longest Day,* Simon &

Schuster, 1959. A really exciting retelling of the story of D-Day and the invasion of Normandy.

John Steinbeck, *The Grapes of Wrath,* Viking, 1939. The Joad family are sharecropper victims of the Dust Bowl in the 1930s. Piling everything they own onto their decrepit car, they set off to look for work picking fruit and vegetables in California. This famous book helped bring home the plight of the "Okies" to the rest of the country. It is a great read.

Mildred D. Taylor, *Let the Circle Be Unbroken; Mississippi Bridge; The Road to Memphis; Roll of Thunder, Hear My Cry,* all published by Dial. Cassie Logan and her family live in rural Mississippi in Jim Crow times, when black people who got "uppity" could be risking their lives. Mildred Taylor's four books are about the racism of the Deep South in the 1920s and '30s and how it affects the Logans at different times during Cassie's childhood and youth. They are very well written and sometimes hard to take.

Jade Snow Wong, *Fifth Chinese Daughter,* U. of Washington Press (first pub. 1945). Jade Snow Wong's parents owned a small overalls factory in San Francisco in the 1920s, when she was born. Until she was about 10, Jade Snow led a very sheltered, Chinese life—looking after little sister, learning to cook rice perfectly, and discovering that grown-ups thought boys were more important than girls. Jade Snow decides to work hard in school; eventually she must convince her parents to allow her to be the first girl in her family to go to college. This is a splendid true story of the growing up of not just one Chinese daughter, but a whole family.

Construction Worker on the Empire State Building (c. 1930), by photographer Lewis Hines, a picture popularly known as "Sky Boy"

Picture Credits

AP / WW: Associated Press / Wide World Photos
CB: Corbis-Bettmann
FDR: Franklin D. Roosevelt Library

LOC: Library of Congress
NA: National Archives
UPI: United Press International

5: Joy Hakim; 6: Freelance Photographers Guild; 7: FDR; 8: NA; 9 (top): detail from Nathaniel Currier, *The Way They Go to California,* 1849, Oakland Museum, Museum Founders Fund; 9 (left): NA; 9 (top right, middle right): Bowdoin College Museum of Art, Brunswick, Maine; 9 (bottom right): Museum of Fine Arts, Boston / National Portrait Gallery; 10 (top): U. S. Senate Collection; 10 (bottom): LOC; 11: NA; 12: Monticello / Thomas Jefferson Memorial Foundation; 13–14: NA; 15 (left): AP / WW; 15 (right): *The New York Times;* 16: Culver Pictures; 18: NA; 19 (top): Sir William Orpen, *The Signing of Peace in the Hall of Mirrors, Versailles, 28th June, 1919,* Imperial War Museum, London; 19 (bottom left): Harding, *Brooklyn Eagle,* 1919; 19 (bottom right): *Chicago News,* 1919; 20 (top): Harris & Ewing; 20 (below left): Holmes Papers, Harvard Law School Library; 20 (bottom right): LOC; 21 (top): National Library of Medicine, Bethesda; 21 (bottom), 22 (top): Sy Seidman; 22 (bottom): CB; 23: LOC; 24: Marcel Duchamp, *Nude Descending a Staircase, No. 2,* 1912, Philadelphia Museum of Art, Louise and Walter Arensberg Collection; 25 (bottom): Ben Shahn, *Women's Christian Temperance Union Parade,* c.1934, Museum of the City of New York; 26: UPI / CB; 27: Ben Shahn, *Bootleggers,* c.1934, Museum of the City of New York; 28: Ben Shahn, *Speakeasy Scene, Interior,* 1934, Museum of the City of New York; 29 (top): Brown Brothers; 29 (bottom), 30–31: LOC; 32 (lower left): Brown Brothers; 32 (bottom): LOC, French Collection; 33 (top): Douglass County Museum; 33 (bottom): League of Women Voters of the City of New York; 34: Culver Pictures; 35 (top left): Brown Brothers; 35 (top right): AP / WW; 35 (bottom right): Ben Shahn, *Bartolomeo Vanzetti and Nicola Sacco,* Museum of Modern Art, New York, gift of Abby Aldrich Rockefeller (photo © 1998, Museum of Modern Art); 36 (top and bottom): UPI / CB; 36 (right): *Philadelphia Inquirer,* March 13, 1919, New York Public Library; 37–38: LOC; 39 (top): Underwood & Underwood; 39 (bottom): Brown Brothers; 40 (top): Ellison Hoover, *Life,* March 6, 1924; 40 (bottom): Jacob Lawrence, *Migration Series, (No. 1),* Phillips Collection, Washington, DC; 41: Culver Pictures; 42 (top left): Brown Brothers; 42 (top right): UPI / CB; 42 (bottom): LOC; 43: Culver Pictures; 45: CB; 46 (bottom left): Metropolitan Museum of Art, Gift of David A. Shulte, 1928 (28.127.1); 46 (bottom right): Brown Brothers; 47 (left): LOC; 47 (right): Paul McFarlane—Mary Broderick; 48 (top): Culver Pictures; 49 (left): Bronx County Historical Society: 49 (left): Brown Brothers; 50 (bottom): John Springer / CB; 51 (left): National Baseball Library; 51 (top middle): collection of Phil Dixon; 51 (top right): James Bell; 51 (bottom): Mike Anderson; 52 (top): National Baseball Library; 52 (middle): National Baseball Hall of Fame; 52 (bottom): *Kansas City Call;* 53 (top): Don Rogosin; 53 (middle): National Baseball Hall of Fame; 53 (bottom): Mark Rucker; 54 (top): UPI / CB; 54 (bottom): *New York Daily News;* 55: Hogan Jazz Archive, Howard-Tilton Memorial Library, Tulane University; 56: collection of Leonard V. Huber; 57: Archibald Motley, Jr. *Blues,* 1929, collection of Archie Motley and Valerie Gerrard Browne, photo courtesy of the Chicago Historical Society; 58 (above left): LOC; 58 (bottom), 59: Hogan Jazz Archive, Howard-Tilton Memorial Library, Tulane University; 60–61: CB; 62 (top): *The Razor's Edge* (20th Century Fox, 1946); 62 (bottom): *The Little Colonel* (Fox Film Corp, 1935); 63–66: Clark University Archives, Goddard Library, Worcester, Massachusetts; 67: Minnesota Historical Society; 68: NA; 68 (inset), 71, 72 (top right): Culver Pictures; 72 (top): LOC; 72 (bottom): Granger Collection; 73 (bottom left): CB; 73 (top right): NA; 73 (bottom right): *The New York Times;* 74: Granger Collection; 75: Underwood & Underwood / CB; 76 (top): UPI / CB; 76 (bottom), 77, 78: LOC; 79: Milton Brooks, *Detroit News,* July 1930; 80 (top): William Gropper, *Migration,* Arizona State University Art Museum, Tempe; 80 (bottom): LOC; 81: Dorthea Lange / LOC; 82: Alexandre Hogue, *Drought Stricken Area,* Dallas Museum of Fine Arts (1945.6); 83: LOC; 83 (bottom): Special Collections Division, University of Washington Libraries; 84: Herbert Hoover Library; 85 (top): CB; 85 (bottom): NA; 86 (top): Granger Collection; 86 (bottom): Herbert Hoover Library; 87 (top): *Literary Digest,* November 21, 1931, New York Public Library; 87 (bottom), 88–93: FDR; 94 (top): CB; 94 (bottom left and right): FDR; 95 (top left): CB; 95 (top right): FDR; 95 (bottom): AP / WW; 96 (left): Special Collections, Van Pelt-Dietrich Library Center, University of Pennsylvania; 96 (top): UPI / CB; 96 (bottom), 97 (left): FDR; 97 (right): UPI / CB; 98–99: FDR; 100: CB; 101 (top): FDR; 101 (bottom left): John Tinney McCutcheon, *Chicago Tribune;* 101 (bottom right): LOC; 102 (top): UPI / CB; 102 (bottom): FDR; 103 (top): UPI / CB; 103 (bottom): Miguel Covarrubias, *The Inauguration of FDR,* 1933, *Vanity Fair,* National Portrait Gallery, Smithsonian Institution; 104 (top left and right, bottom): FDR; 104 (below left): LOC; 105: UPI / CB; 106 (top): Peter Arno, *The New Yorker,* 1936; 106 (bottom): LOC; 107 (top): Granger Collection; 107 (bottom): AP / WW; 108 (right): UPI / CB; 109 (bottom left): collection of Kenneth W. Randell; 109 (top): NA; 109 (bottom): Otto Rösner / NA; 110 (left): UPI / CB; 110 (bottom right): AP / WW; 111 (top left): John Erikson; 111 (top right): Otto Hagel; 111 (bottom left): AP / WW; 111 (lower right): FDR; 112 (top): L. M. Muller; 112 (bottom): Hulton Picture Service; 113: Leo Baeck Institute, New York; 114: NA; 115 (top left): Yivo Institute for Jewish Research; 115 (top right): Peter Hunter, Rijksinstituut voor Oorlogsdocumentatie, Amsterdam; 115 (bottom): Lenni Sonnenfeld, University of the State of New York; 116: Wiener Library, London; 117 (top left and right, bottom): NA; 117 (middle right): Henry Beville; 118 (top): UPI / CB; 118 (bottom): Granger Collection; 119: courtesy of Liane Rief-Lehrer; 120 (top): General Electric; 120 (bottom): U. S. Immigration and Naturalization Service; 121 (top left): Los Alamos Historical Museum Photos Archives; 121 (top middle, top right, bottom): Los Alamos National Laboratory and National Atomic Museum; 122 (top): NA; 122 (bottom): *Washington Star,* 123 (middle): AP / WW; 123 (bottom): U. S. Air Force; 125 (left): NA; 125 (top right): CTK, Centralna Agencja Fotograficzna; 125 (bottom): UPI / CB; 126: Charles Cundall, *The Withdrawal from Dunkirk, June, 1940,* Imperial War Museum, London; 126 (bottom), 127: NA; 129: UPI / CB; 130 (top): Fox Photo; 130 (bottom): *Detroit News;* 131 (top): LOC; 131 (bottom): Roger-Violette, Paris; 132 (top): Bildarchiv Preussischer Kulturbesitz, Berlin; 132 (bottom), 133 (bottom left): NA; 133 (bottom right): Gillon Photo Agency; 134 (top): Bundesarchiv, Koblenz; 134 (middle, bottom): Sovfoto; 135–137: NA; 138 (top): Imperial War Museum, London; 138 (bottom): collection of Kenneth W. Rendell; 139 (top): NA; 139 (bottom left): UPI / CB; 139 (bottom right): Naval Historical Foundation; 140 (top): NA; 140 (bottom): American Red Cross; 141 (top right): German Bundesarchiv; 141 (right second and third from top, bottom left, bottom right): NA; 141 (top left): UPI / CB; 142–143: NA; 144–145: Dorthea Lange / NA; 147: from Miné Okubo, *Citizen 13660,* Columbia University Press, 1946; 147, 148 (top): NA; 148 (bottom): Toyo Miyatake; 149: U. S. Navy; 149–150, 151 (top): NA; 151 (bottom): Dwight Shelper, *Fighter Scramble—Guadalcanal,* Naval Historical Foundation; 152: Joy Hakim; 153: NA: 154 (top left): Frank B. Elam Photo; 154 (top right): NA; 154 (bottom right): Planeta Publishers, Moscow; 155, 156 (top left and right): NA; 156 (bottom): Ullstein-Birnback; 157 (top): UPI / CB; 157 (bottom): Bildarchiv Preussischer Kulturbesitz, Berlin; 158–159: NA; 160 (top): Dwight D. Eisenhower Library; 161 (top right): Robert Capa Archive, International Center for Photography; 163–164, 165 (top left and center right): NA; 165 (top right): *Arizona Republic,* 1943; 165 (bottom left): Dmitri Baltermants, Moscow; 166: NA; 167 (bottom): Ullstein-Bilderdienst, Berlin; 168–169: FDR; 170, 171 (top left and bottom): Harry S. Truman Library; 171 (top right): Stan Cohen; 172 (top): UPI / CB; 172 (bottom): FDR; 173–174: NA; 175: UPI / CB; 176, 177 (top left): AP / WW; 177 (top right): Keystone, Hamburg; 177 (middle left): Hulton Deutsch Collection, London; 177 (bottom left): NA; 177 (bottom right): Sovfoto; 178 (top right): CB; 178 (center left): Frederico Patellani, Milan; 178 (bottom right): NA; 179: Harry S. Truman Library; 180: NA; 182 (top left): UPI / CB; 182 (top right, bottom), 183 (top): NA; 183 (middle): Eiichi Matsumoto; 183 (bottom): Naval Historical Foundation; 184–185: NA; 186: George Wesley Bellows, *Cliff Dwellers,* 1913, Los Angeles County Museum of Art; 187: Edward Hopper, *Nighthawks,* 1942, Art Institute of Chicago, Friends of American Art Collection (photo © 1998, Art Institute of Chicago); 188 (top): Alfred Stieglitz, *Flatiron Building,* 1903, Metropolitan Museum of Art, New York, Alfred Stieglitz Collection (photo © 1998, Metropolitan Museum of Art); 188 (bottom): Alfred Stieglitz, *Georgia O'Keefe: A Portrait—Head,* 1922, National Gallery of Art, Washington, DC, Alfred Stieglitz Collection (photo © 1998, Board of Trustees, National Gallery of Art); 189 (top): Imogen Cunningham, *Magnolia Blossom,* 1925, courtesy of Christie's Images, New York; 189 (bottom): Georgia O'Keefe, *Cow's Skull: Red, White, and Blue,* 1931, Metropolitan Museum of Art, New York, Alfred Stieglitz Collection (photo © 1994, Metropolitan Museum of Art); 190 (top): Arthur Dove, *Fog Horns,* 1929, Colorado Springs Fine Arts Center, anonymous gift; 190 (bottom): Elie Nadelman, *Women at the Piano,* c. 1917, Museum of Modern Art, New York, Philip L. Goodwin Collection (photo © 1998, Museum of Modern Art); 191: Stuart Davis, *Landscape with Garage Lights,* 1932, Memorial Art Gallery, University of Rochester, New York; 192: Joseph Stella, *Battle of Lights, Coney Island, Mardi Gras,* 1913–1914, Yale University Gallery of Fine Arts, bequest of Dorothea Dreier to the Collection Société Anonyme; 193 (top): Charles Sheeler, *American Landscape,* 1930, Museum of Modern Art, New York, gift of Abby Aldrich Rockefeller (photo © 1998, Museum of Modern Art); 193 (bottom): Charles Henry Demuth, *The Figure 5 in Gold,* Metropolitan Museum of Art, New York, Alfred Stieglitz Collection (photo © 1996, Metropolitan Museum of Art); 194: Grant Wood, *American Gothic,* 1930, Art Institute of Chicago, Friends of American Art Collection, all rights reserved by the Art Institute of Chicago and VAGA, New York (photo © 1998, Art Institute of Chicago); 195 (top): John Steuart Curry, *Tornado Over Kansas,* Muskegon Museum of Art, Muskegon, Michigan, Hackley Picture Fund; 195 (bottom): Thomas Hart Benton, *Cradling Wheat,* 1938, The Saint Louis Art Museum, purchase; 196: Dorthea Lange / LOC; 197 (top): William H. Johnson, *Li'l Sis,* 1944, National Museum of American Art, Washington, DC / Art Resource, NY; 197 (bottom): Aaron Douglas, *Aspects of Negro Life: From Slavery Through Reconstruction,* 1934, Art and Artifacts Division, Schomburg Center for Research in Black Culture, New York Public Library, Astor, Lenox and Tilden Foundations; 201: Lewis Hines, *Construction Worker on the Empire State Building,* c.1930, Avery Architectural and Fine Arts Library, Columbia University

Index

A Aaron, Hank, 49
ACLU. See American Civil
Liberties Union
African Americans. See blacks
airplanes, 17, 67–71
air power, 123, 129, 135
Alien law, 36, 118
Allies: in World War I, 14; in World
War II, 123, 130–34, 154, 163. See
also World War II
amendments. See constitutional
amendments
American Civil Liberties Union
(ACLU), 45
anarchism, 35
Anderson, Marian, 96
Anson, Cap, 52
Anthony, Susan B., 30, 32
anti-Semitism, 112–19
Arendt, Hannah, 118
Armistice Day, 13–15
Armory Show, 24, 187, 188, 191
Armstrong, Louis, 55, 56, 57–58
artists, 24, 46, 105, 186–97. See
also specific artists
"Ashcan artists," 186–87
atom bomb, 120–21, 179, 180–83,
184
Auschwitz (Poland), 116, 164–65
Axis powers, 124, 130, 131–34, 154,
163, 166. See also World War II

B Barber, Red, 44, 48
baseball, 47–54
Battle of the Bulge, 164
Bearden, Romare, 46
Bell, James, 51, 54
Bellows, George, 186, 187
Benton, Thomas Hart, 46, 194, 195
Bergen-Belsen (Germany), 177
Birkenau (Poland), 116
blacks: African heritage of, 58, 73;
as artists, 196, 197; as athletes,
51–54; as doctors, 23; and Jim
Crow, 56; migration of, 40; in the
military, 135; and music, 55–59;
rights of, 41
Bonus Army, 84, 85, 96
bootleggers, 28
Bradley, Omar, 161
Britain. See Great Britain
Bryan, William, Jennings, 45

Buchenwald (Germany), 117, 176
Burns, Lucy, 29, 30
Byrd, Richard E., 67

C Capa, Robert, 161
Cassatt, Mary, 46
Catt, Carrie Chapman, 32, 33
Cézanne, Paul, 24, 190
Chagall, Marc, 190
Charleston, Oscar, 53, 54
China: inventions, 64, 65, 66; in
World War II, 179
Churchill, Winston, 124, 130, 131,
165, 168, 179
Civilian Conservation Corps
(CCC), 96, 105
Civilian Works Administration
(CWA), 105
Clemenceau, Georges, 16, 18
Cleveland, Grover, 89
codes, military, 137–38, 154
communism, 34–36, 86, 111
concentration camps, 115–17,
164–65, 176
constitutional amendments, 27;
1st, 20, 36, 45; 4th, 146; 14th, 41,
146; 18th, 26–27; 19th, 31–33;
20th, 101; 21st, 28
Coolidge, Calvin, 37, 41–42, 46, 76,
103
Copland, Aaron, 46, 61, 190
creationism, 44–45
Cubists, 191
Cullen, Countee, 46
Cunningham, Imogen, 189
Curry, John Steuart, 194–95
Czechoslovakia, 125

D Dachau (Germany), 176
Darrow, Clarence, 45
Davis, Stuart, 24, 187, 191
D-Day, 159–63
de Gaulle, Charles, 131
Demuth, Charles, 193–94
Depression. See Great Depression
Didrikson, Mildred "Babe," 50
Dihigo, Martin, 51
disease, 21–23, 41, 150
Douglas, Aaron, 197
Dove, Arthur, 188, 190, 191
Drew, Charles R., 140
Duchamp, Marcel, 24

Dunkirk, Belgium, 126
Dust Bowl, 80, 81, 82

E Eakins, Thomas, 186
Edison, Thomas, 192
Einstein, Albert, 120–21, 191
Eisenhower, Dwight D., 85; in
World War II, 141, 149, 156, 159
Ellington, Duke, 46, 59
England. See Great Britain
Enola Gay, 182
eugenics, 114
Evans, Walker, 196
evolutionism, 44–45
Expressionists, 196

F factories: automobile, 193;
during war, 14, 155, 156
farmers: economic conditions of,
80, 81, 196
Fascism, 111
Faulkner, William, 46
Fauve, Les, 24, 191
Federal Deposit Insurance
Corporation (FDIC), 105
Felton, Rebecca Latimer, 32
Fitzgerald, F. Scott, 46, 59
Ford, Henry, 43, 87, 193
Founding Fathers, 9–12, 27, 113,
118
Fourteen Points, 16–18
France: in World War I, 14, 18; in
World War II, 126, 131, 157, 163
Frank, Anne, 177
fundamentalism, 44–45
Futurists, 191, 192

G Garvey, Marcus, 73
Gauguin, Paul, 24
Gaulle, Charles de. See de Gaulle,
Charles
Gehrig, Lou, 53, 54
George, Lloyd. See Lloyd George,
David
Germany, 86; armed forces of, 124;
Nazism in, 107–109, 112, 113,
114–19, 120, 124; in World War I,
14–15, 17, 18; in World War II,
125, 130–34, 140–41, 155, 156,
157, 159–64, 166, 176–78
Gershwin, George, 46, 61
Goddard, Robert, 63–66, 137

Gogh, Vincent van, 24
Great Britain: in World War I, 14; in World War II, 126, 130
Great Depression, 62, 76, 79–87, 100–101, 102–103, 111, 196
Guadalcanal, 143, 149–53
Guthrie, Woody, 81

H Harding, Warren G., 37–40
Harlem Renaissance, 46, 196
Hartley, Marsden, 188
Hemingway, Ernest, 23, 46, 190
Henri, Robert, 187, 188, 190, 191, 192
Heyward, DuBose, 61
Hirohito, Emperor, 184, 185
Hiroshima, 182–83
Hitler, Adolf, 54, 86, 107, 109, 111, 114–19, 130–34, 159, 164, 177
Homer, Winslow, 186
Hopper, Edward, 187
Hoover, Herbert, 72, 73, 84–87, 101, 103
Hoover, J. Edgar, 146
Hoovervilles, 83, 84, 85
Hopkins, Harry, 127, 134
hospitals, 22, 23. See also disease, medical schools
Hughes, Langston, 46
Hull, Cordell, 127, 128, 129
Hurston, Zora Neale, 46

I immigrants, 36, 115, 118–19, 146. See also Alien law
imperialism, 168
influenza, 21–23
internment camps, 115, 144–48
isolationism, 20, 122–24, 129
Italy, 86, 110; in World War I, 14, 18; in World War II, 130, 156–57, 158
Ives, Charles, 60, 61
Iwo Jima, 166

J Japan, 109; armed forces of, 124; in World War I, 14; in World War II, 126–29, 139–40, 142–43, 149–53, 166, 168, 179, 180–83, 184, 185
Japanese Americans, 144–48
jazz, 55–58, 191

Jazz Age, 46, 59. See also Roaring Twenties
Jefferson, Thomas, 12; as architect, 10; on religion, 113
Jews: persecution of, 112–17, 144
Johnson, William H., 196, 197
Joyce, James, 194

K Kendall, Ada Davenport, 30
Ku Klux Klan, 36, 72, 111, 118

L Lange, Dorothea, 81, 144, 145, 196
Lawrence, Jacob, 40, 46, 197
League of Nations, 17–20, 39, 118
Lenin, Vladimir, 34
Leonard, Buck, 54
Lindberg, Charles A., 66, 67–71, 86, 111
Lloyd George, David, 18
Louis, Joe, 54
Luce, Henry, 194
Luftwaffe, 131, 176

M MacArthur, Douglas, 85, 101, 141, 166
McKay, Claude, 46
McShane, Elizabeth, 30
Maidanek (Poland), 117
Marin, John, 188
Maris, Roger, 49
Marshall, George C., 141
Martin, Anne, 29, 30
Matisse, Henri, 24, 190
medical schools, 23
Mitchell, Jackie, 53
Mitchell, William "Billy," 123, 135
Modigliani, Amadeo, 190
monkey trial. See Scopes trial
Morey, Katherine, 29
motion pictures, 41, 46, 62
music, 46, 55–61
Mussolini, Benito, 86, 110, 111, 130, 157, 177

N Nadelman, Elie, 188, 190
Nagasaki, Japan, 180–82, 183, 184
Native Americans, 55, 138
Navajo Indians, 138
Nazis, 109, 111, 114–19. See also Germany

Negro Leagues, 51–54
Nevelson, Louise, 197
New Deal, 100–106
New Orleans, Louisiana, 55–58
Nisei, 146, 147
Normandy, 159–63
North Africa, 156

O Obata, Haruko, 144–47
O'Keeffe, Georgia, 188–89
Olympics, 54
Owens, Jesse, 54

P Pacific theater. See World War II
pacifism, 123
Paige, Satchel, 51, 52, 53
Palestine, 118
Palmer, A. Mitchell, 35–36
Patton, George S., 156
Paul, Alice, 29
Pearl Harbor, 125–29. See also World War II
Perkins, Frances, 104, 175
photography, 161, 188, 189, 196
Picasso, Pablo, 24, 190
Poland, 125, 131
poliomyelitis, 92, 97, 99
Pollock, Jackson, 197
Porgy and Bess (Gershwin), 61
Potsdam conference, 179, 184
Precisionists, 193
Prohibition, 25–28, 43
Public Works Administration (PWA), 105
Pyle, Ernie, 158, 161, 163

R racism, 72, 73, 112, 114, 118–19, 140, 146
radio, 10, 44, 48, 102, 129
Rankin, Jeanette, 32
Regionalists, 195
Reif-Lehrer, Liane, 119
Roaring Twenties, 41–44, 193
Rockefeller, John D., 165
rockets, 63–66, 137
Rogers, Will, 86, 103
Rommel, Erwin, 156, 157, 159
Roosevelt, Eleanor, 88, 93–96, 169, 171, 172, 173–74, 185
Roosevelt, Franklin Delano, 87, 100–101, 120, 121, 164; achieve-

ments of, 174–75, 196; child-hood of, 88–91; death of, 171, 172–74; family of, 88–89, 101, 169; final days of, 167–69; fire-side chats of, 129, 172; health of, 92, 95, 96, 97–99; and Japanese Americans, 146, 147; marriage of, 92, 95; and New Deal, 100–106; and Pearl Harbor, 125–29; and Truman, 170; and World War II, 141, 165
Roosevelt, Theodore, 91, 92, 100
Ross, Nellie Taylor, 41
Rushmore, Mount, 43
Russia, 86, 110; in World War I, 14, 34. See also Soviet Union
Ruth, George Herman "Babe," 47–50, 53

S Sacco, Nicola, 35
Scopes trial, 44–45
Seabees, 135, 153
Securities and Exchange Commission (SEC), 75, 105
Sedition Act, 20, 36, 118
self-determination, 17, 168
Serkin, Rudolf, 118
Shahn, Ben, 25, 27, 28, 197
Sheeler, Charles, 193
Sicily, 156–57
Sloan, John, 186, 187
Smith, Al, 72, 73
Smith, Bessie, 58
Social Security, 104, 105
Soviet Union, 110; in World War II, 131–34, 154, 155, 165. See also Russia
space age, 63–66
Spain, 110
speakeasies, 28, 57
Spender, Stephen, 87
Spirit of St. Louis, 68–70
sports, 47–54
Stalin, Joseph, 34, 86, 111, 131, 132, 155–56, 165, 168, 179
Stanley, Thomas J. "Stumpy," 152
Stanton, Elizabeth Cady, 32
Stein, Gertrude, 190
Steinbeck, John, 80, 81
Stella, Joseph, 192
Stieglitz, Alfred, 188, 189, 190

stock market, 44, 105; crash, 74–78, 101
suffragists, 29–33. See also women

T Taylor, Frederick, 193
Teapot Dome, 38–39
Teller, Edward, 121
Tennessee Valley Authority (TVA), 105
Thompson, Florence, 196
Thompson, Marguerite, 190
Tojo, Hideki, 127, 130, 139, 184
Tokyo Rose, 148
Toomer, Jean, 46
totalitarianism, 34, 111
Truman, Harry S.: in World War I, 14; as president, 170–71, 178, 179, 180, 185

U U-boats, 136, 140, 154
Ulysses (Joyce), 194
unemployment, 84, 87, 100, 105. See also Great Depression, New Deal
United Nations, 165, 185
U.S.S.R. See Soviet Union

V Van Gogh, Vincent. See Gogh, Vincent van
Vanzetti, Bartolomeo, 35
VE Day, 178, 184
Verne, Jules, 64
Versailles treaty, 18, 19, 108, 124
VJ Day, 184, 185

W Walker, Moses (Fleet), 51–52
Walker, Welday, 52
Wall Street. See stock market
Wallace, Henry, 171
warfare, 13, 123–24, 135–38, 140–43, 150–53, 154, 155–57, 180–83
weapons, 13, 135–38, 140–43, 180–83
Weber, Max, 188
Wells, H. G., 64
Western theater. See World War II
Wiesel, Elie, 116
Williams, Smokey Joe, 53, 54
Williams, William Carlos, 193, 194

Wilson, Woodrow: and women's rights, 30, 32; and World War I, 11, 13, 15, 16–20
Woman's Army Corps, 147
women: athletes, 50, 53; doctors, 23; equal rights of, 24, 29–33; as flappers, 42–43; in the military, 13, 147; penitentiary for, 37; and war effort, 155
Women's Christian Temperance Union, 25
Wood, Grant, 46, 194, 195
Works Progress Administration (WPA), 105, 196–97
World War I, 13–20; veterans, 84, 85
World War II: Allied and Axis pow-ers, 130–34; end of, 184–85; home front, 144–48, 154, 155; Pacific theater, 126–29, 139–40, 141–43, 147, 149–53, 166, 168, 178–79, 180–83; Pearl Harbor at-tack, 125–29; Western theater, 140, 154–64, 176–78
WPA. See Works Progress Administration

X xenophobia, 119

Y Yalta conference, 165
Yoncalla, Oregon, 33

Z Zaharias, George, 50
Zorach, William, 190

A Note from the Author

It was the best of times, it was the worst of times, it was the age of wisdom,
it was the age of foolishness....

Charles Dickens was thinking about the 18th century when he began a famous novel with those words. But he might have been describing the first half of the 20th century.

The best of times? The worst of times?

Which was it? It was both.

Take that bomb, for instance. It was horrible to think of its hellish, destructive force. But there was another side to atomic energy. Wisely used, it held great hope for the future.

Wisdom and foolishness in modern times? You bet. And sometimes it was hard to tell them apart. Should the bomb have been dropped? The answer was obvious: of course not.

It was outrageous, and barbaric to bomb children and other civilians with any kind of bomb. The bombs dropped on Hiroshima and Nagasaki were the terrible outcome of a misguided idea—strategic bombing (which meant bombing of any targets, including civilian, that might aid the war). Strategic bombing was first tried in Spain in 1939 by Fascist forces. Hitler took the idea further when he bombed Britain. The Allies went still further.

But there was another question that had to be asked. What would you have done if you were Harry Truman? If you had a weapon that would end the war quickly (and save lives on both sides), would you have used it? Of course you would. In 1945, hardly anyone even thought of hesitating.

There was a lesson in all this. It isn't easy to be a citizen in a democracy. It takes work: reading, listening, and questioning. And yet, after the war, some people were still crying out for simple solutions. They were looking for leaders with slogans, not thinking explanations. They weren't willing to take time to become responsible citizens. A good citizen needs to be well informed, to get involved, and to know history.

Why history? Because it helps us make judgments. And history shows us that ideas set in mo-

tion sometimes head in unforeseen directions. They may lead to places we wish they wouldn't go.

The people in Germany who followed Hitler didn't expect his ideas to take them into the sewers of evil and destruction. But they didn't examine those ideas carefully. They didn't protest while they still had a chance. They didn't consider other people's feelings. They listened to simplistic messages, and they let others think for them.

The people in the United States who were racists and bigots didn't usually mean to hurt others. But they didn't do much thinking. History tells us that disgusting, ugly ideas are sometimes accepted by ordinary (but unthinking) people.

Did we learn anything from the history of the first half of the 20th century?

Yes. We learned of the horror and stupidity of totalitarian rule. (In totalitarian governments, a powerful leader is usually in league with the military, the police, and sometimes with business interests. Once they seize power, the ordinary citizen doesn't stand a chance.)

We learned of the waste of war. What if all those 20th-century children who died of violence had lived? What might they have accomplished?

And what of the waste of resources? Destroying a million dollars' worth of city buildings and streets usually costs the other side a million dollars in planes, bombs, and equipment. (Imagine if that money were spent to make life better for people.)

We learned something else: in a time of crisis, the best in people often appears. There was much real heroism during those years of war and depression. People worked together, and sacrificed, and felt good about that, and about each other. Is there some way to bring that sense of shared emergency to today's problems? How can we work together to make our cities safe? To improve our schools? To help all our citizens pursue happiness?